GW00546569

AMERICAN ECSTASY

LINDA LUNDY

MINERVA PRESS
MONTREUX LONDON WASHINGTON

AMERICAN ECSTASY
Copyright © Linda Lundy 1996

All Rights Reserved

ISBN 1 86106 187 0

First Published 1996 by
MINERVA PRESS
195 Knightsbridge
London SW7 1RE

2nd Impression 1997

Printed in Great Britain by
Antony Rowe Ltd, Chippenham, Wiltshire

AMERICAN ECSTASY

This book is dedicated to a cat named George who was my very best friend and lives for ever in my heart.

To a man named Adil - my superstar of the seventies.

And to my beloved sons Tashi and Monty and to their sister, Etoile, who is shining down on us from heaven.

Angel Hunting

Angel cries are lost in
the roar of the dashed seaside;
the last moonbeams fled the morning tide,
their telltale, silver footprints having dried.

They came from where the silence
sucks word-husks of all meaning
where "is" is not "seeming"
where earth is air
where even the tallest star
peaks only at its nadir. There

clouds, like gossamer blotters,
absorb color and sound:
the ink of the night,
grief, drowns
and the screaming stops
and eternity begins
and you are no longer afraid of heights
nor being alone with the Alone - or its Twin.

Thomas B. White

Have you seen those who are led by their own appetites?
They are all like beasts and even more misguided.

The Koran

Chapter One

The first thing she thought of that morning when she woke up was Eric. His long, slender legs floated into her memory and connected themselves with his perfectly formed chest. The golden, graceful muscles of his shoulders and arms rippled through the haze of drugstore tranquillisers that she took each night in order to sleep. She stretched and yawned happily, then turned her head to the pillow next to her and smelled it to see if she could detect a trace of his tanned brown cheeks and curly hair. She moved once more, then groaned. The bed she lay on was long and narrow, like the room she was in. Eric had spent the previous night with her for the first time, jamming himself up beside her in the uncomfortable bed and wrapping his long legs around her body like growing vines, then pushing his hard dick into her tanned body at dawn. She smiled as she recalled their conversation from last night.

"Let me come up," he had said.

"No," she had replied.

"Why not?"

"'Cause I don't want to get into anything heavy. You know these dates of ours are just pleasant props, and that's the way they've got to stay."

"I won't make love to you," he had said earnestly. "I just want to sleep with you."

"Oh, Eric," she had sighed.

"You're just a bitch!" he said, pounding on the steering wheel while they sat in the parking lot of her apartment building.

"I'm not," she said, clinching her shapely knees together tightly.

"You are," he accused her again.

She turned and looked at his warm pouting lips, at the firm line of his jaw, and said, "OK, you can come up, but we aren't going to screw."

It was the first time she had slept with anyone since she had left her husband a few weeks before.

Suddenly her big, striped cat crawled out from under the bed and meowed loudly, interrupting her recollections of the night before.

"Shhh, Porgy darlin'. You know they'll kick us out of here if they hear you, so be quiet, honey," she cautioned her cat.

The cat looked at her solemnly with his great yellow eyes, blinking as if he had understood.

She lay in the bed a few moments longer, fighting the inertia that the tranquillisers produced in her body. She gazed up at the ceiling dully and saw long shreds of old paint peeling off.

"Jesus, this is a far cry from the Hilton in New York! God, and I thought the Silver Spring Holiday Inn was a comedown! Shit," she said to no one, and ran over to her large blue suitcase. She stood looking down at the contents while yawning, then began to search around for some cans of cat food and the opener she had hidden under her new clothes. Porgy began rubbing himself furiously against her long slim legs in anticipation.

"You certainly are intelligent, darlin'."

She clutched the cold tin can opener in one hand and leaned down to massage Porgy's thick, blunt head with the other.

"Come on then."

She walked into the pitch blackness of the bathroom and switched on the blue-white neon light, shivering from the touch of the cold bathroom tiles under her feet. She opened the cat food and stood watching Porgy gulp it down noisily, then turned to the bathroom door and blinked sleepily at herself in the full-length mirror. Her body was tanned dark brown from sunbathing at the Hilton pool, so that she wore the white print of her bikini on her nude body.

As she turned the tap on to wash her face, her long, dark hair hung down into the round white water basin. She soaped her face vigorously with the stinging, creamy lather, trying to focus her attention through the constant waves that spun through her brain from the tranquillisers.

Brrinng! She heard the phone and cursed, but ran hurriedly to the old black receiver.

"Hello."

"Eric, darling, where are you?"

"Where am I? Get your brain together, kid. I'm at the Hamburger Hostel, natch. That's where I work, remember? I gave you a big, beautiful greasy hamburger – heavy on the onions, remember? You met me there when you checked out to go to the dump you're in now."

"Oh, Eric," she said, smiling through the soapsuds and rubbing them into her eyes. "It's just that you sounded so close."

"What a compliment. Listen, luv, there were about a billion hundred dollar bills lying on the dresser when I woke up this morning, so I took the liberty of putting them in your suitcase. I guess your 'friend' left them there last night before I came."

"You're so thoughtful, Eric."

"Ha! Outta sight. What a dame."

"Eric, when can you come?" she asked, and sat down on the woolly material of the dresser chair, feeling it prickle her behind.

"You're going to the Hilton, natch?"

"Yeah, I mean I guess so. There's nothing else to do." She gazed towards the bathroom door and watched as Porgy sat cleaning himself carefully with his paw.

"Well, I'll be there about three – okay? Three-thirty at the latest."

"Oh, Eric, so late?"

"Cybele, it just happens to be twelve-thirty right now."

Porgy leapt up onto the dresser in front of her, swishing the black tip of his tail under her nose voluptuously.

"Darlin', darlin'," she mumbled and sank her face down into his body, sniffing his fur.

"Are you kissing that damned cat again?"

"Are you jealous?"

"He's not the only one I'm jealous of."

"Oh, Eric, Eric Star, let's not get started on that again. You knew about Hadrian. You agreed to be the 'other man' when my husband's detectives were following me, remember?"

"That was before last night."

"Well, Eric, I'm not going to give up Hadrian. I love him."

"And your husband, and me, right? Got any others I don't know about? How about a stray giraffe?"

"Eric, I've gotta go. I was washing my face and the soap's killing me."

"OK, have a nice day until I see you at three." He paused and then added, "Put all your hundred-dollar bills in the bank and then go lay your pretty little fanny in the sun until I get there."

"OK, I love you. Bye."

She ran back into the bathroom and began rinsing her face.

Brrinng!

"Goddammit," she shouted, and ran back to the phone.

"With whom have you been talking?" She heard Hadrian's rich, sensuous voice say. "Your hippie boy?"

"Well, yes," she responded breathlessly, waiting for his every word.

"How was your date last night?"

"Oh, okay I guess." She heard him blowing smoke from a cigarette, and thought of his massive chest and powerful arms in one of his expensive jackets.

"And what have you done?"

She could see his curving, sensual mouth as he spoke in a pronounced foreign accent and she could feel it pressing against her body; imagine the roughness of his beard exciting her as it scratched her nipples.

"Oh, we went to a few night-clubs, a couple of places where my husband might have seen us." She gazed at herself in the mirror and made a face. 'I'm too brown,' she thought happily.

"And then?" She heard the click of his lighter as he lit another cigarette. She wanted to touch him when she heard him inhaling the pungent smoke from his English cigarette.

"I was sad."

"Why?"

"I missed Pierre."

"Then why did you leave him?"

"You know."

"What do I know?"

"Why I left him."

"Never mind about Pierre. What have you done with Eric after your nightclubbing?"

"I came back to the hotel room."

"Alone?"

She hesitated. "Yes."

"Cybele, don't lie to me. I drove by your hotel parking lot this morning, and Eric's car was there."

She thought quickly to figure out if he was bluffing. She knew that Eric went to work early – too early for Hadrian to check his car, unless he had come to work extra early on purpose.

"Hadrian, you didn't see his car. Don't pick on me. Why did you tell me to come here anyway?" She gazed around the stark room. "It's awful in this place."

"Never mind, there are lots of nice retired people from the State Department there. You must be more conservative. Now answer me – did Eric spend the night there last night?"

"No!"

"I don't believe you."

"OK, believe me or not. This was *your* idea, you know."

"It's not my idea for you to spend the night with any other man, Cybele."

"You said to be seen with him around my husband. Well, I'm being seen. I'm going all around with the guy to keep Pierre off your back. What else do you want?"

"I want a faithful cunt."

"Oh, you're crazy. Damn, you know it? There you are over there in Bethesda with your wife."

"I don't fuck her."

"Yeah?" She slipped up on the glass-covered dresser and winced when she felt the cold glass on her behind. "Well, everybody tells me I'm nuts to believe that. I've seen her. She's young – and not bad."

"She's awful." He sighed deeply.

Cybele giggled. "You sound so sad when you mention her, Hadrian." She looked happily at her flat belly in the mirror.

"Uh oh, London's on the other line. I want to see you tonight. Be in your room about six. Be sure and go to the bank with all the money I brought you. And don't see Eric anymore. Finish up with him, okay?"

He clicked off before she had a chance to answer. She was left holding the receiver. She spread her toes out on the chair and pushed until it fell over backwards onto the bed. All of the voices were gone and she was left alone. Beside her round, curving hip, a vase of red and yellow carnations sat wilting.

She walked back into the bathroom and began running her bath water. She was frightened to admit to herself how dizzy she still felt from the medicine she gulped down each night in order to sleep. She sank her slim body into the hot bath and lay back in the cold, white porcelain of the tub, trying to think of what she might be doing if she were still with her husband. It was the middle of the day now. She would be out in her little sports car on some contrived errand in order to escape his presence, or else meeting Hadrian in the secret apartment he had rented for them. She sighed and used her foot to turn more hot water into the bath. She lay her head back on the tub once more. She felt a terrible ennui, a weariness for remembering her past when she thought of her husband and tried to understand what it had all meant. Yet when she concentrated on their marriage, all she could remember were the horrible, macabre fights.

She hadn't been feeling well when they had awakened one Sunday a few weeks before she had left, she remembered as she lay back in the hot water of her bath.

"I hope you aren't going to keep this up all day," he had said.

"Oh no," she had answered, "it's just a bad headache. Give me an hour or so."

They had gone into the sunroom and sat on the yellow velvet sofa. He had said something and she had answered back. She couldn't remember what, then she had felt a crushing blow to the side of her head. She had turned her head painfully to look at him, dazed from the blow, then reached up and felt something wet. She had brought her hand down and saw it covered with blood.

"Pierre, Pierre!" she had cried. "This is incredible." She had looked at her hand again. "I thought we were through with all of this."

"You bitch! You lousy, ugly bitch!" he had yelled, and began kicking her shins over and over with his boots. She sank down further into the hot, steaming water, but trembled as she recalled the ugly, twisted expression of anger on his face.

"Pierre, Pierre!" she had screamed, and ran into the living-room. "It isn't *me* you're mad at," she had said, cringing against the wall she had painted pink. "Don't you understand?" She had looked at him, terrified, thinking, 'This is it, this is the last time. He's insane.'

He had slapped her over and over before collapsing into a chair. Then he had begun his old familiar weeping, begging her to forgive him as he sobbed.

She yanked the plug out of the old bathtub and stood up, trying to put an end to her disturbing memories of the past.

"Oh, God, it's so shitty," she said aloud, and began to whimper. Porgy ambled up to her wet feet.

"Brrutt," he said, and blinked his large owl-like eyes.

"Yes, I love you," she said, and scooped him up to her wet body. "But you've gotta hide, Porgy." He blinked up at her innocently. "You've gotta get under the bed and hide, darlin', but don't worry – it's just for a few more days. Then we're gonna get an apartment here." She looked at the old-fashioned room. "We'll get an apartment in this damned old mausoleum, and then. . ." – she crammed Porgy under the bed – ". . .and then, I don't know what the hell we'll do."

She walked over to the closet and opened one of the boxes of clothes she had bought before she left the Holiday Inn. She got out a shorts set and pulled it on over her semi-dry body. She looked down at the money Hadrian had left her, then threw a lot of panties over it and shut her suitcase.

Knock! Knock! She heard someone rapping insistently on the door.

'God! Who can that be?' she wondered, and began hopping around, trying to pull on the new outfit as quickly as possible.

"Who is it?" she called.

"Mr Masters, your landlord," she heard a muffled voice say.

"Oh. . ." She finished pulling on her shorts hurriedly. "Be right with you," she called, then made a frantic rush around the room, throwing things in the closet and under the bed. She crouched down by the bed. "Now, Porgy baby, *please* stay under there."

She ran to the door and unhooked the chair she had wedged under the door handle, then looked through the peephole to ascertain that it *was* definitely the landlord, and not her husband. Sure enough, she saw the old bald head of Mr Masters covered like an ageing oak tree with white, moss-like hair on each side. At the sight of the yellowing ends of his hair hanging into his dirty, wilted collar, Cybele felt the same foreboding she had had when he touched her elbow in the lobby the day she had rented the room. But she shook the feeling off deliberately. "He's just a harmless old man," she told herself. "I don't like him because. . . his clothes are so dirty, and he stinks! Wonder why he doesn't wear clean clothes, since he owns the whole joint?"

She opened the door slowly. The same sickening odour she had encountered upon their first meeting flooded her nostrils as she confronted the landlord. Unconsciously she stepped back from the smell.

"How'd do?" he said, and smiled at her with his false teeth that looked like old crockery.

"Why, just fine, Mr Masters, just fine," she replied, and looked at him nervously. The skin of his face was white and puffy. Its spongy, flabby quality was redolent of death and disease.

'Maybe he's sick,' she thought, while she stood waiting to see what he wanted, 'and that's why he stinks. Yes, that's probably it. Poor old goat,' she thought, but cringed and shrank back when she noticed the nearness of his horny old hands propped on the door facing.

"I thought you might want to see the apartment we fixed up for you."

"Apartment?" She stared at the big brown liver spots on his hands and thought of leprosy spreading, spreading. . . "Oh, that is, I'd *love* to see the apartment. Just let me get my key."

"Oh, t'won't be necessary," he said in the old-fashioned slang of an elderly person. "It's right down at the end of the hall. You can just leave the door open."

She looked anxiously at the bed where Porgy was hiding. "God, I hope Porgy doesn't come out," she sighed, but prepared to obey the landlord's instructions. 'After all,' she thought, 'he is sort of the boss around here.'

"Oh well, okay," she said, and followed his tall, stooped frame to the locked door at the end of the hallway. His bent posture belied the massiveness of his back and arms. She watched him unlock the door and was reminded of the wiry, powerful arms of an ape hanging onto the iron frame of a zoo cage.

She walked behind him into the spacious living-room of the apartment. She immediately noticed the french doors that led out onto the balcony.

"Oh, Mr Masters, it's delightful," she exclaimed, feeling the apartment's spaciousness acutely after being in the cramped room.

"I got you one with a balcony," the old man said, observing her slender body hungrily.

She looked all around happily, oblivious to his *carnal* stares in her excitement.

"There's a bedroom suite in here you might want to buy," he offered. "It was left by another tenant."

He had seen a lot of money in her purse when she had first come into the apartment building and had decided she must be the daughter of a rich diplomat or government official. He knew that she was running from something, and presumed rightly that it must be an unwanted husband. At any rate, he had resolved to get as much money from her as possible.

She followed him into the bedroom, aware of his old body and hands all the more as they stood in the room's intimate atmosphere. She could hear his heavy, breathing and see the grey bristles of his beard sticking out vulgarly from his cheeks. A certain sensual greed emanated from his stance and his eyes. All of this she kept brushing aside in her desperate desire for an abode of her own – a real home, instead of the countless hotel rooms of the past few weeks.

"Oh, Mr Masters, this furniture is gorgeous."

"I can let you have it for seven hundred fifty dollars plus fifty apiece for the lamps."

"Oh, perfect, perfect. I'll take it."

He sucked his breath in sharply. "And the apartment is seven hundred and eighty-five dollars a month, not including utilities." He fished in the pockets of his baggy trousers and came up with a large, rumpled handkerchief. Cybele tried not to watch while he blew his nose into it over and over.

"Great, great," she said absently, accepting any terms he offered.

"I'll have to have six months' rent in advance."

"Of course. I'll get it for you tomorrow," she said, wanting to hurry back to the room and close the door before Porgy came out from under the bed.

"Well, fine, fine," he said. He rubbed his old dry hands together, and made a gumming sound with his mouth.

She walked hurriedly back to her room.

"You must have a lot of business to attend to today," he said with curiosity shining out of his eyes like a wizened weasel. "You seem in such a hurry."

"Oh, yes," she said nervously. Her eyes darted ahead to her open door. "I have to go to the bank."

"You getting a divorce or something?" he asked when they came to her door, purposely detaining her.

"How'd you guess?"

He smiled shrewdly. "It's a shame. Bet you were a good wife. Do you like to cook?"

"Oh yes, I love it." She hung in the doorway apprehensively.

"So do I," he said. "How'd you like to come to my apartment tonight and have dinner?"

She must have looked at him with an expression of incredulity because she saw his face grow hard and hateful before she refused him – an honest expression of emotion at last plainly showing on his weather-beaten face.

"Why. . . I . . . Mr Masters, how nice of you to think of me," she stuttered. The more she faltered in embarrassment, the more he pinched his thin lips.

"But I have other plans for tonight, unfortunately," she finished lamely, still staring at his obscene old mouth. *Suddenly she felt Porgy's furry body between her ankles and she gasped.* The old man followed her gaze to the cat.

"We don't allow pets here."

"Oh yes, yes, I know. My sister is just in town for a few days and she begged me to keep her cat for her while she's here," Cybele explained hastily.

"We don't like animals in the rooms," he said ominously, as impolite now as an illiterate farmer.

"Yes. . . well, my sister is staying with my aunt who loathes cats – so it's only while she's here. Probably a couple of more days." She looked frantically into the old man's beady, cold stare, desperate that she might actually lose the lovely apartment, the long sought-after haven.

"As long as she won't be here much longer then. By the way," he said pointedly, "we don't supply parking for overnight guests of the tenants."

"What?"

"Your friend had his little sports car in one of our tenant's parking spaces last night."

She felt her cheeks grow red, but maintained her composure, trying frantically to keep her chance for the apartment open.

"Of course, of course," she acknowledged apologetically.

"Well, just so you understand."

"Oh yes, I do."

He turned and walked off abruptly.

"Thank you," she called after him. He grumbled some inaudible reply, sounding like an old, cranky dog as he lumbered away.

"God!" she said as she closed the door. She walked over to the night table and lit one of Eric's cigarettes. She didn't smoke, so the nicotine made her dizzy when she inhaled. "Shit, Porgy, you may have fucked up the whole deal." She took another deep puff of the cigarette, reeling as she fell onto the bed.

"Oh, well, I'll ask Eric about it," she decided and stubbed out the cigarette. She stuffed Porgy back under the bed, then gathered up her purse and left the room. As she passed the various closed doors of the apartments, she had an eerie feeling that from one of them Mr Masters was peering out at her with his beady stare. She trembled with apprehension, afraid of what she might encounter in the long empty hallway, and ran toward the elevator.

When she slid out of the air-conditioned cab in front of the Washington Hilton Hotel, the summer heat hit her like the blast from a furnace. She strode through the sleek, modern lobby and walked down the steps that led to the pool, descending them two by two. She put her hand on the wide, heavy glass door that opened out onto the patio surrounding the pool and started to push it open, then hesitated. She walked back over to a row of pay phones that were lined up on the wall like look-alikes on a quiz show, then dug inside her purse and pulled out two thick nickels. She lifted the receiver and dialled the Hamburger Hostel. People in the lobby passed by her like paper dolls.

"Good afternoon, Hamburger Hostel."

"May I please speak with Eric?" she asked as officially as possible.

"Certainly, one moment."

She heard a long buzz, then Eric's voice said, "Hamburger Hostel
– hamburgers all the way – Eric speaking."

"Eric."

"Cybele. What's up?" he asked. His voice cracked a little from
the seriousness that he tried to impart to it when he heard how
desperate she sounded.

"Oh nothing." She looked around the Hilton lobby and shivered in
the icy air-conditioning. "I miss you, Eric. Please come."

"Only another half an hour, Cybele, and I'll be there. OK?"

"OK, Eric." She held onto the receiver like a drowning person.

"Well?"

"Well," she answered.

"Go on out in the sun and order some orange juice. When I get
there, we'll have a couple of cheeseburgers." He waited for her to
answer. "Cybele?"

"Eric, I'll die if you don't show up."

"Shut up and do what I told you. And don't dive off the
swimming board! Have you got that? You'll never surface."

"Oh, Eric, I love you. You're all I depend on."

"Yeah, me and a lot of US currency. What'd you do with all that
bread?"

"Hid it in the suitcase."

"What?" he exclaimed, his youthful voice cracking again with
surprise.

"Well, the landlord showed up, and I got so busy trying to keep
him from finding Porgy." She looked at the black pay phone in front
of her. Its curving chrome head of change slots had the appearance of
a little mechanical man. Row upon row of them sat beside one
another along the phone shelf.

"God, Cybele, you're crazy! Anybody could get that dough. The
maid – anybody."

"They won't, Eric."

"They won't, huh?" She heard him sigh deeply. "Christ, do you
realise I couldn't make that much money in months!"

"Eric," she said, disregarding his exasperation, "if that money
disappears, Hadrian will give me some more."

"God, you talk like the dude's Onassis or something."

"They're very good friends," she said matter-of-factly.

"What?" he exclaimed.

"They're in the same business, remember?"

"Oh, yeah," he said. His voice seemed to fade away under the impact of the name Onassis and people who really knew him, of large amounts of money lying in suitcases.

"Listen, Eric, the thing I'm *really* worried about is the landlord."

"Whaddaya mean?" Eric said. His voice went into a high, whine of impatience. The sound of it reminded her of a schoolboy who has dropped his books and begun to scream with a childish exasperation. Sometimes the circumstances of Cybele's life fell on top of Eric's consciousness like a deluge of bricks. He was intimidated by her high-flying lifestyle. Her strong dependence on him emotionally made him frantic at times.

"Well, he's like a big mangy bear," he heard her soft southern voice drawl.

"What does that mean?"

"Well, he's old and big. . . and sorta loose. Know what I mean? I mean his body's kind of mammoth like a bear, but the flesh hangs in folds."

"Don't get fancy on me, Cybele. Anyway, we'd better talk about this later."

"The thing that scares me is that he asked me for a date—"

"A date?" Eric screamed. "That old dude must be eighty!"

"Nah, couldn't be more than seventy-five."

"That's right, you're a specialist in old men."

"Anyway, Eric, when I turned him down, he got real nasty and said that you shouldn't park your car in the parking lot, and all that shit."

"Don't tell me two old dudes are going to be after me?"

She heard someone yell, "We got an order for two double cheeseburgers, Eric. Are you working today?"

"Huh? Oh, gotta go. See you soon," he said, and hung up abruptly.

Chapter Two

She walked out into the blinding sunlight, blinking until her eyes accustomed themselves from the gloom of the hotel lobby. Wicker-backed chairs stood around multi-coloured patio tables like straw hats flung about in immobility. She passed by them absently. Everything became vague in the sunlight, like the shadowy images on film negatives.

"Could I have a glass of orange juice?" she asked a man standing behind the yellow striped awning that stretched over the food and bar stand.

The man smiled at her. The thick flesh of his face bunched in wrinkles around his eyes as he did so.

"Miss, you can have anything your beautiful little heart desires," he answered, looking at her long tanned legs propped up on the bar stand.

She smiled back at him, deciding that his appreciation of her was more approval than the lust she so often encountered in her meetings with strange men.

"It's a beautiful day, isn't it?" she observed amiably, to pay him back for his honest admiration.

"As beautiful as your eyes, darlin', " he said, and bent down to open a large jar of orange juice.

She gazed out at the shimmering, aqua-coloured water of the pool. People were lying on long *chaise lounges* like brown filleted fish. She was so glad that the Washington Hilton had a pool, unlike the one in New York. One of the lifeguards waved at her, thinking that she was staring at him as she stood gazing in his direction at the long, luxurious pool.

"Here ya are," the bar attendant said, and he put a glass of orange juice on the black leather bar.

She put her hand around the icy glass and said, "Thanks."

The bar attendant looked closely at her eyes.

"Turquoise, aren't they?"

"Huh?" she said, sucking the cold liquid into her mouth in small greedy gulps.

"You've got turquoise-coloured eyes, sweetheart."

"Oh yeah," she said vacantly, becoming irritated at the sound of 'sweetheart' on his lips.

"A guy would have to be able to buy a dame like you emeralds to go with those eyes."

"Um hm," she said and walked over to one of the tables. She sat staring out at the sparkling pool, waiting for Eric to show up. Finally she walked out to one of the *chaise longues* and peeled off her shorts and top that she wore over a bikini, then flopped down on the plastic of the *chaise*'s plaited material. She closed both eyes tightly and waited for the perspiration to begin. As it started to bead on her lithe, curving body, she smiled, and turned one shoulder a little, trying to escape the *chaise*'s abrasive material. Finally she gave up and just let it cut into her flesh. The sun beat down on her face and legs more fiercely, and she thought of a short story she had read in high school called "The Hunger Artist."

'I'm being purged here by the sun and this god-awful contraption I'm lying on,' she thought. She shifted one leg up, then down, like a horse discouraging flies. "It's good to get purged," she said out loud. A very corpulent man lying nearby rattled his *Wall Street Journal* angrily when he heard her remark, glaring at her from under his wiry, black and grey eyebrows.

""The Hunger Artist" was right," she said aloud again, forgetting the few stray, sweating bodies near her. Since she had been alone so much in the past few weeks she had begun comforting herself with her own conversation.

"What's happening, Cybele? Is the sun making you delirious?" she heard a masculine voice say.

She opened one eye and squinted up casually at the tall lanky lifeguard standing in front of her. Her composure belied the icy fear his voice had poured over her before she saw whom it belonged to.

"Nah, just reciting a few formulas for a course I'm taking," she lied coolly. 'God, I'm beginning to stay on the defensive,' she thought.

"Oh neat," the guy said, impressed. He squatted down by her, holding one side of the *chaise* with his long arm. Its muscles looked like toughened leather under his tanned flesh. He looked tired, although he was probably in his mid-to-late twenties. The whites of his eyes were red from their constant exposure to the sun.

"Ever read anything by Lawrence Dickey?"

"Nah," she said. "Oh, wait a minute – I got some of his stuff from the Discount, but never read any."

"I'll bring you some of his books if you'll be here tomorrow." He looked down at her with curiosity.

"Sure, I'm always around."

The other guard whistled at him shrilly. They both turned to see Eric standing at the entrance to the pool. His thick, unruly hair curled tawnily in the breeze.

"That your husband?" the guard asked.

She leapt up and waved at Eric. "He wants me to sign him in," she said, without answering his question.

She ran past the lines of *chaise longues*, oblivious to the stares directed towards her from the other bathers. All she could see was Eric standing like a golden mirage in front of her. His long muscular legs curved gracefully from under a pair of cut-off khaki trousers he wore as a bathing suit. Each part of his body was so fresh that she wanted to sing about it! Instead she ran along with her feet stinging from the hot sidewalk, chanting, "Eric, Eric, Eric Star" under her breath.

"You shouldn't run so fast in this heat," he said. His brown eyes gazed playfully into hers.

"Oh Eric!" she exclaimed. She looked at his broad muscular shoulders, hypnotised by their swelling mounds of flesh, then she leaned down and kissed him on his slim, naked waist. The lifeguards watched enviously, fascinated by her enchantment with Eric.

"Hey!" he exclaimed happily, jumping slightly from the touch of her lips. "Right here afore God and everybody, Cybele?"

"Oh Eric," she sighed again. She put both of her hands into his tawny, curling hair. It felt feather soft and emitted a sweet grassy fragrance.

"Down, girl," he said, and leaned down to kiss her on one cheek. A group of fortyish ladies watched them hungrily, temporarily abandoning their novels and knitting.

She felt his warm, full mouth on her face. Her tongue yearned to suck its apple freshness into her own.

"I *adore* you," she murmured, walking along beside him in a daze. "Hey, you came up here to sign me in, remember?" "Hmm?" she said, pressing her shoulder close to his arm. She turned her face up to his so that she could gaze at his tapering cheeks and face once more. "Oh yeah," she said.

His words registered late in her brain through the sensations with which the smell and touch of his fresh young body had dizzied her. She ambled over to the large grey book and wrote his name down, feeling the crisp white page under her hands as she did so. The print waved before her eyes in a melting blur. The heat and severe sunlight etched objects into its own reality, confusing her, frightening her a little, while she stood before the large, meaningless book. But she saw Eric waiting for her when she looked up from the book. His presence was good and real and magical. She ran back to him happily, linking her fingers in his.

"My, aren't we affectionate today?" he remarked, and drew her arm around his waist.

A lady who had been knitting resumed her activity, looking over her knitting needles at them with two hard, round eyes. Cybele punched Eric in his lean stomach like a tomboy. The lady clattered her needles while she watched them intently.

"Don't be too flattered," Cybele said, and pushed him into the pool. He pulled her in after him, laughing.

"Oh m'gosh, you idiot!" he yelled. "My wallet. . . my glasses!" He fumbled up to his temples, searching for his glasses.

"Oh, Eric. Ha, ha. You look so funny with your glasses like that," she said, looking at his thick, round steel-rimmed glasses which hung precariously over the tip of his nose. "And what about all of your money?" she giggled.

He strode swiftly through the water's heavy weight, then hoisted himself up nimbly on the side of the pool.

"I'll be back, witch," he called as he walked over to put his glasses and wallet on the chair.

She swam to the other side of the pool and waited, feeling a delicious sense of excitement from his mock threat. She watched the supple muscles of his back ripple enticingly when he bent over the chair. She had unconsciously clenched the muscles of her stomach at the sight of his body as she held onto the side of the pool.

"So beautiful, so beautiful," she whispered to herself again, and floated her hand along the surface of the water. She turned it palm upwards and enjoyed the pinkness of her flesh in contrast to the turquoise water. "Just like a little seashell," she said, looking at her hand as he splashed up to her.

"Now, Mrs Tashery," he said, and grasped her shoulders menacingly. Without glasses his eyes looked strangely naked.

She touched his eyebrows and eyelids gently.

"You mean you aren't terrified?" he asked, showing his white teeth as he squinted against the sun.

"In the most delightful way, darling," she said, and grabbed his legs with her own, pulling his body close to her.

"You're outasight today, Cybele." He laughed self-consciously, shy suddenly at the intimacy of their bodies. Until the previous evening their relationship had lacked the powerful, serious quality that making love carries with it.

He looked down into the translucent water that separated his chest from her breasts. He seemed reluctant to look at her, yet happy to have her body touching his. His quietness made her solemn. She felt her hand on the flesh of his shoulder and held it there formally, not daring to move her fingers. She didn't want to move her fingers because her movement would make them both aware of their bodies. If they were aware of their bodies, they would have to be conscious of what had happened between them the night before. And that seemed so sacred to both of them that they were loath to realise the responsibility of their newly-formed relationship.

She stirred in front of him, trying to get a better hold on the side of the pool so that she could buoy them both up.

"Hey," he said, almost inaudibly.

"Yes?" she asked softly, afraid to speak in a normal tone.

"This," he declared, then kissed her slowly and deeply. His full warm mouth pressed onto hers like a red, ripe plum. The smell of his flesh and breath mingled with the chlorinated water, and overwhelmed her nostrils with his nascent, boy smell. A wild thrill ran through her hand from the touch of his shoulder on her fingertips. Her body vibrated all over from his touch. She relaxed her knee on the hardness of his leg, allowing it to be seduced by his flesh.

"Oh Eric, Eric," she said, burying her nose in the ladle-like dip of his neck. She put both hands up to his chest like a small child, forgetting to balance herself and Eric in the pool water.

"Watch out!" he cried, and grabbed the side of the pool. "Trying to drown a great relationship?" His eyes were warm and sparkling. Their brown colour danced with the gold of the sun. She dived down deep into their beauty with her own, almost drowning.

"I love you so much that I can't catch my breath!" she declared. She grew afraid as she watched him in front of her. He gazed at her smilingly, placid with pleasure from the moment.

Suddenly she splashed water in his face, wanting to dispel the enchantment that had literally taken her breath away.

"You witch!" he cried, spluttering from the water. "Now whatd'ya do that for?" he asked, looking like a perplexed puppy.

"Because I couldn't breathe," she replied, and batted her eyes at him. They glinted sea-green at him from under her dark lashes.

"I love these drops of water on your face, Cybele," he said, then licked the tiny drops from her chin. "They look like diamonds," he exclaimed.

"Oooh, that tickles!" she giggled. "Listen," she said breathlessly, "let's go and have a bottle of champagne."

"OK," he said. He put his hands around her waist and lifted her up deftly onto the side of the pool.

"Gosh! You're so strong!" she proclaimed. Behind her, two older men watched them with jealous and longing eyes.

"Hi," she said to them awkwardly, embarrassed by their stares. Their mouths wrinkled into weak smiles that resembled eroding earth. Eric leapt up beside her like a strong young weed, shaking and dripping the chlorinated water in pools around his feet.

"Come on," he said. "Let's go and get our champagne." He grabbed her around the waist with one strong, wet arm, and pulled her along beside him. She felt his bathing suit sloshing against her body. Its stiff, corded material stung her sunburned skin. It was like his arm – rough and new, bearing the inexorable resilience of growth and freshness. It cut her flesh with a savage newness. Underneath his hip she felt the sharp bones of his body thrusting into hers.

"What are we celebrating anyway?"

"The beginning of our love," she said, and leaned her face on his arm. Their pleasure bounced around the faces of the pool like a huge beach ball, upsetting the other bathers' novels and knitting needles with its impetuous affections.

They sat down at one of the heavy wrought iron patio tables and waited for a waitress to come over. Cybele slouched down in her chair and flung one foot up on Eric's chair beside his hip. He sat staring at her fixedly like an admiring cat.

"Eric, I adore you when you look torpid." She dug her toenail into the side of his thigh.

"Ouch!" he said, with the same perplexed expression he had had when she splashed water in his face.

"Now you look like a dog again," she giggled, and threw a dirty straw from the table at him.

"You little shit," he said. He grabbed out at her wrist, and missed it. "How can a person look like a dog?" he asked, while rubbing his thigh in pain. A long red welt had appeared under his sunburn.

"When a person looks torpid, he's like a cat," she informed him, and drew both knees up to her chin.

"That's not a very modest pose," he said, looking at the slight bulge of her bikinied crotch.

"You know, Eric, sometimes you're positively conservative."

"Come on," he said persuasively. He drew her legs down and rested her feet on his knees. He looked at her patronisingly, imitating his idea of sageness so intently that one of his eyes almost closed.

"Ha ha, now you look like somebody out of a comic."

He kept on gazing at her like a simpleton sage.

"Anyway, let me tell you, Eric, that when a person looks puzzled and sort of stupid, he looks like some dogs I've seen."

"That's a lie! Dogs are much smarter than cats."

"That proves it," she said, and lifted her feet off his legs scornfully. "You're a dog!"

"Shit!" he said. "This conversation is for the birds."

"May I help you?" A fat, round-faced girl asked. She stood beside Eric like a little doughnut, holding a check pad against her tiny, ruffled apron, and looking at them with curiosity.

"Yes," Eric said grandly. "We'd like a bottle of champagne."

"Anything else?" the girl asked as she wrote on her pad methodically.

"Yes," he said, disappointed that she hadn't reacted a little more to his request. "We'll have one salad – with two plates."

She looked at him briefly, then began writing again.

"God, Eric, you're a scream," Cybele said as the girl walked off.

"Now just *why* am I a scream, Mrs Tashery?"

"Oh, when you try to be sophisticated and everything." She began kicking his ankle softly with her foot.

"Well, everybody can't be like your illustrious Hadrian. That old dude's had a few more years to go at it than I have." His eyes glowed hurt and lambent through his thick glasses. "Why are you picking on me, anyway?"

She compared the circumstances of Eric's life with Hadrian's mentally when she saw his wounded expression.

"Oh Eric," she said. She ran over to his side and flung her arms around his neck. The waitress returned and sat a bucket of ice, with a bottle of champagne nestling inside, down beside them. "You're just as good as Hadrian." She kissed him on his ear. The curls of his hair tickled her nose. "Better!" She sat down again in her chair.

"Why better?" he asked, and began twirling the champagne bottle deeper into the ice.

"Because you don't want power."

"Who told you that? I want power and money and everything else."

"Yes, but you have the capacity to forget about those things, and Hadrian never does."

She watched as he lifted the long green bottle out of the ice and twisted off the cork.

Ice fell from its plump bottom onto the sidewalk, and melted swiftly in the burning summer sun. The cork popped out and landed in her lap.

"Hey, that means good luck, Eric."

He poured the icy, bubbling liquid into the champagne glasses. They lifted the glasses and toasted one another.

"To our love," she said.

"To you, luv, and to bigger and better tab bills," he said, signing her initials on the check.

"Eric, what do you think of my toe?" She pressed her big toe onto the firm flesh of his leg and smiled at him over her glass of frothy liquid.

"Whaddya mean?" he said. He looked at her foot. "It looks like a big fat toe."

"Do you know that I'm usually very sensitive about people looking at my feet?"

She dragged her toe down towards his kneecap. He caught her ankle with his hand and squeezed it, looking meaningfully into her eyes. She felt the hairs of her cunt under the wet bikini she wore. She remembered his dick from the night before, thought of its sharp hard thrusts inside her warm body, and longed to have it there once more.

"So?" He gazed at her with his distinctive, warm look. She felt herself swimming through the brandy colour of his eyes.

"Every time I get a train of thought with you, Eric, something else seems to take over."

"Ha!" he said, then grabbed both of her feet with his hands and placed them on his legs. "We were discussing toes."

"Oh yes. Well, anyway, remember when you swam up to me in the pool?"

"Yeah, yeah," he said, running the tip of his finger over her feet. Its light, teasing touch made her want his hard, thrusting dick even more.

"I was looking at my hand." She held her hand out to him. "And it seemed to be apart from me. When I saw how pink the inside was, it seemed to be a seashell. It was so lovely in the water that I became hypnotised by it."

He ran one of his smooth, firm palms along the calf of her leg. The contact of their flesh made a rustling sound as he rubbed her leg back and forth, back and forth with strong, swift caresses. Two men walked by, clad in pale summer slacks, stopping momentarily to watch his motions on her legs. They walked away hurriedly when they realised that they had stopped to look so blatantly.

"Then you came, and touching your legs with mine was so sweet. . . so dizzying that I lost my breath," she continued. "I really grew afraid that I might not be able to breathe."

"So that's why you splashed me," he said, and squeezed her inner thigh.

"There were so many sensations coming all through my body," she told him, "and it was so pleasant, and then they became like my hand." He took her hand and began kissing its soft, pink palm.

"Things get in the way, you know," she said inexplicably.

"Things?" he inquired. "I'd like to put something in your way."

"Things get in the way and hypnotise you or make you so you can't breathe. It's then that I want to run away." She dipped her tongue into the champagne, allowing it to sting her tongue.

"Have you ever thought about materiality, Eric?"

"Sure, the materiality of this hotel is getting in the way for me to make love to you!" he said, and smiled at her with his desire for her showing frankly in his eyes.

"Oh, I love you!" she said. She pushed her head into his stomach, butting him like a baby calf. She touched his nipple shyly. It felt like a tender brown berry.

"But maybe materiality takes people to other things," she said, pressing up and down on his nipple with her fingertips.

"I guess you just have to concentrate on getting past the things," he said.

"What do you mean?" she asked.

"Well, the other day I read about a man. He drove up to a service station for some gas. When the attendant told him they were closed, he said, 'Oh yeah? Okay, then.' Then he took out a can of gas he had in the trunk of his car and poured it all over the car. He lit a match and said, 'There!' and walked away."

Eric gazed at her, letting his lips glide over his teeth in a slow smile. "You might say he was trying to get rid of the encumbrances of materiality."

"Eric, sometimes you amaze me," she said, and drank the last of her champagne thirstily. She held her glass out to him. He filled it deftly, pouring just the right amount. She leaned back in the hard wrought iron chair and sipped it slowly, savouring its stinging taste.

"Yes, but Eric, after he set the car on fire he was probably arrested. Then think of all the legal rigmarole he had to go through. Maybe they even put him in jail." The bubbles of champagne drifted up into her nose. She wrinkled it automatically from the sensation.

"Maybe," Eric said. "But at least he had the guts to try and beat the system. He drank the champagne quickly, like Coca-Cola.

"The other day I was rushing everywhere," she said. "I parked my car in a parking lot and ran to get some things from a delicatessen. When I came back, my car was blocked by about five other cars. I paid the girl at the counter, then went and sat in my car, waiting for the attendant to move the others. I sat there, dressed in a lot of uncomfortable clothes, with a heavy purse full of stuff I had been lugging around all day beside me and began to think about the solidness of the cars in front of me and the time it took to move them. I began to wonder what it would be like if somehow my car had no mass – materiality – and how I could just drive gracefully forward, maybe even fly if the car and myself and everything weren't substance."

"You probably do have wings, Cybele. They're just hidden," Eric quipped.

"Anyway, Eric, do you think material things lead one to spiritual ones, or do they hamper that journey?"

"They say everything is illusion," he answered lamely.

"Like my hand in the water, and my feeling of suffocation when you swam up?" she persisted.

"If we ran through a field of daisies that might transport you," he said.

"You know, Eric, the other night I dreamed I saw Marlon Brando. He was fucking the corpse of Marilyn Monroe."

Eric sputtered champagne onto his chest. "Eek! That's cold!"

She stood up and started walking away from the table. Eric ran behind her hastily, visibly upset by her erratic change of mood.

"What the hell's wrong with you?"

"Nothing. I just got sick of champagne." She walked along beside him sullenly, then flopped down on the *chaise* where her clothes lay in a little pile without looking at him. He lay down in the chair next to hers and they began baking silently. She turned her head away from him and started to remember her husband again.

The she looked back at Eric, deriving pleasure from his tanned young face and perfectly proportioned body. 'This is the first time I've ever allowed myself to be seduced by the sheer physical beauty of a man,' she thought.

He turned his face to hers and looked solemnly at her with his warm, brown eyes, looking like a subdued puppy. Silently they linked their fingers together and let their arms hang down from the chairs. Their clasped hands brushed the sun-wilted grass under the chairs. They turned their faces back to the scorching sun and began baking slowly in a ritual of sun worship. She returned to her traumatic memories.

"Pierre!" she had cried. "Please don't kill me!"

"Oh, shut up, you dumb bitch," he had said. "Stop being dramatic." He had drawn back from her, looking at her face. "You're so ugly right now," he had said, and spat in her face. She had felt his saliva trickle into one eye, and she turned her head a little to make it run the other way.

"Don't move your head," he had said through clenched teeth, and he had slapped her with a hard, stinging blow. She had ceased her movements, letting the spit run into her eye. "You're so pasty-faced right now," he had said. "God, you're ugly. I can't believe I ever married you, you worthless, stinking bitch," he had said, and pressed his fingernails into her fingers like a knife. Her very existence had seemed to incense him. She had lain in utter dejection under him.

"I've gotta go and get wet," Eric said, looking at her speculatively and trying to determine if her mood had changed. "Wanna go?"

"Nah," she said, without looking at him. She heard the *chaise* creak when he lifted the weight of his body from it, and then his subsequent splash into the pool. Her mind went back to the apartment and her husband.

She remembered holding herself still as a dead person under the weight of his body, wishing somehow that she didn't exist anymore. His eyes had gone past her and stared into the slate-grey landscape of winter that spread outside the window like a Breughel etching.

"I'd like to go home," he had said, and stood up abruptly. She had lain motionless on the floor, waiting to see what he would do next. He sat in one of the kitchen chairs and drummed his fingers irritably on the table. "Could I have some orange juice?" he said.

She sat up slowly, painfully, then stood up and walked towards the refrigerator. Inside were a few dried devilled eggs and a half-eaten ham. The grease from its fat had congealed into a glue-like substance. She took a jar of juice out of the refrigerator and poured some into a glass, then handed it to him.

"There's not enough ice in here," he snarled, and flung the glass down on the floor. She stooped down and began cleaning up the sticky liquid, sobbing with a hopeless despair.

"You bitch!" he had said, and kicked her in the side. The toe of his shoe had grazed her breast, producing a sharp stabbing pain down her side. She fell over into the sticky liquid. He jumped up from his chair and began kicking her legs.

"Bitch, bitch!" he had said, pummelling her relentlessly with his feet. She staggered up and ran to the door, trying to escape. He caught her by her hair and pulled her into the other room.

"Trying to get away, huh? Well, I'll show you." He had looked all around the room. His eyes darted in every corner like a rabid dog. Finally they lit on an old black umbrella in the corner. He rushed and snatched it up, then turned back to her.

"Now I'll show you," he had said. He raised the umbrella like a huge bat. She shrank back against a mahogany chest and put her hands over her head to protect herself.

"Put your hands down," he had said, and flung them away from her head.

"Pierre, please don't. *Please* don't," she had pleaded. "What's wrong? What have I done?"

"I'll show you," he had said. He brought the wooden cane of the umbrella handle down on her head.

She had screamed shrilly as it splintered apart on her skull. A thick, wet stream of blood poured down the side of her face.

"Shut up!" he had said savagely, and clamped his hand over her mouth. She bit his fingers as hard as she could, and struggled away from him, trying to reach the door again. He ran after her, catching her with both of his arms around her waist. He squeezed her until she lost her breath again.

"Oh God, oh God, I wish I were dead!" she had wailed.

He had picked the umbrella up and beat her over her back with it until its steel spines were bent apart like the limbs of a tree that has been struck by lightning, then stood panting over her.

"Bite me, will you?" he yelled. he reached down and took her hands and bit her fingers methodically.

Cybele shifted her weight in the broiling sun, and groaned. She had begun to cry in dry, jerking sobs.

He wanted to go home after that fight, she remembered. 'Wanted to see his father, "The Great French Aristocrat",' she thought bitterly. She turned onto her stomach and watched Eric as he floated calmly on his back in the pool. She stood up abruptly and walked over to the pool.

"It's great in here," Eric called.

"Is it?" she said. Her eyes were clouded by sadness.

"Yeah, come on in."

"Okay," she said dejectedly, and slipped into the icy water. She swam up to him and placed both of her hands on his shoulders, letting her forefingers trace themselves along his collar-bone. He saw the tears in her eyes.

"What's the matter? Do you miss your husband again?" he asked.

She giggled hysterically.

"C'mon, let's get outta here," he said, looking at her, worried.

They got out of the pool and gathered up their belongings that lay in wilted little heaps on the chairs. The sun blinded them as its rays slanted across the elaborate chrome and glass of the hotel.

"Ready, luv?" he asked, studying her expression and trying to handle her mood with delicacy.

She shrugged, and walked off without answering. He followed her, not trying to make any further conversation. He knew from the short experience of their relationship that she was thinking about her husband.

They climbed into his dusty little car and roared off down Connecticut Avenue.

"Hey, stop here," she yelled above the engine's noise. He pulled over to the side of the street.

"What now?" He rested one elbow on the steering wheel and squinted at her through his thick glasses.

She could see his bare toes pressed down on the brake pedal. The length of his leg stretched long and curving, down to the black, furry carpeting of the floorboard. Its line mesmerised her for a moment.

"Gotta go to the laundry," she said, while staring at the flowing curves of his bare chest and shoulders.

"Is this your old dry cleaners that you had with Pierre?"

"Yeah, why?" she asked.

"I guess you'll leave him a note or something dramatic like that?" He said and pinched his handsome mouth into a scowl.

"Sure, why not?" she said, and flung open the door. "Say, this must be your 'animal time'." She looked pointedly at his bare chest as she leaned down by the low-slung car door. "You usually keep yourself all covered up, like it's just too good to let anyone see. Such vanity there is in modesty, my dear friend!"

He reached for his shirt. She kicked the car door and said, "If you put that on, I'm not getting back in this car!"

He looked at her bitterly, then threw the shirt behind his seat with contempt.

"See ya," she said, and walked into the dry cleaners.

She came out of the laundry with a package of blue sheets. When she got back into the car, Eric didn't say anything. He jerked the car into gear and sped along down Connecticut Avenue.

"Eric, what time is it?"

"Fuck it all," he yelled. "Why do you always ask me that same question? You know my clock's in your apartment.

She watched as he sat looking at the red light in front of them, waiting for it to change. His cheeks were burning with excitement under their sunburn, and his hair seemed to explode around his face in snarled curls. She glanced down at his groin automatically, feeling the heat of his desire on her legs as if it were the sun above them. The trees in Dupont Circle swayed heavily with their summer burden of leaves, enclosing the splashing marble fountain like green, undulating arms. Men trudging home from work had taken off their ties, and fat housewives sat on benches watching freaks walking and sitting in the grass. A young girl with long blonde hair sat on a bench near the shell-white fountain, wiping dripping ice cream from her little girl's dress.

"Oh Eric, let's not argue," she entreated and touched his kneecap with her fingertips affectionately.

"Yes, let's not," he agreed. His face was alive and angry with emotion. He switched on the car's sound system as loud as it would go. It blared through the stifling afternoon heat in a cow-like moan.

"Eric!" she screamed when he jerked the car to the side of the road suddenly, trying to avoid hitting an old man. The decrepit man turned his head dumbly towards their car and peered at them with fear. He raised his cane and began waving it angrily.

"Hippies, bums!" he shouted.

A siren whined up behind them.

"Oh fuck," Eric said, and reached for a cigarette. "This is all I need."

A patrol car roared past them, narrowly missing the same old man. The man stopped in the middle of the street, stretching and craning his neck as if he were in a wild jungle beset by unpredictable beasts.

"Shit," Eric said. "The whole world's fucked. I've gotta go by my place soon. Whaddaya wanna do in the interim?"

"Why do you have to go to your place soon?"

"Very simple. We've got a load of dope coming, and I've gotta be there to cut it."

"Why don't we go and get Porgy some shrimp?"

"Shit," he said.

"No, shrimp." She corrected him, and ran her fingers through his tangled hair while they sped along in the hot summer air.

They wheeled down M Street and on into Georgetown over the old cobblestones of the street. Eric purposely steered the car into defunct streetcar tracks, making it sway violently back and forth, laughing at her squeals of protest as they jostled along. He pulled up to Cannon's seafood market and waited while she ran inside. In front of him the street plunged down into a steep hill to K Street. He watched bikers walking their bikes across the bumpy stone sidewalks of the canal pathway. A stream of gaily clothed hippies poured in and out of the yellow façade of health food store, bearing bags and boxes of strange looking foods.

She came running back to the car carrying a plastic bag full of shrimp. Her brown legs moved nimbly as she picked her way over the dipping stone sidewalk.

"I hope that shit ain't going to smell up my car," he complained.

"Listen, Eric, why don't we walk down to Brandon's place?" she suggested.

"Brandon who?" he asked, sounding bored.

"He's a really neat friend of mine," she said persuasively.

"Okay, c'mon, but I gotta be back at my apartment soon."

"I'm supposed to be home for a call at 6:30," she volunteered.

"From the big H, I guess," he replied sarcastically.

"C'mon," she said, ignoring his reference to Hadrian, and opened his door.

"Stick the shrimp under the seat then, so nobody'll take them." He got out and watched her stoop down to his seat. The sight of her slender back evoked a protective, almost fatherly expression on his young face that was incongruous with his youth and touching in its tenderness.

"Hi," he said when she stood up, and began kissing her softly by her temple, feeling the silky hair that grew there in little secret whorls with his warm soft lips. She glanced at him with curiosity, wondering at his unexpected expression of tenderness.

"I can't wait for you to meet Brandon," she said as they walked along Wisconsin Avenue.

"I'm sure he's terrific," he replied, jealous and hostile again.

"Oh Eric, please," she protested, and linked her arm around his sweaty body. "See how much I love you," she said, and smeared his perspiration on her hand then licked it.

"Very impressive," he said, still looking sullen.

"Oh, you're impossible!" She picked his arm up and let it flop back abruptly on his side. He walked along silently beside her. His semi-naked body looked like an untamed, tawny lion set loose in the streets.

"God, you're beautiful, Eric!" She began stroking his arm playfully.

"Get off the shit, will you?" he complained and spurted ahead of her in irritation. His long, muscular legs pulled him through the streets in great gallops. She ran behind him, panting from the heat.

"Hey, this is like caveman – I follow you! OK, caveman, you lead and I— Ow!" she screamed, and grabbed one foot, hopping up and down on the other to keep her balance.

Eric stopped walking and turned around to her reluctantly, looking at her with a feigned disgust. The expression on his full, inviting mouth gave it the appearance of an exotic flower.

She concentrated on his mouth as he walked up to her. She wanted to touch every part of it with her fingers, then suck its red, warm flesh between her lips.

He took her foot in his hand and scrutinised it well. The nail on one toe was torn and bleeding.

"You know, if you'd just wear shoes, Cybele, you wouldn't have these problems."

She looked down at his well shaped feet, at the shell pink nails of his toes placed so perfectly by nature in his tanned flesh.

"But Eric, *you* don't have any shoes on."

"Hey, watch out!" he cried and jerked her out of M Street onto the sidewalk as a car rushed by.

"C'mon," he said, pulling her along by one hand.

"Where're we going?" she asked, hobbling behind him.

"Shut up and just follow. Me Tarzan – remember?" He looked back over his shoulder at her, smiling and showing his white teeth in a dazzling, gopherlike grin.

"Me Jane," she said, hopping on one foot after him.

He pushed her into a dimestore and went up to a shelf containing aspirins and ointments. She watched him pick up a bottle of alcohol.

"Where's the cotton?" he inquired, studying the rows and rows of items.

She looked back wistfully at the embroidery counter. 'I need some red thread,' she thought suddenly, and went running down to the shelf of brightly coloured threads and imported linen doilies and pillowcases.

"Here it is," Eric said. He plucked up a weightless, medicinal smelling box of cotton from the shelf, then stood up, expecting to find her standing behind him. Instead he saw her several aisles in front of him, studying the fat, colourful bodies of thread packets.

"What the hell are you doing?" he demanded. He carried the alcohol and cotton over to her as if he were a hospital orderly.

"Just getting some thread," she explained, without turning around.

"Christ, you gotta be kidding me," he said, exasperated.

"You know that I do embroidery, Eric," she said, turning back to him with three packages of red thread.

"I know." He jostled his packages importantly. "But at a time like this?" He raised one eyebrow sternly, looking like a bleary-eyed idiot through his thick glasses.

She started to giggle.

"Ha, ha, oh Eric, we're crazy, far-out insane. You know that, don't you?"

"Hold still." He uncapped the alcohol, and sponged some of it onto her toe.

"Ow!" she yelled while he blew furiously on her injured toe to avert the pain.

"Say, didn't you kids see the sign on our door?" a stout man with deep furrows in his forehead said. "No one is allowed in here barefoot."

"They must have just started that," Eric said belligerently.

"Have you paid for those items?" the man clamoured. His white shirt crinkled like starch around his sloping fat shoulders.

"Don't worry, we're going to pay," Cybele said. Her green eyes stared at him like a fierce cat.

"I merely wanted to apply a little first aid to the lady's foot," Eric explained with grandiose chivalry, and daubed gently at Cybele's foot.

"Better pay up and go then," the man said. The furrows in his forehead resembled the wrinkles on a fat dog's head.

Eric and Cybele stood up and sailed past him, knocking their hips against one another rhythmically as they walked along.

"What an ass-hole," Eric said.

"He looked like an old dog, with his forehead all wrinkled like that."

Cybele agreed, feeling the chill of the store's gelid air-conditioning penetrate her flesh.

"Gosh, it's nice to be back outside," she said when the heat washed over her limbs like a warm tide as they came out of the store.

"Where is this joint we're going to?" Eric asked, bobbing beside her in long, erratic strides.

"Oh, just down the road a piece," she told him, emphasising the traces that were left of her southern accent. "Eric, I wish I had a leash and collar. I could put it around your neck and give Brandon a real gas."

"Cut the crap – you Jane, me Tarzan, remember?"

They walked up to Wisconsin Avenue and turned right by an old, gold-domed bank building. People hovering in front of stalls filled with gaily coloured clothes, with labels that read "MADE IN INDIA", slowed down their pace. She darted across the street unexpectedly and halted in front of an old music store.

"Now listen, Eric, this is one of my best friends, and he's definitely not used to shit – OK?"

"Look, Cybele, one more word and I'm not even gonna go in."

"I just want to warn you what a great guy he is – I mean, he's even written music for concerts. He was a professor, his aunt has oil wells, and. . ." She elaborated, her eyes getting wider and wider.

"Oh Christ," Eric protested, but he was secretly impressed. "Don't hassle me, will you?"

"OK, come on in then," she said, and walked cautiously through the doorway of the shop.

Brandon sat behind a large wooden desk, holding a phone receiver.

"Now, Margaret Lee, I know it's going to be a great party," they heard him say. His curly blond-haired head was inclined severely with the evident strain that the conversation was producing on him. He reached for a package of Lucky Strikes lying on his desk and took one out and put it between his lips.

"Yes, of course, Margaret Lee," Brandon said, and glanced up at Eric and Cybele. He raised one eyebrow inquiringly at Cybele when he saw Eric, then motioned for them to sit down. Cybele led Eric over to a big rocking chair and sat down in it like a silky, satisfied cat. It reassured her when she felt its smooth wood under her body. She pointed to a small wicker chair, indicating to Eric that he should sit there, then held her fingers to her lips and turned all of her attention back to Brandon. Eric scowled at her, intimidated by her obvious respect for the young man in front of them, but he obeyed her command and sat very still. With his hair curling out in every direction, Eric looked like a comet halted in flight.

"Margaret Lee, there is just no way I can make that party tonight. Now get that out of your head." Brandon's unlit cigarette wiggled up and down in his mouth when he talked. Cybele saw that he was searching for a match and leapt up to get a packet of matches from the far side of his desk. Brandon's green eyes crashed together like marbles during his conversation. His decisive, well-shaped mouth was partially hidden by the phone. She leaned over and lit his cigarette, admiring his red and white plaid shirt and the tan, cowboy-style pants he wore as she did so. She touched his shirt and whispered, "That's cute."

"Thank you," he mouthed at her while listening to the rather rasping voice on the other end of the line. He pointed at the receiver and rolled his eyes to the ceiling. Again she noticed a gold, antique ring that he wore on his finger.

"Given to me by my grandfather, whose grandfather gave it to his father," he had told her.

She sat back down in the old rocking chair and began rocking methodically while she watched Brandon. Eric looked around uncertainly in the deep gloom of the shop. Assorted golden harps sat like gilded personages beside dark red mahogany violins and other musical instruments. Stacks and stacks of sheet music were arranged on wide, wooden shelves.

"Yes, you can bring me some left-over *hors d'oeuvres*, Margaret Lee," Brandon said.

He looked like a slim cowboy as he drew deeply on his Lucky Strike. A multicoloured tiffany lamp hung just above his desk. Its yellow and red glass was like scalloped butterfly wings.

"God!" Brandon exclaimed after he had hung up.

He viewed Cybele with a practical, discerning gaze, then glanced at Eric. Cybele watched Brandon's expression with satisfaction. She knew that he understood that she had brought Eric by for his inspection. She also knew Brandon was busy trying to figure out what she was using Eric for. He walked out from behind the desk, saying "old witch" in reference to the caller, laughing as if it were a situation the three of them shared, but observing Eric and Cybele closely with his serious, penetrating eyes.

"What are you up to?" Brandon asked Cybele, and ran his fingers through his matted hair. He looked at Eric again with curiosity.

"Oh, swimming. . . running. I'm injured," she said, and held her foot up. Brandon looked down at the bulky white bandage on her foot.

"Looks like you've had a little first aid," Brandon said.

Eric shifted his weight in the straw mesh chair and drew his legs closer together. He desired to be neater in the presence of Cybele's interesting friend. Brandon's eyes again darted back to Eric when he heard the mesh of Eric's chair creak.

"But I always live, now don't I?" she said, not realising that her face betrayed a strange expression. She was too busy concentrating on Brandon's pale green eyes staring into hers.

"Who's your friend?" Brandon asked finally, after having waited for an introduction that was not forthcoming.

"Oh!" she exclaimed and looked at Eric. "This is my slave, Eric. Eric, this is Brandon."

"Hi," Eric said. He sat awkwardly in the chair. His tanned muscular body overflowed its confines with a healthy, animal-like vitality. He looked like a golden stallion at bay in the shadowy interior of the music shop.

"Nice to meet you," Brandon said, accepting Eric because he was with Cybele. "Looks like you two've been having fun. I guess you've been swimming?"

"Yeah, it was really great in the pool," Eric volunteered, then clammed up again.

Cybele looked at Brandon's long, pencil-thin legs in front of her, enjoying the tan colour of his slacks and the bright red and white checks of his shirt.

"You're lucky," Brandon said. His soft-syllabled accent soothed Cybele and reassured her of the old stable culture they had both left in the South.

"You know I always invite you, Brand," Cybele said, and batted her eyes at him coquettishly. "But you just never will come.

"Who's going to stay in this shop?" Brandon asked.

"You know *I* would – anytime. I've been reading a book about Dvorak. I just might get knowledgeable on music."

Brandon squeezed her knee with a brotherly sort of affection.

"This is a nice shop," Eric said, trying to enter the conversation. He looked at a gothic, piano-like instrument with chimes on top of it. "What's that?" he asked.

"A Lyrasluger, German made – a real collector's item," Brandon explained. "Why don't you look around?" he said affably.

Cybele realised that he was being exceedingly accommodating to invite an unknown person to view his collection of instruments so openly. He had a strong sense of property and ownership, ingrained from his southern upbringing, and did not easily open his domain to strangers. But his affectionate relationship with Cybele lowered his self-protective instincts towards Eric.

"Where did you find him?" Brandon whispered when Eric had reached the far end of the shop. "Oh, there's some interesting things in the back room," he called to Eric, trying to get him further away from their conversation.

Eric floated into the other room in a mass of long tanned legs and curly hair. His makeshift khaki bathing suit had dried and clung tightly to his firm, round muscled rump like clay.

"He's 'the other man'," Cybele explained, crossing her legs prettily in front of him. Her long sexy calves were positioned together like tapering fruit.

"I don't even have to guess who's idea that was," Brandon surmised.

Cybele flung her head back against the back of the rocking chair. Its rich brown wood curved smoothly behind her and framed her head with its carved flutes.

"Can't really blame Hadrian though," Cybele said. "What with Pierre running around looking for me with a gun."

Brandon looked out the door of his shop with a mechanical apprehension. His cheek moved suddenly with a nervous tic. Her words had affected his strict sense of social propriety. She noticed his reaction immediately, and felt a little like a gun moll sitting in an eighteenth-century painting. She resented vehemently being cast in the role.

"How do you like him?" Brandon asked. "Doesn't seem your usual type."

"He's beautiful – like a young stag, or something like that," she smiled. "It was just supposed to be a casual thing. I mean, Hadrian wanted Eric to take me around to places where Pierre might be." She clutched the sturdy handles of the rocking chair, feeling the bones of her fingers clasped on the flowing undulations of its wood. "And he's been doing just that. We've been having a lot of fun." She felt a slight dampness under her thighs and sighed. The shop was not air-conditioned, and her head had begun to ache in the stifling heat. She looked out of the door of the shop, searching hopefully for storm clouds.

"God, it's hot," she declared.

"You look tired," Brandon noticed sympathetically.

"I don't know, I shouldn't be," Cybele said. "I sleep ten hours a day."

"That doesn't count for emotional tiredness. You're sleeping that long to escape," he said.

"How do you know everything?" Cybele asked.

"I've been through a lot." Brandon put his foot up on one of the sharp rockers of the chair. The soft leather of his boot gave a little on the jutting wood. She put her bare foot, with its bandaged toe, on top of his foot and pushed at it with her injured toe. She looked up into his eyes ironically. The seriousness of his gaze waved like a grey-green sea in front of her, one that had recently been turbulent in a storm, but now moved strong and silent, still swollen from its fight.

"You're in a destructive mood today," he said.

"My moods vary," she sighed.

"Yeah, from bad to worse," Eric said, having overheard part of their conversation as he walked up.

"Ah, here it comes," she said sarcastically. "My beautiful little puppy dog."

"Look," Eric said heatedly, "I'm not going to take this shit."

"Why don't you take off then?" she said, challenging.

"You really wait me to? 'Cause for five cents. . ."

"You'll do anything, right?" She smiled condescendingly at him, enjoying controlling his reactions like a yo-yo.

"Now, children," Brandon said. At thirty he made a poor father substitute for the two of them.

They both lapsed into a sulky silence.

"Eric, want to see some stuff Pierre did?" Cybele asked and walked over to three pieces of sculpture sitting on an old desk.

"No!" Eric said, looking at the sculpture avidly.

Cybele touched a large, Robin Hood-like figure of a man archer, then picked up another sculpture of a girl playing a harp. Her smiling, pearl-glazed face and gaily flung-out arm seemed to be symbolic of a person saying, "Follow me! I know the way!" But the emotion in her position near the harp suggested an unnatural confidence, as if the girl somehow knew that her quest might prove impossible.

"Wonder what she's trying to tell us?" Cybele mused, making more of a statement than a question as she looked at Brandon.

Brandon took the statue from her hand and contemplated it seriously. He ran his fingers over her jutting breasts and thrown out hip. "I don't know," he said, still touching each part of the sculpture. "I used to like it. I even had it upstairs for a while."

"And everyone knows that not many things or people are allowed up there," Cybele commented. Her voice was sharp with irony.

"No, they aren't, are they?" he replied. The dignified tone of his voice warned her not to be sarcastic with him. His eyes frightened her a little. They told her: "No, my dear, I am not the puppy type – so *don't* go too far."

"I think it smells," Eric said, transferring all of his frustration to the object Brandon held. "Looks inhuman," he continued, "Like death. . . ugh!" Small flecks of spittle had gathered in the sides of his mouth with the intensity of his speech.

"It does have a decapitative quality, doesn't it?" Brandon agreed, still staring queerly at Cybele. She stopped rocking and shivered in the heat. She wanted to leave, to get away from the gaping smile of the strange, ethereal girl.

"I've gotta be back home for Hadrian's phone call, Eric," she said and stood up from the chair, averting her eyes from Brandon's. She wanted to escape from his expression. His words had skilfully conjured up a mood of dread in her. She wondered if he had worked this particular magic on her purposely, in order to get rid of her and Eric.

They left Brandon standing with the piece of sculpture still in one hand. His crisp, slender form was outlined by the darkness of the objects around him. His softly murmured, "Take care, glad to meet your friend" wafted out behind them like feathers.

"You're late for your call," Eric said as they walked along the burning hot sidewalk.

"How do you know?" she asked.

"There were only about thirty clocks in that place," Eric said with a ferocity that was comic.

"Oh yes, Brand *does* have a penchant for clocks – musical clocks. Time and music are related, you know. Well, what'd you think of him?"

"Who?"

"Brand, of course."

"He's OK," Eric muttered. "But you were awful in there."

"Well, Brand understands. I'm often like that around him. We're like cousins. I mean, both being from the South and all."

"You sure seem to love him," Eric said.

"He's written music for several Broadway plays." She looked at Eric, waiting for him to be impressed, but he just opened the door of the car and waited for her to climb over to her side.

"Gosh, we got here quick," she said. She stepped over the car door into her seat and sat down. He cranked up the car brusquely. The little green car careened through the heavy traffic as they sped back towards her apartment.

"Have you ever heard of the American Chili Company?" she yelled over the car's engine and the five o'clock traffic that had grown even thicker at six o'clock. Although Eric didn't turn his head or make any comment, she knew that he had heard her. "His family owns it! He's probably one of the richest bachelors in the United States!"

"Why don't you marry him then?" he said, cryptically. He pushed the car gear into third, hurling them faster and faster down the street.

"Are you kidding?" she screamed. "He's gay, Eric – couldn't you tell?"

"No. I mean, how the hell should I know?" He wheeled around into the parking lot of her apartment building. "Listen, if old fuck face doesn't call, me and a bunch of my friends are maybe going to a rock concert at about ten tonight – interested?"

"Sure, great," she said, hopping out of the car. She was anxious to get Hadrian's phone call, to hear his gruff accented voice in her ear telling her what to do, orienting her somehow. She started to walk away when Eric caught her by one arm.

"Hey," he said, smiling at her.

"What?" she asked.

"C'mere," he said, and pulled her back down to him.

They kissed as they had in the pool. Their fresh warm lips clung together with a tender, sweet pressure. The scent of growing summer leaves filled her nostrils and combined with the smell of his flesh until she swayed like the gently moving tree boughs that hung over them.

"Eric, Eric," she whispered.

"What is it, Mrs Tashery?" he whispered passionately.

She heard a clattering sound behind her, and twisted back to see where it was coming from. Above the back entrance was the landlord's apartment. Her eyes travelled upwards to the source, stopping when she saw Mr Masters' bulky figure in the window motioning angrily to Eric and herself. He shook a blunt finger at them like an outdated schoolmaster and scowled down at them from under his bushy, grey eyebrows.

"Whaddaya looking at?" Eric asked. He followed her gaze upwards to the old, gnarled looking man.

"Nobody," she said, still studying the landlord and his menacing gestures.

"Looks like Boris Karloff," Eric commented.

She stood up from their position of embrace. The languid summer air of early evening gave her a particular sort of strength with its grassy, leafy perfume.

"Okay, maybe I'll see you later," he said.

"Yeah, maybe," she replied and walked desultorily towards the apartments' back entrance way.

The landlord yelled down to her again, but she couldn't understand what he said – only that he spoke angry words, because of his garrulous tone.

She remembered the first day she had come to the old hotel and apartment building. She had gone out for her daily sunbathe with Porge. The grounds behind the antiquated building were green and spacious with large, graceful trees spreading cool areas of shade over daffodils and tulips.

She took a deep breath of fresh air and lay down on the thick green grass near a lovely rose garden. Porge gambolled about the yard, delighted with his freedom from countless nights in a hotel room. She watched him from under her sunglasses as she lay peacefully under the rays of a late May sun. Soon she fell asleep.

She was awakened by clumps of soft, cool dirt falling swiftly on her legs and feet. She saw Porge digging frantically under one of the yellow rose bushes as if he were after a mole.

"Porge!" she cried, and walked over to see what he was doing.

Suddenly the old landlord sprang out from nowhere with a big rusty shovel. He pushed Cybele backwards and yelled out:

"Get away from my flowers, you derned cat!"

He swung the shovel down with all his might, aiming for Porge's back.

"Noooo!" Cybele screamed. "Porge, look out!"

The cat looked back at the old man, and spurted ahead just in time for the shovel to land in the dirt behind his last paw track.

"Oh Porge, Porge!" she cried and rushed over to her cat. But the old man blocked her way.

"There're things under them rose bushes that nobody knows and nobody ain't gonna know," he mumbled dementedly.

He leaned down swiftly and picked up Porge, who cowered under a red rose bush. Porge wasn't used to violence, so he didn't comprehend that the man was really after him.

"Now get out of here, you old alley cat." the tall, big framed old man yelled, and threw Porge viciously out into the driveway.

Porge ran under a bush and hid.

"You shouldn't be sunbathing out here with clothes like them on," the old man told her and looked meaningfully at her bikini. "You might be seen by some bad people that way."

She only stared at him, unnerved into speechlessness by his menacing manner. He looked at her a moment more, then turned and walked back into his apartment complex through the back entranceway.

She ran over to Porge and grabbed him up to her breasts.

"Oh Porge, you poor darlin', he could have killed you!" She felt the large cat trembling in her arms as she walked over with him to gather up her things. The sunlight winked and dappled itself invitingly on the rose garden near the place where Porge had been digging. Cybele stood looking for some evidence of his passionate interest. She stood for a few moments longer, looking at the mounds of earth, then started to go on inside and wait for Eric. Suddenly, her gaze fell on a small white object. She leaned down and picked it up.

'A bone?' she thought, and turned the small bone around in her hand. 'It looks like a little animal's backbone,' she concluded, puzzled.

She looked at the bone curiously. There were two joints that bent.

"My gosh! Could it be the bone of a little finger?"

She felt a strange chill go down her back and prickle up the hair under her neck.

"Ugh!" she shuddered. "I'll show it to Hadrian," she decided.

"C'mon, Porge," she said. "We don't want any part of the old fart's rose garden!"

Chapter Three

Eric wheeled out from under the cumbrous old oak trees after she had walked away, thinking happily of the new load of dope he would receive that night if everything went as arranged. He turned his sound system back up and sat waiting for a red light impatiently, working his mouth back and forth over his teeth and gums in a habitual, nervous reaction. Commuters going back to homes in Maryland glanced with curiosity at him as he sat half naked in his little green sports car, making odd movements with his mouth. A burly truck driver pulled up beside Eric and studied him for a few minutes, then spat almost into his open car. Eric looked towards the red, shiny doors of the truck, startled by the slight spray of spittle he felt on his naked shoulder. He heard the driver chuckle and stared up into his wide, brown-toothed smile.

"Whereya going, boy, dressed up so fancy and all? To the wars?" the man asked sarcastically. His mean eyes inspected Eric's slim young torso enviously.

"No, I've already been," Eric said, contemplating the truck driver's dirty face. A belligerent, comical expression of ignorance shone out of the man's eyes.

"Oh, you one of them Vietnam veterans, eh?"

"You might say that," Eric said and turned his eyes back to the stop light.

"Sheeut! You hippies get shipped over to 'Nam, walk around in the bushes a few months, step in some mud puddles, and phhtt. . . you're back in beau-ti-ful America. Life's just a big party – right, pal?"

The light turned green and Eric stepped down hard on the gas pedal. The man's nasty, leering expression stayed in his mind. His whiskered, perspiring face took Eric back to the days when he had walked around in bushes and stepped in mud puddles. To the days when he had seen sweaty, unshaven faces scream as he blew their stomachs open and their insides fell out into the mud that they stood in.

Five other guys were sitting around in the living-room waiting for him when he arrived at the apartment that he shared with Jeff. Their faces were tense with excitement, even though they passed a joint around and dragged on it with an exaggerated casualness.

Eric recognised all of the signals and knew that the dope had arrived.

"Where is it?"

"Right outside, under the air-conditioner. They loaded it in at 3 a.m. last night," an agile, thin guy dressed in faded Levis and a Levi jacket said. His dark hair hung down in whimsical wisps around his collar-bone and curled in bangs over his forehead.

"Great," Eric said. He flexed his fingers a few times to get ready for the feel of the dope in his hands, for the measuring process on the small, metal scales in his bedroom.

The dark-haired guy stood up, pushing at his beaded Indian headband nervously. The seat of his worn Levis wrinkled in two tiny tucks on his flat, bony behind.

"Sit down, Danny," Tom said, adjusting the black cowboy hat that he wore with his large hands and moving a pair of elaborate silver boot spurs against a black lacquered coffee table in front of him to punctuate his remarks. Tom scowled out from under his hat, looking carefully at the other three guys in the room. Finally he shifted one long, black-clad leg like a lengthy piece of liquorice and said, "Raymond, you're it, fuck-face!"

Raymond stood up uncertainly, grinning sheepishly for no reason. His extremely long legs pushed him up to such a height that he had to stoop when he entered the low doorway of the kitchen.

"Where ya going, ass?" Tom said.

"Orange juice," Raymond called from the kitchen.

"Shit, that orange juice fed brat," a stubby legged fat guy sitting on a rug in the corner said.

"I like to drink something else," his red-haired companion on the rug said, and sniffed loudly. Everyone guffawed. The boy's freckled, pug nose made him seem more of the age to sniff candy instead of cunt.

"OK, let's cut the shit," Tom said. His black shirt and black pants gave him the appearance of a modern-day Hopalong Cassidy as he sat on the black leather couch.

Raymond emerged from the kitchen carrying a tiny glass of orange juice. He raised it in a small salute, then downed it and sat the glass on the floor. He leaned over and picked up his cream-coloured, Spanish-style hat and cut the air with it in reference to Tom's remarks. Everyone laughed again.

"Come on, meat-head," Eric said, and walked out of the room. His fingers tingled with excitement, and his stomach felt icy inside over its tightly clinched muscles.

Raymond adjusted his hat with the thumb and forefinger of his hand, pulling it down decisively over his blond, curly hair. He looked around at the others with his sea-green eyes and smiled capriciously.

"Butt-hole," Tom muttered.

"What say, Hopalong?" Raymond asked drolly as he followed Eric out of the beamed ceiling living-room and into the long hallway.

Danny got up nervously and stood by a wooden table that stretched its long slatted top in front of two sweeping windows. The branches and leaves of wilting wild flowers and pussy willows in a tall vase sitting on the table brushed the sleeve of his Levi jacket. He fumbled in an upper pocket of his faded blue jacket and pulled out a long American cigarette. His pocket was embroidered with a bright red and yellow butterfly.

"Ain't nervous are you, Danny boy?" the freckled faced, red-haired boy mocked him again and laughed shrilly.

"Shut up," Danny said irately. He wheeled around to the guy so suddenly that he upset the vase of flowers.

"Flower boy, flower boy!" the boy chanted.

Danny sat the vase back up and began picking up the flowers, disgusted.

"Better cut it," Tom advised, grinning. "He may be little, but he's sure as hell mean."

Danny stuck one hand up and made the peace sign. He squatted with his back towards them, still gathering the flowers.

Eric led the way down the darkened hallway. The shadows on his golden shoulders were burnished and glowing in the dark like fine old furniture. Raymond loped along behind him with swift, sure strides. The silver braid of Spanish coins on his hat glinted in the dimness.

Had he had guns on his hips, he and Eric might have been going to a showdown.

High noon had long since passed when they walked out into the lengthening shadows of early evening. Eric pushed the door open and stood for a moment on the threshold, looking guardedly about at the street in front of them. Raymond hung behind him like a well-oiled gun. Eric clinched his fingers, then let them go loose, allowing their maddening, jangling tingle to vibrate upwards from his fingertips and shoot through his whole body. When he could stand the vibration no longer, he made fists of his hands and walked out of the door.

The mellow rays of sunlight were still sharply hot at seven o'clock that July evening in 1971 as Eric strode casually down the slanting stone steps. The triangular blades of the clipping shears he had brought with him were balanced in his hand like the beak of a metal parrot. Their black lacquered handle was sleek and polished. He opened and closed them mechanically, deriving a sense of rhythm and the beginning of a plan from their movement.

"Gotta go cut a few bushes, my man," he said to Raymond, hearing his own voice echo hollow in his ears. Raymond snorted, feeling a little nonplussed by their play acting. "Why don't you stay here and fry your brains in the sun, son?" Eric punned as he strode out towards the bushes growing around their apartment building.

Raymond stood on the steps, using a toothpick to clean his fine white teeth with expertise. His incredibly tall frame was slouched gracefully on the iron railing of the porch. His movements were indolent, blunted deliberately with an elaborate casualness, but from under his wide-brimmed hat his eyes skirted the street and windows of the houses around them with the acumen of a hawk. From time to time he scratched the back of his head, disturbing his fancy hat. He shifted the toothpick in his mouth from side to side like a cow masticating its cud. The fatuity of his oral actions belied the shrewd alertness in his sea-green eyes.

Eric pushed the knifelike blades of the pinking shears into the stubby green bushes and began cutting their tops and sides with quick, superficial motions. He eyed the humming air-conditioner under his bedroom window cautiously, allowing himself to glance at it for a moment, then jerked his eyes back to the long clicking blades of the shears. His eyes darted back and forth between the air-conditioner and the shears like a horse's wild glance when reminded of its duty by a stinging flick from its master's reins. He began to perspire in the heat. His arms ached from their interminable motions. As he drew near the bushes around the air-conditioner, Raymond gave a low, trilling whistle. Eric looked over at him quizzically, unaware that he had got so close to his destination. When he saw that he was almost in front of the air-conditioner, he remembered the prearranged signal immediately.

"Coast must be all clear," he muttered under his breath, then called out to Raymond, "Hey, how about a box for some of this stuff?" He pointed down at the fallen branches and leaves around his feet.

"Sure thing," Raymond said, and he picked up a cardboard box sitting in the doorway. He carried it out to where Eric was standing. Their eyes met briefly, then they both kneeled down and began gathering up the short branches and leaves.

"Hold the box over here a minute, will you?" Eric said, nodding at the underside of the air-conditioner. Raymond placed the box of leaves directly beneath the air-conditioner, hiding the large package of grass and dope that was taped there. Eric took out a pocket knife and cut the tape that held the package, allowing it to drop into the mass of foliage. He quickly dug a hole through the branches and secured the dope deep inside the box, then covered it over hastily with leaves.

"Stay cool," Raymond muttered, "There's an old bag behind us."

An elderly woman walked towards them, squinting in the sunlight through a pair of horn-rimmed glasses.

"You boys keeping the place up, I see." She held one arthritic hand over her eyes like a shade' to protect herself from the glare of the waning daylight. Its back was dappled profusely with large brown liver spots.

"Yes, ma'am," Eric said, patting the leaves over the dope and smiling at her happily.

"Well, it's nice to see a fine young man like yourself fixing things up," she said and touched her grey hair that she wore crimped in a style reminiscent of the twenties with a wan gesture, as if she had suddenly remembered her own appearance. She was afraid that she might not be suitable for the situation somehow, as old people often feel around much younger people. She stared with curiosity at Raymond's hat and clothes and said, "My goodness, boy, you look like something straight out of a Roy Rogers' movie."

"Ha, yes, ma'am," Raymond said and flushed. He jiggled the box of leaves self-consciously under Eric's hands.

"Watch it fu— meat-head," Eric warned. He smiled sheepishly at the woman and nervously wiped a heavy, sliding drop of perspiration from his temple.

"We want to keep this operation neat," he explained to the woman.

"You boys keep up the good work," she said, and began walking away. "It does a body good to watch the likes of you." She shifted her packages, trying to get a better grasp on them, and walked on towards the bus stop. Midway to the bus stop sign, she halted and waved at them. "I'm proud of boys like you," she called.

"Kinda sweet, ain't she?" Raymond said. He tipped his hat to her ceremoniously.

"Yeah, just as sweet and stupid as a mother," Eric remarked.

"You sound like you have a great respect for the institution of motherhood," Raymond remarked.

"I only know about one particular mother," Eric said with a smirk. "My *own*."

"Don't care for the lady much, eh?" Raymond said.

"You might say the feeling was. . . *is* mutual on both of our parts. Now, if you don't mind, butt-hole, I'd like to get this load of shit inside."

"What's happening, man?" a spindly-legged guy with long, stringy blond hair asked as he stood in the doorway of the living-room.

"Not much, Carot," Eric answered, pulling the drawstrings closed on the last fat pouch of dope and sitting it down with satisfaction by the other plump pouches lined up on the couch.

"Not much, huh?" Carot queried again. He smiled broadly, pulling his thin lips into an alligator-like grin. He crossed one bowleg over the other and reached into his black leather jacket for a joint. He had on knee-high boots, pulled up over black pantaloon trousers, and a necklace of wooden charms around his neck. He patted a pencil-thin joint before putting it between his thin, smiling lips.

Eric stood up, balancing the small silver scales in one hand and carrying the cardboard box of leaves in the other.

"My compliments, Raymond," he said, and dropped the box of leaves and branches into his lap.

"What the hell?" Raymond said. He stood up foolishly with the box of trash.

"Dump it in the garbage, will ya?" Eric asked. He walked towards his bedroom with the scales. Carot followed like a scruffy-headed Puss 'n Boots.

"Looks like you're in the shit tonight, my friend," Carot said. Eric sat the scales down on the black lacquered chest of drawers carefully. "When's everybody coming for the pick up?"

"What time is it now?" Eric asked. A white, Indian-style shirt that he had donned for the upcoming appointments had come untied on his chest, revealing the honey-coloured hair that whorled there in fine tender curls.

Carot consulted a Mickey Mouse watch and said, "Quarter to nine."

"In about half an hour, I guess," Eric answered.

"Why don't you come up to my pad about ten-thirty then? Like I told you last night, if you've got twelve bucks we're renting a limousine to hear a good group tonight." He sucked on the joint deliberately and tapped the toe of his boot against the door facing in a mind rhythm that was unique in his brain. "Bring a chick if you want, but everybody's gotta bring their own bread, OK?"

Eric flopped down in the overstuffed armchair that stood beside his cot-like bed.

"I dunno, man. I might, might not, okay?"

"OK," Carot said, slipping the burned-down joint into an elaborate roach clip. "Frank's the chauffeur, in case you're interested."

"He's always the driver, Carot," Eric said, and pushed his hair back in a whirling, hypnotic gesture of nervousness.

The front door banged loudly and Danny entered, treading lightly like a soft-shoed Indian.

"Hello, goodbye," he called into Eric's bedroom, and walked hurriedly by, leading several other people who stared with a keen interest at Carot and Eric.

"Well, here's your suckers," Carot drawled. "Go sell your shit."

"I'll try to come," Eric said, and rushed past Carot into the living-room.

"Do you want your cock now?" Hadrian asked, squatting on his knees in front of her.

"Oh, yes," she said, staring at his huge, bursting organ that he had thrust into her face. She put out her hand to touch it.

"Take him then," he commanded, and he pushed her mouth down on his overly thick cock. It surged her mouth like a swollen weapon.

"Umm, tastes so good," she said, looking up at his flushed, swarthy face.

"Do it then," he said. "Do it, darling. You do it so well."

She grabbed his large fat balls in one hand and gently massaged them while she slid her mouth up and down on his cock, sucking it greedily with her tongue.

"Oh yes! Yes!" he exclaimed, and lay back on the bed groaning. "That's it. That's the way." His legs were taut under her soft, round breasts, straining intently before his orgasm. She moved her mouth faster and faster, feeling the end of his thick, blunt dick hit the back of her throat.

"I want to swallow you," she said, ceasing her movements for a moment and looking at his stiff, purple cock. She sniffed the end of it and tasted it lightly, lapping at the tiny hole where the semen jetted out, like a cat taking its milk.

"Hadrian," she cried, and looked more closely at the end of his cock.

"You have *two* holes!" She put the tip of her tongue in one, then the other.

"Yeah," he said, "double-barrel. Now kiss him. Kiss him, please. Shut up to talk and suck me, darling."

She encircled his dick with her mouth again and began sucking it passionately.

"Oh, Cybele, oh darling. Oh yes," he sighed. The creamy semen of his cock filled her mouth. She reached up and felt the silky black hair on his chest under her palm to enhance her voluptuous feeling of pleasure that his expression of ecstasy had given her, then she swallowed every drop of his juice gratefully.

"Oh, that was good," he said.

She lay back into the crook of his powerful, thickly muscled arm. Her cat had come out from under the narrow bed. He stood watching them intently from the top of an old, scarred dresser. His green-yellow eyes blinked like two caution lights. Cybele stared into his eyes like a diver contemplating the depths of a pool, then sank down into a light, troubled slumber. She began to dream about her husband. In her dream she was sixteen years old again, and Pierre was twenty-two. They had been married only a few months.

"I'm gonna blow your brains out," Pierre said, in her dream.

"Oh God, oh God," she whimpered when she felt the cold steel of the gun barrel on her temple. She looked down at his hand on her naked breasts, and began to cry.

"Shut up," he snarled, and pummelled her ribs with his knee. "You make me sick, sick!" he said. His voice hissed through his tightly clinched teeth like a viper. "Do you get that? You ugly bitch!"

She grasped at her torn blouse and wrung it despairingly in her hands. She could smell Pierre's cigarette-stained breath. She stared at his expression of rage with curiosity through her torment. He danced around the room erratically, as if possessed by an unknown devil. Each time his clear blue eyes focused on her, his motions grew more agitated.

"You're crazy," she whispered fearfully.

"Don't you dare call me crazy," he cried, and slugged her on the back of her neck. She fell forwards onto the floor, hitting her head on the rough wooden boards.

"Oooh," she groaned.

"You're not hurt," he sneered. He put the revolver back to her temple.

"Now, I'm gonna get rid of you," he said, and cocked the hammer of the gun back.

"Pierre, Pierre, *don't*! It's loaded, you know."

"Of course it's loaded. You think I'm going to waste my time playing with a silly, ugly bitch? I intend to get rid of you – you and all of my problems," he said, with a strange, demented logic. He grasped her shoulders frantically. She felt a frenzied tension in his touch that emanated from the lithe muscles of his body. It filled the room with a foreboding feeling of dread, a horrible menacing feeling of anger and ultimate despair.

Click! She heard Hadrian's lighter slam shut after he had lit a cigarette and she started up out of her dream, screaming.

"What the hell?" he exclaimed and clasped his large sensual hands over her mouth in surprise. "Don't make noise."

She awakened from her nightmare to see Porgy bustling down off the dresser.

"Oh Hadrian," she said, nestling up to the solid, comforting warmth of his body. "I had a bad dream."

But he pulled away from her abruptly. "You made a lot of noise. I don't want any scandal. What time is it?" he asked, looking at his heavy gold wrist watch. "Quarter to ten. Oh m'gosh. I told my wife I was going to the drug store. I have to get out of here."

She watched him slide wearily to the side of the bed, and felt a smothering desolation sweep through her like a wave swishing voluminous quantities of sand in its wake.

"Ooh, I'm tired," he sighed. The heavy jowls of his face were suddenly more pronounced by his obvious fatigue. "I have three charter parties tomorrow."

She sat up in the ruffled bedsheets. Her almond-shaped eyes looked at him like a saucy-eyed kitten who had just finished its play.

"Charter parties?" she asked, and looked at him blankly.

"For the ships. The ships," he said, looking around for his socks. "I told you a million times."

"Oh," she said, and flopped back on the pillows dejectedly.

"Okay, darling, we'll have a nice dinner tomorrow night," he said when he had finished dressing, and patted her knee.

"And what do I do until then?" she asked.

"What?" he said absently, adjusting his tie.

"Oh nothing," she said. "Just zero, I guess."

"Okay, darling, come and lock your door," he said. He was fully dressed now in his cream coloured suit. He paused by the door with his hand on the doorknob.

When she got up from the bed, she felt an uncanny familiarity with the situation, a haunting feeling that all of this had taken place before. She shook her head as she walked towards him, feeling an unusual dizziness in her brain.

"Goodnight, dear," he said, and pressed his lips to her cheek with a prim tightness. She felt his perfunctory kiss on her flesh and sank backwards into a more intense remembrance of an event she couldn't quite recall.

She walked to the dresser and sat down nude on the prickly material of the chair in front of it, pushing her finger along its glass top dully. A haunting feeling that the same situation had once existed in her life surrounded her in the narrow hotel room. It was a disturbing, familiar consciousness of a pattern she had begun long, long ago. Her mind wandered back to the first memories of her life that she could recall. In her memory she was a little girl five years old again, living with her parents in a small southern town on the Louisiana coast. She remembered the cramped, bleak apartment they had lived in.

Inside the little apartment everything was quiet – she didn't hear a sound. Even her small bare feet were silent as she walked slowly over to the window. Her hair hung lank and trailed down on the white cotton material of her dress, silky and black on the rough cotton material. Outside, the grass was burned and ugly, brown and sparse. Row upon row of stark, brick apartments sat in the sweltering summer sun. The afternoon was like an ugly blister. She clutched her wiry black teddy bear by her knee, staring, staring while she rubbed the teddy bear's short, thick arm. His fur irritated her fingertips so pleasantly that she squeezed his plumpness harder. She wondered where they had all gone. Suddenly she was left in a vacuum.

The teddy bear's black, coal-like eyes stared back into her sea-green eyes. She loved him. His body was so thick and solid. His eyes were black and his expression always remained the same. Behind her she felt the afternoon. She felt the silence, the heat. All of the chairs were waiting behind her. They were thinking. They were sitting. She felt them behind her. The floor was under her feet – cool and slick. The window in the dining-room was also watching her. Its cool grey light was calm behind her head and body. She rubbed her neck. The perspiration there was so sweet. She rubbed it on the teddy bear's eyes.

"Teddy bear, teddy bear," she sang as she slowly rubbed his back against her leg. Then she turned towards the stairs, lifting her eyelids heavily and fingering the end of the teddy bear's squat, fat arm, stopping the tip of one finger on his cold black eye. Now she was climbing the narrow stairs and looking at the landing in the hall.

The door of her bedroom was partially open. She saw the bed bathed in the light of the sun. She pushed the door open slowly, looking at each object in the room before she entered. The bedspread was white and slightly rumpled, soft and inviting. She felt the delicious coolness of the air as it fanned her hot little face. She laid the teddy bear down on the bed very carefully, then turned to shut the door. She closed it deliberately, firmly. She wanted it to be secure. She wished that there had been a key to lock it.

The teddy bear looked so black on the white spread. The soft spread rippled under his wiry, rough body. Suddenly she heard a noise and frowned. It was an aeroplane. She watched it glide past impatiently. After it was gone, she lay down on the bed beside her teddy bear. She cradled him in her arm while she lay quietly, thinking. She felt the round little balls of the bedspread and stroked them gently with her small child's hand. She wanted to think of her father.

She put her other hand on the cold iron bars of the brass bed's headpiece – so cold, so hard. Now she watched the door. *She had to stay inside. The door was locked.* Her father had locked it and made her stay there. She was delighted when he did that. She was happy when it was quiet. Now she pushed her small fingers between her legs and smiled. She looked at the teddy bear's black silent eyes. . .

The shrill ringing of the phone shot through her childhood memories and brought her back to sitting nude on the chair. She picked up the black, sharp-looking receiver and said, "Hello," cautiously, as if it might be some unknown god calling instead of a human being.

"What's happening, Cybele?"

"Nothing. What's supposed to be happening except what always happens around here," she said, pushing her toe dejectedly along the leg of the chair that she sat on.

"Christ! You sound really down. Did the old dude show up? I mean, or is he going to show?"

"He showed."

"Jesus! I hope he ain't still around."

"Nope."

"Yep, nope. Will you cut the Gary Cooper act?"

"Nope."

"Shit. Wanna go to a rock concert tonight? It'll cost you twelve bucks."

"Why?" she asked.

"Because we're hiring a limousine."

"Why?"

"For kicks. Everybody'll think we're somebody. But we won't be, and that's part of the fun. Got it?"

"Yeah," she said, staggering up out of her mental fog. "I like that."

"Yeah, I like that," he mimicked. "Be out back in ten minutes."

"Why in back?"

"You remember what the landlord said about my car?"

"Oh yeah," she drawled.

"Jesus, what happened to you while I was cutting the shit? You sound like you got mowed down by six platoons," he asked, exasperated.

"I'm OK. I just fell asleep, that's all."

"OK, but get your shit together and I'll see ya."

She hung up the receiver and looked around the room. Porgy sat on the pillow washing his face. She went over and hugged him, pushing his wide furry face to hers and rubbing her nose on his.

"Darlin', darlin'," she said.

"Meow," he answered.

The night enveloped her skin like a dark ripe grape when she came downstairs. Eric's white shirt loomed out of the darkness with a neon brightness while he sat in his little green Triumph waiting.

"Eric, Eric, Eric Star," she called, and ran up to the side of the dark green convertible, surveying the graceful curves of his ample shoulders under the thin, gossamer material of his shirt happily. Its criss-cross pattern of strings that zigzagged over his collar-bone and down the hair of his chest made her salivate automatically. Her tongue moved under her teeth, contemplating the sweet taste of his golden chest hair.

"Ready to swing some, luv?" He grinned happily at her.

"Eric, you look so young!"

She buried her face into the grassy fragrance of his wildly curling hair, then stared again at the creamy smoothness of his face.

"I *am* young," he said. "For a twenty-five-year-old dude, I'm young."

"Sure you are, my one and only star I've found in this lifetime," she said, and hopped into the little car. He swerved out of the back driveway slowly, keeping the car's motor as low as possible, then he roared up onto Wisconsin Avenue.

"Gosh, Eric, do you have a muffler?" she asked. She brushed a strand of her long, thick hair back from her face and sniffed the humid dampness of the night.

"Of course not, Cybele." He put his hand on her knee and squeezed it, grinning at her impishly as they rode along the neon-lit avenue.

She flung herself on his chest and kissed his smooth shaven jaw, then put her fingers to his moustache and said, "Oh Eric, Eric, Eric Star," sighing. She nestled her head near his ear, inhaling deep draughts of his hair's natural perfume.

He put his arm around her slender shoulders, working his mouth back and forth over his gums in an expression of happy nervousness.

They roared through the hot, humid air that hung over the city like a damp blanket, whizzing past the lights of Wisconsin Avenue. She looked over at Dart Drug as they flew past a yellow caution light, and felt comforted to see its darkened interior, knowing that it sat pregnant with many supplies that she could go and buy the next day when it opened. She stretched back against Eric, arching her back in a voluptuous movement of release before sinking back completely into the bracelet of his arm. She thought of the smooth, creamy bars of Nivea soap sitting in stacks on the shelf of the Dart Drug, of their little bodies wrapped in crisp wax paper before being smartly encased in neat, blue and white coloured boxes marked NIVEA in large blue letters. They were about forty cents a bar, and she marvelled at the cheapness of such a luxury. She began rubbing the filmy material of Eric's shirt while she thought of rows and rows of Johnson's Baby Oil bottles lined up on the shelf. She thought of how she could scoop up three or four enormous plastic bottles of it, along with at least five bars of soap, and hustle to the counter like a scavenger and lay down that part of her "cache", so that she could go back for more articles of shampoo – oh yes, at least four huge plastic bottles, and if there was a sale on, maybe eight.

'Oooh,' she thought, and longed to be in the store right at that moment. She contemplated an orgy of large plastic bottles full of rich oils and lathers, cans of fragrant, highly pressurised sprays, and the winey smell of cheap colognes.

"Where's your head at?" Eric asked. He geared down for a red light, using the same hand on the arm he had encircled her waist with to change gears, pushing her forward slightly and closer to him.

"Huh?" she asked foggily. She rubbed the material of his shirt more insistently back and forth between her fingers, as if the soothing, smooth texture of it might carry her back into the world of her thoughts that he had interrupted.

"Where's your brain travelling?" he asked again.

"Your shirt is like a magic door to my own marvellous, private world," she answered as she gazed dreamily into his eyes. "I love your moustache," she added.

He turned to her while they sat waiting for the red light to change. The warmth of his brown eyes blurred out at her through his especially thick glasses. They sat on his small, pug nose like the "other" eyes of a strange, friendly animal.

"I'll accept that shit, Cybele," he said, and kissed her on her left eyebrow. "But which private world are you in right now, at this moment?" he asked.

The light changed, and they careened over the beginnings of the old streetcar tracks that shot down through the bumpy cobblestones of the road like swift silver wings.

"I was in the Dart Drug having a ball!"

"OK, OK, I can dig on that. Yeah!" he yelled out into the night from their topless car. He clutched the ripply black steering wheel with both hands in his excitement and shook it. "I feel like I could just pull this fucker right out of here," he said, as he tugged at the wheel.

"Could you still drive like that?" she asked simply.

He glanced at her candidly trying to determine if she were really serious.

"I mean, Eric, I really think you could. Of all people, that is."

"Sure, with my big toe. Fuck!" he shouted, and laughed.

She pulled away from him and flung her head back on the cracked leather of the bucket seat, gazing at the gemlike array of stars that winked and blinked their brilliant light over them like myriad beacons from another world.

"I feel like I could fly up into the stars," she said.

"You'd look cute up there," he said. He pulled over to the side of the road and parked.

She looked across the street at Clyde's.

"Hey, we're on M Street," she said, looking puzzled.

"I know," he said.

"But we were on Wisconsin," she drawled. "I don't remember. . ."

"Turning onto M? That's because you were flying up in the stars at that particular time," he said, then reached across her and opened her door before getting out himself.

"Alight, m'dear. Ole fairfoot be here! Ha! I made a poem."

"I know, Eric. You're my star, my own poetic star," she said, and hopped out of the car, stepping on one of his dirty bare feet.

"Ow! Christ," he yelled. "Do you have to mutilate me?"

"Oh Eric, Eric darling. Are you hurt?" she asked. She reached down and touched his foot.

"God, what's he got?" a young guy asked his companion as they walked by Eric and Cybele.

"Lookit, she's kissing his feet!" he added. They both stopped to watch while Cybele stooped over Eric's foot. Her clinging hot pants rolled past the beginning of her ass when she bent over him, making their eyes goggle.

"Will you cut the crap and stop showing your ass to every creep in the fucking road?"

"What?" she asked, looking up at him stupidly.

"I said, get up, will you? I mean, how much do I have to go through anyway?"

She stood up, looking at him in bewilderment. She slipped her feet out of her brown leather sandals and held them out to him.

"See how much I love you?" she said, smiling sweetly at him.

"Luv, you don't even need dope. Get in here."

He pushed her through a narrow doorway that led into one of the rows of buildings lining M Street. A staggering height of wooden steps loomed before them like a pyramid. They began a *giggling* ascent, pushing their hips back and forth against one another in a seesawing, carefree rhythm.

"Up we go. Ho, ho, ho," he called, and lifted her over three steps with one strong young arm.

"Wheee!" she laughed, and licked one of his ears.

"Halt! Who goes there?" Carot asked. He stood at the top of the stairway with an unsheathed sword, looking like a modern-day cavalier in his black pantaloons and knee-high boots.

"I'm Robin and she's Hood," Eric said, halting before the long, gleaming blade of a sword that Carot had stuck into the floor in front of them.

Carot pushed a large, plumed, purple hat back from his stringy blond hair and peered down at them with small, round eyes that glittered glassily from under his bushy blond eyebrows.

"Show one of your arrows as proof," he demanded, and guffawed.

Eric swept Cybele up in his arms magnificently. She clasped her arms around his neck, sighing happily like an expectant virgin.

"Let me pass, mate. Me bride n' me's gotta make it for the first time!" Eric joked.

Cybele giggled and bit his ear, feeling herself go wet between her legs when she felt his strong arms under her legs and back.

"*Elle est très joli,*" Carot confirmed. "You may use my water-bed," he offered. He pulled his sword from the floor and stepped aside grandly for them to pass.

Eric swirled Cybele into a room filled with large, multi-coloured cushions that lay on the floor like spongy mushrooms. He had to step down to enter the room because the door level had sunk into an odd, slanting incline from the seeping, relentless humidity that suffused the seasons of Washington, DC.

Carot sidled up to Eric, directing his eyes at Cybele's feet and moving them slowly up the side of her calf and thigh.

"Got a lot of hot ice tonight, Eric?" he queried. His green, beady eyes darted up and down Cybele's flesh like pale, nervous fish. "Why don't you drop it over there?"

He pulled Eric by his gossamer-thin shirt to the water-bed. The black material of his full pantaloons swished like a tomcat's heavy tail as he did'so.

Cybele clasped her arms tighter around Eric's neck, rubbing her breasts into his hard ribs. "Oh yes. Put me there, Eric," she said, looking at the bed's wide expanse.

"God, she's affectionate," Carot exclaimed. "Dammit, Eric, where do you get these rabbits?" He touched the toe of his razor-sharp boot on the water-bed. It began to undulate under the mussed quilt.

"It's moving, Eric," she shouted. "Oh look!" she exclaimed, watching the heaving, jelly-like movement of the bed.

"It's moving, Eric," Carot mimicked. "Fifty *Hail Marys* – what have you been feeding this dame? You must have given her the *crème de la crème* of your shit tonight."

"Wheee," Eric exclaimed and flung Cybele onto the bed. She landed on the bed's soft, elastic support, sinking deeply into the watery, plastic-covered mattress.

"Oh, I love it! I love it!" she exclaimed. "Why don't we ever do this on Jeff's water-bed at your house, Eric?"

"Christ, what a dizzy broad," Eric muttered. He retreated back to the other side of the room. He watched Cybele's machinations on the bed as if she were a captive lioness that he had momentarily set loose.

"*Mon dieu, mon dieu. Cette une très belle jeune fille,*" Carot whispered, "*très belle jeune fille.*" He stood beside Eric. His black pantaloons were like graceful smudges next to Eric's cream-coloured khaki pants.

"That's right," she called, bouncing up and down on the water-bed, feeling her body float on its jelly-like support. "Stand there and admire me. I love to be admired. I like to think I'm performing a duty, and that I don't take it personally," she said, and turned a somersault in the pillows. "But I do, I do!

She looked down at the pillows rapturously. "Just look at all these things," she exclaimed, and spread her fingers out on the brightly coloured cushions that surrounded her. "They're all around – all around," she marvelled. She sat contemplating the many-shaped cushions lying about her body like heaps of confetti. Her eyelids felt heavy over her eyes. She stared down hypnotically at the pillows. "Their shapes are so mysterious, so mysterious, so mysterious. . . They want to take me somewhere." She shook her head and giggled. "I don't understand that," she said, knitting her brows and pouting. Her eyes strayed absently over to Eric and Carot, halting at the rich, black colour of Carot's pants.

"I like that! I like that!" she exclaimed, and pointed her finger at Carot's pants. "Come, come!" she commanded Carot. "I want to touch your black pants and tell you about the cushions."

"Certainly, certainly, *madame* – *à votre service,*" Carot said, rolling his green eyes at Eric, then upwards, as if contemplating paradise. He hustled over to her, flicking the long ash from his cigarette with a nervous, expectant movement.

"Oh your pants, your pants!" she screamed, and shoved some of the pillows away to make room for him. "Listen to the noise they make!"

"Shit!" Eric said. He walked over to a shiny tin bucket fresh from the Army Surplus store, that had been filled with punch. He began taking out the strawberry coloured punch with a cracked cup. "Anything in this stuff?"

"Just a little Speed," Carot answered, and sat down beside Cybele gently. He surveyed her long, tanned legs almost furtively, feeling guilty for looking at her - for looking at something he perhaps shouldn't be seeing. "Why don't you bring us some?"

"I'll bring you some, old sport, but she's flying without anything," Eric informed him.

"So I see, so I see, " Carot agreed. He slipped his hand around her ankle and squeezed the delicate bone there under her smooth, warm flesh. Again a feeling of guilt washed over him, warning him that he shouldn't be touching this woman. He let it fill his chest with its sweet, sickening sensation until he hardened in his black pants, then released her ankle.

"Enjoying yourself, pal?" Eric asked with an exaggerated expression of disdainful indulgence.

He handed Carot a glass of strawberry coloured brew. The punch moved in small waves inside the fragile wineglass, like thin jam.

"Merely a mixing of wills. . . a twining of thoughts," Carot replied as he extricated his last finger from Cybele's ankle.

"Right on, right on, friend," Eric replied. He drifted like a cotton-clothed moth to the side of an old, massive chest. It sat on the inclining boards of the floor like an overweight nun. He studied the inanimate structure of dark wood with a drifting, dreamy sort of concentration, wondering how it ever been transported up the steep, cliff-like ascent of the stairs.

"I know. They built the house around it," he mused to himself.

He gazed at the puppet-like motions of Carot and Cybele ensconced on the lightly lapping water-bed. Cushions began to fly through the air, and a light, feathery giggle from Cybele floated up with them.

"Such marvellous shapes," she shouted, delighted with each soft, plump body she hurled into the air.

"Yes, er, that would be so. . ." Carot muttered over the rim of his painted crystal glass while he contemplated her super-thin hips on the delicate material of the bedspread. A splotch of gay orange embroidery woven there peeped out from under one of her thighs.

"Hark!" Carot said. He turned his head towards loud clumping sounds on the stairway of his apartment and cupped his ear dramatically.

"Oh Christ!" Eric said, and smiled foolishly at Cybele. He drank down the cold pink punch in deep draughts and raised both eyebrows meaningfully, looking like a cartoon sage.

"Eric is silly! Eric is silly!" Cybele began to chant.

"Whhaa! You rats!" A miniature girl dressed in a long blue jeans skirt shouted. She sprang into the room with an etiolate boy trailing behind her.

"Brenda!" Cybele screamed, and waved a pillow, conking Carot on the head.

Brenda jerked her head in Cybele's direction, carrying a mass of luxuriant, chestnut coloured hair that had been bound in a black, sturdily woven hairnet across her bird-like shoulders.

"Lookit her! Lookit her!" Brenda exclaimed. She turned the brim of her British jockey hat from the left side of her head to the back in an abrupt motion of delight. "Lady Bathesheba!" she shouted. "Oh God, ha, Cybele, you're perfect there, don't move. Lookit!" She pulled her insubstantial companion behind her like a loosely wound string ball.

"Brenda, darlink," Carot sighed, and sank back idly in the pillows. "Come, join my harem!"

"Love it. Love it," Brenda cried as she sat down beside them. "Well?" she said, looking at her companion impatiently and patting the bed. "Don't you want to be a member in our harem?"

The boy sat down with a sniff, pressing the faded, holey knees of his jeans close together in a nervous clutch.

"Join our famous cavalier," Brenda shouted at Carot. "And our illustrious mistress and girl friend, Cybele!"

"Hi," the boy said.

"This is Slim," Brenda announced. "He's pocket change," she added and started laughing.

"Oh Brenda, you're so silly, really," Slim lisped. He pressed his bony knees closer together, then he took a wilted petunia out of his pocket and presented it to Brenda. "I almost forgot," he prefaced, with a sly, elf-like smile playing about his lips as he handed her the flower.

"Ohhh – you're too tender, Slim," she said, taking the purple and yellow flower in her hands. She cupped them maternally around the dying blossom.

"Brenda always gets the sweet ones," Cybele protested. She drew her fingers petulantly over the coarse material of Brenda's black hairnet.

"Oh, don't complain, you exotic bird!" Brenda laughed at Cybele while she studied her with curiosity and frank admiration.

"Compliments of the house," Eric said as he handed Brenda and Slim two glasses of punch.

"Super," Brenda said. She took both glasses authoritatively and handed one to Slim. "Watch out or it'll skin your gizzard," she warned him. She grabbed at Slim's bony chest. "You got a gizzard in there?" she asked.

"Isn't she amazing?" Cybele drawled.

"No, *you* are," Brenda countered, turning her brown, vital eyes to Cybele. "You and that savage beast cat of yours!"

"Oh, you mean Porgy? Oh, dear sweet Porgy," Cybele crooned and began stroking the back of Carot's head.

"Hey, watch that shit," Eric shouted from a corner.

"Have you met her cat yet?" Brenda asked Carot.

"I'm just having the pleasure of meeting her. . . initially, tonight," Carot replied. He drank his punch in greedy, satisfied little sips and stared over the rim of his crystal glass at Cybele with two large, pale green eyes. "Superb," he muttered under his breath. He swept his gaze up and down her legs, fanning his eyes back and forth over her body in a fluttering, voluptuous motion. Cybele batted her eyes back at Carot coyly, responding happily to his attentions.

"Well, I met him the other night in the hotel room. He was chewing a huge, bloody steak bone," Brenda told Carot.

Slim watched Brenda like a contented mouse, basking in the generous magnanimity of her personality. He hooked his bony fingers around her tiny, plump hand like a little rodent taking hold of a fat, sleek chipmunk.

"My God," Carot whispered admiringly, still lost in the depths of Cybele's turquoise, black-lashed eyes. "A creature from the South seas."

"Oh Carot, you express yourself like Hadrian," Cybele said, caressing pillows with the backs of her legs, moving them back and forth, back and forth over the satiny material. "But you're not European?" she asked, and lowered eyes, smitten by an unexpected shyness from her own observation.

"This huge, hulking cat. . . crawling along the floor and dragging a bloody bone in its teeth," Brenda continued before Carot had a chance to answer Cybele. "I was terrified!"

"Oh Brenda, your skirt has a circus on it," Cybele interrupted. She sat up suddenly, upsetting Slim's punch when she reached across him to touch the bright yellow, green and red pattern of a circus scene that had been sewn in patches on Brenda's skirt.

"I adore circuses and elephants," she told them.

"Especially green ones," Carot added, smiling like an indulgent parent at Cybele.

Slim sat with his crotch saturated in cold pink punch, not moving, and smiling weakly, as if he hadn't felt the icy liquid on such a sensitive part of his anatomy.

"She runs up to the beast," Brenda resumed, "and coos, 'Porgee, Porgee', like he's some sort of king or something."

"That fucking cat!" Eric said jealously.

"Don't you dare say that about Porgy!" Cybele called from behind Carot's back. "You know I can't bear anyone to say mean things about him, Eric."

"Shit, what time does the concert start anyway?" Eric groaned and lit a fresh, thickly packed joint.

"Then Eric made her read me her diary," Brenda said, looking speculatively from Eric to Cybele, as if estimating how far she could go into the intimacy of their relationship they had allowed her to enter for some reason that evening the previous week.

"Oh Eric!" Cybele shouted. She leapt up spontaneously from the water-bed, stepping over Brenda and Slim as if they were pillows. "I love you so," she proclaimed, and hugged his reed-like hips to her slender brown body. She had been reminded of their newly-shared intimacy of the night before by Brenda's personal remarks.

Carot watched the two of them, transfixed, and not moving his punch cup that he held in mid-air.

"They're beautiful, aren't they?" Brenda captioned the two twining figures in front of them. "They're like this all the time," she added, and studied them as if her remarks had given her power over the situation, some sort of entrance into sharing the euphoria of their relationship.

Cybele clung to Eric's back, unable to stop the sweet, sharp sensations that pierced her stomach and breasts like little, poignant arrows. Eric shrugged his shoulders happily, helplessly, at the three figures on the water-bed, overwhelmed by her embrace.

"She's been doing this all day," he explained to them sheepishly.

"Oh Eric, Eric, when are we going to bed? I want to go to bed!" Cybele demanded, seizing Eric's firm, well-moulded shoulders.

"My Lord," Slim said, staring at Brenda's flushed cheeks that were effused vicariously from the blatant display of passion before them. "You shouldn't pay so much attention," he added lamely.

A car horn yodelled in three deep, melodious blasts outside the apartment building. Suddenly Carot stepped up on the bed and leaned through the window. His black pantaloons fanned out behind him like a ruffled black peacock. "OK, Kreeger, be right down," he shouted.

A beefy, dimpled jawed man waved back to him from a shiny black limousine, then turned his large fat head back to the stream of people milling past him on M Street.

"My God, it's a hearse," Cybele cried. She peered out the window at the long black car. "I'm not getting in that thing!"

"You'd well know she was never a President's daughter," Slim muttered, and placed his cup carefully on the sloping punch table.

"Yes," Cybele answered, "I can always say my father is a son of a bitch without worrying about publicity."

"*Is* your father a son of a bitch?" Carot asked carefully.

Cybele leapt off the bed and ran towards Eric's disappearing figure.

"No, not really," she called. "Just sort of insubstantial, but gentle and kind. He is even. . . noble, but I guess he's nobody I could really idolise," she told Carot as she followed Eric down the stairs.

"Hadrian is Cybele's father," Brenda screamed up to Carot from the bottom of the stairs. "You should see the picture of him sitting on her vanity table. He's up there like a god she worships at an altar. He's being pinned with a medal and is grinning from ear to ear."

Cybele lassoed Eric's waist with her arms and inserted her finger into his small, tight navel while they clumped down the stairs.

"Oh, I see. A sort of glory hound, eh?" Carot inquired, and drew out a long thin cigar.

"Thanks," he said when Slim opened the door for all of them.

"Nah, he's a man," Brenda confirmed. "A real man. The first thing he did when he came into my apartment was press the mattress of my bed to see if it was hard enough for making love."

They trailed out into the humid night air, surrounded by its dense, porous darkness that was interrupted by the glittering lights of car lamps and flower-like patterns of pedestrians' summer clothing.

Kreeger stood solidly beside the elaborate car, bowing and smiling facetiously while he held open the limousine's wide door. People gathered around the car and stared when they entered. They settled into the cushy brown seats like candy being poured into a different bowl, adjusting gracefully next to one another's bodies in the car's freezing coldness. They heard the door slam shut, and sat contained and waiting in their new atmosphere.

"Good evening, children," Kreeger addressed them. His fat, thick neck wrinkled like red mud under the greasy black hat of his uniform. He looked over at them and asked, "Where to, same place as last time?"

"The very same," Carot answered. He slipped an envelope out of his red velvet vest officiously and began counting a wad of bills in lower denominations. A small gathering of onlookers huddled about the car, peering in at intervals through the limousine's dark, smoked glass windows. Their faces were like the masks of clowns representing various expressions of anger, delight, and curiosity.

A great burst from the car's powerful motor sent them careening away from the kerb, dispersing the crowd like weightless leaves. The lights of M Street shimmered in front of them. Their long, sleek car nosed out to join the twinkling parade of lights and noises from the cars and voices of people along the street. Cybele snuggled close beside Eric's jean-clad legs, and murmured, "Oh, too cold, Eric." She stared down at the goose pimples that had covered her thighs and arms.

"Country girls should be in barns, not limousines," Slim piped up, watching Eric and Cybele with colourless, glittering eyes.

"You remind me of a bird I had once," Cybele said, noting the pathetic thinness of Slim's arms and chest and his bony white neck that disappeared like a turtle inside his thin T-shirt. "He was black, and I called him Rathbone. Had to keep him in the bathroom away from the cats."

Slim smirked at Brenda while they listened to Cybele's rambling tirade. "Cuckoo," he whispered.

"Took us a hell of a time to fasten his cage up on the shower bar," Cybele continued, ignoring Slim's bitchiness. A slight, cruel smile played about her lips. "Well, no matter what I did good for that bird, all he did was peck and scatter seed on the floor and into the bathtub. Finally, one night I came into the bathroom and saw what a mess he had made. I looked at his bony black back and fussy-looking feathers, then took him out onto the patio and let him go. Never saw him again," she sighed. She leaned her head back contentedly on Eric's sinewy chest. "But I always hoped that nothing ate him. He was such a poor miserable thing."

"Listen to er, Jeez. Sounds like my grandmother's tales," Brenda exclaimed.

"Oh really, Brenda," Slim whined irritably. "How you do go on."

"A definite presence," Carot opined. He tapped on the opaque plastic partition that separated the driver's section of the car from the passenger's. Kreeger pushed it back with one bearlike hand, allowing billows of pungent smoke from his cigar to invade their spacious, icy cubicle.

"I think you'll find the right amount in there, Kreeger," Carot said. He settled back into his loveseat beside Slim and Brenda. His eyes fastened onto Cybele like a bee realighting on a flower it had lost momentarily.

"I can't believe we're really going to see the Starlights," Eric exclaimed. "I mean, just think of how famous they are! How do people get that lucky?" he asked no one.

"My dear man, you're more lucky than the Starlights. Look what you have beside you," Carot said.

"Oh God," Slim groaned. "How much further?"

"Just a piece over the bridge," Carot intoned towards Slim, not bothering to look at him. He flicked the lacy cuffs of his blouse meticulously away from his wrists.

"Just look at us!" Brenda exclaimed, surveying the coffin-like interior of the limousine excitedly. "We're stars!"

"Don't you just wish," Eric whined. "Think of all that dough."

"Oh Eric, Eric," Cybele sighed. "You're divine."

"Shit!" Eric answered.

"No, love," she countered, and began kissing his pouting mouth. She sucked at the tender tip of his tongue with her lips while listening to the heavy tread of the car's enormous tyres on the pavement underneath them.

Kreeger steered the long car slowly past a mass of shouting, running bodies which peered hungrily into the limousine's darkened windows.

"Hey man, over here!" one shouted.

"It's them, I think!"

A thin smile spread over Carot's mouth like a razor blade. He studied his nails deliberately, while a group of screaming, pushing kids shoved their faces anxiously up to the car window.

"Jesus, I think it's really them!" a young girl shouted before stumbling near one of the car's large tyres.

"Lookit 'em – there's a couple in back balling!"

Cybele and Eric had reclined down into the back seat, touching one another's bodies like expectant farmers gathering their crops.

"Eric, Eric, you're so neat in this car. We feel thinner in here, don't you think?" She looked dreamily up into his closed, bronze-lashed eyes, enjoying the pink flush that had covered his face and softened his features in a rainbow-like glow. "Aren't we, Eric? Thinner?"

"Umm," he murmured over her lips.

"Wow, an X-rated right on the way," Brenda said.

"Strictly third rate," Slim sneered.

"But charming," Carot laughed.

"You want me to pull it up back like last time?" Kreeger asked through the smoky partition.

"That's right, Kreeger, my man," Carot directed. He sat forward on his seat, holding the handle of the car door and looking out into the crowd with an excitement he was enjoying controlling.

"Enough, m'dear. I'm suffocating," Eric's muffled voice said.

"Such protestations," Carot said," amused when Eric rolled to his knees and into a sitting position.

Cybele sat up abruptly, upsetting Eric onto the wide floorboard. She peered out the window at the paperdoll-like people who had once more surrounded the car, and asked, "Where are we?" Then she blinked wide-eyed at the grinning, shouting faces.

"This is it, kids," Kreeger called. He pulled over beside a steep incline of wooden steps that led up to a wooden platform surrounding the back of the auditorium.

"OK, gang, get ready," Carot commanded. He sprang out of the car like a cavalier alighting from his horse.

"It's them! It's *them*," several people shouted and ran towards Carot.

"Quickly," Carot called, pulling Cybele, then Brenda, out of the car and guiding them hastily towards the sloping steps of the platform. Cybele stumbled and he lifted her up deftly like a feather while still mounting the steps.

"Jesus!" Eric exclaimed, when several people grabbed at his clothes. "They're like locusts!"

"Still want to be famous?" Carot called as he disappeared into the back stage door.

"Just a damned minute!" Eric yelled when he heard the sleeve of his shirt rip. Slim hunkered close behind him. His small mean head was like a nut as he sought cover from Eric's torso.

"For God's sake, Eric, don't antagonise the beasts," he panted.

"But this was my best shirt," Eric complained, running blindly up to the closed back door. "Just cleaned at the laundromat today." He pushed desperately at the grey steel door.

"Gad, don't tell me it's locked on us," he cried. He jerked frantically at the door's long metal bar.

"How about an autograph?" someone asked, touching the sleeve of Eric's torn white blouse.

"Would you mind?" Eric asked, and extricated the boy's dirty fingers from the jagged tear in his shirt.

"This is my best shirt. I ain't got another one, pal!"

The boy blinked in confusion at Eric while he continued yanking at the door.

"May I?" Slim asked. He pressed down with both hands on the door handle, opening it immediately. Eric fell forward inside. Slim muttered over his shoulder at the bewildered fan, "Get lost, snot face, we ain't nobody. Just a bunch of fakes!" and slammed the door brutally in the boy's face.

"Oh Eric, Eric," Cybele cried, looking all around at the crowd. "I'm so enchanted!"

"Well, I'm not!" Eric snorted. "I was almost ripped to pieces by those creeps." He held up the blouse-like sleeve of his torn shirt.

"Poor baby," she sympathised and began kissing his elbow through the tear.

"This way, this way," Carot called in a loud stage whisper, leading them through row after row of seats on the side of the stage.

Before them, musicians sat blowing, twisting and tuning their guitars and musical instruments on a honey-coloured, circular stage. A ponderous black curtain hung down in front of them, blocking them from the audience's view.

"OK, gang?" Carot asked. He pointed at five seats near the back of the stage.

"Oh, neat," Brenda said. She hustled down into the row of seats. "Just like a school auditorium, isn't it, Slim?"

"Exactly," he answered grimly.

"What happened to Eric?" she asked as they slumped down in the wooden seats.

"Attacked by a fan," Slim quipped.

"You guys OK?" Carot asked, and settled in beside Eric and Cybele.

"Oh, we're just perfect, Carot," Cybele said. She squeezed his knee happily. She followed his gaze, then Eric's, down to her hand on Carot's knee and hastily removed it.

"I mean, I'm just devastated. Aren't you, Eric?" she crooned, nuzzling her cheek into his arm.

"Yeah, far out," he said, glaring at the hole in his shirt.

"Oh, my gosh, here he is," Brenda cried. "Oh God. I'm dying!"

The sumptuous black drapes parted to screams from countless, featureless faces that made up the audience.

A young man of medium height and long, sandy-coloured hair rushed out onto the stage in a blur of white buckskin jeans that flashed gaudily with rhinestone ornaments. A bejewelled, matching jacket opened to his lean waistline. With each movement he made, an elaborate gold chain bounced against his hard, rippling stomach muscles.

"Oh God, I'm dead," Brenda declared, slumping dramatically onto Slim and clutching her throat. She held the brim of her jockey hat as if she were in pain, knotting and unknotting her faded brown shawl in nervous, twitching motions with her other hand.

"He *is* rather attractive," Slim whispered. His eyes were riveted to the vibrating figure in white moving before them.

"Even from the back?" Eric asked, and laughed.

Cybele strained forward trying to get a glimpse of the singer's face.

"Oh Eric," she said when the singer walked back over to the drummer and flashed a smile in their direction. "He makes the nape of my neck feel like a cup of fire."

"Oh balls!" Eric groaned.

The crowd moved forward visibly, seething and rustling like leaves on the branches of a massive old tree caught in a violent storm. In the singer's hand, a parabolic microphone glinted and flashed dazzlingly from the glare of the footlights. The rich, honey-like croon of his voice poured through it and flooded out in a thousand heady, hypnotising sounds into the ears of the hungry audience.

Cybele grasped Eric's hand with each throbbing beat of the music while she sat staring straight ahead at the man singing. Soon she became aware of the enchantment that the shape of Eric's hand brought her. She felt as if she might be holding the compact, sensual hand of an animal instead of a human being. The touch of his fingers clasped around her own drew her knees close to his legs. Her whole body followed soon afterwards, straining to touch all of her flesh with all of his. A stabbing, sweet sensation of pain-like pleasure laced itself through her chest and pushed her face close to his, drawing her warm red mouth to the side of his cheek. He looked down at her through his thick glasses. His amber-coloured eyes brimmed with golden lights.

"Oh Eric, kiss me! Kiss me, please," she said, and rubbed her lips lightly over the roughness of his whiskers.

He moved his mouth onto hers and pressed its ample lips to her lips. She felt his mouth burning hers and couldn't remember where his stopped and hers began.

"We're fused together, Eric," she gasped at the end of the kiss. "Hold me now, Eric. Hold me!" She clung to his shoulders and waist, pushing her head hard against his ribs.

"Luv, what's happening?" Eric whispered. "Don't you want to dig the singer?"

"Of course, Eric. I love him. But I need you to hold me, Eric. Hold me please, because I'm so afraid." She looked around at the auditorium's brilliant lights, then back at the twisting, wailing singer, pondering the inexplicable magnetism pouring out of him.

"I'm so lonely sometimes, Eric," she sighed. "I'm not used to being alone so much."

"But there's only fifteen million people around, dummy."

She continued to kiss and touch his arms, keeping herself as close to him as possible.

'Why couldn't Hadrian do this with me now?' she thought. 'Why couldn't he hold me when I need to be held? And why couldn't I feel this fantastic happiness with Pierre that I needed so much? Life is so weird. Does one really have to go to so many different people to get what they need? Can't it all come from just one man?'

The curtain whisked to a close, and the figure in white dashed from the stage like a flash of premature lightning.

"Want to go out to the car?" she heard Eric's voice say over the horrendous din of applause and catcalls.

"Sure," she answered and smiled at him delightedly. "But what about Kreeger?"

"Kreeger's a nice fellow," Eric said confidently. "Come on."

He pulled her up from the battered wooden seat and led her through the long row of chairs. The pattern of embroidered daisies on her beige shorts showed up blue-white in the psychedelic lighting of the auditorium and made them appear almost detached from her body, like unnatural flowers floating in the air.

"Eric, Eric, you're so beautiful! Did you know that, fair prince?"

"Where're ya going?" Brenda yelled when they walked by.

"I'm taking her to the bathroom," Eric answered. "She can't go alone."

"Sickening," Slim drawled to Brenda.

"Slim, you're so bitter sometimes, it makes me shiver," Brenda said. She wrapped her shawl around her small, plump shoulders as if she had felt a gust of cool air. Her tiny, well-shaped hands clattered the rings she wore on every finger of her hand together noisily.

Eric pushed open the weighty metal door of the auditorium as they stepped out into the moist night air. A peaceful silence lay over the car tops and motorcycles parked in slipshod rows in the parking lot. Kreeger stood by the old limousine, smoking his fat cigar.

"Kreeger, old man, why don't you go and watch the show?" Eric asked, and handed him a ten dollar bill surreptitiously.

"I think I will. Why don't you two sit in the car and rest a while?" he answered. He winked theatrically at them while he held the wide car door open.

They slipped inside the dark upholstery of the car's interior like two nimble deer, laughing and touching one another's sides with fingertips made icy from anticipation. She stared at his shirt, watching it buckle open from his hard, curving rib cage. She thrust one hand forward and touched his chest.

"Hey, that tickles," he protested. He pushed her backwards in a heap of legs and arms.

"Ha! Ha! Ohh," she gasped. She fell back on the cushiony car seat, grasping his arms like a tiny person riding the wings of a giant moth.

His hand fell on her stomach like a warm, cupped paw.

"I'm gonna get you now," he panted, laughing excitedly, and averted eyes from hers with an adolescent embarrassment at the nakedness of his desires.

"Just wait," he continued, and pinned both of her wrists down to the seat as if she were struggling to get away. She twisted her face from side to side and tried to escape from his hard young body. The rough material of his khaki pants rubbed the flesh of her thighs, heating her skin like a stinging whip.

"Eric, Eric, be careful. I can't breathe," she whispered. She struggled up on both elbows until she managed to sit pressed against the cold of the car window.

"Umm, mmm, mm," he said as he kissed her warmly on her pretty mouth.

"Just let me breathe, please, Eric," she sighed. She moved her fingertips over his berry-like nipples and felt the teats grow hard as B-B gun pellets under her touch. "You are like a wild, gay animal!" she exclaimed. She traced the line of his jaw with the fingers of her hand lovingly. "Maybe you should have a horn in the middle of your forehead – one single, graceful horn," she whispered. "Extending up from your nose," she continued, and pushed her forefinger along his nose and up into the air.

He grabbed her hands again and sank them into the car seat behind her back, kissing her neck with swift, short endearments.

"Oh God, I love you, Cybele," he murmured from the hollow of her neck. The muffled sound of his words reverberated on her flesh like a man in pain.

Even though she struggled in his clumsy, insistent grasp, she shifted her hips up under his thighs smoothly, instinctively, stopping when she felt his hard, sabre-like dick jutting on her thigh.

"Eric, Eric," she said softly, caressing his cheek with the palm of her hand. "You can't be a unicorn. You have to be my minotaur – my wild man. You deserve two horns, *not* one." She pressed him tightly to her breasts, squirming rigidly up to his body until her nipples grew hard from being ground into his chest.

He pulled one of her legs apart and thrust his hand into the warmth of her body. "Ohhh, Cybele. Oh!" He pushed himself into her lustily, like an oar hitting the water of a rippling stream.

"Oh God, oh God, I love my dick in your cunt, Cybele." He moaned in pleasure and he jabbed himself up into her soft, wet flesh with the fast mechanical strokes of his hard dick.

"Oh Eric. Oh God. Do it to me good," she panted, and grasped his thick, curly hair with both hands.

"I'll love you good," he whispered savagely. He thrust the tip of his hard, insistent dick higher into her body until she felt a searing pain on the outside of her womb.

"Oh yes! Yes! You do. You do it good," she wailed, still holding onto his hair.

"Pinch my nipples, you cunt. Pinch them," he ordered, and pushed her up to his chest. She twisted the soft, brown-purple flesh of his teats in her fingertips and gloated at his expression of ecstasy. She felt his hard cock in her cunt and his tender nipples between her fingertips.

"Eric, Eric. I love you! I love you! Love me forever," she said urgently, and flung her legs wildly around his tapering back.

"Oh, oh, gonna come now," he sighed. He drew his narrow hips back from her belly and held her perfectly still and even for the piston-like strokes of his dick. The expression of his face mirrored his petit mort, changing in the way a film goes slightly out of focus.

He sank over her like a stilled bow, breathing into her ear.

"Oh Star! Oh Eric Star," she sang happily into his curls, draping her long slender hands over his heaving shoulder blades.

They fell asleep blissfully in one another's arms. Their bodies lay together like two Raggedy Ann dolls. Both of her hands were drawn up under her as if in prayer. Their breathing clouded the massive glass of the car windows. It obfuscated all but a tantalising view of her legs and the side of her face on his shoulder.

The concert ended and a slow stream of people made their way out to the parking lot. Some of them drifted past the limousine, then stopped to examine its fogged-up windows with curiosity. One of them noticed the white flowers on Cybele's shorts in the car's darkened interior and drew closer to the window. He peered down at Eric and Cybele greedily. His breath came in short little gasps on the car's steamed-up windows.

"Hey – lookit," he shouted. Several of his companions came running over beside him and followed his gaze into the car.

"Wow!" one of them exclaimed, without taking his eyes from the pair inside. "Right here in the parking lot?"

"Yeah, man," another joined in, jostling sweatily up to his companion.

"Hey, you wanna have some fun?" the seeming leader of the group asked. He unrolled a packet of cigarettes that he had twisted up into the arm of his T-shirt, Marlon Brando style. "Go get the flashlight," he grinned wildly at his companions.

Kreeger stepped outside of the auditorium and relit his cigar almost immediately. He took a deep breath of the muggy night air and gasped, then clamped his teeth down on his well-chewed cigar butt. The shrill vibrations of the music still seemed to be pulsing themselves through his protruding belly. He grasped his wide black belt between one fleshy thumb and forefinger, hitching up his pants as if to steady himself while walking towards the car. He remembered a strident, ringing sensation that always coursed through his whole being when he came out from one of these affairs. His body felt unusually light and floating. The sounds that had flown through it had detached it from its actual heavy weight.

"Eric, Eric!" Cybele shouted, blinded by the startling glare of the flash light that the people had shone into the window. "Wake up, wake up!" she moaned and twisted her body out from under him.

He came sleepily back to consciousness, looking into the light dully, then all of the muscles of his body tensed. He sprang off her and rolled the window down a few inches.

"What the fuck do you dudes think you're up to?"

"We just want to see the stars make love," a skinny guy with large brown eyes drawled.

"Yeah, how about an autograph?" the boy smoking a cigarette asked. "How was it, anyway?" he leered. The rest of his companions guffawed.

"Oh Eric, this is *awful*," Cybele cried, mortified by the boys' sweaty, hungry faces.

"I wanna beat their asses, but I'm afraid to open the door," Eric told her. "They might try to grab you or something dumb like that." He sat on the edge of the seat with his naked buttocks visible, then leaned forward in agitation, flailing his arms menacingly at the boys and girls surrounding the car.

"Can't you dudes think of something to do with your own chicks?" he taunted them, exasperated by their persistent inquisitiveness. One of them took the flashlight and bashed it against the car window.

"Eric, they're going to hurt us!" she screamed. She clung to his arms with both hands, whimpering.

"Goddammit, that tears it," Eric shouted. He crawled past Cybele and flung open the car door.

"Eric! Oh Eric! I'm afraid," she cried. "Oh no! Oh no!" she protested, clutching his arm so hard that her fingernails scratched his flesh.

The light from the flashlight blinded her. She became panic-stricken when she felt his arm slip away from her grasp. The odour of the boys' sweating bodies swept into her nostrils like an overwhelming flood. A nauseating, icy fear gripped her stomach. She felt like a rabbit caught in the ruthless glare of a car's headlights. She stared into the flashlight's dazzling beam, hypnotised.

Somehow, she was once again on a pitch-black, deserted country road just outside New Orleans. She was running, stumbling in front of the elegant white snout of Pierre's Jaguar, trying to escape from the blinding headlights of his sports car.

"Run, you bitch," he had shouted, racing the car motor violently.

"Pierre, Pierre!" she had screamed. "Please don't hit me. Oh! Oh!" she had panted. She ran along in front of his car. On either side of her the night had stretched, endless and black like a pit in the swampy Louisiana night.

"Run, bitch! Ha. Ha. Run! You look so funny running in front of my car. Why didn't we think of this game sooner?" he questioned her gleefully, and speeded the car up a little.

"Oh Pierre, Pierre, I'm tired. I can't keep running. God. God!" she had wailed, then stumbled before the relentlessly bright headlights.

"Help! Help! Don't hit me with the car, Pierre! Oh no. Oh don't!" She felt herself wrestling with two ropey muscular arms. "No!" she screamed, and threw her hands over her head, trying to protect herself from the car.

"Will you cool it a minute?" Eric asked. He grasped her around the waist and then threw the large flashlight into the crowd of running boys.

"Thanks, Kreeger," Eric grinned. He thrust his hand into Kreeger's beefy palm and shook it with relief.

"T'wasn't nothing," Kreeger smiled. He leaned over to pick his train conductor-like hat out of the dirt. A footprint showed itself plainly on the crown.

"Hey, man, you're bleeding," Eric exclaimed. He touched the front of Kreeger's ear.

Kreeger put his fat finger up to the side of his face, then drew it and stared at the blood there.

"Must've nicked me when he went down," Kreeger supposed. He winked at Eric conspiratorially, looking like an aged, high school tough. He dusted his hat off and carefully replaced it on the dome of his egg-shaped head, then stepped back shyly when he noticed Cybele crying on Eric's arm.

"What's going on?" Carot shouted as he ran up to them, pulling Brenda and Slim along behind him.

"My God, Cybele, you're as pale as a ghost," Brenda exclaimed, and rush up to her side.

"Maybe it's the company she keeps," Slim observed sourly. He trailed behind Brenda like a disillusioned ballet dancer. In the revealing brightness of the parking lights his face looked wan and hollow-eyed. Great, dark circles had grown under his pale grey eyes like strange delicate fruit during the concert. He kept his body close to Brenda's with a bitchy, nervous urgency, like a sickly child complaining constantly to its mother, yet never wanting to lose the comforting security of her closeness.

"Everybody in the car," Carot commanded. "We'll talk it over inside."

He jerked open the door to the driver's seat and looked meaningfully at Kreeger. Kreeger pushed his cap further down on his fat head and shuffled in the car seat like a hired hand, his bulky figure acquiescent under the authority in Carot's voice.

The engine of the oversized car roared up with sound like a bear growling from an awakened sleep. Eric and Cybele followed Slim and Brenda into its cavernous interior. Carot stood just outside the car door while he waited for them to enter, glancing warily at the straggling group of kids milling near the car in small clusters.

"Sir. . ." one called, and took a few steps forward, tentatively holding out an autograph book.

"Don't get too close!" Carot shouted. He held his hand out so menacingly that the boy dropped his autograph pad and fled.

"Ha. . . ha. . . ah ha – fools, fools," he gloated. He swept inside the car beside Brenda and Slim like a latter-day Bella Lugosi. Cybele viewed him with mistrust, while she clung to Eric like a tattered doll.

"Drive on, Kreeger, my man," Carot shouted harshly. "Get us out of the hordes. . ." He brushed violently on his maroon velvet jacket. "These hordes of locusts," he finished. He adjusted a small antique brooch pinned just under the nape of his shirt and returned Cybele's frightened, suspicious look with surprise.

"My dear girl," he said, touching her hands sympathetically with his long tapering fingers, "whatever happened to you?" She drew her hand back from his touch, shuddering involuntarily as if a lizard had landed there.

"You look positively broken," he continued. "Eric, what have you done to this child?"

"Look, you over-aged glory hound," Eric snarled. "Your little act tonight almost got my ass kicked, and Cybele could've been raped. Not to mention poor Kreeger's car. So you just cool it. I don't feel like carrying on any trashy conversation at the moment." He finished in a rush, turning his face sulkily to the window. Cybele continued to lie beside him like an expired flower.

"Wow, what a strange evening this has turned out to be," Brenda said in a small, embarrassed voice.

"Turned out to be? Humph," Slim said. He drew his bony knees together so tightly that had they been toothpicks they might have snapped.

"Never mind, there's a tremendous party going on right now at a friend of mine's. We'll just get Kreeger to drop us by and hitch a ride home later."

"We will not," Eric protested sharply. "That is, Cybele and I will not be going to any fucking party. I've had enough of your parties for one evening, Carot."

"Oh, goody," Brenda said. "A party!" Slim's sunken eyes drank in her enthusiasm.

"Sure, party time again," Carot said, smiling his thin smile. He began rolling a joint. The thin white paper folded itself neatly over the marijuana. He licked one long finger and ran it down the edge of the paper, moistening it with a sleek, polished motion. Then he pressed it securely around the grass. The hiss of his match sent a flare of bluish-orange light up around his face when he lit the joint. One fluffy white puff wafted out from his thin, wise mouth and up into their nostrils. They heard a sharp intake of breath, and sat waiting to see who would be the first to be offered the next drag – the accepted protocol of courtesy among all grass smokers.

"Good stuff, lady," Carot said, and handed the joint to Cybele. "Good for the soul," he added, searching deep into her memory-ridden eyes.

She reached out for the joint with her eyes fastened onto his like a drowning person grabbing at a stray piece of flotsam floating in the ocean.

"Nah, don't give her any more," Eric said wearily, and pushed Carot's hand away.

"Pleasesee, Eric," she whined. She leaned forward so swiftly that she fell onto the floorboard and landed on her knees at Carot's feet. "I need some."

"Balls!" Eric groaned. He slumped back against the black leather car seat, letting his chin droop down to his collar-bone in dejection.

"Yes, you need some. . . solace," Carot decreed, stroking her shiny black hair, and he put the joint to her lips.

"Hold it deep, little girl, this is some special stuff," he advised.

"Hurry up, Cybele, don't be such a spoiled person," Brenda said. Her broad, Philadelphia Jewish accent rounded *person* into *poyson*.

"Patience, Brenda. All things come to those with it," Slim said wryly.

"What are you giving her anyway?" Eric asked suspiciously, and snatched the joint from her mouth. "If this is what I think it is, one puff is plenty for her," He dragged the smoke down deep into his throat and held it searchingly in his lungs.

"Columbia Red, you bastard," he said, choking slightly when he exhaled.

"Really?" Brenda said, clapping her ring-encrusted hands together. "Pass it on over, and I hope I meet somebody beautiful at the party." She took the joint between her tiny fingers and rolled her eyes around comically, then inhaled gratefully.

"Oh brother, just what I need," Slim said self-consciously.

"That's *exactly* what you need," Brenda said, putting the joint into his mouth.

"Brenda, you're so sloppy. Really!" he sputtered, but inhaled deeply on the mushy-tipped cigarette.

Carot smiled at them with amusement as they sped over Key Bridge and back into Georgetown.

"We want out at your place, Carot. I've probably got a ticket already," Eric said.

"Are you sure about that, old man? This's really a swinging place. They got a trampoline out in the backyard and everybody'll be swimming 'as is' in the pool.

"What if I don't feel in the mood to get wet?" Eric asked unsociably.

"Then you and lady love can go hop on the water-bed. Give her another hit on that and you might have to leave the water-bed to go swimming," Carot drawled and squeezed Brenda's shoulder with affection.

"Carot, you're a master party-man. You're my style, baby," Brenda squealed. She grasped his hand and pulled herself playfully under his arm.

Carot patted her head like a person throwing peanuts to a small animal in the zoo and said, "You'll fly, little wee one, don't worry."

"Oh Eric, Eric, let me have some more of that stuff. I feel so. . . swinging," Cybele exclaimed, starting up out of her depressed stupor.

"Oh God, now you've got her going," Eric groaned.

"Sure, beautiful butterfly. Just fasten those warm tender lips on this and fly away," Carot prescribed to Cybele like a witch doctor.

She brought her mouth up to his hand and dragged on the joint, giggling and choking from the strong smoke.

"Here's where," Carot said as they slid to a stop in front of his apartment. "Last chance to continue the enchantment." He looked longingly into Cybele's shining eyes, that sparkled like pellucid mountain streams in the bright neon lights, and blew a kiss to her inviting smile.

"Oh Eric, let's go to the party, *please*," she pleaded.

"Christ!" he muttered. "I knew it. I knew it."

"But Eric, maybe we could spend the night together there without having to worry about Hadrian. Carot said they had a water-bed." She looked at Carot entreatingly.

"She's always thinking for you, my man," Carot said. His voice was tinged with envy, yet admiration showed in his eyes for Cybele's enthusiasm.

Eric hesitated a moment, like a horse trying to refuse sugar lumps.

"Ah, Ericson – you know you wanna come now," Brenda coaxed.

"It's the event of the year," Slim intoned sarcastically.

"Eric, I just can't wait to hop in a pool, nude!" Cybele squealed.

"Whatever gave you the idea, luv, that you were going to swim nude?" Eric asked, looking at her so sternly that she felt herself blush.

"Well. . . Carot said. . ." she began.

"OK, OK, let's go to the party. But only if I get to lie around in my birthday suit with a blonde," he said teasingly.

"Oh Eric, I love you!" Cybele cried and she clasped her arms tightly around his neck.

"Onward, Kreeger," Carot shouted.

"Right-O," Kreeger said. He spurted the big car forward, turning off M Street and onto Wisconsin Avenue. They sped through the moist summer night like a special joy train. Leafy trees were pregnant in a lacy canopy over the hood of their car. Carot switched on a tiny transistor radio and a singer wailed out "Good golly, Miss

Molly, you sure know how to ball!" Brenda began singing along in a nasal voice. Her words were slurred noticeably by the marijuana.

The car nosed its way down the width of Massachusetts Avenue, past the half-moon-shaped driveways of embassies that stood like corpulent, self-satisfied men under the grand branches of ancient oak trees, and came to a halt before a large private home.

"We have arrived, children," Carot announced, then sprang out of the car.

"Wow, what a joint!" Brenda exclaimed, looking at an impressive, stucco-covered home. It sat at the top of a terraced rock garden that rose in specially landscaped tiers to the black wrought iron front door of the elaborate house.

"Eric, it's a *castle!*" Cybele whispered, looking up at the house without moving from the car.

"Yeah, it ain't bad," he agreed. "Are you getting out of the car or not?"

They watched Carot leap up the steps in bouncing, catlike steps, then followed like the clan of an unknown superman. A girl with hip-length, silky blonde hair opened the door and smiled sweetly at Carot.

"Enter," she said, then stepped back from the doorway. Her pale hand rested on the black wrought iron door gracefully. Its delicate nails were tinted pink underneath with her fresh warm blood.

"Charmed to be met at the door by a real live sea nymph," Carot said, glancing at the girl's shell-pink nipple that nature had painted feather soft on the white, shining flesh of her breast.

"My name is Anna," the girl said in an aristocratic British accent. She drew her other hand down by her firm, tapering thigh in a protective gesture, yet opened the door wider. She stood staring at Carot with large blue eyes.

"My heavens, she's like the goddess Artemis," Slim said in spite of himself.

They followed the girl inside a spacious darkened foyer. Their shoe heels clattered sharply over the parquet floor. Under their feet were puffy Chinese plum blossoms that had been hand painted on the ivory-coloured tiles. Large, pear-shaped urns with green, hissing dragons sculpted on their sides stood by walls that disappeared into the blackness of the shadows. The girl's pale hair shone like the silvery slime of a snail's progress on old stones from the moon's oblique beam slanting through the sweeping patio doors. She led them through rooms filled with white draped furniture like an apparition.

"Joe's parents have evacuated for the summer to their home in London," she explained as they traipsed past inanimate mounds of covered furnishings. On a rose marble mantlepiece, a Meissen statue of a delicate-cheeked man stood in halted promenade. The cold porcelain of his turquoise jacket rippled open casually over dark red flowers scattered across his yellow vest in designs of fleurs-de-lis. A lion that had been carved about the round, sly face of an old clock stretched its paw out a few inches away from the statue's gold buckled, high-heeled shoes. Behind the *objets d'art* a wide glistening mirror hung, reflecting the statue's graceful stance. His hand was inclined over a rose like Byron remembering his favourite poem. Through the still dark air, tiny motes of dust floated upwards into the ceiling like bodiless, silver spirits.

"This way," Anna called, walking through two crystal glass doors and out onto a tree-shaded veranda. They followed her uncertainly, abashed into silence by the obvious vastness of wealth displayed so simply about them.

"My God," Brenda exclaimed when they came in sight of a lighted swimming pool. It was shaped like a swan's wing in the deep green velvet of the lawn. Figures darted in and out of the pale blue water like strange shining nightfish, their limbs luminous in the pool's bright lights. In the distance, darkened bodies bounced up into the treetops like high flying gas balloons from the trampoline below. And in the highest branches of the trees, a waxy yellow moon burned through the hazy summer night:, its edges blurred with indistinct rings of a yellow and pink halo.

Anna led them to a group of people sitting in *chaise longues* and white patio chairs around an ample matching table.

"Joe, some more friends," she said to the back of a man's shiny, dark-haired head.

The young Eurasian turned his head back to her partially. A small smile of anticipation showed on his full, pouting lips while he studied them with his brown, slightly-slanted eyes.

"Welcome to the night," he said, for want of some other expression which he didn't feel like making the mental effort to think of. The lapel of his robe buckled over the initials *J.Y.*, that had been stitched in dark blue silk on the pocket, when he turned towards them.

"This is Joe Yang," Anna said, resting her small, fragile hand on the thick, white towelling of Joe's bathrobe.

"Hi," Joe said. His blunt, flat nostrils flared outwards like the dragon snouts on the urns in the hallway. Small drops of pool water trickled down the sides of his handsome face as water courses off the impervious feathers of a duck's back.

"And I don't know your names yet," Anna continued in a voice barely audible over the splashings from the pool.

"What would you like to drink. . . er?" Joe said, waiting for Carot to give his name.

"Carot Edwards, here," Carot said.

He took off his plumed hat and swept it down to the floor with a flourish. Everyone chuckled appreciatively. "I'm partial to Bloody Marys," he stated.

"Hsi, Hsi," Joe called, clapping his hands together. A short, bald Oriental standing at a portable bar on the far side of the patio came running over. He bowed seriously to Joe three times. Each time he did so, Carot bowed after him.

"Bloody Mary for him, Hsi – how about everybody else?"

"A little glass of sherry for me," Slim said timidly. His large grey eyes mirrored the pool's lights like a mouse looking out furtively from its hole.

"We're just smoking tonight," Eric explained and clasped his arm around Cybele possessively.

"Most marvellous stuff," Cybele giggled.

"Yes, looks like it," Joe agreed. He looked closely at Cybele as if he might be appraising a statue suitable for his parent's house.

"You've got a grand place," Brenda observed, looking all around. "Could I go and hop on the trampoline?"

"Of course," Anna replied. "Come on, and I'll take you over there." She took Brenda by the hand. Her long slender legs were half hidden by the flounces of Brenda's full patchwork skirt.

"Brenda, you can't jump up and down in that outfit," Slim yelled, running along behind them, agitated. "You'll be killed!"

"Want to go swimming?" Joe asked Eric and Cybele. "Since you're only smoking tonight, someone passes around the edges of the pool every half an hour with something good to sniff."

"OK, great," Eric said. He started walking off to the pool.

"You can change in there," Joe said, nodding to a room next to the patio.

"Into what?" Eric asked.

"Anything you'd like," he replied. He turned back to continue his conversation with a blond young man who had draped his slender torso over one of the *chaise longues*.

"I'll just wear my shorts," Cybele said.

"Better save them for later. You'll need them," Eric cautioned. "Here, take my T-shirt and just wear your underpants."

"But Eric, I don't have any panties on!"

"OK, pull the damned shirt down over your ass then, and stick close to me."

They walked across the sloping yard, away from the patio and into the musty little room Joe had directed them to.

"Eric, I just can't believe that you're going to strip down to your underwear. As modest as you are and everything," Cybele protested, laughing.

He scowled at her for a moment, then began laughing crazily.

"OK, Mrs Tashery. Whatever you say, it's just a bunch of shit and I'm not listening cause I'm going to have fun with your bare little fanny in that pool tonight. You got that?" he said, and took another drag from a joint he had lit.

His eyes shone brightly at her. Their unnaturally bright glitter excited her in the room's darkened interior. She rushed over to caress his bare legs when he stepped out of his khaki pants.

"Oh Eric," she whispered, "how *divine* you are!"

"Lick my toes," he commanded.

She stared at his dirty, pleasingly-shaped toes and began kissing one obediently.

"Ha. Ha. Far out! You're really a loving woman." He knelt down and put one hand on her backbone, tracing its subtle imagery tenderly. He pressed his hard groin against her head while she kissed his foot. She tore off her blouse and began rubbing her breasts back and forth on his feet.

"You love to fuck, don't you?" he asked, smiling at her gleefully. "C'mon over here on this thing, whatever it is. I want to put something hard and good in your cunt."

He pulled her over to a wing chair and pushed her slender body back on the velvet upholstery.

"Open your long, lovely legs, sweetheart, if you want my dick," he commanded.

She opened her legs and lay back in the arms of the chair. The stillness of the room was interrupted by their short pants and rippling laughter. He shoved himself up into her swiftly, like a man cutting off heads with an extra sharp sword.

"Oh!" she gasped.

"Like it?" He smiled down at her, his eyes glistening with passion and grass.

"Eric, Eric, push your dick in me. He feels so good in there. Oh!" she screamed. "Don't come up too far. It hurts when you do that. No, don't!" she cried. He purposely thrust his dick further up in her body, using his long, supple legs to give the hardest impetus to his strokes.

"You love that and you know it, damn it."

She smiled at him silently, watching his rhythmic motions, watching his dick.

"Did you come?" he asked, looking avidly into her eyes. He returned her smile when he saw a surfeit of pleasure brimming in her blue-green irises.

"Yes, you came," he recognised, kissing her nipples tenderly with his tongue. "Sometimes you don't scream," he murmured into her ear. He continued to move smoothly in her body.

She wondered what he and Hadrian would both do if they knew that she only faked orgasms.

"Oh, oh God. Yeah, me too," he gasped. She looked swiftly up to his face before he buckled over her, hungry to watch his expression change with the sudden explosion of pleasure coursing through his body.

"Oh Eric, you're so beautiful when your face crumbles," she whispered.

"Cool it," he said, then sprang off her. "Somebody's coming! Put this on," he told her, and threw his T-shirt over her breasts. He stood in front of her like a recently displaced mannequin while she hastily pulled on the shirt. His dick was still semi-hard and bulging inside his cotton jockey shorts.

Her eyes lit on a white object stuffed down in the chair. She thrust her hand between its velvety cushions and pulled out a filmy, pair of panties.

"Look!" she exclaimed, holding the panties up for Eric's approval.

"Yeah, someone's been using this spot for our same labours. Put 'em on."

She pulled the panties on over her thighs, grinning at him as if she had just been outfitted in Saks, Fifth Avenue.

"Got the T-shirt pulled way down?" he asked, still panting from his past activities.

"Uh huh," she said in assent. "Why don't we go?" she asked, then leapt out of the chair and onto his back. "Piggyback," she shouted. "Go piggy! Ha. Ha."

He looked merrily over his shoulder at her, working his mouth wildly back and forth over his gums in a habitual expression of excitement. He hooked his arms tightly under her legs and galloped past two startled figures out onto the luxurious lawn.

"Faster, faster, strange beast," she giggled as they hopped along down the rolling green slope.

"I know your ass is hanging out, " Eric said. He galloped to a halt by the pool's side.

"No, it isn't," she answered primly. "I've got the shirt clamped down with my fanny muscles."

"Strongest muscles in the world," he confirmed and dumped her into the pool over his shoulders.

She plunged into the warm lap of water, opening her eyes to thousands of shooting, aqua-white bubbles as she floated to the top. Eric dived in after her, jumping through the velvety night air like a springy-legged grasshopper. She lay on her back and absorbed the light of a million blue-white stars in one glance. Her arms pushed her body smoothly through the champagne-coloured water and close to two nude figures on a floating *chaise longue*.

"Humph! Gotcha," Eric said. He grabbed her around her small waist and lifted her up into the air.

"Oh! Really, Eric!" she said demurely, batting pendulant, crystal drops of water from her mascara-blackened eyelashes.

"Oh, really Eric," he mimicked, and dropped her back down in the water.

She surfaced and followed his gaze to a couple in front of them on a floating chair. The girl's long, silky hair hung down on her Titian-like breasts in heavy, golden ropes. Her girlish laughter tinkled enticingly over the heavy swish of the pool's water. She plaited and

unplaited one pale gold piece of hair into a long braid. Her dainty
white hands disappeared like lustrous pearls into its silken mass.

"Wow!" Eric exclaimed.

A dark, curly haired boy drew the girl closer to them by the rim of
her floating-pool boat.

"It's Anna," Cybele whispered.

"Hello," Anna called, pressing one rosy knee against the other,
and shifting her legs up for more balance and modesty on the gliding
chair.

"This is Omar," she said, holding her small hand out in the boy's
direction. She smiled at them sweetly through brilliant red lips.

"'Lo," Omar said. His deep voice vibrated mellowly through the
light splashing sounds that the movements of their bodies produced in
the water.

"Hi," Eric and Cybele said shyly. They both still gazed at Anna's
Dresden-like figure floating before them.

The boy followed their stares, then smiled disarmingly at them.

"I know," he said, as if they had already spoken. "She's
beautiful, isn't she? A real classic. A piece of porcelain. Maybe like
something you'd have on your bedside table," he stated reverently and
kissed a gold medallion that read "Allah" in Arabic from a chain
around his neck.

"Omar is our chief scribe around here," Anna said, letting both of
her long, slender legs slip down from under her arms. She touched
his hand with one toe and revealed a golden thatch of curling hair on
the 'V' of her cunt.

"He travelled all the way from Kuwait to record for us."

"He's a writer?" Cybele asked, her voice a little shaky at the sight
of another girl's cunt so simply displayed. She glanced automatically
at Eric to observe his face, her natural cunning for hiding her jealousy
overridden by a feline curiosity.

"Yes," Anna replied, kicking her delicate shell-pink toes in the
water's fluorescent glow. "Of fantasies," she added, smiling at them
mischievously.

"Fantasies?" Cybele repeated, bewitched. "Can we read some of
them?" she asked, with a childlike candour that was so credulous that
they all burst out laughing.

"Under the water, fairyhead," Eric said. He pushed her down into the pool to relieve his feelings, looking furtively at the empyrean creaminess of Anna's face and body.

At that moment Anna turned her golden-haired head to a figure leaning over various indigo silhouetted bathers along the pool's side. Leaning her graceful body forward and grasping Omar's vigorously curling hair like a languorous odalisque, she cried, "Steer to poolside for our dearest perfume, oh satyr mine," in succinct British tones. Her smooth, moon-white hand grappled in his dark hair as if seeking two hard, miniature horns to grasp.

"Ohhh," Cybele gasped, springing up out of the water and gulping for air.

Omar had already turned towards the direction of the pool's side. He guided Anna and her feather-like "boat" with his brown, sturdy arms like a dusky slave of ancient times.

"C'mon," Eric said, excitedly, and pulled Cybele after them.

Anna stepped off the boat into Omar's waiting, thickly muscled arms that glistened from the pool water. The lightly blushing pink of her nipples brushed the hard, bunched muscles of his forearm as he lifted her carefully down into the water beside himself. She placed her pale hands on both of his darkly tanned shoulders, smiling angelically while he manoeuvred her to the side of the pool.

A boy leaned over and held his cupped hand to her nose. She reached up with both of her hands and clasped his hand more firmly to her face, then breathed deeply. The rouge on her lips shone as red as crushed berries against her small white teeth. Behind their white, sharp-looking tips her tongue moved wetly, pressing itself against their backs with an anticipatory pressure.

"What is she doing?" Cybele asked.

"Sniffing cocaine, ignorant one," Eric said scornfully.

"Hurry over," Omar called. He motioned sportively to them. "Participate," he encouraged.

He reached out and grasped Cybele's hand. She let herself be pulled up alongside him and Anna, feeling the closeness of their bodies to her own. She was startled by Omar's overly muscled arms and Anna's golden pubic hair submerged in the water like golden seaweed. She wanted to stroke the hulking flesh of Omar's arms, to feel the furry, delicate hair between Anna's legs.

"How beautiful your nipples are, Anna," she exclaimed.

"Kiss them, then," Anna advised. She held one full round breast up to Cybele with her small hand.

Eric sped up behind Cybele. He clasped her around her slender waist and stuck his forefinger in her navel.

"Shall I?" Cybele asked, looking at Anna's breast admiringly.

"It's ever so delectable," Omar recommended.

"Here, come and have a whiff first," Anna told her and pulled her through the water to her side. The boy standing over them held his hand to Cybele's nose.

"Breathe deeply," Anna instructed. "Don't let any get away."

Cybele took a deep breath, and coughed.

"No, no, " Omar exclaimed. "Take another and hold one side of your nose."

She took another deep breath from the boy's cupped hand.

"You've never had cocaine, have you?" Omar asked. He smiled engagingly at her darkly tanned face and gleaming green eyes. His white, still adolescently rough front teeth showed charmingly under his rubbery, thick lips.

"Uh uh," she grunted through tightly pressed lips, motioning to her mouth. She began laughing, letting her breath out in a whoosh.

"Yes, she has," Eric said in a surly, contradictive manner. He was torn between his lust for Anna and the jealousy that stabbed him while he watched Omar's trenchant brown eyes on Cybele's lithe, water-moulded body. "She just doesn't remember it."

"Yes, I do, Eric. I remember lots of things," she replied, pouting.

She splashed him tentatively with water to see what he would do. He swam up beside her and grabbed her hands. His shoulder brushed Anna's breast as he did so and made it tremble like jelly. A pang of jealousy swept through Cybele when she saw his flesh touch Anna's. But a desire to have this same flesh that stoked her jealousy so much in her mouth formed in her brain and shone in her glassy, drugged eyes.

"Kiss me now," Anna asked Cybele again.

Cybele looked at Eric with a questioning expression. He shrugged his shoulders and kept watching her attentively to see what she would do. She stared at Anna's long flowing hair floating in the water and surrounding her shoulders like liquid honey. Her crystal blue eyes looked into Cybele's green, curious gaze with expectation. Slowly Cybele drew her lips to Anna's delicate, pink nipple and tasted its tender flesh.   She rolled Anna's teat around on her tongue, then clasped her own nipples hungrily.

"Ummmm, you kiss so well," Anna moaned.   She pressed Cybele's dark-haired head closer to her white breast with one graceful, imperious hand.

"She's like an Indian, Omar.   Why don't you fuck her?" Anna asked.   Cybele clasped Anna passionately around her waist.

Cybele felt Omar's thick, ample cock press itself between her round, taut buttocks.   She unconsciously relaxed their muscles, trying to facilitate the pressure of his cock on her body.   She put her hand down to Anna's cunt, exploring her plump, fresh pubis with her fingertips.

"I've never felt another cunt before," she said, and put her fingers between Anna's soft, tumescent lips.

"Mmmm," Anna said.   "She knows how to play."

Eric watched the three of them jealously, held back by a dated but subconsciously binding conventionality.   Finally he leaned down and kissed Cybele's high puffy breasts, while holding one of Anna's bosoms in his hand.

"Oh Eric, do that, darling," Cybele cried.   She felt his mouth sucking fiercely on her nipple and Omar's club-like dick pressing back and forth on her ass.   Eric's hand passed over her hand with which she held Anna's cunt and moved her fingers away.   He thrust his fingers up into Anna's golden fleece and began jabbing them back and forth in Anna's body.

"Ohh, ohh, they're terrific, Omar," Anna cried, grasping Eric's cock in one hand and touching Cybele's cunt with her diminutive fingers.

"Oh, oh," Cybele sighed.   "I want to be with you!"   She thought longingly of Omar's wide cock almost in her ass now.   She wanted its savage width inside her body.   She wanted to try something new, just for the moment.   She longed to suck his fleshy lips between her teeth and tongue.

"Well, well, what an inspiring sight," a detached, accented voice said.   They looked up to see Joe Yang standing by the side of the pool, smoking deliberatively from an ivory, Meerschaum cigarette holder decorated with carved flowers.   "It's enough to make a fellow want to hop in his own pool," he commented dryly.

"Why don't you?" Anna asked invitingly. A small cloud of vexation veiled the lust in her eyes.

"Oh no, my dear sweet pet. I'll just sit this one out," he replied cryptically.

The white towelled robe he wore fell back to reveal his elongated, barrel-like chest and rather high, narrow hips. His body was slender and his legs long. He looked like a good sprinter or soccer player.

"Are you having fun?" he asked Cybele drolly.

"Oh yesss," she slurred. Her hand was still on Anna's body.

She looked at him with fascination. His eyes met hers with all the mystery of the Orient. Suddenly she saw his expression change when he shifted his gaze to Anna. A terrible agony of outrage and pain contorted his youthful features. He clenched his hands into fists. She could see him exerting a superhuman control over his emotions

"I know you are," he laughed. "You're on the rule of five.

"The rule of five?" she repeated, looking at his tall, warrior-like figure speculatively. "What's the rule of five?" she asked.

He placed the elaborate cigarette holder between his faintly stained teeth and smiled sagaciously in the soft purple dusk of the night.

"You'll understand that when and if you ever escape from it," he answered mysteriously and walked away.

She stared after him, trying to assimilate his remarks. Her brain's machinery was ponderous from the heavy drugs, and her body tingled from its many stimulated sources of sensation. His tall, imposing form disappeared into the trees, leaving her with a disturbed curiosity, a longing to speak, but no words came to her mind. Soon she became aware of Omar's cock between her legs and Anna's lovely breasts floating in the water before her. Their globular mounds of flesh had the texture of opaque, creamy pearls. A sharp, stinging sensation shot up from Cybele's nipple and down into her belly when Eric resumed his tongue's caresses on her breast.

"Oh, ha, ha, ha," she exclaimed, then grabbed Omar's cock. "You're so big and thick down there, Omar."

She turned back from Anna's languid, exquisite face and laughed merrily at Omar, squeezing his spongy, substantial cock in her fingers. His brown eyes shone like a farouche tiger when she touched him. His eyelids closed partially in pleasure each time she squeezed his cock, making him resemble a lumpy green frog being stroked.

"I love you, Omar, I love you," she cried, and turned to kiss his full lips. "I taste figs on your mouth," she cried. "Your mouth is a firm, plump fig." She studied his face carefully. "And your nose and mouth, your eyes. . . look Egyptian. Ha ha ha," she cried deliriously. His mouth descended on hers and pressed its rubbery flesh onto her own in a firm, determined kiss.

"You don't look like any Anglo-Saxon I've ever seen, sweetheart," he breathed excitedly in her ear.

"Oh goody. I want to be different people, Omar. Let's create a fantasy tonight." She pulled back from his massive, armour-like chest and put her hands in his wiry black hair.

"Can you be an Egyptian tonight, Omar?" she asked.

"I'm your very own, Cybele. Whatever you want me to be, we'll make it come true right over there under the trees."

"Just where the fuck do you think you're taking her?" Eric demanded.

She turned back to Eric as if startled by the screech of a mawkish parrot, her tanned brown arms still encircling Omar's darker, exotic skin.

"Don't be upset, Eric," Cybele said. "We all love each other." She pressed her nose back and forth on Omar's sideburns, itching it confidently.

"Hey man, you got business to take care of right beside you," Omar instructed him, looking pointedly at Anna's slender, voluptuous body.

Eric scowled at Cybele and crossed his arms stubbornly.

"Eric," Anna crooned, encircling his neck with her long white arms like a graceful swan. "Could we get out of the water now?"

Eric hesitated a moment, then lifted her out of the water and onto the pool's side. In the distance forms of trampoliners bounced up and down in springing, perpetual jumps. Their shouts of laughter echoed mellowly through the night's dark, intoxicating air. Anna stood waiting before them, her pale shoulders and long white back surrounded by her golden tresses of hair.

"Oh, she's beautiful!" Cybele gasped. "I love her."

"I love you, Cybele," Omar whispered. "I love the way you love. Now upsy-daisy," he cried, and lifted her onto the side of the pool.

Anna stood in the deep indigo of the night. Away from the pool's glow, her body was bathed only in the light of the moon. Its waxy whiteness embodied the same stillness of large, willowy petalled irises that grew in clumps near her bare feet. She moved her arms torpidly through the heat of the night, raising long wet locks of golden hair off her neck. Eric leapt up beside her and took her hand shyly. She clasped her hand in his. The motions of her body and hands were removed from the natural movements of a human being. She was Persephone reincarnated, standing alive and warm blooded in the dark green grass.

She took Eric by the hand and led him into a copse of bushes. Her white feet moved swiftly as a fleeing doe through the grass. They huddled down on the soft dust and cool grass under the bushes. A pleasant smell of decayed plants and mouldy lichens wafted into the air and entered their nostrils. The perfume of oxygen and decay intoxicated their inner thighs and plunged them into sprawling attitudes on the grass.

Eric felt the smoothness of her skin on his roughened palm and imagined fleecy clouds in the sky that he had never before touched. Her silky flesh acted like a magnet on his loins, and his cock sprang up like a bumptious peasant between his legs. For once he wished he weren't so quick to be aroused. He wanted to go on touching Anna's arms for at least an hour before he moved to her pendulous, swaying breasts. The skin of her white, supple arms was like the newest baby chick's down under his fingertips. His lips trembled in an ardent kiss on the faint blue vein of her neck.

"Anna," he said reverently, watching her body in his arms as if he were holding a precious treasure.

"You are so tender, Eric," she said, and smiled at him again through glossy, red-rouged lips. Her blue eyes were wide and bright, like two periwinkles in the deep green darkness of the bushes. When she turned towards him, the scent that wafted out from her drying hair on her neck made him almost come. He clutched at his groin, moaning.

"Are you always this gentle? she asked, still smiling into his eyes with her clear blue eyes.

"No, never," he admitted, and moved his hands to her exquisite breasts. Her nipples were elastic and pink under his fingers. The heavy flesh of her breasts that filled the palm of his hand was like a plump, exotic fruit growing in the night; being plucked and stroked and fingered by his blunt, paw-like hands.

"Be good inside me. Be like a swift sword, Eric."

The sound of her words in his ears came like the inexorable splintering apart of a wave, releasing his body from its control that had halted him heretofore. He turned onto her stone-smooth belly and pushed his cock through the soft springy wound of her golden-haired cunt. Its creamy liquidity paralleled the softness of her breasts in his palm.

"Wow, you really *are* a fire-dick, Eric," she moaned, and lifted her lofty legs around his heaving back.

He felt the sharpness of his hard flesh inside her soft, warm cunt and had a frightening sensation of drowning.

"Oh," he cried, and flooded the essence of his body inside the convoluted trap of her vagina.

He breathed deeply several times, then moved his hands down to her hips. Their velvety solidness made him think of the tallow composing long, slender candles he had made in high school. His cock immediately regained its potency, and he began his motions anew.

"Eric, you fantastic dick," she crooned while she hugged her legs tighter around his shoulder blades. "How much longer can you keep this up?" she asked, looking wonderingly over his shoulder at his slim buttocks bobbing up and down over her.

"About four more times," Cybele answered cryptically as she and Omar approached into the circle of the bushes' enclosure. She purposely lay down very close to Anna, clutching her own breasts with jealousy and excitement, while she watched Eric shove himself up into Anna over and over.

Omar advanced to Cybele with determination. The chocolate glow of his skin shone mutely in the darkness. His rigid, dark cock hung before her eyes. Its emerging flesh had grown swollen and huge.

"Oh gosh," she exclaimed, amazed as she watched the size of it grow and grow. It had swollen up like a wild ungovernable plant, tumescent and dangerous to behold.

"Kiss it, Cybele," Anna instructed. "He loves to have it sucked."

Cybele reached out for Omar's cock, startled and frightened at the way it overflowed in her hand. She put its large, purple head into her mouth and began sucking its tip with a swirling motion of her tongue. He fell down on his knees before her, moaning, and tried to shove his cock up into her mouth.

"Oh no, I can't," she gasped. "I can't take that thing all the way!"

He placed one hand on her head and pushed her mouth gently over his cock.

"Relax, baby. I ain't going to do nothing you don't like," he consoled her.

She kept what she could of his cock in her mouth, lapping underneath at the small cut flesh of circumcision that Hadrian had taught her to concentrate on.

"Oh baby, I'm so glad to see you know right where you are," he whispered. His voice was filled with a husky ecstasy."

"She's good, isn't she, Omar?" Anna smiled dazzlingly again, watching while Cybele sucked furiously on his cock. "He's good too," she said, and opened her legs wider for Eric's swift thrusts.

"Why don't you come while she sucks me, Anna?" Omar asked. "I want to watch your beautiful face then." He shifted his hard rod further up into Cybele's mouth.

"With this action I can accommodate your wish very soon," she gasped, laughing happily.

Her blue violet eyes deepened their colour with her pleasure while Eric kept pounding into her submissive, pale flesh. Omar increased his thrusts into Cybele's mouth, inspired by Eric's lightning-like strokes and Anna's dangling, dimpled knees about his waist. Cybele tried desperately to keep his cock in her mouth without choking.

"I see your eyes, Anna," Omar cried. "It's going to be soon, now. I can tell."

"Yes, yes, soon, Omar. Oh, it's so good, so fantastic. He moves so fast. God! God!"

Eric kept up his rapid thrusts like a highly-fuelled fucking machine. He kept his face turned away from Omar and Cybele, still locked in a half-remembered conditioning of decorum.

"Your nipples are hard, Anna!" Omar cried. "I know you will come now." He sank his huge cock into Cybele's mouth until its head probed the back of her throat. She gagged painfully, but kept on sucking his cock faithfully.

"Oh, it's now," Anna said with helpless surprise. Her pale blue eyes clouded into the deep blue colour of the night that surrounded them.

Cybele turned her eyes away from Omar's cock and stared hungrily at Anna's face. A soft flicker of light had suffused the alluring whiteness of her cheeks and lit them like the luminous underbelly of a firefly. They were lambent, disturbing and poignant in the deep purple darkness. A small drop of spittle had formed outside her petal-like mouth. Her tongue flicked back and forth over her dry lips, searching for the moisture that passion had robbed her of.

"Then it's now for me too, doll-face," Omar said. Cybele felt a hot, thick cream shoot into the back of her throat.

"Ahhh," she heard him cry, and tried to swallow his juice to keep from choking. He bent over Cybele's thin shoulders like Apis praying, with his cock still rammed up in her throat. Anna's supple legs descended around Eric's buttocks in an attitude of ravished satiety. She threw one pale arm back on her blonde hair and turned to watch Omar's creamy semen gliding down Cybele's neck in slippery, clotted chunks.

"God, baby, *that* was good," he said, looking at Anna passionately as if Cybele had never existed for him.

"For me too," she smiled and took his hand from her lying position while he kneeled, straddling Cybele.

At last Eric stopped his movements and lay silently over Anna. After a few moments he turned his face to Cybele and Omar, and he looked at them curiously. Torment painted a vital glow in the whiskey-coloured irises of his eyes as he watched Cybele push Omar's large cock from her lips.

"Don't you want to see how happy you've made me?" Anna asked Eric, pivoting his face back to her own with one aquiline finger. He looked down into the fragmented blue colour of her eyes and smiled weakly.

"You have the fastest cock I've ever experienced," she complimented him. "Really, Cybele, you are a lucky girl."

Eric got past Anna's milky white cheeks and shoulders, past her masses of silky, golden hair that had inspired such new-found tenderness in him, to the turquoise stare of jealousy filling Cybele's narrowed, almond-shaped eyes. Her pouting red mouth twisted itself into an expression of anger. She brushed a strand of her gleaming black hair away from the wetness of Omar's juice on her mouth in an abrupt movement of irritation.

Eric felt his cock hardening from the sight of her dusky brown body so recently used by Omar's even darker body before her. He felt his passion differently towards Cybele. Her tense brown limbs and jealous, angry eyes excited him into a more overt action than he had experienced with Anna. He looked down at Anna's soft body sprawled under him and remembered the sensation of bottomlessness he had felt in her cunt. "Maybe I could drown in her," he had thought, frightened for the first time while he fucked a woman.

"Yes, it's the first time I've shared him," Cybele said resentfully.

"Oh, Omar, look at her face," Anna laughed. "She's jealous! Oh, isn't she precious?" Her gay laughter encompassed the four of them like a careless garland of flowers, but a hint of the bee's sting shone on her sharp, white teeth.

Omar looked down at Cybele's pinched, lovely face and felt his cock hardening.

"Yes, she's like a spiteful cat," he observed, tilting her chin upwards with his broad hand. "*Une chat noir*," he pronounced in a heavy Arabic accent.

"Makes you want to tease her," he laughed, and kissed her brutally on her mouth.

"Or fuck her," Anna added. Her silken limbs glowed again with an inner light of desire and rustled like satin under Eric's legs.

Cybele stared at Omar's purple cock. It grew larger and larger, lifting his ample balls away from his hairy brown thighs. A little knot of fear and anticipation formed in the pit of her stomach while she watched his flesh extend in front of her. She put her hand on it tentatively, thinking she might understand how it had become so big by touching it. The muscles of her cunt drew themselves together protectively, realising instinctively that this cock would hurt it.

"Don't try to fuck her with that," Eric warned. "She's got a super tight cunt, and it'll never take it."

"Relax, Eric," Anna advised. "My little love nest tells me that you're still packing something for me." She moved her hips under his hard cock several times and smiled. In spite of himself, he began to pound at her soft flesh again.

"You're so soft, Anna," he murmured, sinking down into her like water draining into a basin. The cloying quality of her cunt submerged his energies again while she coiled her arms and legs around him like a pallid snake.

"Easy does it," Omar said, and spread Cybele's legs wide apart on the dusty carpet of the ground. He put the tip of his cock on her clitoris and began massaging her flesh rhythmically, softly, until she began to moan with pleasure. She lifted one leg over his brawny shoulder and pushed the mouth of her cunt to his prick.

"Easy, easy, little pussy," Omar cautioned, and bent over her breasts, taking her nipple in his mouth excitedly. He sucked it so gently that she strained upwards into his mouth trying hard to feel each light flick of his tongue on her teat. Every faint sensation whetted her appetite until she was begging, him, "Please, oh please screw me with your big cock!"

He pushed the head of his cock into her cunt an inch and moved it back and forth, back and forth in light, teasing strokes, while still kissing her nipple in the same manner.

She felt the probing, plunger-like width of his cock tip enter her cunt and spread her legs wider apart on the warm dark earth.

"Oh, you're a sweet pussy," he moaned. "A real delight." He moved nimbly inside the tight flesh of her cunt. "Just takes a little time."

"How beautiful you are inside her, Omar," Anna called. "I can see your cock pushing her cunt apart. Oh, move faster, Eric, faster. I'm going to come now with your new dick." Her eyelids fluttered closed when she came under Eric's hasty, plunging cock.

Omar forced his a few inches deeper into Cybele's compact opening and waited to see how she would react. He felt her hips straining forward to take more of his cock and heard her hot little pants in his ear, but the flesh of her cunt was tight around his cock like a knotted string. He moved back and forth, restraining himself from shoving his cock all the way up to his balls into the inviting warmth of her cunt, as he desired so hotly to do.

"Umm, mm, so good, so big. Thicker than Hadrian's," she said, forgetting Eric's ears in her ecstasy.

The sound of her words and her tense, firm cunt made Omar come faster than he had climaxed since high school.

"Omar, you look shattered," Anna exclaimed, looking ardently at his expression.

Omar's brawny shoulders shook convulsively over Cybele from his laboured breathing. He extracted his cock from her cunt so swiftly that Cybele gasped.

"Oh no," she moaned. "Don't take him out. I can come. I want to!"

"Relax, my dark star of love," Omar ordered, and dipped his skilful tongue to her clitoris. He began sucking her slowly hardening flesh with his wet, warm tongue. She wrapped her legs around his neck and sucked her breath in sharply.

"I love it. Oh, do that. Kiss me, do," she begged. He sucked her clitoris with soft insistent caresses until she screamed like a wild night bird under the bushes.

"Now," he said, and inserted his cock into her dripping cunt, shaving it in until he could go no further.

"Hey, this cunt is unique," he exclaimed. "I feel the end of your vagina. You're tight all the way up," he said wonderingly.

"Now! Now!" she exclaimed while he moved harder and harder. The motions of his dick inside her body shook her breasts and sent a hot warmth up from her cunt and into the vein of her neck. A fiery, surging pleasure flushed her face and breasts while he pounded the solid meat of himself inside her.

"Omar, you super cock. Oh God," she cried. The juice of her cunt sprayed itself around his heaving organ.

"Oh no, no more, no more," she pleaded, but he moved on and on inside her. "It hurts!" she protested again.

"Here," Eric said, hopping off Anna and pulling her cunt to Omar. "Take this one. It's looser, old man!"

Omar stared dazedly at Eric with perspiration running in small rivulets between the furrows of his brows. Eric pushed him off Cybele and mounted her with effortless grace, beginning his pistol-like movements almost without interruption in her cunt. Gone was the feeling of drowning he had had with Anna, when he felt his cock hit the top of Cybele's cunt. It was sheathed in her firm, tight vagina. The more it grabbed at his cock, the more he wanted to fuck it. And the firmer it felt, the fiercer his movements became.

"Pinch my nipples," he demanded. His fully salivated mouth slurred his words.

"Oh, I will, Eric. I will," she said and twisted his flesh in her old, familiar fashion. "I will if you'll hurt me. Hurt me good!"

"Breakfast is being served," someone called.

Cybele started out of her satiated sleep with a low, animal-like cry. The bushes surrounding the four sprawled figures had begun to pale with dawn's filtered, insubstantial light. It revealed shadows of dust on the lustrous skin of Anna's legs which lay across Cybele's tanned calves. Eric yawned sleepily into Cybele's ear and stood up unsteadily. Omar slept on beside Anna, breathing in deep, peaceful draughts of air. The sound of his breath filled the air around them like the rustling summer leaves surrounding them. He shifted his hand in the dust and sighed lethargically. A rounded, cooing sound escaped from his lax lips that were bubbly as a sleeping baby's mouth from saliva. Anna turned her head and smiled happily at Eric and Cybele.

"What a heavenly night!" she exclaimed, putting her small, expressive hand daintily on Omar's burly shoulder. "You'd never believe this one was alive a few hours ago," she remarked wryly.

"Wake up, Omar," she shouted, and tugged vainly at his arm. "I need my robe."

"Where is it?" Eric asked. "I'll go and get it for you."

"OK, 'Lightning'," she replied saucily and looked pointedly at his groin that he had already covered with a pair of khaki pants. "Better bring back a bucket of water from the pool to get Omar up with."

She drew one of her long legs up to her breasts and inclined its thigh over her golden pubic hair and lower belly to protect her nakedness from the probing dawn light. A soft stirring of wind rustled leaves borne by the venerable trees surrounding their copse of bushes. It mixed the smell of fresh dew and grass with the odour of their bodies that were redolent of sexual emanations.

"I wish I had a Bloody Mary," Cybele piped, and flung herself backwards, squashing Omar's nose down in the dirt.

"Aww shhitt!" he groaned. He turned his face towards them dully, affixing the group with one unfocused, bleary eye.

"C'mon, Cybele," Eric ordered, warily observing Omar's ample body sprawled lackadaisically on the ground. He remembered the equipment Omar packed, and what he had done to Cybele a few hours earlier.

"Why?" she asked stupidly. She grinned at Omar and Anna like a silly, unthinking child.

"Because, luv," he said, and plopped her panties onto her bare crotch, "it's time – that's all."

She looked down at her panties, then back to Anna and Omar. She began pulling her panties up slowly, like a person sleepwalking.

"Bye, y'all," she called. She held out her hand and waved goodbye, opening and closing her fingers twice in a private salute, then stumbled into Eric when she turned to go.

"Christ, you dope," he said. "You're still flying! That's the only problem with her," he apologised to Omar and Anna. "She's overly susceptible to all the fun things." He pulled a still soggy T-shirt over her head.

"Go to my bedroom – to the left of the hallway where we came in – and get her into some dry clothes," Anna advised. "You're welcome to a bath and anything you find of mine to wear. OK?"

She turned towards Omar's relaxed form, dismissing them without looking back. She rolled over onto his back, covering it with her soft white belly, then locked her supple, enticing legs around his hips and calves.

Cybele and Eric made their way up a wet, dewy slope of grass. They passed the abandoned, undulating pool, and stepped onto the sweeping flagstone patio of the rambling mansion. The steady, rhythmic night noises of splashings in the pool and thumpings on the trampoline had given way to the discordant echoings of crickets and scraping *chaises* by weary, debauched party-goers; to the tinkling of half-melted ice cubes in thrice-refilled gin and tonics and Bloody Marys.

"One more time," a weary, hoarse voice called.

They turned around to the pool and watched a nude figure plop into the turquoise water. A young, blonde-haired girl leapt up and screamed, "Howie! Oh my God!" she wailed, poking at a multi-freckled, red-haired man lolling beside her on a *chaise*. One of her eyes stared away from the other in a strange, unfocused gaze. There was a fierce dynamism in her movements. Her long, well-shaped legs and sexy buttocks were not only taut from a perfect muscle tone: but also from the ideas in her head. "For Christ's sake, Ralph, get him outta there. He can't swim!"

Ralph burped loudly and rolled back over on his paunchy belly. There was a pleasing sensuality in his large, bearlike form. He lay in the *chaise* apathetically, with his eyes closed. A bored expression tucked the corners of his mouth under.

"Hsi! Hsi!" they heard a clipped, authoritative voice say. "Please take care of it."

They turned towards the commanding voice and saw Joe Yang, now clothed in a black silk smoking jacket with red, plumed birds painted on its darkness like a Chinese silk screen. Still in his mouth was the elaborate cigarette holder. Pale grey smoke from his cigarette furled up evanescently into his shiny dark hair. Cybele noticed the tip of one wooden sandal peeping out from under his dark green slacks, and again felt greedy curiosity for his foreignness and obvious sophistication.

"What's going on?" Brenda called.

She and Slim climbed, tired, up the grassy slope leading to the patio. They watched Joe's servant, Hsi, put his serving tray down and strip to his underwear. His bowed, muscular legs appeared like sturdy rubber bands from under his trousers. His unclothed body appeared like something apart from the figure he had been in uniform. Cybele started to laugh while they watched him hastening down the slope in a bumpy, ape-like gait.

"Oh, thank God," the tall, skinny girl shouted as she ran over beside Eric and Cybele. Her strange, unfocused eye gazed in one direction away from them. The other more natural one, piniomed them with its fierce, black pupil, making Cybele's giddy laughter choke to a halt.

"Whatever could be so funny?" she demanded, and swung her long mane of hair haughtily back in Hsi's direction as he plummeted into the pool.

"C'mon," Eric said, tired, not evincing much interest in the happenings around them or the girl's remarks. "Let's go and find Anna's room. You look sort of cold."

Cybele remembered her apparel for the first time, and rubbed her chilled arms vigorously. She began to tremble with her body's sudden consciousness of the cold dawn air.

"Doesn't that girl have a funny eye?" she asked in a loud, unmodulated voice. Its unsophisticated wonderment echoed indiscreetly across the still, damp lawn.

"One of em's glass, dummy!" Eric said, pulling her along after him onto the patio like a rag doll.

"Just a second, dammit!" she cried, and stopped to pull her soggy T-shirt over her French lace panties. Her elbow bumped Joe's sleek, silk-clad elbow, making her realise that he was standing in close proximity to them for the first time.

"Ha ha," she laughed, embarrassed, clutching at the lace of her drawers like a misbehaved child.

"You look terribly uncomfortable, Cybele," Joe noted. "Why don't you have a nice hot bath in Anna's room?" He drew on his cigarette reflectively, like an Arab ruminating slowly over a water pipe. The bone of his jaw showed firmly in his rounded oriental cheek from the pressure of his teeth that he had clamped down tightly on the cigarette holder. Again she noticed his high breast bones and his large brown nipples under the buckling material of his robe. The length from his high, parabolic rib cage to his waistline intrigued her. She stood holding the sides of her panties, mesmerised by his aloof tranquillity. The bulk of his broad shoulders had lifted the material of his tailored smoking jacket within a fraction of an inch too short around his wide wrists. Cybele guessed rightly that he must lift weights to maintain such perfect muscle tone.

"We were just going," Eric said abruptly, glaring at Joe with a comic pugnacity.

Joe puffed silently on his cigarette, ignoring Eric's puerile impoliteness and remarked stonily, "I believe Hsi's managed to save a drowning man."

They stood on the blue-grey flagstones of the patio and watched Hsi lug a drunken looking bather from the pool. A stocky woman appeared from the doorway behind them and ran down to Hsi, carrying a red kimono. The way she held the kimono in her tensely bowed arms paralleled the legs of Hsi's wiry, bent stance on the abrasive concrete surrounding the pool. The pool's pastel colour had softened in the pale violet light of early morning. A rosy pinkness from the rising sun's rays had begun to suffuse a sheaf of innumerable, congealed pebbles that made up its sides as they pulled the unconscious man to the soft, wet grass. His lanky, tanned limbs and sharded, yellowish hair touched their own sturdy bodies like a drowned crane brushing against dredging barges.

"Oh my God, oh my God," the askance eyed girl screamed. She ran up beside Hsi and his companion in lifesaving. "Save him, please!" she entreated, holding her bony knuckled hands up to her equally bony chest melodramatically.

Hsi turned the blue-faced man over on his stomach and mounted his frail, unsatisfactory body with his short, powerful legs.

"I've never seen anyone saved before," Cybele whispered, taking Eric's hand to gain comfort from her fear.

They followed Joe down to the figures around the poolside and stood watching while Hsi administered first aid. His tightly knotted back muscles clinched and furled themselves like a coiled machine as he pressed down on the man's scrawny frame, then deftly lifted his chest from the ground with a clean expertise.

"Howie, baby," the skinny, hysterical girl cooed. She knelt down beside Howie and pleaded, "Speak to me! Oh Howie, how could this happen?"

She glared up at Joe and Eric and Cybele accusingly. Her glass eye seemed to train its own singular gaze specifically in Cybele's direction.

"If anything happens to this man, I shall never forgive myself," she declared, staring critically at the absurd prettiness of Cybele's lace panties.

"Can't you put on something else?" she asked, irritated, and turned back to Howie's bedraggled form.

A mushy, squeaking noise emanated out of Howie's lungs from the constant pressure, then release of pressure from Hsi's strong, knowing hands. He spluttered painfully, and turned his face from one side to the other. The thin, pinched jowl of his cheek pressed into the grass like a desiccated starfish.

"Howie! Howie!" the girl cried. "Oh my God."

The pale, saved man opened his eyes, and burped loudly. This he followed with a long volley of farts.

"Come," Joe said, noting the animal-like noises issuing from the man with distaste. "Let's go and get some warm clothes for you two."

Their long brown legs were like those of two deer as they turned to follow Joe's vermilion-clad back up to the patio.

"Have the decency to bring some brandy for this poor man," the kneeling girl's strident voice pursued them.

"Ahhh!" Joe said, flinging his hand down in a gesture of annoyance. "Goddamned woman. Hysterical bitch!" He knitted his brows so fiercely that Cybele began to laugh. He turned and saw her prettily curving thighs in the lacy panties, her long dark hair around her wide shoulders, and he began laughing too.

"Oh, you're a beautiful girl, Cybele. I can't ever imagine you being bitchy or hysterical," he stated with genuine admiration.

"Oh *yes*, she is – both – plenty of times," Eric contradicted, angered again at Joe's appreciation of Cybele.

"Then it must be that you don't know how to direct this girl, Eric," Joe said astutely.

"Direct her? Shit!" Eric exclaimed. "That's not my bag."

"But it's certainly hers," Joe observed shrewdly. He clamped his teeth down on his cigarette holder, again emphasising the taut muscles of his jaw and the hard roundness of his face and high cheekbones.

"OK, OK," Eric said impatiently. "You mentioned some dry clothes, a shower?"

"Of course, right this way," he said accommodatingly, and strode through the partially open patio doors.

His heavy wooden sandals clunked smartly over the hallway's tiles. They had to trot to keep up with him. He turned out of the gloomy hallway and into a light-filled bedroom. Its ceilings and walls were resplendent with Waterford chandeliers and wall sconces.

"Oh!" Cybele gasped. "I don't believe this place!"

Slabs of pearl grey marble decked rosewood furniture sitting two inches deep in oriental rugs. Behind a mammoth bed, white silk wallpaper shone in the early morning light. The bed's headboard consisted of a gold, antique mirror from the Baroque period, composed of scrolled cupids. Everywhere, in the large yellow vases standing in corners of the room, in the feather-like patterns of plants and peacocks painted delicately on the yellow bedlamps, in the sumptuous golden brocade drapes and bedspread, the impression of Anna's hair and lustrous, creamy skin dominated the room. Everything, even the gold-rimmed, hand-painted mirror lying on the yellow vanity table, signed its name 'Anna' on the décor.

"Oh, I especially love these!" Cybele cried, and ran up to two statues of a man and woman bowing to each other.

"Yes, from the Tang period," Joe offered. "My father was given those by an American ambassador who admired his collection of silk screens. I believe that Father rewarded the gentleman with his favourite screen in return." He looked at her reflectively for a moment. "I wish I could give them to you since you admire them so much, but. . ." – he shrugged his shoulders – "they're really quite priceless."

She scrutinised the tiny hand of the woman, who held a black lace fan in her minute fingers. Each part of the sculpture was perfect. There had been no mistake. One could even detect a suggestion of infatuation in the bowing man's face.

"The bathroom's right in here," he said, clicking on a chandelier with spear-shaped prisms. It hung over a sunken bath of black and lavender marble shining like a fallen star in the bathroom ceiling.

"Oh, let's bathe together, Eric," Cybele decided immediately.

"She's fabulous, Eric. Always ready to play," Joe said. "Well, I'll leave you two now."

"Where are you going?" Cybele asked, with unconcealed disappointment. Eric groaned in irritation.

"I'll be in the room adjoining yours, should you need me," he added sceptically.

"Are you going to bathe?" Cybele asked Eric after Joe had left.

"Nah," Eric said, exhausted. "I just want to lie down. Hang these up somewhere to dry, will you?" he asked, and handed her his damp pants.

"OK," she said, and took his pants in one hand. She held them away from her as if they were a dead rat.

She walked into the many mirrored walls of the bathroom and waved hello to her reflections, then stooped over the bath and turned on the water in the tub by large, gold-filigreed knobs. Around the tub's dark marble sides stood a collection of exquisite crystal bottles filled with pale pink and green liquids. She opened each bottle and tipped part of its contents into the bath, then stepped into the steaming, perfumed water. She sank down in its depths with a low moan of pleasure and lay back against a spongy headrest. A specially muted light from the chandelier spun myriad reflections in the water, dappling her with a lace patterned coverlet of water.

"Sponges are dunges," she rhymed meaninglessly.

She lifted a cake shaped sponge up from the water and squeezed its contents onto her face. The warm water was medicinal on her chilled, exhausted flesh. She lay drowsing in its soapy perfume for a number of minutes.

"I wonder why that singer made a hot flash come in the pit of my neck?" she asked no one, squeezing the sponge again, and listening to the pattering sound that its released water made on the bath water, as if trying to answer herself with the sound.

"I never had that experience before," she said aloud. She lifted her long, tanned leg from the sudsy water and watched sleepily as a rainbow-coloured bubble glided down her foot.

"What power a guy like that must contain in his body, to produce such a strong, hot warmth in my neck by my merely looking at him.

She stepped out of the tub uneasily, dizzy from the hot water and her own exhaustion.

"Why, he could be a priest if he used that power in a different way," she mused, following her mind's groping logic.

She wrapped herself in a large, luxurious towel. The letter 'A' had been embroidered on its upper half.

"Anna the adored," she mocked jealously. She trailed into the immense bedroom and curled up beside Eric in a wilted heap. Once during the night she woke and wondered where she was.

The next day she awakened, still in Anna's elaborate bed, but alone.

"Eric?" she called groggily. She jumped out of the bed and ran into the bathroom to see if he might be bathing. Only the singular chandelier hung over the opulent marble tub like a glass being that existed as well as herself. She heard a noise in the bedroom and ran back out of the bathroom, calling, "Eric!"

The same oriental maid who had helped Hsi earlier that morning was placing a glass of orange juice, along with a bowl of warm buns and fruit, on her bed table.

"Wow!" Cybele exclaimed.

She examined the bowl of abundantly stacked fruit as if it were a box of assorted gems, while sitting nude in the middle of the bed. Soon she began guzzling orange juice and hastily eating the sweet iced buns,

"How did you sleep?" she heard Joe say from the doorway.

She turned to him, smiling happily, and said, "Oh, great," mindless of her bare breasts and body. She sank her teeth greedily into the bun, waiting to see what he would do next.

"Er, your friend told me he had to leave. He said he had a 'big load in', whatever that means. He said to tell you he'd see you at your apartment tonight."

"Oh," she said, still dull-witted with sleep.

Joe stood in the doorway, watching her with curiosity and enjoying vicariously her unabashed pleasure from the food and drink. A golden sunlight filled the room, etching her limbs like bronzed gold against the ochre sheets. Her green eyes shone like two bright jewels in the early afternoon light that filtered in slanting beams through the honey-coloured drapes.

"Want some?" she offered and held a bun out to him, uneasy from his constant, albeit admiring, scrutiny.

"I never eat until dark," he declined, without taking his acute brown eyes from her face. His obvious enjoyment of her pleasure gave her courage.

"What did you mean when you said we were on the rule of five last night?" she asked pertly.

"Ah ha – ha! ha! ha!" he laughed loudly. His voice echoed down the cavernous hallway behind him. "That's the last thing I thought you'd remember about last night."

"Well, it was such a strange thing for you to say," she replied, licking her fingers absently. "What did you mean – rule of five?"

He walked up to the side of the bed and sat down close beside her, then took her hand lightly between his thick-skinned palms.

"If I kissed you on your lovely, sugar-smeared lips right at this very moment and enjoyed it tremendously, and you did also – well, we'd be on the rule of five."

"Oh, you mean *sex*," she said, relieved.

"No, not just sex. I mean that humans follow certain rules. All life on earth follows inescapable premises, and when you descend into humanity and other forms of materiality, you are subject to ineluctable laws," he finished, running his short, blunt fingers through his brown hair. "Unless you discover how to control the 'centres'."

"But why should one want to escape?" she asked, puzzled. "Why not just enjoy kissing my lips and I enjoy yours? It's a beautiful day. Look, the buns are good!" she exclaimed, smiling at him with deceptive simplicity.

"There's no reason to try and escape from the rule of five," he said. "Unless it starts failing to satisfy you. That's when one begins to suffer."

"I hate to suffer," she said, draining the last drop of orange juice from her glass.

"Do you?" he asked, studying her face with a dogged wiliness. "When do you suffer, Cybele?"

"Oh, when my boyfriend ignores me. When he only makes love to me and then leaves me."

"You mean the guy you were with last night?"

"Oh no, not Eric. I mean Hadrian. You don't know about him," she said with an innocent confidentiality. "Hadrian controls me."

"*Controls* you?" he asked, his eyes shining brightly with interest.

"Yes, he does. He's the only man who ever made me suffer – mentally, that is. My husband used to beat me."

"When this man – Hadrian, you said – controls you, does it excite you?" he asked, watching her face with a calculating, expectant demeanour.

"What do you mean exactly?" she asked, surprised by the nature of his questions.

"Exactly what I said. Do you wait for him for hours sometimes, and cry when he doesn't come? Do you cry after he leaves? And do you wait for him over and over in a half stupor, not even able to use your brain properly?" he asked, clutching the sheets around her thighs tightly.

She paled under her tan and dropped a half-eaten cake onto the plate.

"How do you know this about me?" she whispered.

"Because Cybele, I know *you*. I knew you from the moment I saw you slinking in behind that fool you came here with, like a lean, hungry alley cat, looking up from under your brows and pretending to be shy." He grasped her wrist until she cried out in pain. "You're a sensualist and a masochist. You came here looking for something bizarre, because something out of the ordinary is the only thing that will ever turn you on. But you never found it – yet. You looked at me hopefully, but unfortunately, for me and you, I don't think I could meet your requirements for pain. · Because you, my dear little masquerader, groove on mental pain. I'll bet your Hadrian, or whatever his name is, gets turned on when you attack him in anger. Doesn't he?"

"My God. No one's ever said any of this to me before," she said, astounded. "How could you know this about me? And about my boyfriend, for that matter?"

She looked at his smooth, youthful face and asked, "How old are you, anyway?"

He smiled calmly.

"Twenty."

"Twenty! But that's only three years older than me! You talk like a man Hadrian's age."

"Because my father, like your Hadrian, is also my mentor." He breathed slowly, deliberately, as if he were controlling his breathing.

"I listen to everything my father says. I do everything he asks me to. My father, as ambassador, represents China in this country. Everything we do in this country must show respect and command respect. I have been taught these premises since I was five years old."

He looked at her indulgently, viewing her as an oriental man comprehends a geisha.

"My father is my God," he said.

"And your mother?" Cybele asked with a feminine curiosity.

"My mother is a flower my father picked in France," he said, and smiled at her boyishly.

"She's French?"

"*Oui, madame*," he mocked playfully.

"We are French also," she told him. "French Jews."

She looked at him with a new understanding and a feeling of warmth and compassion.

"I studied ballet and pointe dancing from six until I was sixteen," she told him. "I practiced several hours four afternoons a week. I also know what rigid discipline means."

He tweaked the nipple of her breast playfully. "You have an oriental style, Cybele. And I'm not one of your foolish American men who is unable to recognise your approach to life. You play a lot of games to amuse yourself. But the one that amuses you most makes you the weakest. And that's this strange debilitating game you play with your main man."

She sighed and fell back into the sheets dejectedly. "Everything you say is true. One night in Geneva we went to a dinner party thrown by a famous Swiss banker. I'll never forget him. His name was Ludwig or something like that. I remember thinking that he would have been capable of murder without spilling a drop of blood. Freaked me out, too, because he resembled my father so much physically. That was the only resemblance, though. God, was he loaded – one of his businesses was with the Japanese, and old Ludwig was making most of the money. If you can imagine that. . ." She halted momentarily, afraid that she might have offended his sense of culture.

"And?" he asked impatiently.

"Anyway, I got all dolled up in a very expensive dress. At least one that these older business types consider chic. Personally it made me gag, it was so contrived."

Joe smiled indulgently at her.

"Hadrian was in terrific spirits that night. He had just swung a big sugar deal in Bangkok. He brought me back a pin – of a rooster covered with rubies and diamonds – and said, 'Here's my cock, darling. He's yours forever,' and he kissed me. Everything went like a breeze until Ludwig started to zero in on me. He was fascinated by my youthful simplicity. Ha. And like I told you, he looked as mean as hell in a calculating way, and that always turns me on. But I kept getting freaked because he looked like my father. So Hadrian began a little game designed to blow my cool in front of Ludwig.

"'Pick out something to eat, Cybele. The menu's in English,' he'd say, very condescendingly.

"By twelve that evening he had me so fucked over I couldn't think straight. I felt like clawing his face down to his cheekbones. And that's just what he loves. Poor Ludwig gave up hope on his attentions to me, and I finally stalked out of the living-room of our suite in the hotel and into the bedroom. I slammed the door so hard that everyone else left pretty soon too.

"Hadrian came into the bedroom with a sullen look on his face, but I could tell that he was very excited. I was already in bed. I usually sleep nude, but that night I had put on one of my elaborate night-gowns. I can't stand showing my body to anyone I'm mad with," she explained.

118

"He lay down far away from me," she continued, "and began telling me what an awful impression I had made on everyone. Jealous bastard! I just lay there waiting for the antihistamine I had taken to put me to sleep.

"All of a sudden, he gave a little cry and gasped, 'My heart! My heart!' He's always talking about dying at any moment while he whoops down ten pounds of caviar or balls me five times a night, but I rushed over to his side anyway and grabbed one of his hands."

She paused and stared out the sweeping french windows.

"His eyes were so beautiful then, so. . . warm and brown. And the black, glossy hair on his chest. He has such wonderful arms, you know, from all of the rowing championships he won in the Olympics in Istanbul."

Joe smiled tenderly at her, observing the softened expression that had relaxed her features.

"He pulled my hand down on his cock." She shrugged ironically. "It was as hard as a brick bat!"

She trailed her fingers along the silken border of the sheets.

"He is my master," she said, almost inaudibly. "The one I've been searching for since I was a little girl. And I know I'm using him, casting him in a role, as it were, to make myself feel ruled. . . but. . ." – she began to cry weakly – "I can't give him up. A normal relationship with a man, without any tricks, frightens me to death. I'd be bored out of my mind. Besides, I wouldn't want the responsibility of a normal relationship. I need my father," she ended obscurely.

"Your *father*? Is this an older man you've been telling me about?"

"Yes, much older. He's my father with a cock. Ha. Ha!"

"You are a choice specimen, Cybele. You should be in one of Papa's china cabinets."

He touched her inner thigh with his fingertips lightly. "Umm, like silk, just as I had expected."

"I don't hold any surprises for you then?" she asked coyly.

"I am an oriental man," he replied, ignoring her question, "and I know the power of gaining another person's essence through emotional suffering. Especially with a woman. Once you get her addicted to it, she's your slave forever. And that's what you are for this man, Cybele. An exquisite harp he plays for his own luxury. He must be a very sophisticated person – he's not an American, I can tell by his name."

"No, he isn't," she admitted. Her face had become drained of all its animation. "Please let's don't talk about it anymore. You're like a Mimir I read about in my mythology book, and it's making me dreadfully unhappy to be analysed by you," she concluded dolefully.

"Oh, you mustn't feel badly, Cybele. You should be proud that you are sensitive enough to indulge in such play. But," he took her hands carefully, "I hope this man never abandons you. Because, my dear," he said, kissing her fingertips tenderly, "you are madly in love with him. I've never seen a woman so utterly possessed by a man before. What you have left, what you gave here at the party, and even right now, is just an empty, unreal shell. You're only biding your time until your Hadrian's next visit."

He dropped her hands onto her legs, and stood up.

"Now I must leave you. Anna is waiting," he explained. "She's always so depressed after these orgies with Omar."

"No, please stay a while longer," Cybele begged, pulling him back down beside her. "I need you to explain this rule of five more."

She repeated the words slowly. They sounded unfamiliar in her ears. She sighed dejectedly.

"Sometimes I think I'd rather just live with my cat. He's so honest and faithful and—"

"And they don't operate on the rule of five like humans, Cybele dear. They live without the burden of knowledge. They haven't made that first fatal choice like man. No apple has tempted them. They don't see the duality of things. That's what makes pets so charming for people. They have no knowledge of death, because they haven't advanced. . . or deteriorated to knowledge. Oh, they can kill, but they don't have the burden of murder in their realm of consciousness. It's much easier to be honest when there's no choice. Humans have advanced to the responsibility of decisions.

"Each time you get into life with other humans," he continued, "you start following what I call the rule of five. They've got it all set up. You do certain things to get specific rewards, and it's an endless sort of game, really. When you get tired of their idea of satisfaction, you may begin to embrace the negative in order to gain a better sense of awareness. But very few people have the courage to do this. And even if they do, they usually get all muddled up in their own idea of what they are doing."

He sighed. "Modern man has no teachers to show him 'the way', as in olden days. People don't realise the value of being a simple, good carpenter."

"Eric's a carpenter," she said vivaciously. "At least, when he's not cutting dope."

Joe laughed. The energy in his body emitted a sort of electrical discharge with each of his words, making her aware of his long, tense back and arms The sanguine material of his robe fell over the bare flesh of her breasts like contained slides of blood.

"Everything you talk about sounds like something I'm trying to escape from," she said, puzzled.

He smiled enigmatically at her with full, bow-like lips. "And are you escaping, Cybele?"

"I. . . don't know," she faltered. "How does one get off the rule of five anyway?"

He held up the statue of the little bowing figures that she had become so enamoured of the previous evening and said ponderously, "Perhaps when creating something like this, someone escaped for a period of time," he mused.

"Oh, you mean *art*? Sure, I understand. That's what I do too – I paint, and then it's my world, and doesn't have to follow your hideous rule."

"So you paint." He gazed silently at the diaphanous sheen of the white silk wallpaper in front of them for a moment. "Then you understand how free it feels to escape from this contrived world. And how much more inspiring it must have been for humanity in the days when all art was an instruction instead of just an escape."

"Last night I saw a singer," she stated out of context, holding the toes on both of her feet self-consciously. "As soon as I saw him, a red warmth flooded the base of my throat."

She brushed her hand back and forth along the pleasing texture of the perfumed sheets. "It was like a hot coal in the middle of my throat. Do you understand that?"

"Yes," he replied.

"I guess it was almost like a mystical experience, since I immediately understood that this man carried a tremendous power in his body. Because just by appearing he inspired this terrific reaction in me. I thought of how the same warmth floods the whole of my chest and breasts *sometimes* when I'm having an orgasm."

She looked shyly at the clean, graceful sweep of Joe's white forehead into the black line of his hair and fell silent.

"Please go on," he implored. "I find this fascinating."

"Well, I saw what the man was doing – I mean he wasn't trying to hide it, of course – exploiting his talent and good looks and making every female wet between her legs. Even the guys didn't seem to mind the inspiration he might be working up in their chicks for them later. Then I started to wonder: what if this guy were in Tibet or somewhere like that?" she asked, blushing at her clumsy expression of philosophy in the presence of his obvious sophistication. "And he had been trained since he was a little child to somehow use this thing he possessed – to use it somehow," she ended searchingly.

"I'm amazed," Joe said. "You've been into some good books. Who led you to them?"

"A friend of mine."

"A woman?"

"Yes, funny how you guess everything."

He smiled again, and rubbed the satiny skin of her knee.

"Anyway, I also wondered is it possible for him to use his power this way for material and egoistic gain, yet retain that same power and use it in a higher manner?"

"Whheewww," Joe whistled. "Kill to eat, but know what you are doing," he captioned her statement easily.

"Joe," she said earnestly. "I want to use whatever energies I have outside the rule of five. I've been running from that concept all of my life. And I don't even have a starting point."

She lay back, tired, in the sheets.

He studied her intently for some moments, then bent over her with the solemnity of an immobile statue given movement, and kissed her navel.

"You've already begun," he said quietly, then stood up to go. "Come anytime you'd like and tell me more things you've discovered." His fierce dark eyes glowed softly at her like the flames of burning candles.

She clasped her hands around her knees and sat watching his retreating back. Halfway across the room, he hesitated as if he had remembered something. He walked back to the bed and picked up the intricately carved statue from the night table. He turned it around slowly in his long fingers, then threw it on the soft flesh of her belly.

"Have this," he said. "May you stay on the rules of this statue forever, dear Cybele."

She looked into his vital brown eyes and asked, "Tell me, why don't you make love to me?"

He came over beside her and lifted her hand to his lips. He kissed it lightly on the knuckles, then pressed her palm to his groin.

She took his cock gently and squeezed its limp, but substantial flesh, and watched his warm, red mouth as she waited for him to harden in her caress. She moved her hand back and forth across his cock, but nothing happened.

"You don't like me?" she asked, pulling her hand away from him in embarrassment. "I know I'm not like Anna."

"To the contrary. You delight me more, infinitely more than Anna."

He drew her up to his fine, silk robe and held her in a tender embrace, averting his head so that his eyes were turned away from her puzzled gaze.

"I'm impotent, Cybele."

"Oh. . . I'm, well, I don't understand. . ." she stammered.

"Anna broke my heart. She was. . . she is unfaithful." He paused. "She brought me so much pain, I can't take pleasure."

"How long have you been like this?" Cybele asked.

"Eight months."

She looked at him gently.

"Perhaps it will pass," she said.

"Yes. Perhaps. When we marry - when she becomes more mature. When she learns that sex is sacred - as are marriage and children. I must leave you now," he told her. "Till another party," he said and smiled at her boyishly, then strode out of the elegant bed chamber.

Chapter Four

Vrrroom! Vrrroom!

She looked up from the motion of her long brown legs, past the thick lace of green leaves and sap-glutted July growth to the silver mirage of a Corvette.

"Wanna ride?" the driver asked.

"Nah, there's no room," she said, looking at a blur of high cheekbones and thick blond hair, while she kept on walking swiftly down the street. She noticed a bag of golf clubs fallen over on its side behind the black leather car seats and felt an automatic aversion since it had been her hated father-in-law's favourite game. Her eyes travelled from the golf bag to the driver's companion.

She glanced away from the two young men quickly and kept on walking. She felt the muscles of her legs pulling her through the oppressive heat. They were strong, sure and intent with their constant forward motion. The pace of her walk seemed more real to her than the cardboard figures who hung momentarily in the haze of the early afternoon, then vroomed away.

She thought of Eric, Eric, Eric Star, and felt a flinging of pinpricks through the veins in her arms and stomach.

'Incomparable, inimitable, idiot Eric,' she thought, and increased her pace almost to a run.

'Joe said he got a load in,' she remembered to herself. 'That means he'll be in a great mood and we'll do something fantastic today. Oh goody!"

She began to run along the uneven sidewalk, dodging tree stumps from huge old trees that had pushed their roots up through the concrete like the limbs of a giant. She passed by a heavy wrought iron fence that surrounded one of Georgetown's venerable old mansions in a daze of anticipation. Even though she knew that Eric had slept with her for a few hours after the pool party, she felt upset that she couldn't really remember his presence with her during the previous night.

"I was doped out of my tree," she said out loud. She trailed her finger along the black iron fence, watching its blurred motion with pleasure.

'But he's gotta be with me,' she thought illogically. 'I mean, I can't lose him, I just can't.'

She rushed on down the sunny, tree-shaded avenue in apparent agitation.

Vrrrommm! the car's motor roared.

'Shit!' she thought.

"Hey, wait a minute," the young handsome driver said. He had stopped his car right at her knees and stepped over the door of the low-slung car with great agility.

She turned and waited as he walked up to her. He was very tall.

'The all-American image,' she thought cynically.

"Hi. You've got beautiful eyes," he said, looking down at her from the height of his super long legs.

"Why, thank you, honey. I'm just real glad y'all think so," she responded sarcastically. 'Big overgrown lug,' she thought, while appreciating his high, chiselled cheekbones and the rich brown colour of his eyes. 'Sorta like Eric's,' she thought, 'but with a difference.'

This man had the eyes of a Hun – a Tartar. They were sharp and piercing with intelligence. Eric's eyes were pretty, but weak behind his glasses. When he wasn't wearing thick, steel-rimmed glasses, they were soft and lambent, like those of a sweet puppy. It was her season for sweet puppies – lithe – bronzed teddy bears of twenty-five.

'Still,' she thought, glancing quickly, secretly at the driver's face and body, 'one could always throw in a Hun for variety.' She looked past him to the car. 'Yeah, I dig that car.' She felt jolted suddenly by her thoughts. 'And I'm just a teenager,' she thought, and grinned. 'Yep, that's me.'

She felt the driver's hand grab hers.

"Come on, get in," he said.

His perfectly pressed, grey knit slacks matched the low-slung body of his silver grey sports car. A red plaid shirt he wore was tastefully muted with grey stripes in its pattern.

His square, decisive cheekbone carved out the golden brown jaw of his cheek. The vital scrutiny of his dark brown eyes excited her with their intelligence. She noticed the mocking expression on his handsome mouth and decided that she liked him immediately.

"But look, there's no room," she protested.

"You can sit on the golf irons. Come on and meet Kevin. What's your name?"

"Cybele. Cybele Tashery."

"OK. Kevin, this is Cybele. Where ya going, Cybele?"

"Hi, Kevin. Er, just to a friend's place on Q Street."

"OK, I'll take ya there. Kevin and I were just out hittin' a few golf balls. Kevin here's a dentist."

She wedged herself into the thick foam and leather of the bucket seat and looked at the smiling guy beside her. Her legs were pressed next to his because of the small space in the car. A golf club lay coldly against her thigh.

"You look so young to already be a dentist, Kevin."

"I try harder," he said, and scratched his curly brown-haired head. He glanced at her quickly, trying to size her up. 'Another one of Sherman's waifs,' flitted through his mind. 'Poor Sherman,' he thought. 'He likes to collect people – likes to feel popular.'

"Not only a dentist – oh yeah, my name's Sherman Stein – he makes a fortune on the stock market." He swerved the car suddenly onto Wisconsin with a strong turn of his wrist. The power of the motor under her body excited her.

She noticed Sherman's hands on the steering wheel. They were slender and square, still boyish in appearance. They were different from Eric's, more dextrous and sensitive. She looked back shyly at his face. He returned her attentions with his piercing Hun look. Then he laughed absurdly, as if he were mimicking an idiot, and she loved the sound. She giggled back.

"What do you do?" he asked suddenly, trying to catch her off guard.

"Well, er, not anything really. I mean, I don't have a profession. What do you do?"

"I'm a promising young man in white," he said. "I'm going to go for plastic surgery, to be more specific." The white of his cigarette between his lips fascinated her. All at once she was aware of the powerful, heady odour of the two men surrounding her. She looked up at the treetops that whirled past them over the open sports car.

"Ooooohhh," she sang secretly to herself. "I feel so alive, so alive!" She stuck her arms straight forward over the windshield and felt the wind whoosh through her fingers.

"Oh, a doctor," she said. "The doctor in a silver Corvette. Ha, ha – well, that means you're legitimate."

"Legitimate?" he asked with a puzzled tone. "Why do you use that particular term? Aren't you?"

"What?"

"Legitimate?"

"No," she said and grinned at him teasingly.

"Cybele, Cybele," he said, and squeezed her knee. "I bet you play a tough game, honey." He looked at her with mounting interest. She kept grinning at him in the sunlight as if to say, "Try me."

"Here's a piece of paper," he said. "Write your name and number down there."

She took the paper and wrote down her address and phone number with a pen that Kevin handed her.

"What's a sweet young thing like you doing in a place like that old mausoleum?" he asked when he saw that she lived in Lancashire Place. "You're near my parents, sort of."

"Well, you could say I moved to this mausoleum under duress, and now I'm on ice there," she said.

He frowned at the tone of hysteria in her voice. 'Neurotic bitch,' he thought impatiently. 'Don't mind those legs, though.' He looked at her breasts. 'Big and high,' he thought. She must be really young to have tits that sit like that.

He liked big breasts. They emphasised her wafer-thin body. She was an extremely pretty girl with a feminine, fragile air, yet her attitude was like a tomboy, and this excited him. She was a peculiar combination, all right.

"Oh, here we are," she said with the same abrasive hysteria in her voice.

"Well, wait for me to stop the car," he told her irritably.

"Oh, thank you, thank you," she said with a vague sweetness that made him want to capture her voice.

He was a typical, practical Capricorn and could be charmed by nebulous, personalities that were so different from his own. But he was also a scientist and he abhorred sloppiness. He observed her closely as she crawled over the golf bag, past his silent companion.

She turned back to them and waved goodbye in a disarming manner. Her green and white shorts suit looked like a mint against her brown skin. The make-up around her eyes had been carefully applied. She was wearing a pair of expensive pumps when she should have been wearing sandals. The note of incongruity intrigued him.

'Nah, she isn't sloppy,' he thought. He saw her turn and noted the thinness of her shoulder blades underneath the white material. 'She is vulnerable,' he concluded. He felt protective towards her instead of experiencing the familiar impatience he usually had for women who weren't strong and competent like his mother. He looked at the note she had written her address down on.

"I'll pick you up at 8:00 tomorrow night. OK?" he said.

"Sure, OK," she agreed.

She kept waving goodbye to him as he roared off from the kerb. He saw her in his rear-view mirror and waved back.

She stood blinking in the blinding sunlight, trying to define objects through its sharp, metallic glare. She could smell little plants and the earth as she strode happily up the steps to the door of Eric's apartment building. She heaved open the solid new door and ran down the hallway. She rang the doorbell and stared at the sign RING TWICE AND ASK FOR PAUL. "Eric, Eric," she sang with anticipation.

A tall, slope-shouldered guy yanked open the door.

"Hi? Goodbye? Eric ain't here."

Cybele smiled at him, enjoying the black, wide-brimmed hat he had on his head and his old scuffed boots that he had crossed one in front of the other before her.

"Where is he?"

"Out getting some dope. Wanna come in?" He paused amiably in the doorway. The easy grace of his body was ready to move aside so that she could enter. She studied his loose, flowered shirt and the flowing position of his legs with a sensual pleasure, enjoying his decorativeness.

"I don't know." She hesitated another moment. "That is, no. I'll go back," she decided, as if he knew where she had come from.

"Suit yourself." He lounged in the doorway with a waiting casual tension. His eyes never left her face.

"Will you tell him I'm there?" she asked.

"Sure, I guess he knows where 'there' is?"

She grinned and turned around to leave without answering.

'Fuck,' she thought as she plodded down Wisconsin Avenue. She considered hailing a cab, but she began to feel exhilarated with the exercise of her legs and decided to continue walking back home.

When she reached the old apartment building, she was so hot that all she could think of was tearing off her clothes and sitting by the inadequate air-conditioner. She stepped into the elevator and shivered happily in its delicious coolness, anticipating a release from her clothing.

She walked into her apartment and pulled off her outfit immediately. She stood there naked for a moment, trying to figure out what to do until Eric came.

"I'll go out in the backyard and 'bake' some," she decided. She grabbed a bikini and pulled it on over her heated, damp body.

Outside, the pavement burned her feet when she walked across the parking lot to the grassy backyard. She flung the blanket out, then flopped down onto it, placing her portable radio within reach. She covered her eyes with two round leaves from little plants that grew nearby and lay back to relax, purposely blocking all thoughts from her mind. Soon she fell asleep in the smouldering, relentless sun of late afternoon.

She was awakened by the silly 'toodleloo' sound of the horn on his car. She heard the large, heavy tyres swerving over the gravelly concrete of the driveway and she lifted one leaf pad off her right eye. She saw him sliding out of his long white Continental hurriedly. His stocky body was clad in a cream-coloured linen jacket. His tie and pants were brown. He had on dark, silver-rimmed sunglasses that he sometimes wore in bed.

"C'mon," he said in his pronounced foreign accent. He even snapped his fingers at her, as if she were a waitress he was summoning to serve him. Overhead the mammoth oak trees shaded him, fanning him with their large, leaf-laden branches. His skin was swarthy and exotic, contrasting attractively with the light, expensive jacket he wore. The deep creases on each side of his nose emphasised his darkness, outlined the curving, camel-like foreignness of his nose. She often licked the skin between it and his mouth. He put a cigarette to his mouth, and when she saw the whiteness of it between his lips, the muscles in her stomach gripped her with a sweet ache of longing and desire. She felt herself drawn towards his body as if she were being pulled by a giant magnet. "Hadrian!" she whispered to herself with delight. She sat up on one elbow and squinted through the sun's white haze.

"Well?" he said impatiently, then turned and walked to the back entrance of the old apartment building.

She watched a drop of perspiration as it ran like a miniature river down the black-brown tan of her belly into a small pool at her navel.

"You have a beautiful nombril," he had said the last time they made love. She remembered him sucking her navel slowly, looking up at her from under his heavy black eyebrows with his smoky brown eyes full of adoration for her.

She grabbed her blanket and radio and ran to catch up with him. She heard a loud clatter overhead and looked up to see Mr Masters, the old landlord, pulling up his blinds in order to spy on them. He scowled down at her through rheumy eyes, with his mouth set in a bitter expression in his pallid face. She waved and smiled at him impudently, then stopped to turn on the outdoor faucet so that she could cool herself off before going up to meet Hadrian. She wiggled happily under the iciness of the cold water and pulled her bikini bottom away from her belly to let the crystal stream pour down over her. She looked up at the old landlord once more, then gazed down pointedly at the dark brown hair of her cunt.

"I told you not to run around in my backyard naked," he yelled down at her. "I've done things to tramps like you before and I can do it again!"

"Old goat," she muttered. "Bastard."

Suddenly she heard the raucous motor of a sports car. "Oh God," she groaned. She peered quickly through the gloom of the back entranceway, trying to figure out whether Hadrian had gone on up to her apartment. She didn't see him anywhere, so she assumed that he was on his way upstairs.

"Cybele! Why aren't you at the Hilton?" Eric grinned at her like a forsaken playmate in the hot summer sun. His eyes were pleasantly blurred from his thick glasses. One of his tanned, muscular arms was hanging over his little green Triumph.

"Eric, darling!" she exclaimed. "I got tired of the Hilton so I left and went to your place, but you weren't there." She ran over and grabbed his curly hair with delight, burying her nose deep in the grassy fragrance of it as if she wanted to drown in its perfume. She pinched the muscle of his shoulder with a hungry sensuality.

"Hop in, luv." He uncapped a bottle of orange juice and began gulping it down happily.

"Later, darling." She looked back anxiously over her shoulder.

"Oh, I gotcha. The big H is here, right?"

"That's right," she smiled. "Call me in two hours." She looked back up at Mr Masters. He railed one arm at them angrily. She gave him the peace sign, then the high sign.

"I got a better idea," he said, drawing his finger slowly down her arm. "Take a cab over, cause I'm busy cutting some dope in a couple of hours." He leaned his head back on the seat and gazed up into the sky lazily.

She kissed his Adam's apple impulsively. "OK, I'll try to get some more money from Hadrian too so we can go to a movie – anything. OK?"

"Seeya later," he said, accelerating the car abruptly. She jumped back from the compact sports car as it spurted forward, and ran into the apartment building.

She felt the coldness of the elevator floor under her dirty bare feet and smelt the salty flavour of her skin freshly burned by the sun. In her hands she clutched many articles, but she was oblivious to them all. She was conscious only of her body and its yearning, almost sickening fever, for the man who waited for her upstairs. She watched the numbers appear in lights on the elevator as if hypnotised. When the number five appeared, she stepped off onto the dark red carpeting of the hallway. She crunched her feet down fiercely into the thickness of it, trying to feel it to the very end of its fluff. She reached out to touch the bumpy white surface of the old corrugated plaster walls as she walked down the hallway to her apartment. Intermittently, after each three or four doors, there were signs of the zodiac in raised mosaics. She touched them also. Her fingertips were almost raw with the tingling sensations that the walls had produced on her hands. When she got tired of feeling the walls, she looked at every other one of the small, luxurious chandeliers that hung overhead in glittering rows down the long hallway. Their yellow light permeated the hallway like old, forgotten suns, casting strange shadows on the red carpeting under her bare feet. Their antique prisms had grown yellow with age. Their fine, delicate designs were rotting in loveliness.

The hallway stretched endlessly. It lived there before her like a long-remembered dream, a dream she had had as a little girl. The mouldy air of the hallway penetrated her nostrils. She sniffed it hungrily. The walls were cold on her hot, sunburned hands. The coolness of the stagnant air fanned her face as she increased her hurried pace to a run. At the end of the long hall, she reached the door to her apartment. She felt her key hit the gold lock with a metallic clink and she shoved the door open.

When she entered the hallway to the bedroom, she saw that he was already nude on the bed. He was in a half-sitting position with his legs crossed very casually. His large, intelligent eyes burned through the peaceful darkness of the bedroom at her. His mouth was set in its characteristic expression of logic and sensuality, and he had crossed his arms over his massive chest with the easy, concealed power of a lion. He inclined his head to one side with a shrewd expression of understanding at her obvious adoration for him. She saw his lips part slightly with anticipation as she approached the side of the bed. A cigarette was smouldering in his hand.

Soon she would feel this same hand on her legs, on her stomach, and on her breasts. The palm would be a little rough from the gardening he did – sometimes even in the dark – to soothe himself after working twelve or fourteen hours a day. She saw him there like a miraculous form of slowed-down energy. It was as if Einstein's theory of mass and energy had suddenly settled for a time on her bed, waiting to envelope her, as if it had waited and slowed down just for her and had become tangible in the form of a mature man – slowed down, but only temporarily, from the beauty of its fluid energy into a big, thick dick.

"Hadrian," she said softly, singing his name into her ears. "Hadrian." She looked at him again, seeing once more the black, black hair on his chest, seeing once more in her imagination the way it became beaded with perspiration after he had made love to her. "So silky," she whispered, "so silky."

"C'mon," he ordered her again. He patted the bed with his fleshy hands. She noticed the way his thumb fanned out at the nail and wondered if he had ever stuck that in her. "Where have you been all day?" he asked, not listening to her answer.

"Out in the sun," she replied, knowing that he didn't care what she answered.

"What is this?" he asked, and tugged her yellow bikini. She thought of his fingernails and the way they sometimes tore her when he put his fingers into her cunt. "Why do you put this on when I'm here?" he asked. "It hurts my hand."

She slid the uncomfortable suit down her legs, looking at the bulging muscles of his arms, at the black hair covering them, and his stocky masculine body with excitement as she did so. His dick was already hard.

"Oh, Hadrian," she said, looking at him with a slavish reverence. "I'm *so* glad you could come. I was miserable after you left last night," she said unthinkingly, forgetting where she had spent the previous night. "Why did you leave me? Why didn't you call me? Why don't you love me like I love you, Hadrian? Why? Why?"

"C'mon," he said again calmly, snuffing out his cigarette in a small, white Chinese ashtray. She looked through the red and yellow brocade curtains and was amazed that the six o'clock traffic had not relented yet, but was still moving by in an impersonal parade.

She put her knee down on the edge of the mattress near him and held her other leg hard and straight behind her, feeling the tautness of its muscles as it supported all the weight of her body. She stood there, poised for an instant, staring intently at his face and into his eyes.

"C'mon," he repeated, and patted the mattress as if she were a little pet.

She lifted her leg up on the mattress and moved into a sitting position on the bed.

"Why did you leave me?" she demanded insistently. She clasped her hand into hard, clammy balls on her soft warm thighs. "Why?" she persisted and beat her legs softly with her fists.

"Shaddup," he told her gently. He leaned his head forward and licked her navel casually.

"Mmm, smells good. Lie down," he commanded, and pushed her down on the pillows where he had been. She fell back onto the coolness of the sheets, watching him intently as she did so, observing the top of his head and the way it moved while he kissed her stomach. She lay immobile, watching him in the cool gloom of the bedroom with its heavily draped windows. She held her body very still so that she could see everything he did. She only dared to grasp one of his powerful shoulders because the sight of it excited her so. He pushed her legs apart and moved his mouth to her cunt.

"No!" she exclaimed.

He stared up at her, smiling, and said, "No?"

He dropped his head to her body and began kissing her slowly with his warm, wise mouth. She twisted her head into the pillow, trying to bear the sweet ecstasy that his kissing brought her.

He looked into her eyes once more, stopping his activity for a moment. "Do you say no to me?" he asked her again with an ironical smile on his wet mouth that glistened from the juices of her body.

She gazed down at him in a delirium of aroused sensuality, throbbing with pleasure from the touch of his tongue on her clitoris. He kept his eyes locked with hers.

"Do you?" He grabbed her wrists and held them tightly. Still she gazed at him rapturously.

"I said, do you?" he repeated. He thrust her wrists down in a demanding movement with his large, powerful hands, pinning them to the bed over her head.

She began to move her head back and forth against the pillows to say no.

"What do you say then, darling?" He kissed her once more between her legs, then stopped again, smiling teasingly at her.

"Oh," she signed. "Do! *Do!*" She pushed his head down to her body. He dipped his head between her thighs and lapped her cunt gently.

At the end of the hallway Porgy sat watching the two twisting bodies on the bed. Behind him the Chinese mobile tinkled softly in the summer breeze that blew in from the french doors.

She began to scream with pleasure. The more she screamed, the more furiously he kissed her – as if he were greedy to hear the sounds of her pleasure. He felt her body go limp and looked up at her.

"Was it good, darling? Was it?" he asked, and pulled himself up over her. She felt his dick on her belly. She felt its thickness as he moved it voluptuously across her stomach. He moved almost frantically inside her.

"Oh, what a beautiful pussy you have," she heard him say. He pulled her arms back from her breasts. "Don't cover them. Show me your breasts. I'm fucking them now." He thrust himself inside her several more times, then shuddered to a stop.

"It was beautiful, beautiful!" he exclaimed and began to kiss her softly on her temples, looking carefully into her eyes while he did so.

"Are you appraising me?" she asked self-consciously.

"No, darling. I'm loving you," he murmured. He held her head tenderly in his hands, as if he were holding a precious possession of his, one that he wouldn't want to break.

"I don't just love you, Cybele. I *adore* you."

She went into the bathroom and ran a tub of water. She stepped into the bath, watching the hot, steaming water cover her body slowly. She began to think of Pierre, of being married and having to call him and lie to him. She leaned her head back on the wall as she relaxed in the bath, frowning at the water.

'I hated that,' she thought. 'I hated those lies. I'd like to get out of lying ever again – yet, that's what I'm starting all over with Eric and Hadrian.' She began soaping her body vigorously, still staring at the lapping bathwater hypnotically. 'I'd like to get out of everything, really.'

When it grew very dark, she had finished dressing. She studied herself carefully in the mirror, as if Hadrian might have left a trace of himself on her. She felt angry when she realised that he hadn't – that he had come for a few hours and then left her as usual.

"Bastard, bastard," she said to herself, and thought of him longingly. She sat in the yellowish light of the high ceilinged old bedroom, inert and unmotivated. She felt a pleasant languor steal over her limbs and body as she sat there remembering the way he had kissed her. Then she heard the desk clerk buzzing her to let her know that a cab was waiting. She grabbed Porgy and her purse.

"You didn't think I'd let you stay here alone again, did you?" she asked and squeezed him to her body affectionately. She ran down the hallway, panting from the weight of the large cat. She noticed the desk clerk scowling at her from behind a battered brown desk and thought of an outmoded clock.

She sat in the cab stroking Porgy, mindless of the other cars in the street, concentrating only on what awaited her at her destination. She seemed to alight from the cab without being aware of it, and then she was standing in front of Eric's apartment building.

She came into the musky, wood-smelling hallway, up to the black door with the sign that said RING TWICE AND ASK FOR PAUL. She had never met anyone in the apartment named Paul; however, it was always reassuring to her that the sign read RING TWICE AND ASK FOR PAUL. Porgy struggled in her arms. His long, racoon striped tail flicked about her darkly tanned arm like a furry snake. She pressed the doorbell and felt her heart pounding with anticipation. She stood wondering who would answer the door, hoping it would be Eric.

"Cybele, hi!" he piped in a happy tone. His eyes were filled with pleasure and anticipation from seeing her.

"Hi, Eric." She looked at him standing in the doorway as a child does when its eyes alight on its favourite toy. His white, Spanish-style shirt was embroidered with a design sewn in black silk thread, and opened far down on his chest. His pants were black and tight on his slender hips. She saw the bulge of his groin and felt her face flush warmly. She looked up slowly to his eyes. They were brown and puppy-like. She looked like a child-girl as she stood gazing at his face while remembering his body as it had lain beside her the previous afternoon in the sun.

"Are you just going to stand there and gaze at me all night or do you plan to come in, m'lady?" He giggled. "Come on in, you little masochist – my little masochist. I'm going to let you in this time. What'd you do when I left you this afternoon? Suck Hadrian's dick?" He reached out and pulled her through the doorway.

Behind him Danny slouched in the doorway like a miniature Christ. He liked to dress in blue. He smiled whimsically at her through a haze of smoke from a joint. "H'lo, Cybele," he said.

"Danny, oh Danny, how are you?" She hugged him. She felt the sharp ribs of his chest pressing into her breasts.

"Oh fine, child. Fine. Here, take on some of this, babe."

Cybele held Porgy back from the smoke of the marijuana as she sucked the bouquet of warm, pungent weed deep into her lungs. She was immediately aware of the surging quality it gave to the blood in her veins, of the instant euphoria it puffed into her brain. Her hands tingled and her stomach flooded with a flow of juices. She felt like whipped cream. She leaned dizzily on the cool clay of the wall, contemplating the white shirt Eric was wearing and the firm bulge that sat on his upper thigh like a smart pistol.

Eric watched with admiration as she took drag after drag on the joint. "Ha, glad to see you're getting ready for the night, kid," he said.

Danny pulled at his black beard, smiling and listening to the two of them like an imp, like a deft-footed Indian from one of the classics. An elusive smile played about his lips.

"Oh God," he groaned pleasurably. "Oh God, am I stoned!"

The word "stoned" echoed down the hallway as he walked towards the living-room. She stood looking after him, expecting Indians and blue, smoky mountains to appear at any moment, forgetting Eric completely.

"God, what a dude," Eric said. "Come on, come on, Cybele. Cybele? Are you there, m'girl?"

"Oh Eric, dahling. Oh, Eric. Hhaa, haa, I love to say your name. Can I say your name?" She turned and looked at him with renewed delight.

Porgy leapt out of her arms and inched cautiously around the corner to the next bedroom. When he saw that the water-bed was sans Maria and Jeff, he hopped up uncertainly onto its ripply support, turned around three times, and began to lick himself thoroughly.

"Of course you can say my name, m'girl. Ha ha, come on in here in my little room and say my name. Come on now, let me lead you in here like a little baby. You bitch, you beautiful bitch. See how fun it is to sit on my tiny bed? He sat her down as one would do a small child, caressing her bare arms tenderly while he did so, and touching her hair possessively.

"Eric, Eric, don't be mean. Please don't be mean," she entreated him weakly. She held on to the blouse-like sleeve of his shirt. "Oh, I'm so glad to get to come here. Really, Eric, I am. Thank you."

"Oh, you're welcome, Mrs Tashery. If you're real nice, I might let you keep coming. Just don't show up with your husband."

"Oh Eric, please don't be mean. Please." She lay her head on his chest and looked up at him through the blur of floating sensations that the grass had produced.

"I won't be mean to you tonight." He kissed her softly on the nape of her neck. "Here, let me undress you." He began to undress her as if she were a little girl, lifting her arms one by one while she sat dutifully and silently on his narrow, cot-like bed.

She gazed dully at the collection of Chinese books in the corner of the room which he had bought at an auction. She smiled hazily to herself when she remembered the first afternoon she had come there, rushing up to the books and saying wonderingly, "Chinese? Eric, can you read these?" He had said, "No, but I'm going to learn how to some day. Some day, luv – it's a future project." He had asked her to come over and do laundry with him, and she had rushed over, excited, as if he had invited her to a grand event.

"Of course you'll learn Chinese, Eric," she had said while watching him sort out his clothes that lay in a heap in the tiny closet. Overhead hung the dark blue navy jacket he had been wearing the day she had met him.

She clung to him, feeling suddenly afraid when she realised where she was and who she was. "Oh Eric, Eric, I miss Pierre." She was conscious of hearing her own voice. It sounded strange and unreal. She thought that she sounded like a little girl talking.

Eric let his head drop down on his chest and sighed. His head was a mass of tangled curls as he gazed down at the Persian rug he had thrown over the dark, scarred boards of his bedroom floor. "Are we going to start that shit again?" he asked in a tight, controlled voice.

"Oh, Eric, no. I won't. I won't. Please don't be mad."

"OK, dammit." He stood up and strode over to the door.

"Eric, please, please come back. Oh, Eric, if you don't sit here with me, I'll just die. Really I will. Eric?"

He turned around slowly. "OK," he grinned. "I can't help it if you're crazy, Mrs Tashery. I love you. It just so happens that I love you. You cunt. Come here."

She smiled and walked over to him self-consciously. They hugged one another tightly. "Oh Eric," she said. "You're so beautiful. Really you are."

"And you're not bad yourself," he told her.

Suddenly the door flew open. Danny stuck his head in briefly. "Uh oh," he said, "Just checking. Yep, things look good in here so I'll get out." He smiled slyly at them, vicariously enjoying their embrace.

"Yeah, it's good in here, Danny, m'boy. So get the hell out and shut the door – pronto."

"Aye, Aye, sir, over and out." He made an ironic peace sign with his fingers as he exited backwards from the bedroom.

She awoke in a wavering haze. The grass she had smoked still made her brain float.

"When did we come back to my place?" she asked Eric. Her eyes alighted on Eric, her hippie toy, her sad child through the sensations of the marijuana. The situation focused with one-dimensional unreality. She was again mistaking fairy tales for reality – but after all, what reality was there in life? Even a human's eyesight could merely. guess at substance – in actuality it never saw more than the surface of each object it gazed upon.

'Yep, old Ouspensky was right,' she thought. 'Good old P.D., and if one *has* to live with surfaces, Eric isn't half bad." She stroked his head as if he were a cat. He rolled over beside her, breathing heavily, and. put her hand on his hard, sabre-like dick. "Oh Eric, Eric. Do! Do! Do!"

He began to kiss her breasts. "I love your breasts," he said. "They're so white and soft. They tell me you're a white woman after all!" he teased her.

She laughed softly. "And I love for you to kiss them. Oh yeah, oh yeah, oh yeah, yeah, do. Kiss them. Oh, hurt me, hurt me some, please."

He pushed her back on the bed while stroking her legs rhythmically. "I love your legs, I love your legs," he murmured and pushed them apart. "I love my dick in your cunt," he said as he pushed himself into her.

She felt the slice of him in the warmth of her body.

"You feel like silk, silk! Pinch my nipples," he demanded.

"I will. Oh, I will," she said, delighted, pinching the delicate whorls of flesh that sat so new on his chest. She let her hand rest lightly on the reedlike slimness of his youthful torso, and breathed the pungent, natural perfume of his body, enjoying its sweet healthy smell.

"Cybele, Cybele. Oh God, can you come?" He looked at her and paused briefly in his perfect movements. "You're beautiful. Did you know that? You're used to that though, aren't you? – being beautiful?"

"Make me beautiful, Eric – oh your dick, your dick!"

"Oh God, you love to fuck, Cybele." He fell over her like a devouring, possessive animal, moving like lightning inside her cunt with his sharp, quick dick. His long, muscular back was smooth and golden over her breasts. The thrusts of his cock sent sensations of pleasure up inside her body like a field of daisies being rippled by a summer breeze. "Oh God, let me fuck you always, Cybele! Let's not stop," he said as he pushed himself into her over and over. "Can you come? Can you come? Oh baby, oh! You came," he declared, looking at the expression on her face with delight. "I'm going to fuck you all night."

He looked down at her admiringly. She was wet on her belly from him. Her black hair clung to her face from the heat of their bodies. Her eyes gazed at him in a fever of sea green. In the long hallway the bells of the Chinese mobile tinkled musically from the breeze that wafted through the balcony.

"Eric," she asked. "Are you on Speed?"

"No, why? Ooh, ha, I gettcha – no, that was last night! Come on, you witch, let's go fuck in the living-room." He sprang off the bed, leaving her in the rumpled yellow sheets. "Cybele," he said, "you look like a pretty butterfly lying there."

"And you look like a beautiful praying mantis. Eric, darling, turn around. Let me look at the golden fuzz on your thigh."

He turned and struck a Roman-like pose. He looked a little uncertain, and a bit silly, like a dignified statue with a bird perched in its hair.

The warm, marble of his body was poetic instead of cold, inspiring as a summer day. He ran over to the mirror and looked at himself with curiosity, then smiled with satisfaction as he grinned at his reflection. "You good looking dude!" he said to it. "Come on now, butterfly, I'm tired of it in bed – to the living-room!"

She jumped out of the bed, giggling, then suddenly screamed. He ran back from the front room and peered at her with alarm. "What now?"

"Oh, Eric, Eric," she said.

"For Christ's sake, what's the matter?" He walked back to the bed, tangling his hair in the mobile as he approached her. "God dammit, why do you hang this fucking thing here anyway?" He swung at the metal balls irritably, inadvertently tangling them more in his hair. "I *know* why you do it. I know," he said accusingly. "You do it because you think it'll stop a burglar the same way it has me. *That's* why."

She ran up to him. They clung together naked, rocking one another in the dark lavender of the night. "Oh Eric, do you love me like I love you?" she asked. They huddled together closer.

"Oh Eric, please, please," she said while she clung to his arm. "Please, Eric. Oh God, I'm so afraid – so afraid. Will you save me, please?"

"Now, don't start that shit – just don't – or I'll leave." He kissed her. "Don't you want to fuck anymore? Huh? You like that. Come on and let's fuck in the living-room. It's cooler there."

He looked towards the bedroom where the old air-conditioner that he had laboriously hauled over to her apartment in his little green Triumph was humming noisily, making more heat than coolness in the spacious room.

"OK, Eric, but first let's go in the bathroom and talk. Let's do. I've got to tell you something." She pushed him an arm's length away. He looked down at her and smiled indulgently, putting on his "sage" look that she loved so much.

"All right, Mrs Tashery. Let's go into the bathroom and have a discussion."

"Oh good, isn't this going to be groovy – outasight?"

"Oh, it'll be outasight all right – it'll be outasight because I already got it figured that you're crazy."

"Oh, that's right, Eric. Isn't this just marvellous? I mean, ain't it great? Sit down now. Come on," she said and pulled him down by the bathtub.

"Great, great. Ha ha – what now?"

"Feel it, Eric."

"Yeah, I feel it. That bathtub's fucking cold against my back all right."

"But Eric, doesn't it feel good under your ass? So cold and all. Haahaahaa, I just love these cold tiles."

"Yeah?"

"You know what it reminds me of?"

"I don't even want to hear it."

"Reminds me of when I used to sit on the crypts down in Louisiana. Once Rachel ran right up into one of them. I reached in to pull her out and came up with a leg bone – ha! I was waving it around in the air when suddenly I thought, 'This is a *human* bone.' It was a sobering thought."

"Who was Rachel?"

"Oh, she was a cat, you know? My only other real cat."

"Oh God."

"Yeah, she was, Eric. She was orange and skinny and bitchy like I was."

"You're still bitchy, and I don't know how you were before, but you sure aren't fat right now."

"OK, OK. But anyway, Eric, I had come over to this guy's house who worked at the university with Pierre and was keeping Rachel because we weren't allowed to have pets. It was over a hundred degrees, which is just normal for New Orleans in July, and I took her out for a walk after I had given her a bath in cold water to keep her cool in that horrible heat. We went to walk in the graveyard across the street."

"Shit."

"I'll never forget that afternoon. Everything was white. Everything! Heat makes things that way. I kept saying, 'Albert Camus, Albert Camus', and looking for the Arab's blood to be running red at my feet over the white walkway. Instead, all I saw was Rachel's yellow tail. Every once in a while she'd look back at me with her green eyes and whine."

"What Arab?"

"Anyway, Eric, please listen to me." She took his face with both of her hands and turned it towards her. "The other day I met the ghost who lives here." She stopped talking abruptly and stared at the commode.

"Well, I hope you two plan to be friends."

"Oh yes, I think so. He's an old man."

"Oh well, that ought to be right down your alley."

"I suppose you're referring to Hadrian?"

"He's the only fifty-year-old dude you're fucking, isn't he? Or is he older than that?"

"Oh, now, Eric, don't be jealous of Hadrian. Now, about this ghost. I forgot what I had been doing that afternoon – oh yes, I came home from the pool early because you hadn't shown up, and it was hot – really extremely hot. Everything I had on was grimy. As soon as I came in the door I began to peel off all the clothes I had on. I wasn't thinking about anything, but when I reached the hallway a strange sensation went through my body. For some reason I looked out of the doors of the balcony. The light was so austere, so white and dead, that I was startled. I rushed into the bathroom and turned the water on as hard as it would go. I still felt uneasy, but I slipped down into the coolness of the water and relaxed. As soon as I lay back, my night-gown fell down from the bar of the shower curtain. I had hung it up there to dry," she explained. "It fell down exactly as a person would if they had been knocked down or something – straight out – with the arms flung out on either side. God, Eric, when that happened, I jumped out of the water and ran into the bedroom. There was the most bitter, cynical presence standing there. I even thought of running out the door in the nude to get away, but I had an intuitive feeling that if I started towards the door something disastrous would happen to me. This ghost was old and I was sure he hated me. He had lived in this apartment and died here. I swear, Eric, when I think of it a little I am convinced he can come back. He viewed me very steadily, his eyes toyed with me over and over. Oooh, hold me! Hold me!" she cried.

"Oh shit! You've completely broken my back against the tub."

"When I leapt up from the bath I was frantic, terrified. And it was all so real, Eric, can you imagine? Yet there was nothing there – nothing except the hate. A feeling of hate that made my hair stand on end. That's another thing. When I came into the bedroom, Porgy shot out from under the bed and, Eric, every hair on his body was standing on end down to his tail."

"Ha, that must have been a sight – here, do you want any more of this or not? It's burning my fingers."

"Nah, you smoke the rest. I want to concentrate on this ghost. It was a feeling of hate," she continued, "and the fact that I had invaded something that he considered his. I ran to the closet and grabbed a dress to wear and came back over to the bed. All the time I was still without any clothes. Suddenly I looked at myself in the mirror across the room. The light was flooding behind me so soft and yellow. The leaves by the window were a dark, deep green. My body seemed so lovely to me, golden like the light behind it, and my face was pretty. I seemed to be admiring someone quite apart from myself. It was then that all of the hate in the room disappeared, and with it my terror. The old ghost sat on the bed watching me. I believe it was the naturalness of my body, the poetic light filtering through the drapes that began to charm him. Everything had become rather ethereal, and

I felt completely sensual with this ghost. He sat on the side of the bed and I began to sense that he liked me. As a matter of fact, you might even say—"

"That the dude wanted to fuck you, right? Oh God, I'm getting out of here."

"Eric, no, please. I'll kill myself."

"OK, OK, I'll stay until eight o'clock tomorrow morning."

"Eric, why do you leave at eight o'clock every morning?" You don't go to work until twelve."

"You don't know what I do all the time, Cybele, m'dear. For instance, sometimes it's better to cut dope in the morning than at night. It's less suspicious that way, shall we say."

"Eric, when are you going to get a straight job? Every time I come to that place I'm in danger. You cutting that shit and all. It's so depressing really. Every time I come in and see you with those foul little scales."

"That cuts it. I'm leaving. I mean it." He ran into the bedroom, working his mouth back and forth over his gums the way he did when he was laughing a lot or very upset. "It's just all I can do to get my own life together, much less yours," he protested as he pulled on his pants.

"Oh, Eric, you've got a hole in the back of your pants. Oh, your ass looks so cute. Eric, don't leave. Have pity on me."

"I don't care if my balls are hanging out. I'm going."

She sat motionless on the bathroom floor, waiting to hear the front door bang, which it soon did. She began to cry. One of her tears tickled down her nose and irritated her. She ran out to the balcony and waited to see when Eric would ride past in his car. She peered into the darkness of the night intently.

"God, it's still out here," she said to no one.

Massachusetts Avenue wound through a tunnel of green, leafy trees like a deserted ribbon. Suddenly she gasped. The bushes beneath the balcony rustled a little, then more and more.

"Don't be afraid, little girl. It's just your old ghost come back to haunt you."

"Oh, Eric, you've come back. I knew it. I knew it!"

"Have we got any orange juice left?"

"Yes, we do. Please come out of the bushes and talk, Eric."

"OK, m'dear, I can do even better than that." He began to climb the evergreen growing by the balcony.

"Oh, Eric, I'm so touched. Nobody has climbed a tree for me since I was a little girl."

He swung over the balcony like a springy-legged ape. It was so quiet in the darkness that she could hear gravel dropping from the soles of his bare feet.

"My Romeo, my hero. . . Oh, my star, my star!"

"Cybele, get the orange juice."

"Oh yes, master, anything you say."

She ran into the deserted kitchen where everything was white and sharp and antiseptic-looking except for bottles of liquor and a few stray peanuts. Porgy came hesitantly around the corner and whined. In the corner of the hall, pillows still lay on top of the telephone.

"Here you are, prince," she said and handed him the juice. "Hold Porge a minute, will you?"

"OK, if you promise he won't get hair in my drink."

"Oh, Eric, what do you care anyway? It's only Porge's hair. And he's a magic cat."

"All of your cats are magic."

"Eric, there's the phone. Now be quiet." She ran into the hall, throwing the pillows that covered the phone frantically aside.

The voice on the phone said, "Cybele dear, how are you?"

"Oh, I'm just fine, Hadrian. Just fine. But missing you horribly. Why don't you come over a while?"

"Are you crazy? It's two o'clock in the morning."

"Well, where are you?"

"In the garden."

"You have a phone in your garden? How neat!"

"Yes, aaaha, it is. Cybele, my dick is so tight. He misses you so badly."

"Really? Where does your wife think you are?"

"Oh, don't mention her to me. She's asleep. Have you got your cream? Go and get your cream. Will you? Put some cream on, dear."

"Oh, Hadrian."

"Don't you want to come with me?"

"Of course, but—"

"But what?"

"Let's wait until tomorrow."

"That's different. Tomorrow's different. Tomorrow is another time. Have you got the cream? Now open your legs. Open your beautiful legs, darling. Is she wet? How is my cunt? Oh, she's beautiful. The best pussy in the world. Are you caressing her?"

"Yes I am," she said, looking towards the balcony at Eric. He was playing with Porge.

"Caress her well, darling. Oh, I'm so big, so tight. Oooh, I'm wet, I'm wet. Are you caressing her?"

"Oh Hadrian. I'm so hot, so hot. I wish you were here."

"Never mind, never mind. We can come this way tonight. Cybele? Cybele? Oh my beautiful cunt, my beautiful pussy, come! Come! Are you coming?"

"Yes! Yes! Oh Hadrian, Hadrian." She pretended.

"Me too. Me too. So good, so good. Isn't it good? Isn't it?"

"Yes Hadrian, yes, it's so good."

"You are my only one, my only sex," he sighed.

She heard him rustling a Kleenex and imagined that he must be cleaning his semen off himself. Somehow, the sound was comforting to her. She didn't bother to make any reply to his declaration, feeling that she had been given something that fulfilled her miraculously from the black phone receiver in her hand. She sat dreamily by the phone, glancing absently out at Eric on the balcony. His long, willowy form was silhouetted in the purple darkness like a strong fern plant. It was cut out in the night like a still-life painting. She felt an unreality in his figure and was relieved by the seeming flatness of his body. She wanted him to be a still life while she was with Hadrian on the phone. She knew that when she hung up, Eric would assume his natural dimensions and become real once more.

"Oh, Cybele. The more I fuck you, the more I want you, darling," she heard his husky voice say.

"Open your legs again, darling. Open your beautiful legs. The legs that I masturbated for."

The soft, sexy hoarseness of his voice had a powerful effect on her cunt. Her long legs opened voluptuously.

"Now touch her," he commanded. "Touch your beautiful pussy for me, Cybele. Ohhh!" His sensual voice sighed luxuriously in her small, whorled ear and sent a cascade of tingling chills down from her ear onto her slender neck and jutting breasts, hardening the teats of her pink-brown nipples.

She put two long fingers on the silky brown hair of her cunt and stroked its plump, beaverlike pelt and warm, fleshy lips. The clitoris swelled under her probing touch like a hard, miniature man.

"Are you touching her, Cybele?" he whispered. His clothes rustled suggestively against the receiver, evoking memories of his sweeping back and hulking shoulders, exciting her mind's eye.

"Yes," she said, moving her fingers down to the creamy warmth of her cunt. "I'm touching her, Hadrian."

"Oohh, touch her well, Cybele," his voice said with a rushing, wave-like sound. "Caress her, darling. Caress your beautiful pussy," he whispered huskily. "She is the best in the world. Are you caressing her?"

"Yes, Hadrian, she loves for you to touch her."

"Smell your fingers now!" he whispered excitedly. "Isn't it well? Isn't it the best pussy in the world? The wonderful cunt smell of your pussy, darling. Oh, she's so clean, Cybele. The cleanest cunt I ever fucked."

Again she heard the suggestive movement of his powerful arms in the background, and thought of his hard, wiry legs, of his dick's club-like thickness, and she pushed her fingers inside her vagina.

"Oooh Hadrian," she moaned. "Pussy's so hot. Oh, she wants to be fucked by you. She wants your big, thick dick, Hadrian."

She strained her slender, round hips up to meet the inadequate jabbing of her fingers. A fine whine of yearning and half-fulfilled ecstasy laced through the flesh of her hot, tight cunt.

"Yes, yes, me too. He loves your cunt, darling. He wants to fuck her always. Are you fucking her well, darling?"

She heard the movements of his hands through the phone receiver and imagined his swollen, thick cock, saw its engorged, purple head ready to enter her, and moaned with desire.

"Yes, yes, Hadrian. I'm fucking her. But. . . she needs your thick dick. Oh, I want to suck you now. I want your fat cock in my mouth. Oh, it'd be so divine, Hadrian. To suck him until your juice shoots in my mouth."

"Get your candle, darling,. Fuck yourself with the candle," he advised her. "Oh, my cock is so big now," he told her, almost cruelly. "I've smeared my hand with Vaseline and he's imagining that he's inside your silky, tight cunt."

"Oh Hadrian, you're torturing me. Why don't you come over?"

"Impossible. I cannot leave the house right now. Go get the candle."

She glanced through the door of the hallway to see what Eric was doing and saw him immersed in play with Porgy.

"OK," she said, and ran into the bedroom. She grabbed one of the long, orange candles from its holder that sat on the night table and then ran back into the darkened hallway.

"You got it?" he asked sexily.

"Yes, I did," she answered, embarrassed.

"Put it in your beautiful cunt, darling, like it's my cock fucking you. Oh, he loves you so much, Cybele. Are you fucking her now?"

She moved the thin candle inside her cunt, and felt a searing sensation of pleasure fill the inside of her vagina, like gold gilding a silk screen.

"Ohhh," she sighed. "So good to fuck with you, Hadrian. I wish I could touch your big wide shoulders. Oh, they feel so nice in my hands. I love to hold them when you're over me with your cock inside," she said, moving the candle vigorously back and forth in her cunt.

"Yes, yes. Me, too, darling," he said, panting softly through the receiver and into her ear as he masturbated his cock. "I wish I fuck her now too. But never mind. Come this way with me tonight. Is the candle way in?" he asked.

"Yes, it's way down, down in my pussy, Hadrian."

"Oh, I wish *I* was there. There in your hot cunt, darling."

"Oh Hadrian, oh. I love you. The candle isn't like your thick cock, darling," she said, thrusting the candle faster and faster into her cunt.

"I know, I know. My hand isn't like your cunt. But, oh," he sighed into her ear. "We can come like this tonight. Come with me, Cybele, come!"

"Oh, I will, I will," she said, and jabbed the candle harder and harder up between her thighs.

"Oh! Oh, darling, I'm coming! Are you coming too? Come with me, please," he cried.

"Oh yes, Hadrian. I do. I do!" she said. Her legs collapsed around the candle in pleasure. She could only experience orgasm with the control masturbation gave her.

"Oh, that was good," he said, smacking his lips in her ear. "Are you all right?" he asked.

"Yes, yes. Perfect," she said.

"Oh, fucking with you is so beautiful, Cybele. Even when we have to masturbate."

"Hadrian, why don't you leave your wife?"

"What? Don't talk about her right now. Don't spoil this beautiful fucking."

"OK," she said, looking anxiously towards Eric.

"Oh Cybele, my cock is tight again. He wants to fuck more. Oh God, I wish I come there now."

"Me too," she said, still gazing at Eric's naked, beautiful torso on the balcony, apprehensive that he might come and find her with the candle stuck up in her cunt. The soot-black tip of Porgy's magnificent tail lodged itself teasingly in his armpit as he held a matted string up in the air and dangled it playfully before Porgy's wide, green eyes.

"Oh let's fuck again, darling. Huh, Cybele? Once more? Once more, darling?"

She stretched her legs out wide and thrust the candle up inside herself testingly. A warm flame of desire flooded her cunt again and she began pushing the candle back and forth, back and forth.

"Can you come like this?" he whispered, breathing heavily.

"Yes, yes, I can. I'm so hot for you, Hadrian. I can't wait to have you inside me tomorrow."

"Yes, yes. But come now, come now! Fuck yourself well. Oh!" he cried, and came again.

"Did you come too, Cybele?" he asked.

"Yes, I did," she lied. Eric had slipped off the side of the balcony just before she was about to climax, and startled her so that she had pulled the candle out of her cunt and thrust it into the pillows that lay around the phone.

"OK, darling, it's getting cold here in the garden. Take me around your beautiful legs, around your arms."

"I do, Hadrian, oh, I do. I kiss you."

"Goodnight, dear."

"Goodnight, Hadrian."

She ran back out onto the balcony. "Hi, Eric."

"I guess that was the one and only Hadrian."

"Yes, it was."

"Are you going to get any money from him anytime soon? I have to pay for the rest of that air-conditioner if you don't. Damn thing doesn't even work either. Then there's the Jesus robe you promised to buy me for the party Friday."

"Oh, Eric, let's not talk about money. I didn't talk about money with Hadrian. He always takes care of me. He left five hundred dollars this afternoon."

"Wow, I wish somebody would take care of me like that."

"Well, you do happen to be a man, Eric."

"What does that mean?"

"Oh, nothing. Listen, Eric, let's have a baby. Please."

"I didn't even hear that."

"You're so good looking, Eric, and I am too. It's bound to be a terrific baby."

"I can't even take care of myself, much less a baby," Eric said. Besides, you're a baby yourself!"

"Eric, have you ever read the part about Mary?"

"Mary?"

"You know, Jesus' mother. She's sitting all alone in the temple, pregnant – to all intents and purposes really fucked up – and each day food and drink somehow appear. Then this guy comes up. I forgot his name, but he's very well known also in connection with the story. And he says, 'Mary, where is all of this food coming from?' and she answers, 'God.' I have a distinct picture of her in my mind sitting there placidly, smiling sweetly and saying with the most simple faith, 'God.'"

"Look, m'dear. You know very well that it's old Hadrian who's taking care of you, and if he stops you're going to be screwed, and don't try to hassle around with me and tell me that if he stopped giving you money you wouldn't be fucked over. You love his money too – more than him. What would happen if he wasn't loaded? Be honest."

She stroked Porgy contentedly, sniffing the pleasant summer air deep into her nostrils like a person appreciating the bouquet of an expensive brandy. 'It's so much fun to talk late at night,' she thought.

"Naturally I love Hadrian's money, Eric. But I also admire Hadrian. He inspires me more than any man I've ever known. He's dynamic. He's also good looking, Eric, and he's got a nice fat dick that he fucks me with as much as you do. Outside of money, inspiration and dick, what is a man good for anyway?"

"Oh Christ, let's discontinue the conversation. Let's go to bed."

"What about the idea you had for the living-room, Eric darling? Making love by candlelight has always been so beautiful for me. Here, let me get the candle from the bedroom." She jumped down from the balcony. Porgy sprang ahead of her like a mechanised Jack-in-the-box.

"You love to fuck, dontcha?" he asked her.

"Yes, I do. Don't you?" she said, and walked towards the candle that lay submerged in the pillows, still wet from her cunt.

Chapter Five

She sat in front of the little vanity mirror, perspiring as usual from the heat in the large, spacious bedroom. She leaned forward, hearing her breath in slight little gasps when she bent her body towards the mirror, and began lining her eyes with a black mascara pencil. She could feel the shiny red wood of the pencil between her fingers, sleek and plump, as she guided it across one eye, then the other. She watched the creamy black line appear over each eye, then drew back from the vanity mirror and studied the effect. She smiled at herself in the mirror when she saw how green and gleaming her eyes had become with the black kohl of the eyeliner to enhance them. Every once in a while, she had an uncanny feeling that there was someone in the room with her – someone that she couldn't see. She remembered the afternoon that the "ghost" had invaded her apartment, and she shuddered. But she was so excited about her date with Sherman and the game she was playing with Eric, that she lost touch with the disturbing, unseen presence.

She looked down at the old cracked clock that Eric had brought over when he had started sleeping with her. The numbers on its face looked black and hateful. Its shiny, silver alarm button sat on top like a preserved ostrich egg. She smiled at it when she thought of Eric's firm, pink ass showing through a hole in his old jeans as he rushed around after the alarm had gone off. She felt a momentary pang of guilt when she thought of him sitting on the black leather couch in his apartment, watching television with the other freaks who lived there and didn't live there, waiting for what he thought was her date with Hadrian to be over, waiting for her to call him so that he could tear over in his little green Triumph.

'Oh well,' she thought, and threw the mascara pencil into her purse impatiently. She thought of Hadrian and felt her hands go icy. 'God, it would be awful if he doesn't have a dinner with the Pakistanis tonight and shows up here.'

She kneaded her stomach with one hand until the thought went away.

'Nah, he wouldn't miss a business deal,' she decided.

She thought of his large, massive head, of the slightly greasy quality his high forehead would have taken on with the life juices that had flowed through him during his busy day, of the shrill phone calls, and the thick, blunt fingers of his hand drilling on the glass of his desk.

"Yes, yes, that's right," she heard him say in her imagination to someone in London or Paris, or Hamburg, or. . .

"Oh, I don't give a damn about any of this shit," she said aloud to no one. "I'm gonna have fun tonight – with old Sherman the shark."

She looked down at the simple cotton material of her dress. Purposely she had chosen the cheapest dress she owned because she assumed Sherman was from a wealthy family and she didn't want him to think that she was trying to impress him. She looked back in the mirror and was surprised again at how skinny she had grown. She thought of her husband and wondered what he was doing as she sat there dressing for Sherman.

'There are just too many people to think about,' she thought, and swallowed laboriously. 'Goddamned pills make my throat so dry – but I gotta have them to sleep.' She gulped down the rest of her tenth glass of orange juice that day, then padded into the living-room barefoot. She stood silently in the doorway, leaning on the cold white facing of the door and staring as if hypnotised out of the long french doors of the balcony. The skin of her ankle itched from under the thick layer of baby oil she had poured into her bath. She scratched it savagely with her toenail.

The sombre quality of the living-room delighted her the way the deep, dark colours of an El Greco's *Christ* might enchant an art collector. She had placed an old sofa covered in olive green velvet by the wall under an ornate mirror. Both of these items she had bought from a thrift shop and she felt very satisfied with their old-fashioned charm. "Just like Grandmother's," she had fantasised.

"Gotta paint that gold," she said, looking at the mirror. She put one large, bare foot on top of the other when she had stopped scratching her ankle.

In the corner her oil paints stood beside a picture she had begun of a woman holding a baby. The woman looked like herself; the baby resembled Hadrian. Another picture she had painted before she left Pierre stood propped on the radiator. Its pastel flowers spilled out of a large blue vase onto the rough texture of the canvas, like pieces of silk and lace. She stood enjoying the cool blueness of the dusk that had descended on the room, leaving the balcony before her in darkness.

A knock on the door clattered in her ears. She tensed from her reverie and drew herself to attention like an animal on guard. She waited until he knocked, once more, then opened the door.

"H'ya, babe," Sherman said, and looked down at her from his towering height with his dark, piercing eyes.

He stood tall and modern looking in the backdrop of the old hallway behind him. His legs were extremely long. The crease of his maroon knit slacks made them appear knife-like. He had slung his jacket over his arm and stood with one hand propped on the doorsill.

She looked at his hand touching the door so casually, trying to escape from the glowing curiosity in his eyes. She was struck again by the fine, tapering quality of his fingers. Even in the deep gloom of the unlit room, they seemed almost translucent at the tips.

She put one foot on top of the other and said, "Hi," without inviting him in.

"Do you always stand around in the dark like a goblin waiting for someone to knock on your door?" he asked sarcastically.

She couldn't stop looking at him as he stood silhouetted in the doorway. His dark navy jacket hung in just the right angle over his maroon slacks, and his plaid shirt was in the most correct style of the day. She followed the line of his long legs down to his shoe. They were mod-type loafers of a deep maroon colour with gold bars across the top. 'Gucci shoes,' she thought, with the part of her brain that was still southern. Her eyes swept back up to his face, absorbing his high, chiselled cheekbones, his alert intelligent eyes and attractive mouth hungrily.

"You look beautiful," she said, smiling at him.

"You're not supposed to call men beautiful," he said, emphasising the 'p' in 'suppose'.

She detected a modified New York-gone-DC type accent from the way he pronounced this word.

"That's what my brother says," she agreed, still gazing unabashed at him. "But he's beautiful, too. So I have to call him that."

"You're also not supposed to keep people hanging around in your doorway before you ask them in."

"Oh, my deah, do come in," she said in affected southern drawl. "I was just admiring you so while you were standin' theah, that I plumb forgot to ask y'all in."

He walked certainly into the room, trying to assess its contents in the darkness.

Porgy came rambling past his leg and yowled softly.

"What the hell?" he said, and drew back quickly from the cat's soft, furry touch. He glanced at Cybele surreptitiously when he saw the cat, embarrassed that she might have detected his initial fear. When Cybele saw his secret glance, she wanted to touch him ever so tenderly. Since he had tried to hide something, however trivial, she could identify with him.

"Are you trying to save on electricity, babe, or did you just forget to light the candles?" he asked. His succinct accent cut across the shadowy room like print in a textbook.

"Oh. . ." She looked around the dark room absently. "That is, I was just going to turn on the lamp." She had been enjoying the room's darkness so much that she had forgotten how strange it might seem to anyone else. She ran up to the lamp that was sitting on top of a bright red shawl she had thrown over the radiator.

"There," she said, looking over her shoulder and smiling at him as the lamp lit up the stately old room.

He blinked from the unexpectedness of the light, then looked carefully around.

"Did you paint that?" he asked, nodding towards the picture of flowers.

"Yes," she said vaguely, still smiling at him. She was anxious to call his attention away from any clue to her real self.

"It's very good," he told her. "You have talent." he looked at her curiously. "Why don't you go to school so you can use it?"

"Why don't we go out on the balcony?" she suggested, feeling her fingertips tingle with excitement at the sight of his confusion. "Come on," she urged.

"Why?" he asked, trying to hide his hungry curiosity.

"Oh, I just want you to see the whole domain."

"It's grand, alright," he said, looking around the old-fashioned room.

"It could be," she said. "Maybe it even was in its better days." She wondered how far she could go with her flamboyance before he called her bluff.

His firmly-chiselled jaw and perfectly pressed slacks kept cutting through the atmosphere of the aged walls and architecture of the building. She enjoyed the sight of his disciplined young body on the balcony as he leaned against its mouldering stone facing.

She hopped up on the balcony in front of him, happily showing off her slim figure. All the while, she was thinking, 'Wonder what he'll do? Wonder what might happen?'

"Isn't it green out here?" she said. "I just love summer. Reminds me of the South."

"Is that where you're from?" he asked. Again she felt his sharp glance on her face and person.

"Can't you tell?" she asked, and looked deeply into his eyes, allowing herself to savour the full pleasure that they brought to her.

"Yeah, I guess so." He put his hands on her shoulders, as if trying to hold her still for his appraisal. "Sometimes you sound southern, but other times—"

"But other times?" She hopped down in front of him, using one of his shoulders to balance herself as she did so. Suddenly they were both aware of the proximity of their bodies, of a strong, invisible force that drew them towards one another.

"Other times," he said, letting his hands rest lightly around her waist, "you could be from anywhere."

"Or anyone?" she said, delighted.

"No one can be more than one person," he said deliberately.

"Why not? I mean, if they really tried and went about it the right way." She touched the crisp, new material of his shirt.

"Why would you want to be more than one person?"

She rolled her eyes to the side dramatically as she had seen many movie actresses do, unconsciously imitating them. "Because it's so limiting to be just one person all the time, always following the same rules, the same routine things – you know? You might have all sorts of unknown capabilities – things that might never surface if you were always the same person."

"You could also get pretty confused going around being more than one person, Cybele." The tone of his voice was indulgent, slightly mocking. "What if you got your roles mixed up and you did one thing as one of the people you were pretending to be that another person you were also pretending to be should have done?"

She looked at him suspiciously. "Don't try to confuse me, Sherman honey, with your bedside manner. Come on, I've gotta go and put on my shoes, my feet are cold." He looked down at her feet, surprised that he hadn't noticed that they were bare before that moment, or had he forgotten?

He followed her into the bedroom, feeling uneasy but curious. 'Strange dame,' he thought.

When she clicked on the light, he looked around the room. It was furnished more completely than the living-room, with an elaborate French Provençal bedroom suite.

"Looks like you live more in here than in there."

"Huh?" she asked, hunting around on the floor of the closet for a pair of shoes. As she stood up, she saw Eric's old leather belt with its buckle that was shaped like a butterfly, and felt a strange giddiness once more.

She came out of the closet with a silly smile on her face, holding her shoes like a pair of dead rats. Sometimes, as Sherman had warned her, she lost touch with one role and became confused.

She sat down on the little round love seat and began putting on her shoes.

"Who's this guy?" he asked, pointing to a picture of Hadrian.

"Guess," she challenged him, and pulled the tiny strap of her shoe over one big toe.

He crossed his arms and held them with his hands in a habitual gesture of concentration. His young face narrowed with an intelligent, almost aged shrewdness, while he studied the picture.. His hair stuck out from his neck in a peculiar way as he inclined his head to observe the photograph more closely.

"He's either your father or your sugar daddy."

She stopped fumbling with her shoes for a second. The old air-conditioner droned loudly in the spacious room. Its sound was like a palpable barrier between them.

"You're cool," she said, grinning up at him like a tomboy.

She stood up. "Well, I'm ready. Where're we off to?"

"I thought we'd have dinner at my parents' apartment. We're going to be the guests of my mother's maid since my parents are in Europe right now."

"Is she a Negro?"

"Yes.

"And I thought the Jews were so liberated."

He still stood with both arms crossed. She felt chastised by his stance.

"You know, Cybele, you seem to have a constant need to challenge me." Again she heard his distinct New York accent when he enunciated 'constant', and the sound of his voice excited her ears. "And the manner in which you do this suggests certain things to me."

She looked at him petulantly. She was excited and intimidated by him. She felt the way that small children do when their father scolds them about something the child knows he has done wrong but still resents the authority of the parent.

"And what's that, Doctor Stein?"

"Did you go to college?"

"I'm only seventeen years old," she answered.

"My God, you're jail bait," he exclaimed.

"You seem to have a terrific inferiority complex for some reason."

"Christ, the way you stand there looking at me like I'm under a microscope gives me the creeps. You'd think you had a degree in psychiatry, the way you try to psyche me out."

"I *do* have a degree in psychiatry, as a matter of fact," he said.

"I'm really impressed," she said honestly. She started to laugh. "Hey, this'll be fun. Let's see if you can figure me out."

"You must think you're terribly fascinating," he said. "Maybe I should have said 'superiority' complex."

His carefully chosen words amused her. She thought that they sounded like the language of a well-educated peasant. But his clean, good looks and brilliant eyes were not those of a peasant in any way. "I suppose I just feel prejudiced against the New York accent," she assessed her feelings correctly.

They walked towards the apartment door and out to the long, softly lit hallway. The light from the fine old chandeliers reflected down on them in dappled patterns.

"Ha, ha!" Her laughter echoed through the tomblike hallway as their feet sank into the plush, red carpeting. "You're already mixed up," she goaded him, and clasped his hand happily.

His car was parked under thick-trunked oak trees. She ran up the side of it and looked down into the black leather interior.

"I just love your car," she said, running her hand along its low-slung door.

"Do y'all now?" He smiled at her, appreciating her genuine spontaneity. He lifted the sunken chrome door handle easily, and opened the car door. She watched him fit his long legs and torso under the steering wheel with interest.

"Why don't you get in, Cybele? Or are you just going to stand there admiring me all day?"

"Ha," she said, and stepped over the car door without opening it. "I bet your mother tells you how great you are every hour."

The splendid trees swayed over them, perfuming the air with a leafy, acrid smell, while they sat like two children playing in the low-slung car. Their leafy branches made a chiaroscuro of constantly moving patterns on the shark-shaped hood of the Corvette.

She saw him draw his shoulders together defensively when she mentioned his mother. 'Oh goody, a weak spot,' she thought, and slipped her arm through his, smelling the healthy odour of his flesh under his shirt like a friendly predator. She felt the stringy, tough muscles of his long arm as he put the car in gear. 'Hadrian's are thicker,' she thought, but still she clung to Sherman's arm. The motor roared up in their ears.

"Oh man, this is great!" she exclaimed.

"Is it?" He smiled and slung the car around the corner. The motor backfired with the sudden decrease in speed when he did so.

He put one hand on her knee as they rode down tree-lined Cathedral Avenue. She lay back on the soft leather seat, relaxing for the first time since their meeting. Before she knew it they had come to a large complex of tall, luxurious apartment buildings.

"This is it," he said, and swung the car into an underground garage. His jaw jutted forward in a more authoritative manner when they sped past parking attendant. She took her arm from his and straightened her legs away from his hand as they roared past many parked cars.

"Where're you going, Cybele?" he asked, when she pulled her knee away from his hand.

"Well, we *are* at your parents' place," she said, looking around the starkly lit garage.

"Cybele, you're a smile," he said. The neon lighting played harshly on his tanned face, but its illumination only emphasised his youth.

The garage was cold and seemingly air-conditioned. She followed him, feeling subdued and cautious. Her hands were cold against her sides.

He swung open the heavy metal door that led out of the garage. The sharpness of his shoulder blades jutted out from under his shirt. They excited her and made her forget the cold, austere parking lot.

"Here, wanna hold this, Cybele?" he asked, smiling warmly at her and plopping his expensive sports coat into her arms.

She felt anger rising at his command, but forgot about it while she contemplated his engaging mouth. Its full, lush flesh invited her own.

"You always want me to do something for you," she said, feeling the pebbly material of his knit jacket on her arm and following his swift strides up the concrete steps. The length of his legs intrigued her as they mounted the steps. It creased his pants like a blade.

"How do you know I always want you to do something for me?" he asked. His voice echoed down the bleak concrete corridor.

"Oh, I can tell," she said, panting laboriously from the climb.

They came out into a lavish, richly carpeted lobby flanked on either side by heavy sectioned wall mirrors. A desk clerk sat behind an extravagantly large desk.

"This is it, Cybele," Sherman said, leering slightly. "Home, sweet home." He strode over to the desk importantly and asked if there were any messages for Stein.

She leaned against a huge ormolu pot and stared at her sandalled toes in the deep French blue carpeting, then gazed out the wide, floor-length windows that led onto a courtyard. Around the courtyard were several buildings of the same size that she stood in.

'Thousands and thousands of 'em,' she thought, as she read a few names on the vast expanse of mailbox slots.

Sherman walked back up to her, brushing his thick blond hair away from his forehead self-consciously. Again she felt about him a curious vulnerability that drew her towards him. At first she wanted to touch him gently, then she felt a perverse need to wound him.

'His blood might be so sweet,' she thought happily and followed him through the ridiculously sumptuous corridor towards the elevator.

He seemed to stay on the defensive with her, and this flattered her. It made her feel that she was important enough for him to feel intimidated by her.

"Like the place, Cybele?" he asked sarcastically.

"I bet I'm the only gentile in sight," she said.

"Shhh!" he said mockingly, and pushed the elevator button. "They might think you're prejudiced."

"Not really," she said. "More like interested – I mean, take the Italians. . ."

"Yeah?" he said. "Who'd want a dumb old greasy Italian?"

"See?" she said. "Who's prejudiced? It's just that the Jews get so paranoid about people pointing out *their* particular ethnic qualities. Always afraid that someone's going to poke 'em in a gas oven."

He guided her onto the elevator, looking at her well-moulded calves and tapering ankles.

"Little Cybele," he said, and pushed down on her shoulders until her knees buckled underneath her. "Bow," he commanded, and forced her to the floor.

"You know, for somebody who's going to be a doctor, you sure do seem to lack tenderness at times," she drawled, batting her eyes and biting at his fingertips that rested on her shoulder.

"Ah ha!" he exclaimed, and jerked his hand away. "So you're vicious?"

The elevator came to the fifteenth floor and stopped.

"What would you do if I bit your finger?" she asked. "I mean, really bit it?"

"I'd probably have to lay you out," he grinned, putting his hand in hers and pulling her up gently from the floor of the elevator. They walked out into a long hallway flanked by rows and rows of impersonal doors.

"Where d'you get all this biting shit from anyway?"

"My husband," she said glibly, and felt a sinking feeling when she heard herself say 'husband', knowing that she had revealed herself. "See, I've got his whole mouth print on my elbow," she said, and held her arm up to him. He took her elbow and scrutinised it well. She felt an icy thrill of pleasure rush through her as she observed his high cheekbones and the pulse she saw beating faintly in the vein of his neck.

"Umm, real psycho eh?" he said casually, but he stared alertly at the teethmark scars on her arm.

"Don't worry. I bit him back – almost paralysed his thumb once. His typing thumb. That ruined him for a week," she added.

"What kind of work is your husband in?" he asked, and unlocked the door to his parents' apartment. She looked past him into the living-room's soft pastel-coloured furniture of white and light blue. A silken, intricately designed oriental rug covered the large room's already carpeted floor. In front of them a modern, gold-rimmed mirror reflected his youthful face when he stood aside for her to enter.

"He's a professor – of literature," she added, and walked warily into the foyer of the apartment. She glanced down at a group of unopened envelope marked *Dr Myra Stein* that were neatly stacked on the foyer's desk.

"Who's Myra?" she asked with her back to him, pretending to be still looking at the envelopes, but secretly watching the expression on his face from the mirror. The name Myra on her lips visibly jolted him. Its personal intimation obviously surprised him, especially with the insinuating tone that she had used.

'What game is she playing anyway?' he thought and shook his head suddenly, feeling the fatigue from his long day at the hospital steal over him. 'Whatever she's got on her mind, I can take care of it,' he thought and flexed his finely shaped fingers. He remembered the scalpel under his hand earlier that day when he had deftly scraped out an elderly lady's cheeks and pulled the skin back behind her old, withered ears, remembered the satisfying plop when he had flung the unwanted flesh from her face into a plastic covered trash can at his elbow.

"A little suture here, a little suture there," he said. "And right under the eyes," Sherman said aloud to Cybele. He pushed the flesh under her eyes up so hard that she took on the appearance of an oriental, then drew himself back from her and studied the effect.

"Hey, you look good like that, Cybele."

"How about Myra?" she asked, putting both of her hands on the pockets of his slacks and carefully clamping her palms around the chiselled bones of his hips. "Is your mother oriental or Jewish?" she asked brightly.

"Why don't you let me do your first face lift, Cybele?"

"Free?" she asked and rubbed her hands back and forth on his hips, studying his reaction like a cat waiting for a mouse to make its move. "Or wouldn't Mother approve? I'm sure she wants 'her son the doctor' to make lots of money." She smirked at him prettily with one tanned brown leg crossed pertly in front of the other.

"Cybele, I believe you've got a real bitch on tonight. Bet you haven't had an orgasm in two weeks."

"Umm, feels nice," she continued, still stroking supple his hips.

"Think you could give me one?" she asked, and laughed mockingly, into his dancing brown eyes.

"Here comes the maid," he said, glancing into the luxurious living-room.

"Why don't you lay some southern comfort on her, Cybele?"

He gave her a little push forward. She reached back and pinched him on his knee.

"You must be Mr Sherman's new friend," an emaciated Negro woman said and she held out a black, bony hand to Cybele.

"Yes, I must be," Cybele said, and shook the woman's hand, looking at its rheumatic joints as she did so, and remembering, for some reason, the long, etiolate fingers of her tubercular grandfather's hand.

"Well," the black woman said, wringing her ropy, veined hands, "you're a very, very pretty girl. I can see how Mr Sherman likes you so well."

"Yes, she's pretty all right, Mary," Sherman said to the maid. "But what else is she?" He looked down at Cybele from his height, studying her with an uncharacteristically tender expression on his handsome face.

"How do you know what I am or who I am?" she said savagely.

"Why don't you go on in the kitchen and watch Mary make shrimp curry, like a good little girl?" he said, touching the soft, bare flesh of her shoulders.

"I've made shrimp curry millions of times," she retorted hotly.

"Yes, but do you know how to make it with kumquats?" he asked, following her and Mary into the kitchen.

Mary led them into the ultra-modern, gleamingly clean kitchen. Cybele watched her long black fingers reach up for cans of grated coconut and kumquats, and remembered watching the Negro cooks her mother had employed years ago down South.

'They never could eat with us,' she thought with a sort of puzzlement at why they had eaten separately, until she remembered the social reasons for their being segregated from Whites.

All the while, Sherman caressed Cybele's slender, tanned arms with a relaxing, reassuring motion.

She felt the sensitive touch of his fingers on her flesh. Their caress dissolved her many conflicts for a long moment, as she watched Mary stir the curried shrimp. The careful, deliberate movements of her hands lulled Cybele into a superficial calm.

Sherman dipped a spoon into the boiling mixture and startled her out of her reverie with his abrupt gesture. He blew on the liquid for a minute and said, "Here, have some of this. The curry will wake you up. You look like you're about to go to sleep, babe." She looked into his fierce brown eyes, and was shocked into consciousness by the clarity of his glance, the positiveness of his manners.

'He gives things like this to people all day,' she thought as the hot, spicy liquid filled her mouth.

"Umm," Cybele said, "I like you."

Mary grinned down at the bubbling liquid while she stirred the mixture. The fine creases and wrinkles in her dark face reflected a gentle and honest struggle with life.

"You like me?" Sherman said. "Just because I give you food? Would you like an orang-utan in a zoo who stuck a spoon in your mouth?"

Mary glanced up from the soup and saw Cybele glaring at Sherman like an angered cat, as she licked a smear of curry from her lips.

"You children go on in there and sit down," she said. "This is right ready now."

"All right, little Mary," Sherman said and patted her on the head. Even though he towered over the maid, her gentle dignity made his gesture seem like one of an overgrown schoolboy. Cybele felt a comfortable affection between the two of them that again reminded her of the South and maids that her family had had.

She followed Sherman back into the spacious dining area.

"Wow, you've got a terrific view," she said, looking out of the windows that surrounded the whole apartment. The tops of trees spread out beneath them like clouds.

"Not bad for what it is," he said. He stood close behind her, holding her arms just above the elbow. She felt a particular lonely tentativeness from the delicate touch of his fingers – a searching, bitter quality.

"What do you mean – 'for what it is'?" she asked, still looking into the hills of trees. Black crows were swerving and dipping in the growing dusk. Their blue-black wings were flung out in graceful arcs against the clouds. She could hear their piercing, "Caw! caw!" cries faintly through the insulated environment of the apartment.

"Well, what I mean is, it's a nice penthouse apartment but. . ." His voice trailed off.

"Here it is," Mary said, coming out of the kitchen with a large silver tray of bowls and plates. "Please be seated," she said with a mildness that showed she was in complete control of the situation.

They both turned to survey the rich, inviting array of food the woman had begun to lay before them on the elegant dining-room table. Sherman pulled a chair out for Cybele and said, "Madam." She glanced back uncertainly at him, enjoying the pleasant strangeness of her surroundings as she sat down. She looked into Mary's smiling eyes and felt at home once more.

Sherman began ladling curry onto her plate. He held out a bowl of exquisitely cut crystal brimming with white fluffy coconut and said, "Want some?"

She nodded happily and said, "Yeah, lay it on me!" Their eyes met once more. He leaned over impulsively and brushed his full, warm lips over hers.

"You sure do know how to make a guy feel good, Cybele." He put the bowl down and picked up another one. "And now for the kumquats," he said, grinning moronically at her. "You like kumquats, Cybele?"

"I never had any."

"What? Never had any kumquats?" he exclaimed, and placed several small orange sections over the coconut. She stared at their spongy, plump bodies on the white bed of coconut, taking pleasure in their bright colour.

"Ah, I think you like to say the word better than eating them," she said and put a large spoonful of the mixture into her mouth with gusto.

"That's the spirit, Cybele. Gobble it up!"

"When you say 'kumquats', it sounds obscene," she mumbled over a mouthful of food.

"That's it," he said, eating fast also. "That's it exactly. Like 'em because they sound obscene!" He pushed two kumquats into his mouth and smiled at her as some of their juice dribbled down on his chin. She started to laugh.

"And what did you mean about this apartment being OK?" she said, looking around at the collection of original oil paintings that hung in perfect taste on the walls. "It's lavish, by most standards."

"Uh yes, by most standards, yes. He studied the white wine in his glass, then drained it greedily. "Uh, Mary, could you please pour us a little more wine?" he called. Mary appeared like a friendly apparition with a tall, thin bottle, poured more wine, then disappeared. Sherman lifted his glass to hers.

"Skol, my dear. To our first date." He winced with mock horror at his choice of words, then gulped down half of the wine in his glass.

She sipped a little wine and said, "How about Mary? How'd you like to live where she does?"

He froze over the hot curry momentarily, then calmly began to eat again.

"I happen to know where Mary lives," he said. His New York accent came out again when he pronounced 'know'.

"I'll bet it's bleak too," Cybele said.

"Yes, it is," he said cryptically. "You're a funny chick, Cybele. I bring you over here for a nice dinner and all you do is worry about my maid's living conditions."

"Oh, I'm not worried," she said, chewing on the tender body of a shrimp. "I was just comparing." She looked around them meaningfully at the Impressionistic oil paintings of tender green hills rolling gracefully into cerulean blue skies.

Don't you know I've thought of all that before, Cybele? I've taken her home, been invited inside, and got the whole first-hand report. She lives a very quiet life with her son. Most people would consider it stark. I guess my parents do because they've tried to help in a lot of ways. They offered to send her son to school and so forth, but they seem perfectly content to stay the way they are."

"What are your parents like?" she asked.

"Well, my mother's a psychiatrist and my father's a businessman."

"He must be a pretty good one," she said. "I mean, you've got the typical Cadillac and penthouse."

"I'll take that as a sincere statement on your part and answer you this way. We used to have money – I mean, *real* money." He finished the rest of his wine and looked at the empty glass for a moment. "But my father made a mistake in his business – a very bad mistake. It didn't leave us penniless as you can see, but it changed a lot of things." He pushed at the empty bowl in front of him. As if by an unseen cue, Mary came to take the plates away. "Maybe even for the better. My mother went back to school at almost fifty, and now she's a doctor. I worked for my father and did anything else I could to get through medical school."

"All's for the best in this best of all possible worlds, as old Pangloss would say, right?" she philosophised. She paused for a moment, fingering her long, dark hair. "I guess you're really sort of a very straight guy," she said, as she ran her fingers along the satiny finish of the elaborate tablecloth. "But you have a lot of anger in you from somewhere."

"Look, Cybele, *I'm* the psychiatrist, remember?"

"Among other, things, I guess," she said drolly and smiled.

"What about you," he asked. "You don't look so gentile to me. There's some Latin blood or something exotic in there somewhere – French?"

She smiled. "You've got part of it – how did you guess?"

"With that black hair. Besides, I've travelled with my parents, Lou." He took another bite of shrimp curry.

"What's your maiden name anyway?"

"Lundi."

He looked at her with surprise.

"That's a Jewish name! I know that family. They've got a lot of meat packing and garment companies in Philadelphia. They owned a big restaurant up in Sheepshead Bay in New York."

"Yes," she said. "We're French Jews."

She lowered her eyes to her hands. Sometimes her hands seemed alive, apart from herself.

"My grandfather came down south from Philadelphia. He was a rich cotton broker."

"Well, well, little Cybele – the cat's out of the bag."

He brushed his sexy mouth with a heavy freshly pressed linen napkin.

She felt depressed.

"No game – just life – *my* life."

"Well, what happened? Where is your grandfather? Why isn't he or your family helping you, instead of this weird old Turkish dude?"

He looked at her angrily, jealously noting her large green eyes and her rosy, full lips.

'God, what a fuck!' he thought. 'A fucking knock out.'

"My grandfather is dead." she said tonelessly. "Died penniless at fifty in a cheap hotel room – ran off and left my dad and his mom and ten sisters flat broke when the Crash came."

"God!" Sherman exclaimed. "That wasn't very kosher of him."

"No, it wasn't, was it?" she agreed with a bitter, sad smile. "Guess he couldn't take it, though – suddenly being poor after having been such a big deal. I saw pictures of him. He was a good looking man. He had black curly hair and vital black eyes, a wide sensual mouth. He seemed always to be smiling. He was short – about 5'7" and stocky."

Sherman got up and came around to her side suddenly.

"Don't be so down – don't be so afraid. No one's going to bite you here. Can't we stop fighting verbally?"

"I'd like to trust you,," she told him, and put her hand over his. "I really would."

He turned her face up to him.

"You know you're fucking gorgeous, don't you?"

"Ummm," she said, but her eyes drifted around the room.

"If you like to be different people, study acting. You could make a million bucks as an actress, Lou."

She smiled at him, not really paying attention to his words.

"You seem so out of it – so asleep," he complained.

"I'm just tense," she told him.

"Shalom Aleichem," he said suddenly in Hebrew, looking at her expectantly.

She shrugged her shoulders.

"Haven't you ever been to Temple?" he asked incredulously.

"No," she said flatly.

"But why?" he asked, his boyish face flushed with exasperation.

"Because my father never went to Temple."

"But his father was a Jew."

"I know, but when my grandfather came down south, being a Jew was like being a Nigger. He hid his religion. My dad took us to a Protestant church – when we went."

"So you've never had any instruction?" He stroked her silky black hair tenderly. "Do you have any religion at all?"

"Not really," she told him.

"Don't you believe in God?"

"Yes, remotely. It's just he seems so far away."

"Because you didn't get to be friends when you were a little girl."

"George is my only real friend," she told him.

"Didn't your mom teach you anything?"

"She's Gentile."

"But still she must have believed in something."

"Yeah, she did. She's a good woman – but she's always talking about gruesome murders. She was always reading me terrible stories from the newspapers every day when I came home from school."

"Christ," he muttered. "That's strange."

"She's strange – very antisocial and strange, but sweet."

"You're ambivalent about her."

"I know. I mean, you have to think of a person's life experience. She's never travelled. All she knew was a very loving family and they were their world together. There was no real need for socialising for her. Her relationships with her parents and brother and sisters was so deep and loving, she didn't need others."

She looked around the opulent room.

"But why this fixation with murder – with horror?"

"I don't know. That's the odd part, isn't it? Do you think people can be possessed?"

"Possessed?"

"By evil spirits. By spirits who lead them into horror and sin."

"Wow, Cybele – you *do* believe in the supernatural, if nothing else."

"Of course I believe in spirits."

"And mainly evil ones," he surmised and grinned at her impishly.

"Well, a gypsy said that I was under a curse brought on by a love of money. Coming from my father's side – down to the fifth generation."

"How about your father – was he pleasant?"

She smiled at him.

"Tippy toeing around old Sherman? Stepping lightly around the shit?"

"You *are* bitter, aren't you?"

"Yeah, I'm bitter. All I can remember are bad things – my father reading Nietzsche while getting smashed – beating my mother from rage and frustration at his life."

"Actually he seemed to hate everyone a lot of the time. He was devastated when his father ran off and left them. Then he resented his mother – that she wouldn't marry a wealthy man to alleviate the situation. I mean, he was working at two jobs when he was only fourteen. I saw a picture of him then. He looked like a child boy with his large sad eyes over his wide gentle mouth. He was tall and slender. Said he asked his mother to beat him with a shoe to wake him up at five a.m. every morning."

"You love him?" Sherman said.

"Of course I love him. I love all the good in him. He's a very handsome man – very hard working and caring about his family – a frustrated man with rage boiling out of him at any emotional moment, yet he used to take me to all of my ballet classes."

"Ballet? Were you good at that, too?"

"Too?" she asked.

"You're very talented with your painting, Cybele. Maybe you could go to the Corcoran."

"Yes, maybe. What's that?"

"One of the best art schools in the country."

Her hand brushed the heavy damask linen of the tablecloth. She saw her fingers around the sparkling crystal wineglass. Her eyes swept around the lavishly furnished room, and she remembered another rich man's home she had visited as a child. She began to speak slowly, as if in a half-remembered dream, as if talking to herself.

"Once, I went to a friend's house. The living-room was carpeted in white – like the carpet under your oriental rugs. It was large and filled with satin and velvet sofas. When we went into her kitchen, I gasped. It was so large, so clean and full of the most modern appliances. I'll never forget how I felt in that kitchen. I was only seven years old, but the first thing my brain registered was – how did they get the money for all of this? Then I thought of her father."

"What does your father do?" I asked.

"He's an electrical engineer," she replied.

"It seemed to me that specifically, at that very moment, I wished with all my heart that this little girl's father could be my father – that my father could be brilliant, successful and charming instead of frustrated, poor and dense mentally. He had no good idols – only the prophet of hate – Nietzsche."

Sherman watched her smooth, creamy skinned face with hungry interest. He took her slender brown hand into his larger square hand.

"I followed Michele down into their family room. They had two TVs – elaborate stereos! I touched one with a type of awe.

"Michele smiled at me. 'They're my dad's hobby – he builds stereos!'

"I tried to think of a hobby my father had – I couldn't think of one. I couldn't think of any books he had read, except for Nietzsche; friends he had, or my mom either.

"And I remember I came home. . . my father was sitting in a small, mean looking rocking chair, rocking my baby sister to sleep. The tiny living-room floor was bare. Cheap plastic furniture was the furnishing. An old oil stove stood in the middle of the room, ugly and black.

"My father's eyes lit on me and his features contorted with anger. He had found an object for his immense frustration and rage at his long, miserable day.

"'Where've you been?' he yelled.

"I just stood there looking at him with disgust.

"He jumped up and grabbed me, holding my sister in his other arm.

"'Leave me alone!' I shouted and wrenched my hand from his. I ran past him and locked my bedroom door, shaking all over as I did so.

"He began pounding on it over and over.

"'I hate you! I hate you!' I cried. 'If only you weren't my father!'"

"If we don't get out of here, we'll never get to the fireworks in time," he said and stood up from the table.

"Mary, we're leaving now," he called.

Mary came out of the kitchen, untying a neat white apron from around her meagre waist. Her gnarled black hands brushed its fluffy ruffles like an ape touching lace at Versailles. Cybele felt her dark, haunting eyes on her face and said, "Mary, thank you for the dinner."

"Oh, you're real welcome, Miss Cybele," she said. "You're just a real pretty girl."

Sherman made a face at Cybele in reaction to Mary's compliment, then held his hand out for her. She took it solemnly, feeling his strong hands in hers with pleasure.

As they walked down the long corridor to the elevator, she noticed rows and rows of small chandeliers hung at intervals on the ceiling that gave the hallway a planned, contrived look of luxury. "You have chandeliers on your ceiling just like at my apartment building," she observed.

"Yeah," he said, and reached up towards the ceiling, almost touching one of the dimly lit fixtures. "I used to think of smashing all of them with my umbrella handle when I came home from school on rainy days." He raised an imaginary umbrella and began smashing at the lights.

"Ugh," she said, remembering how Pierre had broken the heavy cane handle of an umbrella on her back and head during one of their innumerable fights.

"Ha, what's the matter, Cybele?" he asked when he saw the expression of disgust on her face. "Everybody's got hidden aggressions. I didn't actually do that, you know."

They walked into the elevator. She stood behind him shivering, feeling the iciness of the air-conditioning numb her scantily clad body.

The trees were dark and all-encompassing around the Lincoln Memorial, and a winey, sappy fragrance from their leaves permeated the still night air. He stopped the car near an old stone bridge. They alighted from the black interior of the Corvette and ran across the wide, circling street.

"Look, Cybele," he cried as they ran together, and pointed to a flying, sparkling light that had suddenly spurted up into the opaque darkness of the sky.

"Oooh," she gasped, transported by the shooting spray of pink, blue and red colours ripping across the warm darkness of the summer night.

The fireworks lit up their eager faces and led them on through the night like ancient Roman torches.

"Here, sit up on this," he told her, lifting her onto a thick slab of marble that served as a base for an enormous lion statue. She felt the cold marble under her legs and settled back between the lion's paws. Long fallen dew from the grass settled onto her bare legs and arms and made her shiver again.

A penetrating dampness from the murky Potomac River added to the night's chill. Sherman leapt up beside her and massaged her arms briskly, then he began rubbing her legs. She stared down at his hands on her legs, enjoying watching them there. Her skin became an open receptacle for the night, revelling in every touch from the air and every drop of dew that beaded on the thick, grassy park.

"Oooh," she sighed when another fiery flash of colour burst into the sky. An answering echo of exclamation emitted from thousands of other throats near them. People were perched like bees around an artificial honey pot of colour in the Washington DC parks on that July 4th, 1971.

She studied Sherman's excited, almost childishly pleased expression of delight in the brilliant light from the fireworks.

"See there, Cybele. The best things in life are free," he philosophised.

"Are you trying to tell me that or yourself?" she asked through the magic of the night's brilliant colours. He grasped her chin and turned her face to him. His dark, fierce eyes burned passionately into hers, lit up intermittently by the fireworks like the glow from a flickering flame. His lips parted to form a word, then closed back together into a warm, curving fullness. She touched his lower lip . The white, lacy flowers of a dogwood tree hung over them, spreading their creamy designs of light into the night like a fantastic snowqueen. The shadows of the flowers dappled their warm flesh in an exotic pattern of chiaroscuro. His intense eyes seemed to be diving down like a wild bird onto her face. He pressed his lips to hers for the first time, searching, moving, trying to find an answering flame on her mouth to match the one she had seen in his eyes. The warm flesh of their mouths shot a surprising thrill through their bodies and they drew back from one another like two startled, healthy animals, wary of the uncontrollably sweet sensations their kiss had created. He grasped her head as if to steady them and they gazed at one another with red and green cheeks coloured by the spurting colours of the fireworks. He grabbed her body roughly and pushed her back against the extended forepaw of the lion's leg, looking greedily into her eyes before he kissed her once again.

"Oh, babe," he said.   His breath trembled into her ear. "Goddammit, you're good!"

She pressed both of her hands onto his shoulders, feeling their hard, slender shape, comparing them to Hadrian's muscular arms. She wanted both of them, or did she? She needed Hadrian more than anyone, but he always left her and then she got lost.

"Don't try to hold me off," he said, shoving himself up to her body. "You don't want to, you know." He kissed her cheeks softly and began nibbling at her ears.

"No!" she protested. "I can't bear it."

"You love it," he said. He rubbed his forearms up and down her ribs, lifting her arms as he did so and brushing the sides of her creamy high breasts. She felt the hardness of his dick on her leg and pressed her knee against it a little to judge its size better. The tip shot up, answering the pressure of her knee.

"Ummm," she moaned.

"Oh, babe," he whispered and pushed her further back on the statue of the lion, letting his hands touch the contours of her body.

"Hey, just a minute," she protested and pushed his hands away.

"Why don't you try to be pleasant with me?" he asked. His breath rushed onto her cheek and his slender fingers pressed into the flesh of her thigh.

"I *am* pleasant, aren't I?" she asked, and moved her knee against his body again. "Why don't we walk somewhere? I want to move," she said impatiently.

"OK, Wonder Woman – where to?"

She slid down off the marble pedestal of the statue and stood with her shapely hips in front of his pencil-thin waist and tapering thighs, staring at his hard, bulging dick.

"Come on," she said, and grasped his fingers with her own, digging her fingernails into the flesh of his palm.

They began walking along, swinging their arms back and forth in a lackadaisical, seesaw motion. Suddenly she wrung her hand away from his and darted forward, running joyously through the lush grass.

"Catch me if you can," she called, and ran faster and faster under the wide boughs of the trees.

"Ha, Cybele, you're a smile," he yelled as he passed her easily. His long legs moved like a cantering thoroughbred through the dark, grassy night.

"Come on, come on, babe," he laughed, running backwards in front of her like a sleek racehorse. "You can make it."

She ran on with him in front of her, panting swiftly from the movement of her legs.

"Oh, Sherman," she whined pitifully, feeling a searing pain in her lungs as the night air forced itself inside her chest.

"Huh? Huh?" he taunted, and lolled his tongue out at her.

"Don't go so fast," she panted.

"Ever play any touch football, Cybele?" he challenged her, still running in front of her with an easy, graceful gait.

"No."

"I didn't think so." Get ready for a tackle," he said, and grabbed her around the legs as she ran by.

"Oh!" She screamed in surprise and fell down onto the loamy black earth.

"That's a tackle, babe," Sherman said, gasping for breath beside her on the ground. She held the weight of her chest off the ground with her elbows, and looked back at his hands holding her knees.

"Damn it, you hurt my foot," she said. She turned around under his hands and drew one leg up. "See? It's bleeding."

"Ah, you're gonna live."

"Yeah, maybe. Well, I've gotta go anyway," she said, thinking of Eric waiting at his communal apartment and wondering if Hadrian was going to stop by that evening or not. Things were getting too complicated.

"Can I come in?" Sherman asked when they got back to her apartment. He stood in the dimly lit doorway. The sleek precision of his person faded into a Renoir-like softness from the light of the dirty old chandeliers that hung over them in the hallway. She stood in front of him, shortened by his unusual height, and fingered the shiny gold key to her apartment hesitantly.

"I don't know," she said. Her expression was like a hard, tight acorn just dropped on a pre-winter ground. "I mean, I don't have much time."

"Oh, you've got time, babe," he said, and tucked his hands under her armpits.

"I do?" she asked. "Well, since you know everything, come on in."

Her handsome, striped cat greeted them, yowling and rubbing his thick, sensual body against their legs. She stood surveying the gloomy old living-room for a moment.

"Would you like a cognac?" she asked, without turning around. He touched her shoulders lightly with his long, graceful fingers.

"Sure, why not?" he answered.

She flicked on the kitchen light and walked past the cat's feeding bowl that sat encrusted with a hard, cement-like residue of cat food. She looked into one of the bleak white cabinets for a couple of glasses and slid the fat bottle of brandy across the formica tabletop. The harsh black and white pattern of the linoleum floor almost crossed her eyes when she caught sight of it from time to time in the neon lighting of the room.

She splashed the golden brown liquid into a cheap crystal glass and recapped the squat bottle.

She handed him one of the glasses. He took the glass and sampled the tangy liqueur, looking at her with his avid brown eyes.

She lifted her glass and said, "Here's to it." She downed her brandy like a sailor, then took the bottle and refurbished her glass. "Think you'll need more?" she asked, standing with one perfectly chiselled leg crossed in front of the other and smiling scoffingly at him.

"Why don't you bring it, babe," he said, "just in case." He raised the tiny glass to his mouth.

"Would you think I was trying to seduce you if I changed into my kimono?" she asked.

"No, why? I see more than that every day in the hospital," he said and walked towards the living-room.

"But not in such an atmosphere," she said and smiled confidently. She took him by the arm and steered him towards the bedroom. "Would you mind if we sit in here? I'm not in the mood for the other room tonight."

"Sure, babe. 'Whatever that means."

They walked into the spacious old bedroom. He sat down uneasily on the bed. She stepped inside the walk-in closet, took out a kimono and went into the bathroom to change.

When she emerged, she saw him standing by her vanity table, holding the photograph of Hadrian.

"Well," she said, and smiled.

"This dude here – he's your sugar daddy, isn't he?"

"Rather archaic term for a guy like you to use, isn't it, Sherman?" She walked gracefully over to the bed and picked up her embroidery. All she could think about was getting rid of him and feeling Eric's hard dick in her body all night.

"You say Hadrian is a weird old guy – I don't think so. He's a diplomat as well as a businessman. He was decorated for valour in the Korean War. He has hundreds of friends that he enjoys. They are all over the world. They help one another in business, and yet are close like a family with him socially. He grew up with a strong faith in God, praying five times a day as all good Moslems do. His father was like an Onassis in Istanbul and taught Hadrian everything he knows about the shipping business. He sent Hadrian to school in France giving him the best education that money could buy. Hadrian has a doctorate in international economics from Grenoble."

Cybele offered him a challenge in her flashing green eyes.

"You really worship him, don't you?"

"He'll do anything for me – he'll never let me down. Never!"

"Why are you so sure of that?" Sherman asked.

"I don't know – but he never would. I'm something for him. He sees me as himself when his father died suddenly. He knows I'm all alone, like he was – and he wants to protect me from what he went through." She paused. "He's the father I've been looking for all of my life. The tycoon I want to grow up around. I want a man I can worship."

"But you can't really enjoy sex with him, Cybele, can you? I mean, the guy's at least sixty. His body must be old looking for you."

She smiled. "I don't come when I have sex unless someone licks me – except through masturbation. I just pretend."

"Most young girls don't."

"For me it's enough that Hadrian adores me. That he chooses me over his wife – and she is young and lovely, a blonde, so different from me. He offered to buy an apartment in Paris for me."

"Why not here?"

"Oh, he will. . . he will."

"I hope you're right, Lou. You're so young – so fragile."

He caressed her arms and kissed wisps of her hair.

"I just want to be with someone who'll let me paint and relax – who won't be beating my brains out all the time."

Suddenly Sherman's handsome face and powerful body brought her back to the present. She smiled at him coyly and said, "I like to do this," she said, and began pushing the bright pink thread into the thick linen material, like a spider spinning a web, watching as he tried to impart a casual quality to his reclining pose on the bed.

"It's very decorative," he noted, and extended his hand to touch the material. She noticed that his hand trembled when he touched the embroidery hook.

"I wonder why you wanted to go to the fireworks tonight?" she asked, pushing the delicate, silver embroidery needle into the material again.

"What do you mean, Cybele? Why does anyone want to see the fireworks?"

She felt his dark, passionate gaze on her face as he watched the petal of a pink flower emerge from the thread.

"I mean, you seem so far removed from that sort of. . ." – she bit the thread and tied it neatly under the embroidery pattern – ". . .sensuality," she finished, and smiled coyly at him, touching one of his perfectly moulded knuckles.

"I know what you're trying to say, Cybele," he said. His eyes gazed about the room, mirroring his feeling of confusion as they groped through the room's enigmatic atmosphere. "And you're right. Sometimes it is harder for me to get into things like that." He stopped with an expression of irritation crossing his face. "You know, this place could be the set for some sort of kooky play."

"I know," she said, and grinned impishly at him.

"That delights you, doesn't it?" He grasped her wrist, causing her to drop the embroidery.

"If you seek fantasy, you will have your pleasure," she said portentously. Her dark hair fell over the pale green and orange colours of her kimono's pattern, framing her face like a misplaced Egyptian queen.

"But if one seeks knowledge?" he asked, and brushed his lips against her neck.

"They'll have to be like you – skirting all crude pleasures and hitching up their pants at 7 a.m. every morning. Having beefy-armed nurses wake them at 3 a.m.. . . ." Her voice trailed off as she relaxed on the pillows. "But you will learn the truth. . . on your path, anyway."

"I believe in spells and curses, don't you?" she asked suddenly. "My cat and I saw a ghost in this apartment."

"It's spooky enough to have a ghost here. God, why don't you move?"

"Oh, I will. I've gotta get away from that old landlord anyway."

She looked at Sherman, speculating on how much more he could take.

"Do you want to see a bone my cat dug up in his rose garden the other day?"

"A bone?" Sherman looked at her with alarm, then laughed. "What kind of bone, Lou – chicken, dog, or cat?"

She walked over to the French Provincial dresser and slid open a small drawer. She brought the small white bone back to Sherman and plopped it in his hand.

He looked at the bone closely, turning it over and over in his hand. "This is a human bone, Lou – looks like the little finger."

He looked up at her solemnly. His tanned, handsome face was grim in the glare of the overhead light.

"You should get out of this place, Cybele," he repeated. He looked all around distrustfully. "This landlord sounds like a psycho."

"You're scaring me, Sherman." She thought of Eric and hoped he would show up soon.

"I'm sure that if you tell Hadrian the landlord's coming onto you, he'll let you move."

"We'll see," she said, wishing he would leave so that Eric could come and protect her.

"You know what I'd like you to do, Cybele?" he said, pushing one of his arms behind her and encircling her waist.

"No, what?" She crossed one of her legs over the other. The filmy material of her kimono parted, revealing the side of her curving thigh.

"I'd like for you to put down your embroidery and seduce me."

"Wouldn't that be a little redundant?" she asked, and slid sleekly off the bed.

"Where're you going?" he asked, looking like a well-oiled, modern machine on her bed.

"Phone's ranging. Didn't you hear, Doctor?"

She ran into the hall and threw the pillows off the phone.

"This is your friendly service bureau, luv," Eric said. "Do you need my services now or later?"

She giggled into the receiver.

"I'll be right over," he said.

She giggled again, and he hung up.

"Sounds like a very primitive conversation, babe," Sherman said. He stood by her in the dark hallway, holding his sports coat over his shoulder by one finger.

"It's what I need." She looked up at him defensively. "What I want."

"OK, Cybele. I'll call you," he said, and opened the door. "Be careful, little girl," he told her and looked at her meaningfully.

"Bye," she said as he kissed her lightly on the cheek.

She ran back into the bedroom and began hastily checking the room for any tell-tale signs of her little masquerade. She didn't see anything that Eric might find unusual, so she walked back into the kitchen and began making herself a drink.

"Ha, ha, Porge," she laughed. "Didn't we have fun, child? Didn't we?"

She picked up her apartment keys absentmindedly from the formica kitchen cabinet top, where she had thrown them when she had walked into the room with Sherman.

"Yes, we did, old Porge," she said, and raised a glass of liqueur to her lips.

"Hey! What the hell!" she exclaimed when she felt a sticky substance on her keys and key chain. She stared down at the key chain, then ran her fingers over them with surprise.

"Feels like glue!" she exclaimed.

She stood in the middle of the silent, stark kitchen holding the wet keys. Her ears began to tingle, and she found herself listening for a sound in the next room.

"Oh, m'God. I wonder if this shit's in the keyhole too?" she said aloud, then ran over to the solid white doorway. She jerked it open and looked at the large gold keyhole. It was completely filled with a white, hardened substance.

"Oh no," she cried. Her eyes darted up from the keyhole to the empty hallway in front of her. It stretched long and silent past all the unopened doors, harbouring the secret of whoever had glued up her keyhole. Suddenly she remembered the glue Pierre used in making various forms of sculpture, and shuddered.

"Uhh!" she gasped, and slammed the door. An icy fear stole over her body, making her almost swoon. Her knees felt weak as she walked into the darkened living-room. She quickly switched on all of the lights and flopped down on the old green couch.

'I wonder why I didn't notice the stuff when Sherman and I came in. God, it must have been done just before we got here to still be so soft! Maybe he's here now.

'No, it's impossible for him to know where I am," she decided. Her hands trembled as she pressed them up to her temples. "I know him – he'd do something more than this. He'd wait for me in the hall – he'd have a gun or. . . Oh, God, Eric, please come!' she thought desperately.

'But what if Pierre's around? He might hurt him.' She bit her fingernails nervously. 'Maybe I'd better call Eric and warn him.' She stroked Porgy anxiously, and stared out onto the darkened balcony. She ran to the french doors and slammed them both shut. "There!" she said senselessly as she thrust the small bolt through its slot to lock the doors.

The wall-like branches of the fir trees hovered threateningly beside the long screens of the windows. Their dark, dense foliage terrified her. 'Oh God, oh God. He could be anywhere!' she thought with an increasing paranoia.

Suddenly there was a rap on the door. She jumped up from the couch and ran to the door. She looked through the little round peephole and saw Eric's grinning, tanned face.

"Eric!" she cried, and flung open the door with relief.

"M'dear," he said. He stepped back a little, startled by her desperate greeting.

"Oh Eric," she wailed and threw her arms around his hard, muscular chest. "I'm *so* glad you're here."

"To say the least," he observed dryly, looking past her head, that she had huddled into his shoulder, to the tightly closed doors of the balcony.

"Did you and the old guy have a seance in here or something?" he asked ironically. "Or do you just like to sit around and stew in the heat for no reason?"

"What?" she asked with fear and confusion distorting her perspiring face.

"What the hell have you got this place all closed up for?" he repeated.

"I. . . Eric, look at the keyhole," she said in a whisper, and pointed towards the doorknob dramatically.

"Yeah, it's a keyhole. So what?"

He looked at her with exasperation. He had begun to perspire in the stifling, unventilated hallway. "Christ, let's open those doors or else go in the bedroom where the air-conditioner is," he begged her.

"But Eric," she said, agitated. "Look what's *in* the keyhole!"

He bent over the keyhole and scrutinised it through the thick lenses of his glasses. A surprised, baffled look passed over his face.

"*Glue?*" he said, puzzled.

"Yes, Eric. Glue like Pierre used to use in all his sculptures."

"Jesus!" Eric exclaimed. "I wonder if the dude's still around?"

"I don't know," she faltered. "That's why I was so glad to see you."

"I can imagine. Shit! You put me in some close situations sometimes."

He felt her body trembling under his hands and realised how terrified she was.

"Now, now. Come on in here and let old Eric Star take care of you," he reassured her. She followed him into the bedroom like a child who had been terrified by a horror movie before bedtime.

"Hmmm, looks like you two had a good time tonight," Eric said. He strode around the bedroom like a swift antelope who had purposely left his domain and had now come back to claim his sovereignty. She saw his eyes brush over the room's contents like an all-encompassing lighthouse beam. They stopped briefly at each wineglass standing on the night tables as if he had spied two small silvery fish in the ocean's billowing foam, then he moved on relentlessly to the disturbed pillows on the bed that bore the indentations of bodies.

"Been doing your embroidery?" he asked, looking at the white linen doily lying between the pillows like a partially decorated butterfly. He leaned over and picked up the embroidery. "Looks like you didn't get much done," he said, and smiled knowingly at her.

"Eric, you're all wet," she said, wiping drops of perspiration from his brow. "Did you ride your bike over?"

"Nah, I came in a Porsche," he jeered. "How do you think I got here?"

The grassy fragrance of his thick, curly hair wafted through the room's musty atmosphere and enveloped her senses with his own particular musk, drawing her towards him.

"Oh Eric," she sighed, hooking her arms up under his elbows and rubbing her firm, round breasts against the virile flesh of his back. "You are so divine," she said, and wetted his faded navy T-shirt with her tongue.

"Sure, I'm divine all right," he said. His amber eyes seared into hers as he turned his face to hers. "Putting up with your old dude and all."

"Please, Eric, I don't want to talk about my old dude! Believe me, I'm bored with the subject," she said and spread her fingers out on his arm like a fan. She touched the sinewy muscles and pale green veins there experimentally, trying to probe the depths of his arm through touch.

"Yeah, you're so bored that you fucked the guy not more than twenty minutes ago," he said, grabbing her hand that rested lightly on his arm and twisting it cruelly. His eyes glittered dangerously at her through his thick glasses, and he squeezed her hand with an insistent, pumping motion. The pulse in his neck beat swiftly as she pushed her body up to him.

"Oh, Eric," she whispered, feeling his hard dick on her upper belly. His height brought it almost up to her ribs. "Ummm!" she murmured and relaxed next to the swift pounding of his heart.

He jerked her chin up violently to his face and pressed his lips onto hers until she felt blood on her tongue. She let it glide down her

throat while he thrust his tongue deep into her mouth. She opened her
eyes and saw his feverish gaze on her face.

"Wench!" he rasped, and pulled her head back by her long dark
hair like a bow, then pushed his mouth into the hollow of her neck.

"Oh, I love you, Eric. I love you. Hurt me some," she moaned.
"Hurt me a little." She twisted her breasts against his sharp ribs, and
rubbed her bare legs on the rough material of his jeans.

He thrust her back on the vanity table and began twisting her
breasts until tears came to her eyes.

"Pinch my nipples," he said, pressing her hands on his firm,
muscular breasts.

She seized the tender flesh of his nipples in her fingertips and
squeezed it hard, then put her soft wet mouth to his breasts. She took
his teat gently between her teeth, and watched him smile a languid,
sensual smile of satisfaction, enjoying controlling his pleasure, then
clamped her teeth together on his soft flesh in a vicious little bite.

"Owww!" he grimaced through clinched teeth. He grabbed her
head and pushed it harder to his chest. "Why don't you really hurt
me?" he dared her. "Why don't you taste my blood between your
teeth?" he asked, and thrust his hard dick against her stomach, using it
like a stiff weapon on her flesh. She bit down harder on his nipple,
and heard him gasp. The rush of his breath inside her ear sent an
electric charge down the whole side of her body, and chill bumps
sprinkled her flesh like fine pebbles from the violent sensation.

"Oh, Eric. I want you now," she said.

He picked her up and carried her to the bed. "How would you
like to land?" he grinned.

"With you on top!" she smiled, looking at his flushed cheeks and
shining eyes, at his crown of taffy-coloured hair with adoration. She
sank her nose into his neck and sniffed his body's fresh, sweet
perfume deep into her lungs.

"Umm, you're a heady draught," she sighed, dragging her nail
down the bulging muscle of his arm while he held her.

"Down onto the bed where a good cunt belongs," he cried, and
threw her onto the pillows.

"Take off your clothes!" he ordered her imperiously and
unfastened his gold butterfly belt buckle. He flicked open his fly and
let his dick burst out like a proud, impressive weapon.

"Like it?" he asked and grinned merrily at her.

"*You* take my clothes off," she asked submissively, looking hypnotically at his dick. She studied its pink, delectable colour and sturdy young head while licking her lips hungrily.

"OK," he said, and jerked her kimono over her hips. He lifted her up by one arm like a rag doll and took off her kimono.

"How's that?" he asked, staring at her nubile, virginal-looking body. "Whew," he whistled, and bent down to kiss her breasts. "You don't have the body of a woman, Cybele. It's more like a little girl with tits."

He drew back and studied her flat, tanned belly, then slapped it playfully. "Hard as a rock," he observed admiringly.

"How about you?" she smiled, and grabbed his cock in her hands. "Aren't you hard too?"

"Want to find out?" he asked. He shoved himself inside her and moved wildly back and forth. "How's that?" he queried. "Better than your old dude?"

"My old dude?" she asked stupidly. "Oh," she said absently. The memory of Sherman flooded her consciousness and interrupted the mellifluous chain of sensations between her legs.

"Oh?" he repeated. He stopped his motions and looked at her suspiciously. "That *is* whom you saw tonight, isn't it?"

His vital brown eyes burned into hers with a farouche puissance, freezing her blood with a familiar dread – the dread of guilt and having to lie. The scam of her married life with Pierre flooded into her brain like a polluted river and left her limbs limp and numb under his body. She saw Hadrian's stiff cock in her mind and remembered the sensual venality of their lovemaking as she pictured his cock in one of her hands and his hundred-dollar bills in the other. She turned her head dully to the scalloped arabesques of the bed's headboard, trying to blot out Eric's exigent, inquiring demeanour.

He grabbed her shoulders and shook her roughly. "Answer me, bitch! That is who I sat around watching dumb TV programmes all night for, waiting for you to get laid and paid, isn't it?"

She lay under him like a spent cartridge.

"No," she answered laconically, still staring at the wall.

"Whaddaya mean?" he exclaimed, and leapt off her as if he had found himself in a patch of poison ivy.

"I mean no, that isn't who I went out with tonight," she said, feeling a cloying deadness suffuse her body, an almost pleasurable negative emotion being let loose like a dangerous, escaped animal.

She glanced slyly at his expression, grooving on the sharp pain that had etched itself in a few fine lines between his eyebrows, watching for the beginning of anger in his eyes and on his mouth, anticipating it excitedly.

"Who *were* you with?" he asked, shaking her violently.

"A guy I met," she said, simply.

"What guy?"

"A young doctor," she answered, hoping to produce more pain with the man's professional accomplishments. She wetted her lips like a hungry panther stalking a scent of fresh blood, and waited hopefully for his reaction.

He appeared stunned for a moment, then slapped her almost automatically.

She looked maliciously at his face that had become distorted with anger, feeling a curious elation from the stinging pain on her cheek.

"You bitch," he said softly, and rolled over beside her like a wounded animal.

"Did you fuck him?" he asked, staring up at the ceiling to avoid exposing his expression of pain to her further.

"No," she answered honestly.

He lay beside her, breathing heavily, with his cock still jutting up in the air.

"What'd you go out with him for?"

"For kicks," she said.

"Kicks? Where d'you meet him?"

"On the way to your pad. I was walking along and he pulled up in his big corny Corvette."

"Spare me the details," he groaned contradictorily. "Do you like him?"

"No, Eric, not really. Just curious, that's all."

"Curious? Shit, man. You're just a whore and that's it." He lay still beside her for a while, then got up and switched off the bedroom light.

"Come on," he said, and pushed his cock back up in her cunt. "I'm gonna screw you until you scream." He moved his cock up in her violently. "Until you can't walk, m'dear."

"Eric, Eric, you know I love you. You know I do."

"You don't love anybody, Cybele. But you do love to screw," he said, fucking her with hard, abrupt strokes. "And I love to screw you. Oh!" he cried, and fell down on her, pressing his hot face to her neck.

"You're all lovely and wet," she murmured, as he lay panting by her ear.

"Damn it, damn it," he sobbed. "Why did you do this, Cybele?"

"Eric, you're crying!" she exclaimed. "How awful!" She kissed him tenderly on his temple and felt the soft curls of his hair tickle her lips.

"You like to tease men, you bitch," he said, pinning her by her neck with his forearm like a crossbar, and pushing his again hard cock up inside her.

"Oh yeah, oh yeah," she said huskily. "Fuck me again, Eric. I love it when you stick your dick in me." She clasped her legs around his long back and thrust her body up to his stomach, trying to take the full length of his dick.

"You've got a fabulous cunt," he said. "The tightest I've ever had."

She saw the pale blue light of dawn filtering through the curtains and felt a languorous pleasure seep through her body like the nascent light of morning and sighed happily.

"It's so nice to have your cock in me, Eric, when the day is just beginning to happen and all." She yawned sleepily.

"Tired?" He looked down at her, grinning. His face looked ravaged.

"Oh yeah," she sighed, and dropped her legs around his waist.

He leaned over and opened the drawer of the bedside table.

"Here," he said and threw a tube of cream on her breasts. "Put some of this on, cause I'm not going to stop.

She looked at him wanly. "But Eric, I can't take any more."

"Oh no?" he asked, looking at her cruelly. "We'll find out." He uncapped the tube and took his cock out of her for a minute. "Here," he said, squeezing the cool, creamy liquid onto her cunt. "This'll make it easier," he said, and mounted her once more.

Chapter Six

When she woke up, the sun's fierce heat was flooding behind the
heavy bedroom drapes. She lay on her side, trying to remember when
he had stopped fucking her.

'I must have fallen asleep with him still in,' she thought with
amazement. She rolled over on her back, then gasped as a sharp pain
coursed up her stomach from her cunt.

"God, he killed me," she groaned.

She sat up on the side of the bed like a person just awakening after
being beaten in a street brawl. Her thighs had small blue bruises on
them from Eric's hip bones and his furious activity in her body.

"Oooh, my head," she moaned, trying not to blink her eyes. She
stared insensibly at the elaborate brocade drapes hanging by the
bedroom window.

'Jesus, I've got to stop this,' she thought desperately. All of the
thought waves coming from her brain seemed to be passing through a
violent storm before they reached their proper processing in her
different brain centres. Their interrupted thought patterns left her
dizzy. She stood up uncertainly. She was afraid of falling as she
walked towards the living-room.

"I've gotta call Brand and ask him about things," she reasoned
foggily. "That's what I'll do. I don't know why I didn't think of it
before." She picked up the phone and dialled Brand's number.

"Brand, I've gotta talk to you," she said, when he answered the
phone.

"Sweetheart, you sound a little desperate," she heard his pleasant,
boyish voice say. It crackled sexily in his throat from all of the Lucky
Strikes he was constantly smoking.

"Oh, Brand. I think I've been doing some things wrong," she said
plaintively.

"Now don't get so upset, Cybele," he said calmly. She heard his
lighter click shut and imagined the aromatic smell from his newly lit

cigarette. His masculine voice in her ear was like the pungent aroma of his cigarette that she had imagined.

"But Brand, I lied to Eric."

"About what?" he asked, with amusement.

"I told Eric I had a date with Hadrian, when I really had a date with Sherman."

"Who's Sherman?"

"He's this new guy I met. Really good looking. A blond, Jewish intern."

"You and your Jews and Arabs, Cybele. One could fight the Arab-Israeli war right in your bedroom."

"Oh, Brand. Don't be a prejudiced Southerner," she reprimanded him.

"I'd just as soon be a prejudiced Southerner as a prejudiced Jew, or Arab, for that matter."

"Anyway, Brand, are you listening?"

"I'm all ears, honey."

"I told Eric about the lie last night."

"What'd you do that for?" Brand asked.

"Because. . . I. . ." she faltered. "I didn't want to get back into the same game of deception I had to play when I lived with Pierre. You know. . . lying and all."

"But why do you have to lie at all now, Cybele? You aren't with Pierre anymore. I mean, you aren't divorced yet, but you're free to date different people. Why couldn't you just tell Eric that you wanted to go out with someone?"

"Brand, you sound so logical. But you know things aren't really all simple. I mean, Eric and I love each other. You know he doesn't want me go out with other people."

"But what about Hadrian?"

"Well, Eric knows I love Hadrian and. . . you know Hadrian takes care of me. I don't have any money, and neither does Eric."

"Things are complicated in your life, Cybele," he sighed.

"Well, what should I do now, Brand?" she asked.

"I guess you'd better try to stick with one person – or one person who'll accept Hadrian also. From what you've just described to me, Cybele, I gather you enjoy playing games with people – er, men people especially. I don't where you've got this from. It seems a little too sophisticated a thrill to go with the rest of your personality.

But I'd say you're going to end up a very lonely girl if you don't stop juggling these men for your amusement. Also, some people get mad when you do things like that, Cybele. Especially men.

"And I can warn you. A man's ego is a fragile thing, especially when a beautiful girl like you starts playing around with it. You seem to get a perverse pleasure from hurting men's egos. You're courting disaster like that, you know."

She trembled in the heat of the hallway. Again, she had the feeling that there was an unseen presence in the apartment with her, a very strong, watching spirit. It hovered in all parts of the apartment, omniscient and watching.

"Gosh, Brand, I'm afraid here."

"What do you mean?" he asked. The soft Southern tones of his voice became more alert.

"I – promise me you won't think I'm crazy if I tell you this?"

"I promise."

She could imagine him smiling indulgently when he said "I promise."

"Well, I saw a ghost in this old place I'm living in." She paused, waiting for some sort of negative reaction.

"Go on," he said.

"He's an old, mean man, and he was watching me bathe the other day. Porgy ran out from under the bed with all of his hair on end when the ghost showed up."

"I can imagine," Brand said.

"Well, I was terrified, Brand, just terrified. I haven't told anyone else about this but Eric, you know. Anyway, I know he lives here, Brand. And I'm not sure whether he likes for me to be staying in his place or not. Does this sound crazy to you, Brand? I mean, some people don't believe in ghosts. Do you?"

"Oh yes, honey. I've seen too many of them not to."

"You've seen ghosts, Brand?" she said with relief.

"Of course, honey. Anyone from the South especially has seen ghosts. I've seen them in old castles in Europe too. I mean, a ghost is a pretty run-of-the-mill thing, Cybele. But there are good ghosts – and bad ones."

"Brand, that's what I'm worried about! I think this one is a bad one," she whispered.

"Well, you've got trouble then, honey. Maybe you'd better get out of that place anyway. You say the landlord there hates you?"

"Yeah, that's true. Can you imagine the old dude asking me for a date?" she asked incredulously.

"Well, a man's a man, no matter haw old he is, Cybele."

"Yeah, I guess so. But ugh, how could he suppose that I'd want *him*?" she asked with a naïve perplexity.

"Well, you probably let him know by your reaction, inadvertently, that you didn't want him. And you are so lovely, Cybele, that this is a double insult for the old goat. That's why he's picking on you so much now."

"Oh," she said simply.

Brand laughed. "You're incredibly innocent, Cybele. And you don't seem to understand what a strong effect your extreme good looks produce on people. I guess it's because you aren't conceited. And also, you're just one of those Southern girls who's been taught through the culture down there to love everybody, and people up here don't know how to take that sort of thing, Cybele. They just aren't like us Southern people," he ended. "God, I've got a customer right now, Cybele. Can I call you later?"

"Listen, Brand. Can I come over a while?" she asked urgently. "I know you're terribly busy and all, but I need to see you," she pleaded, revealing her anxiety without knowing it.

"Sure, come on over, Cybele. We'll go and get some pizza when I close up."

"When you close up?" she asked with surprise.

"Yeah, it's already three thirty."

"You're kidding me!" she exclaimed.

"No, I'm not kidding you, you dizzy dame. You've slept all day as usual."

"Yeah, yeah," she agreed vaguely. "I must have." She yawned, tired.

"See, that's the only trouble with games, Cybele. They take a lot of time, and you lose yourself too."

"So?" she questioned stupidly.

"So, since games do that, and all of life is a game, the best thing to do is make sure that the one you're playing is working for you."

"Oh, Brand, you're so sane. Listen, I got a new pack of the Tarot. I'll bring it and we'll tell one another's fortunes. OK?"

"OK, Cybele. Goodbye."

She hung up the old black receiver with a bang and ran into the bedroom to get dressed.

"Shit, I just don't feel like taking a bath today," she said to herself. She uncapped a bottle of expensive French perfume that Hadrian had brought her and dabbed it generously on her body, then pulled on an old pair of jeans over her naked thighs.

"Come on, Porge," she called as she tied on a halter top. "You gotta go with me."

When she walked into the musty, pleasant-smelling music shop, the light had fallen in soft purple shadows on the oversized viols and ornate, gleaming harps. Brand had already begun peremptorily closing the mahogany cabinets that contained stacks of old sheet music placed in a prim, orderly fashion between antique musical clocks and old metronomes. She saw the slightness of his slender shoulders under his Western-styled shirt and felt jolted by their fragility. His extra thick, curly, blond hair was unruly about his youthful face.

"Brand! You're so skinny today," she exclaimed.

"Huh?" he stuttered in surprise, and almost dropped an old clock he had been holding. "God, don't creep up on me like that, Cybele – scared the shit out of me!"

Her fat, tiger-striped cat struggled violently in her thin, brown arms. His insistent vitality almost flung her over. She staggered towards Brand, trying to balance the large cat in her arms.

"Look out with that monster," Brand warned. He shrank back against the cloudy glass of the old cabinet.

"Oh, Porge is so full of energy, Brand. Don't you wish we could be like him?"

"Well, I wouldn't mind some of his pizzazz. But I could do without the tail."

"Really? I think Porgy's tail is one of the nicest things about him."

"Yes, tails do have their function," Brand agreed and laughed. "Come on over here, you crazy girl," he said, and led her over to an old rocking, chair she often sat in when she came to his shop.

"Of course tails have their function, Brand. Hermann Hesse said that if people had tails like animals, and could just swish them around when they got upset about things, there would be no madness in the world. Do you believe that?"

"Sure, why not," he agreed. He sat down in front of her behind the old wooden desk he had constructed. He lit a Lucky Strike cigarette and smiled tiredly at her.

"You know, you remind me of my grandfather when you smoke those things," she said.

"Yeah?"

"Yeah, you remind me of him and the South, and a lot of things in my life, Brand. The way you made that desk and all – that's like Pierre. The wonderful, building part of Pierre. His creativeness – his sculpture," she reminisced, then scowled when she remembered the glue in her keyhole.

"Cybele, it's amazing to hear you reminisce so fondly about a guy who's held loaded guns up to your forehead and tried to run you down with a car. Not to mention the bite marks all over your arms."

"Well, maybe Pierre had reasons for doing those things to me!" she explained defensively.

"Oh, I know you can be a maddening person, Cybele. But I wouldn't exactly react that way if you made me angry."

"But maybe your father never used to beat you like Pierre's father did him. You know, any time Pierre did anything wrong, his mother would wait all day until his father came home from work and tell Pierre's father his 'sins'. She would promise Pierre not to tell, but she always did. Can you imagine the type of anxiety *that* must have created in a little kid, to wait all day, knowing your own mother was going to be like a Judas to you and use your father as King Herod against you?"

"God, Cybele, how'd you get into such a family?"

"Only in America – down South in America," she replied.

"Oh no, honey, that sort of thing goes on all over the world," he told her.

"Anyway, Pierre's mother was this real puritanical, hung-up type who creamed every time she reinforced her husband's image in her mind as a big tough. Each time he asserted himself with Pierre she got bigger and better orgasms. Pierre began to believe that everyone got a golf club to the head when he didn't make the football team. And old Calvinistic 'mammy mine' was back in the kitchen with her cunt cocked for the whole thrilling showdown. She got more 'comes' that way later when Big Daddy came to her strange, hot altar!"

"Whew, what are you on today, Cybele? Cocaine?"

"No, just my own juices. They're strong enough."

"You know, you remind me of my great aunt down in Kentucky. She used to live in a sixty-room mansion that was over two hundred years old. Anyone who ever stayed at her house had to wake up at five o'clock in the morning because she'd bang on their door with a long, wicked-looking cane."

"How awful!" Cybele replied, settling comfortably into the large, accommodating rocking chair. "I would have never put up with that!"

Brand laughed and sat down wearily in the little strawbacked chair behind his desk.

"You wouldn't have had any choice, honey. When she started banging on that door, you would have had to wake up. No two ways about it!"

He picked up his lighter that had American Chili Company written on it and turned it round and round in his strong, young hand.

"Shhh, Porge!" Cybele said when her cat meowed to protest being forced to sit so docilely in the large rocker with her.

"There were sunk-in places in the wood of the door where she pounded on them with that hickory cane of hers," Brand said to emphasise the fact that she would have had to have got up at such an early hour. His Southern accent became more pronounced also, the way it often did when he spoke about memories of his childhood.

"Hmmm, well, I bet we would have had a fight," Cybele said, and stroked Porgy placidly.

"Ha ha. I bet you would have too. But my Aunt Bertha would have tanned that little fanny of yours with her hickory stick, Cybele!"

He looked out of the opened door of the shop at the lines of five o'clock traffic beginning on M Street NW..

"Once you got up, though, it was worth it," Brand said. His green eyes shone with fond memories of his aunt. "She ate filet mignon and eggs with molasses every morning for breakfast, and biscuits – honey, you ain't tasted biscuits like that, ever!" he exclaimed, smacking his lips with gusto. "Mmm, makes me hungry just thinking about it."

"Oh, yes, I have too tasted good biscuits, Brand. At my aunt's house down in Georgia. She made hot chocolate to pour on them.

Oooh, I wish I could go over to her house right now. I'd take you with me!"

"We'll go and get a pizza pretty soon," he said.

"Oh, but not until we tell our fortunes with the Tarot," she begged excitedly.

"After my aunt had breakfast, she'd go ride her horse up on her mountain."

"Gosh, she rode a horse?" Cybele said incredulously. "My aunt was too fat to ever ride a horse. Besides, she would have been afraid!"

"Well, Aunt Bertha wasn't afraid of man or beast. That's how she died one day – out riding her horse. She just fell off of him, dead as a doornail. She was one hundred and four years old!"

"A hundred and four years old! Wow, Brand!" Cybele squealed.

"That's right," Brand said, looking at her triumphantly from behind his handmade desk. "She was fifty years old when they discovered oil wells on her property. Made her mad as hell. She said it ruined the landscaping of her estate." Brand lit a cigarette and propped his scuffed leather boots on the desk. "She owned half the State right in her backyard – four hundred acres."

"God, Brand, this sounds like tales from Münchhausen." Porgy had crawled up onto her slender legs and sat there quietly like a huge, striped mushroom, staring at Brand with his owlish eyes.

"Yeah, 'cept that these are all true," he said. His unfiltered cigarette looked like a joint between his lips.

"Gosh, Brand, why do you think people used to live so long?" she mused.

"I don't know, Cybele. Maybe it's cause they ate steak and eggs for breakfast."

"And molasses," she added. "My mother says molasses is full of iron."

She stroked Porgy, watching her hand as she did so.

"But I'd hate to live that long, Brand. Think of how old I'd look!" she said with a shudder.

"Oh, you'll want to live, Cybele. Just as long as you can. You won't give a damn what you look like after a while."

He studied her with an X-ray scrutiny, then laughed.

"And you'll be as mean as hell, just like her."

"Ha ha," she laughed, enjoying his mental word pictures. "Where's my cane, sonny?" she said in the crotchety tones of an old woman.

"You know, people in the Bible used to live a long time, Brand. I mean, some of them were supposed to have lived for hundreds of years. How do you think they did that?"

"Maybe they were as mean as my aunt!"

"Maybe they were just wise, like Solomon and all. I mean, Solomon even knew how to talk to the birds."

"You're beginning to sound like an old philosophy teacher of mine, Cybele."

"A philosophy teacher! Wow, I've never been compared to one of those before."

"She used to tell us that man no longer lived for long periods of time because he had regressed."

"Regressed? I thought we were in the space age, and all that jazz."

"Oh, well, we were in the space age millions of years before now," Brand said mysteriously. "And probably much better at it then too. Witness the monoliths and other things that have been proven to be placed in designs by people who had to have studied the earth from some sort of plane in order to put them down the way they did."

"I wonder why they put these things down anyway, Brand? I mean, it must have been a lot of trouble."

"They did it to teach people the knowledge they had learned, Cybele. Knowledge that it took them maybe a thousand human years of life to learn."

"You're saying that these guys lived a thousand years, Brand?"

"Well, that's what this teacher of mine convinced the philosophy class of, anyway. She said that man lived this long because he hadn't lost contact with the oneness of the universe. That he had not become as primitive as modern-day man and did not go through the emotions of fear, greed and lust – emotions that put a person on a certain level, and make him react mechanically to things."

"Oh," she said simply, and continued listening with a peaked interest to Brand's conversation. "You mean, they were like Mary when the people asked her where all the food and drink was coming from, and she just said, "God." Cybele sighed. "She believed like a little child. But I never really believed anything when I was a little child. I mean, I liked to get gold stars for going to church and all, and I can still remember the church bells. But the most I can remember about church is the damp smell of the old basement where they sent us for Sunday school lessons and walking with my father in the pure, sunny day, dressed in one of my two dressy dresses." She began to rock back and forth in the chair. "I remember. It was a taffeta dress with white, black and lavender stripes. I loved that dress. But I was always so afraid that somebody might remember it. Because 1 only had one other Sunday school dress to alternate it with.

"Well, want to go get a pizza now, Cybele?"

"Not before we tell fortunes, Brand," she said, and drew out the Tarot from her red leather purse. The black bulls that had been carved on her purse sank into butting positions when she took the cards out of it.

"I don't know, I've always been afraid of those darned things," he told her. "They always come true, you know."

"I know, Brand. That's what makes them so great." She drew the old rocker up to his desk and laid the cards down.

"And terrifying," he added.

"Now pick up the cards, Brand," she ordered. "Pick them up and handle them slowly. And while you handle them slowly, think of what you want to know about your life.

She watched him with unabashed curiosity as he picked up the cards and began shuffling them. His face had taken on a characteristic seriousness that enlarged his eyes and made his normally boyish good looks frightening to her. His cheek began to jerk with a nervous tic that she found most disturbing. She felt like reaching out and shooing away this "new Brand" that had appeared in his face as he concentrated on the cards. Instead she picked up the cards and said, "Now! The first card will signify who you are."

A young, blond-haired page was the first card that appeared.

"Oh – the diligent, serious young man," she exclaimed. "How like you, Brand! See? We can't go wrong with these things."

Brand studied the card with an obsessive concentration.

"The next card shows something that has been in your past long ago."

She turned the next card over and said, "Hmmm, I'll have to look that one up."

She flipped back to the index of the book. Brand lit a cigarette nervously as he watched her look up the card.

"It says here that you have known great riches – that an abrupt rupture came in your life and changed it completely." She looked at him closely, trying to understand what the card might conjure up to him. He sat in a stony, cautious silence with his eyes trained on the card.

"Well, aren't you going to say anything?" she demanded.

"Go ahead," he said cryptically.

The position of the next card was upside down and it was woman with dark hair.

"Oooh," she exclaimed excitedly. "Now who could this be?"

Brand looked surprised.

"This card is your immediate past," she said. "Upside down this is a young woman of bitter experience. . . I. . ." she stammered. "Don't you look at me," she warned him.

He dragged deeply on his cigarette and pushed at his blond curls nervously.

"Oh, don't worry, honey. I've met worse than you."

"Porgy, do sit down," she scolded her cat, and pushed at his large, furry backside with irritation. "Damn it, Brand, I know that card is me."

"Look, we can discontinue this if you want to," he told her.

"Oh no! I want to see what's in your immediate future," she said, and turned over the next card impatiently.

"Ah ha! A cavalier," she said. "I don't remember which one he is – so I'll have to look him up." She flipped through the pages of the book so fast that she tore one of them.

"Oh drat. Here he is," she said triumphantly. "Only, remember, he's reversed," she cautioned, pointing to the upside-down card.

She didn't notice it in her excitement, but Brand's face had taken on an excited, apprehensive look.

"This man is a very dashing, daring person of accomplishment right side up. But when he's reversed, he is avaricious, petty and cowardly. He can even be dangerous at times."

"Let's go and get a pizza," Brand said abruptly.

"But who could this be, Brand?" she asked.

"I know who it is," he said.

"Well, whoever he is, he's going to appear in your life pretty soon because the Tarot never lies."

"That's the worst news I've heard in months," Brand said, stubbing out the butt of his cigarette in the ashtray. "Let's go, gypsy girl."

"Wait a minute, don't you want to know your long-range future?" she asked, and held up the next card enticingly.

"OK," he acquiesced. "Lay it on me, you little clown."

A young blonde woman surrounded by stars was the next card.

"Brand! Who could that be?"

He pinched her arm affectionately. "Stick around, child, and you might find out!"

"This is a young woman of beauty and accomplishment, about to be married," she said. "Gosh, I wonder who she could be?"

She looked at the card reverently. A deep longing had charged her perfect features with an intensity that accentuated them like the lines of a Gauguin painting.

"Maybe she's you, Cybele," Brand said tenderly.

"Me! How could she be me?" she asked. "I'm getting a divorce." She slumped back in the old chair dejectedly. She remembered her wedding dress suddenly, and the white brocade shoes she had worn. 'I dyed them black later on,' she thought. 'So I'd be able to wear them around. Dyed the dress too – so I could wear it to night-clubs in New Orleans. Huh, we were so poor. He didn't even have a ring to give me. His parents could have given him a diamond as big as The Ritz for me, but they hated me cause they couldn't control me.' She looked down at a large green emerald surrounded by diamonds that Hadrian had given her and sighed.

"See, you are tired, homey," Brand said. "Let's go and eat."

"OK, but will you tell my fortune at the restaurant, Brand?"

"Of course I will," he assured her, and put his arms around her in a brotherly fashion.

"Oh Brand, you're so sweet, really," she said plaintively. "I just don't know what I'd do without you, green eyes."

"I like you a lot too," he said, and kissed her cheek lightly.

"Oh goody," she said, feeling her spirits revive from his caress. "We'll eat pizza and listen to records – just like down South in high school."

"Yeah, man," he said, and locked the shop door behind them.

"Gosh, it's lighter out here than in there," she remarked.

'Wonder why he's too tight to air-condition the place or put a light inside since he's supposed to be so rich?' she wondered. 'Oh well, guess he's part Scottish, like Mama.'

She trailed along beside him, surprised when he encircled her waist loosely with his arm as they walked across the street. He was usually very careful not to play the part of a boyfriend around her. Her sexiness frightened and intimidated him. He wanted to make sure that it didn't end up entangling him with her the way he had seen it do to Hadrian and Eric and Pierre. Sometimes she felt impatient that he didn't act like more of a lover around her, but mainly she was relieved to have a purely platonic relationship with a man – especially one from her own background.

"Here we are," he said, and pushed open the door to the pizza parlour.

"Oooh nooo!" she exclaimed, and began to shake. "It's air-conditioned in here."

"That's OK, you'll get used to it," he said, and steered her towards one of the little wicker-backed chairs. "Sit your pretty fanny down here, and I'll bring back some pizza."

"Uh, OK. But I think I'll play some records."

Brand walked over to the crome-rimmed counter and got in line behind a tall slender Negro man with an Afro haircut. Cybele thought he looked dwarfed and out of place next to the young Negro's modern appearance.

'That's silly for me to think that,' she thought to herself. 'Brand's had orgies when he lived in New York with all sorts of people.'

She dropped a few quarters into the rainbow-coloured jukebox and punched in several wide, waxy-white buttons.

"I'm being followed by a moon shadow, moon shadow, moon shadow", by Cat Stevens, began blaring out into the icy, air-conditioned pizza parlour.

"Moon shadow, moon shadow," Cybele sang along with the light, lyrical voice of the singer.

"Don't this look good, child?" Brand said as he approached the greasy, littered table where she was sitting, carrying two large pieces of pizza.

She looked at him and laughed.

"Brand, you'd make the screwiest Italian I've ever seen!"

He looked confused for a moment, then returned to his joy over the two pieces of pizza in his hands.

"Well, it ain't filet mignon and biscuits like at Aunt Bertha's, y'all – but we's a long way from Aunt Boither's," he said, mimicking a Southern Negro dialect.

"True, true, so true," she said. "But we don't wanna be back down there anyways right now, do we, Brand? I mean, I just don't think those people would understand us at all, do you?"

"'Shut up and eat de meat', as old Scott Fitzgerald would say."

"Yep, bread's the thing. Thank you, dear Lord, for this bread," she said.

"Walkin' and talkin' with a moon shadow, moon shadow, moon shadow," Cat continued.

"Gosh, I love that song," she sighed, and took a big bite out of her pizza.

Brand gulped down his pizza and ran back for two more pieces so quickly that when he said, "Yeah, you're one of the few people who might actually be being followed by a moon shadow, Cybele!" she hardly knew that he had been gone.

"They were playing it everywhere when I was staying in New York at the Hilton. I felt lonesome unless I heard it at least five times a day. I don't know why it makes me feel so great every time I hear it – I was even more miserable then than I am now," she said whimsically.

Brand studied her seriously, then put his square, boyish hand over hers.

"Where's Hadrian tonight, anyway?" he asked.

"Huh? Oh," she said foggily, as if she had just thought of him for the first time in several weeks. "He really is with some Pakistanis," she told him, and smiled slyly.

"Ha, you're crazy, girl. Far out, insane. You almost had me feeling sorry for you before I remembered all your crafty games."

"Oh, yeah," she said. "Let's continue with the Tarot."

"You'll have to show me how to do it," Brand told her, and popped the last piece of pizza into his mouth.

"Sure, it's easy," she said, and began shuffling the cards deliberately. "Be quiet so I can concentrate on what I want to know," she ordered him. He rolled his green eyes around in exasperation and took out a Lucky Strike.

"Now," she said, "I've thought of everything." She set the deck of cards down in front of him carefully. "All you have to do is turn the cards over," she explained. "I look up whatever we don't know. The first card will be me."

She looked at the cards as if her life depended on them. Brand turned over the first card.

"Oh, one of the queens. She's blonde, fair and chaste – how the hell could that be me, Brand baby? Honourable, etc. etc. See, I'm a good poirson," she said, mimicking a Jewish accent when she pronounced 'person' to devil Brand.

"Not when you sound Jewish," Brand admonished.

She wondered suddenly what it would do to their friendship if he knew the secret she had been taught by her father to hide.

"You know, I think we're prejudiced, she said. The next card will be my present circumstances."

A devil with a forked spear appeared on the next card.

"Christ, let's discontinue the game," Brand shuddered.

Cybele felt an icy chill ripple up her backbone.

"I'll have to look that one up, just to make sure," she said barely audibly.

"I don't know why you want to play this stupid game," Brand complained.

"Shhh. . . This card means bondage, enslavement, physical dissipation, black magic. Oh, Brand," she cried, and clutched his hand.

"Goddammit," he said, and threw the cards into her purse. "I'm not keeping on with this shit anymore."

"Brand! You idiot. . ." She stood up angrily from the table. "Now I'll never know what's going to happen to me!"

"Cool it," Brand said, and steered her calmly out of the pizza parlour.

"Look, don't get upset about that card, Cybele," he reassured her. But his eyes looked worried and the expression on his face showed that he was upset.

"Don't be worried, huh?" she sneered. "You're not the one who has to go back and live in a haunted apartment!"

Brand shuddered. "Listen, Cybele. I think you'd better get out of that place. The people are too old for you there anyway. You'll be a lot happier in a building with some young people around."

"Oh, Brand, you don't understand. A person can't escape from the Tarot," she said, and stared desolately at the debris of cigarette butts and various empty cartons and paper wrappers littering the kerb.

"I understand it very well," Brand said harshly. "I've studied those cards, Cybele. I've known all along how to tell a fortune with the Tarot tonight." He looked at her sympathetically in the harsh light from the streetlights. "You look tired."

"Yes, I'm so tired, Brand. Let's go back to the shop and get Porgy so I can get a cab home."

"You aren't afraid to go back, are you? 'Cause if you are, you can stay with me tonight," he said, still holding her around the waist protectively.

"Oh no, Brand. As long as ol' Porge is around, I feel safe."

"You and that damned cat," he said as they ran across Wisconsin Avenue.

"Listen, Brand," she said, as she slid into a yellow cab, "everything's going to be OK so don't be worried. Get over there," she ordered Porgy, and pushed his large racoon-like back to the farther side of the cab. Porgy glowered at her like a sullen, spoiled child.

"Call me," he said and made the peace sign as her cab drove away.

"See, Porgy, we've got to get some normalcy back into our lives," she said as she looked around the spooky, half-furnished apartment.

"Number one, I've got to stop playing my kooky games, and number two we've got to get some food in this place," she said, and switched on the light of the stark, empty kitchen.

Porgy yowled happily, pushing his fat body between her slender legs affectionately.

Of course, of course," she said with a desperate decisiveness. "Why haven't I thought of it before? I'm a terrific cook – why, just think of all those dinners I used to give when I was with Pierre," she exclaimed and slung open the door to the large old refrigerator.

"Ugh," she said when she saw a rotting cucumber and a half-full bottle of orange juice inside.

"Meow, meow," Porgy cried.

"Yes, kid. I'm going to the Safeway right now – I'll get scads and scads of stuff. It'll be like the old days again."

She grabbed her purse and ran out the door, leaving Porgy looking startled and disappointed that she hadn't given him anything to eat.

Downstairs in the parking lot, little white, naked lightbulbs shone weakly overhead, lighting the grim stone walls with a dim, yellowish light. She walked swiftly past a few groups of parked cars, trying to smell the pleasant night air through the stale stillness of the garage.

"Cheez, even the cars are old fashioned here," she muttered with disgust. She looked happily at the shiny white car Hadrian had just bought for her.

"I'm really so lucky, and now I'm going to try to start living a normal life."

She cranked up the car and felt a thrill when she heard the noise of the new engine crash through the mouldy interior of the garage.

'Hadrian's so good to me,' she thought as she shifted the gear of the Jaguar down into first. 'And I really should be more faithful to him.'

The car skittered back into the wall of the garage.

"Ooops! Don't do that, car," she exclaimed, and twisted its red leather steering wheel to the extreme left in order to extricate the car from the wall. She heard the bumper scrape against the old stone wall.

"Ugh," she groaned. "I really should drive this baby more often."

She swung out of the garage and out onto the driveway. The car's engine roared like an unruly animal under her slim thighs. Each time she pressed down a little on the gas pedal, the car spurted forward as if on its own volition.

"Wheee, this is fun!" she cried, and revved the motor several times while she halted before a red light. "But those tranquillisers make me so dizzy, I'll have to be careful."

She switched on the car radio to keep herself company as she flew down Massachusetts Avenue.

"Don't pull your love out on me, baby, 'cause I think if you do now, maybe I'll just lay me down and cry four hundred years," blared out into the velvety blackness of the night.

'Gosh, I hope Eric isn't going to stay mad about Sherman,' she thought anxiously as she listened to the words of the song.

Her hair blew around her forehead like fine black whips when she bent forward to get a package of cigarettes on the dash of the car. She put one long white Benson & Hedges between her lips and lifted the burning orange lighter to her cigarette. Suddenly the car swerved sharply to the right.

"What the hell!" she cried, brushing hot, stinging coals from the cigarette off her arms with one hand, while trying to hold the car in control with the other.

People began honking their horns impatiently when her car slowed down in front of them.

"Okay, okay!" she cried. "If I were lying dead in the road they'd just want me to hurry and move so that they could get by."

She clutched the steering wheel frantically, trying to control the direction of the car. She felt its large, powerful tyres weaving crazily under her and looked around desperately for a place to stop. She saw a street to the right leading up into a neighbourhood of quiet, large brick homes, and tried to steer the car off Massachusetts Avenue, but the wheel of the car jerked out of her hand when she tried to turn the car.

"Help!" she cried pitifully, as she felt the steering wheel being wrenched out of her hands by the sudden spinning motion of the tyres.

The long, sleek car jumped the kerb like an escaped animal and rolled down the sidewalk.

"Oh, Christ," Cybele cried. "What did I do to deserve this?"

The car crashed into a black steel lamppost.

"Haven't I been good to you, tell me what you're going to do?" the singer's pleasant, whiny voice still crooned on the car radio.

She lit another cigarette, and turned off the motor of the car. In the Jaguar's rear-view mirror she saw an elderly couple approaching her, and she sighed.

"Some people go to the race tracks for this sort of thing. All I have do is go to the grocery store," she lamented.

"Are you hurt, hon?" an old gentleman asked her.

She looked at his friendly, concerned face and smiled.

"No," she said and shook her head. "Just puzzled, that's all."

"How did it happen?" the man's wife asked. "Did you hit something?"

"No, I didn't," Cybele replied. "That's what's so scary. The car just spun out of control suddenly."

The familiar wail of a police engine flooded the night. Cybele sighed.

"I'm so tired," she said, almost forgetting the presence of the old man and woman.

"Of course you are, dear," the woman said. "Why don't you come on over and sit in our car?"

"Nah, I think I'll just stay right where I am," she said ungraciously.

The woman looked at her husband in surprise, and backed away from the gleaming white sports car.

"Here come the police, Mary," her husband said nervously. "Well, miss, if you're OK. . ." He looked at her suspiciously. 'Wonder if she's drunk?' he thought, and felt anxious to escape the situation.

"C'mon, Mary," he said abruptly. He took his wife by the arm and led her back to their car.

"Let's see your driver's licence, miss," a young, glossy-cheeked officer said.

'Shit,' she thought, and handed him her licence.

He shone his flashlight down on her plastic-covered license plate and papers, then glanced at her with curiosity.

"What caused this accident?" he asked. "Somebody run you off the road?"

"Officer, I was just on my way to the grocery store when my car veered of to the side of the road. . . It was almost as if someone had taken the wheel out from under my hand."

"Hmmm," the man said sceptically. "Have you been drinking today?"

"Just Coca-Cola, straight up, with a pizza," she added.

"You're cute," the officer conceded. He walked around the car, inspecting it closely.

"Your right front tyre is almost completely off," he remarked dryly.

"God, maybe that's what did it," she cried, and jumped over the car door.

"It's a good thing you weren't going any faster," he told her. "Being in a convertible and all. If you'd have turned over – well, that would have been the end of your pretty little head."

She blinked at him in shock.

"But, Officer, how could my tyre be off? My car's been sitting in the garage for a week now. And I just bought it!"

"Maybe this lamppost knocked it off," the policeman said, and stooped down by the tyre.

"Whewww," he whistled. "This is something weird!"

"What?" she asked, and squatted down beside him.

"The bolts on your tyre have been unscrewed almost off all the way around," he told her and pointed to the tyre.

"But – I don't understand," she said, puzzled.

"You got anyone who doesn't especially care for you?" he asked.

She looked at him grimly. "I don't know. I mean. . ." she faltered.

She looked up at a fat songbird chirping happily on a long, curving branch of a rosebush. He trilled out several stanzas of a song, then honed his black beak a few times on the branch.

"La, la, la la!" she trilled back at the bird. The officer smiled.

"Maybe my husband hates me 'cause I left him, but I'd picture him more like blowing my brains out point-blank than doing something this sneaky."

She grinned at the young, handsome officer impulsively. The songbird began trilling "Chirree, Chirree, Chirree" again. His insouciant, lilting voice lulled Cybele back into a happy, carefree mood.

"You know, that bird's trying to tell us something," she said.

"Maybe I should ask if you've been smoking anything?" the officer asked.

"Never touch the stuff," she vowed. "Why, are you onto something good?"

She pressed her hand back on the pavement behind her to steady the weight of her bent thighs as she knelt beside the officer.

"Ugh," she gasped, and pulled her hand up from the sidewalk so quickly that she fell over onto the policeman's long legs.

"What's happening?" the young officer asked.

"Chewing gum," she said, and held out her hand for his inspection. She spread her fingers out, stretching the dirty, pink gum like a duck fanning out its flippers.

"It's dangerous for a woman like you to be alive," the man remarked.

"I'm beginning to think the same thing myself," she said, and began slinging her hand to get rid of the gum. Suddenly it flung off her fingers and plopped onto the officer's cheek.

"Oh m'gosh," she said hastily, pulling the gum from his face. "No offence intended."

"Dangerous woman," the officer said, shaking his head and thoroughly enjoying himself.

"Ha ha ha," she laughed as she cleaned the last bit of gum from his face. A little bit of it had stuck to his moustache, and she tugged at it gently, trying not to pull its red-gold hairs. She rubbed this last little speck around on her finger until it turned into a tiny ball, then threw it out into the grass.

"Chirree, Chirree," the bird called, then flew away.

The policeman stood up, and she followed his example as she might have done an ex-schoolmaster.

"I'll just make a little report on this so you won't have any hassles with the Department. Then I'll drive you to a station where we can get a wrecker to haul your car in. Shouldn't take 'em too long to fix it up." He opened the door of his squad car for her.

"Gosh, you're so sweet," she drawled.

"Ma'am," he replied, grinning. He looked appreciatively at her round, shapely hips encased so firmly in her faded blue jeans.

She looked at her beautiful car with sadness as they pulled away from the kerb.

"And to think of how happy I was only a few moments ago," she murmured half to herself.

"What, miss?" the officer said, and started the squad car.

"Oh, nothing," she said. "I was just thinking of how you can't really trust anything these days."

"That's the truth," he said. "Cigarette?"

"Nah, I've got my own." She groped in her purse for a Benson & Hedges. "Damn it, I left them in the car."

The officer offered her his package of cigarettes again. She pulled one from the crumpled package and sighed. The cigarette paper stuck to her fingers as she took her hand away from the cigarette. An unpleasant sensation swept over her when she felt the gummy stickiness of the chewing gum on her fingers. The startled expression on Eric's tanned, handsome face when he had looked at the glued-up keyhole of her door flashed into her mind.

"Gosh," she said, "maybe somebody really *is* trying to kill me."

"What?" the officer asked over the blare of the police radio.

"I said maybe. . ." The meaning of the officer's uniform imposed itself on her consciousness and shut off her flow of conversation.

"Maybe I can get to bed early for a change," she amended.

"Oh, yeah. Ha," the young man said.

'Christ, I've gotta be careful,' she thought. 'What if he comes snooping around. He could get Eric in a lot of trouble, what with the grass and all.' Her brain began to work coolly, like a small machine.

"You know, I bet I can guess who was fooling around with my tyres," she said, looking at the officer slyly.

"Yeah?" the man said, and pulled into an Esso station.

"Yeah, some little kids I saw playing around the lot the other day. They were real mean. Even threw broken glass at me and everything," she fantasised.

"That's an idea," the officer agreed and got out of the car.

"Damsel in distress," he called to one of the attendants, then leaned his head back through the squad car window and asked, ironically, "But what about the irate murderous husband?"

"Oh, him," she said with a strained nonchalance. "He's just a mild-mannered English professor – would a man who loves F. Scott Fitzgerald and reads *Bury My Heart at Wounded Knee* kill anybody?"

She smiled sweetly at the officer, and pulled her tight jeans away from her clitoris, feeling a pleasant, sexy sensation of pleasure as she did so. 'God, Eric blistered me with his cock last night,' she thought with satisfaction.

"You smile so sweetly when you say that, one can hardly keep from believing you."

"Could a girl who went to church with her father every Sunday *ever* lie?" she asked demurely.

"Yeah, OK," the officer said to the station attendant. "I'll give you the location of her car. Be right back," he told Cybele.

'Great,' she reflected. 'I've gotta get back home to Porge and go to bed,' she thought impatiently. She looked down at her legs on the black, braided car seat and felt afraid suddenly. 'God, what am I going to do?' she thought hysterically. 'What's happening?'

"You can pick your car up here tomorrow, OK?" the officer said.

"Huh?" she asked, and jumped a little at the sight of his face so close to hers at the window.

"It's going to take a while for them to get a wrecker to tow your car," he explained. "So I'll drive you back."

"Oh, great," she agreed simply, taking what fate decreed with as little resistance as possible.

"Could you do me a favour?" she asked, as they rode along.

"Sure, anything – within reason," he added.

"Could you let me stop at this Seven Eleven and get a few cans of cat food for my cat?"

"It's done," the man said, and stopped by the kerb. "Why don't you get yourself a sandwich?" he asked. "You look like you could stand two or three."

She walked, tired, through the gaudy, worn-looking lobby of her apartment building after the cop had dropped her off. The desk clerk scowled at her as usual. She didn't bother with any response, but looked straight ahead at the grey, bland door of the elevator. She was grateful, for once, for something mechanical, and devoid of any human response to fasten her attention onto.

Her cat attacked her ankles ferociously, but she hardly bothered to stroke him as she opened a can of Tabby Treat.

"I'm just so tired," she whined, and looked around the dark, empty apartment. "Fucking place," she sighed.

"I think I'll call Juliette," she exclaimed suddenly. She thought of her tall, beautiful sister with pleasure. Juliette's large blue eyes floated into her mind like Monet's enormous purple water lilies.

'Gosh, maybe she'll come up,' Cybele thought, and dialled her parents' number in Louisiana.

"Hello," she heard a breathy, feminine voice say, and thought of tall lilies brushing their petals together.

"Juliette!" she cried. "I'm so glad you answered."

"Cybele, is everything alright?" her sister asked.

"Sure, great, great. Listen, why don't you come on up? I've got some real crazy people for you to meet. You'll get a kick out of them. I'm going with a terrific young guy."

"What about Hadrian?"

"Oh, I'm with him too. But more seriously, you know."

"Yeah, I know," Juliette said and laughed.

"Listen, Juliette. I'm kind of scared."

"I knew something was up," Juliette sighed apprehensively.

"If I send you a ticket, can you fly up? We'll go swimming every day at the Hilton. The pool's enormous. You can go out with some of Eric's friends – and of course Hadrian will take us out to dinner all the time."

"Hmmm, I'm tired already," Juliette said.

"You have such beautiful hands, Juliette," Cybele exclaimed craftily. "I've always envied your hands – and loved them too. The fact that I've envied them makes me love them infinitely more! And your boobs are so big! So much bigger than mine. You're another Sophia Loren!"

"Ha, ha! Cybele, you're trying everything. You must be desperate. Why don't you come home?"

"You know I can't."

"Why can't you?"

"Oh, you know." She thought of Hadrian and began stubbing her toe in the old carpeting.

"No, I don't know, really," Juliette replied.

"Hadrian might not like it," she explained.

"Is he your keeper, Cybele?"

"Well, sorta – you know. . ." She lapsed into a waiting silence.

"Pierre called Mama," Juliette said finally.

"Yeah? What'd the bastard want?" she snarled.

"Oh, Cybele, don't be so dramatic. He just wanted to know if we'd heard anything from you. He sounded sad."

"Sad, huh? Well, you can feel sympathy for him. You've never been bashed in the head and—"

"I know the details," Juliette replied cryptically.

"Well, look, can you come or not?"

"I'll come," Juliette said, "in a few days."

"Oh, Juliette, terrific. You can take the late morning flight. Eric and I'll pick you up. I'll send the ticket tomorrow. What day will you come?"

"Monday."

Chapter Seven

'God, I'm pissed,' she thought as she dodged the cobblestones on Q Street, slipping in her high heels and cursing intermittently when she turned her ankle. She tugged at the zipper on the front of her dress, feeling rivulets of perspiration course down the sides of her legs in tiny lines. She looked down the front of her dress with irritation.

"So smart the way they fixed the zipper on this dress. Doesn't even show. Ain't I cute? Ain't I neat?" she said, yanking off her shoes as she strode up the steps to Eric's apartment building.

"I get dressed up in this monkey outfit and all he gives me is a hundred bucks. Shit! And I have to come down to his office to pick it up. Wait around the whole night for him last night and he doesn't even show until eleven – could've screwed Sherman – could've screwed Eric – could've gone to Hawaii. Who the fuck cares anyway? Well, at least Juliette'll be here Monday."

She clumped into the dark, narrow hallway and rammed her hand down on the bell, then shrieked when she felt a sliver of wood from the floor slide into her heel.

"I've always known I had a devastating effect on women," Danny drawled as he pulled the door open slowly. "But for them to greet me screaming – well, that comes later, babe."

"Oh Danny," she said, flinging herself into his arms and clutching at the soft, damp material of his T-shirt. "I've wounded myself." She held up one large, dirty foot comically for his inspection.

"I'll kiss it if I get to kiss something else," he joked.

"Danny!" she screamed, and hit him lightly.

"What's going on?" Eric said from the bedroom. "I thought I heard a bitch! Is it mine or not?"

She pushed past Danny and stood in the doorway of Eric's bedroom. Danny kept his hand linked in hers like a loose bracelet.

"Hi," Eric said. He was sprawled in a big, overstuffed chair that stood at the end of his narrow bed. He looked at her with moist, lambent eyes through his thick glasses. His long colt-like legs were askance on the broad arms of the chair. She studied his curly, tousled hair, the lazy, ironic expression in his eyes and his wide, full mouth, then dropped her eyes automatically to the apparent bulge of his groin. She felt a warmth surge into her breasts and a flame of desire heat up her stomach. She studied him more closely to make sure that he really delighted her as much as she had thought. When she felt the tips of her fingers tingling, she ran to him and sat on his knee and curled herself against the golden fuzz of his chest.

"Far out!" Danny said from behind her. "Now that's what I call hypnotic power."

He walked to the chair where Eric and Cybele sat, and touched Eric tentatively. Eric smiled hazily up at Danny through his glasses, then began nuzzling Cybele. She sighed and hooked her legs firmly around Eric's knees.

"Just thought if I touched you some might rub off on me," Danny explained. His fingers brushed Cybele's knee as he dropped his hand from Eric's hard, round shoulder.

"Cut it out, Danny," Eric said softly, "or we'll confiscate your headband." He reached up and yanked Danny's beaded Indian headband off.

"That does it," Danny said. He lunged out at Eric and grabbed at his hand, then lost his balance and fell into the big chair with them.

"Get outa here, fart-face," Eric said, chuckling.

Cybele slipped out from under them and ran over to the bed.

"What is this anyway – a Boy Scout meeting?" she asked, and flopped down on the bed. Danny and Eric wrestled on the floor until Eric took his knee and pushed Danny against the door.

"Now here's ya band," Eric said and placed the headband carefully on Danny's head.. Danny stood up and looked in the mirror.

"I hope you know you put it on crooked," he complained.

Cybele began to bounce up and down on the bed. "Oh my heart belongs to Daddy!" she sang.

"Dame's flipped out," Danny said, and walked towards the door. "You two try not to injure one another, will ya?" he cautioned them as he walked out of the room.

Eric came back to the bed. Cybele spread her legs out as wide as her dress would allow. She put her thumb in her mouth and began sucking on it, then sang out again, "So I want to warn you, laddy, although I think you're perfectly swell." She rolled her eyes idiotically, then turned over on her stomach and began kicking her legs.

Eric lay down on top of her, pressing his hips into her round, soft ass. "That my heart belongs to Daddy," she mumbled up from the mattress that he had pressed her face into. He ground his dick harder into her ass.

"'Cause my Daddy treats it so well." She sang and wriggled out from under him.

"Hey, luv," he said, "if you think Daddy's so good, look what your son's got for you!" He sat back in the pillows with his dick sticking up from his jeans like a lollipop.

She laughed, then looked at his face. "Eric, you look like a real idiot right now." She glared at his silly, laconic expression.

"Ummm, hmmm," he drawled and batted his dick back and forth on his flat belly.

"Look what I've reduced you to," she smirked and slipped off the bed. "Just another dick."

"Oh, so we're gonna play games? Well, speaking of being reduced. . ." He stood up and put both of his hands on her shoulders, then slowly unzipped her dress. "What is this shit you've got on anyway?" He pulled her dress open and kissed one of her breasts.

"It's my street outfit."

"Street outfit?" Eric exclaimed. "You're a freak!"

"Yeah, I'm a freak. It's the sort of outfit I wear when I go down to Hadrian's office for bread." She looked into his smiling sunburned face and concentrated on his lips, imagining them on her nipple once more. "I mean, you gotta play the role."

"Aren't we tough today?" he jeered tenderly at her. "Come on over here and let me get that splinter out of your foot." He picked her up suddenly and took her dress off completely. "I hate you in this fucking thing."

"How did you know I had a splinter, Eric?"

"Oh, word get's out," he said.

She hugged him tightly as he lay her down on the bed.

"Eric, I love you. I love you so simply it hurts me."

He tightened his grip on her foot while he peered at it intently, looking for the splinter. "This might hurt," he said, and started to pick at her heel.

"Eric, please don't!"

"Whaddaya mean? I'm trying to help you." He pushed her back on the pillow. His short, plump fingers pressed on her stomach.

"But I hate for people to look at my feet," she whined, feeling a pleasant sensation in the pit of her stomach from the touch of his hand.

"Shut up. I've seen your ass-hole and that's pretty too."

"Eric!" she screamed. "No man has ever said that to me before."

"Yeah," he said, giving a final pluck to her heel and bringing out the splinter. "I'm a real flatterer."

She sat up, rubbing her heel. "Thanks, Eric." She put her hand on his hair. It sank into his thick, spongy curls. She kissed the bone of his cheek. Her hand dropped to his hip, brushing the material of his pants. She could feel his heart beating swiftly on her knee.

"Oh man, I wanna fuck you, but I'm afraid I'll come too quick," he said.

"You can come quick, Eric, I don't care. I can come quick, too."

He heaved himself up on her. "Ohhh – ohh God, Cybele. I've gotta fuck you. I'm going. . ." His breath rushed inside her ears in frenzied pants, and his cock shoved itself back and forth in her cunt like a piston.

"Move a little more. Do it once more," she whispered. Then they both shuddered to a stop.

They lay riveted to one another. Both of their bodies were wet with perspiration, in spite of the apartment's central air-conditioning. He blew into the nape of her neck lightly, making her shiver beside the warmth of his body. She felt the sides of his deer-like legs and hips and drew the smell of his hair deep, deep into her lungs.

"Eric, what would you do if you didn't cut dope?"

He groaned.

"Eric? Answer me."

"Oh, I guess I'd be an old cocksucker who gave young girls money so I'd get to fuck them."

"But since you're a young man with no money to give girls to fuck you. . ."

"I fuck them free." He sat up and accidentally banged his head on the wall. "Ow! Goddammit – can't we discontinue this ambitious conversation?"

"But what *would* you do, Eric? I wanna know."

"I don't know. Guess I'd be a carpenter."

"Eric!" She seized his hands in hers with enthusiasm. "I like that." She continued holding his hands. "Mary was married to a carpenter."

"Mary who?"

"You know, Mary, mother of Jesus."

He leapt up off the bed. The sun gleamed dully on his virginal body, moulding its contours with highlights of burnished gold. She looked at him, enchanted with his perfect physique.

"I need a hit on that statement. Let's get high."

She sat up, still staring at him. "Oh Eric," she whispered. "I wish I could just look at you nude for the rest of my life."

"Wow, you're freaking me out, luv." He went over to his jeans and pulled out a little white pouch and some papers, then turned around and began pouring grass onto the onion-thin paper. He propped one foot up on the old chair and squinted through the gloom of the curtained bedroom at the amount of grass he was siphoning out. Then he pulled the string of the pouch closed with his teeth.

"You look so barbaric when you do that, Eric," Cybele sighed. "Your teeth are so white and sharp looking."

"All the better to. . ." – he lunged onto the bed, making one of the slats clatter down with a loud bang – ". . .eat you with, luv." He began biting her nipples.

Danny pounded on the wall. "Down in there!" he hollered.

"Eric, please," she implored, and took the joint from his hand. "Don't be so obvious." She laughed and started to pound back on the wall with her feet.

"If you aren't the picture of subtlety!" Eric countered and took a big hit from the joint.

She leaned over and kissed his knee. "Even your kneecaps are pretty, Eric." She looked back up at him with her eyes gleaming.

He stuck the joint between her lips and said, "And I told you even your—"

She put her hand up to his lips and took a deep draw from the joint and held it for a moment.

"If you say that word again," she said, choking from the grass as she exhaled, "I'll have to consider you a very vulgar person."

"Ass-hole!" he screamed, and grabbed her. He turned her over and pretended that he was about to inspect her rectum.

"Help!" she screamed.

Danny pounded on the wall again.

"Shit!" Eric said. "Let's get outta here. Ya wanna take a ride?" He pulled the window curtain back. "It's gorgeous outside."

"Oh, Eric," she cried, "Let's do. Let's do!" She stood up and began jumping up and down on the bed. Eric watched her like a lazy, satisfied animal. She flopped down on the bed suddenly with the grass making her brain explode in euphoria. "Ya wanna walnuto?" she giggled.

"Ya wanna get raped before we go?" He put his finger in her navel. She pulled his head down to her mouth and began sucking his chin, then rolled off the bed.

"Nah, I want to do it in the grass." She walked over to his dresser and picked up his old black hairbrush.

"Don't lose that!" he said rudely.

"Oh fuck you," she replied and smiled at him from the mirror while she slowly brushed her hair. "How can you be so niggardly with your possessions, Eric?" she asked, as she rummaged around in the old dresser for a pair of her shorts.

"Whaddaya doing?"

"I'm trying to find something to wear. Do you mind?" She threw the brush at his dick. "I mean, I was 'given' this drawer for my stuff, wasn't I? Or was I dreaming the other Saturday when you definitely went so far as to 'give' me a drawer in this chest?" She pulled out some shorts and a top and began hopping around on one foot and then the other while she put them on.

"Cybele, I do believe you're making fun of me." He walked over and grabbed her breasts. "You get two twists for that." He grinned and twisted her breasts gently.

"Oh goody!" She laughed and pulled her top down over his hands.

They ran out to the little green Triumph and flung themselves into the hot, cracked leather seats.

"Oh fuck," Eric said, and pushed himself out of the seat with one bare foot. "Be back in a minute, m'dear. I forgot the orange juice!"

"OK, precious love," she drawled and took the joint carefully from his fingers. The street wavered before her in the heat. She studied the STOP light in front of her as it blinked its red, yellow and green colours in the brilliant, summer sunshine. She flung her head back and dragged on the grass over and over until her whole body seemed to be floating in the shimmering sunlit leaves of the trees towering above the little green sports car.

She was hardly aware that he had jumped back into the car beside her until she felt a cold jar of orange juice against her thigh. She stared at it dully as it lay on the sun-bleached hairs of her tanned legs.

"Oh man, Eric's got the all American dream," she heard Danny yell over the roar of the motor. She lolled her head back dizzily and smiled at him and Tom while they stood on the steps of the apartment building watching them. Tom cocked his cowboy hat down over his eyes and drawled, "Yep. A beautiful girl, a sunny day, and a joint. What more could a man ask for?" She stared at him more closely, then realised that it was Tom. He stood like a towering sentinel beside Danny's slight frame, his hair dark and gleaming under the oversized hat.

"Hi ya, Tonto," she yelled back at them, and waved the big, slippery bottle of orange juice at them precariously. It fell into her lap. "Take care of the Lone Ranger."

"Cybele, I love you," Danny called.

"Lucky thing it had a top," Eric mumbled, then gunned the motor of the little car over and over. Raymond ran out onto the steps when he heard the noise.

"What's going on?" he asked. The spurs on his boots glinted in the sun. Under his Spanish-styled hat his blond hair curled out in thick, careless waves.

"Nothing. We're just watching old Eric here, with a beautiful babe on grass, a summer day—"

"Knock it off, Danny," Eric smiled. "A jug of wine and—?"

"And thou!" Danny finished and clasped Tom around the waist. Tom pushed him off the porch. "Careful there, boy," he said and creased his black hat. "Ya don't wanna end up a dead Indian!

They roared off around the curve onto Wisconsin Avenue.

"Eric, I'm stoned, but I'm sure the light was red."

"It's a nice colour, ain't it?" he agreed, and laughed idiotically.

"Oh God, oh God," she groaned happily as she watched his Adam's apple bob up and down while he chug-a-lugged the orange juice.

"I love to watch your throat move while you do that." She rubbed her hand up and down his leg, watching his toes squash against the black rubber pedal when he pressed down on the accelerator.

"Cybele, you're a right-on girl."

"Yeah, I'm right on," she replied, hopping onto his lap and grabbing the bottle of orange juice.

They flew down Wisconsin Avenue in the little green car.

"Just what I need – to be wrecked by a nice piece of ass and a bottle of orange juice."

She leaned over and kissed him, passing some orange juice from her mouth to his as she did so.

"Yeah?" she gasped. "We should both die this way every day." She ground her fanny into his lap, laughing.

"Cool it until we get into the country. We don't want to be interrupted by the Feds before we hit the clover."

She slid back into her seat. "Oww!" she screamed.

He grinned over at her. "Kinda hot on that little fanny of yours?"

"Like you?" she laughed.

They swung onto M Street, up through the glistening line of traffic that shifted sluggishly in the torpid afternoon heat. Yet the breeze that stirred through the trees rippled their leaves in a light, dancing movement. The grass on the hillside that rolled down to the Potomac seemed to repeat this same carefree undulating movement as they spun around the curves of Canal Road. Everything swayed and sparkled – even the polluted waters of the Potomac shimmered like a blue gem in the breeze. The wind stung her cheeks and whipped up through her thighs, blowing the ruffles of her blouse her neck. She studied the firm, blue-green ropes of Eric's veins protruding on his arm as he grasped the steering wheel, and she thought of strong young plants, of how they bore the same, sap-like veins while whipping in the wind.

"I'll bet you've got the reddest blood, Eric," she said, and touched one of his veins with her forefinger, watching the plump flesh of her finger push it out of shape. She felt the strong, vital current of his blood under her finger.

"Help, a vampire!" he yelled above the wind. "Here, reach in my jacket and get that extra joint I brought for the ride, will ya?"

She took his rough, blue denim jacket that he had wadded into a ball and got the joint. She held the fat little cigarette up to him tauntingly and grinned.

"Gimme," he said.

She stuck it in her mouth and shook her head. "Nah."

"You broad."

"What a term, Eric. Sounds like the Army, or something gross like that. Which would you choose, Eric – me or grass?"

"Both," he replied, and jerked the joint out of her mouth.

She watched as he lowered his head to the flame of a match. His brown and gold hair blew in the wind. His square, paw-like hand held the steering wheel easily while she buried her head in his neck and nibbled at his flesh.

"Cut it out, will ya, or I'm gonna have a wreck," he protested, giggling.

"You're all brown and gold, Eric – you make me think of amber. I want to drink you like brandy."

He took a deep drag on the joint, then handed it to her.

"Luv, you're poetic today."

"'For they were young and could never die,'" she quoted.

"Huh?" he asked.

"Quote from a favourite book of mine – when I was young," she sighed.

"Don't get literary on me. That's your husband's bag."

"Eric, it isn't my bag either – I can't even remember the author who wrote that. Someone from the twenties most probably."

"Most probably," Eric babbled, and turned up the sound track of the stereo. They wound deeper and deeper into the lacy green countryside.

"You know, my sister's coming."

"Yeah? Why?"

"Oh Eric. Because I want her to."

"Whatever makes you happy, luv."

She thought about the way her tyre had been purposely unscrewed and she frowned.

"Don't scowl, Cybele. I'll be nice to your sister."

"Oh Eric. You're so sweet to me!"

She threw her arms around his neck and sighed as a feeling of safety pervaded her being.

"Hey," he exclaimed, swerving the car back into the right lane. "You keep trying to wreck us!"

"Sorry," she said, still snuggling near the comforting strength of his body. She decided not to tell him about the incident with her car. 'After all,' she thought, 'the glue was weird enough. He might get spooked out by me altogether.'

"You should be sorry – about a lot of things," he admonished her resentfully when he remembered her date with Sherman. "I am nice, you know.

His voice cracked in a boyish, adolescent tone that charmed her ears with its youth. The contrast between Eric and Hadrian constantly freaked her out.

"And you should remember stuff like that before you decide to play games with me."

"Oh Eric. I – little me play games with you?" She raised her brows incredulously.

"You broad," he said, and rested his hand on her knee.

"Oh Eric. Eric, look at the cow! Oh God, what a beautiful cow!"

"Yeah? It's the first one I've ever seen too." He slowed the car down and pulled onto a gently sloping shoulder of the road. "This is it," he said. "All out." He jumped over the side of the car and stood waiting for her in the piercing sunlight. She got out and ran up to him, flinging herself around his wiry, narrow waist.

"Oh Eric, it's beautiful here!"

He grasped her hand and pulled her after him as he ran across the highway.

They ran up the hillside and crawled under a rambling white fence, smelling the rich heat of the field as they slid under it on their knees. He stood up before she did and held his hand out to her once more. She took it, feeling its hard, firm shape in hers as he jerked her up on the other side.

"Oh, Eric," she gasped. In front of them lay garlands of white and yellow daisies that rippled gaily across the endless meadow. One lone dogwood tree stood at the foot of the hill. "It's a paradise, Eric," she whispered, looking as far as she could see into the blowing grass and flowers. He leaned down and kissed her tenderly.

"*Our* paradise, Cybele. Come on!"

She ran along after him, panting in sharp little gasps through the heat.

"There's no one around, Eric!"

"Natch."

"Oh, God!" She ran in front of him, dancing in circles, around and around, then threw herself down in the flowers. He flopped down beside her and began kissing her ears. She turned her head and quoted Thomas Wolfe once more. "'Come up into the hills, oh my young love.'"

Eric blew into her ear.

"Tickles!" she said happily.

He stared down at her solemnly. The skin on his face and arms seemed to have become more tawny, more burnished in the golden sunlight. She stopped laughing when he began to rub the sides of her ribs slowly. The tips of his fingers touched her breasts.

"Are you like this all over?" he asked.

"What do you mean?" she said.

"Creamy."

"It's bath oil," she explained.

"I know."

"Then why d'you ask?"

He pulled her shorts down slowly, then pushed himself up into her cunt. The pungent grass smell surrounded them as he pounded himself into her body. She felt the grass under her hips and ceased thinking. When he stopped moving, she was conscious of a singular dogwood tree at the end of the hill.

"Hey, Eric, did you ever kill anybody?"

She looked down at her panties sprawled around her ankles. She heard his heavy breathing and turned towards him on one elbow, smelling the sharply bitter odour of grass that she had squashed with the bone of her arm. He was squinting into the field of windswept grass and flowers. All around them the leaves and grass heaved in an opulent green sigh of summer. River Road lay behind them like a careless, winding ribbon. Its white-columned mansions and sleek-backed horses stood in bas-relief against the pregnant land. She grasped out at tiny, flying bugs that hummed in the summer heat, enjoying the feeling of clasping her fingers to her palm.

Eric remained silent, looking straight ahead, as if wanting to disappear into the sloping hillside.

"Well?" she asked, and began pulling up her pants.

He pushed her over on her stomach and began kissing the back of her neck.

"Why do you ask such stupid questions?"

"Because I want to know. You were a man – an American like me – and sorta my age, and you were in Vietnam. And I want to know what it was like. I mean, if you did it?"

He caressed her long, slim legs that lay brown and firm in the tender green grass. His hand touched her skin with a soft, childlike insistency. He kept touching her inner thigh with urgency, as if he were remembering but trying not to.

"*Did* you, Eric?"

"What?" he shouted. His mouth was rosy and full with emotion.

"Kill anyone?"

"Yes!" he yelled.

"What was it like?" she persisted.

He still stared into the field, refusing to look at her, but touching her legs all the while. The flesh of his thumb was like soft, sanded wood. She felt anger welling up out of him like a sombre, forbidden pool.

She decided not to say anything more. The subject had been a mistake, she thought. She touched her hair almost primly, and unconsciously began to collect herself to leave.

"See that tree over there?" he asked. She looked at him immediately, startled by his tone. The ruddiness of his cheekbones and the golden colour of his sunburned hair belied the suffering that his voice implied. She followed his eyes to a dogwood tree that he was looking at in front of them. Its green branches were swaying like a delicate bird caught in the torpor of the afternoon heat.

"Yeah," she responded.

"It's like going over and chopping that tree down for no reason. You might be sitting here looking at that tree and just go over and. . ." He cut the air with his hand, then looked at Cybele with a strange smile.

Then he rolled away from her down the hill, giggling. She rolled down after him, over and over, feeling the dirt stick to her face and clothes. When she stopped by him, she climbed on top of him and laid down on him as if he were a mattress. She laid her cheek next to his and pushed her stomach hard against his slim, muscular buttocks. She could feel the backs of his legs through his jeans with the muscles of her thighs. The dirt on both of their cheeks mingled until he turned his face into the grass. She began biting him on the back of his neck, sucking his flesh between her teeth and breathing the grassy fragrance of his hair.

"Hey Eric, Eric, I love you – I really love you, Eric." She tried to turn his head around to her mouth. "Kiss me. Kiss me or I'll die!" She tried once more to turn his head. Suddenly he jerked around, pushing her off him.

"Fucking female." He brushed at his arms and hair furiously in a flurry of grass and dirt.

"Eric, Eric, what did I do?" She looked at his face. Tears had made streaked patterns across his cheeks.

"You'll die! You'll die!" he cried. He pulled abruptly at his boots. "Yeah, you'll die. Just like they did. I used to watch them. They'd be playing craps, or whatever the hell those Orientals do when they play with dice." He flung himself back on the hillside and kept talking, as if to the clouds. "We'd be sitting there in the bushes watchin' 'em, with lice crawling around our asses, bugs bitin' our balls. They'd be laughing, talking, then whop – we'd blow their heads off. One guy was washing out his underwear when we got him. He kept trying to wash it even when his brains came out in the washbowl."

Cybele froze beside him. She no longer dared to look at his face, but stared hypnotically at the dogwood tree.

"You wanna die?" he asked, taking the palm of his hand and chopping her arm with it so that she fell back beside him. "I can kill you, baby. Just tell me how you wanna die."

He was crying when he began to kiss her ears softly, then her temples, blowing the dirt away gently in a gesture that was like a caress.

"Yeah, Eric, I want to die with you," she said plaintively. "Can we die together?"

He groaned and unzipped his jeans. His stiff dick jutted out through the silver zipper of his pants.

"I'm gonna ram it in up to your throat." He pulled her shorts down brusquely scraping her thighs with the dirt that was still on his hands.

She leaned her head over his dick and licked it tentatively, tasting it slowly.

"You cunt! I'm gonna kill you – gonna stab you to death with my dick."

She still sucked at his nipples while holding his dick in her hand, feeling its spongy, delicious quality with her fingers.

"Come on," he said, and rolled over on top of her.

"Eric!" she shrieked, "Eric, you're cutting my back on a rock. Oh God, oh!" She felt his hard, long dick inside her body and she forgot about the rock.

"I love my dick in your cunt. Oh, Cybele!"

She looked up at Eric. His face was framed by his thick, curling hair. His head blocked the sun from her eyes as he plunged into her over and over.

"Hurt me! Hurt me!" she screamed, and tore at his hips with her nails. He slapped her over and over while he pushed into her. She smiled, feeling her lips tight over her teeth and her cheeks stinging from his slaps, while his hard dick thrust deeper and deeper into her body.

"Oh God, oh God!" she cried.

"Are you dyin', baby?" He laughed down at her, never ceasing his movements. He slapped her once more, hard.

"Twist my breasts, Eric. Oh hurt me, hurt me! Make me come. Hurt me so I can come." She drew her knees back to her breasts. "Oh God," she said again.

"That's right. Call on God when you're about to die."

She saw his eyes roll back under his lids before he fell down over her in a heap.

Now she was aware of the rock under her back, and moved painfully out from under him. He didn't kiss her again as he usually did, but continued staring into the sky while breathing laboriously.

"Ohhh," she groaned and touched her back. When she looked at her hand, she was surprised to see blood on her fingers.

"Look!" she said and thrust her hand into his face.

"Yeah, when you die, you gotta have blood." He still didn't look at her. She felt cross that he was ignoring her. She had always felt especially helpless when a man didn't seem enchanted after making love with her.

"Oh, Eric," she said, grabbing at her shorts a little desperately. She faltered as she stood up, almost falling. "I'm not going to mention Vietnam anymore," she said, and pulled her shorts up. "Come on," she said, knitting her brows bitchily.

"OK," he said. He stood up unsteadily. "You're fucking me bowlegged, m'dere."

She tried to smile at his crude joke, but felt irritated when she saw how easy it was for him to zip up his pants and be ready. She felt the painful scrape on her back once more.

"M'dear, m'dear," she said with impatience, and she scowled. She plunged up the grassy hillside without looking back. "Sometimes I feel positively married when you call me that!"

He ran to her side and pretended to trip her. "Ha ha, Cybele's fucked up. Ha, ha. Bet she's even pregnant!"

She stooped down and grabbed a rock to throw at him.

"Oh, now you're getting violent with me! I've got your game, m'lady." He twisted his graceful, sunburned body close to hers, teasing her with the litheness of his movements.

"Where're you gonna wound me, huh, huh?"

She threw the rock down and began to cry.

"You shit, you're just a shit," she said for no reason, and began to run towards the car.

He caught up with her. The heat of his body kept her company with the steady rhythm of their legs as they ran.

"Hey, Cybele, just look at us. We're in America – see all the cows? Look at that big mansion over there – capitalism and all that. . ."

"Shut up!" she screamed. They both stopped running. He was staring at her with his mouth set in a guarded, bitter expression. "Just because you kill a few guys – just because. . ." She swung on angrily towards the car.

"Yeah? Yeah?" He ran up beside her, panting from the heat. "Well, you didn't have to kill 'em – you weren't there. You were home with your husband while he wrote poetry."

"I wish I hadn't asked you about it, Eric. Let's just skip it." She put her hand on the car forlornly and slunk down into the cracked leather seat.

He got in beside her and lit a joint.

"Christ, let's don't fuck up the afternoon," he said, and put his hand on her knee.

"I'm just so tired of people saying that America's decadent," she explained, rubbing her fingers on his faded old jeans. He kissed her lightly. "I mean, even if it is decadent," she said, looking back at the waving field of daisies, "I just don't see why it has to be."

He smiled at her. "Here, take a drag of this and get some sweet inspiration."

She took a lot of smoke into her lungs and felt the old familiar scraping at her throat.

"Don't forget the party," he said, and spun the car off the side of the road onto the black, sweating pavement.

"Oh yeah," she said. "We've gotta buy your Jesus robe. I forgot all about it, Eric." She pulled his arm around her shoulders tightly and closed her eyes.

Chapter Eight

"Eric, for God's sake, help me. We've got to hurry, you know." She stood in front of the old stove naked, then stooped down to the boiler. " Oh, Eric, we've had it. There's no broiling pan in this fucking stove. How will we cook the damned steak? And we don't even have the meat yet. Do you know how to buy good steak?"

"Listen, you little cunt. I happened to be the butler for one of the best families in Connecticut one summer. You just go and get dressed – make yourself beautiful for the old dude."

She squatted down beside the stove miserably and watched a cockroach crawl across the floor. "Fucking place," she said. "No dining table. Eric, where'll we eat anyway?"

Eric abandoned his determined pose by the doorway and walked over to her. He swooped down and picked her up gently by her elbows. "Why, the bed, of course, Cybele. Now go in there and fix your make-up. The rice is ready, so's the salad. I'll go and get the steak and your sister."

She leapt back against his chest happily and dug her skinny shoulder blades into him. "OK, Eric, but for Christ's sake, hurry. Hadrian will be here soon. It would be hell if the two of you showed up at the same time."

"Am I stupid? Now shut up and get out of here before I spoil everything."

"What?"

"Rape you, that's what – if you don't get out of here with your pretty little ass."

She went back into the spacious bedroom and walked up to the long closet full of clothes. She took out a yellow pants suit and began to pull it over her body. It clung like yellow elastic over her firm brown legs and belly, leaving her belly button exposed. The top tied just under her breasts. She pulled open the mirrored closet door and studied the effect that she would have on Hadrian. She thought she looked sexy and even a little gay.

"Eric, Eric, how do I look?" she asked as she walked back into the kitchen. She found it empty. The rice was pre-flavoured with many spices and she sniffed it hungrily. She walked across the kitchen to the big old refrigerator and pulled open the door. Inside were three bowls of salad that had been carefully arranged by Eric. She thought of his legs in his worn jeans, of his handsome chest in his simple cotton shirt and of the beginning of golden hair at the bottom of his V-necked shirt. She looked down at her toes and felt a strange aloneness once more. She felt as if her playmate had left her with the stage set and readied, but that it was she who would have to play the real scene.

She ran into the bedroom to see if everything was OK. What did 'OK' mean? She didn't know. 'OK' had to be a feeling about things. Maybe everything wasn't OK, but it had possibilities at least. She walked down the woolly carpeting of the hallway, feeling it under her toes, feeling the ribbed material of her outfit stretched across her body. She thought of her sister and felt apprehensive. Why did Hadrian want her here? In her heart she knew. He wanted to use Juliette, as he was using her, the way he manipulated everyone in his life. She tried to understand this. When she understood it, she decided that in her deepest being she felt sorry for Hadrian, and afraid of him at the same time. He had never run through a field of daisies without any thought. She couldn't imagine that he had ever made love to anyone in a meadow and smelled how sweet the grass could be when it was crushed underneath a lover's body.

She felt a sharp pain in her left side and remembered that she hadn't had a period for two months now. She knew she wasn't pregnant. She just didn't bleed. 'It's my own business not to,' she thought.

Then her thoughts returned to Hadrian. She wanted to show him the careless beauty of love. She wanted to show him the innocence that it brought to a person. To love simply.

She gazed out at the leafy green trees, wishing that she could disappear into their colour. She wanted to be absorbed by something – to escape. Then she heard the key click in the elaborate gold lock and saw Eric's pawlike hand emerge around the door. Her sister's soft, nebulous voice was answering the boyish tones of Eric.

"Hi," she said uncertainly to Juliette. "Ready for the party?" Cybele looked at her sister. Juliette stood watching her with curiosity shining in her wide blue eyes. Cybele found herself regretting the situation that she found herself in with Juliette profoundly. 'But I'm letting it happen,' she thought guiltily. 'I'm responsible.'

"Hmmm, well, I dunno," Juliette said, and laughed nervously. She was holding a brown leather bag in her tanned hands. Cybele noticed that it was worn out, and felt a wrenching pain shoot up into her throat. She saw the fragile collar-bone of her sister and thought of porcelain or a bird's wing.

"Whaddaya mean? Of course she's ready. You're not the only lady around here who's a sexy dish," Eric said. He put his arm around Juliette's waist and smiled. "What say, kid?" he asked, and squeezed her while winking at Cybele.

"Eric, you're sweet," Cybele said lamely, and hugged him back.

Juliette walked into the semi-empty living-room without any conviction for the agenda. Cybele watched the way she walked from the hallway. Her style of moving was like their father's. She bent down to some books Cybele had stacked on the radiator, and Cybele winced again when she noticed the thinness of her shoulder blades in her little cotton top. Juliette was tall and slender. Her legs were long and prettily shaped. She stood by the bookcase in a charming, casual stance that was still redolent of adolescence.

"You've got some pretty good books here," Juliette said, turning back to Cybele as if she had felt her eyes from behind. Her cheekbones were high and well moulded. Cybele noticed Juliette's large blue eyes peering at her from the gloom of the living-room. They were so large that they startled Cybele. She thought of the time when Juliette had fallen from a platform and cut one of her eyelids when she was a little girl, of the way she had looked lying in a crib in the hospital. She had been so round and tanned, like a little berry – with one large white bandage over her eye. Cybele shivered.

"Yeah, not bad. I just bought a dictionary. That's a hopeful sign." 'Why does it have to be this way every lousy time?' she thought. She longed to have a wholesome atmosphere around her sister. "Just for once, dammit. Just one damned time.'

"OK, Cybele, get in here if you want to see something good," Eric called.

She went into the kitchen and saw Eric holding two large, livid pieces of meat, smiling foolishly between them.

"OK, OK, Eric. You did good, baby." The red, vibrant meat made her feel tired suddenly. "I feel like I need a cup of blood." She thought diabolically of cutting a plug in Hadrian.

She walked into the living-room and picked up a book of Hesse's poems to show Juliette that they shared the same literary tastes, at least.

"I read these when I was drunk one night," she told Juliette. "Smashed out of my mind. All I remember was that they were very sad."

"Hey, they look really neat," Juliette said, holding the thin book of poetry in her slender, graceful hand. Again Cybele noted Juliette's shoulder blades. She hugged her impulsively. They looked at one another in confusion, then parted shyly.

Cybele smelled the steaks cooking from the living-room and regained her composure for the evening ahead of them.

"Why don't you take them back to read on the plane with you?" she told Juliette.

"Thanks a lot. I've got Roshalde, so I'll bring it to the pool for you when I see you tomorrow."

"OK, ladies," Eric announced, poking his head around the kitchen door. "It's getting shipshape in here. The dude couldn't ask for more." He glared at Cybele through his thick glasses. "Still can't figure out what he wants with your sister?" Cybele met his blurred stare defensively.

"We'll have fun," Cybele said defiantly. "Now get out of here before he shows up, will you?"

Eric smiled at her crookedly. "OK, luv. Y'all have a nice evening." He lingered in the doorway another half second, then disappeared.

Cybele walked into the kitchen, and Juliette followed. "Do you want me to set the table," she offered.

Cybele leaned down to the improvised boiler. Eric had propped the broiling pan under the fire with two bricks.

"Table? Well, in a manner of speaking. Actually, you can set the bed, 'cause that's where we're gonna eat." She looked at her sister carefully, wondering how she was going to hold up under the situation. "And Juliette, remember, be nice to Hadrian. He's taking care of me, and he's a very sensitive guy. Don't worry about anything tonight. I know the situation is bizarre, but I can handle it. Don't worry," she repeated, trying to derive comfort from her own words.

Juliette went into the bedroom with some plates, walking delicately like a young doe. Cybele saw her feline, careful steps and smiled to herself. "Another cat. Maybe that's the only kind Mama ever had."

She heard Hadrian's unique tapping on the door and felt the usual wild beating of her heart, the frozen excitement in her limbs.

She switched off the oven and ran to the door. She saw his broad thick face through the peephole, then flung open the door.

"May I come in?" he asked. He smiled coyly and looked up at her engagingly from under his eyebrows. She thought of a large gorilla in the zoo trying to be subtle.

"I'll die if you don't." She smiled back at him ardently, standing with her scantily clad body directly in front of him, wanting to excite him, longing for his approval. He leaned down and kissed her navel. She put her hand on the top of his head while he lapped gently at her stomach.

"Where is Juliette?" he asked, still looking at her with his distinctive expression.

"Why don't you go in and talk to her while I finish the meat?"

"I'm not hungry."

"Dammit, you'd better be, Hadrian, because I went to loads of trouble to make this dinner. Besides, I know Juliette is."

Juliette came into the hallway. "Hadrian, how are you?" she asked. She walked to his side uncertainly, but was nevertheless making a timid effort to follow Cybele's request. Juliette liked Hadrian's evident sensuality and his brilliant, cunning intellect. She was also fascinated by his complete sophistication.

"Juliette, how are you too?" Hadrian asked, and kissed Juliette on her cheek. He used his nasal, British accent for the occasion – the one he always cultivated when he wanted to be especially charming.

"Oh fine, just fine," she replied.

"Tell me, why haven't you any date tonight?" he asked.

Juliette looked swiftly at Cybele, who said, "She did have a date, but you asked me to have her here tonight, remember?"

"Well, Juliette, what do you think of your sister's new life?" Hadrian said smoothly, ignoring Cybele's accusation.

"I think it might work out."

"Might?"

"Well, she'll have a lot of changes. I mean, she's used to living with someone." Juliette propped herself against one of the kitchen cabinets and waited for his reaction. She viewed him carefully. It was obvious that she didn't trust his relationship with Cybele.

"Have you talked with her husband?" he asked, as he steered her into the bedroom.

"No, why would I do that?" Juliette asked.

"Well, you know him."

I know you too, Hadrian," Juliette said, and smiled.

"Do you love me, Juliette?" he asked her in a nasal voice, trying to court her – to charm her with his feigned British tones.

She studied him carefully. "Sure I do, Hadrian. You know that." She put her hand on his shoulder tentatively, afraid of his insistent sexuality. Her lithe, voluptuous body was tense by his side.

Cybele came back into the bedroom with some food.

"What's going on? I can't even turn my back on you before you've put your hand on my man!"

"What's this?" Hadrian asked, looking at the food while he sat lightly on the bed. He drew one leg up and lay back casually on the pillows. He was watching both of the girls with an amused, yet alert stare.

"Dinner, darling, dinner. I suppose you've heard of breakfast in bed – well, this is dinner. . . in bed, so to speak." Cybele looked back at Juliette as she put the plates on the bed. She had to watch two people that night and it made her nervous. She was less graceful than usual.

Juliette sat down at the foot of the bed and lay back on her elbow. Her orange halter draped back away from her breasts, exposing one almost to her nipple. Cybele looked quickly at Hadrian. She knew that he was staring at Juliette's breasts. She felt happy that Juliette was giving him pleasure, but was also jealous of his enjoyment of her sister's body. His darkly glowing eyes excited her as they stared at Juliette's breasts. His stocky body resting so agilely on the bed thrilled her, but her hands were cold and trembling. She hurried back to the kitchen and got the remaining dishes.

"Here, Hadrian," she said, handing him an uncorked bottle of wine and a corkscrew. "You do that."

"OK, I'll do that," he said, emphasising the words "do that", and smiling secretly at her.

"Hey, great," Juliette said. "I love wine." Her voice sounded thin and alone in the musky atmosphere of the room. The muscles of Hadrian's arm rippled under his coat as he struggled to uncork the wine. His yellow shirt was wet with sweat. Rivulets of it ran down his cheeks. Juliette looked helpless and frozen sitting across from him. The room swam in a dark, glow from the dim lamplight.

"And you will love this even more, my dear. It's the best – from Tunis," Hadrian said, and slowly twisted the corkscrew into the pliant new cork. It made a soft, squeaky sound. He was perspiring profusely under his cream-coloured jacket. His thick brocade tie buckled a little under his wide, strong chin.

Cybele noticed its satiny material and wanted to touch it. She put one finger on his tie, bringing her hips close to his elbow as she did so.

"Yes," she said. "This is Hadrian's own special wine." She pushed her finger back and forth along his tie. "He gets it by the case from the Tunisian Embassy because he is the Honorary Consul there."

"What are you doing?" he asked impatiently, and drew away from her finger.

"Trying to caress you," she replied, and felt a violent hatred for him momentarily. She walked back into the kitchen to get the wineglasses, feeling her body tremble from the intensity of her emotion towards him.

From the bedroom she could hear them chattering gaily, and knew that he was unaware of how she felt. When she heard her sister's laughter, she was glad and reassured to know that Juliette was relaxing a little bit.

'She's pretty cool,' Cybele thought. 'Once she gets the situation in place, she can handle it OK.' She held the wineglasses in one hand and reached down to draw Porgy close to her with the other. "Brutt," he purred softly, and looked at her with his large yellow eyes. "You little owl-eyes," she said, and clutched him closer to her until he struggled away.

She stood up and started back into the bedroom. For a moment she contemplated the door in the hallway and thought of just walking out. But she knew that she would return to the bedroom. Her whole body was alive only for the man who sat in there. She walked back into the room and smiled gravely at Hadrian as she handed him the glasses. He looked around the room swiftly. His eyes hunted for something like a hawk.

"Ah yes," he said, putting each glass carefully on the night table. "Turn off the light and start the candle, my beautiful girl, while I pour the wine." She looked at his darkly handsome face, at his wavy hair. It gleamed black, then silver in the light as he bent his head over the wine.

She walked swiftly to the dresser and picked up the large orange candle she had lit so many times before. She stared down at the wick as she lit it, smelling the acrid smoke from the match.

"Cheers," Juliette said as she raised her glass to Hadrian, then handed Cybele hers. "To a romantic couple," she said, and watched both of them suspiciously. They sipped their wine in the gloom and looked uncertainly at one another while they sat together on the bed.

"To both of my beautiful girls," Hadrian said, raising his glass in a toast. He turned towards Cybele and said, "Did you get the grass?"

Cybele slid the door of the night table open. Inside lay two fat white joints twisted tightly at one end. Hadrian smiled. "Good girl, darling." They began to eat. The plates were unsteady on the bed as they cut the thick steaks.

"Ummm, I like this rice," Hadrian said.

"Of course you do. It's Far East rice. Just like home," Cybele said sarcastically. She took a large bite of steak and glared at him.

"Ooops! Oh darling, here." He leaned towards her and wiped her chin gently. "You're spilling the blood."

Juliette started to laugh. "Do you two do this every evening?"

"Do what?" Hadrian asked, and smiled.

When the last piece of meat had disappeared, Juliette and Cybele got up quickly and began to gather the dishes. They looked at each other furtively, one looking at the other when the other one was unaware of the other's glance.

"What now?" Juliette asked when they got into the kitchen.

"Smoke the grass."

"And then?"

"You can always split, you know. Anytime. Smoke a little and then leave."

Cybele shoved the dishes down into the sink, squashing a cockroach as she did so. Juliette hovered near her. One of her thin, tanned arms brushed Cybele's shoulder. She pinched Cybele suddenly and laughed.

"You rat!"

"Oh God, ha ha. I don't know about this set-up," Juliette laughed nervously.

Hadrian was waiting for them like a Buddha on the bed. His belly was full and round. The smile on his face softened his blunt features. He had already lit the grass.

"Here," he said, and handed the joint to Juliette. "You can be first after me, since you are our guest tonight." He pulled Cybele close to his knees and rested his hand on her hips, grasping her flesh in a hard pinch until she gasped. She lay back on him and watched Juliette drag deeply from the joint. The walls of the spacious old room danced with eerie shadows from the large candle. Their bodies were etched in soft, charcoal-like lines by the darkly golden light. In the dresser mirror she saw their reflections. Some flowers that she and Eric had bought several days before were wilting prettily in a vase beside the candle.

"Here," Juliette said. The bell-like tone of her voice brought Cybele's eyes back to her and Hadrian on the bed.

"You know, this is a special type of grass," Cybele said, and sucked a big swallow of smoke into her lungs. She handed the joint back to Hadrian as she held the smoke tightly down in her lungs.

"What do you mean – special?" Hadrian asked.

She pointed to her closed mouth and motioned for him to go ahead and smoke before she answered. He looked at the joint again, then drew it to his mouth. She watched, fascinated by his lips pressing tautly on the cigarette.

"It's an aphrodisiac," she said, letting the smoke flood out of her mouth. She took a gulp of her wine, drinking it like lemonade. "And we have to be careful not to smoke too much. It's very strong."

Hadrian started to answer her, but she quickly pushed her hand against his mouth. He had forgotten to hold the smoke inside.

Juliette was dragging slowly on the joint. Her eyes grew pink from the smoke. She shifted one of her long legs into a better position and leaned back on one arm. Her breasts swayed voluptuously when she shifted her body.

"Juliette, show us your breasts," Hadrian said.

Juliette held onto the smoke a little longer. She gave Cybele a questioning look.

"You can already see her breasts," Cybele said.

"Yes, but I want to see all of them. Please, Juliette, show us. You have such beautiful breasts. Cybele and I just want to look at them." Hadrian inclined his head until the tip of his chin touched his chest and looked up at her from under his shaggy brows.

"Oh now, Hadrian," Juliette said, looking tense and bleary eyed from the grass. "You know I can't do that."

"Oh, why not? Just for a second." He leaned over and deftly pulled her halter open. Juliette grabbed at her top.

"I don't like that," Cybele said.

"Now you mustn't be jealous, darling. I only want to look at them – not touch them." He looked back at Juliette hungrily. "Please," he said again.

"Oh, I'm getting out of here," Juliette said and slid off the bed.

"No, don't go yet," Cybele pleaded and stood up also.

"Well, I want to smoke, but nothing else," her sister told them. She held her hands in firm little fists by her sides. Her knuckles were whitely translucent as she gripped her fingers. "I mean, let's just play, Hadrian," Juliette said and giggled nervously. She ran over to one corner of the room and began to slide up and down on the wall with her back and ass. Suddenly her face contorted. "Cybele! Cybele!" she whispered. "What's that awful thing over there?" Cybele followed her sister's incredulous gaze to the other side of the room.

"What?"

"Don't you see it? Ugh! So black. No, now it's turning green. Oh God, it looks like a sore. It's going to cover the whole room!" Juliette twisted her face to the wall and began to sob.

"Juliette, Juliette," Cybele said. She stooped down and began to stroke the top of Juliette's golden-haired head. "Don't worry," she told her, feeling her own head whirring with a loud, roaring sound. "We won't let it bother you." But at her sister's suggestion she turned her head and also saw the mass of seething matter. It was thick and black and horrible.

"Ahhh! Ahhh, it smells." Juliette writhed up against the wall. "Can't you smell that awful odour? Oh God, oh God, we're all going to rot with it."

"What's going on?" Hadrian asked. He moved slowly up from the bed like an aroused beast.

Juliette darted away from the corner suddenly. She ran to the light switch and flicked it on, then started to run out of the door.

Hadrian turned the light off again and ran after Juliette. He caught her and pushed her back on the bed. He began to kiss her knees. "Your legs aren't as good as Cybele's," he said. "Your breasts are better, but your legs aren't."

Juliette sprang off the bed and ran to the light switch. She seemed frantic to have the room lit.

Hadrian jumped up again and ran over to Juliette like a football player making another touchdown. As soon as she turned the light on, he turned it back off again.

This time Juliette managed to escape from him. She ran back over to the corner of the room near Cybele. Cybele stared unbelievingly at Hadrian as he lumbered towards them.

"Wrrrowwoww, I'm a cat," Juliette said, laughing hollowly. She held one thin arm out to stave him off.

Cybele slinked over beside Juliette and fanned her fingers out on her hip. Her other hand was stretched towards the candle and shook in the air so that her bracelets clattered noisily. "And I'm a gypsy," Cybele said, lifting a scarf off the vanity table and covering her face up to her eyes. "I tell all of my fortunes behind this veil." She reeled back to Juliette. "My first fortune tonight will be on this slinky cat in the corner." She hovered beside Juliette with one hand raised over her head and the other clutching the veil to her mouth.

Juliette pawed the air with her hands and hissed at Cybele. They both shot glances at Hadrian during their play acting.

"This slinky cat in the corner is really a young princess," said Cybele. She looked at Juliette. The lines of her body hinted at voluptuousness, yet they were still fragile and slender with youth. "This princess has the power to cough diamonds from her lovely throat, and when she—" She gasped when she felt Hadrian's strong arm around her naked waist and she looked down in horror at his large hands clutching her belly. "No!" she screeched, and jerked away. "The gypsy cannot be disturbed during a fortune." She held herself between Hadrian and her sister, who still crouched in the corner.

"Now, what can this man be?" she asked, to ward him off. She felt her knees sinking. She fell down to her knees, holding his trouser legs tightly as she did so.

Juliette moved swiftly out of the corner, but Hadrian grabbed her wrist. "Let go!" she cried, and hid herself behind Cybele.

"You bastard!" Cybele said, but the room had melted into different moving angles, like the planes of a Picasso painting.

"Picasso, Picasso," she shouted, and began to dance around in a circle, dodging Hadrian's hands.

"No, no! Rouault, Rouault," Juliette sang back happily. They joined hands and began skipping in a circle.

"Ring around the roses," Cybele sang, feeling her blood pulse in her temples. She leaned over and took a gulp of wine from her glass.

"Pocket full of posies," Juliette sang back. Their eyes met, shining gaily from the grass. Their bodies were wet with the heat from the room. She felt her sister's graceful fingers in her own and clutched them tightly. They were united at last in a weird, desperate dance.

"Come here, you cunt," Hadrian said. He reached out violently for Cybele and began rubbing his hands over her breasts. He pushed his mouth on hers brutally.

"Oh, you've broken the circle," Cybele cried, and began to sob wretchedly. "No, no," she cried when he grabbed her thin body and held it close to his. "Don't do this in front of my sister. Please respect me. My sister. . ."

"Oh, come on, come on. Juliette, take your sister in the bathroom and undress her."

"You're mad – mad!" Cybele cried.

"Juliette, you can kiss your sister. Why not? Go and take off her clothes."

"I don't believe this," Juliette said. Her eyes had become deep blue pools. Their pupils were dark with terror. She started out of the room, but Hadrian grabbed her once more. They began to move in a circle, one after the other, with Juliette trying to escape.

Cybele saw the vase of dying flowers that stood limply beside the mirror. The sweating forehead of Hadrian and her sister's curly blonde hair were going round and round, dissolving into a mass of shapes and colours. The lamp seemed to be sitting on the floor.

Juliette bent close to Cybele and whispered, "Cybele, Cybele, do you see that light?"

Cybele stopped and followed Juliette's eyes to the corner of the room. "Where?"

Juliette clutched her shoulder. Her fingernails bit into her flesh. "There," she pointed, and turned towards her vision. "It's going round and round," she whispered again.

Hadrian stood watching them uncertainly. He looked dizzy. Cybele strained towards her sister's pointing finger. Juliette whirled around and around, as if trying to follow some unseen presence.

"It's going round and round the room – swooping," she said, puzzled. "It's flicking in and out. It wants to attack us." She ran to the opposite side of the room to escape. Cybele ran after her.

"I don't see it," Cybele said. "I want to see it."

Suddenly the features of her face underwent a strange transformation.

Her body became rigid against the wall.

"Don't do it! No! Pierre, Pierre, please don't." The agony in her voice stopped Hadrian from his amorous pursuit.

She grasped her head tightly, then gave a piercing scream. She sank down to the floor and held her hand out in front of her, looking at it with disgust and terror. "Oh no! Oh no!" she moaned. "The blood. The blood is all over my hand."

Hadrian stood looking at Cybele apprehensively.

"Oh God," Juliette said. "This is awful – awful!" She sank back against the end of the dresser, staring at Cybele in distress. Cybele's mental agony had dispelled Juliette's demon.

Hadrian kneeled over Cybele. "Come on, darling. Come and lie down." He lifted her up into his massive arms as if she were a small child. She clung to his neck and stared back at Juliette. Juliette gasped when she saw her sister's face. It was the face of an eight-year-old girl! In the past hour it was as if Cybele had lived several parts of her life.

Juliette followed them uncertainly to the side of the bed and watched as Hadrian lay Cybele down on the bed. Cybele was staring up into the bright ceiling light of the room that they had switched on in order to alleviate the uncanny atmosphere of the room. But it lingered as she lay trembling and moaning in the rumpled yellow sheets.

"Oh no, oh no," she moaned faintly at intervals, turning her head from side to side, but never letting her eyes leave the blinding light.

Juliette sat down beside her and stroked her forehead. "Close your eyes, Cybele. Please don't look into the light like that." But Cybele continued to stare desolately into the lamp. Her face was pale and ravaged by her emotion.

Hadrian got up and turned off the ceiling light. He picked up one of Cybele's hands and rubbed the back of it consolingly.

"Who does she think is beating her?" Hadrian asked. "Her husband?"

"Yes."

"My God," he said, aghast. He looked down at her again. His eyes swept up and down her body hungrily, then peered into her face. He bent down and began kissing her neck. "My beautiful girl, my beautiful girl," he whispered. He began to rub her thighs as he moved his lips to her mouth. Juliette slid off the bed and walked out of the room.

Cybele felt him tugging at her slacks, felt them being slipped down over her hips and legs. He pushed himself into her immediately.

"Darling, darling, I'm going to fuck you all night," he told her. His voice swam in her ears. The sheet under her neck felt like newspapers. She put her hand back to see if that was what they were. He was moving inside her with an unrelenting motion. His dick seemed thicker than usual because of the grass. She felt as if it were the only real thing in her life. It was alone and moving in her. His whole body was like a boulder over her. She looked up at him and cried out, afraid of his face and body over her.

"What's wrong?" he asked, but never ceased his pounding strokes. He bent his head to her nose and began sucking her nostrils. "You can't be afraid of me. We fucked too many times." She put her hands to his chest and touched the black hair there.

"Yes," he groaned, "touch my breast. I like that. You taught me that."

She twisted his large purple nipples between her fingers with pleasure, then put her mouth to one of them and sucked it fiercely. She rubbed her cunt on his leg furiously as she did so.

"That's it, darling. Suck my breast while you come."

"I will, Hadrian. Stick your toe in my cunt while I come so I can pretend two cocks are fucking me."

He pushed his big toe up in her cunt carefully.

"Like that?"

"Oh, yes! Just like that. Now, now move it good and hard," she told him while moving back and forth on his leg. "Ummm, mmm. So good. Oh!" she cried.

"Darling, your ass is so beautiful in the mirror. Oh, I wish you could see her!"

He turned her over and began biting her ass. She spread her legs wide apart and he jammed his fingers up in her cunt.

"Come this way, darling. Come while I eat your beautiful ass."

The sharp, stinging pain that his teeth produced on her backside made her cunt open wider for his big, thick fingers. Her brain whirred from the drug. Her cunt was on fire with desire.

"Oh, I just want to fuck, Hadrian. Oh God. Oh, you good, good dick!"

"Sure, sure, Cybele. We'll fuck the whole night like this."

He turned her onto her back and guided his ample cock back up into her slippery cunt.

She murmured incoherently. Her legs felt like spaghetti. She could feel them dangling limply by his thighs. He stopped at intervals, then began again. He seemed like ten different men, yet he was only one. She noticed that the bedroom door was ajar and wondered where Juliette was. She was sure that she could hear them. She tried to reason why she hadn't thought of this before, but the marijuana clouded her mind.

"I'm sure she can hear us, Hadrian."

"Oh, forget about it. What a fucking we're making. Ohhh." He dropped his head onto her shoulder. She saw his face change. It crumpled out of focus with his emotion. His deep pleasure lit up his handsome face like a light, and the smile of satisfaction that Cybele saw on his mouth thrilled her like nothing else had in her life. Then at last he stopped. She could hear only their breathing in her ears.

"When I'm fucking you, your body becomes entirely cunt, darling," he said. He kissed her over and over by her temple and forehead, holding her head tenderly in his fleshy hands. She felt enveloped by him. His dick was still hard inside her. It had become the centre of her. She only felt his dick. She hardly felt her legs. She had actually become only a cunt. He thrust his cock far down into her cunt again. She moaned with pleasure.

"You want more?" he asked. "You want?"

She reached up to his neck and pulled him down to her.

"Tell me. Tell me," he demanded. "Tell me 'fuck me'."

He began to move in her furiously. She felt a hot pleasure build up with each stroke that he made inside her body. The drug lengthened every sensation that she felt.

"Oh good, good!" she cried. She began laughing. "Yes, do it. Do it!"

"Do what? Tell me."

"Fuck me. Oh God, fuck me with your dick. Oh, he's so good."

She woke up abruptly in the dark room. For a second she couldn't remember where she was. She often had this sensation upon awakening because she had lived in so many hotel rooms in the past few weeks. She saw Hadrian lying stolidly on his side, as if he had passed out. She slid quietly off the bed and ran into the hallway. Juliette was sitting on the floor near the kitchen.

"Juliette, have you just been sitting here all night?"

"Yeah."

"Oh God, Juliette. It's awful, awful."

"I know. I crashed too. There's some sort of evil in this apartment. I don't understand it. I've never been so certain of anything before."

"Yes, I knew that before you came," Cybele said. "That is. . . I was afraid that you might not come if I told you."

"Told me what, Cybele?"

"About the ghost who came here one afternoon."

"Ghost! Cybele, what's happened to you? Are you cracking up?"

"I dunno. What do you think Eric gave us anyway?"

"Whatever it was, I know he did it on purpose," Juliette said, and stared at Cybele's naked thighs. Cybele followed her gaze.

"God, I don't have any pants on!"

Juliette began to giggle. "Natch. For what you've been doing, you don't need them."

Cybele slumped down on the floor, making no effort to cover herself. She put her hand to her cunt. "Oh, I'm wet. I'm wet. Oh no!"

Juliette stared at her with curiosity. "Are you still high?" she asked cautiously.

"Oh yeah. I'm flying. Really."

"This is as bad as acid," Juliette declared.

"Is it? Yeah, I think you're right" She looked towards the bedroom. "He's so still. God, what if the dope killed him? He's an older guy, you know."

Juliette's eyes opened wider as she followed Cybele's gaze into the bedroom.

"We'd really be in a mess then!"

"What do you mean?" Juliette asked. She looked as if she were ready to run away at any moment.

"Well, we might even go to jail. Oh God, Juliette. It's starting again. It's pulling me. Oh, my arms feel like they have razor blades in them."

"Do you want me to call an ambulance?"

"Huh?"

"Do you want to go to the doctor?"

"Well, I can't stand it. Oh, Juliette, I'm in hell, hell! The sex was fantastic, but it just wasn't worth it. Call a doctor."

Juliette picked up the phone and began dialling Information.

"No, no," Cybele said. She took the receiver away from Juliette. "Hadrian would have a fit. There might be a scandal. He'd be ruined. Oh, what can we do? Oh, Juliette, I'm in agony. My head feels like it's being split apart." She sank back down on the dirty carpeting. Its woolly material felt like burrs in her behind.

"I know. It's the same with me," Juliette replied. "I'll take a cab over to Eric's apartment. OK? She stood up, anxious to leave.

"OK, that's a terrific idea. Maybe he'll know what to do," Cybele said desperately.

"Yeah, maybe he'll know some antidote."

"Juliette, you *will* come back, won't you? I feel as though I'm flying apart." She grasped her sister's arm frantically.

"Of course I'll come back. Maybe you can persuade Hadrian to go home." She looked back towards the bedroom. An expression of pain crossed her face.

"OK, OK, hurry. Remember I can't make it without you."

"OK, Cybele." They hugged one another fervently.

"Are you still floating, too, Juliette?"

"Yeah, it's going up and down – the whole room. Isn't it freaky? I'll never smoke this shit again."

"Be careful then," Cybele cautioned her.

Juliette walked out of the door and into the musty odour of the hallway. She clutched her leather handbag. Her fingernails cut into her hand. She looked down at her handbag. She had forgotten what she was holding. She ran down to the elevator, panting like an animal in the heat. The hallway moved in weird angles. She had to keep shaking her head in order to clear her vision. When she got down to the lobby, she had to stop once more and hold onto one of the old, elegant chairs to keep from falling.

"Shit, shit!" she kept saying with her mouth clenched. She looked out at the driveway. The cab hadn't come yet. She reached down into her purse and pulled out her wallet.

"God, Daddy said that I might need an extra five bucks for a cab," she said to no one, and started to laugh. The man at the desk frowned darkly at her.

"Good evening, sir," she said, and bowed so low that she almost fell forward into an old gold sofa. In the mirror she saw herself falling, falling. The furniture seemed to be moving around the lobby. It was covered in red and gold velvet and built in the twenties style. The big, overstuffed chairs looked like the furniture in a whore's boudoir. She looked up at the massive chandelier and screamed.

"Oh!" she exclaimed. "That was close. I mean, it really seemed like it was falling on me."

A cab careened up into the curving driveway. "Cab's here," said the deskman. "If you don't get outta here screaming like a fool, I'm gonna call the cops. Bet you're with that black-haired girl."

The dullness of his voice shocked her. She ran out into the night like a frightened animal.

"Hi," she said to the cabby, and yanked open the door of the cab.

"Be careful," he said. He turned his strangely shaped head towards her and met her eyes with a beady stare. "That door don't work too well."

She looked at him closely when she had got in. One part of his back seemed to be caved into his behind. The front of his chest jutted out like a broken mirror.

'God,' she thought, 'it must be the grass.' She hung her head out of the window as they pulled off, trying to clear her brain with the fresh air. She looked back at the cab driver, hoping to see a normally shaped human being, but he looked the same. She kept the door unlatched, ready to spring out of the cab at any unexpected movement he might make.

"Where to?" he asked, looking back at her nervously. He noticed her hand clutching the door handle, but didn't say anything.

"Oh, it's a house on Q Street. Don't worry, I can show you how to find it," she assured him.

He made a growling noise and turned around. She looked at him more closely and shivered. 'He really is a cripple – it's not the grass. Oh well, I would get one like that,' she thought, then felt ashamed of her pitiless assessment of the man. But she kept the cab door open the whole way down Wisconsin Avenue. It seemed like two days before she heard him say, "OK, lady. Dis is Q Street. Where to?"

"Right over there," she said, looking frantically at the outside of the apartment building, worried that she might have forgotten how the place looked.

He swerved to the kerb with such an abrupt movement that the cab door swung out of her hand and crashed against the kerb.

"Tear it up, tear it up," he mumbled.

She handed him the five-dollar bill and hopped out of the cab, hitting her toe on the hard pavement of the sidewalk. The heat of the night was around her like a heavy blanket. She had to wade through it. She blinked her eyes constantly because they still stung from the grass.

She yanked open the heavy wooden door of the white brick apartment building and ran into the harshly lit hallway. The black lacquered door of Eric's apartment was at the far end. She ran up to it and pushed the bell, still panting from emotion and the night's fetid heat. Soon two dark, coal-like eyes appeared and blinked at her through the peephole.

"Cops!" a black guy yelled in a deep Southern drawl, then flung open the door.

"Hi ya, babe." He grinned at her as he propped himself in the doorway with one long black arm.

"Where's Eric?" she asked.

"Why, Eric is in there learning the pleasures of wine, my sweet, tawny chick." He put his finger out and lifted her chin up. "My, my, de good Lord sure laid a pair of blue eyes on you, darlin'."

"Please, it's a matter of life and death," Juliette entreated him.

"In that case, my lovely lady," he said, and led her down the long hallway of the apartment. They passed Maria and Jeff in the bedroom next to Eric's. They were asleep on the water-bed, looking like two limp dolls. Clothes and books and shoes were scattered about them like confetti. An old kite lay at the head of the bed.

"This child is worried, Eric," the Negro guy said when they walked into the large square living-room.

Eric smiled at Juliette with a dazed, beatific expression, looking like Rodin's *Eternal Spring* brought halfway to life.

"Juliette, m'dear, where's Cybele?" he asked, still sitting in his trance-like position with the pneuma of a child.

Juliette ran up to him breathlessly. The other faces and shapes in the room were a blur to her.

"Oh God, Eric, you gotta come. Cybele's in trouble."

Eric sat for one instant longer on the black leather footstool that extended out from under his narrow hips like a spongy mushroom. Then he leapt up with his wineglass still in his hand.

"What's happened?" He looked down at his hand absently when some of the wine sloshed over his wrist.

"She's sick. Oh, Eric, she's really bad off!"

"Goddammit, I'm going to kill that bastard!" Eric threatened. He stood in a state of immobilised passion. Little flakes of marijuana fell from his jeans and sprinkled down around his feet.

"Where is she?" he asked.

"At her apartment."

"Goddammit, let's go," he said again without moving.

"OK, OK!" Juliette said, yanking him by his arm.

At her touch he seemed to come alive, and they both ran out of the apartment and into the hallway. "Is he still there?" Eric asked.

"I don't know. I think so."

"C'mon, then," he said, pulling her towards his dark green Triumph.

Juliette felt as though she were in the hands of a rash child. Eric wrenched the emergency brake out of its upright position as he gunned the motor, then pushed down hard on the accelerator. The car bolted off with several jerky movements. Juliette held her old brown leather bag tightly in one hand, the other she used to clutch the "sissy" bar. She looked over at Eric. His hair was blowing wildly in the wind, and his eyes looked demented behind his thick glasses. They were reflected by the glare of the street lights like spreading amoebas.

"Eric, please don't go so fast. We'll get stopped by the cops."

"Fuck 'em, fuck 'em," he said as they flew through a red light.

She stared at the side of his face. He was working his mouth furiously back and forth over his gums. She began to laugh. Her body felt light and tingling, as if she had turned into a string of bells.

"Are you hysterical?" Eric asked.

"I think so," she replied and giggled again.

"Well, don't go off on me now. We've got to save your sister."

The car idled in her ears like the strong healthy wings of a summer bug while they stopped at the Wisconsin and Massachusetts intersection. She saw Eric squint up at the old apartment building where Cybele lived. The name of the building appeared in blue lights which were strung eerily across the entranceway. Several of the letters were not lit, and the irregular pattern of the lights gave the building a foreboding appearance.

"I'm going to beat the shit out of that old dude," Eric said, squeezing the steering wheel as if he wanted to break it. He shot off again across Wisconsin Avenue and careened into the back parking lot of the building. He yanked open the car door and said, "Look, you wait for me in the hall. I'm going in there and see what's up."

Juliette ran up beside him apprehensively. She stared at the golden brown hair around his tiny nipples. He had on a denim jacket that was left unbuttoned and showed most of his bare chest. Both of their faces gleamed white from the parking lot lights. They lit up their fear and uncertainty in small shining patches.

"Eric, are you sure you'd better go in?"

"Whaddaya mean? Of course I'll go. I'm going to tear his ass."

She ran along beside him, still holding her old brown bag. "I don't know, Eric. If there's a fight, the cops might come. Then they'd find the grass and we'd all get it."

They stood by the grey elevator door at the back entranceway. Stacks of old newspapers were lined up on the side of the hall and tied with thin wires, ready to be hauled away. Juliette watched dully as an extraordinarily large cockroach crawled towards them. 'Probably his favourite bed for the night,' she thought. She pictured Eric's narrow little bed in his curious den-like room, the stacks of books on his dresser and the clothes tumbling out of his closet. She sighed. Her long, beautiful legs hurt and she yearned to sit down.

They got on the elevator and slumped against its cold walls.

"I wish you'd stop mentioning cops," he said. "You're beginning to give me the creeps." He pulled out a small pouch of grass and began rolling a joint. "One for the road," he laughed, and handed the joint to her. She took it, then handed it back quickly.

"Oh, no, I've had enough."

They got to the fifth floor and padded out onto the thick red carpeting. The silence of the hallway filled their ears like a thick plug. Their bodies were encased in its cool air. They walked along carefully, like men on the moon getting used to a new stratosphere.

"Eric, really, why don't you let me go in first? I'll just see what's going on. Maybe Hadrian has even left."

"That old goat."

"Shhh," Juliette whispered when they heard an apartment door being opened.

She shrank back against the wall involuntarily.

"Well, okay." But one word," he said, working his mouth back and forth over his gums again, "Just one word from you and that old dude's screwed his last tonight."

"Ha ha. Oh, Eric, you're a riot." 'If you only knew,' she thought to herself, 'how 'that old dude' can screw.' She remembered the sounds from the bedroom, remembered creeping around the corner and secretly watching Hadrian and her sister about twenty minutes before the room began to swim before her eyes again.

"Pssst!"

"Huh?" She whirled around and saw Eric holding out a key to the apartment. She ran up to him and clutched his arm apprehensively.

"Eric, please, you scared me."

"Stay calm. That's what me old platoon commander always said."

"Platoon commander? Oh, Eric, you can't have been in any war! I mean, there hasn't even *been* a war in the past five years or so."

"One so minor it's probably slipped your mind – Vietnam."

"Oh. . . were you there?"

"*Oh, were you there?*" he mimicked her voice. "Here, take this key, will ya', and get going. This show's gotta get on the road. I can't stay up all night. Got some really 'classic stuff' coming in early tomorrow morning." He handed her the key and then slumped back into a corner to wait.

She put the key in the big, oversized gold lock and opened the door. She trembled as she walked back into the dreaded hallway once more, then closed the door softly, listening for any sounds.

"Hey," Cybele said. Juliette peered into the gloom of the living-room.

"It's just me," Cybele said. "I'm sitting here talking to my toes and the ghost of this establishment."

"What?" Juliette asked, and walked cautiously over to her sister. She smelled a strong disinfectant. Its fumes made her aware of the polluted atmosphere in the apartment.

"Oh, he's here all right," Cybele said, looking up at Juliette. The whites of her eyes were bloody from grass and there were dark circles underneath them. She kept trying to pull her short yellow top down over her naked hips with her toes. Juliette felt a wave of impatience at the spectacle of her on the sofa. 'Always fucking up her life,' she thought.

"Where's Hadrian?"

"I think he passed out."

"Well, Eric's here." She studied Cybele's reaction carefully, hoping to jolt her out of her unattractive apathy.

She leapt off the loveseat. Her top bounced up to her breasts, leaving her nude from the waist down. "Where?" she cried. She seemed to have forgotten about her nakedness.

Juliette found herself easily ignoring her sister's body. Cybele had taken on the aspect of a child again, one totally immersed in the moment.

"Hiding in the hall," Juliette said, and they suddenly began jumping up and down like two mad rabbits from *Alice in Wonderland*, screaming and laughing as they used to do as children.

"Oh God, oh God," Cybele groaned as she stumbled out of the living-room, still laughing. "This is the best scene yet, isn't it, Juliette? Much better than anything we could have got with my husband!" She turned back around to her sister. Juliette's face looked ravaged in the brightly lit hallway.

"It's far out all right." She looked at Cybele sadly. Her blue eyes were large and haunting in the shadow of her face.

"What should I do?" Cybele asked her. She stood in front of Juliette, twisting the tie knob of her blouse, still ignoring her nakedness. Her hair was tangled in black, wild-looking snarls. She looked like a sea nymph as she stood there with one foot placed over the other.

"Why don't you persuade Hadrian to leave?" She stared at Cybele again with chagrin, letting her mind float away from the reality of their predicament on the heady waves of grass, dreaming for a moment and trying not to think of the bizarreness of the situation.

"That's a great idea!" She ran up to Juliette and kissed her. "You're really helping me." When she turned and ran towards the bedroom, Juliette couldn't keep from laughing again at the sight of her naked ass that jiggled like Jello with the movement of her legs.

Cybele pushed the bedroom door open cautiously with one finger. She peered into the darkness of the room until her eyes became accustomed to its shadows, then she tiptoed over to the side of the bed where Hadrian lay woodenly on one side. He was completely still, and his stillness was forbidding. It preserved his presence there as if he were awake and watchful.

"Hadrian," she whispered softly, touching him as she might touch a dangerous animal. He kept breathing deeply and smoothly. "Hadrian." She pushed one of his thick, muscular arms. He groaned. "Please, Hadrian, you have to go." She shook him more vigorously, all the time looking at his curling black hair on the yellow pillowcase.

He rolled over and stared up at the ceiling. "What time is it?"

She crawled over him and sat on his stomach. "Why do you always ask me that when you're the only one around this place with a watch?" She leaned down and kissed him.

"Oh, you want more?"

"Hadrian, darling, if I get any more, they'll have to pour me into a jar."

He fumbled on the night table for a cigarette.

"No, Hadrian, it's time for you to leave."

"Leave? Are you serious? I told my wife I was going to New York tonight."

She stared at his large sensual head, then leaned down to kiss him. "Well, you'll just have to tell her you got back 'cause Juliette's ready to go to bed."

"But Cybele, darling, I shall have a wreck. I'm dizzy. Let's all sleep together."

"You know we can't do that."

"But why not? You sleep between us."

"No!" she shouted.

"Don't scream. I'm going." He slid off the bed and began to dress. "There's a reason why you want me to go. I know you."

"None except that we're sleepy."

"Don't play with me, Cybele."

"Oh shit, let's not talk anymore. You call me tomorrow and we'll start planning another orgy." She sat on one of the pillows like a sad-eyed cat, weary from the various battles of that particular night.

"Oh, I hate that," he said with his voice becoming very nasal. "I hate it when you start to be sarcastic with me."

"Hadrian darling, *please*. I'm just *so* tired. Can't you understand that?"

"You're tired because you're lying to me." He pushed his hair back with one wide, blunt hand, and slipped his gold watch over his wrist. "Has Juliette been here the whole time?"

"No." She looked at him steadily.

"Ha! What I thought exactly. *How* did she get back here? Eric brought her?"

She kept looking at him while still sitting on the pillow. He flung himself across the bed towards her and grasped one of her arms. "Eric is here, isn't he?"

"No. Dammit. Get out of here, will ya?"

He stood up, folding his tie carefully and putting it into one of his pockets. "I'm going, Cybele, but don't think I don't know what's going on."

"Oh, you don't know anything."

"I know," he said wisely. He walked back to one of the night tables before he left the room and pulled out his wallet. She watched as he put several bills into the drawer. At the sight of his perfunctory movements she felt a rage boiling up within her. The money incensed her. She ran over to the table, still naked, and grabbed the money out of the drawer.

"Don't leave me this!" she screamed.

"Keep it, darling – to pay your gigolo with." He drew his cigarette up to his mouth swiftly and smiled ironically at her. "You'd better go to bed, you look awful."

She clenched her fists, trembling. Her hair was wild and tangled. She smelled of vomit that she had thrown up earlier in the evening.

"You see! You see!" she cried.

"What, darling?" He pressed his hand to her face and smoothed her hair back from her hot temple in a gentle, cruel gesture.

"You see that you *knew* what was going on. You knew where I was going to get the grass." He began walking towards the bedroom door. She ran after him. "Aren't you going to talk to me, you bastard – you *old* bastard?" She felt her whole body vibrate with rage and frustration.

"Oh, I have had enough. I have had enough," he said, and picked up his briefcase.

"You knew we had to ask Eric for the grass," she screamed at him, following him out of the room like a wild cat. "You didn't give a damn – just so that you could come up here and turn yourself on at the expense of me and my sister.

"I wouldn't fuck your sister, darling. She's not my type."

"Whaddaya mean, you old goat?"

He turned his face back to her, looking as if he had been struck by her physically. "Who taught you to say that? Old goat? Those aren't your words. You never insulted me like this before."

"What do I mean?" She stood slumped against the wall, feeling all the hatred and anger dissolve inside her as she contemplated the stricken look on his face. "I mean, my sister wouldn't *want* to fuck an old man – *that's* what I mean. I mean, you're *repulsive* to her."

"You whore!" He reached out and grabbed at her, pinching her shoulder as she struggled away from him.

"Oh yeah? Well, maybe your wife would like to know about your little whore?" She laughed hysterically.

He stood with both of his fists clenched. "You do that and I'll break your neck."

"Yeah? Well, you'll see. Bright and early tomorrow she'll get my call." She walked past him with an exaggerated swagger. He hit her between her shoulder blades with his fist. She fell down at his feet, staring dismally into the matted, dirty carpeting. He had begun to speak in another language, his rage was so great. She listened with curiosity, trying to understand which language it was. All the while, she was trying to get her breath back from the stunning blow. 'Turkish,' she thought smugly. He stepped over her and walked out of the door, carrying his expensive leather briefcase smartly by his side.

After she heard the door close, Juliette ran into the hallway. "He hit you!" she cried in dismay. She looked down at her sister lying on the old carpeting like a crumpled sack. "Cybele – my God. What have you got into now, if he hits you just like your husband did when you were married?"

Cybele staggered up and looked down at her naked body in horror. "God, I'm nude!"

Juliette remained silent. Her clear blue eyes pierced Cybele's consciousness, rejuvenated her. "Where's Eric?" she asked.

"Guess he's still out in the hall."

"Go get him, will you? Oh wait, let me take a shower – oh, well, just go and get him and I'll get ready in the bathroom." She stared down at her toes. They were tanned brown from the summer sun. She felt as if she had become a child again in her little Southern hometown – always barefoot and tanned, usually scantily clad. "You know, Juliette," she said, "I used to be like a little Indian – innocent and carefree. . ."

"Get in there, Indian," Juliette said, laughing again in spite of the situation. "Believe me, you're still an Indian." She watched Cybele shed her top and step into the bathtub. "You just grew up physically, that's all," Juliette said to herself as she walked back to the door. She flung open the door and called, "Eric, get in here!" She saw a mass of curls sticking out from the trash shute door. "All's clear, as your old platoon leader would say."

Eric smiled beatifically and floated out from the trash closet like an insubstantial angel.

"I know. I know, I saw him leaving."

"Why didn'tcha come out then?" She observed his face and body, with pleasure. It seemed to shimmer like diamonds under the lights of the old chandeliers in the hallway. It was fragmented and moving softly from one place to the other. She had the feeling that if she reached out her hand to touch him, it would go through one of the illusionary holes.

"I don't know – doesn't pay to be too quick, m'dear. . . in anything."

He winked at her meaningfully. "I mean, maybe the dude was going to forget something and come back." He let the trash closet door slam behind him and jumped at the sound of it.

Juliette thought of him racing over wildly to save Cybele. 'Maybe I shouldn't have cautioned him so much,' she thought. She studied his khaki pants, quickly bypassing the bulge of his groin that showed so prominently, trying to forget how horny she was – how she hadn't had a man for over a month now. She started when she understood how akin she was physically to her sister.

"We even smell the same," Cybele had told her as they had sat on the bed together studying French one afternoon many years ago.

'God, she says the most intimate things,' Juliette thought. 'And so casually – as if it were the weather report.' Juliette hovered over the vast enigma of her sister, touching down and then soaring off – puzzled.

"Is she OK?" Eric asked.

"Huh? – oh, yeah. Come on in. She'll be waiting for us."

She followed Eric as he stalked along the hallway.

"Cybele, luv," he called uncertainly after she had opened the door. He saw her standing in the doorway of the unlit bedroom.

"Hi," Cybele said. Her voice shook with fatigue.

Eric rushed up to her and grabbed her thin arms with his short, blunt fingers. "M'god, you look awful," he said, pushing her hair back from her wet brow.

"Thanks." She tottered backwards a little, setting her mouth in a pitiful, resolute expression.

"Get in here," Eric said, assuming a protective role. She followed him, with her hand linked loosely in his, then she leaned down to pick up the cat.

"And leave that Goddamned animal alone." He pushed her onto the bed. She fell back on the pillows like a broken doll. "You looked so great when I left you," he said, and peered into her face with chagrin.

"*What* was that stuff you gave us anyway?" Juliette asked, leaning on the chest of drawers, tired. She looked at the piece of furniture with detachment – like someone remembering the events of a dream.

'A dream,' she thought with disgust. 'More like a nightmare,' she decided.

"Ha ha – that, m'dear was an aphrodisiac. Used under the right circumstances and with the right people, it's a jewel of a weed." He put his hand on Cybele's tangled hair. "Obviously, both were lacking in this case."

"Horrible," Cybele mumbled. "Oh, Eric, I wish you had been here. Oh, I missed you."

Eric turned to Juliette. "Your sister's a strange bird. She's with one dude and she misses another guy."

Juliette laughed. "Maybe she just uses one for one thing and the other for another."

"Yeah, but she told me she was trying to get out of that."

Cybele wobbled up into a sitting position. "Please stop talking about me as though I'm not here."

Eric leaned down to her face. "Oh, you're here. We're well aware of that." He studied her eyes, relaxing in their shining green colour. She felt his soft lips on hers. They were fuller and softer than Hadrian's.

"You have a mouth like a baby's ass, Eric."

"You fucking female."

"Hey, Eric, better take me back to the apartment," Juliette said, impatient that it was her sister who ended up with a man again, and not herself.

"Oh, OK, don't get your ass up on your shoulders." He grinned and kissed Cybele once more. "I'll be back."

Juliette and Eric walked towards the door. As Eric opened it they heard the bed creak.

"He's the only one who makes me feel secure," they heard her say in a slurred, weak voice.

Eric and Juliette turned to see Cybele standing up nude on the bed. They stopped, frozen with the spectacle of her. She swooped down to the night table and yanked open the drawer.

"Money, baby, money!" She waved the bills that Hadrian had left threateningly at them. "Well? Well?" She threw the green bills towards them. "Ain't it what counts?" Her mouth twisted unattractively with her emotion. "I mean, it counts so much with Hadrian, and he's so wise. So. . " she said, falling down into the pillows. "So it must be."

They walked out and left her mumbling to herself. They were both unusually silent.

When Eric came back to the apartment, he found her sleeping peacefully. The light was still on. He peeled off his clothing completely, then slid into the bed beside her. He began to kiss her ears. She smiled, then scratched herself violently. "No," she said, without conviction.

He kissed her breasts, holding the hand she had used to scratch herself with away from her body. "Always so self-destructive," he whispered. He moved his hand to her cunt. "Hey! you're wet." He began to slide his full, wide mouth over her mouth, over her body, as he hoisted himself up on top of her.

Chapter Nine

The next morning she awoke to the alien glint of early morning sunshine trying to pierce its way through the new brocade drapes. Inside the bathroom she heard Eric splashing water around. He came back into the bedroom hurriedly. 'Off for his latest business conference,' she thought ironically as she watched him pull at his tangled curls, using his fingers like a comb. She closed her eyes and licked the outside of her mouth. It felt numb and dry. Her eyes burned. She moved her limbs slowly under the cool sheets, feeling their soreness. Then she lay still, waiting patiently for him to leave. Soon she heard the click of the lock.

She sprang out of bed and ran into the living-room. Her cat blinked sleepily at her in the sunshine from his bed that he had made on the old green sofa. Even though it was only nine o'clock in the morning, the room was hot and burning from the sunlight that streamed through the french doors. She stretched her arms up and touched the chandelier, pushing it gently to make it go round and round.

Then she walked to the pillows that covered the old black telephone. She threw them around the hallway and picked up the receiver. After she had dialled the number she slid down to the floor and squatted by the phone.

"Halloe," she heard his nasal, foreign voice say. She carefully replaced the receiver, rubbing her swollen eyes with one hand as she did so. She trailed into the kitchen and opened the heavy door of the refrigerator. She looked into it vacantly for several seconds, then slid a large jar of Safeway orange juice out. She raised the big heavy jar to her cracked lips and gulped the juice greedily. Porgy mewed hungrily behind her.

She opened some cat food for Porgy then strolled back to the phone. She lifted the receiver up wearily and plonked the jar of orange juice down beside her leg as she seated herself on the floor.

258

She dialled Hadrian's home number again, then waited, hoping that his wife would answer.

"Heelooo?"

"Mrs Abdullah?"

"Yes?"

"Mrs Abdullah, you don't know me, but I know your husband. He's been supporting me for the past two years." She paused, waiting for some reaction.

"He bought me a new car this year."

"Oh really? What kind?" she heard the cold twangy voice say.

"You know, Mrs Abdullah, your husband is over here almost every day. He even comes in the afternoon." She waited breathlessly, furious and blinded by her anger for Hadrian.

"Really? Well, you two have fun," the woman said in a stunned, but defensive tone.

"Oh, we do. He kisses me all over my body," Cybele retorted.

"Oh good," she heard her say calmly, but she could tell that Hadrian's wife was surprised.

"Tell me, are you sure this isn't some gag? Are you really real?"

"Oh, I'm real, Mrs Abdullah. I'll even give you my name. It's Cybele Tashery, and my address is 1600 Massachusetts Avenue."

"It's hard to believe you're real."

"Last night Hadrian came home at 3 a.m., right?"

"I was asleep."

"Sure, you're always asleep. He says he hates to sleep with you. He says he never touches you."

"Oh, he touches me," she said. The woman's voice was trembling now. Cybele noticed the crushed tone of her voice with satisfaction.

"Well, he says he never does." Cybele felt dizzy from the sound of her own words echoing in her ears. She felt as if she were delivering mortal blows with a knife to another human being. But she kept on and on, drunk with the misery that she heard in the other woman's voice. "Anyway, he must be the world's sexiest man if he does touch you, because he comes here at least four times a week, and it's never just once when he makes love."

"Having fun? Having fun?" Hadrian's wife asked. Her voice was tight and choked.

"He made me come to your house during the holidays. I can describe your bedroom to you. I didn't want to come there. He made love to me right in your bed. Tell me, Mrs Abdullah, aren't you curious about the way I look? Wouldn't you like to see me?"

"Describe yourself to me."

"Well, I have dark hair."

"What colour are your eyes?"

"Why do you ask me about my eyes?"

"Because he always likes the eyes."

"They're green. Don't you have green eyes?"

"No, I do not."

"Well, I have beautiful green eyes. Hadrian worships my eyes."

"How old are you?"

"I'm very young."

"How young?" the woman asked sharply.

"I'm twelve years younger than you, and I'm very slender. "You're. . . more fat."

"What do you suppose Hadrian will do when he finds out that you've called me?"

"He'll get rid of me, of course. That's what I want. I'm sick of the situation. I just thought you should know. I mean, my husband knows, and Hadrian said I was his wife No. 2."

"He said that?" she asked angrily.

"Yes, he did. So I thought that wife No. 1 should know about wife No. 2."

"You're right. Wife No. 1 should now start looking for husband No. 2."

"If you want to meet me, you can come here."

"No, I don't think I'll do that." Her voice had become cool again, remote.

Cybele thought quickly, trying to make up another remark that would melt the woman's iciness.

"I saw your books lying on the table at Christmas when I came to your house – math books. Hadrian says that you took French for five years and still couldn't speak a word.

"Oh, you know so much. Yes, I'm not very linguistically inclined."

"I know your mother was sick. I prayed for her."

"You sound like a very nice person."

"You know, I tried to get away from your husband. But he was after me every minute. I left my husband for him." She hurried on with her conversation. Her words tumbled out of her mouth like ABC blocks. She said everything that came to her mind. "Tell me, how do you live, Mrs Abdullah, without any love?"

"Well, we have an arrangement."

"You sound so cold. Yet you're young. You're pretty. I've seen you before. I feel sorry for you."

"And I feel sorry for you, dear. You sound just like I did ten years ago – and now I really must go."

"OK, go. But think about seeing me. I know you won't forget my call." She clunked the receiver down and stood up, staggering slightly. She went back to the bed, but knew that she would be unable to sleep. She lay for about an hour in a semi-conscious state, drifting between dreaming and waking intermittently. Finally she sat up, seeing an explosion of stars when she did so. Her head pounded, and inside her stomach strange animals seemed to be eating one another. She weaved into the bathroom and stepped inside the tub.

'Where can I go?' she thought. She turned the water on and squatted under it, watching it rush over her thighs. Suddenly she thought of Brandon.

"Of course! I'll go to Brandon's. Maybe he'll be in a good mood. I'll go there and tell him everything."

She washed herself hurriedly, dropping the soap often in her haste.

"I gotta get out of here. I gotta go somewhere or I'll go nuts."

She started to cry, but kept on washing her face furiously. She turned the shower on full blast, then decided not to catch any water for an oil bath the way she usually did after she had bathed. She didn't want to take any extra time.

On the way to Brand's music shop, she glanced anxiously into the cabby's mirror. She was surprised to see that her face looked fresh, as if untried by the events of the night and that morning.

'God, I hope he's in a good mood,' she thought, and lifted the backs of her legs up a little from the sticky plastic seat of the cab. It was eleven in the morning but already ninety degrees.

She walked slowly into the music shop, looking hopefully into its gloomy interior for Brand. He appeared behind his rough, wooden desk almost like a mirage.

"Brandon," she sang out, like a little bird.

"Yes, dear," he said wearily. He put on one of his wide, syrupy grins. "I'm here – for one and all." He bent his head over the old tin ashtray as he put out a Lucky Strike. She stared at the thick curly blondness of his hair, then looked at his fingers mashing out the burning coal. She was amazed that he didn't burn his fingers, since the stub of the cigarette was so short. She saw about twenty other small white stubs in the ashtray, all crushed to the nub in the same way.

"Brandon," she sang out again. She touched him lightly on his arm, as if she were afraid to actually make contact with him.

"I don't like the sound of that sweet voice," he said and looked at her with his grey-green eyes unblinkingly for a full minute.

"Brand, I'm innocent," she protested. She opened her eyes wide and held her hands out imploringly to him.

He stood up from the desk and walked towards the door. She followed him outside of the shop. His legs were long and slim in his blue denim pants. The shirt he wore looked Southern. It was a blue and red plaid.

"You look like a fancy farmhand, Brand."

He put his arm around her loosely and laughed.

"Now don't try to change the subject, angel-face. You may be innocent, Cybele, in fact I *know* you're innocent. But you're dangerous, baby."

"What would you do if I told you I'm *not* innocent?"

He leaned back on the black pipe fence that divided his shop from a basement stairway next door, never taking his deep-set eyes from her face.

"Don't stare at me so solemnly, please," she begged. She shifted her weight from one foot to the other nervously. "Besides, it makes you look kinda strange with that expression in your eyes." She leaned back on the fence next to him in order to escape his gaze.

"Oh, honey, I'm just waiting to hear this next little tale you're about to lay on me."

She glanced back at the side of his face. It looked boyish in the sunlight of late morning, framed like a choirboy by his curly blond hair. He kept looking straight ahead as if waiting for something.

"You'll never guess what I did this morning!" she said with a rush.

"You're right. I probably couldn't," he agreed, and looked at his watch. "As a matter of fact you're usually not even up at this time of day." His face registered surprise.

"I know. I couldn't sleep." She took a deep breath that stretched her lungs out to their maximum extension and filled them suddenly with so much oxygen that she almost fell backwards over the fence.

Brandon placed her back into an upright position and said, "Steady there, my little mare. They shouldn't have let you out of the stable this morning."

"I couldn't sleep," she continued, "so I called Hadrian's wife." She looked at him quickly.

"That must have been a lovely conversation," Brandon said, twitching one side of his nose spasmodically. She thought of a rabbit when he did this – a nervous one.

"Well, you could say it was interesting. I mean – gimme one." He handed her a cigarette, then put one in his mouth. The match flared up blue in the stark sunlight. "She's not going to forget me for a long time." She dragged on her cigarette like a drunk Indian.

"Yes, you do have that ability – to make people remember you, Cybele. The question is, *how* they remember you!" He twisted his hand on her kneecap. "May I be so bold as to ask what *did* you talk about?"

"About Hadrian, of course."

"Oh, of course. About what a great guy he is?"

"In a way, yes. I told her what a lover he is, about how generous he is – things like that." She slid up onto the fence and held herself there by clenching her legs on the railing. "Then I invited her over for a cup of tea so that she could see what I look like." She swayed like a swan on the fence, laughing at Brandon's expression with satisfaction.

"What a cup of tea that would be, sweetheart," Brand remarked wryly.

"Yes, if I were her I'd be dying to meet me." She swayed some more. Brand grabbed her around her waist and lifted her down from the fence.

"You've got a small waist, Cybele."

"Sure, are you just noticing? Your timing is all off, Brand."

He squinted at her from under his bushy blond eyebrows. His hands still rested lightly around her waist. The brilliance of the early sunlight made his eyes glint like two green marbles as he stared at her steadily.

"Oh, I've been noticing a lot of things," he said.

"What things?" She put her arms around his neck and hugged him impetuously.

He pinched her on her thigh. "Stick around and you'll find out."

"Oh, don't kid me. You'd pay more attention to me if I were a violin."

"Cybele, you're so funny. You really look petulant. Put your lower lip out a little more and you'll look like a nigger!"

"Nigger! Brand, honey, I do believe you're from the South." She dropped her arms from their tentative embrace around his neck. "What *do* you think about my phone call?"

"There you go again, honey, asking me those questions. What do you think Hadrian will do about it?"

"Who gives a damn?"

"That's a switch."

"If you knew what he did last night. . ."

"Honey, I wouldn't be surprised at anything Hadrian might have done to you."

"He wanted to have an orgy with me and my sister!"

"I think I'll have a Lucky Strike on that," Brand said, laughing nervously.

"Well, he did. He got Eric to get some grass for us even."

"I've never doubted that Hadrian has always used everyone – unsparingly," he said, and put his cigarette up to his mouth in a gesture that reminded Cybele of her husband. "He's got a slight problem with his usual game this time though."

"What's that?"

"Well. . ." Brandon languished the word in his soft, Southern drawl. "He just happens to adore you, that's all. I don't think he realises how much."

She whirled around to Brandon, grabbing his hand and kissing it. "Oh, Brand, Brand, you say the most wonderful things! What would I do without you?" She kissed his hand again.

"Hey, cool it, sweetheart." He glanced anxiously at two guys passing by them on the street. "People are going to think we're running an indecent show around this place. Let's go back inside the shop and talk this situation over."

"Oh Brand, Brand!" she exclaimed again, holding his hand as she might have done with one of her cousins while they played years ago. The sound of his soft-spoken voice drawling "situation" comforted her, made her remember once again her small home town where all of the people in her life were essentially like Brand. There had always been an answer – some sane, logical plan to follow. Nothing had floated then as it seemed to do so often these days. She skipped along happily beside him, trying to figure out why he was so solid for her. Why could she sit for hours in the cool gloom of his music shop with nothing more to do than swat at an occasional fly and rock in an old rocking chair, and feel perfectly contented? Her thoughts drifted back to her grandmother's house and the way she had ridden her bike over to the steps of the rambling white veranda as a child. Again and again she returned there in her memory to sit in the slatted green swing that had hung at one end of the porch. She imagined the leafy pecan trees whose branches surrounded the wide, sloping porch and poked their way between the tall white columns of the veranda. At any moment she could run into the house and find her grandmother cooking something delicious in pots that seemed larger than she was, or showing a maid how to do a chore that she would later do herself.

Brandon sat down behind his wide, wooden desk. The youth of his face was accented by the old cash register sitting on one side of the desk.

"Now, honey, listen to me," Brand began.

She settled back into the thick, curving arms of the rocking chair. Its richly gleaming wood was warm under her hands.

"He's hung up – maybe for the first time in his life. And he's going to play every trick he can think of to get out of it, believe me."

"But why does he want to get out of it?" she asked.

"Cybele, you're so naïve. That's another thing that gets him. He knows that you're completely different from anyone in his life."

"What do you mean by that?"

"I mean, sweetheart, that he's used to everyone using him for money or to gain something, and he's a master of playing the same game back at them and beating them."

"But Brandon, what does that have to do with me?"

"That's exactly what I mean, dear. You're totally different from all the other situations he deals with every day, and I'm surprised he has anything to say around you. But he knows that his love for you gives you a certain amount of control over him – and he wants complete control over people."

"He doesn't talk much. I mean, when I ask him to tell me his secret thoughts he tells me he doesn't have any." She looked perplexed.

Brandon laughed. "I wish I had a tape of a conversation between the two of you."

"But Brandon, I've got to explain it properly to you. That's one of the things I like about Hadrian – his silence, his foreignness, you know?"

"Oh, I know. I'm as masochistic as you are. Why do I sit in this shop all day and put up with the drivel that slops through here?"

"I mean, when he's angry and shouts at me – it's the strangest feeling, but that's when I feel loved more than any other time."

"Oh, I know. I know." His voice trailed off as he stubbed out another cigarette. The phone rang so shrilly that he jumped. He stared down at the old black receiver as if it were alive and dangerous. It rang once more before he carefully lifted the receiver.

"Hello," Cybele heard him say. When he heard the voice on the other end of the line, she saw his face change into a worried, excited expression.

"C.W., you're as drunk as a skunk," he said, hastily lighting another cigarette.

"Um hm, um hm. Well, just don't bother coming to see me. There's no money here." Cybele listened in amazement as she heard Brandon's voice disintegrate from its boulder-like calm into an agitated whine.

"Oh, don't tell me, C.W! Just don't try to tell me. You just want to come here to get some money out of me and then leave on one of your trips."

Brandon was more excited than Cybele had ever seen him. His face was flushed. His whole body stood at attention from the sound of the voice on the phone. She felt a curious stab of jealousy and began to rock nervously in her chair.

"Oh, don't tell me, Crag. Where are you? Oh yeah? Well, you may as well take right on off on another plane." Brandon glared down at the phone. His eyes were like flints striking sparks. "Don't you *dare* come here!" he shrieked. Cybele stopped rocking. She felt as if they were about to be attacked.

"I'll lock the door of this shop if you come. I swear I will, Cragmont!" He hung up abruptly. His face looked haunted. All of the blood had drained from it, leaving it like a limp paper cup.

"Gosh, Brandon, what's going on?" He looked past her with a wild, distraught expression in his eyes. His mouth jerked with a spasmodic tic. Then his eyes locked back into focus with hers.

"Ghosts, darling. Old, forgotten skeletons jumping out of their closets."

"It must be quite a ghost."

"Oh, he's a winner – as far as ghosts go."

"Is he coming?"

"I'm afraid so," he replied and sighed.

'He's so peculiar,' she thought, 'protesting, yet pleased.' She glanced at him again. He wasn't paying any attention to her. She felt forlorn, like a child who has had one of their toys taken away.

"Well, what will we do when he gets here?" she asked, trying to get him to answer her. His confusion and excitement made her giddy. The floating sensation came back and bore her away.

They sat in an apprehensive silence. Brandon had forgotten Cybele completely. Her body had assumed an abandoned attitude in the rocking chair. She didn't bother to hold her legs in a provocative position. She felt like leaving, but in her situation even his confusion was something for her to grasp. Besides, she felt that he might need her to protect him.

The jangling bell on the door of the shop invaded the silence and made them sit upright. Brandon stood up uncertainly when he saw an impassioned young man stride through the door. Cybele studied the intruder carefully. He was deceptively tall. The bulk of his muscular body diminished the length of his legs. She saw him look at her furtively from under his bushy, eyebrows. His eyes were hazel-coloured and ridged with plentiful black lashes. They looked as if they had been kneaded under his brows like dough. His hair was steel grey and brown, tossed together in a mass of curls that he had tried to tame. His failure on this point lent a British touch to his appearance. She thought of a Welsh Frankenstein as she watched him standing by a large viol. But most of all, she couldn't stop looking at Brandon. His face had changed radically into a sweet, mincing expression. He looked as if he were fawning.

"Now Brandon, cool it," Cragmont said gruffly.

"Cragmont, you can get right out of here."

"I'm not going anywhere. And you know damned well you're glad to see me," Cragmont said. He smiled brokenly at Cybele.

Brandon crossed his arms and remained silent. Cybele felt unnerved by his display of weakness, but she concentrated her attention now on Cragmont exclusively. His shirt was opened almost down to his belt. From the angle of the room where she was sitting in the rocking chair, she could see one part of a strange-looking scar on his chest, just above his left nipple. She leaned forward, hoping to glimpse more. She was consumed by curiosity.

Cragmont spun around to her and said, "I hope you aren't being moved by this pitiful display on Brand's part."

"Well, no. . . I mean, whatever Brand thinks is right," she finished lamely. Brand had put his hands together and stood twisting them against his chest.

"Well, everything's OK – I mean, it's really all right." Cragmont glared at her with his sunken grey eyes. She thought of a cypress tree in the swamp, wet from rain.

Cragmont lit a cigarette nervously. He couldn't stop moving. He was like a whirlwind trying to blow things into place.

"Are you drunk?" Brandon asked him.

"Why would I be drunk?. Just answer me that!" Cragmont demanded.

"I wouldn't be surprised," Cragmont mimicked back at Brandon. "Shut up and bring me something to drink." Cragmont drew his hands up on his slim hips and bent forward in an ape-like stance. His open shirt buckled, revealing more of the purplish, swirling scar on his breast.

Cybele was startled to see Brandon walk towards the door that led to his apartment over the shop. She had never seen him so obedient before. "Excuse me, Cybele. I'll be right back," he said.

"Don't worry, she won't *be* here much longer," Cragmont told him authoritatively.

Cybele sat doe-like and alert, accepting everything Cragmont said because Brandon was so obliging to him. Her inquisitiveness had also gripped her. She barely noticed his insult. It was inaudible to her consciousness compared with her interest in him and his obvious power over Brand.

"I suppose you're Cybele?" Cragmont asked as he sat down behind the rough wooden desk Brand had constructed. His grey and brown hair curled wirily about his high cheekbones. His face had changed from the fine flush it had sported on his arrival to an ashen, olive colour. The colour of his complexion looked unhealthy, yet his body was obviously powerful and young.

"How did you know?" she asked, acutely aware that they were alone together.

She studied him with an unconcealed fascination as he sat in front of her. His head and shoulders loomed before a sombre landscape painting hanging behind him on the wall, making the paleness of his complexion more disturbing.

"Oh, I know all about you – and that jackass husband of yours."

She remained silent, curious as to what he would do or say next.

"You're prettier than I thought you'd be. I'll say that for you," he admitted.

Brandon came back slowly into the room, carrying a tray with cups of coffee and pastries. As he set the tray down in front of Cragmont, Cybele understood that Cragmont had already taken authority over the shop and Brandon. Brand smiled mincingly at Cybele and handed a cup of coffee to her. He appeared almost apologetic. Cybele balanced the hot cup carefully between her fingers while she watched Brandon and Cragmont.

"Coffee? Cheez!" Crag protested.

"What'd you expect – a cocktail?" Brand admonished, and raised his cup deftly to his lips. His voice retained the peculiar lisp it had affected upon Cragmont's first appearance in the shop.

"You know, my dear boy," Crag said, "when you hold your arm just in that particular way and your mouth in that particular expression, you'd be amazed at how much you look like your worried, warty old mother!" He finished the last few words in almost a yell.

"Let's not get started on that subject, Crag," Brand protested, but he looked almost pleased with the intensity of Cragmont's passionate outbursts.

"Oh why not?" Crag clattered his cup down into the saucer. She saw his eyes glint like hard slate when he looked up at Brand.

"After all, she does seem to have a great deal of influence over you."

"What do you mean by that, C.W.?" Again Cybele noticed a gratified tone in Brand's voice, despite his protestations.

"Oh, just that little matter of your will."

"That's none of your damned business," Brand sniffed, and began picking at lint on his shirt.

"Oh it isn't, is it?" responded Crag, his voice becoming shrill and nasal. "I suppose someone who lived with you for ten years never had a thing coming to him? And a mother who lies around and drinks all day while your father. . . Oh well, I won't even mention that old bag of bones. Anyway, I suppose that old cunt merits your whole estate while I—"

"Crag, you shut up. We do have a guest in this room, you know!"

Cybele felt unnerved at being referred to as a guest. The word mobilised her. She stood up.

"Brand, I really do have to be going. Hadrian may want to come over and beat my brains out for that phone call. So I'd better be around."

"If Hadrian is your replacement for that maniac you were married to. . . well, cheez, looks like you've picked another winner," Crag said.

"Goodbye, Cragmont," she said softly, ignoring his remark. "I'm glad I met you. I'll see you tomorrow, maybe."

"Yeah? Well, just make sure it isn't every day."

Brandon walked out of the shop with Cybele. She felt as if she were walking beside a skeleton.

"Are you going to be OK, Brand?"

"Oh sure. If he gets on my nerves too much, I'll call the cops."

"Who is he anyway?"

"Just an old friend, dear. A very old friend. He's back to get all he can but he's going to be disappointed. There ain't nothing here."

"Well, I'll call you tomorrow."

"Let me know what happens with Hadrian. Don't worry about that phone call to his wife. She won't dare do anything."

"Really?" She looked at him dumbly. "Hard to believe she won't even throw something at him."

"That's when you love somebody, honey," Brandon smiled. "You think everyone's like you are."

"Well, OK. I'll see ya, Brand. Take care of your new friend."

Brandon looked grim and sighed, then walked into the shop. She looked up hopefully at the scudding clouds, then thought balefully of the empty afternoon looming ahead. She decided to go by Cannon's Seafood Market and get Porgy some shrimp.

The phone was ringing when she came back into her apartment.

"Hello?" Hadrian's deep, masculine voice said.

"Yes?"

"Fortunately I managed to get rid of your insane phone call."

She stood holding the receiver dumbly, not saying anything.

"Are you there?" he asked.

"Yes."

"Where is your sister?"

"She flew back home this morning early."

"You didn't see her before she left?"

"No. Eric took her to the airport at 8:30 this morning."

"But you were up. You called me before ten – er, I mean my wife."

"Oh Hadrian, please, I'm so tired. She just went home, that's all. You scared her away."

"I haven't done anything," he said indifferently.

"Oh no? Just everything! I hate you! I hate you!" She started to cry from exhaustion. "I'm so tired."

"Darling, rest now. I've got tickets for Bermuda. We'll leave tomorrow afternoon."

"Bermuda!"

"Yes, you need to get away from Eric – from Washington – and just relax."

"I don't know, Hadrian. I'm fed up," she warned him without conviction.

"Fed up! With what? I give you whatever you want, put up with your hippies, suffer your insane phone calls to my wife. . ."

"Why don't we just cancel this whole affair?" She stared at her toes dejectedly.

"Go to bed now. Rest. I'll call you tonight. I don't want you to go out. Go to a movie – but don't see Eric. I kill you if you see him again. Damn it – I have enough!"

She sighed. He clicked off and she was left holding the receiver. She staggered into the bedroom and flopped down in the rumpled bed sheets and fell asleep.

Chapter Ten

The next afternoon was hot and brilliant. The clouds she saw from the plane's window were scattering like fleecy, plump sheep. Every once in a while, when the plane dipped sharply from an air pocket, she could actually imagine that they were on the backs of white, temperamental animals. The drink glasses on the stewardess's tray tinkled with a metallic sound, and Hadrian kept squeezing her knee enthusiastically. For some reason she had put on hose, and the mesh cut into her flesh each time he pressed his fingers on her leg. She smiled painfully at him, and reached up to touch his smooth shaven jaw, smelling his intensely sweet cologne as she leaned forward to kiss him. A brilliant sunlight flooded the pastel blues and creams of the plane's interior décor. She saw a pretty stewardess smiling approvingly at them. Her champagne blonde hair looked like another colour that had been designed expressly for the plane's colour scheme.

"She likes you, darling."

"Who?" Cybele asked.

"The blonde who was smiling at us."

"Oh Hadrian," she said crossly, and withdrew her hand from his cheek.

"You should be proud, darling." He put his hand back on her knee possessively, staring at the stewardess with his dark, hawk-like eyes. "Another Scotch old fashioned, please," he commanded the stewardess as she walked briskly past them. He handed her his glass demandingly, as if to show her that she existed only to perform this service for him. He had created an imaginary desire in her for Cybele, and just as quickly had taken things back into his control by handing the girl his drink glass.

'Always playing his little power politics,' she thought, sighing as she turned back to contemplate the clouds again. She felt nervous and tense. She thought that she detected cramps in her stomach, but as soon as one came it disappeared so quickly that she couldn't be sure.

They were like the scattering, bunched clouds – inconstant and ephemeral. Only Hadrian's solid body beside her seemed to intervene, to take shape and guide her.

When the heavy door of the plane was flung open and they stepped outside, a warm, humid wind whipped their summer clothes against their bodies and flung Cybele's hair across her face. She kept reaching for his hand, wanting to feel its strength in her own, afraid for some reason. He strode along beside her, as if what they were doing was the most natural course of events. Her breasts and hands tingled and for a moment she felt as if she might fly apart. So many things kept happening that she had no control over.

"Oh God!" she exclaimed.

"Yes, darling. We're going to have a wonderful relaxing weekend," he said, misunderstanding her exclamation of confusion for one of exhilaration, the way he often did with their language barrier.

The cab pulled up to an enormous hotel. She waited while Hadrian gave instructions to the bellhop about their luggage, impatient to tear her clothes off and swim in the turquoise waters she had seen from the cab window. She kept feeling hot, then cold and a familiar dryness in her mouth from the tranquillisers. All the while, Hadrian was smiling at her and patting her arm or leg until she felt like she might run off down the hill screaming.

They entered the lavish hotel lobby with an obsequious black bellhop hauling their suitcases behind them. In the elevator Hadrian stood far away from the sweating Negro and held his nose secretly behind the boy's back to show Cybele how foul he smelled to him. Cybele started to laugh and the boy looked nervously over his shoulder. The whites of his eyes looked tropical against his chocolate-coloured skin. He staggered into their hotel room under the weight of their baggage. Cybele walked hurriedly past him and out onto a large stone balcony that resembled an old fort.

"It's marvellous out here," she called back to Hadrian.

"We have the best suite in the hotel," he said.

She ran back into the large, spacious room and flung herself into his arms, kissing his ears and biting the back of his neck.

"Ooh, darling – let's fuck!" he said, wrinkling his nose and laughing as her kisses tickled his ears.

"You maniac," she giggled, and felt his dick. "Let's see – yep, already hard."

They began to kiss one another slowly, seriously.

"Oh Hadrian," she said.

"I adore your body, Cybele," he said, and began unbuttoning her dress. He drew it down just over her breast and began kissing it. "Are you wet?" he asked and thrust his thick, powerful fingers under her silk panties.

"Oooh, what is this?" He held his hand up to his nose and smelled his fingers. "Your pussy is smelling so well, Cybele." He put his fingers to her nose. "Smell it. Isn't it good?"

"I like what I have in my hand," she said, and squeezed harder on his large, bulging dick.

He pulled her dress off and began kissing her on her stomach, then pushed her down on the bed.

"Oh darling," he said, and began kissing all of her legs as he drew her stockings down.

She lay moaning with pleasure, watching his mouth on her thighs intently. She pulled his zipper down and reached into his pants, bringing out his hard, swollen dick.

"Oh, how lovely he is, Hadrian." She smiled and began kissing his dick slowly, savouring its taste. "Oh, I can't wait for him to be in me," she said, and sucked him harder and harder.

He pulled his clothes off as he watched her mouth glide back and forth on his large, bursting dick.

Then he was beside her, kissing her breasts, thrusting his fingers into her cunt.

"Oh, this cunt wants to be fucked, darling. Oh, she's hot!" he said, pushing his fingers harder and harder into her cunt. "Oh, let me be inside now," he said and pushed his thick, angry-looking dick into her cunt.

She felt the muscles of her body separate to make room for his wide, insistent cock and she opened her legs wider to take as much of him inside as possible.

"That's right, Cybele, take it all. I'm fucking you with my balls now."

He held her by her shoulders as if she were his captive and pressed himself into her over and over. She felt his dick go deeper and deeper, until she screamed with an orgasm.

"Oh, you beautiful girl," he said admiringly. He kissed her forehead and held her hips under him with both hands, still moving inside her.

Beside their bed was a basket of fruit. His eyes fastened on it as he pushed himself into her. Cybele, let's use the banana!" he said and reached over to the basket.

"Huh?"

"Let's fuck your cunt with a banana." He cut the end of the banana carefully so that it wouldn't hurt her.

"Oh God, you're crazy!" She smiled languidly at him. "It'll melt."

"Then I shall eat it and your cunt. A pussy split. Ha! Ha!"

He pushed the banana slowly into her cunt. "Same size, Cybele, don't worry. Same size as my dick. You can take it."

She drew her legs back to her breasts, enjoying his eyes watching her cunt as he pushed the banana inside.

"Can you come?"

"I don't know," she said, holding both of her knees with her hands. "Oh yeah, yeah! Push it. Harder! Harder!"

"Oh darling, oh darling," he said, and pushed the banana harder and harder into her cunt.

"Oh, oh! Yeah! Do!" she said.

"Cybele! You came." He stopped, looking at her delightedly.

"Your cunt came with the banana! Oh, I adore her," he said, and heaved himself back up on top of her. His dick was even harder and bigger from watching the banana as he shoved it back into her with savage, quick movements.

"Oh. . . oh. . ." he said, and shuddered to a halt inside her. Perspiration poured down his black chest hair and dripped from his forehead onto her cheeks and into her eyes. Its salt stung them shut. "Oh, I came well," he said. Beside them the soggy banana lay in the rumpled sheets. They looked at it and began laughing.

She left him lying on the bed and went to put on her yellow bikini. It was the same one she always wore in the backyard of the apartment building for sunbathing. 'At least I won't have to put up with the old Mr Masters staring at me today,' she thought happily.

"Hadrian, hurry, let's go swimming."

"Oh, Cybele, I want to sleep," he protested. "I'm tired."

"No! Absolutely not. You're going to swim and get some sand on your back, you old fucker!"

She ran to the bed and hopped in beside him, where she began bouncing up and down on her knees until he groaned and sat upright.

"Come on, Hadrian, do something with me for a change instead of just fucking. I get the feeling you'd like to lay a couple of hundred down and tell me to get lost while you sleep."

"Sleep with me," he asked.

"Not now.

He studied her carefully.

"You're extra nervous today. Are you about to have your period?"

"Huh? Oh yeah. I think so. But I don't know. Come on," she said.

They walked out on the beach and sat down in the ghostly white sand.

"Oh, it's so great – so great," she sang merrily and ran to the water, splashing it all over her hard slender body. Hadrian sat watching her, enjoying her pleasure vicariously.

"Come on," she coaxed him.

He walked out to her, then lay down and floated on his back. She swam around by his legs and grabbed his toes, then began pulling him through the emerald green water.

"Ha ha, ever had a woman pull you around by your toes, Hadrian?"

"First time," he said, bobbing around in the water like a saucy cork.

After a while, they flopped down on the large white beach towels. He lay on his stomach with his face turned towards her. The cool sea water flowed down his face from his black, waving hair.

"Hadrian, you look like a big baby lying there." She sat propped on one elbow, looking at him with adoration. "I just love you when you look like that." She grabbed his big, powerful shoulders with both hands and began sucking between his shoulder blades with loud, slurping noises. People on the beach stared at her as she kissed and fondled him. With her hair wet and all of her make-up washed away, she looked like a fourteen-year old.

He reached into his yellow beach robe and brought out a box of raisins. He began poking them between her lips, watching the black spongy raisins disappear into her warm red mouth.

"Where d'ya get those?" she asked, pushing her wet black hair back from her face and scratching her nose from a sudden itch that the sea water had caused.

"From the fruit box in the room," he said, and they collapsed over one another, laughing hysterically. The other bathers stared at them with frank curiosity. They were creating a mild sensation lying there without even noticing.

Soon they gathered up their beach towels and walked back to their room. They turned the shower on extra hard and soaped each other under the burning hot water, still giggling. She came out of the bathroom with him swaddling her in huge white towels.

"Sleep now," he said, and pushed her down on the bed, then crawled in beside her.

"No, wait a minute."

"What now?" he groaned. "Can't you be still for five minutes?"

"I want you to do something," she said, reaching for the bottle of perfume he had given her on the plane. She handed him the bottle.

"Put this on me," she said, and smiled at him, rubbing her fingers through his black chest hair. "I want to smell wonderful while I sleep."

He opened the bottle of Cossack and began rubbing the sweet perfume on her legs and breasts.

"Put some on my hair. I especially love for my hair to smell good," she told him.

He dribbled some perfume in her hair, then capped the bottle. It was almost half gone.

"Now sleep," he commanded.

She slept fretfully beside him, waking several times and imagining large, purple bats flapping through the heavily draped french doors. She finally awoke to hear him breathing rhythmically beside her, his body bathing the back of hers in sweat from his own. His perspiration mixed with the perfume on her skin and wafted through the soft lilac darkness of the high-ceilinged room.

'Everywhere I go the ceilings are high and there are french doors. It's a conspiracy,' she thought vaguely, and slid off the bed. She darted into the bathroom and put her mouth to the faucet, letting the cold water that tasted of minerals pour down her throat and keeping the water on low so as not to make any noise.

She slipped on an elaborate white night-gown and walked out onto the balcony. It was still very light outside. The white lace of her filmy gown etched itself like a seashell on her darkly-tanned arm. She pulled up a chair and waited in the vivid colours of the late, tropical afternoon for Hadrian to awaken.

That night they went for a lengthy dinner. Again she felt the eyes of the other guests on them as they walked to their linen-covered table beside a spacious window in the opulent dining-room. She gazed into Hadrian's sparkling brown eyes over a crystal vase containing two red roses. He raised his wineglass and toasted her regally.

After dinner they went to the Steel Pier night-club. Dancers went under a flaming bar held so close over their bodies that she gasped.

"Do that again," he said. "It excites me when you're afraid and make that noise."

When they got back to the hotel room, she was in a dream-like state of happiness. At last he was all hers for a whole night. He wouldn't leave to go home to his wife or his business or any of the things that usually took him away from her.

But then the phone rang.

"It's probably just Room Service with the bottle of champagne I ordered," he said. "Why don't you go out on the balcony and wait for me?"

He lit a cigarette and picked up the receiver. The muscle of his arm bulged under his cream-coloured jacket in a hard, masculine swell of flesh. She looked at his swarthy face once more as he put the receiver up to his ear, then left the room.

She walked to the edge of the balcony and gazed at the winking lights in the distance. She breathed in a deep sigh of the sweet night-time air. It seemed permeated with the sap and pure oxygen of a thousand green plants. It sank down into her lungs like a special perfume.

"Oh, everything is wonderful, wonderful!" she half sang through the cool, soft air. She leaned back on the pebbly stone railing and purposely let it grate against her thighs.

After a while, the air began to chill her bare arms and she wondered why he hadn't come to join her.

"Hadrian?" she called. She waited a few more minutes, then went back into the room.

He was lighting another cigarette and talking animatedly into the phone.

"What?" she heard him say. "Impossible! How could she know where I am? Detectives? Oh m'gosh!" He dragged deeply on his cigarette.

"Hadrian, hang up!" she said, feeling the blood rush to her temples without warning.

He put his fingers to his lips, silently warning her to be quiet. His cool, detached gesture made her head throb with anger.

"Hang up, Hadrian," she repeated loudly.

He clasped his palm over the receiver. "Will you please shut up?" he asked impatiently.

"No!" she screamed. "I will not shut up." She grabbed the phone and slammed it down on the hook. "I will not be dismissed by you in such an insensitive way."

He glared at her with his fists clenched. "That was my secretary, you little idiot."

"I don't give a fuck!"

"Oh, you're vulgar!" he said with disgust.

"I'm *vulgar*? *I'm* vulgar?" she yelled, stamping her foot impotently.

The phone rang again shrilly.

"Get out of here if you can't be quiet." he warned. "My wife is having us followed. I have to hear about this, don't you understand?"

"I understand," she said bitterly. "And I am getting out of here." She grabbed her purse and slung past him.

He picked up the phone and said, "Just a minute," hurriedly, then jumped up and reached out to stop her. His hand caught her wrist like a bear grabbing at a small twig, but it was slippery with baby oil and she twisted out of his grasp.

"Cybele, Cybele!" he cried, looking pale and drawn under his tan as he stood at the door of their hotel room.

"Always something!" she complained, running down the hallway away from his dark, burning gaze.

She fled down the hotel corridor panting, feeling the skin of her body pulling with the motion of her bones underneath it. The thud of her feet on the carpet frightened her. The music of the dance that they had left behind in the night-club only an hour before still rang in her ears – the curious frenzy of the drums and xylophone, a mystic cacophony of sound floating through the tropical night. "Matilda, Matilda" had pulsed through the silk-like quality of the air and joined the high-pitched song of piping tree frogs that sang over the whole island. She remembered how they had watched the cascading waves of a crystal, night-time sea, swirling and undulating under the moon's glow from an outdoor balcony at the night-club as she ran past the numbered hotel doors. She had pressed back against the balcony in a fever of passionate excitement. She hadn't been able to keep her fingertips from brushing the roughness of his linen jacket. She couldn't stop holding the thickness of his muscular arm, of touching his mouth with her mouth, of feeling his whole solid body with the front of her legs. She couldn't stop saying his name over and over. To hear it echoing from her throat, to see him turn his head, to watch the beautiful texture of the skin on his cheek, to see his eyes, warm with life and love, rich and brown, was to feel him loving her. His look had caressed her whole body and she had begun to move as a plant under the warmth of the sun until there was a searing heat of desire in her blood, throbbing in her head, in her heart, and hot between her legs.

"I want to fuck you, darling," he had whispered. "Can I fuck you here?" he had asked, biting her ear and pinching her thigh.

"Oh Hadrian, I love you, I love you," she had sighed and tried to encompass the whole of his chest with her arms. The width of his shoulders and back delighted her. His hair delighted her – his eyes. The smell of him in her nostrils was a perfume too rare for anyone else to ever again match for her. She wanted to suffer for him, be ravaged by him, torn by him, beaten by him, hated by him – anything as long as he still wanted her, as long as she could hear his voice saying, "I want you". *I want you* was like honey he poured into her mouth, into her body.

"Open, open," she heard him say from only a few hours before when they had made love that afternoon. "Open, open more! Take me all – take all."

She had suddenly become aware of the other people around them, dancing, moving, drinking like pale pastel shadows in the silk of the night's jacket.

"Oh Hadrian, Hadrian!" she had whispered. She loved his name. It was the most private song in her heart. She had begun to dance. Her arms were brown, her dress was pink, her hair was black, and her green eyes were fastened onto his face, his mouth, and her body was remembering his body.

He had followed her dancing with his large brown eyes, smiling while he looked at her passionately. In his eyes she had seen him watching her with a shy curiosity, a curiosity that had excited her, flattered her – a shyness that had made her want to open everything to him. She had wanted him to see the core of her. "Look at me, look at me," she had said that afternoon.

"Oooh, so pink!" he had exclaimed.

She recalled all of the afternoon and evening as she stood panting by the elevator door. Looking at herself in the mirror, she saw a girl desperado, a renegade, a victim of euphoria – a euphoria that rang in her brain and seared her nostrils when she smelled the viciously sweet perfume that he had brought her – Cossack.

"Rider, rider," she whispered dementedly and smiled. "Night rider." She thought of Hadrian grasping at her in the hall, pale under his tan. 'Why did I run away? Why did I leave?' she wondered. 'I love him,' she thought. 'I really love him. Then why did I leave – what am I seeking? But why did he have to get that phone call?' she thought angrily.

She stepped out of the hotel lobby and into the silken air of the Bahamas, feeling suddenly bereft and miserable at her flight, at the madness inside of her that had taken over as once again she fled a situation, seeking, looking, feeling perverted and afraid. The tree frogs sang in a trilling, pipelike din, melodious with the silver light of the moon that shone down on the thickness of the green date trees and overgrown vegetation surrounding the island.

She remembered the sign they had seen – CAUTION, POISON IVY AND WILD CATS. "Really, it was a jungle here," she whispered to herself. She thought of the slinky black cats that she had seen from the window of the dining-room. They had been wild looking – taut, muscular, and skinny. They had been looking, hunting and prowling about like evil spirits. A shiver of recognition ran up her back. This was what she had always felt in common with cats – their predatory nature and their sensuality – easy, quick, yet with a sliver of the claw lurking beneath.

She stood by the hotel door and stared at the whiteness of the small British cars, at the whiteness of the chairs that sat against the whiteness of the hotel, at the white uniforms of the cab attendants, stunned by the thought that she was truly mad.

She paused for a moment, then, with a sudden feeling of hopelessness, as a soldier who trudges on over corpses, feeling only the cold steel of his gun barrel on his shoulder, she plunged ahead into the romantic night, perverted now for her by her anger and strange physical tension.

She came to the same steps that they had walked up the day before. They were wooden, powdered now with luminous dirt that was lit by the moon.

"O moon, moon!" she sang reverently.

She sat down on the third step. She was afraid to go very far. She had a horror that one of her flights might lead to the end of her. She could feel the crush of her skull in her ears – it was a wild thought. But when anyone actually began to beat her, she wanted them to stop, wanted to reverse it immediately, even though she might have done everything possible to bring it on. She stared down the moonlit valley of the golf course. Flowers were blooming everywhere.

"The flowers love each other," he had said, with his accent enhancing the poetry and mystic quality of his remark. She had looked at him with delight and then back at the multitude of white and purple morning-glories blooming in the night like bunched lace as they sat in the garden after dinner.

"In the night, flowers are more alive, aren't they, Hadrian?"

"Oh yes," he had said, with no further explanation.

She had looked at his profile. She adored his head; the foreign shape of his mouth and nose enchanted her. Once again, when her eyes travelled to his eyes, he had suddenly looked at her as if he had just discovered her and leaned over to kiss her. She had reached up to touch his hair that was wavy and black, to stroke the silver of his sideburns that were the colour of the moon.

In front of them a waterfall had splashed constantly as the sea moving by the cliff. Past the waterfall was an elaborate pool. At the end of the pool was an arch of white stone, an arch framing the palms and oleanders behind it, making almost a circle. She had looked at the waterfall and then at the arch. She imagined Tunisia and Egypt.

She had always wanted to go to these places – to Morocco, Istanbul and Egypt especially.

"The flowers love each other," she heard his voice saying.

"Hadrian!" she had exclaimed, burying her nose in his hair and breathing the smell of it that she so loved. "You are innocent."

"Yes," he had said, "I am. Be good to me because I am innocent."

Now she sat there, evil and perverted on the step, bereft of his presence. She knew that he was back in the room feeling angry and frustrated.

Suddenly she saw the figure of a young man down at the end of the incline. He appeared before her almost as a mirage. She stirred as if she were a hunter and the game had come into her sights. She couldn't see herself, but if anyone had, they would have told her that the whites of her eyes were brighter than the moon and that the green of her eyes paralleled the trees she sat under and could have matched the green of a wild cat's eyes. She waited, motionless and taut, tense as the skinny black cats she had seen prowling the courtyard that lay under the large, luxurious windows of the hotel dining-room.

"The flowers love each other she heard his voice saying in the tropical night. "And when the wind blows they kiss each other."

She watched as the oleanders stirred gently against their leaves in the dark lavender of the night. The tips of their blossoms touched one another, caressed each other. 'They are making love,' she thought and smiled there alone in the moonlight.

"But they die soon. Why, Hadrian? Why do they die?"

"Because they love each other so well, they have to die in a few days."

"Oh, I see," she had said, not understanding, but feeling the truth of the remark.

All at once the figure at the end of the incline attracted her attention again. His leather jacket reflected the moon in shards down his back and shoulders. With each glint of the moon, each movement of his long legs under the jeans he wore, and the sight of the boots on his feet, her lips parted, and the top of her body began to lean forward towards his form as one of the flowers did to another in the wind. She was ready to fuck him without saying a word, in fact she felt desperate for him *not* to speak. Her fingertips tingled at the thought of touching his back, her fingernails flexed back and forth in the sweat of her palms, alive at the idea of sinking them into the sweet flesh of his arms. She sat shivering as the man slowly climbed the hill.

"Good evening," he said. "Are you alone?" He propped one long, coltish leg in front of him and fumbled into the pocket of his leather jacket.. A whiff of its leather hit her nostrils and mixed with the strong, pungent aroma of tobacco smoke from his cigarette.

"Cigarette?" he offered, as if recognising her pleasure from the smell.

"Umm? Oh. . . yes," she said softly, inadequately, irritating him a little. She took the cigarette mechanically and sat waiting placidly for him to offer a light.

He looked at her hungrily, feeling an alien urge to grab a woman and rough her up. His eyes darted to the clumps of bushes surrounding them that were thick and green and secluded. He felt her glance on his face and looked more closely at her eyes – but they had gone suddenly past him.

She sat as in a trance-like state, staring at the moon. The vibrant pink colour of her dress and the whiteness of her shoes in the darkness startled him. Her legs were tanned dark brown, and the way she had stretched them out in front of him so casually, yet somehow guardedly, excited him. He trembled to touch her. He felt his hand unsteady as he raised his cigarette to his mouth and was mad when he saw that she had noticed.

"Isn't the moon lovely?" she said.

"Yes, 'tis a bit, isn't it," he answered her in a clipped Scottish brogue.

The sound of the words on his lips charmed her. She let her ears listen and leaned back on one of the steps. She thought of Hadrian and sighed. Their present hassle with one another was beginning to make her feel married. The worst aspects of her marriage began to flood her consciousness – that hateful, confined, bitchiness of living too closely with another human being. She hated to be invaded. She was a fanatic about privacy. When someone opened a bathroom door on her or watched while she made up her eyes, she could shoot them – literally, for one moment of hate, she could blow their brains out to get rid of them. 'Yet, yet,' she thought and drew on the cigarette, 'to have a man that I love watch me bathe gives me almost as much pleasure as fucking.'

The boy sighed again, bringing her back to the star-cluttered night. Her eyes were peopled by the lush jungle growth once more, by the tiny white cars. The golf course still lay rolling it her feet.

"It's wonderful here for a vacation, isn't it?" she said, feeling the need to say something.

"Yes, 'tis an idyllic spot. . . for millionaires," he quipped, looking at the heavy ropes of pearls around her neck meaningfully. "My wife works here at the hotel as a waitress. Forty more minutes before she's off." he added.

The sullenness in his voice was something she had to escape.

"Yes, I must go back now, too," she said lamely, feeling a tiny knot of misery at the thought of the scene awaiting her upstairs. 'But Hadrian isn't like Pierre,' she assured herself. 'He won't beat me – will he?'

She rubbed her arms with her palms, trying to warm herself from the damp night air as she strode back into the hotel lobby. They stuck to her skin like sandpaper. Somehow they felt clammy and lizard-like. Her pink dress was the colour of sea coral. The heels of her white shoes sank all the way down into the soft, turquoise carpeting of the hotel corridor. Two maids moved lightly on their rubber-soled feet out of a room. They smiled at her courteously. The atmosphere was ultra-polite and pleasantly detached. She was almost at their hotel door. In the room next to theirs she heard many voices from a party. She saw that the door to their hotel room was ajar. She pushed it open slowly. Hadrian was dressed in a robe and stood at his suitcase, hastily putting something inside it. He crossed back over to the bed swiftly.

"Where have you been?" he asked.

"I went for a walk," she replied and sat down on the edge of the bed. She felt heavy, dizzy, and ill. Her ears were ringing.

"Fix me a drink, please." The expression on his face was hateful. It had paled from his intense emotion and was even more dramatically handsome with the deep wrinkles sculptured by his impotent anger on either side of his sensual mouth.

She picked his glass up deftly from the dark mahogany night table. The curtains hanging at the french doors leading out onto the balcony were blowing like white, twisting ghosts. She dipped her hand into an ice-filled plastic bucket, enjoying the pain that bit into her fingers from the coldness. She crossed the room back to him with the glass of liqueur. Its Scotch odour made her nostrils tingle. She stood over him silently for a long moment, memorising his constrained posture on the bed, noting with satisfaction the pinched quality his exotic face had assumed. When she stretched out her arm with the drink in it, she was terribly excited. She had the urge to throw off his dark silk robe – to banish its sophistication, to rip it, to scratch his body. She shuddered.

"Why are you trembling?" He looked at her sharply. "Have you seen anyone?"

"Yes, as a matter of fact, I did. A Scottish boy."

"Did you fuck?"

"Oh, for Christ's sake, no!"

"Are you sure? I don't believe you." He sank back on the pillows. He was frowning at her in a strange way. She had never seen him at this point before. It excited her. The worse it became, the happier she felt. His suffering, his ugly expression made her feel loved by him, as if she mattered enough for him to have this much feeling for her.

"I hate you now," he said. "You are ugly for me – a snake." His hand was trembling as he raised the glass to his mouth. "I masturbated while you were gone." He looked at her steadily. She was amazed by his statement. "So that I would have no desire for your body when you came back."

She drew into herself more. She imagined herself a ball of rope that she had poured water on and made shrink. Her eyes wandered out into the sultry night through the balcony's opened doors. She felt stabbed by the stars, and shuddered with fear and excitement. Part of her was in the room, the other wandered without form out into the night.

"Don't sit with your back to me," he admonished, grabbing her arm and twisting her back towards him. "I said I don't believe you." The sound of his voice was like a fine violin being played at its highest, most difficult note. "I know you," he said. "I know you.

His eyes were smouldering like dark, golden oil. His skin glowed in the half-light of the lamp. She looked down at the hard, curving muscles of his forearms. She felt her body straining towards the masculine smell of his body. She ached for him, yet she wanted to hurt him.

"You can fuck anybody when you are like this – anybody," he continued. "You bitch! You bitch!"

He clutched her arm until she felt as if the bone would give way.

"Let me go," she said and she twisted away. "I hate you! I hate you!"

"I hate you too," he said darkly. "Bitch! Whore! When we get back home, I'm going to hang a red light outside your door – you whore!"

"Yeah? Well, at least I don't have to lie around and fuck myself!" she replied and slung a glass of ice water she had been holding into his face. He sputtered and blinked his eyes rapidly from the icy water, gasping with surprise. Then suddenly he raised up like an incensed black bear and struck her on the nose. It was a blow like none that she had ever felt before. She felt the bone go soggy. He ground his knee into her side, punching her ribs like a sack. She turned her head to look back at him with shock. He had never hit her with such a brutal abandonment before.

"Hadrian! Hadrian!" she cried, terrified. "Don't hit me any more. Please don't beat me any more."

Suddenly he stopped his attack. The room was quiet except for their sharp, animal-like pants. She felt splintered. He got up suddenly and went for some more liquor.

"I hate you now," he said again. "I hate you."

"You hate me?" she asked. "You hate me?" She was sitting in the rumpled sheets. She had changed into a pleated shortie night-gown. It was also pink like her dress. She felt something hard under her hand and lifted the empty water glass from under her pillow. She thought of what might have happened if she had broken it with her body during the fight. She felt her nose again. The squishy quality of the bone was interesting. Then she dropped her hand to her belly and began rubbing it. She needed to have her period, but it wouldn't come.

"You thought I was going to say, 'Oh, that's OK, Cybele, that's OK,' but you went too far, dammit. I've had enough," he protested.

She listened to him intently. The sound of his voice scolding her was satisfying to her through her desolation. Even the trickle of her tears, translucent and diamond-like, over the swollen side of her eye was comforting. She felt the muscles of her thighs surrounded by the gauzy material of her night-gown.

"You hate me?" she asked again, looking at him coyly through her tears. She flung herself back against the pillows. All the while, she was aware of her body in the night-gown and his body in the silk robe.

"Yes, I hate you, but I want to fuck you. In spite I masturbated, I want you now." Suddenly he was at her side again, rubbing her arms and legs with his powerful hands. She held on to the back of his forearm happily, lifting the tips of her fingers slightly to feel the texture of the black hairs on his arms. "In spite I hate you, I want your cunt. You have such a sexy pussy, darling. Open your legs."

She opened her legs and relaxed, watching him move over her like a massive bull.

"Come, darling," he said. "Can you come? Your cunt must come."

"Yes, Hadrian, make me come. You make me come."

She woke up aching. Her mouth was dry and she could smell stale cigarette butts in the ashtray. She turned slowly in the darkness and groaned from the bruises on her body. He lay immobile beside her, remote and still. She clutched her belly again, rubbing it and feeling its swollenness. Her ears still hummed and she could not sleep. She lay quietly for about half an hour, listening to the rasping sound of his breathing and looking at him carefully in the darkness, feeling the familiar strangeness that lying beside him brought her, the comfort that he alone could sustain. She traced his nose with her eyes.

"Oh, Hadrian," she whispered into the pitch-dark night-time hours. "You are my whole world, my only identity, my blood, my breath. Master, master, I adore you, Hadrian."

She felt a violent twinge in her stomach. 'What is it? What is it?' she thought. 'I feel so nervous, something is pulling at my arms from inside.' She felt the skin of her face tight across her high cheekbones from sunburn. She was perspiring. She put her hand on Hadrian's arm, trying to join herself to him once more. She was so afraid. The dampness on the sheets under him comforted her. She loved the way he perspired each night, as if a giant motor was slowly cooling itself down. But she couldn't stay. Her body made her get up. None of its nerves would stay still.

Out on the wide stone balcony the night stretched before her in an endless expanse of blue darkness. The sea heaved in a soft swish of foam and waves. She leaned over the tall stone wall and stared down at the row of motorcycles lined up neatly for the next morning's rentals. She turned and stared at the white patio table. Its lacy white chairs were turned towards one another. Their positions reminded her of the afternoon's conversation they had had in the brilliant, stinging sunlight.

"You see, Cybele, when I was in Istanbul, all I ever dreamed of was to come to America," Hadrian had said. "But to come here and live as my family had lived in Turkey – as one of the first families there."

He sipped his Scotch like a connoisseur.

"Well, I'm for that, Hadrian – sure, why not?" She darted over to his side and clasped his muscular arm in adoration.

"It's not so easy, you know," he protested.

"But for a man like you, Hadrian. . ." she said, looking at him slavishly. "An entrepreneur of the shipping business. And you even talk to Onassis. Oooh, Hadrian, you are my hero! Why, I've never met a man like you in my whole life. You know I'll probably *never* meet another man like you!" she declared, grasping his arm more firmly.

"Ah yes," he said, patting her head as if she were a faithful lap dog. He pulled his arm away from her clutching fingers in order to pick up a package of English cigarettes on the table.

"I wanted to do it the 'American way' so badly, Cybele – to be accepted in all the best clubs,, meet all the best people." He inhaled the cigarette savagely. "And when I came to America, my father had died, and his two business partners had cheated my mother out of her share of the business. I had to drive a taxi and sell insurance policies – can you imagine? *Me*, whose father had owned one of the greatest shipping businesses on the Mediterranean, who had lived like a prince, going to the best schools in Europe? And here I was, landscaping rich people's gardens after my two other jobs!"

"Oh Hadrian, how spectacular," she drawled, and kissed him on his large ears.

"Please, don't do that, huh? It tickles," he said, and pushed her back into her chair.

"Yeah, what you talkin' about? It wasn't easy, I tell you the truth."

"Oh Hadrian, I just admire you more and more," she swooned.

'How different from Daddy,' she thought as she recalled her father sprawled on the sofa watching television before going to his dull, mechanical job.

"Plus the fact that I could hardly speak English. I read the newspapers every day to learn, and practised writing some of the editorials even. I did everything, everything," he repeated, and drained the last drop of his Scotch. "But I always sent fifty per cent of my earnings home to my mother, always!" he said proudly.

"You are a god, Hadrian," Cybele said reverently.

"Yes, I wanted to do it right, darling," he said, and began caressing her legs. He looked at her body and blew her a kiss. "What a bootiful body you have, darling. Ummm," he sighed, and began rubbing her bare shoulders.

"But. . . Hadrian," she began.

"And I wish I met you ten years ago," he told her emphatically. "Yes, I wish I met you instead of that bitch I married. Ugh!" he shuddered.

"Then why *did* you marry her, Hadrian?"

"I guess I was lonely. I had a new home, and in the American suburbs one must have a wife."

"Gosh," she said. "Have you ever thought about what a straight life you lead, Hadrian?"

"Before you, my little nymphomaniac!"

"But you got into such a trap, honey, the all-American trap."

"What can I do, darling," he smiled, and began kissing her breasts through the gauzy material of her night-gown, "except love you? My only, only sex. My only love!"

She stretched her long legs out on his muscular thighs, purposely arranging them so that they appeared before him in their most attractive shape, then asked, "And am I *so* different from your wife, Hadrian?"

"Oh yes, you are," he declared. "As different from night and day."

"Oh Hadrian, how I love to be loved by you," she exclaimed, and dropped down to his knees and began kissing them. "It's like an addiction!" She lay her head on his leg and demanded, "Now tell me, tell me how I'm so different from her."

"Well, you are beautiful and she is not," he said and laughed with embarrassment.

"But she's pretty. I've seen her."

"But cold," he sighed.

"What is her body like?" she asked, and lay down on her back at his feet, hoping that she looked beautiful. "Is it good?"

"Nah. Her hips are too big."

"But she has long legs. You love her legs!" she exclaimed, and began to cry.

"No, I do not love any legs like I love your legs. I masturbated for your legs when I saw them on the bicycle one day, you remember I told you that?"

"And her breasts?"

"Not good, not good."

"Her nose is too big, isn't it? Oh yes," she said with delight. "I remember that it was big, and her hips are fat! Ha ha. But what about her cunt? Is it as tight as mine?"

"No, too dry," he said, and smiled at her indulgently.

"But you must have fucked her a lot when you first got married," she persisted. "I know you, Hadrian. You love to fuck!"

"Well, first couple of years, yes I did. But it was just because I thought I had reached my ideal, my dream for this country."

"But what happened, Hadrian?"

"Oh darling, let's not talk any more. I got bored with her. That's all. It was an illusion. She was like the American woman – cold and too practical. She had a very mathematical brain, as a matter of fact. C'mon now – let's go inside. The chair is hard here," he said and motioned to his ass,

"Oh, OK, but first let me finish painting my toenails."

She gazed past him at the pastels of the coral and white balcony, feeling its bleached, grainy surface under her foot. The other foot she held with her sunburned hands while painting her toenails a rich, bright red. Her night-gown blew in the breeze and kept getting in the way. It was filmy and its gauzy white material gritted against the stinging sunburn on her arms and back.

"I don't know what to do about my brother," Hadrian said suddenly.

"What about your brother?" she asked as she placed the brush of the polish carefully on the nail of her little toe.

"He needs me to help him," he explained, and took another deep drag on his cigarette with a mature, sensual pleasure.

"Then help him," she said with her characteristic forthrightness.

"Ha," he laughed. He smiled at her ironically. His eyes were like glinting brown pools. "It's not so easy. It takes time. Besides, I don't trust my brother. He always has these big deals brewing that don't materialise."

He raised his tall glass of Scotch and sucked on the ice, viewing her with interest, as if by some miracle she might advise him correctly. Her different approach to life startled, yet pleased him. He watched her, waiting for each new thing she might do. His inner being wondered if she knew things by revelation. It was a novelty for him to be so interested in a woman's words for whose face and body he held such a violent passion.

"It's amazing how dark you get in only one day, Cybele."

"Yes, my mother used to put me in the sun on a blanket when I was only a few weeks old. I loved it," she said, "even then. At night when my father carried me out into the yard, I'd look over his shoulder and cry for the moon."

"What an imagination you have, darling."

"Really, my parents told me I used to scream for it." She squinted up through her black eye make-up at the turquoise dusk, seeking and seeing the full, thin outline of the moon. "You see, there it is now, waiting for the night. Tonight the moon will be very white and big, Hadrian," she said, staring at his dick.

"You son of a bitch, you're not looking at the moon." He grinned at her. She laughed back at him gaily, then dropped her gaze down to her toenails.

"Anyway, go on about your brother. You need to help him, but it's too much trouble."

"Not too much trouble, but it takes so much time. He needs a lot of money also. And he's greedy – he's become more greedy with the years."

"But he's your brother, Hadrian. You must help him – for your soul. Besides, you're both in the same business. Perhaps he may make you rich." She grinned at him impudently, knowing that he would hate the idea of anyone but himself making him rich.

'Always has to be in control,' she thought to herself, and slashed at her nail with the red paint savagely. She stared at him through her lashes. He had on a white towel robe. His hair was black and curling around his leonine face and neck. He kept swishing the liquid of his glass and dragging on his cigarette at intervals, then drumming his blunt fingers on the patio table.

Intermittently a large gathering of Jews screamed and laughed, interrupting the lambent dusk like exotic parrots with their voices. Hadrian smiled at her cynically.

His eyes drew the remark, "Straight from Noiw Yoik," out of her. She was happy to have the "king" confide his mild distresses to her.

Suddenly she looked at him impatiently, irritated by the sound of his drumming fingers. "Why don't you relax? Just shut up and be still. Always thinking, always plotting. Some people just lie around and relax!" she said and slammed the bottle of polish down on the table. She looked at the side of his face and felt weak in her stomach and hot between her legs. She felt happy and sad as she stared at his languorous, catlike sprawl in the chair. 'Relaxed, but ready,' she thought.

"I mean – I saw you happy and not thinking when I pulled you around in the water today. Wasn't it heavenly, Hadrian? Have you ever had a woman pull you around by your toes, Hadrian? Ha!"

He blew her a kiss. "Darling," he said.

"I loved it when you fed me those raisins, Hadrian. I felt like your queen. But back to your helping your brother."

"Yes, but Cybele, I can lose a lot of money."

"You're rich, Hadrian."

"I'm rich, huh? Ha. Pooh."

"You're rich and you should help your brother by giving your money and time to help him."

"My time, huh? How much longer do you think I shall live?"

She looked at him closely. "At least ten years."

"I don't think so."

"I do. You've got a strong heart and a powerful body, and you fuck like you're twenty-five. I'm sick of hearing about your impending death and then having you fuck me four or five times a night all week. That's smacking of incongruity, Hadrian, luv," she said, employing one of Eric's terms of endearment, thinking of him briefly and how he would have loved the beach and weather on this tropical island as she did so. "Look, Hadrian, you're gonna make money, you're gonna fuck, you aren't going to die for a long time, and this is just another one of your chances to do good for your soul before you die."

He drained the last of his glass. "Let's get ready for dinner," he had said.

She had put the bottle of nail polish down on the table and looked at its tall white top screwed tightly onto the fat red body that it sat on. Then she had jumped up and followed his wide back through the open french doors.

But that conversation was gone now. How had it gone? She looked back at the chairs and tables once more. They were still in the same attitudes that had held their bodies that afternoon, turned the way they had been turned. Even the glasses remained in the same position. The nail polish had blown over. It rolled around on the table like a little red and white ghost.

She shivered as she fingered the pale ribbons that hung untied from her shortie night-gown while still looking at the table and chairs thoughtfully – feeling their whiteness, feeling a part of her and Hadrian that had remained there with their words somehow. The french doors were still slightly ajar. The filmy white curtains still blew and undulated with the wind, as if they had a life of their own. She looked down at her hands. They were familiar to her. They were hands she had known a long time. She saw them as being detached from herself, yet being hers also. She smiled, touching her hands with her eyes. They had a life of their own, like her arms and her eyes. She felt happy at the thought of this, and touched her legs with her hands softly, then brought her fingertips to the rims of her eyes, to feel their shape. Then she looked once again at the doors – at how they were opened partially. She could feel Hadrian's presence on the other side of them. She imagined that she could hear his heavy breathing. The bulk of his body lived for her under the white, white sheets, under the cool, blue-white sheets. Sometimes she imagined that he was calling her. She wanted him to call her. She wanted to see him standing in the frame of the doors, to see his face and have his eyes on her, to hear his voice. She desired him so. She desired his feet and hands. There was nothing on his body that she did not desire, or about his brain and personality that she did not desire. *And she desired to be controlled by him.*

She turned quickly, pulling the virgin air of morning deep into her lungs. "So pure, so pure," she whispered, touching the tips of her nipples and feeling the tender, pebbly quality of her shell-pink teats. "Ohhh! Ohhh!" she whispered in exhilaration. She stood on her toes, stretching the back muscles of her calves and thighs. But why did she wake up? 'Why can't I sleep?' she wondered. 'I want to sleep. I'm so tired.'

She yawned, then hung over the wide stone balcony. The sea was blue and green. The light of the evening was tinted with a powdery purple hue, a lavender shade, the colour of large flowers she had seen blooming around the island. She studied the clouds, looking intently at their shapes.

'They might tell me what to do,' she thought. 'I'm so afraid, I'm so afraid. Why am I? Why am I?' She turned away from the balcony, still hanging on it, but looking back at the patio and their room, so as to know it was behind her. 'That's behind me. That's there. I have it there in back of me.' Thinking this, she turned back to gaze at the sea and the clouds.

She began to pray in her old desperate fashion. "Help me. Help me, God. God, please, please help me. Help me, oh please, please." She was crying but the tears were sparse and felt more like a thin mucus from her nose. All at once, her eyes lit on the nebulous motion of what looked like smoke. She strained forward, feeling the stone balcony against her stomach, cold and hard.

"Is smoke coming from that house?" she asked no one. She peered through the gloom. The left side of the vista was covered with lush green shrubs and trees. It covered the mountain-like hills in moss green growth. Sunk into one of the hills she thought she saw smoke wafting up from one of the white frame houses of the islanders. "No, no. It's a woman!" She shook her head and shifted her gaze back out to the wide expanse of the sea, studying the clots of high ground covered in coral and green undersea growth closely in order to clear her sight, then brought her vision back to the hillside – back to the secluded green and blue nook. The smoke was whirling and twisting itself into the green earth.

"It's a woman," she whispered. "I wonder what she's doing there at this time of night?" She thought of the tall Scotsman she had met in the moonlight hours earlier. "Maybe she's an island woman. A woman who knows this countryside and isn't afraid."

Then the form sank back into the grass. Cybele could see only her seductive outline. "Why is she doing that?" she whispered. Then she saw the shapes of four different men appear. "She's going to fuck them – all of them!"

Cybele turned her head to one side, straining to see if this was actually happening. The bright, blue-and-green tinted clouds were scudding by over the heaving sea. To her right the pool and lounge chairs sat like a finely drawn immobile sketch. It was the same pool she had swam in that afternoon. She turned back to the hillside. Her body was cold all over from the clamminess of the chilly air. She saw the shapes mounting the woman. One after the other came on top of her, moving fiercely, as if they did this often, met this way many nights. Cybele stared at them intently, waiting for the last one to leave the woman. As she looked, straining every nerve in her body to see those people, the forms turned into smoke from a chimney on a small, squalid-looking house.

'But that happened,' she thought frantically. She shook her head, feeling the lankness of her hair cold against her cheek.

"Cybele, Cybele, what are you doing?" Hadrian called out in an alarmed voice.

"Spying," she said happily.

"Thank goodness he woke up," she whispered to herself. But she was afraid to look at him. She was afraid to show him herself in her present condition. 'He'll hate me, he'll hate me. Once he knows, he'll despise me. I won't turn around,' she thought.

She dropped her gaze to the driveway below, to the black concrete road. "I'll just drop off down onto the pavement and that'll be the end of it. Then I won't have to go through it and neither will he. But then he'd hate me even more, there'd be a scandal. Shit."

"Get off that balcony!" he called. "It's dangerous up there."

She heard the elegant, sophisticated tone of his voice. It filled her ears and caressed her body, but she didn't turn around.

"I want to hear him say those words again. It's so beautiful to hear his voice. Then I'll turn and I'll see him and that'll be even better."

"Get down, damn it!" he demanded.

She turned around, feeling her pulse beating near her collar-bone and proceeding up into her neck, then throbbing in her cheekbones at the sight of him in his blue and purple silk robe. He was already smoking a cigarette.

"What are you doing out there the whole night?" he asked, exasperated. "Come in right now. Don't you want to rest? You'll be sick."

"I want to rest with you, Hadrian. With you."

"Then – then, why don't you do that?"

"I don't know. I want to – but I can't. It's my body. I'm so nervous, Hadrian." She ran up to him, shivering.

"Do you want me to call a doctor?"

"When does one come? I need to bleed. I beat my stomach to make me."

He pulled her through the doors, rubbing his arms briskly. "Oh darling, you're freezing. Poor girl, poor Cybele."

She glimpsed her haggard, young face in the bathroom mirror and grinned impishly at her reflection, noticing the bluish bruise around her eyes and nose proudly.

He sat her down on the bed, then went over to the closet to bring her a blanket. She looked at the bottle of Cossack perfume, that he had bought in for her, on the dark mahogany night table.

'I wonder what kind of perfume my grandmother used to wear?' she thought. 'It might have been like this perfume – because this perfume smells winey and sweet like the South, like Southern women.'

She stared up at the high ceiling of the wide, expansive room. She saw a circular scar from where a light fixture had once been hung. The mark had been painted over, but still showed.

Hadrian came bustling up to the side of the bed, unfolding a soft blue blanket while he stood in front of her anxiously. He spread it out over the bed. "Now lie back."

She sat very still, perched on the side of the bed like an unclassified bird. Her big feet hung on the frame of the bed, supporting her long brown legs.

He dropped in front of her and put his head on the tops of her thighs. He held the outside of her legs with his warm, strong hands and rubbed them. He kissed the flesh of her legs, letting his tongue prod the blonde hairs on the tops of her thighs.

"Did you know that my grandmother might have used this perfume, Hadrian?"

He stared up at her from underneath his thick black brows, smiling tiredly. He began kissing her legs again and sniffing gently for the smell of her cunt. She put one hand over it coyly, but he pulled it back down to her side.

"Stop," he protested.

"As a matter of fact, Hadrian, this whole room is like my grandmother's house. Look at it. See, on the ceiling?" She pointed to the ceiling. "It's a mark where a fixture used to be. My grandmother's house had a small chandelier in every room, right in the middle of the ceiling, just like that."

He pushed her back against the pillows, holding both of her wrists and pinning them to the mattress. He began to kiss her mouth slowly, softly, studying her face carefully as he did so. He moved his lips on hers determinedly.

"The furniture's mahogany too. Her furniture was always dark. I even remember the bedroom furniture. It was like this, Hadrian."

He moved his body on top of hers, pressing his hips and dick onto her stomach, still kissing her deliberately.

"Ouugh! Get off. You're too heavy." She pushed at his chest, noticing the hair on his chest and smelling his sweet body flesh as she did so. He slid down gently by her side, still looking at her with a grave intensity. He stroked the top of her hair and slid his hand to the back of her head in a cat-stroking motion that calmed her for the first time that evening.

"Oh yes, do that. Do that," she pleaded. "I like that."

He grinned at her sleepily. "That's what you say when I fuck you - 'do that, do that'." He pulled his robe aside to show her his hard bulging dick. She stared at it, as if it were something alive in the bed with them, apart from both of them.

"My uncle used to love me to comb his hair. He was a cook on a boat. He would be gone for a long time, then he'd come home and give my cousin and me a lot of dimes and nickels and quarters. He knew how to make applejacks. Do you like to be tickled?" She dropped her hand to the lapel of his robe, pushed it inside and trailed her fingertips across his chest, smiling at him as she did so.

He opened his mouth to cover hers well. His tongue and lips sucked her mouth greedily. He pulled her hand down to his dick. She grasped his dick and squeezed it, then let it go.

"My cousin and I used to tickle one another." She felt the rawness of her throat. The limbs of her body felt spongy with fatigue. "Oh! Oh! Move. My leg. My leg – it's gone to sleep."

She sat up cross-legged, holding her toes and looking like a child-Buddha. "The most wonderful thing was my bike. Oh, Hadrian, my bike was so great. So great," she said tiredly, yawning again. "That light, Hadrian, look where it used to hang," she repeated as if in a trance. She pointed to the ceiling and flopped back on the pillow.

Hadrian propped himself over her with his elbow. He put his large hand over her breast and squeezed it firmly, making it warm. The skin roughened as he cupped it in his hand and squeezed the teat with his thumb and forefinger.

"Darling, you have the face of an eight-year-old girl!" he exclaimed. He peered at her more intently, looking very surprised. "Cybele, Cybele, I wish you see your face in the mirror. It changed to eight years old. Come on, dear, I want to fuck you as a little girl. Give me your pussy again with your little girl's face."

He mounted her quickly, still holding her arms back by her wrists. His forehead was wrinkled with passion. He was breathing very heavily and his hands trembled when he brought them down to caress her stomach.

She looked at the swarthiness of his face, at the top of his head, feeling his large dick push itself into her once again. The perfume from his robe and neck flooded her nose. She smelled his ears greedily, then looked past him at the old scar where the light had hung. She liked being fucked then, and he was enjoying it so. His panting excited her terrifically.

"Come, darling, come like a little girl. I shall fuck your pussy like your father."

He dipped his head down to her breast, sucking it relentlessly. She screamed with pleasure while he moved inside her harder and harder.

"Keep sucking me. Suck me like that, hard," she said, holding her teeth taut against one another as she felt his dick jabbing inside her cunt. "Suck me while you fuck me. Oh, oh, now!"

The next day was only a few hours away. She awoke before him again and ran into the bathroom hurriedly to pee. When she sat down on the cold white commode, she winced from the bruises on her body. She put her hand up to her eye tentatively and felt its swollen, puffy flesh.

"Oh God, oh God," she groaned. All she could think of was escaping from Hadrian, getting away from him and the elaborate, birthday-cake type hotel. 'To think that I was looking forward to spending last night with him,' she thought, disgusted.

She looked up to see him watching her as she sat on the commode.

"You look awful, Cybele." He put one large hand in his robe pocket and stood with one bare foot over his other foot.

"No kidding," she said without looking up. "Wonder why?"

"Hurry, darling. We only have two hours before our flight back. We'll have to separate the minute we land, of course."

"Whaddaya mean?"

"The detectives," he sighed.

"Oh!" she said simply, remembering the phone call from his secretary. "What do you think your wife's up to?"

"Who knows?" He shrugged, and lit a cigarette. "Whatever it is, she'll sweeten up for a little cash."

"Oh, how revolting."

"Yes, revolting that you put a snake like her on my back."

"Oh, get out, will you?" she groaned, and winced when she touched her throbbing temples. She pushed the door closed with her foot.

"Any blood?" he asked from the closed door.

She glanced down at the toilet paper. "Yeah, a little. It's dark brown. Ugh! Shit, looks like death."

"Be home this afternoon," he said. "I may stop by after I get things under control at home."

When they landed, she walked out of the plane wearily, trailing behind Hadrian, but not walking beside him as he had instructed her. As he stood waiting for their luggage, a dark-haired man held up an absurdly large-lensed camera to one sunglassed eye. She pulled her eyes down with her fingers and stuck her tongue out at him.

"Whaddaya want?" she asked, walking right up to his startled face. "Fuck off, buzzard face!" she said. She ran out to a cab, leaving her luggage with Hadrian, without even looking back at her lover.

"Ha ha," she giggled. "First time I ever played James Cagney," she thought as the taxi pulled away from the kerb.

She flopped down on the old green sofa when she got back to her apartment and sat stroking Porgy, while contemplating the events of the past two days.

"Shit, Porgy. Shit!" she said over and over, staring about the room as if she were a shell-shocked soldier.

Suddenly the phone rang.

"I ain't gonna answer it, damn it," she said, and ran over to the phone.

"Get your cunt over here immediately," she heard a precise, youthful voice say when she put the receiver to her ear.

"Who is this?" she asked, sinking back down to the floor.

"Never mind who this is. I want you here this instant so I can shove my big, palpitating organ up your delectable, pink cunt."

"My Lord," she said. "I'm gonna hang up."

"You hang up and I'll call that jackass husband of yours and tell him where you live!"

"You must be crazy. Don't you know he'd murder me if he found out—" She stopped in mid-sentence, realising at last whom she was speaking with. "Where is Brandon? This is Crag, isn't it?"

"How did your moronic brain ever come to such a brilliant deduction?"

"You're the only one strange enough for this conversation," she replied.

"This isn't me talking actually," he said, and laughed. The sound of his masculine laughter in her ears conjured up memories of his open shirt, of his slim hips in an old pair of Levis with their sharp pelvic bones like two razors under the worn material.

"Who is it then?" she inquired, intrigued.

"It's Basil."

"Basil?"

"My trademark, dummy!"

She remembered the large, livid scar she had seen etched in a strange cross on one side of his chest.

"Hey, you're neat," she said.

"Then get your ass over here."

"Well, I dunno." She looked vacantly around the room.

"Whaddaya mean? You've got nothing else to do but sit around and finger fuck your pussy all day."

"God, you are awful," she said, listening eagerly to every word.

"And you just love it, don't you?" he snarled into the phone.

"How do you know what I love?"

"I know all about you."

"From Brandon?" she asked.

"Nah, just by looking at you. You'd love for me to burn your ass with an iron, or beat you with my belt."

"You're crazy!" she screamed.

"You love it, Cybele. Now get over here."

"Maybe," she said. "Where is Brandon?"

"Fuck Brandon. Now get over here." He clicked off and she stood holding the whining receiver in one hand.

"God," she said. "It's a nutty world." She yawned and went over to the mirror to study her greenish black bruise. She gazed at it proudly, fingering it with care. She sank into the still unmade bed and slept for an hour. The phone was ringing again when she woke up.

"And don't bring that fucking, farty cat," Crag said, and clicked off again in her ear.

She went into the kitchen, yawning, and opened the refrigerator door. A large jar of Safeway orange juice was the most prominent thing in there. She yanked it out and started chug-a-lugging the stinging, citric liquid, staring at a head of wilted lettuce leaves in a salad bowl. 'The remains of our very infamous grass dinner,' she thought.

"When was that?" she mumbled. "I'm getting so confused." Then she remembered Crag. "Gosh, Brandon really came up with a weirdo."

She thought of Brandon's tales about his life in Paris at the Sorbonne where he had studied music, and his roommate there who had killed himself in front of him.

"He begged me to watch his suicide," Brand had told her. "Claimed it would redeem him from past sins. I finally agreed. He did it Japanese style.

"How awful," she had replied. "Didn't it gross you out?"

"Well, there was a lot of blood – ruined everything in the whole apartment."

She shivered from the cold air of the open refrigerator and from her thoughts. "Brandon is strange," she said out loud to no one. "He likes that shit. He's got some sort of hang-up about it. Gosh, maybe he's in trouble or something. He never answers the phone over there anymore." She visualised Brandon chained to one of the twin beds in his dark gothic bedroom and trembled again, then slammed the refrigerator door shut. She looked down at the jar of orange juice. It was all gone except for a swallow. She gulped that down, then looked at Porgy. "All gone, Porgy," she said.

"Meow," he whined.

"There ain't nothing left but some old dead lettuce leaves and lots of Scotch," she told him. She reached up and got a can of cat food from the cabinet.

"Except this, of course."

Porgy howled, recognising the shape of the can.

"Ain't eaten in two days, have ya?" She opened the food hurriedly. "Well, you need to diet some." She put the food down for him and went back in the bedroom to dress.

She walked into the slope-roofed music shop, blinking as usual through the gloom inside. No one was sitting at the large, wooden desk behind the black antique cash register. She walked up to the desk as if she were treading on eggs, looking suspiciously around the shop. Something was different. She turned and looked about the room uneasily. Then the loud music registered in her mind.

'Brand never has that sound system up like this,' she thought. She stood before the desk uncertainly, and contemplated ringing Brandon on the intercom that connected his apartment upstairs with the shop below. For some reason she felt afraid to do so, as if she might be intruding into his privacy. She knew what a fanatic he was about his privacy. "God, how they love to invade you," she heard him say. He had pronounced the word 'they' as if he were speaking about insects.

She walked through the shop to the door of the back room. It was partially ajar. As she drew near she heard men's voices over the sound of the loud music. For some reason she did not enter, but halted before the door and listened quietly.

"Comere, Comere," she heard Crag say. Someone panted and groaned. She thought that Crag must be tussling around with some guy. She didn't think of sex because it was two men that she heard.

"Oh Crag, that thing is so hard."

"You love that cock up your ass! And you know it," she heard
Crag snarl. "Say it, you little ass-hole. Tell me how much you love
it shoved up your ass!"

"Oh Crag, I do love it. I do!"

"I'm gonna tear your ass until it—"

Cybele stumbled back against a table and knocked over an antique
violin. "Oh m'gosh," she said, as it clattered to the floor.

Crag kicked the door open with one foot when he heard the noise.
His dick was still sunk deep inside a skinny blond boy's ass.

"I thought that might be you," he said, glaring at Cybele. "You'd
better get the cash for that violin, you little whore – pronto too, or I'll
call the cops."

She stared at his enormous dick with amazement, stunned into
silence at the spectacle before her. Crag had the biggest dick she had
ever seen. She just couldn't believe it.

He laughed diabolically at her expression.

"Some cock, huh? Bet you've never seen one this fierce," he
gloated at her.

The boy under him twisted his head around and looked at Cybele
with surprise.

"But Crag, you've got your cock ring on," the boy whined.

Cybele noticed a silver-looking ring around Crag's cock and balls.

"That's right," he said when he saw Cybele looking at the silver
cock ring. "It's sterling silver, baby." He pushed the boy's head
down and kept right on with his movements in front of her. She stood
there in a paralysis of shock a few moments longer, then fled out of
the shop.

"God, God, I've just got to get out of all this crap," she wailed
aloud in the hot, mellow afternoon. "Everybody's crazy, including
me."

She ran wildly along Wisconsin Avenue until she realised that
everyone had begun to turn around and stare at her. She slowed to a
fast pace as she headed on down the Avenue, licking her dried,
parched lips nervously and wishing desperately for something cold to
drink.

Ice Cream Parlour in large, antique lettering appeared before her
eyes almost as a mirage, and she turned impulsively into the narrow,
high-ceilinged ice cream parlour.

"Yesss maamm," a tall red-haired boy said. His pale blue eyes twinkled healthily. "What'll it be?"

"Oh, er. . ." she stammered, and stared in confusion at his angular, pleasing hand on the counter. Large pale freckles on his fingers and knuckles were splotched pleasantly between other smaller ones.

"Peach, strawberry, chocolate, vanilla, raspberry, lemon, orange, lime, chocolate chip, almond, pecan, rum. . ." he chanted happily.

"Oh, strawberry," she decided. "Uh, I mean chocolate," she amended. The wide old floorboards of the shop felt rough under her bare feet.

The young man smiled at her indulgently, then leaned down over the large vats of ice cream.

"Here ya are, miss," he said and handed her a cone heaped with ice cream. "One chocolate-strawberry."

"Gee, thanks," she said excitedly, and began licking the chocolate, then the strawberry dip of ice cream.

"There's a catch though," the boy said.

"Ummm?" she asked, with her cherry-red lips encircling the ice cream greedily.

"For you, 25¢, sweetheart. For anybody else – 50¢."

"Oh, sure," she said, and handed him a dollar. "Here, I'm loaded!" She laughed at his startled expression and walked back out onto Wisconsin Avenue.

The icy, satisfying cream trickled down her throat and refreshed her mouth. She could feel her cheeks tingling from the cold ice cream. A few drops fell onto her brown thighs and dribbled down the calf of her legs. She brushed them from her flesh and licked her fingertips happily. But when she came to the end of the ice cream and began crunching on the crisp, golden cone, a dismal feeling swept over her again. She saw the pale, agonised face of the young boy in her imagination as Crag hovered over him like a hulking beast.

"Ugh, such barbarity," she whispered, and watched the rhythmic pace of her tanned feet on the golden shadows of late afternoon that patterned the pale grey sidewalk like opulent, colourful ghosts.

'Like everything else in my life,' she thought angrily, and snatched a flower from a bush impatiently.

"But trees are so gentle," she murmured wistfully, and looked up at the all-encompassing canopy of sweet-smelling leaves bunched on branches of trees like the dollars in a successful bank vault, then back down at the light, feathery shadows that they made along the sidewalk.

"And flowers are so delicate and sweet," she sighed as she smelled the fragrant white lily that she had stolen. The tip of her nose was covered with yellow pollen when she drew it back out of the blossom.

"Oh, if only I were a plant," she pined, and sighed mournfully. She kept the long white flower up to her nostrils like a gas mask against noxious life odours. "If only I were anyone but who I am," she concluded dolefully.

Suddenly she stubbed her toe in one of the cracks of the sidewalk that jutted up over a large tree root.

"Ooww! Dammit." She stooped over her foot and clutched at her toe in pain.

"Oohhh! That happened because I'm ungrateful. That's it. I know it!" She gasped from the pain as she hopped up and down on one foot, holding her injured toe as if the pressure of her fingers might stop the hurtful sensation.

"I'll just go right home and hop in my beautiful Jag and go for a ride through the countryside," she decided, and hobbled joyfully down the street at her sudden decision. "Why didn't I think of that before? All these cabs I take and everything when I have that gorgeous car at home. What's wrong with me anyway? I mean, gosh, just because I hate to drive. Everyone can't have a chauffeur like Carot. . . I mean, after all. I've gotta stop being such an ingrate and do something with my life."

She hunted around on the avenue for a cab. Only the long, sparsely-populated avenue stretched down towards Massachusetts Avenue.

'Saturday's are a bitch for a cab,' she thought, 'and that's a fact.'

Suddenly the face of Anna Karina loomed up on the marquee of a theatre that she was passing by.

'Gosh,' she said, and stopped to gaze admiringly at the actress's high cheekbones and round, heart-shaped face.

'If only I were her. If only I could act like that.'

She stood before the picture for a few minutes, scrutinising every feature of her beloved actress's face and costume.

'Maybe I should go in here and rest a little before I go for the drive,' Cybele thought. She looked all around for a cab before going up to the ticket counter. 'I may as well,' she decided as she watched a crisp, yellow ticket emerge from the metallic silver slit after she had laid down a few dollars.

The faint moustache on a Greek woman behind the ticket counter lingered in her memory as she wended her way down the thickly-carpeted aisle of the theatre. She groped blindly for a place to sit, and settled wearily into one of the prickly, comfortable theatre chairs. As her eyes became accustomed to the theatre's darkness, she saw the pale face of Anna Karina framed by her long dark hair on the screen. Her almond-shaped eyes looked imploringly at the stern, unyielding countenance of an attractive older woman.

"God," Cybele whispered.

"Shhh," several people around her admonished.

It was very dark when she emerged from the theatre. The night was soft and fragrant as a deep red rose. Its silence assailed her ears like birds that had ceased to cry. She stood in front of the brightly-lit marquee and stared at the hard finality of the pavement under her feet. She saw Anna Karina throw herself from the window of a stately apartment and onto the cobblestones of a street in eighteenth-century France, saw the silky flounces of her formal dress spread out around her legs like a fallen swan.

'She didn't want to be a nun and she didn't want to be a whore,' Cybele thought. 'But she just couldn't find her place.'

She looked down the long, wide avenue. Music from a topless go-go joint blared out from a pink stucco building. Beside it a bakery filled with young freaks sent out its spicy perfume.

"Even when she escaped from the convent, she just couldn't find her place," Cybele said sadly. A pale, fat-necked man looked over his shoulder at her suspiciously while she stood whispering to herself.

A yellow and black cab pulled up to her bare legs almost as if it had been appointed. She slid inside and gave her address to the cab driver like a person in a trance, her actions never once interrupting her thoughts about the film of Denis Diderot's novel, *The Nun*.

'I'll get into my Jag and ride through the park,' she thought hysterically. 'That'll cleanse me of all these terrible experiences.'

She leaned back on the sweaty cab seat and tried to relax. But she saw vivid pictures of Hadrian chasing Juliette around her candlelit bedroom, saw his powerful hands on her sister's delicate wrists.

"No, no," she moaned softly.

"You told me to go to Massachusetts Avenue, lady," the cabby said nervously when he heard her moaning.

"Huh?"

" Massachusetts Avenue, right, mam? But what address?"

"Yes, yes," she said.

The cab driver looked back over his shoulder at her quizzically. His bushy black eyebrows were knitted together severely, giving his face the appearance of an angry crow.

Crag's oversized cock appeared in her mind as it pounded into the frail flanks of the slender boy who was hunched over on the floor of Brand's music shop.

"I've got on my silver cock ring," she heard Crag's deeply masculine voice say.

Lights glittered down Wisconsin Avenue like reflections on fine silver in a jewellery window. Cybele clutched at her chilled thighs in the cab's air-conditioning, trying to derive some manner of comfort from her own flesh. But the silken flounces of Sister Sainte-Suzanne kept spreading themselves out on the pavement in her imagination.

"She was so beautiful, so innocent," Cybele whispered to herself. "How horrible, horrible!"

"Do you see that tree down there?" she heard Eric say. "Imagine that someone saw it, went over, and for no reason, chopped it down. Well, that's how it is when you kill somebody. . ."

"Here we are, Massachusetts Avenue. Now where to?"

"Oh, er, 3895 – The Lancashire Apartments!"

Cybele sat with her head still lying back on the cab seat and her eyes closed, even though they had reached her destination.

"Hey, miss. You all right?" the cabby asked.

She opened her eyes to the sombre lights of the hotel-apartment building driveway, then closed them tightly against the stinging sensation that their brightness brought to her eyes.

"Yeah, sure," she assured him. "How much do I owe you?"

"Two and a quarter, miss."

"Here's three from me," she said.

"Are you sure you're OK, miss?" the man inquired again, looking at the distraught expression on her face.

"Of course, I'm great. Now you just take it easy yourself," she advised and pushed both buttons down on the taxi's doors as she got out.

The electric bulbs glowed dimly in the hotel lobby, lighting the brocaded wallpaper like yellow stains. Stuffing popped up from old sofas and red velvet chairs.

"He just kept right on washing his clothes for a minute while his brains fell out in the bowl," she heard Eric say. "First I blew his guts out, then I went for his head. They suffer more that way."

"Oh God, I've just gotta get outta here!" she wailed aloud as she walked up to the elevator.

The desk man's pale face scowled at her like an ill-done Halloween mask.

"You too!" she shouted at the man accusingly before she stepped into the elevator.

She pressed 'B' for basement and waited impatiently for the elevator to descend. She stepped out of the refrigerator-shaped elevator and stumbled into a stack of newspapers.

"What the fuck?" she screamed, and kicked at the old papers. "Always got this crap stashed around. What for?"

She thrust open the black steel door to the garage and peered through several rows of large Lincolns and Chryslers before she spied her sports car.

"Same reason he lights the stupid place with naked light bulbs," she observed truculently as she walked to her car. Its long sleek door opened stiffly under her fingers. She slid into the unfamiliar luxury of the car's interior like a stranger entering someone else's automobile.

From the corner of her eye she noticed two men sitting in the back of a faded blue car. For some reason she pressed the LOCK button on her car door down after she had seen them. As soon as the tip of her finger left the button, one tall, long-armed man began yanking on the door handle of her car.

'Oh God, this can't be really happening!' she thought as she looked up the long, wiry length of the Negro's arm.

"You may as well get out, lady," the man said. "We got you."

Cybele shook her head "no" like a stubborn little girl as she looked into the leering face of the tall Negro. He began pounding on the window of her car with the butt of a long silvery knife.

"God! God!" she screamed.

The other man swerved his car up behind her white Jaguar like a shrewd predator. The man at the window of her car pounded harder and harder on the window glass. A tiny crack appeared in the glass like the incision of a mad surgeon.

"Help! Help!" she screamed.

The man at her window smiled wider and wider at her terror. Small rivulets of sweat coursed down his greasy, mindless face.

Cybele hit the horn of her car and drew her keys up to the ignition slot with a hand that shook like a person fighting the freezing inertia of fear in an Arctic storm. She felt the key glide into the slot and turned on the motor as if with an energy that was not her own. The powerful engine of her car roared up like a disturbed lion under her slender thighs. She thrust the gear shift into first, and the car spurted forward like an unruly cat. The man's long black arm was displaced from her window like an extra-large toothpick as she shot forward into the old stone wall of the parking lot. The horn of her car wailed like an incensed animal as she rammed the round leather gear handle back into reverse. The sleek chrome bumper of her car clunked against her assailant's blue Chevrolet with a triumphant clink.

The black man at the window jumped back into position at her door and began yanking on the car handle again.

She froze with terror when she heard the metal of the door handle tearing off its slot like a breaking icicle. She looked into the black bucket seat next to her for a gun almost as a reflex action.

'If only I had one,' she thought savagely, looking into her harasser's sweating face with a violent hatred born from her intense fear.

She pushed the gear forward into first and prepared to ram the bumper of her car back into theirs again. From her rear-view window she noted the startled expression on the face of the man in the car blocking hers with satisfaction.

Her car hit his with a resounding thud. The strength of her car intimidated them, and the noise from her horn made them nervous. The driver of the old Chevrolet pulled back several inches from her car. As soon as she saw this, she forced her car backwards more and more until the man relented and moved further away.

'Gottcha!' she thought dementedly and took advantage of his shock by ramming her bumper onto his softer one until she could turn her car and flee out of the garage.

'God, am I fierce in the face of danger!' she thought proudly. She turned the air-conditioning on in the stifling, tightly-closed compartment of the new Jaguar. She started to stop for a red light, but decided to speed as fast as possible away from the two men.

'God, who could they have been?' she wondered. Her hands shook as she reached for a cigarette on the dash of the car. Perspiration from her fingers wetted the delicate paper around the long Benson and Hedges. She glanced in her rear-view mirror as her car tore across Massachusetts Avenue. The men were nowhere in sight. She lit the cigarette and sighed with relief.

'Maybe Hadrian's wife hired them,' she thought suddenly with alarm. 'She had those detectives waiting for us when we came back from the Bahamas and I told her where I live!'

She trembled in the coldness of the car's air-conditioning. Since she had only driven it several times before and was unfamiliar with the gears, it spurted and jerked along in the wrong gear. She put the long cigarette to her lips and dragged deeply on its firm, satisfying cork tip. The aromatic smoke filled her lungs and dizzied her brain. She coughed painfully as she flicked the car's air-conditioning off and rolled down the windows.

"Of course," she whispered with fear. "That's got to be it! The frigid bitch is trying to have me killed."

She flew by stately embassies lining Massachusetts Avenue in a flurry of haste and indecision. Anna Karina's pleading dark eyes kept invading her memory. Crag's large dick popped up in her memory as he jabbed it into the frail, excited boy on his knees in front of him over and over. The sound of the butt handle of the Negro's knife pounding on her car window still reverberated in her ears. She clutched the gleaming black plastic of the steering wheel and pressed down harder on the accelerator.

'Lucky thing I'm in a Jag,' she thought. 'They're the only car that can take the curves at this speed.'

The white snout of her car nosed around the graceful curves of Massachusetts Avenue like a high-powered machine, sleek and inspiring in its perfect synchronisation of motor and body style.

'Just like our Jag in Louisiana,' she thought wistfully. 'Screeching around those flat curves on the way to Biloxi at 130 mph. Wow!'

She shook head sadly when she remembered seeing Pierre's gleaming blond hair in the light from the red dashboard of intricate tachometer and speedometer dials. She saw his crystal blue eyes glance over at her whitened knuckles as she grasped the "sissy" bar in apprehension, saw his small white teeth bare themselves in a sensual smile of pleasure at her fear.

"Oh Pierre, Pierre," she moaned, and lit another cigarette in despair. She inhaled the strong nicotine deep into her lungs and sputtered it back out of her throat in convulsive little gulps. Its unfamiliar effect made her so dizzy that she swerved over the yellow dividing line of the road and narrowly missed an oncoming truck.

"Fuck!" she exclaimed hysterically.

"What happened to us, Pierre?" she cried out desperately. "What happened to everything?" She thought longingly of their bike rides along the George Washington Canal.

"This is my little pirate box," he had explained to her one afternoon when she had walked into his workroom and found him holding a small black leather box of rough design that he had made.

"Oh Pierre, Pierre," she sobbed. "I need somebody! I need somebody!"

She turned the car up into the driveway of a large stone house and clicked off the lights. Tears blinded her vision, and the smoke that she kept inhaling nauseated her.

"What a joke this all is," she whispered brokenly. "What a big joke." She stubbed the long cigarette out desolately in the small tin ashtray and lay back, tired, in the luxurious leather seat.

"I thought I was escaping from just this sort of crap when I left." She shook her head and stared glumly at the lofty exterior of the large stone house whose driveway she had invaded.

'I just hope one of those special guards they have around here doesn't show up and have his dog bite me,' she thought warily.

"What now?" She sighed with exhaustion. The tops of her shorts had rolled up like shrunken brown paper around her thighs. She pushed at their rough material until she felt the moistness of her cunt underneath.

'A little animal alive in my pants?' she thought wryly. 'And what trouble it's caused me. . . and pleasure.'

She sat in the comfortable bucket seat until she dozed off from sheer exhaustion.

She awakened to the clear, plaintive chirping of a cricket and stared up at lacy, circular patterns of fan-shaped plants which had been gracefully planted along the driveway.

"Oohh, my head," she groaned. She shifted her legs around under the steering wheel and groaned again. "Oohh, my body. Oh, my lungs hurt. God, why couldn't I have woken up dead?"

The long white hood of her car gleamed new in the dark greenery of bushes growing around the lavish house, untouched by human suffering or fatigue.

"I wonder what time it is?" she wondered, and switched on the radio.

"WMOD," the radio chimed. "Eleven forty-five."

"How thoughtful. Is there anything I ask for and don't receive?" she decided cynically. She turned the key in the ignition and gunned the motor gently with her foot. It purred softly in the deep velvet night, like a lion controlling its growl.

"Now will someone just tell me where to go?" She thought of the old stone walls of the garage she had escaped from earlier and shuddered.

"I can't go back there tonight. Never! Never!" she exclaimed, and pulled out of the driveway that circled the front of the house like an arc, with her lights still off. She wheeled back onto Massachusetts Avenue and turned at random down a street that led to Connecticut Avenue.

'My old stomping grounds,' she thought sadly.

She remembered walking slowly down Connecticut Avenue when she had still been living with Pierre, of long, timeless afternoons when walking Porge and contemplating her dinner menu had been the greatest of her distractions for the day.

'I wonder if Pierre's still awake? Wonder what he'd do if I showed up?' she thought.

She circled down the street where he lived and glanced up into the windows of the sunroom of his apartment that overlooked Rock Creek Park. The light from Pierre's desk lamp glowed yellowly through the diaphanous white sheers she had hung between sumptuous red velvet curtains.

"Uhuhh!" she gasped when she saw the vibrant reality of the light. "He's home. . . or else he left the light on just to scare away burglars like we always used to do."

She nosed her car into a parking space along the winding street and sat staring hypnotically at the lighted room. Tips of pendants on the chandelier sparkled from the high ceilinged living-room.

'My chandelier,' she thought sadly. 'Why did I have to leave it? I loved it so. I loved my doll's house so.'

She twisted the steering wheel back and forth in agitation.

"I think I'll go up and see him," she decided suddenly.

She jumped out of her car and ran across the street to the apartment building before she could have a chance to think and maybe lose her courage. She watched her finger press down on the intercom button as if it were guided by a force other than her own body.

"What apartment, please?" she heard the desk clerk ask.

"Apartment 518 – Mr Tashery, please," she added, hearing his name pass from her lips like a frightening news bulletin on the radio.

"Hello," she heard Pierre say,

"Pierre, it's Cybele," she said, and cursed her voice for trembling so.

"Cybele?"

"Cybele Tashery."

"Cybele! What are you doing here?"

"I came to see you, Pierre."

"To see me? But aren't you afraid for your life?" he asked drolly.

"I don't know. Do I have to be?"

"What do you want, Cybele?"

"To talk to you for an hour. I'm fucked up."

She heard the sharp whine of the buzzer on the lobby door and grasped the cold chrome of the door handle. She strode into the frigid air-conditioning of the lobby and smiled sweetly at the desk clerk.

"Good evening, Mrs Tashery," he greeted her. She felt the comforting security of respectability and marriage wash over her in the tone of his voice and her married name on his lips.

"Christ, what a difference from the joint I'm in now," she lamented and pressed the elevator button.

She felt her legs trembling as she walked down the long corridor to the door of their apartment. Pierre was standing in the doorway smoking a cigarette and looking at her rather curiously when she arrived. His hair had just been washed and shone golden in the soft light of the hallway. His slender physique was clad in a Scott Fitzgerald-like pinstripe jacket and dark slacks. The way he put his cigarette to his lips, with his knuckles touching his mouth, turned her on immediately physically.

"Pierre!" she cried, and flung herself into his arms. He clasped her tightly against his youthful body, yet there was something maddeningly detached about the tenderness she felt in his embrace.

'When I'd really like to be raped, he always ends up treating me like a newly hatched egg,' she thought impatiently. 'Besides, his body is so different from Hadrian's. It isn't the body of a strong man somehow.'

"You look great," he said, and stepped back from her embrace, the way one does from an apparition.

"You do too," she said. She looked all around the apartment as if she were revisiting an oft-repeated dream.

Exactly as she had imagined over and over since her flight from Pierre, now she was in the hallway, on the red carpet that she had vacuumed so many times before. Everything in the apartment was familiar, haunting and *hers*. And he was standing before her just as she had pictured him, with his head inclined slightly over a cigarette that he raised more in a gesture than in any desire. Below his dark pants, she saw that he had on a pair of black boots that they had bought together. She remembered how he had kicked her over and over on her shins with these same boots and trembled. The shirt that he wore was pale blue – or was it white?

"Come on in," he said strangely.

She looked past him at the brightly lit kitchen, then back at his youthful face with suspicion.

"You won't hurt me, will you, Pierre?" she asked.

"Oh God, Cybele, please don't use that tone of voice with me. Just to see you right now is the greatest joy I've had since you left!"

He dragged on his cigarette deeply. The muscles of his body were tensed so rigidly that he could have been snapped like a twig by a strong wind.

"Oh Pierre," she said for want of anything else to say. As she studied his face and body, she felt a familiar attraction for him, but it was ultimately an unsatisfying feeling.

'He just seems too young,' she thought, incongruously forgetting Sherman and Eric's youth. 'And he always gets mad. He'll always get mad for some dumb reason and beat me,' she realised with a sinking sensation. 'Still, still, he loves me so much, and he's so brilliant and charming.'

"Oh God," she said aloud, as he took her hand and begged, "Come on in," again softly with a gentleness that struck her as being newly added to his character.

The kitchen light was on and she saw the cabinets there that she had painted orange, the matching orange linoleum that he had laid down on the floor. 'I wonder if all my little spice pots are still there?' she thought, and remembered the dinners she had made for their friends longingly.

"Could I look at the kitchen a minute, Pierre?" she asked. "I just want to see all the little salad bowls and stuff." She looked past his glance of curiosity and shrugged with embarrassment.

"Of course, Cybele. If you only knew how many times I've pictured you there." He put his arm around her waist and hugged her like a brother. "I haven't had a cherry pie since you left. This is still your home, you know. You can go anywhere you'd like here," he said as he led her into the kitchen.

"Of course," she agreed with no conviction in her voice.

She stood in the kitchen with him and looked through the doorway at the sparkling elegance of the dining-room chandelier. The windows of the room were partially covered with green ivy, making the room look like a lush hidden arbour. She looked at the white linen tablecloth she had chosen that dressed the long mahogany table and felt an ache in her chest.

"Would you like something to eat?" he asked.

"What. . .? Oh, no thanks, Pierre." She turned back to him with a puzzled look on her face, then glanced down at a little red serving table by the sink.

"Oh, look! It's the little red table," she exclaimed, with her eyes lighting up as if she had seen diamonds.

"Yes, and here are all of your cooking utensils, Cybele," he said and pointed to the neatly arranged knives that he had always kept sharpened so well for her as if he had found a new, secret way of attracting her interest.

"Oh, yes, there they are – gosh!"

"Oh Cybele, Cybele, please come back," he begged, and began crying by the kitchen sink.

"Pierre, Pierre, please don't cry," she pleaded, and put her arms around him.

"Come look at our scrapbooks," he said, "then you'll realise everything you just threw away."

She followed him back through the hallway. She glanced into the oval mirror she had dragged home from a thrift shop and saw herself and Pierre as two forms – two "others".

'We're very young,' she thought to herself. 'We shall always be young together because I left before we got old.'

She shook her head in an attempt to dispel her thoughts. Balloons were going off again in her brain. She began to have that disturbing familiar feeling of being about to rise and float at will. She giggled hysterically, but he didn't turn around at the sound. He seemed intent also in living out something here with her.

"Here they are, Cybele," he said and began to lift a large box filled with papers and scrapbooks from a shelf in the hall closet.

She watched him lug the large cardboard box down as if he were unearthing a long-buried treasure.

"See, here we are down in New Orleans," he said, and held up a picture of them standing in front of the black lace-pattern of an iron balcony on a building overlooking the French Market. Her hair had been cut short and she held some books that she had just bought from the book shop at Tulane University where Pierre had been teaching at the time. Her large green eyes stared at the camera like a cat that had noticed the eyes of another cat in the lens of the camera. Pierre stood beside her in the picture with his blond hair gleaming like pale silk.

"Oh Pierre, how adorable we were!" she exclaimed. "Like two little dolls."

Pierre squeezed her happily and said, "Yeah, they used to call us Scott and Zelda, remember?"

"Oh yes, they did," she agreed vaguely. "I remember that. There was a famous writer who haunted the Press Club – I forget his name. . "

"Randolph Post," Pierre coached her.

"Yes, yes, Randolph. Anyway, he especially loved us, Pierre, and he especially called me Zelda and you Scott."

"That's right, Cybele," he said with delight. "See how glamorous we were together? So you really must come back. You must!" he said, and seized her imploringly.

"Pierre, please. You're crushing my ribs. I. . . I have to sit down somewhere."

"Come with me to the sunroom, Zelda," he play-acted.

"But I don't want to be Zelda," she protested as he led her through the lofty-ceilinged living-room. "Zelda ended up in an institution where she burned to death and she didn't accomplish anything she set out to do artistically. Her husband stifled all of that!" she rambled on in a daze of fatigue and punchiness.

"Yes, but she loved Scott madly," Pierre said smugly. "Just as you love – loved – me madly before you met that old goat – that old foreigner who's cast some sort of spell on you! Don't you see that, Cybele? He has you there at his whim – it's ridiculous – a beautiful girl like you, with a young husband who adores you."

"You know so much," she said cautiously.

"Of course I know. My father hired the best detectives for me in order to track you down, Cybele. We know everything – everything."

"Yes, you always relied so much on your father, didn't you?" she mocked.

"Don't get smart with me!" he warned, and shook her suddenly.

"Oh now, I guess you're going to beat me," she challenged. "I was wondering when all of the sentimental slop was going to end!"

He stopped shaking her abruptly, sobered by her cold tone.

"Well, what's wrong with my father helping me? You must understand someone wanting their father to help them, especially since everyone says that you're using this old Turk as a father figure," he accused. "And that guy is older than my father, Cybele," he added.

"Please, please let's not quarrel, Pierre. Haven't we had enough of that?" she said and sank down on the couch in the sunroom. "It's just that whenever you wanted to quit one of your innumerable professorships, you could always call old moneybags to tide you over until you finished the great American novel."

"You bitch!" he exclaimed, and slapped her with the back of his hand.

"Uuuhhh!" she gasped, and shrank back on the couch. She looked up at the wild expression in his blue eyes, panic-stricken when she realised that she was at his mercy again physically.

She saw his eyes dart around the room for some object to hit her with, and leapt up from the couch.

"No!" he cried. "Don't try to go. Don't, or I'll kill you," he said, and pulled a gun out of the desk drawer.

She sat back down on the sofa limply.

"Just sit there a minute and let me get my head together." he cautioned her. "I have to think a little. The things you say are so hard for me, Cybele," he said, training the barrel of the gun on her unconsciously.

She waited on the sofa apprehensively. A great dejection swept over her spirit. She felt like a person who had come seeking flesh on the bones of old skeletons.

He sat down in his desk chair, and laid the gun on the desk in order to light a cigarette.

"Want one?" he asked.

"Sure," she said, and reached out for the cigarette. He grabbed her hand and kissed it, then fell down to her knees, and began sobbing.

"I love you, I love you, Cybele," he declared.

"Yes, Pierre, we've loved one another," she said with a shaking voice, still looking at the gun on the table warily. She let her head drop back on the couch in exhaustion, and looked out the open, long glass windows at the trees in Rock Creek Park. They were large and puffy with fragrant leaves. Their full outlines were smudged like the marks made by purple pastels in the night's soft darkness.

"It's so beautiful in this room," she sighed.

"Yes, yes," he agreed. "It's just like you left it. But I threw your embroidery basket away," he said quickly. "Couldn't stand to look at it."

He raised up on his knees and began kissing her face. She turned her head to the warmth of his cheek. He seized her face and looked intently into her eyes with his brilliantly blue eyes. Their whites were a little red from lack of sleep. She touched his sideburn tenderly, ruffling the red black and blond hair that grew mingled there.. She directed her gaze to the silky blondness of his hair to get away from his eyes,

"Oh God," he said, and pushed her hand down on his dick. "I want you, Cybele. Say you want me too."

All around them the morning sent its coolness into the high-ceilinged room. The yellow velvet sofa was like a daffodil under their bodies. The green rug was like deep summer grass on the floor.

He kissed her again on her mouth. His lips were thin, and she felt repulsed by his small tight mouth. She realised how unattracted she had always been to him with intensity at that moment.

"Oooh, your hands hurt," she protested, feeling them tough and callused on her breast.

"Tell me anything you'd like," he said, and cradled her in his arms. "Just don't leave again – ever."

She still felt his eyes on her, on the top of her head, as he carried her through the living-room. He touched her hair lovingly, then pulled it away from her face and tilted her lips to his. She felt the firm litheness of his body against her thigh, felt her loins against his, her hands on his back, his cheek against her neck, and the prickly stubble of his beard.

She looked up at a portrait she had done of his grandmother, handing above a gold velvet chair. She was wearing an elaborate black straw hat that made her look like one of Toulouse Lautrec's ladies and holding a Dixie cup. Cybele had even painted in the brown liver spots on her hands.

"*Grandmère*," she whispered, feeling dizzy with exhaustion. Her throat was painfully dry.

"This is just the way I carried you over the threshold when we were first married," Pierre said happily.

'Yeah,' she thought. 'The threshold of that dinky little apartment where you beat me up three days later because you thought I was flirting with our best man when he came over to visit us.'

She gazed into the antique mirror hanging in the hallway over Pierre's shoulder. Her eyes burned with curiosity and there were dark blue circles underneath them. She looked like a strange child.

He walked into the bedroom with her and flicked on the light. She looked at the fine white Provincial furniture she had bought and said, "Still white in here."

He held her so tightly. There was a hysterical touch from his hands on her body. She noticed a substantial glass jar that had filled with candlewax during all of his fuckings since she had left. She glanced down at the fawn-coloured oriental rug. It was a little soiled under his feet. On the dresser she saw pots and jars of creams and perfumes that weren't hers.

He sank down onto the bed with her. She was so tired, so tired. She lay back on the pillows voluptuously and put her arm around his neck.

He kissed her cheek softly, then felt the right side of her temple. His fingers were trembling from exhaustion and his emotion.

"*There* they are," he mumbled. He found two moles at her temple and pressed them, as if their tangibility proved that things didn't disappear.

"Why do you like them?" she asked, pulling her face away from him and smiling sleepily at him.

"Because they're real. Because they're still there. See?" he said, and touched them again. "They didn't disappear like you did. I can count on them."

He propped his head up on his elbow and looked at her searchingly.

"Cybele, why did you leave? You've been the most precious treasure of my life." He buried his head in her hair and began kissing her all over her face.

"I adore you. I adore you."

"Yes, but Pierre, besides being your precious treasure and being adored by you – which I always loved, don't get me wrong – I want to be a human being."

"Of course you're a human being, Cybele, one of the most beautiful people I've ever known," he replied.

"You say I'm a human being, but you used to throw my philosophy books at me. You hated the ideas that were so important to me, Pierre – don't you remember that? A person has the right to develop her own concepts about life."

"I'll buy you any book you want, Cybele. Who cares about a fucking book when it comes down to you and me?" he cried in an agonised voice.

"But my books are important to me. I loved the ideas of my philosopher as much as you sometimes, Pierre. You could never accept that."

"And what else do you love – or *whom*, should I say?" he demanded, and gripped her wrist cruelly.

"Pierre, you're hurting me," she gasped. "You're not going to hurt me again, are you?" she whimpered. A strong fear swept over her whole being as she looked into his cold blue eyes.

"Oh no, no, I'll never hurt you again, Cybele," he declared, still grasping her wrist in his excitement.

"But you are hurting me right now," she said, and looked down at his hand on her arm. 'And you would still hurt me if I came back,' she thought. "You would! It's all still there between us – the same unsolvable problems. And I don't love you at all." She thought and shuddered. 'In fact, I loathe you,' she thought with horror.

"Oh, I'm sorry," he apologised, and looked down at his hand around her wrist as if it were something apart from himself. He released her arm and began tracing the profile of her face reverently, as if he were touching a sculpture by Rodin in a museum that had erected very precise signs reading DO NOT TOUCH under the artwork.

"You are my ideal woman, Cybele. Even your flaws are endearing to me," he said and kissed her softly.

She was beginning to feel weak from fatigue. Her head ached and she could hardly keep her eyes open. She kept wondering what Hadrian was doing, and worrying that her visit with Pierre might prevent her from getting back to him somehow. The thought began to cut her almost in two as she sat staring at Pierre's pale, ugly face.

"I know that even more than ever now since you left," he continued.

"All of the women I've been seeing are like empty paper cups compared to you. And if it's that old man you love, Cybele, then he can be a friend of ours – together," he emphasised.

"Pierre, you're so tender to me," she exclaimed. "And aren't you aware that I've suffered horribly without you, too?" She lied. "But I love Hadrian not just as a friend."

"OK, OK," Pierre screamed, and jumped up from the bed. "You love him!"

"Maybe I'd better go, Pierre," she said, trembling all over as she lay on the bed.

He towered over her, pale and shaking.

"No, don't go, don't go. I'm not going to do anything else," he said, and reached into his pocket for a cigarette without taking his eyes from her face. "In fact, if you try to leave right now, I might do something."

"OK," she sighed. "Do anything you want. You've already done everything you could do to me except murder me. As a matter of fact, that's one of the reasons why I came here tonight," she told him.

"What do you mean?" he asked apprehensively.

"Two men tried to kill me in my garage tonight. I think they were hired by Hadrian's wife."

"What?" he exclaimed.

"That's right," she affirmed his fears. "Only a few hours ago someone was pounding on my car window with a knife."

"Cybele, what kind of weird life are you leading now?" he asked.

"I dunno," she said, and looked into the open closet. New dresses hung there. Someone's language books were on the shelf with a thick dictionary underneath them. "Juliette says it's always been this way."

"Juliette? When did you talk to her?" .

"She came up here – a week ago. I thought her presence might strengthen me. Hadrian tried to do a threesome with her and me."

"Shit!" Pierre said. "I've gotta go and have a drink. Can I bring you one?"

"Some wine, please," she said.

"Oh God, oh God," she moaned after he had left the room. "What the hell am I doing back here?"

She lay back in a heap of hair and silken sheets and looked all around the room that she had once abandoned.

'I have to think of a graceful way to exit,' she thought craftily. 'Oh God, maybe you can present one,' she prayed. She laughed nervously.

"I'm just like the nun. I'll never find my place. Every situation will always be the same. I wonder which window I'll jump out of?"

Pierre walked into the room with two steaming cups of tea.

"I decided that tea might be better than alcohol at this point," he explained solicitously.

"Oh, yes," she drawled and sat up alertly. She looked at him cautiously as he walked towards her with the steaming cups of hot tea.

"Now, wait until it cools," he cautioned her. "Don't burn yourself."

He put his arm around her and handed her the cup of tea carefully.

"Ummm," she said, and looked up at him gratefully.

"See, I can take care of you, Cybele. I know what you need more than those other creeps you've been hanging out with."

He rubbed the little dip in her collar-bone and kissed her on the cheek nervously. He was being so gentle with her that she was really amazed. She couldn't remember having inspired this degree of tenderness in him before. But in spite of his actions, she felt like a little mouse in the paws of a giant, temperamental cat.

'I don't trust him, I don't trust him,' she thought. 'And all I want to do is get outta here.'

"You can drink it now, I think," he said. "It's Earl Grey – the best tea in the world, in my book."

She raised the cup of hot tea to her mouth. As she brought its boiling depths to her lips, she recalled Pierre telling her that he had once thrown a bowl of hot soup on his first wife, and she trembled.

'And if I do anything wrong right now, he might do the same thing to me with the tea,' she thought. It was the first time in many weeks that she had had to genuinely fear someone physically and the feeling was very disturbing to her.

"Ummm, great," she said, knowing that he was expecting some form of approval for the tea from her. As she drank the tea she glanced at his face surreptitiously. It was suddenly tired looking, also. His young body was slouched beside her in fatigue. She realised that her thoughts were unfair, that her worries were unfounded – for the moment, anyway. She put her empty teacup back onto the saucer, and glanced at him again, still wary of what he might do.

He took the cup and saucer from her hand and said, "Now lie down," without any hint of sexuality – or was there? She was too tired to distinguish any longer.

She lay back on the pillows gratefully and closed her eyes. But the Negro man pounding on her window with a knife flashed across her inner eye. And the end of Pierre's gun followed this disturbing image.

"Oohhh," she moaned. "I'm tired."

"Go to sleep," he said, and lay down beside her.

She found the closeness of his body repugnant at that instant. His form embodied all of her fears and insecurities. She wanted to move away from him, but was afraid to do anything too abruptly, afraid of arousing his feelings of insecurity for her and thus his illogical anger.

"What is that smell?" she asked and looked at him alertly with the cunning of a cat, pretending to be interested in the spicy smell that she had noticed upon her first moment in the apartment.

"Oh, it's Sophia's bubble bath. It's the greatest stuff," he said, taking the bait immediately.

"Yes," she agreed. "It is nice." She rolled over a little bit away from him.

"I'll tell you the name so that you can get some," he offered naïvely.

"OK. Who is Sophia?" she asked cleverly.

"Oh, she's the girl I've been seeing," he volunteered. "Madeleine introduced us."

Cybele thought of the plump, pretty French woman who was their neighbour and laughed.

"Oh, Pierre darling, that woman is seducing you by proxy. The French are incredible, really." She started to laugh. "Pierre, why do you think there's such evidence of Sophia all over the house?" she asked, anxious to enlarge on the subject of Sophia rather than the idea he had for her to sleep with him. She knew that it must be near dawn and that he would have to go to work in a few hours. She propped her head up on one elbow and looked at him with curiosity. He floated in front of her like a lake. The cool, Nordic colour of his eyes and hair, which he had inherited from his mother's side of the family, gave him a distant, elegant manner.

He shrugged. "Guess women are just more personal than men."

"Oh Pierre, Pierre, what a fabulous remark – only you could have said that," she complimented him.

He turned towards her and smiled tiredly. The phone ding-donged. She watched his body tense and smiled a sad smile to herself. "Who could that be?" she asked.

"Dunno," he mumbled, somewhat embarrassed, and not looking at her.

"Could it be Sophia?" she asked. "Answer it, please."

When he left for the phone, she knew that it would be easy to make an exit. She went into the living-room and gathered up her purse, then looked all around the apartment before she had to leave it again.

He put down the receiver. "She's coming over."

"Well, I'd better take off."

"You could stay," he said.

"Nah, I better go. Don't you think that would be better?" she asked, looking at him and feeling half amused with the situation now that her fear of him had subsided. 'Nothing like another cunt to take a maniac's mind off one,' she thought cynically, but with great relief.

"Well," he said, "I don't want any scene."

"Pierre, you will never have a scene from me," she assured him. She walked up to him and hugged him goodbye. "Everything will be OK," she said.

It was dark in the hallway of the apartment. He opened the door hesitantly. She understood how strange he felt.

Outside the door she saw Babette and King, two honey-coloured cocker spaniels that belonged to Madeleine and her husband scurrying along in front of their owners with their silky blond ears and tails waving like golden cornstalks.

'Oh my God,' Cybele thought. 'The last busybodies I'd ever want to bump into at 7 a.m. in the morning.'

"But Cybele, what do you do here?" Madeleine demanded accusingly.

She looked at Madeleine's pale, handsome face and braided blonde hair and thought of wine and French bread. "Well, Madeleine, I just dropped by for a visit with my husband. Lucius, how are you?" she asked Madeleine's husband with a pointed politeness.

They shuffled past Pierre's doorway as quickly as possible. Cybele felt Madeleine's snapping disapproval floating off her well-rounded shoulders as she bustled off hastily down the hallway beside her diminutive husband, and began grinning to herself.

"Pierre, darling, I'm exhausted. I have to go."

She leaned over and kissed him on his ear. He stood silently before her like a well-flogged prisoner.

Cybele ran down the cool hallway and out into the bright morning sunlight. She saw a cab screech to a halt and a tearful, ruddy-faced girl alight and run up to Madeleine and Lucius. The emotional girl turned to watch Cybele as they gestured down the sidewalk at her.

"Sheeut," Cybele said to the squirrels, to the summer morning air. "Sheeut, got out of there just in time."

As she started her car, she glanced over at the apartment and saw Pierre standing by the windows of the sunroom watching her. His arms were flung out against the dark screens like a man on a torture rack.

She couldn't see the pain on his face, but she could imagine it.

"Pierre, Pierre, thank God I'm rid of you!" she said. But he couldn't hear her. Then she noticed Mr Grandin, another neighbour of theirs, pointing frantically at her car door. She looked down at the door, wondering if it was on fire, and saw that one of Porgy's leash and collars had been caught there. She smiled and waved at the dapper Englishman as she pulled the leash back into the car. He lifted his hat politely while his black, overgrown poodle ran ahead of him like a precocious prodigy.

'Christ,' she thought. 'The English are so fucking civilised.'

She glanced up at the sunroom windows once more, but they were empty now. She pushed the stick-shift smoothly into first gear and spurted ahead in her white car through the humid air. The early morning was already collecting the heat of the coming afternoon.

Chapter Eleven

"Cybele, I've got to talk to you," she heard a hoarse, soft-syllabled voice say.

"Sure, Brandon." She yawned sleepily and sank down into the pillows that she used to stifle ringings from the phone with until she woke up. "Shoot," she said tomboyishly. Pierre's blue eyes still wavered in her memory like a Nazi soldier.

"It's Cragmont, Cybele. He's trying to murder me," Brandon sighed raggedly.

"What?" she exclaimed, trying again to stifle a yawn. Her whole body ached from her night-long visit with Pierre.

"Can you meet me somewhere, dear?" he asked.

She heard a match scrape against a wooden box of matches and imagined the Lucky Strike he held tightly in his lips, fresh and firmly packed, its edges crinkling like fast disappearing lava as he dipped the cigarette's pistol-like end into the flame.

"Of course, Brandon. You sound so upset," she said, worried, and dug her big toe into the pillows lying around her like new-fallen snow.

"Can you pick me up in a cab?" he asked.. "I can hardly walk."

"Oh God, Brandon. What on earth has happened to you? I'll be right over, OK?" She blinked uncertainly into the darkened living-room. "What time is it anyway?" she asked, realising with a start that she had been asleep more than twelve hours.

"About nine-thirty. Maybe we can get something to eat," he said hoarsely. "Haven't had anything for ages. I think he's trying to starve me to death too."

"OK, I'll be in front of the shop at 10 p.m. If Crag's trying to starve you, it ain't gonna work," she added, trying to introduce a small note of humour into the grim situation. "'Cause we're going to have the thickest, bloodiest steaks you've ever seen. OK, y'all?" she drawled.

"Y'all'd better believe it," he answered weakly. "But I'm afraid there's more to it than that, dear."

"What are you talking about?" she asked. A shiver of fear rippled up her backbone like the finger of a ghost.

"He's dropping pills in everything I drink."

"What kind of pills?" she asked. Her fingers had become icy with fear around the phone receiver.

"Barbiturates, tranquillisers. Anything he can get his hands on." She heard him drag deeply on his cigarette.

"Oh no, Brand. Oh no!" she repeated.

"Oh yes, sweetheart."

"But we've got to get you out of there, Brand. Right away," she said, staring out at her cat's silhouetted figure on the balcony, lost momentarily in the machinations of his paw as he washed his face with deliberate, rhythmic strokes. Porgy sprang off the high stone railing of the balcony and onto the porch. His heavy body hit the stone floor like a water-filled balloon.

"OK," she resumed, jolted by the cat's sudden movement. "See you in twenty minutes."

"I'll be outside the shop. With a harp," he added.

"Ha. Brand, I think you'd make a joke even if you were going to the gallows."

"Honey, the hangman just walked in," he said, and laughed hollowly through the receiver.

"Crag?" she asked, trembling.

"The very same. But I'll be downstairs at ten – don't worry," he assured her and clicked off.

She ran into the bedroom and switched on the light, looking for the nearest thing to put on. Over the fat, mushroom-shaped seat of her vanity table she noticed the shorts and top she had thrown off after coming in from her visit with Pierre. She brought her hands up to her head in a gesture of confusion and pressed the sides of her temples with her fingertips.

"I've got to keep things straight," she said to no one, and stumbled over the vanity table, bruising her leg.

"Goddammit," she said, as she opened the door of the clothes closet.

"Excuse me, God," she apologised seriously, and pulled out a dress that Eric had bought for her in Georgetown one hot afternoon.

She put it on hastily. Its organdie material scratched her nose and shoulders like fine sandpaper. She grabbed her purse without bothering to look at her face for once and ran to the front door. Suddenly she remembered that she hadn't brushed her teeth. She bolted back to the bathroom and squeezed some toothpaste into her mouth, then ran off through the door.

Brand was huddled in the doorway of his music shop when her cab pulled up on M Street. The material of a cream-coloured windbreaker that he wore was laced tightly around his slender shoulders, blown against his flesh by a whirling, racing wind.

"Brand!" she called.

He spied her after a moment and ran up to the cab, peering at her through the window with dark, sunken eyes. She was so startled by his ravaged face that she thought momentarily of telling the driver to move on before he could enter the cab, then shuddered involuntarily at her cowardice and swung open the car door.

"Thanks for coming, sweetheart," Brand said as he climbed into the seat beside her.

"Of course I'd come," she said, looking at his emaciated face and figure with stunned surprise.

"Yes, of course you would," he said, staring hard at her through his lachrymal, grey-green eyes.

"Oh Brand," she said, and hugged his bony shoulders impulsively. "Er, we want to go to Dino's Steak House," she told the cab driver. "It's only a few blocks down."

The cabby looked at her quizzically, wondering why they didn't walk. When Brand put his hand in hers, she wasn't surprised to find that it was trembling. She stared again at his cachetic face and felt a disturbing sensation of anxiety course through her body like the dangling chord of a bell.

The cab flew down M Street and onto Wisconsin Avenue to the restaurant in an unusually lucky run of green lights. Brand gave the driver some bills with a hand that was visibly shaking, then stumbled out of the cab.

"I'm doped," he explained helplessly.

"Never mind, Brand. All you need is lots of hot food," she recommended, and steered him into the restaurant. A long-legged hostess, whose glistening, red-lipped smile matched her red uniform, led them down to a snug, cushiony booth. They stepped gratefully into its hidden confines and sat looking at one another furtively. Each of them was glad to have the other's company, but they were both afraid to look too closely at the other's face, afraid of what they might divine there.

"OK, what's up?" she asked with mock simplicity.

"Nothing. I haven't been able to get anything up for ages," he joked, and laughed nervously.

"Yeah, downers do give one that propensity," she agreed.

She watched him light another cigarette. Her heart sank when she noted his vitiated face. She felt her last real link with stability dissolving, and stifled a sigh.

"Oh God, Cybele. Where are we all going anyway?"

"How about the zoo?" she quipped, surprised at her unexpected humour.

"That's a good idea," he said. "At least there we'd all have a title."

"Brand the Brave!" she offered.

"And Cybele the Cunt – gosh, what am I saying?" he asked, and blushed furiously.

"No, really," she said. "Don't feel badly. I take it as a compliment."

She put her hand over his to reassure herself of their platonic friendship, but she was jolted by his uncharacteristic lapse into vulgarity. She felt her fingers brush the old gold ring bearing the crest of his famous family that he wore on his index finger, and relaxed with a familiar feeling of security and identity antique, approved things brought her.

"Honey," he said, and pulled her hand up to his lips. You're too sweet."

Once again, the sound of his soft southern drawl gave her a feeling of belonging, and calm descended on her.

"You don't need to shake your head like that, Cybele. I'm not going to rape you – unless you get under the table, that is. And I've already told you, until I sober up from these drugs I'm zero anyway."

"Which brings up the question of food," she noted practically, and began glancing seriously at the menu.

"I don't know if I can eat," he said uncertainly.

332

"Definitely, you can eat. OK?" she assured him, and called the waitress over authoritatively. "Two of your biggest, bloodiest steaks, please," she ordered. "And two Heineken beers."

"God," he exclaimed. "You make it sound like a massacre!" He looked searchingly into her eyes for a moment, then asked, "Have you got a pen, sweetheart?"

She fumbled in her purse and brought out a black ball-point with *Zürich* inscribed on it, that Hadrian had left at her apartment one night. Brand took it and began writing laboriously on an old envelope that he had pulled out of his pocket.

"Shit," he said in a slurred, pathetic voice. "I can hardly write." He looked up at her with tears glistening in his eyes and handed her the note.

"Here," he said, while she tried to read the barely legible scribble. "I want you to have this also." He pulled his grandfather's ring from his finger and handed it to her.

She looked at the ring gravely, then slipped it on her finger. She was stupefied that something she had venerated for such a long time had been given to her so freely. Then she read the note:

"*Cybele, I should have married you two years ago*" he had written.

She kept her eyes glued on the note, trying to avoid whatever might be in his eyes. He was a man she had considered like a brother now offering himself in a new, disconcerting context.

'And how like him to pass me a proposal in a note,' she thought. 'How charming.'

"You would have taken care of me," he went on in a desultory voice.

Her heart sank when she realised that he only wanted her for another mother figure – or did he? A slight pain began to throb at her temples.

"Don't say anything back," he cautioned her a little incoherently. "I just want you to know what's in the note and have this ring before I tell you all this other shit."

"Yes, tell me about everything, Brand," she said anxiously, sentient again of the reason for their meeting when she heard the hoarse whisper of his drugged, unnatural voice.

"Crag is trying to kill me," he stated with startling candour. He's using drugs and liquor to do it. He puts it into my food – everything.

And he thinks I'm so fucked over that I don't realise the shit he's pulling."

"But why, Brand?" she asked, genuinely puzzled. "Why? I know he's a 'fiercey' and all of that, but I thought you two really dug on one another," she finished lamely.

"Why?" he repeated and nailed her eyes with his saturnine gaze. "Because when I'm thirty-one I get forty million dollars from the American Chili Company. And, like a fool, I signed everything over to Cragmont in case of my death when I got mad with Daddy last year – even the music business, which along with the record sales amounts to a good eighty thousand a year from the shop alone. I'll be thirty-one in fifteen days," he added meaningfully.

She sat toying with the crumpled, dirty envelope that he had written his proposal to her on, trying to understand the full value of his statements. The impact of his words frightened her into a confused silence.

"You mean you inherit that much money?" she asked, flabbergasted. "My gosh, Brand, I had no idea you were so rich!" she exclaimed, then blushed furiously at her words.

"Oh, I'm rich, honey," Brand assured her. "In money I'm fine." He drained the rest of his beer and sat looking at her with a wry expression.

"But Brand, you've got to get out of there. Why don't you just leave?" she asked, then immediately remembered why he couldn't leave. 'He loves that monster,' she thought. "Oh God," she said aloud.

He looked at her searchingly, scrutinising her face for a long moment, then said, "Cybele, let's go away together – we'll fly to Europe. Anywhere you say. I can afford it," he added, as if by backing his words up with the power of money he could make the trip materialise.

She sat in front of him, making small knots out of the note he had passed to her like a schoolboy, wondering what she should say. The dark, wooden walls of the restaurant decorated with old cow harnesses and western paraphernalia swamped her thin, tense body. She saw people and events in her life flying back and forth into unselected categories until she felt a great dizziness seize her brain.

'Everything used to have its own slot to fit in,' she thought hopelessly. 'It was OK when I played the games, but now it seems like I'm only another pawn being moved by anything and everyone.'

She began to laugh in self-defence.

"I'm glad I inspired a laugh. But it wasn't exactly what I had in mind," Brand remarked sadly.

"Oh Brand. You know I'll go wherever you'd like, if it would help you any," she amended her statement. She knew Brand was literally controlled psychologically by Cragmont and that she could never have a normal relationship with him because of this. In her mind she saw Crag feeding on Brand's weaknesses like some animals who devour their own offspring.

"Then come with me tonight," he proposed earnestly. Perspiration tricked in a small line from his hair onto his smooth, youthful forehead. "I won't go back to the shop for any of my stuff – I'll just buy clothes along the way," he decided. An insane gleam shone in his eyes.

"You look so innocent sitting there, Brand," she observed. She looked at his slender shoulders in the white windbreaker, at his hands that he held clenched together, and felt a swift, maternal urge to hug him and let him lay his head on his breast.

"None of us are innocent, Cybele," Brand countered. His eyes resembled those of a person sinking in quicksand.

The waitress set plates of steaming food before them and they began to eat hesitantly, each for the first time in twenty-four hours.

"You realise, my dear man," she said, plopping a large piece of meat in her mouth, "that we lead highly irregular lives?" She laughed sillily.

"To say the least," he agreed, and began picking at the food as if it were a foreign substance.

"Let me come back to your place tonight," he asked, grabbing her hand impulsively.

"Sure, Brand. You come back to my pad and figure out what you want to do. We'll solve this problem together," she assured him.

Their words brought both of them a temporary reprieve from their thoughts. They began eating their food earnestly, both feeling a slight queasiness from the meat entering their empty stomachs.

"Yum! Yum!" Brand smacked. "Haven't had an orgy like this in ages."

"Yeah," she agreed and laughed. "Not like this."
"Oh, you're rich, sweetheart."
"I try," she agreed and smiled impishly at him.

A light, misting rain had begun when they stepped out of the restaurant, making the brick façades of buildings glisten with a false cleanness. She pulled Brand close to her side protectively and hailed a cab. He sank inside the car like a collapsed umbrella. His face had a pale, almost greyish colour as he leaned his head on the dark, rain-patterned window in exhaustion. But he managed a strange little smile of sang-froid that attested to the better part of his character.

"Listen to the rain," he said. He moved his knees listlessly and lay his head back on the cab seat that smelled of human flesh and clothes, of baking sun and wintry rains.

"Where to, ma'am?" the cabby interrupted.

"Lancashire Place," she directed. "On Massachusetts Avenue."

"Each little drop is a small chord of music," he said softly. The material of his white windbreaker rustled against her shoulder like dry leaves. "Each rain is a planned concert."

He sighed heavily and lay his head on her shoulder. The golden, burnished curls of his hair touched her cheek like downy feathers. The rain-moistened street lamps glowed through the purple night like lustrous pearls.

"Oh Brand, how lovely to hear you say that!" she exclaimed, enchanted suddenly by the cab's smell, by the soft pressure of his hair on her cheek, and his words in her ear. She listened carefully to the raindrops.

"Which concert would this remind you of?" she asked thoughtfully.

He breathed stentoriously beside her breast. All of his limbs had relaxed, pressing themselves on her body like a doll thrown into a chair by a child. She assumed that he had fallen asleep until he answered quite clearly, "Fantasy in C major, by Robert Schumann."

He jerked his head up erratically, like a puppet reanimated by an unreliable hand. The sound of his own voice had evidently startled him. He looked all around with bleary, unfocused eyes, then flopped back on her shoulder.

"Makes me feel like a plant that sat in some rain forest for a thousand years, absorbing the rain, observing the leaf of every sort of plant around it, noting the exact way that God turned their leaves to the wind and air and sun," he muttered with the uncanny lucidity that sometimes comes during long periods of stress or sleeplessness.

"Perhaps you were a plant, Brand!" she exclaimed joyously. "Oh, do you think so?" she asked, tugging at his arm. "What kind do you think you were?" she asked, waiting expectantly for his next remark.

"Purrppllee," he slurred, and lapsed into a deadened slumber.

She sat close to him, patting his hand, then she turned to observe the wet, glistening street. Hues of the buildings lining Wisconsin Avenue rippled outside the rain-distorted pattern on the cab window like a neon-lit rainbow. Their ribbons of colour echoed through her body as if they carried sound. She thought of a Renoir she had seen in a gallery a few days ago – a pastel of a girl holding an orange up in the air, drawn with soft, apricot-brown chalks. Her lips had been parted slightly, as if struck with wonder at the fruit's creation and of her own being. The whorling, fan-like movement of the etching's strokes had been so intense that Cybele had had the illusion of hearing sound coming from the picture.

"Does one hear with one's eyes?" she wondered, then felt a slight pressure on her shoulder. She turned and saw Brand sleeping peacefully on her arm.

She hated to wake him when the cab pulled up onto the rose-pink tiles of her apartment building's driveway. However, the sombre lights from the old lampposts lining the driveway penetrated the car's interior and awakened him before she had the chance. The whites of his eyes were like the red lines on a road map as he looked wildly about.

"What? What is it?" he asked excitedly. "Where are we?"

He clutched at her hand until she felt the tiny line of his close-cropped nail cutting the flesh of her fingers.

"Cool it, Brand. Just take it easy," she advised him, trying to palliate his wild reaction to the new surroundings he had wakened to. "You're flying on those drugs, old man. Makes you as paranoid as hell."

She saw the cabby's eyes narrow when she mentioned the word 'drugs' and hurriedly pressed some bills into his hand.

'Christ, I'm stupid,' she thought. 'What if he calls the cops or something dumb like that?'

She hustled Brand out of the car, smiling ingratiatingly at the driver while planting frantic little kisses on Brand's cheek.

"Thanks ever so much," she said to the driver and winked, pretending to flirt with him.

Brand stumbled up to the building's big revolving doors and looked about dizzily.

"No!" she shrieked.

He turned around and gazed at her with an expression that was so terrified that she was afraid he might run away.

"That is, Brand honey, I don't want the desk clerk to see me going in with you. They're so archaic here, and the landlord's got a vendetta against me anyway. Let's go around to the back," she said coaxingly.

He stumbled drunkenly as she guided him laboriously to the back entrance. Above them a full moon floated on a sea of clouds. Its brooding white light shone heuristically through the sinewy branches of the old oak trees that surrounded the driveway and onto the gravelly path before them. She shivered from the night's dampness under the dead weight of his arm that he had draped over her shoulder for support.

"Just a few more steps to the elevator, Brand," she said, and looked at him anxiously. "Don't fall asleep on me 'cause I'll never be able to carry you."

"I'm. . . where are we going?" he asked. The slurred quality of his voice was more pronounced than ever.

"To my apartment. Don't you remember?"

She looked around hurriedly, gasping with fright when she saw the wet, dark shapes of the massive oak trees sitting like stern sentinels in the lawn's overgrown grass.

"God, how'd you get so smashed?" she asked, then remembered the beer that they had drunk with their meal.

"How many pills have you had today?" she asked suspiciously.

"Howsha I know?" he drawled, and fell in a heap by her legs.

"Oh m'gosh, Brand. You've got to get up. Please!" she implored him.

"Hee, hee, hee. Aha, aha. I feel so psszazzy. Ha!" He giggled and rolled over on his back, holding up both of his feet and hands like a dog.

"Brand! she screamed. "God, why is everyone I know nuts?"

She picked up a stick and held it out to Brand. "Nice doggie," she coaxed, "come and get the bone."

As he crawled along after her through the back entranceway, giggling demoniacally, a loud clatter like a harsh volley of pistol shots ripped through the moist night. She looked up quickly, seeking the source of the sound, and saw Mr Master's cold, fishlike eyes gleaming chatoyantly through his old, discoloured blinds.

He pushed up the window and yelled, "Don't bring any more bums in here!" A great spell of coughing shook him. "You're no good," he rattled through his phlegmy, aged lungs. "We're going to get rid of you," he threatened and slammed the window shut.

"God, what an old devil," she muttered, while tugging laboriously at Brand.

"Cybele, girl," Brand said, and hoisted himself up suddenly, almost pushing her over. "I'm gonna make it."

"Sure you are, sweetie. Here's the elevator," she said and steered him inside.

The merciless lights of the elevator showed the pale greyness of his face. He looked so wan that she debated whether to call a doctor or not.

'I'll figure that out tomorrow,' she thought. 'All I have to do now is get down that long hallway.'

"Sssspretty swell joint you live in, C.," he said, looking dazedly at the small chandeliers lining the high ceilings of the hallway.

"I imagine you've seen better," she panted, supporting him partially while they walked along.

Finally she felt her key in the lock and pushed open the apartment door. Brand staggered in after her, blinking in the room's partial darkness.

"You've got a chandelier in your living-room," he exclaimed in surprise, and stood gazing dumbly at the solitary chandelier hanging in the almost empty room. It had struck some inchoate chord of memory in his fogged consciousness.

"Yes, I was going to make it very dressy in here – like the place I had with Pierre, but. . ." Her voice trailed off from exhaustion.

"It's strange in here," he observed with a drugged candour. "But pleasantly so," he added, looking at the diaphanous white curtains and red velvet drapes at the windows.

"Yes, it is, isn't it?" she agreed, feeling odd to have him in her apartment. "You've never been here before, I just realised. . ." Again her voice trailed off. She wondered if he should sleep on the bed with her, or on the sofa.

'Oh fuck,' she thought. 'Why not on the bed?'

"Come on in here, Brand. You've gotta get some rest." She pulled him along like a drunken teddy bear to the bedroom and switched on the light.

"Why there's Porgy," he observed very formally.

Porgy blinked his green, owl-like eyes at them, then promptly went back to sleep.

"Come, Porgy, say hello to Uncle Brand," she said, and approached her bed self-consciously.

She began stroking Porgy's large, wide head. Each rhythmic stroke of her hand sent a balm comparable to a tranquilliser through her body. Brand sank down beside her and petted the cat's back with an unguided caress, then flopped onto the bed and fell asleep.

She carefully extricated her cat, then turned off the light and lay down beside Brand. The closeness of his body gave her the same feeling she had had sometimes with Pierre, that of a youthful brotherliness. She lay silently, waiting for a thousand torturous thoughts to assail her, used to their attack in the past month.

But a light sleep descended mercifully over her tormented mind. She lay fully clothed with her hands by her cheek, as if praying. Once during the night she awakened to feel Brand's clumsy kisses on her neck and cheek, and thought of a small child's awkward caress.

"One of these days I'm going to make fantastic love to you," he murmured softly and fell back into a heavy slumber.

Near dawn she heard him cry out, "Crag!", and saw an expression of agony cross his face. She put her arms around him and patted him gently, drawing her body close to his and trying to still his trembling.

"Don't leave me, Crag!" he cried, and began sobbing weakly in her arms.

"Shhh, shhh, darling. I won't leave you," she crooned, rocking him back and forth with the motions of her own body.

When she awakened the next morning, only her cat lay on the bed beside her.

"He's gone," she said to Porgy. "Gone back to Crag. Stupid bastard!"

Chapter Twelve

She heard a sharp rap on the door and ran hurriedly from the brightly lit bedroom, still holding a lipstick in her hand. She peered through the peep-hole of the door and saw Sherman's handsome face pulling itself back from the door to let her look at him, knowing with his usual shrewdness that he was being observed. At the sight of his firm jaw and cream-coloured sports coat, of his fierce brown eyes staring indifferently at the wall of the hallway, she jerked the door open with a flourish of excitement. She stretched her thin body against the pebbly stucco walls in anticipation.

His keen eyes studied her face and eyes, then moved to her body. In spite of herself she felt a thrill in her lower abdomen akin to ice water, a thrill so sharp that she moved back suddenly from his presence.

"Well, Cybele, looks like you've got on your little blue jean outfit tonight." He looked down at her sardonically. His long thin legs were clad in dark knit slacks. His shirt was conservative. The tie he wore was wide and thick – a brocade.

They glared at one another. Each of them was thrilled with the sight of the other. Both wondered if their sarcastic bantering would allow them to fuck that night.

"Why don't you try coming in?" she said, sneering prettily. "Don't you usually do that when you have a date? Or don't I count?"

She frowned as she looked up at him, resenting his youth but loving it, resenting his clothes but loving them, resenting his education but respecting it. Again she stared at his hands and thought of the things he could do with them. It excited her to think that the same hands that could save a human being, which could cut their flesh so deftly in surgery, might also caress her.

He strode into the apartment officiously. Porgy ambled up to him with an expectant meow. "Oh God," he said. "Here's that damned

342

cat again." He glanced around the room hurriedly, as if trying to make a quick diagnosis, until his discerning eyes spied a little glass.

"What've you got here, Cybele?" he held a small wineglass to the light as if it were a test tube, then sniffed it. "Drinking brandy at 7:30 in the evening? You're supposed to *finish* the evening like that."

"Well, you know I never do anything right – just what I feel," she reminded him. "There aren't any hospital rules around here. Why don't you have one, too?"

"No thanks, I've got something better." He sprawled back on the old green velvet of the sofa and took some grass from his pocket.

Cybele grinned delightedly. "Sherman, Sherman, honey, what *do* you carry around with your stethoscope?" Porgy leapt up on the sofa beside them, anxious to be included.

"Goddamned cat," Sherman complained as he sifted a correct amount of grass out onto a thin white paper. "Whew, he's got too much hair."

"Don't scare him, Sherman, please. He's very sad these days."

"God, you're really nuts, you know it? Why would this fucking cat be sad?" He rolled the cigarette paper over the grass.

"Don't even talk about Porgy, will you?" she asked him haughtily. "You could never understand anything about him or me in a million years." She flopped down beside him and pushed her body as close to his as possible.

"Sweet little thing tonight, aren'tcha?" he said, and handed her the grass.

She drew it down into her lungs deeply, then she let her head flop back on the velvet of the old sofa and stared up at the chandelier, noticing that Porgy was watching her all the while from the corner of her eye. She leapt up and ran over to him.

"Darlin', my little darlin' Porgy!" Porgy jumped up into her arms effusively, and sat like a ball of white, black and orange fur.

Sherman walked out onto the balcony to escape. "Looks like your friendly landlord has to do his own maintenance," he remarked as he observed Mr Master watering the lawn.

Cybele ran out onto the balcony with Porgy struggling in her arms. He sprang out of her embrace and pulled the screen door open with his paw so that he could get back into the living-room. She leaned against Sherman's back and looked past his shoulder. Mr Masters was holding an old green hose that sprayed water in a thick, uneven stream on the limp, sun-wilted grass. She stared at the dark liver spots on the top of his head. His shirt was white and wrinkled over his wide, massive chest. Again, she thought of a crumbling Roman statue.

"You should see his rose garden!"

"I didn't see it, but I heard about it."

"Want to see some more bones George and I found?"

"God, this place is straight out of St Elizabeth's, Belle."

She ran to the bedroom and got a large hat box. She came running back to the living-room and out onto the old stone balcony.

"See!" she proclaimed excitedly and handed him the box like an animated child.

Sherman opened the lid slowly as if afraid to understand what lay inside.

He pulled a bone fragment out of the box that was the size of his hand.

"This is part of someone's skull, Cybele. Here's part of an eyesocket. Looks as if their skull was crushed."

He looked at her with horror. "You've got to get out of here. If this is really what I almost know it is, I'm going to report it to the police."

"Better be careful, Sherm, sweetie. They're going to want to know how you found out about it. My husband will find out where I am – he is as bad as old Masters." She looked at him shrewdly. "Wait until I get out. I'm leaving in a few days. You don't want to drag your family and your career in dirt."

"You're so concerned about others' reputations, while your own neck is at stake." He studied her sadly. "This couldn't be another of Hadrian's lessons?"

She smiled at him dazzlingly with her wide full lips shining redly from lipstick. Her white teeth stunned his senses with their pearly perfection.

"How could someone like you be in this situation?"

"I'll be OK. Hadrian will get me out fast."

"I hope you aren't trying to re-enact one of your mother's grisly tales. That happens to people, Cybele. They try to recreate what they've been taught in childhood."

"Christ, what a joint you live in, Belle!" Sherman said.

344

"Perfect, isn't it? It's absolutely perfect for my lifestyle," she answered sarcastically.

"Oh, get off that shit, will you?"

"It's not shit," she said, handing him back the joint. "Just like your parents' penthouse apartment is good for *your* style, this is perfect for *mine*. It's just a seedy hotel," she said, gazing down on Mr Masters like a sorceress. "Replete with old horrors."

"Time to get out of here," Sherman decided wisely. "I'm going to run you around in the grass until you sing."

"You never get tired of playing 'the role in white', do you?" she said angrily.

"Belle, Belle Lady, what am I going to do with you?" he asked, and contemplated her body, imagining his dick inside her as he did so. He felt a mild depression when his mother floated into his mind.

"Darling, you're here to entertain me, naturally," she replied, "and after the past few days I need to be entertained."

She thought of Brand's miserable condition and sighed. "God, and I haven't even had a chance to call him," she remembered.

"You sigh like you just laid open fifty cancer patients," Sherman remarked cynically.

"You don't know everything that happens in my life, Sherman the Shark," she said. She picked the key up from the hall table and took his arm. "Lead the way, lover."

They walked down the long hallway together: Cybele was oblivious to its shabby appearance and Sherman was ignoring it. Crag's rough, large face kneeling over the boy came back to haunt her again.

"Should I call the police?" she wondered.

When they came out of the mouldy lobby into the soft twilight of the early summer evening, Cybele was flying on marijuana. She saw Mr Masters watering the grass by the driveway through a wavy haze of euphoria.

"Hi, Mr Masters!" she shouted, waving at him the way a child at a circus acknowledges a clown. In spite of himself, Mr Masters waved back at her.

Then, realising who she was, he picked up an old rake and shook it at her.

"Belle, you're nuts," Sherman decided. He stared back at the old landlord. "That guy's a real psycho! He looks like Frankenstein."

The old man returned Sherman's stare. "Getta outta here wid that little Jezebel!" he snarled, and waved his rake at them again.

Sherman stopped walking and seized her by her slender arms. "Look," he said, "I'll be glad to put you up in a hotel until you can find another place."

"Yeah?" she said and smiled. "You're nice when you work at it." She gazed up at him for a moment, squinting from the bright daylight, then said, "Where d'you park anyway?"

"You really don't seem to realise how bizarre this old goat's behaviour is," Sherman continued and looked at her, worried.

"I do. . . I do," she said vaguely. "It's just that so much keeps happening and so fast. Maybe next week I'll get a new place. I'm sure Hadrian would let me, 'cause his wife knows where I live now."

"How does she know that?" he asked with surprise.

"I told her," she said and smiled impishly up at him. "God, why d'you do that?" Sherman asked.

"I was mad with Hadrian," she explained.

"Christ! You're such a child!" he said with exasperation.

"Yeah, I think she hired these guys to murder me the other night!"

"What?" He grabbed her by both wrists.

"I was down in the garage, backing my car out to go get Porgy some cat food when these men pulled an old model car up behind my Jag, and another one started banging on my window with a knife."

"This story gets worse and worse, Lou." He looked at her and shook his head incredulously. "I didn't even know you had a car – you said a Jag?"

She smiled triumphantly at him.

"What kind of guy gives a seventeen year old a Jaguar?" he asked with incredulity.

"A man with plenty of bucks to throw around and a lavish lifestyle," she replied smugly. "Also, an old man trying to snare a very young girl."

"You know your assets really well, don't you, kid?"

"I'd better have something to operate on in this situation, don't you think, old Sherm baby?"

He looked at her longingly, passionately.

"I'd buy you one if I were a rich old man," he said with a smile.

"Belle, you're nuts," Sherman decided.

"Yeah? Where d'you park anyway?"

She skipped ahead of him happily. She had changed her blue jeans outfit for a pair of shorts before they left, and her brown legs moved nimbly along in the fragrant summer day.

"Why don't you put your shoes on, Cybele? Why stand there with them in your hand when you don't know how long it'll take me to get this door open? You know, you're gonna get blisters on your feet from that hot pavement." He grinned at her tauntingly.

She grinned back at him over the hood of the low-slung convertible, still holding her shoes.

"Stubborn as an old mule down South, aren't you?" He yanked his door open and slid his long frame into the black leather seat.

She stared down at the gold bars on his shoes. "You know, you always wear the same kind of shoes," she said.

"You do, too. Always the same ones. I started to buy you a pair the other day."

"Well, why didn't you? I'll never get anything out of you, let's face it."

"Oh, you get something, don't you?" He put his hand on her leg with a particular expression on his face. "Legs are a little less spongy, Cybele. Been doing your exercises again?" He started the car without waiting for an answer. Its huge engine roared like a hoarse lion.

"For a Corvette your car sounds pretty good; of course, it's not like my Jag. Doesn't have that English class."

"Like you, Belle?"

She smiled triumphantly and stretched her legs out in front of her.

The wind felt good whipping through her hair. She looked at Sherman's handsome blondness beside her with pleasure. He was a good-looking Jew, but something about his being a Jew made a difference. The difference was a feeling of space, a gulf. It wasn't a bad feeling, but one that she couldn't get rid of because where she was from had inured her to the idea.

'Still,' she thought, 'maybe that's part of the fascination.'

Suddenly Pierre's figure pressed dramatically up against the window of the sunroom flashed into her mind. She remembered his plea for a reconciliation, and frowned.

"Sitting over there mighty quiet, Cybele. We'd better not let you think too much. Here, wanna see something that'll make you laugh?" he asked, and reached down and unzipped his fly.

She stared at his pants in amazement. 'Oh well,' she thought, 'just another first,' wondering if he was going to pull his dick out and why.

"How do you like the underwear?" he asked, and pulled his pants open.

She looked down at the navy and white jockey shorts he was wearing, then back to his face, and she started to laugh.

"Like that, Belle?" He grabbed her knee again and squeezed it hard while he laughed his idiot laugh with his tongue lolling out of his mouth.

"Jesus, I sure am glad you've got me around as your tension reliever!" she exclaimed.

"My little black widow spider, aren'tcha? You and your deadly remarks," he complained.

She noticed fine grin wrinkles around his soft, full lips deepening under his tan. The sight of their pencil thinness cutting into the perfect shape of his face excited her. Her eyes drifted back down to his knit slacks, stopping at his knee and noting the way they were so sharply creased.

She slipped over beside him to kiss his neck and to get his smell, then lay back on his chest and watched the leafy greenness of the day speed by, happy to escape from the apartment and all the unpleasant events of the past few days. He took his hand from the gear shift and held her with his free arm.

"Let's go back where we went for the fireworks. Down by the bridge."

When they arrived near the Lincoln Memorial, she jumped out of the car and ran over to a small bridge.

"I like to dream – to touch things," she said, and ran her hand along the top of the bridge. "I like to feel this bridge against my ribs. I can imagine its graininess cutting my flesh."

She looked at the material of his slacks. It also had a pebbly quality. He pushed her back on the bridge and smiled down at her. She studied the expression on his face as he grinned at her. His eyes were full of an adolescent superiority.

"Oh Belle, Belle, you just like to go around being a strange chick." His voice was husky. It brushed her ears with its sexy timbre. He pushed down on her shoulders and massaged them with his large, firm hands. Again she looked at his hands and thought of what they could do. She felt a controlled violence in him somewhere, as if he were holding himself back from pulverising the bones of her arms. She trembled with delight when she felt his large dick on her legs.

"I like to see the moon," she said, twisting out of his grasp and turning her body towards the bridge again. "I like to watch it there – so high and bright. I can imagine it is pulling me. I can feel that. It is up there and it pulls me harder and harder – a gigantic blue-white magnet that sucks me suddenly through the bridge."

She pressed her fingers on the stone railing, rubbing them hard along its surface. Sherman kept massaging her neck and shoulders in a steady rhythm that made her feel as if she were sailing through the night. He pulled her up to him and began kissing her with his warm, full lips. His tongue tasted sweet between her teeth. When she opened her eyes, she looked into his and saw them glittering darkly in the night. His high cheekbones stood out prominently in the moonlight.

"Ohhhhh, I'm alive, I'm alive!" she shouted, throwing her head back and letting him break her from falling with his strong arms.

"Funny little thing, aren'tcha?" he said, looking at her face and body hungrily. She giggled when she saw his curiosity.

"Come on, moon-gazing time is over," he decided. "Let's go and have a drink in Georgetown." He looked at his watch. "You've got about another hour. I gotta stay in the hospital tonight."

"Oh?" She studied him slyly, relaxing in the lightness of their game. "And I thought you were going to spend the night with me."

"Isn't your place a little crowded these days?" he asked pointedly.

She walked back towards the silver Corvette, shivering from the dampness of the Potomac.

"Ummm, no, I don't think so. I take them one at a time." She set her mouth in a bitter smile. It felt good and tight across her teeth. She clamped her toes down on the carpeting of the car as he started the motor. It whirred in her ears with a whizzing, metallic sound, making her stomach ache with pleasurable shots of feeling. They sped along the George Washington Expressway like people in a fast, mechanically controlled toy. A slight stench penetrated her nostrils from the river, sometimes fishy smelling, other times a strange, sweet pungency of pollution. She saw a good portrait of herself in the car mirror and smiled more grimly when she noted the deep circles under her eyes.

"God, I really don't know how I get into these images. I mean, the scenes I fall into are so third rate," she protested to him.

"What are you launching into now, Belle? Another one of your bitchy tirades? Why don't you just be nice and light a cigarette for me?" He glanced quickly into the car mirror at her face, betraying his nervousness. In spite of his superior position of his money and education, she had the disturbing ability to hurt him. He kept believing in her goodness, but a horrible cynicism boiled out of her in unexpected moments. He looked at her again, and was surprised at how pinched her features had become. 'So different from the dreaming girl on the bridge,' he thought.

"I mean, God, a Jew in a Corvette, a med. student." She sneered every word.

"Why do you always call me a Jew when you hate me and a Hun when you like me?" He smiled at her, and in spite of her anger she pushed herself under his arm. There was a faint smell of perspiration there that excited her. She felt her cunt grow wet, and let the sensation between her legs soothe her brain. As they sped under the brightly lit tunnel, she felt a familiar fear making her hands grow cold.

"Oh, I don't know why I call you anything. You're just a dick, that's all."

"What am I supposed to say to that?" he asked, hugging her closer.

"You make me feel so strange, Sherman."

"I just want to be your friend – so relax, will you?"

The oversized tyres of his car rolled bumpily over the old cobblestone streets of Georgetown. He swerved into a small space, almost jamming the wide snout of his car into a motorcycle parked in front of them.

"How about that for talent?"

"Sure, sure. My boy's got lotsa talent – my son the doctah," she said, with her version of a Jewish accent.

"How'd you like a bust in the mouth?" he threatened. He was still smiling, but she was beginning to get to him.

She didn't answer him, but got out of the car silently. In the city the air was hot and fetid. She saw her face in the one-way mirror of a restaurant called "The Third Edition". It was glistening slightly with grease. She followed along beside him lamely, feeling spent and aimless. Her days were trackless as a desert. She thought that she should live some other way but didn't know how. She looked at him secretly and felt a sudden rush of admiration for him. She saw him fastening his pants hurriedly one morning after they had spent the night together, his fingers clumsy with sleep, as he rushed to be on time at the hospital. She hadn't slept the whole night he had stayed with her. She still couldn't get used to being with more than one man.

"You wanna go in here?" he asked, interrupting her thoughts.

"Yeah, why not?"

They walked into the candlelit interior of the club and sat down at the bar. She noticed the same waiter who had tried to get a date with her a few nights before, trying not to look at her. When he brought the drinks, she smiled at him dazzlingly.

"Friend of yours?" Sherman asked, and lifted his glass to his lips.

"Nah, you're my only friend. You know that." She patted him on his expensive sports coat. "You know, I really like your clothes."

"Yeah? I wish I could say the same for yours."

"Don't tell me you're getting in a bad mood, just when I was coming out of mine." she said, bored.

"Yeah?" he said sceptically. "Well, I'd be pleased to hear about that."

"As a matter of fact, you inspired me. I mean, when I thought of your proposed profession and all that jazz."

"My proposed profession is doing just the opposite for me," he sighed.

"*Pourquoi?*"

"Oh Belle, you're a scream. You're bound to teach me something. You're so different from anyone I've ever known."

"But why doesn't it inspire you?"

He stared into the mirror behind the bar at their reflections.

"It's so sterile. You stay with a patient a couple of minutes, do what you can, then rush on to the next one. Everything moves so fast that you don't even remember their faces – just a series of white beds. The way to make money is in plastic surgery – I know that. But there's the fact that I can't feel involved. I thought of being a gynaecologist, but everybody knows what a rat race that is."

"But don't you want to do something that makes you happy? When we were at the pool, you were playing with some children. I was surprised. I guess you're the only guy I've met who does."

"You know, you're really something else when you try to act nice, Cybele." He leaned over her and lolled out his tongue. "Today I threw half of an old woman's face in a bucket."

"Ugh," she shuddered.

He laughed when she cringed. "It's nothing terrible to get upset about. She's gonna be the happiest old lady you've ever seen in a couple of weeks. She had her face lifted!" He studied her profile in a mocking way and pushed the skin back from her face.

"I'll give you your first lift, Cybele, don't worry."

"Fuck you," she said.

"Fuck you? I mean, Cybele, where *did* you study anyway?"

"Oh, don't get smart with me, you five-minute lay." She experienced a delicious terror when she felt his body grow tense. "What about the stuff you study anyway? So you can slop old ladies' flabby faces in a jar? OK, great, but you don't seem so happy. I mean, you know something? I'd really like to see you happy. I didn't lie when I said I admire you. But look what you're doing with it. I mean, why don't you try to relate to it all? Why don't you stop thinking about money?" She took his arm and squirmed around to his position. "Sherman, why don't you just stop eating kumquats?"

She dropped her head on his arm and secretly rubbed the grease from her face onto his coat.

"I was only trying to tell you how I feel about my medicine. I want to feel warm about it, but there's. . ." – he paused, gropingly – "I want it to be more personal. Anyway, your time's up, Cybele. Gotta go to the big white house."

"I guess I'll get back to my cave," she said wryly.

"Yeah, the animals are all waiting for you," he countered.

Chapter Thirteen

Eric's room was grey and pale green. The light streaming through the long window of his bedroom made each object sit with a curious finality of its own. As soon as she stepped into the room, she could smell Eric and his life there. The room was deserted like never before as she peered into its cosy silence. The hair on the back of her neck prickled, and she felt a spasm of dread in the bottom of her taut stomach. Her kneecaps ached when she turned and walked down the long hall to explore the rest of the apartment.

Maria was sitting on the black leather sofa like a pale flower. Her carrot-coloured hair and breasts hung over the geometrical shape of a clothes pattern lankly. "Hi, Cybele," she said in her wispy little girl's voice.

"Maria, where's Eric?" she asked.

Her heart sank with an intuitive dread as she stared at the transparent quality of the girl's skin. Fragile, feminine freckles were sprinkled like cinnamon across her nose and dappled her complexion like those of a strawberry mare. 'He's left me. I know he's left me because of what I did with Sherman,' she thought with panic.

"Hi, Cybele," another voice echoed into the hollowness that the whole room had taken on for her. She looked up to see Jeff's watery blue eyes. She drifted her gaze flutteringly at the emaciated whiteness of his chest under his open shirt. Beside him the same pussy willows that she and Eric had scooped up a week before at a "rock-folk" wedding outside a church stirred in the early afternoon breeze.

"Where's Eric?" she asked again frantically, scratching one heel against her ankle with the white plastic of her *Evan Picone* pumps until her skin bled. She stared at Jeff with mounting fear.

"Oh, he's with Randolph," Maria said, still cutting out patterns in the lilac-coloured cloth.

Cybele rushed back down the hall to Eric's room. A smothering coldness flooded through her forehead. Her breasts shrank with apprehension. She felt ill. She knew! She knew! He had left her. She dialled Randolph's number.

"I. . . Hi, Randolph," she said when she heard a masculine voice answer the phone. "Is Eric there?" She stared at the veins on her arm. They were so swollen and green. She was like a tree being tugged up from the ground by its roots and trying desperately to hold on.

"Yeah, he's here."

She waited. "Well, can I speak to him?"

"Yeah, OK."

She waited several minutes. She wanted to vomit.

"Yes," a bored tone finally said through the minute little holes of the receiver.

"Eric, it's Cybele. I'm at your place. I walked over from the pool." She waited for his answer. He didn't speak. "Are you going to be here anytime soon?" she asked, hating herself.

"No, I'm not going to be there anytime soon. I'm into something over here and I don't want to stop."

"OK, Eric." She hung up the receiver. She felt dizzy. Back out in the sunlight of the ripe summer day she swayed unsteadily on her feet. She hadn't eaten for two days. She didn't like food anymore. She liked to fancy that she survived somehow on orange juice. She gazed across the street at the red brick façade of "Dorothy Guest", the dress shop where Brenda worked. She felt that she had to get home. She looked down into her soft white leather purse. She could find only thirty-five cents. She thought of walking back to her apartment but knew that she would never make it. Her hunger made her think of her cat, and she remembered the cat food still in Eric's bedroom that she and Eric had bought a few weeks ago when Porgy had stayed with them at his place. She hesitated, wavering with indecision, then thought, 'I have to be responsible.'

She paused for a long moment before turning back into the apartment that was now like a nightmare for her, then she strode through the door again, looking at Eric's room. Maria and Jeff still sat in the living-room. Their pale, untanned bodies looked insubstantial and ghoulish on the black leather furniture.

"I forgot the cat food," she explained to them lamely.

"Why don't you stay a while, Cybele?" Maria asked, still cutting, snip, snip, through the whispering paper of the pattern.

"Yeah," Jeff said, looking up from a comic book and smiling sweetly at her.

"No, I couldn't. I couldn't stay," she replied. She went back to Eric's room and got the paper bag, full of cat food off the old black chest of drawers and ran out of the apartment.

She ran across Q Street and into the clothes shop where Brenda worked. "Hi, where's Brenda?" she asked an Italian girl with long, dark hair and large brown eyes anxiously. Before the girl had a chance to speak, Cybele saw Brenda standing at the end of the corridor, haggling with three teenage girls. She was dressed like a gypsy, with a red bandanna that looked like a sliced pimento tied around her brown curls. She waved her ring-encrusted hand at Cybele, then propped her tiny knuckles under her chin like a fisherman watching a big fish take the hook on his line as she watched the customers' faces. She made a sale and came rushing up to Cybele with an exuberant smile on her lips. But then she noticed Cybele's expression and asked, "What's wrong?"

"Eric ditched me, Brenda. Can you loan me the cab fare to get back to my apartment?"

Brenda walked over to the counter and pulled her floppy Mexican leather purse from under a stack of yellow sales slips.

She handed Cybele five dollars and asked, "Do you need any more, Cybele?"

"Nah, nah. Thanks, Brenda."

She staggered out of the store. She looked at her shoes. They were not shoes that one wore with shorts. And what was she doing wearing shorts on the street? The stores she passed by seemed as if *they* were moving, instead of her.

"What's happening to me? Where is my husband? What have I done? What have I done?" She paused at a STOP sign. "How can I have left? Why?" She shook her head. She thought of the filthy apartment where she lived, of the way Porgy was having to live. She grew hysterical. She fished down into the hollow of her purse for a dime she had seen when she had been searching for some money earlier. When she found it, she ran into a phone booth and dialled the familiar number.

"Hallo," the parrot-like voice said.

"Hadrian?"

"Oh, Cybele. How are you, dear? What a day I had? Are you ready for our orgy tonight?"

She stared at an overweight girl selling dyed carnations. As usual, someone had pissed in the phone booth. She leaned against the cold steel chrome of the phone shelf dizzily.

"Cybele, Cybele, are you there?"

"Yes, Hadrian. I'm here."

"Well?"

"Hadrian, please meet me, right now."

"What's wrong?"

"Nothing. I mean, I don't know – but I don't want to have an orgy tonight."

"OK, OK," he said. "Where will I meet you?"

"In Georgetown."

"OK, at the Carriage House?"

"OK," she said.

"Be right by the restaurant then. We have to be careful these days. I think that my wife is still having me followed – dammit! – and all because of your insane phone call!"

"Well, I think she hired some people to *kill* me, so don't feel so worried just for yourself!"

"Hah? What you talking about?" he yelled excitedly.

"Oh nothing – I'll tell you when you show up, OK? Anyway, I gotta get outta this stinking booth. Please hurry, Hadrian. I'm really crashing."

"I'm there in twenty minutes," he declared and clicked off in her ear.

She stood inside the phone booth in a semi-daze until the acrid odour of urine drove her out. She looked down at her fancy pumps and decided that she would be much more comfortable without them on. She slipped them off and sighed with relief. Her feet were swollen from the heat, and the paper bag filled with cat food that she held was heavy. The bag felt gritty in her hand, and she longed to get rid of it somehow as she had done her shoes. She stared down at her big feet and thought of her childhood. Going barefoot then had never seemed out of place.

"What happens when you get older anyway?" she mused. She stared out into the white dazzling sunlight until her eyes lit on banks of red carnations and yellow roses. She walked over to a fat lady selling the flowers and bought a rose, then she resumed her position close to the phone booth. She held the long-stemmed rose up to her nose and took little whiffs of the flower's fragrance while studying the flower lady more carefully. The woman wore a pair of wide green boots.

'She's older,' Cybele thought, 'and I hate her.' She tried to understand exactly why she hated her. 'I hate her because her hair is coarse and bleached blonde. 'Ugh!' she thought. 'But no, I want to get past the revulsion of my feelings. I want to think with my brain and not just respond with my emotions.'

She-saw the woman digging in a dirty green apron for quarters. She smiled at a man she handed some flowers to, then leaned back against the white brick of the building and squinted from the sun. Cybele could see a vein beating in her thick neck. Her heart was pounding under the weight of her heavy breasts. Finally she glared at Cybele and yelled, "Think you're something, don't ya?"

Cybele stared back into her narrow green eyes, surprised by her attack.

"Buyin' one rose – that's cute, huh?" she hissed through her teeth like a snake.

Cybele looked at the red rose she held. It was wilting in the relentless summer heat. She stood still and silent, waiting for the woman's next remark. She was really amazed that the flower vendor had had such a strong reaction to her purchase. She hadn't thought that it might irritate the woman if she bought only one flower. She had been happy to feel the slender green stem cool between her fingertips. The plump red bud was like the end of a dick. Green leaves that surrounded it were delicately serrated. Each one grew singly and completely on the stem.

"Think you're pretty, don'tcha? Well, you're just a bum!" the woman snarled. "You buy one rose 'cause that's all you can afford! Whadya holding your shoes for like that?"

Cybele looked down at her shoes. She had forgotten about taking them off. She leaned down and slipped them over her dirty feet, then looked back at the vendor for approval.

"Oh, that's smart, real cute. I guess you think you've got a real act going."

Cybele's silence seemed to incense her.

"Are ya deaf and dumb, too? Why don'tcha say something?" she demanded. "You don't need to, though. I had your number the minute I saw ya walking up the street sleep walking. Whaddaya on anyway? Opium? I think I'll call the cops and get you off the street."

Cybele's eyes went out of focus as she gazed at the jabbering figure in front of her. She felt a mild distress at the woman's rage, but outside of that her brain blurred with images of Eric and Pierre, and the stream of whitely glittering traffic moving along Wisconsin Avenue. Tears began to stream down her cheeks from the exhaustion of her body.

"Oh, Brand, we were right. This world is just a big, colossal zoo. And what's happening to you in your cage now?"

Suddenly she heard the abrasive voice of the old woman again – harsh, unreal, something to be stilled. She walked up to the old hag and handed her the rose.

The woman turned pale around her pink, flared nostrils. She trembled with anger. "Stick it up your ass!" she screamed, but Cybele didn't turn around to answer her as she crossed the street through the shimmering chrome bumpers of cars and waded through the pollution and steaming heat of the day.

She stood under the awning of the Carriage House restaurant, waiting for Hadrian and feeling dizzy. In front of her a bearded, tanned guy stood selling Moroccan wallets with camels engraved on their soft leather backs. The leather of the wallets was like the tanned, soft leather of his suede pants. His feet were bare, and she liked the caked blackness of the dirt around his ankles. The colour of the dirt reminded her of the bottom of Porge's feet. Long Indian strings of leather on the guy's pants hung limply by the sides of his feet. All of his body was pliant, like the texture of what he wore and sold. He looked at her with bright black eyes, then scratched between his shoulder blades and grinned slowly at her. She smiled back.

"Hey, babe, can I kiss you?" he asked, and put his slender hand on her hip.

She looked down at his hand on her body, studying its perfectly made bones and the pink colour of the blood under his nails. Her eyes travelled slowly up the line of his hip to the fuzz of his beard and stopped there at the blackness of it. She thought of her childhood teddy bear. "Teddy bear, teddy bear," she whispered to herself. She felt his lips brushing hers and stepped back.

"Wow!" the guy said. "Wow, you're something else."

She stood looking at him in a catatonic daze. Soon she heard the strange chant of the balloon man as he ambled up the street.

"Make the children haaaapppy, make the moother haaapy, make ev-rebo-dy ha-aaapy – with a ballloonn," he chanted. His softly palpitating load bumped and swayed on long beige-coloured sticks in the sky. Behind him she saw Hadrian walking towards her swiftly and determined. He looked like a foreign soldier in some unknown campaign, grown old in a light-coloured jacket. She looked at the dark tan colour of his silk tie, at his swarthy face, at the sensual curve of his lips, at his thick body coming purposefully towards her through the wavering, white light of the afternoon and felt pleased. She wished that they weren't having dinner. She preferred going back to the apartment and fucking without any conversation.. She needed the solid thickness of his body to substantiate her, to pour over her. He was suddenly by her side, looking critically at the boy in front of her.

"Are you talking to the hippie boys again, darling?" he asked sarcastically and loud enough for the guy to hear him. "C'mon, I'm hungry," he told her and took her hand impatiently.

The boy crossed his angular arms over the hard ripples of his flat stomach defensively and began to sneer at Cybele slowly.

"So *that's* it," he said to her as Hadrian turned abruptly to the heavy black door of the restaurant and grasped its oblong gold handle. It curved coldly under his powerful hand. She saw his hand laying hold of the handle again and again in her mind as they entered the cool gloom of the corridor, and she felt wet between her legs.

'I want to fuck. I want to fuck,' she thought happily.

"I'm sorry, sir, but we can't allow the little lady to dine here dressed in that attire." the maître d'hôtel said as they walked into the dining-room. He stared down at Hadrian from his dour, pot-bellied height, pale in the dark, candlelit bar behind him.

The mahogany railing of the bar made Cybele think of a cold beer. She felt her mouth fill with saliva. Her lips anticipated the cool moisture on top of the bottle and then on the side of the glass.

"Oh c'mon," Hadrian said and brushed past the man towards a table, but the maître persisted in his protest with his pallid, biscuit-like face moving like hardening dough. Hadrian glanced at him shrewdly. Cybele watched his look with pride. She remembered this expression of Hadrian's and understood that he would begin some sort of diplomacy to remove the "said" object before him.

"Pleeeease," Hadrian said nasally, affecting a British accent and putting his thick hands together in a deceptively humble way. He bowed his large head and looked up at the man with hangdog brown eyes, making them bleed a little through the whites with his expression. "Please. I bow," he repeated, still staring at the man with his shrewd, wise eyes.

The maître d'hôtel stared back at him with uncertainty, looking like an old, bleached turtle.

"This lady is my niece and just on a vacation. She's staying at the hotel right down the street," Hadrian explained.

Cybele squinched her shoulder blades together and dug the toe of her white patent leather shoe into the carpet with anticipation, listening to Hadrian's words happily.

"And I have only a few hours with her before my flight." He pulled the sleeve of his jacket back and consulted his watch, then looked over at Cybele fondly so that the man could fully appreciate his sentiment. He glanced back at him quickly to understand if his words had got what he wanted. He saw the man waver and hurriedly reached into his back pocket to pull out his thick brown wallet and handed him some money.

Seeing this, Cybele thought of his hand reaching into his pants with the same smooth movement to bring his dick out for her. She squeezed his massive, muscular arm through the coarse linen of his jacket and felt her breasts tingle in the points of her nipples. She stared down at them jutting up under the white material of her blouse. The maître guided them towards an obscure booth with a conquered demeanour. She slipped over the slickness of the booth's maroon-coloured seat like a cat, sliding her thin frame hungrily up to the wide bulk of Hadrian's shoulder.

"Now," he said with satisfaction and smiled slyly as he looked at the wine list. "You look tired," he said while still looking at the list. "What's happening?" His grin increased the heavy folds of his cheek, making him look especially old. "Why don't you want to have an orgy tonight?" he asked, and began caressing her leg.

"Eric left me," she said dully.

"Ohhh," he said softly, still massaging the flesh around her kneecap. She didn't notice the pain that etched itself across his tired face after her remark. She was too miserable remembering Eric.

"I see. So why did he leave?"

"Do I know?" she said, throwing her long, dirty black hair against the seat of the booth in despair. "He's just gone. He's not going to fuck me any more, that's all."

Hadrian dragged deeply on his English cigarette. "If you want to get Eric back, you must pretend not to like him." He let the smoke come pouring out of his mouth in small *o*s.

She looked at him and realised what she had said.

"Oh Hadrian, forgive me," she begged and rubbed her hand up and down his arm hastily.

He shrugged his big shoulders and looked up at her with a sardonic smile. He looked terribly haggard.

"Hadrian, what have you been doing these past few days? You look awful."

"The business is bad, very bad," he said, and sighed morosely. "Let's have a mixed drink instead of wine tonight. I need something strong."

"Oh Hadrian, I guess we're both sort of fucked up today."

"But tell me about this incident you mentioned on the phone. Someone tried to hurt you?" he asked, and popped the cherry from his Scotch old fashioned into his mouth hungrily.

"Oh Hadrian, it was horrible, just horrible."

"When did it happen?" he asked with a speculative expression on his face.

"Right after we came back from Bermuda. I went to see this movie called *The Nun*," she began.

"*The Nun*? What's *The Nun*?" he asked impatiently.

"Oh nothing, I mean it's just the title of a movie I saw – such a profound movie for me, Hadrian," she said and sipped her gin and tonic experimentally. It had been so long since she had drunk any hard liquor that she had forgotten how it tasted.

"Why profound for you?" he asked and squeezed her leg hungrily. "Umm, what a velvet skin you have, darling" He sucked his breath in sharply and made a gusty sound of pleasure. "You don't want to fuck me tonight?" he asked with disbelief.

"Of course, Hadrian," she said. "I always want you. But do you want to hear about the movie, or not?"

"Oh yes, yes, The people and the movie. Continue, please."

"Well, the movie was about a girl who could never find her place in the world. She found corruption wherever she went, and it was—

Ouch! Hadrian, please don't squeeze my leg so hard. It was ultimately unbearable for her, so—"

"So? So? I wish they'd bring the menu now. I'm hungry," he declared impatiently.

"So, she finally jumped out of the window of a fancy apartment in Paris because she had been hired as a whore." Cybele bit her lime and sucked on its tangy flavour greedily.

"But how can a nun become a whore, darling?" he asked, and smiled. "You want meat or fish tonight?"

"Huh, oh, uh, anything – I don't care. I'm not hungry."

"You're never hungry these days since you met your hippie. You're too skinny, my goodness," he complained.

"Oh please, Hadrian, don't nag me," she pleaded. "Anyway, I got so upset by this movie that I decided to take a ride through the park to cleanse myself sorta."

"And?" he asked her. "Er, bring us the meat, and a small salad," he told the waiter perfunctorily. "You want potato?"

"No, I mean, I don't know," she said in exasperation.

"So you went to your car in the garage and they were waiting for you there?"

"That's right," she said in confusion. "But how did you know that?" she asked suspiciously.

"Darling, you keep your car downstairs in your garage, don't you?"

"Yes, I do. Well, anyway, they were down there in a sort of old car – two big niggers, one with a knife pounding on my window, and the other using his car to block mine in with."

"Awful!" Hadrian exclaimed. "And what you did then?"

"Well, luckily I had locked the car door for some reason as soon as I got in. I mean, I had seen them from the corner of my eye and they looked out of place there, being Negroes and all. I don't think Mr Masters allows any Negroes in his building."

"I feel so afraid, Hadrian!" she exclaimed.

"Why?" he asked, and began pouring her champagne. "You mustn't be scared; you must be brave," he told her like a father.

He raised her glass of champagne to her mouth and said, "Here, drink it now while it's cold."

"Hadrian, you're so good to me," she said, and drank the bubbling liquid down like Coca-Cola. "But so many strange things keep happening in my life, I—" She faltered, and thought of Crag again with disgust.

"That's because you live with hippies," he said and lit a cigarette as he filled her glass again. "Your friends are too bizarre," he complained. "Where had you been before the movie?" he asked suspiciously.

"I . . . went by Brand's shop."

"The queer?" he said.

"Oh, Hadrian, do you *have* to talk about my best friend that way?"

"You see? Your best friend is a queer," he exclaimed.

"God, you're so fucking bourgeois!" she shouted. The maître looked over in their direction nervously.

"Let's go," Hadrian said.

"OK, but what about the champagne?"

"That's enough for you," he said knowingly. He stood up and signalled the waiter. "You wait for me in the lobby," he instructed her. "Where will you go now – to The Lancashire?"

"Dunno," she said and walked towards the lobby. She looked out the cut-glass windows of the imposing wooden doors and sighed. She thought with misery of her large, empty apartment and her cat waiting there in the dark for her. A deep feeling of loneliness swept over her as she stood before the door.

'Oh, what am I going to do, what am I going to do?' she thought miserably. 'I'll die if I have to stay in that empty place one more day.' She pushed the door of the restaurant open and walked outside in agitation. 'And now Eric won't be back – he'll never be back – God! I can't bear it, I can't bear it. Pierre's no good either. I. . .'

She put her hand up to her temple in weariness. Heat from the sidewalk and street engulfed her. Across the street the balloon man still walked up and down like an actor in a movie that was continually being shown.

"That old mother fucker, I hate him," she said aloud.

"So may I come with you then for an orgy tonight?" Hadrian asked as he walked up beside her.

"For anything you want," she said, dreading the endless hours of the night that loomed ahead.

She slid into the plasticky smell of his car and took her shoes back off.

"Awful," he said, looking at the dirt on her feet. She laughed happily. She liked for him to criticise her and to touch her as he did so. They rode down the wide avenue under the dense leafiness of its old trees. The day was dying into a smoky, lilac haze of smells and colours. Soft, pregnant bodies of bugs splashed against the wide windshield. Hadrian slid his fingers between her legs. She put her hand over his and leaned back, breathing deeply. His touch took away the traumatic events of the day. He parked his car in the back of her apartment building under the massive oak trees.

She stared straight ahead, momentarily imagining Eric and his green TR, then shrugged her shoulders and pushed open the grand door of the Lincoln. She ran ahead of Hadrian, anxious to see Porge, and feeling guilty about leaving him alone all day. She looked up at the landlord's window from habit. She didn't see him anywhere around.

As soon as they got into the apartment she hugged her cat, then began tearing off her shorts suit. She ran the hottest water she could stand and stood under the harsh torrent of the shower, washing her hair in a brusque, almost brutal way. She did it quickly, then came walking out into the bluish gloom of the living-room. She sat down abruptly by Hadrian, shivering and giggling and writhing under a heavy bathtowel.

"Thank you," he said. "You were smelling really hippie."

"Really, is that true, Hadrian? What sort of smell is that?"

He stroked the wet tangles of her hair. She leaned over suddenly and grabbed her big toe when she felt a flea bite it.

"I dunno," he said. "Just a kind of smell – like marijuana. What is that out there on the patio?"

Porgy had pulled the screen door open with his foot and revealed an old antique mirror that she had bought at an antique shop.

"Heyyy, that's my mirror. I forgot about that." She leapt up and ran into the kitchen, looking around for a can of gold spray paint that she had bought at the dimestore. She watched the slow descent of a thin brown cockroach as it crawled down the cabinet and thought briefly of a parrot she wanted to buy for some reason. Then, feeling the spray can in her hand, she darted back out to the patio.

"Cybele. No! You don't go out there that way."

"Shhhh." She put her finger to her mouth. "Mr Masters is watering the lawn and I can't let him see me." She crept stealthily out onto the patio, bowed over like a naked brown Indian.

"You're crazy," he whispered.

"It's going to be so beautiful, Hadrian. We'll hang it right over there by the sofa." The paint sprayed out of the can with a sharp hiss when she pressed the button. Porgy leapt onto the rail of the balcony to escape the spray.

"Porgy, you got gold on the end of your tail," she said happily. "Ha, ha, ha."

"C'mon now, that's enough – you'll get your feet dirty again."

She reeled back on the balls of her feet after spraying the frame to admire the mirror. "Gorgeous," she whispered, then looked over the side of the balcony down onto the pink-domed head of Mr Masters. She studied the long, wide stains under the armpits of his shirt and shivered. He turned his head slowly, looking in every direction except up at her as he walked around the freshly mowed lawn.

'I wonder what he does all day?' she thought as she stared over the old stone balcony, forgetting Hadrian completely. She watched him move with the slow, awkward grace of age and was reminded again of a once glorious Roman statue mouldering in the ruins. 'Only statues don't stink,' she thought disdainfully.

"What a view I have from here, darling," she heard Hadrian say from behind her. She turned her head around without moving her body. He was reclining on the gold velvet loveseat, smiling languorously at her. His powerful body was relaxed there with a casual, savage strength. She kept staring at him over her shoulder, still hanging onto the balcony with her thin brown arms, squatting there and feeling her cunt open as it hovered over the moistness of the stone floor.

"My beautiful ass, my beautiful, beautiful ass. Bring her to me, darling," he said. "I want to touch her."

She was grinning now as she photographed his face with her eyes. It was dark – dark the way she liked. His eyes were brown – brown the way she liked, and square-shaped. She watched them on her body. The sophistication in his eyes, the intelligence there, was all centred on her, concentrated on her alone.

'Where else could I ever match this priceless attention?' she thought. 'No other man can match you, Hadrian. I want you,

Hadrian. I'm going to go anywhere, live anywhere, do anything, but I'll have you, you old son of a bitch," she said inaudibly to his handsome, aged face.

Hadrian dragged slowly on his English cigarette as she stood up fully in the soft blue of the evening, oblivious now to Porgy and his glowing green eyes behind her. The cat's plump, black-tipped tail swished softly across the stones, while his eyes stared hungrily into the night. Oblivious also to the trickling stream of water spewing out from Mr Masters' hose, she stood up and tiptoed slowly over to Hadrian.

She knelt down by his knees and laid her head on them. She held his thighs and legs with her arms and lifted her hands to his arms. She drew his head down to her mouth. She smelled the pungent oiliness of his forehead and the top of his head. He lifted his head up from her mouth and smoked his cigarette, detached from her vine-like embrace. He smiled down at her coolly.

"I'm hot! I'm hot!" she said.

"Yes, darling, you're hot. You are hot. You are my Cybele now."

"I'm going to fuck *you* tonight, Hadrian," she said, smiling boldly up at him while unzipping his pants and pulling out his big, thick prick. "Oh, look at him! He's beautiful, Hadrian. So beautiful. So smooth. Let me kiss him. Oh, so nice in my mouth, so thick and smooth."

"Kiss him then, darling, he's yours."

"Is he mine, Hadrian? That's hard to believe – a man like you. What about your wife?"

"I told you I don't fuck her. Now shut up and kiss me."

She looked down at his cock again. "Hadrian, your dick looks fierce!" she exclaimed.

She began to kiss him, reaching up for the silky patch of black hair on his chest and stroking it softly with one hand, hearing his voice in her ears, hearing him say, "Oh Cybele, oh Cybele," as he surrendered to her. His pleasure filled her with a wild, sweet pain. She felt tears streaming down her face while she kissed him. She glanced towards the windows while her nostrils quivered over the smell of his flesh. They were full of him, full of the smell of him and the dark rustling evergreens that brushed and surged against the black screened windows in the summer wind. She felt the muscles of her thighs ache as she held herself at his knees, shoved up against his legs and body. His voice and sighs filled her ears. The night was around them – it surrounded them – it echoed around them in soft muted sounds. His body poured itself suddenly into her mouth. She felt the thick cream fill her throat and cover her face. She lay back on the rug and wiped it slowly over her eyes and forehead, then smeared it into her hair, smiling at him while she lay at his feet and enjoying letting him watch her do this.

"Come on," he said. "Let's go to bed now. I want to fuck you now. I want your cunt." He stood up between her legs, letting his pants slide slowly to the floor as he pulled her up with one of his powerful arms.

"Oh Hadrian! Oh Hadrian!" she moaned. She let herself be pulled up by him, let herself rest quietly against the existence of his body. She stretched her chin out over the bone of his shoulder. The feel of his arms under her hands made them hurt pleasurably. He rubbed his hands up and down her hips in a circular motion. They swayed there for a moment before he turned her and steered her into the bedroom with both of his hands holding her ass.

He pushed her down on the bed and stood over her, looking at her as she lay gazing back up at him, fragile and a little broken-looking on the bed. Then he was on her, pushing himself into her with his eyes still fastened onto her face and never leaving her eyes. "I'm fucking your eyes, darling, your beautiful eyes," he said, and she felt his blunt, wide dick shove itself into her.

"Fuck me. Fuck me, Hadrian."

"That's right. I like to hear you say that, Cybele. Tell me 'fuck me'. Be vulgar with me. Be intimate."

"Fuck me, fuck me. I love for you to fuck me with your dick," she said, feeling pleasure as she heard her words in her ears, as she felt his massive body moving in powerful, heavy motions over her.

He shot up suddenly inside her. "Come! Come!" he said, then shuddered over her violently.

The door creaked when Porgy padded into the bedroom and sat on his plump haunches, watching Cybele calmly as he had so many times before. She liked to watch him there, so still and soft-looking in the glowing darkness. She longed to touch his body also. She drifted her eyes along the books stacked on the radiator and saw a book by Voltaire. "Voltaire," she whispered.

"What are you looking at?" he asked, and turned her head back to his face. She studied him sleepily in the candlelight.

"At the cat," she smiled. "He's like you."

"I adore you, Cybele," he declared. "I don't just love you. I *adore* you." He held her head with his hands on each side of her face. He held it while pressing her hair gently under his large hands.

She lay very quietly under him, not wanting to breathe, so that she could feel and see everything he might do or say to her. He studied her face carefully, then kissed her mouth as if he might finally find what he had hungered for so violently about her person on her lips.

"Are you going to your house now?" she asked sadly.

"*You* are my house. My only happiness."

"In my mind, since I met you, you are always present, Hadrian. I never forget you, wherever I go – whomever I see. You've overshadowed them all. I've never had a man do that to me before, Hadrian. But you are my fate. Since I met you it's as if I have no will of my own. You are some sort of strange black magic on me. My body is sick for you. I can sit for hours in a daze just waiting for you – and sometimes you don't come for days." She stopped talking suddenly. She wondered if he had been listening.

"Let me go now," he said.

"Go then," she said. "I'll just wait until you come back."

She sank back into the pillows and watched him put on his clothes. The cat hopped up on the bed beside her and nuzzled her face. She let her hand drop onto his body, kneading his fleshy fur and breathing, deeply. "I'm going to sleep now," she said, and immediately did so.

She felt him shaking her. "You need any money?"

"No, no. Leave me alone now," she said, and rolled over on one side.

"Listen, Cybele, darling," he said, and sat back down beside her on the bed. "We may have to stay away from one another for a while."

She lay on her side not looking at him, and asked, "Why?" in a small, tight voice. An icy numbness washed over her whole being when she heard his words. It seemed that she could predict what he was going to say.

"I'm sure those men were hired by my wife to kill you, Cybele."

"If you can't see me anymore, I wish they had," she replied, still not facing him.

"Listen to me, damn it," he said, and pulled her back over to him roughly. "I don't want anything to happen to you – ever – Cybele. And I can even hire a guard to protect you – I'm ready to do that any day I feel you might be harmed, but. . ."

He lit a cigarette hastily. She stared up into his clever brown eyes with terror.

"Hadrian, Hadrian, please don't leave me. Please don't!" She grabbed his hands hysterically and pressed them into her stomach.

"Don't be stupid. I shall never leave you. I shall always take care of you and protect you," he assured her. "In spite of your call to my wife."

"No, no!" she screamed, and threw herself against him.

"Shaddup now," he said. He seized her by the shoulders and shook her. "Don't be hysterical, Cybele. We must be logical at this point in our lives."

She looked at his dark eyes shining from the candlelight in fascination. The side of his distinguished face gave her the most confidence she had ever had in a man's cleverness and intellect.

'I can't lose him – not him!' she thought desperately. She looked at him shrewdly and immediately drained all of the hysteria out of her body through an immense exercise of her will. The same feeling that she had had when she realised that if she didn't get the key in the ignition she might be killed passed over her imagination.

"All right, Hadrian, I'll do anything you say," she said. She touched his arm lightly with two fingers. The of his skin on her fingertips was like a 10-milligram addict getting only one gram of opium on his tongue, but she purposely made it light, knowing that there was nothing she could do to change whatever he had decided.

"You must get out of this apartment! Look for another place beginning tomorrow. I can send you for a trip to Europe, after that."

"Alone?" she wailed in spite of herself.

He inhaled his cigarette contemplatively. "Cybele, would you like to build a home down in Louisiana on the beach?"

"Huh?"

"You like the South – you could go down there and live, and I could visit you." He looked around the room nervously. "This apartment is awful. I want to get you out of here as soon as possible."

"But Hadrian, why do you keep trying to get rid of me?" she asked and pressed her thin body to his chest.

"Darling, I don't want to get rid of you. . . contrary. I want to fuck you always." He stroked her hair gently. "But I can't afford to have a confrontation with my wife. She'll ruin me, I know," he said. His eyes narrowed like a hunted animal in the dimly-lit room. "You remember what I told you in Bermuda. I've spent a lifetime building back up the empire my family lost with my father's death in Turkey – here in America. Do you know what that means, Cybele?"

"Yes, I. . . I don't know if I do or not, Hadrian," she confessed. She rubbed her hands on his back slavishly, not wanting to take them from his broad shoulders for eternity.

"She will cause the biggest scandal for me, Cybele, and she can get a lot of money. So, please, be patient – for a while, anyway."

He stubbed his cigarette out hastily.

"Come and put the lock on your door, darling," he said, and picked up his jacket.

"How long is 'a while', Hadrian?" she asked fearfully.

"Oh, a couple or three months."

"Oh no – oh no, Hadrian!" she cried, and threw herself around him disconsolately.

"Be brave now, Cybele. "We'll see each other, don't worry."

"But three months, Hadrian," she said incredulously.

"I have to go," he said, and opened the door. "Await my call."

"Await my call, await my call." she mumbled as she walked back into the bedroom. She picked up the bottle of sleeping pills and crammed as many as possible into her mouth.

Chapter Fourteen

When she woke up, the phone was ringing under the pillows she had stuffed over it from the night before. She leapt up from the bed, knocking her knee against the bedroom door as she ran into the hallway.

"Hello, Cybele," a clipped, boyish voice piped into her ear.

"Well, if it isn't old Sherman! How's your mother, Sherman?" she asked sarcastically.

"I tried to get you all day. "I've got something to tell you about those bones."

"Those bones? *What* bones?"

"The rose garden bones. Remember? It's just like we thought – they're *human*."

"Where are you? I'm hungry," she told him petulantly

"Did you hear what I said?" he asked.

"Yeah, I heard. There's no secret about it. This place is creepy. The bad thing is I'm almost used to it."

"I'm still at the hospital. I'll stop by and bring you a tuna fish sandwich. How does that sound, Cybele?" he asked, and laughed at her confusion. "I'm really worried about you, Belle."

"Yeah, me too, worried about the fact that I'll never get a steak out of a cheap bastard like you. But bring it, please. You and your California wine."

"Don't be prejudiced now, Cybele."

"How can one be prejudiced about a racoon, or a cat? They're just like they are and you're just like you are – Sherman, the shark."

"I like the way you say that so sweetly," he countered.

"OK, well, that's good. I gotta go and brush my teeth now. Don't forget the sandwich," she cautioned him.

"Put on something sexy. Your big daddy is coming over."

"Wrong again. He just left." She hung up the phone abruptly, without saying goodbye. "Shit, I hope he shows. I'm lonesome."

She traipsed slowly back into the bedroom, turning on the overhead light and resting her hip against the doorway. She felt very dizzy from all the pills she had gulped down. She smelled the pungent odour of Hadrian's cigarettes from the ashtray by the bed, and stared at the mussed, yellow sheets.

'He leaves his aura, behind,' she thought, 'like an animal.' She ran over to sniff the pillow where he had put his head. It smelled of his hair and of an elusive, faint perfume.

"Oh Hadrian, Hadrian," she sighed, and stretched her stomach and body tautly across the bed. She lay there for ten minutes without any thoughts, hardly breathing. "I could actually just stay this way until he comes back," she realised. "Nothing else I do will matter anyway." She looked at the large yellow candle. He had put it out. "I don't remember that! How long have I been asleep anyway?" she wondered. She picked up two one-hundred-dollar bills that he had left under the candle and wandered over to the vanity table to make up her eyes. She looked at the money distractedly, then put it in a drawer.

She heard a knock at the door and adjusted her face.

"Well," she said, when she had slung open the door. "If it isn't my man in white - stethoscope and all." She stepped back a little, startled again by his height, by the clean lines of his face, and a bit shaky from the burning glance he levelled at her.

"How the hell are you, Belle," Sherman asked and leaned beside the door, surveying her face and body carefully.

"Why do you call me Belle?" she asked, frowning. "To reduce me?"

"Bitchy as ever? You look good." He reached out and grasped the flesh of her inner thigh. "Been working on those legs again, haven't you?" He kept looking down at her challengingly, enjoying his height, enjoying his sharp, well chiselled jaw, and his white intern's jacket, while enjoying her green, stubborn eyes on his face and body, knowing that she was alone and helpless and that she liked to fuck with him. "Come on now, Belle, say something tough. Ha aha ha."

She kept staring at him with her lower lip poked out, still holding the door. He took her chin in his hand and pulled her lips up to his.

"Think you might invite me in tonight, or am I going to stand out in the fucking hall all night?" he asked impatiently. She took his stethoscope out of his pocket and hung it on his ear.

"Come on in," she said, feeling very delighted to see his handsome face and his angular form under the succinct white jacket. He came in guardedly. She imagined that he fairly dunked his head to enter through the door. He sat down on the small loveseat. She was amazed to see how high his knees came up when he sat down. He was very tall. He patted the seat and cocked his head at her whimsically.

"Now sit down here and be a nice girl," he coaxed. He reached down in the deep pocket of his hospital jacket which he had taken off and brought out a sandwich.

In spite of herself, she sat down, looking admiringly at his semitic good looks, and feeling grateful that he had brought the sandwich to her. "I hope this one has a little more tuna in it – not like that other crummy one you brought," she said fussily in order to disguise her pleasure.

"Mumph, Mumph – Grumph, Grumph," he said, and pulled her head back, making his moronic laughter over her face while rotating his head back and forth and thrusting his face into hers. "What did you say, Belle? Did you say something intelligible? Huh, huh?"

He pulled her hair harder, knowing she loved to have him hold her head back tautly in that manner. "Whatd'ya do today, huh, huh? Play with the cat's tail?" He leaned down and kissed her burningly, softly, on her mouth. She felt a sweet ache in her body and relaxed in his embrace. "Good, huh?" he asked. "More later. Go and get something to drink and eat your dinner."

When she came back to the living-room, it was empty. "Sherman? Sherman?" she called anxiously. "Ooohh, my head," she groaned, and put her hand up to her temple. "Those awful pills."

"Out here, bat-brain," he said. She looked towards the balcony and was struck again by his star-like appearance. He was the most perfectly handsome man she had ever dated.

'I wonder what's wrong with him? There's got to be something wrong,' she thought. She stood in the french doors of the balcony, biting into the mushy sandwich with her eyes on him all the time, going up and down his angular frame. She felt her body respond strongly to his there in the darkness.

"It would please me if you brought yourself closer to me," he said. She walked out onto the patio and into the coolness of the night.

The smell of the balcony's old bricks filled her nostrils with a musty, pleasant odour.

"I hope you didn't step on the mirror," she accused him.

"No. I didn't step on your precious mirror," he replied. He lifted her up easily and sat her on the balcony's railing. "Where's that going to go – in the drawing-room? Fixing the place up, aren'tcha? For what, that's what I'd like to know? That carpet in there is straight out of a bus station. Your 'friend' isn't even kosher, Belle."

"That he isn't," she agreed leaning back dramatically and letting one leg hang over the balcony.

"If you fall off, I'm not fixing anything free."

"Big, tough Dr Sherman. Is that the way you are around the hospital? Or do you give them an act for their money? You're so *kind*, really you are."

"But then you never have liked kind men, have you, Cybele?" he asked perceptively. She heard his words and sat up immediately, afraid.

"Why did you say that?" she asked and looked at him suspiciously. His small eyes were burning on her body. She could feel his body and even his brain fucking her, wanting to fuck her. It was the one emotion she trusted from a man. "Trying to use your degree in psychiatry on me? You and your mother – what a lovely pair."

"Relax, I just wanted to get your attention."

"No, you didn't. You meant that – that I don't like kind men."

"Well, do you?"

"Are you kind, Sherman?" she asked, and slid off the balcony railing. She stood very close to him. He held each of his arms just above his elbows and contemplated her.

"I don't know. Am I, Cybele?" He reached out to bring her to him. She felt herself pressed to his hard body, pressed to the smell of his jacket, and had the sensation of a first date, of a high school kiss. He made her feel very small, physically, and she liked the novelty of this feeling. She stared up at his handsome face and enjoyed his youth frankly.

"Some girls have said I'm not kind," he admitted.

"Well, don't be mean to me, Sherman, please. I've had enough of that in my life already."

"Oh, I won't mean to be if I am," he said. He didn't seem to know where to go with the conversation at that point. She had a different way of saying no to him. He never knew if she was going to let him fuck her or not, so he purposely held back a step or two with her, to save himself from too much disappointment.

"Well, since you've finished the sandwich, do you want to sit down, or go for a ride, or—"

"Or go to the 4th of July fireworks," she mocked. "Let's go and lie down," she said, and pulled him through the living-room and into the bedroom, grinning expectantly.

They stalked around each other in the bedroom, aware that their parley of word-warfare had turned into lovemaking. He kissed her again. She looked at his face while he did so and saw that his eyes were closed. They fluttered with his passion so that she could see their whites. This excited her terribly. 'He's lost himself completely with me,' she thought.

He parted from her as if to gain a better footing. He was learning to be tender, and for some reason it embarrassed him for her to notice his effort.

"Come on, fuck me," she said roughly, to relieve him of his embarrassment.

"I'll fuck you any time, babe," he replied.

She pulled open the shirt he was wearing lustily. It was a jersey that stretched apart under her fishy-smelling fingers until she could feel the golden and black-coloured hair on his chest. She rubbed his chest hair hard under her fingers, making it mat up in whorls. She licked it, then drew back to stare at her saliva shining there. She searched for his nipples with her fingers and sucked first one, then the other slowly. He moaned softly with pleasure.

"Which one feels the best?" she asked.

He pulled her away from him and grinned.

"Eric taught me that," she said simply. "He liked me to pinch his nipples. Would you like me to pinch yours, too?"

"I just want to fuck you," he told her.

They began to undress abruptly, taking care not to show any sentiment. It was their unwritten rule. She pulled her panties down, hopping on one leg to keep her balance. When she turned back to him, he was lying on the bed, the same bed she had been lying on with Hadrian a few hours earlier, or had it been a few days? Sherman's body was long and slim, tawny on the mussed sheets. His youth startled her. Her eyes travelled down the beautiful contours of his body reverently, stopping at his very large, erect dick. When she saw how large his dick was, she remembered the pain and the blood from the time they had fucked before, and she frowned.

"How do you want it, Cybele?"

"Slowly," she said. He put himself in her immediately. She gasped when she felt all of him inside her cunt. "Don't hurt me, don't hurt me like before," she pleaded.

He moved jerkily. His breath was harsh in her ear, like his movements. He was breaking himself in order not to hurt her and it was ruining his lovemaking. She felt a rush of love for him. Again she imagined that he was trying to be tender with her.

"Do it! Do it!" she cried. "Now hurt me. Come on, come on, push it hard. Damn!" she demanded, trying to dispel his restraint.

"OK, OK," he said. "You sit on me, you control it."

She forgot when it ended. Only when she heard the phone ringing did she realise that they had stopped. She listened to it ring once more, then leapt up off him to answer it.

"Cybele, m'dear," she heard his familiar voice say.

"Eric, Eric, Eric Star – where are you? Oh Eric, it's so wonderful to hear from you."

"Don't get so agitated. I'm just down at the Pie learning the pleasures of wine. Gramps here is teaching me."

"Gramps?" she mumbled, frantic to go wherever he was.

"You met him at a party, don'tcha remember?"

"Eric, where is this place, please?" she howled. She looked back at Sherman putting on his clothes in the bedroom, hardly remembering that he was still there.

"It's the Apple Pie – on M Street. Don't you remember? You've been here with me before. But I don't want you here now."

"Please, Eric, please!"

"All right, you can come, but no hassling, understand?"

"I promise. I promise. I'll leave whenever you say!" She turned around when she felt Sherman kiss her on her forehead. He had slung his white jacket over one shoulder casually.

"I'll call you tomorrow, Belle."

"Sherman, Sherman, please don't be angry. This guy isn't one-third the person you are, but it's something I'm going through. I have to go through it to get rid of it."

"I'll call you this weekend – if you can get out of bed, we'll go to the beach."

She didn't really notice when he left. She was too busy pulling on her shorts. The elastic-like material slid grudgingly over her tanned thighs like a grasping hand. She pulled the little green buttons together over her big, round breasts and frantically hopped around on one foot, looking for her other shoe. She still wore the incongruous white pumps with narrow gold bands on the side. She finally found her shoe at the end of the dining-room. She wondered momentarily how it had got there, but all she could think of was Eric – that he was sitting in a chair at a place where she could go to and stand near him – not sit with him – just stand three feet away and absorb the essence of him somehow.

'What if he leaves? Oh God, what if he does? He'll change his mind. He'll leave the Pie. I know it! I know that bastard!'

She thought of his thick curly hair in the sun, of his body being slowly bronzed by its rays at the Hilton pool, longingly. She stopped all of her motions when she remembered their life together.

If she happened to awaken from the non-prescription tranquillisers in the morning, she would see his deer-like hips sliding into a pair of old jeans, with his dick up against his navel as he zipped them up. She remembered his paw-like hands brushing his innocent curls into a new mass of tangles as he stooped down to the vanity table in front of the bed, using his fingers like a comb.

Sometimes when he wanted to fuck in the morning, he would roll over on her with one light movement and begin to thrust his cock up inside her without any words – just with a sleepy sort of smile on his face. His dick was like a fire prong. It was young and super-hard, almost too hard, and it never stopped. He could fuck her all night without any great effort. Neither of them had thought it unnatural to spend hours at it.

She stopped getting dressed momentarily and raised her hand to her forehead, staring through the darkness of the living-room and out into the brassy lights of the street lamps. "So hot, so fucking hot in this place," she complained, drawing her hand back down from her temple and looking at the blood she had scratched from her flesh absently. "Always hot, always alone, always nuts – shit, shit, shit," she complained.

Porgy walked up to her and sat watching her very seriously from three feet away. She stared back into his yellow, black slitted eyes, enjoying their wideness and beauty and their concentration on her. She ran over to him and said, "Oh Porgy, Porgy, you are my best friend."

She kissed his broad forehead, smelling the special perfume that his body and fur made there. He held himself still, accepting her caresses patiently, but all the while contemplating what her movements would be and if he could guess what she might do. Most of his whole existence had been centred on Cybele since he was trapped in the apartment with no access to the outdoors anymore.

"Poor baby, poor baby," she murmured into his fur, rubbing his thick, racoon-like body with her hands. "It's all he can do to keep his stripes straight. Oh Porgy, Porgy," she wailed, and began to cry against his back, feeling ashamed to worry him as she did so. He understood very well when she cried, and it made him miserable.

"Come on, I want a Porge-pie!" She held him out in front of her with her hands under his front legs. "I want a pie. It's going to have an orange nose and two yellow eyes, and a long black stripe down the middle." Her mouth formed itself into a strange, cracked little smile. But he was having none of it. He growled and pulled away.

"OK, dammit, I don't believe it either." She let him go and paused for a moment, squatting in a desultory posture in the dirty hallway. "Please don't worry, Porge," she said, and ran over to call a cab.

"The A-p-p-l-e P-i-e," she said, smirking into the black-pitted receiver. "No, it is not a bakery, it's a bar."

She wondered what time it was. Eric had taken his clock back when he had left. "No, that's right – I threw it away," she said, and giggled as she thought of him screaming about his dimestore clock when he had come over to collect his "things" – an old blue blanket, a pair of torn jeans and his belt with a star buckle. She had also gathered up some photographs they had taken of his mother and herself and Eric on the water-bed after they had gone to see *Jesus Christ, Superstar* to give him.

"But Eric," she had said, "it didn't work anymore. It was broken."

"I can't believe the Goddamned thing didn't work anymore," he had said, ranting and raving while railing his arms about in his white, Spanish blouse.

"Eric, take my word for it. Here, use this five bucks to buy another one." He had stared at her with surprise, then stuffed them inside his pocket in exasperation.

The buzzer from the answering service hummed itself through her memories. "Cab's here," she heard the snotty man at the desk say.

She leapt about, looking wildly around for her keys. She finally found them by the large orange candle that stood on the living-room rug.

"Don't worry, Porge," she shouted, as she unlocked the shiny cold lock she had had installed on the inside of the door.

"This is the neatest lock," she said as she struggled to open it, and thought of how happy she had felt when she heard Eric unlocking it every morning when he had left to go back to his apartment and relocking it from the outside. She would snuggle back into the coldness of the sheets, feeling like a little, guarded treasure. She ran down the red velvet carpeting of the hallway, past the zodiac signs that sat in intervals of bas-relief on the white, cake-like plaster of the walls. She thought suddenly of an old Mae West movie. She stared down the hall at the door of an elderly Jewish lady's apartment while she waited for the elevator. "She always wears green," Cybele murmured to herself. "I like that about her."

"Don't let anybody tell you that money isn't the most important thing, dearie," she had said to her one day, looking at her with twinkling, intelligent eyes. "Make green your favourite colour, sweetheart," she had said, and cocked her head to one side like an old bird, trying, to figure Cybele out.

The white, refrigerator-like door of the elevator slid open and Cybele stepped into the stark brightness of the neon-lit cubicle. She felt the skin of her arms grow tight in the coldness of the air-conditioning. "I feel like a lizard," she said, and giggled when the door opened to the lobby. She found herself looking into the sneering, cynical eyes of the night deskman.

"Got a late date?" he drawled.

"Sure, why not?" she snapped. His remark brought her close to tears, but she looked at his stupid, ageing face above his cheap shirt and she felt sorry for him. Don't you wish you did?" she let herself say. Her remark made her feel silly and high-schoolish.

"You're no good," the man said.

"You sound like Mr Masters," she called back coolly over her shoulder. "Not quite as rickety though – yet."

"We're gonna get rid of you!" he shouted after her.

"Ah, fuck yourself," she mumbled. "If you can even do that!"

She grabbed the metallic door of the cab, feeling the chrome handle under her fingers with satisfaction and anticipating the slick coolness of the leather seats under her thighs before she slid inside. She was so used to taking cabs now.

"Where is this place, lady?" she heard the tired, whiny voice in front of the old wiry neck of the cabby say. She sank back into the cushiony back seat of the cab, letting her legs sprawl over the plastic-like leather under them and enjoying feeling the material under her hips.

"It's on M Street. Don't worry, when you get to Nathan's just go straight. I'll show you." She contemplated the back of his neck some more and decided to take advantage of his calmness and not talk much. She rolled the window down and let the damp summer air pour over her face and swish through her hair, that had become oily and lank from the hours of heat and her sexual activity. All of the store windows that they passed peered back at them like glassy, pastel eyes. Their pale green, lavender and white and yellow-coloured glass dotted Wisconsin Avenue like exotic masks in an opera.

Soon they passed the all-night bakery. She glanced over to see if Sherman's silver Corvette might be parked in the wide parking lot. 'Oh, why would he be there?' she thought with irritation, aggravated that she had wondered if he might be there. But still she turned her head to look back at the go-go place next door to the bakery as the cab sped down Wisconsin Avenue.

Young kids were scattered about in front of the place like gay flowers spotlighted by a neon sun. The loud wail of jukebox music flowed down the street after the cab. She rubbed her nose violently and sniffed. 'Fucking weather,' she thought. 'Why am I so bitchy right now?' she wondered, becoming puzzled at her mood.

She looked up at the treetops while they stopped for a red light. Across the street she saw the Georgetown Library that reminded her of the small, brick library in her home town. Streetcar tracks ran down the avenue in front of the cab like pale silver ribbons. The cobblestones were pebbly and smooth underneath the tyres of the car. She saw the blurred, blue sign of the French Market and thought of stuffed snails and liver pâté as they whizzed on down Wisconsin Avenue to M Street.

"Wish I could eat at a table again instead of the floor," she whimpered to herself.

When they got to the Pie, she felt surprised to see it. She reached into her purse and felt a crunchy wad of money in her palm, then and absence of it, and she was alone on the sidewalk in front of the place. She tried to remember which door opened and which didn't. She finally seized the one that usually didn't and walked in.

There was no band that night, so the club wasn't jammed with people as on many evenings. She gazed up at the Tiffany lamps that hung down from the high, rafter-like ceiling. Their black-lined lampshades were studded about the room like colourful butterflies' wings. The bar curved into a haze of purple smoke that throbbed and pulsed with the air from old fans twirling slowly in the gloom.

She cased the whole place, cautiously, then turned her head to the right and saw Eric gesturing and talking loudly with a young Negro guy she had met when he was cutting dope one afternoon. She stared at the Negro's yellow sports coat and tan slacks, admiring the rich colour of the brown leather boots he had propped up on the iron railing near their table. The people passing by floated past the table like one-dimensional beings, accentuating the fullness of Eric's shoulders under his white shirt. She stared at the material of his shirt that was made blue-white by the lights overhead hypnotically. She thought that she could see one of his nipples through the side of his shirt's deep 'V' neck. She dropped her eyes down to his hips. His legs were on each side of the brown wooden chair, firm and taut-looking. His knees hugged the sides of the slatted chair back. She gazed at the profile of his face, then noticed the jugular vein in his neck, prominent from his animated, stupid conversation with the Negro boy.

Again she contemplated Eric's companion, enjoying his dark, chocolatey skin, his yellow coat, and the way it hung askance on the thin material of his sleek pants. He saw her first as she stood by the lower step at the side of the fence with white, clenched fingers. She fairly vibrated there at their feet, at the Negro's shiny brown leather boots, at Eric's scuffed, bubble-topped combat boots. The black man stopped talking and watched her glazed, haunting stare that was directed towards the side of Eric's face. Cybele trembled with a pleasure more profound than if Eric had touched her, lost completely in the bone of his cheek, the curls of his hair. She felt his blouse under her fingers and the texture of his jeans under her hand with her eyes. She could smell the marijuana in his thick, curly hair each time he moved his head as he sat talking and leaning towards the young Negro and lifting the glass of cold, starry-looking liquid to his lips.

Eric followed his companion's eyes to Cybele.. When he saw her, he twisted his body completely around in the chair to stare at her and smiled capriciously. His eyes were puppy-like and brown, blurred pleasantly by his round steel-rimmed glasses that glinted blindly when they came in contact with the light from the bar.

Cybele noticed Ronald, the bartender, watching the scene from behind the bar. His wide, sensual lips were pursed in a slight pout of anticipation. He wiped the glass he held slowly against his soiled white apron.

Cybele twisted from one white, wrinkled pump to the other. She felt the balance of her body change itself while she kept her eyes glued to Eric.

Eric reached out to her and said, "Cybele, luv, this is Gramps. . . from the party, remember? Gramps here is teaching me the pleasures of wine. Sit down, will you?" He looked at her acutely. His eyes became a darker brown, glinting as they did when he came during their lovemaking. He slid a chair under her knees.

"Do you like wine?" Gramps asked her softly. His voice matched the smooth, velvety darkness of his skin and the black pools of his eyes. She stared at his roundly moulded fingers and hand on the slick table top in the same hypnotic way that she had contemplated Eric's face, and smiled into the warm brownness of his smile.

"This is a beautiful girl, Eric," Gramps said, and grinned engagingly at Cybele. She kept smiling back at Gramps, relaxing a little against Eric's arm, and trying to hide the wild thrill that shot through her body from the touch of Eric once more.

"I just thought I'd tell you in case you didn't know," Gramps continued.

Eric opened his mouth and stretched his jaws as if to say something, but merely stared into the greenness of Cybele's eyes. He pursed and unpursed his lips, then slipped his pawlike hand over her large hand. She felt weak in her chair, but strained harder to be vacant and detached. She thought of an old barn somewhere down South and tried to make herself empty like that – hollow – so that she might hide herself somehow. But when she felt his body so close to hers and saw his eyes looking into hers, she was in the present situation so immediately, so fully, that her movements became jerky with the restraint she had tried to impose on herself.

"That's just it, Gramps. Everyone tells me that! After a while it gets to be a hassle. Why don't you drink your wine, Cybele?"

She brought the liquid to her lips and tasted it cautiously. She hated California wine. She managed a grin as the sweet, metallic liquid went down her throat. 'Ugh,' she thought, 'sure isn't like the stuff Hadrian brings me.'

"Really, Eric? It was a hassle when people told you I was pretty?" she asked. She stared at the creamy flesh of his high young cheekbone, surprised by his remarks.

"Sure, m'dear. Anything gets to be a hassle if you hear it often enough." He looked down at her legs with a thin, cruel smile as he pushed the flesh on them back and forth with his hand, then gazed back up at her passionately from underneath his thick glasses. The expression in his eyes made her want the room to disappear. Everyone could go away but her and Eric and the table. 'We could fuck on the table,' she thought and smiled.

"Now, just look at the way the child smiles," the chocolate-coloured Negro said.

"Like hearing 'Eric, Eric, Eric Star' over and over," he mimicked her voice in a high whine, ignoring Gramps' remark. "*That* gets to be a hassle also."

She studied Eric carefully as he sat perched on the spindly, wire-bound chair with his long legs doubled up like a nimble colt.

"Gosh, Eric, I've never seen you vicious before." She gazed at him with interest and raised the wineglass to her mouth again. "It's really sort of neat."

Eric gave her one of his limpid puppy looks. 'Your stupidity is positively enchanting – sometimes,' she thought to herself.

"Hey, Kate, come on over here!" Eric shouted to a young Irish girl with curly brown hair who had just entered the room. Kate looked over her shoulder with a mocking grin and arched one eyebrow theatrically. Her vivacious smile pulled her cheek into a deep dimple. "Cybele – Eric! How are you?" she screamed, and came rushing up to them. Her long, cotton skirt folded itself around the solidness of her legs and hips as she ran. She grabbed Cybele in a strong, affectionate embrace. "How are you?" she repeated, still smiling her wide, happy grin at them.

Cybele noted her creamy complexion and smelled her fresh skin and hair as Kate embraced her. "I'm so glad to see you again! Where have you been, Cybele?"

"Shit, since you aren't going to pay any attention to me, I'll go away," Eric said and stood up, watching Cybele jealously as he did so.

She jerked away from Kate and looked at Eric with fear. The Negro watched her face placidly, sipping slowly from his glass and letting his lips rest on the rim.

"Relax, luv," Eric said, pleased with her reaction. "I'm just going to get some cigarettes."

Kate sat down in Eric's seat.

"I like your necklace," the Negro said to Kate.

"Thanks, I found it at the Goodwill Store! I'm buying a lot of old dresses from there. You know, they're perfect for the 40s style – you should do that, Cybele." She looked at Cybele closely and frowned.

"Can you see Eric?" Cybele asked anxiously.

"Sure, you dope, he just went to get some smokes. What's wrong with you anyway, Cybele? Is this your 'watch Eric night'?" She stood up suddenly, knocking the chair she was sitting in over backwards with her ample rear end.

"Flo!" she screamed, and waved her hand wildly at a tall, bosomy blonde who had just walked through the doorway.

Cybele watched the blonde girl walk into the bar with gliding, light movements of her long, well-shaped legs. The neon lights turned her pale yellow hair into a silvery cap on her head. Cybele stared at the girl's lovely white chest, enjoying the round, fullness of her breasts. She smiled appreciatively at the girl's bright red mouth and sharp, thin nose. Then she remembered Eric and immediately felt her throat grow dry and her stomach tighten when she thought of him looking at Flo.

"Come on over – I'm talking to Eric and Cybele," Kate shouted.

"Don't forget me," the Negro said, and grinned lazily.

Flo propped one of her bright red high heels near Cybele's leg. "Eric and Cybele?" she said. "Thought you two broke up."

Cybele looked steadily at the paleness of Flo's skin, at the newness of it. 'She's so feminine, but her words are cruel – like her mouth and her shoes,' Cybele thought.

"Hey, gimme some wine," Flo said and draped her long torso around Gramps' body. He raised his glass to her red, red lips. Wisps of her hair hung beside the white and pink alabaster of her cheek like tiny knives. Gramps let his hand rest lightly on the pale flesh of Flo's midriff while still staring tenderly at Cybele.

"Oh yeah," he drawled, and looked as if he had remembered something. "I got the whole scene. I got it now."

Cybele lifted her eyes slowly from Flo's bare navel and the dark hand so close by it and smiled charmingly at Gramps. Her body relaxed as she contemplated the broadness of his dark, mahogany face. The yellow of his shirt excited her. She looked at his hand and wished fleetingly that he would stick one of his fingers into Flo's navel. Then she smelt the grassy fragrance of Eric's hair as he ducked his head and nibbled Flo on her white, swanlike neck when he returned to the table. She trembled as she watched his lips so close to Flo's perfect breasts. A current of attention from across the table pulled her eyes back to Gramps.

"Easy, easy," Gramps told her. His words wafted across to her like a soft wind. She wanted to keep his gaze. He made her smile again in spite of herself.

"God, you're spaced out tonight, Cybele," Eric said. His voice had become high-pitched like the strident cries of catbirds. She saw his teeth gleam as he spoke.

"Eric, you're picking on this child," the Negro drawled. "She just came to sip a glass of wine with you."

"What have you been doing, Cybele?" Flo asked.

"Nothing. Lying in the sun, I guess – doing exercises."

"Oh yeah?" Flo said, looking at her blankly and twirling a piece of her long blonde hair between her tapered fingers.

"Are you still working at Clyde's?" Cybele asked, for want of anything else to say.

"Yeah," Flo replied in her flat, blunt tone.

"You're so independent," Cybele said. "So strong." Cybele couldn't understand how such a feminine woman could be totally self-sufficient.

Flo knitted her pale brows into a needle-like frown that looked pretty over her long, thin nose. "I couldn't stand not to make my own money," Flo said.

"And you're so young, too," Cybele echoed.

"Well, everybody isn't helpless like you, Cybele, m'dear," Eric teased her.

"Eric!" Kate screamed, "you're horrible!"

Eric worked his lips happily back and forth over his teeth, looking like a senseless animal.

"Eric, you look like a gopher-star tonight," Cybele said and leaned back happily against his white blouse. He down and kissed her slowly on her mouth, letting the others watch their caress with an innocent exhibitionism. Cybele smelled the sweet liquor on his breath from his mouth, and felt a warm wetness between her legs.

'Oh Eric, Eric, I want to fuck you so. I want to fuck you without thinking, without talking,' she thought, sighing, heavily and audibly.

"Wow, listen to that chick sigh," Gramps said. "Oh man, turns me on all right. Eric, how did you get so lucky to have this child hot for your old body, dammit?"

"I dunno, it's been this way ever since she laid eyes on me," Eric said and grinned down at her, affecting a southern accent when he answered Gramps.

"You really are absurd, Eric," Kate howled again. Her darkly painted lips parted in laughter. She clutched her wineglass with black lacquered fingernails and twisted her heel round and round on the old floorboards with a vital, life-giving energy, touching her fluffy hair with her other hand as she did so.

"Bob," she screamed. "Bob – get over here, darlin'!"

A large, heavyset guy ambled over to their table. Kate grabbed his bulky midriff and asked, "Where have you been all night? That was a great party last night."

"Sure was," Eric said.

"Did you go to a party?" Cybele asked no one.

"I'm hungry," Bob said.

"Ah – you're always hungry," Flo said.

"It was just the event of the year," Kate told Cybele.

"Yeah, we only forgot the Stones, har, har," Bob agreed.

"That's right, Cybele, you weren't there – why didn't you come?" Kate asked, and slung herself back around to Cybele.

"I didn't know there was a party," Cybele confessed.

"Yes, you did, you freak," Eric said. "You just didn't want to come."

"But Eric, I would have loved to come," Cybele protested.

"Well, I figured you might be zooming, around in the silver Corvette with your young doctor," Eric sneered and squeezed her arm tightly with his hand.

"Oh Eric, you know I would have loved to have been with you." She looked into his eyes through his thick glasses longingly.

"Let's not start that shit again," he said softly through lips he held pursed in disapproval over his wineglass.

"I gotta go to work," Flo said. She pulled her red-clad foot away from Cybele's leg and began to dig into a tasselled handbag of red beads for a lipstick.

"Ah, you've always got to go to work," Eric said.

"Yeah," Flo said. "Why don't you try it yourself sometime?"

"Well, listen to this," Eric said. His voice became more passionate with protest. Its shrill tone vibrated in Cybele's ears and made her stomach lurch from the sound of it. She longed to feel his hard, tight ribs under his shirt. Her body strained towards his like a plant in the sun.

"Eric, Eric Star," she said to herself, feeling her heart ache and her cunt burn.

"Hey, Eric, your chick looks sleepy," Gramps said and grinned meaningfully at Eric.

"I like the way you turn your head," Cybele said to Gramps.

"See?" Eric said. "She's not very discriminating – many please her."

Cybele shrank into herself, into her knitted shorts. She felt her juice dry up suddenly as she looked around the smoky café in a haze of indecision. "I've gotta get a cab home," she said softly.

Eric looked at her. She knew that he wondered why she didn't try to get him to come back to the apartment with her. She felt her body grow cold in the clamminess of the café, and with an unusual surge of strength, detached herself from Eric and Gramps completely.

'I have to concentrate on getting back to the apartment – just that and nothing more,' she thought carefully. 'I won't think of Eric as Eric, but just as someone I have to leave.' Her movements felt heavy to her, even though she stood up with agility. She smiled wanly at Eric and then at Gramps. Gramps looked surprised.

"Hey, man, what's happening to the show?"

"Tomorrow," Eric said.

Cybele looked up at Eric's distinct jawline again. She noted his arms hanging gracefully at his sides, then dropped her eyes down to his hips and began enjoying the length of his legs with an aloof fogginess. "Eric, I really do have to go now," she said.

"You certainly are in a hurry tonight for a slow southern girl," he told her. He was still searching her face, puzzled at her composure.

"We'll have to see you later," Gramps said, raising his wineglass in a toast that made him look silly this time.

"Oh, I really hope so, Gramps," Cybele said, leaning down to kiss him on his black cheek and looking at his skin with curiosity as she did so. 'Never kissed a black guy before,' she thought. 'Oh well, what the shit, I like it! I love everything and everyone,' she thought, hoisting her leather purse up on her arm bleakly.

Outside, the air was still moist and damp. She stared down at the cobblestones that showed in patches from under the black, wet-looking concrete, bluish-coloured from the light of the street lamps. She felt the rough, white material of Eric's shirt press against her arm and smelled the new cigarette he lit. A cab rolled up as if by design, and once again she felt the flesh of her thighs on the cool leather seats of a taxi.

"1600 Massachusetts Avenue," Eric said. He leaned through the window and tried to kiss her, but she drew back, smiling emptily at him in her pain. She saw pain in his eyes also. "You OK?" he whispered, as if frightened by what had happened between them.

"Sure," she replied. She still smiled while she gazed at him in the purple neon glare, but she felt anxious to get her eyes on the road ahead. She wanted him to be gone now. He had to disappear so that she could be alone with this sharp, blinding pain that she felt – this pain that prickled her arms and pulled at her legs. He stepped back from the cab, still watching her apprehensively. She turned her eyes away from him as soon as possible.

The iron rods of the street lamps' heavy stems greeted her gaze in a glinting metal relief along M Street. The fronts of stores were still and silent. Their show windows were like blurred, abstract eyes. She didn't see any people. She let her hand drop to one of her kneecaps, touching its hard roundness with her fingertips. 'I exist through my kneecap,' she thought, and giggled.

The big, fat Negro cabby turned around and said, "I swear, you young folks got more energy." He looked at his old metal watch. "Two-thirty in the mornin' and I bet you been dancing all night, and still as playful as a kitten.

"Yeah," she echoed happily, insensibly, comforted once again by the broad old black shoulders of a cab driver. She thought of the apartment and trembled but also thought happily of the bed. 'Wish I didn't have to take those damned pills to sleep, she thought. "I'm starving," she said out loud, and then realised that she had spoken.

"You hungry? Really?" the cabby asked.

"Yeah. I am," she said, surprised that she wasn't embarrassed and that she felt so natural with the cab driver.. "You know where any hamburger places are around here?"

"Was one near where you live." He looked at his watch again. "But it ain't gonna be open now."

"Oh well," she said and sprawled back in the large back seat. "I'll be asleep soon anyway."

"It's too bad. You hungry, you ought to eat."

They rode along in silence to the old Gothic apartment building.

"Listen," he said when they pulled up the driveway. "I got something you can eat."

They both alighted from the cab, and she watched indifferently while he opened the trunk of the car. He was overweight and wheezed as he leaned over to open the trunk. She stared at the greasy black hair on the back of his fat black neck and felt happy. She saw him grasp a can of something in one hand and a loaf of bread in the other as he stood back up. He turned around on his incongruously small feet and held the can and bread towards her. He was grinning at her in the light. She stood there for a moment and smiled back at him. Then she took the can and bread.

"This here's some good ginger beer and that there's some fresh sesame seed bread – just bought fresh from the bakery this afternoon," he declared.

"Gosh, I've never had ginger beer," she told him. "I mean, if I did, I can't remember it." She stared down at the perspiring can, then looked back up at the cabby. "Are you sure you don't need this? I mean, *you* might need it."

"I won't need it," he assured her.

She handed him three dollars and walked through the revolving doors of her apartment building,. The air-conditioning of the lobby surrounded her shoulders and neck like icy fingers. She looked around dazed at the worn, ornate furniture that crowded the lobby like a group of aged, overdressed ladies – ones who could no longer wash themselves properly, but knew how to dress nonetheless.

She stepped into the elevator, without noticing the desk clerk, no longer thinking of her feud with the management, but smelling the fresh bread and thinking of the cabby's thick black neck and small feet, his wide, grinning face and the perspiration that had soaked his shirt and face. She started to hum an old lullaby her father had sung to her when she was a little girl on the ride up to her floor. Then she heard her key click in the lock to her apartment and Porgy howling from the interior of the apartment, and realised with a start, through her foggy emotional state, that she had reached home again.

"Yeah, yeah," she murmured to him, pushing open the door and patting Porgy's large, striped head. "Got some ginger beer here, Porgy," she said. "Don't know what it's gonna taste like, but I bet it's good."

She flicked on the kitchen light. The black and white linoleum of the floor always reminded her of a jail or of her aunt's kitchen in her home town. "Like an old hotel in the 40s," Eric had said. She went over to the wooden drawer and got out an extra-long knife that Hadrian had brought her.

"I hate you, knife," she said as she drew it out of the drawer. "You cut my foot, and you don't even cut good." She popped open the can of beer and took a sip cautiously. "Ohhh, ummm, hey, I told you this was gonna be great, Porgy! Now for the bread."

She felt the plastic covering over the bread under her fingers and tore at it happily, smelling the warm brown body of the loaf as it fell away. She was putting the long, awkward knife into the bread when she stopped and stared suspiciously at the loaf. "I mean, after all, this stuff could be poisoned or something. Maybe he's a weird old cab driver who gives people a ginger beer and sesame bread to kill them."

She thought of the old Negro's face, of the friendly creases that cut into his black skin like slices in meat. "Nah," she decided. "Besides, nothin's been opened."

She put a large hunk of bread in her mouth and walked through the living-room out onto the stone balcony, blowing through her opened mouth at the coldness of the can in her hand. Porgy followed between her legs like a large, thick feather. She sat down on the cold stone of the banister, feeling the rough concrete under her ass. She sucked her saliva in a wet bath over the brown, succulent bread and sighed, letting the taste of the bread go from the roof of her mouth through her nostrils, and enjoying it doubly. The ginger beer was cold and peppery, like a strange champagne.

"Ummm, Porgy, so good, so good," she said, taking, another bite of the bread and leaning back on the brick wall. "This street and me's getting to be good friends," she said, looking down the empty, lilacy Massachusetts Avenue and the trees whose leaves glittered constantly there in the street lights' neon glare.

"Oh, Goddamn. Oh shit," she said, and shifted her backbone, trying to get away from the skinned place she had put on her behind from doing sit-ups. She let one of her legs dangle over the balcony, admiring its slim tautness with her eyes. "I ain't never gonna get fat," she said. "Unless I have a baby."

She frowned, then smiled. "There's old Porgy over there, swirling around, looking at everything," she said in a teasing voice to Porgy. He understood her teasing and swished his tail with a pleased irritation. "Swishing his old tail like a squirrel," she continued. He glared fiercely at her with his yellow eyes. His stripes were black and dramatic on his ample body.

She leaned forward and grabbed him behind his neck, pushing her nose against his wide nose. She raised her lips to his broad forehead and smelled the perfume of his hair and healthy animal body, caressing his generous back with her hand as she did so.

"You've got hieroglyphics on your head, Porge. Hey, you really do!" she exclaimed. "They're all over your body. If I could just read those, Porge, maybe you'd have some secret message for me." She grabbed his front legs and held their meaty bodies hard. "Do you, Porge?" She pushed his head down to study the markings on his forehead, and he growled softly. "Gosh, if I could just figure it out," she told him.

She heard the faint ding-dong of the phone. 'I ain't gonna answer it, dammit,' she said, jumping off the balcony and racing through the french doors to the phone.

"Hello," she said expectantly. She heard a deep sigh through the receiver. "Is this some kind of sex nut?" she asked, "because I'm the wrong person to pick on, believe me! I'm a sex nut *too*." She breathed heavily back into the receiver.

"Cybele," Eric's drunken voice poured into her ear. "Cybelllee? Sis Eric – ol' Eric. How are you, luv?" he said suddenly in crisp tones.

"Is this Eric trying to pretend to be drunk?" Cybele scoffed into the phone.

"Pretend? Honey, have I ever put you on?" Eric protested. Cybele signed wearily and sank down into the pillow that she kept over the phone. "Cybele, m'dear – speak. I want to hear your lovely voice."

"OK," she replied. "You have put me on, and under, and everything else. Whaddaya want, Eric? I'm tired."

He started to mumble into the phone. "I can't be your crutch, I can't – can't take it anymore."

"Oh, damn, who's asking you to? Have I bothered you?"

"You came to the Pie. You came to the Pie," he chanted.

"OK, I came there. I sat with you and had a glass of lousy California wine and then I left in a cab, and now you're the one who's calling and hassling me," she yelled. 'I'm so amazed at myself,' she thought.

She heard the receiver clunk down on something, and then Jeff came on the phone. "He's freaked out, Cybele."

"Yeah, that's what I gathered."

"He just can't bear being your crutch. That's what's freaking him. He can't take it."

Cybele dug the carpet with her toes, watching the old dust that lay embedded in it sift idly. "Yeah, I don't blame him – I wouldn't want to be my crutch either. Hey, you and Maria should come over sometime." He was silent. "I mean, no reason why we can't be buddies."

"Sure, Cybele, we'll do it."

"OK, take care of Eric," she said. "I'm gonna go bed-bye."

"Ciao."

"Yeah," she said, and hung up.

She walked into the brightly lit bedroom. "The centre of it all," she said cynically. She walked over to the elaborately carved vanity table and took a bottle of Quitron out of the drawer. She popped two green and black pills into her mouth and swallowed them with her saliva.

"I'm tired, but I ain't sleepy." She stared around her, feeling suddenly drained. She flopped back on the bed and began lifting one leg then the other in a lie-down exercise she had devised. She felt tears falling into her hair as she slow-motioned the exercise, but didn't pay any attention to them. She heard herself pant with the movements of her legs, then stared as first one leg then the other rose up as if by their own volition. The fronts of her shins and thighs shone dully from the glare of the light overhead.

Soon she drew herself up into a little ball and fell asleep. She awakened momentarily and squinted up at the light, then drew the sheet over her head. The waves that the tranquillisers made in her brain and the coolness of the sheet against her cheek lulled her back into oblivion.

Porgy contemplated the lump under the tangled sheet that was Cybele, then leapt up on the bed deftly and lay down beside her. They slept in the light until she stumbled up to pee, weaving towards the bathroom in a drugged daze. Porgy watched her progress to the bathroom and back apprehensively, then settle his furry body close to her with relief when she had lain down once more. When she groaned, he shot both ears backwards at the sound. She murmured his name softly, stroking his body with each of her hands, and smiled sleepily at the high, wide ceiling before falling back to sleep.

Chapter Fifteen

"Cybele! Cybele!" Crag cried desperately. "You've got to get over here."

"Look, Crag, I'm not in the mood for one of your tirades," she said, tired. "In fact I'm not even going to talk to you right now – OK?" she said bitchily, and hung up the receiver with a bang.

"Fucking bastard!" she said.

"Mrrroowww," Porgy wailed.

"Oh not you, darling," she sighed, and pulled Porgy's fleshy body close to her breasts. "You're my only true love. The only male who didn't double-cross me, baby."

She kneaded his white paws firmly between her fingers, drawing a strong, voluptuous strength from the solidity of his furry flesh and the tiny scimitars of his claws.

"Wrroww," he trilled happily. His meow came from deep within his throat, from deep within his inner, most pleased and treasured-feeling cat self.

"Rowww," he added, revelling in the luxurious clasp of her arms about his shoulders and her massaging fingers on his belly.

"And you ain't even got balls, baby!" she said while pulling his tail playfully. "'Course, you did have. You did have 'em," she said and squeezed the lax skin where his testicles had been.

"Big ones, too. Before your mama had 'em cut off. God, I hated that."

She sank her nose into the sweet-smelling fur of Porgy's forehead and sniffed.

"Ummm, darlin'. You smell so sweet there." She pushed her nose back and forth along the hieroglyphic pattern of black stripes on the cat's forehead.

"That's how I know you're healthy – because you smell so good. You have very good essences, Porge. Did you know that?" She

pulled his muffy, fat cheeks up to her face. Porgy's blue-green eyes
flashed happily at her like sparkling, insouciant gems.

"Wroww," he agreed. he held onto each of her hands with his
paws as she grasped the sides of his jaws.

"Oh, you feel good. Oh, you do," she laughed while shaking his
head back and forth by the sides of his cheeks, and kissing him on his
broad, smooth nose.

He watched her avidly, trying not to loosen his gaze from her eyes
as she twisted his face playfully from side to side.

"Come on in here while I take a bath," she said, and carried him
into the bathroom with her.

She closed the door securely so that Porgy couldn't get out, then
placed him on top of the soft, yellow cover of the commode top.

"Now. You just sit right there while Mama bathes."

Porgy sat swishing his racoon-striped tail back and forth
imperiously along the white porcelain commode. Its black, tapered tip
was like an unscheduled, feline clock pendulum. His emerald green
eyes glowed ferociously at her out of his tiger-striped face.

"You know how your mother loves you to watch her?" Cybele
drawled mindlessly. "So you just sit right there and admire me. It
makes me feel so loved, darlin'," she said, and switched on the bath
water nervously.

"Oh God, I'm crashing," she wailed. "I just can't stand it," she
moaned.

"Oh no, not starting off the day like this. Oh God, God, are you
there?" she asked hysterically, propping one foot up on the bathtub's
cold, white side.

A tear dropped onto her knees like a cool raindrop and rolled down
the side of her leg. "Jesus Christ, if you are, please don't let things
be like this!"

"Wrrrowrw," Porgy cried, and plopped down beside her naked
brown legs with a thud. He began rubbing his head hungrily against
her shapely calves, courting the satisfaction of her caresses with the
pressure of his nose.

"Yeah, yeah," she said, stroking him again and touching the spiky
roots where his whiskers began.

"I know, you just wanna be loved, like me. And you hate it when
I cry. Right? 'Cause then you think that I might not be able to keep
taking care of you – makes you feel insecure. Right?"

She tested the bath water with one foot, then stepped into the tub.
"Anyway, God, if things do have to be this way, could you please give me some guts to bear it?" she asked fervently, and began soaping herself briskly.

"I always feel better after I bathe. God, it was always so filthy at Mama's. All that fucking bacon crease in those little, foul pots! S'nuff to make you wanna be a Jew or a Moslem. Say, Porge, are *you* a Jew?" she asked; and laughed loudly.

"What's your religion anyway? Shit, her food was good, though," she continued, and pressed the soap against her skinny thighs.

"Wish I had some right now," she added longingly. "I forgot when I ate last."

She jerked the stopper out of the tub and stood up languidly, weakened by the hot, steaming bath.

"You know what, Porge, I think I'll call Mama. Shit, maybe we could even go home," she shouted dementedly.

"Rinng! Rinng!" The phone shrilled through her nostalgic reverie.

"Ain't gonna answer it, Porge. Just ain't," she said, and flung a heavy towel around her lissom body.

The phone kept ringing insistently. Each buzz jangled her nerves like onions on a string. She walled determinedly into the bedroom and sat down on the bed, carefully drying each part of her body. She purposely concentrated with unusual care on drying each toe, each elbow, while waiting for the intruding, annoying sound to stop.

"Christ!" she exclaimed when the rings finally ceased.

She stood up from the bed and tried to think about making herself get dressed, then sank back down onto the pillows sobbing.

"I feel like one of those fucking pandas I was sketching in the zoo. Locked up, with no way out. Even the rats can find their way out, 'cause they're smaller than he is. But now I'm identifying, that's right – and you know what Ouspensky says happens when one identifies."

She lay back on the silken bedcovers. Her dark hair emitted a wet, spicy smell of perfume and marijuana.

She thought of Joe Yang when she remembered Ouspensky, of his dark hair and dark, olive complexion, and his firm, muscular hands under the sleeves of his red silk jacket.

"Struck out on the rule of five again, I guess," she mused about herself.

She wandered over to the long white dresser and picked up the diminutive porcelain statue that Joe had given her.

"When you don't like a thing, you just leave it. Right, Joe? Well, answer me this," she demanded, slamming the delicate statuette down so hard that it cracked apart.

"How does a panda get outta a zoo, Joe?" she yelled, tossing the broken, priceless porcelain into the trash basket.

"Turn into one of those little mice that poach food from his tray while he's asleep?"

She paced around the room excitedly with her hands clinched. She caught a glimpse of herself in the mirror and burst out laughing bitterly.

"Or does he circle around in his cage like me, pissing and defecating at will in front of the tourists, jumping up periodically against the sides of the case in exasperated boredom and madness. Shall I peep under the doorsill too, looking at that one stingy ray of light?"

Porgy leaped up on the bed and howled.

"Sure, Porge, you understand. Just be glad you ain't in a zoo, baby."

She sat down at the vanity table and began brushing her long, tangled hair so briskly that tears of pain sprang into her eyes.

"They think he's so beautiful – so black and white and strange," and she continued as the panda popped back into her brain. "So they stand there and coo while he goes mad. Fuck this," she said, and slung the brush down. "Let the damned tangles stay there for all I care."

She pulled on some cut-off jeans and an orange blouse that Brenda had given her.

"If you don't dig a thing, leave it," she repeated Joe's words resentfully. "Well, where do you go, Joe? Back to sweet, violent Pierre – the golden boy? Or how about a fascinating hippie freak? 'My fool,' you called Eric. So his ego can crash on you? Or how about Hadrian? Dear, dynamic, cruel, fragile-egoed Hadrian. Maybe he could bury me in hundred-dollar bills and lonely apartments? Maybe Sherman – how about Sherman, Porge? How'd you like to have him psyche you out every night over coffee? But be careful. He might take off his big toupee when it's dark and frighten you next morning!"

"Ohhh! Maybe I'm just relying on men to solve my problems too much. 1 guess it all started with my father. Tomorrow I think I'll paint – lose myself, Porgy boy, in something besides dick."

She put on her sandals and walked into the living-room.

"Goddammit, is that phone ringing again?" she yelled.

"I'm gonna cut the cord," she declared. She paced into the kitchen and began jerking open drawers erratically.

"If I can just find the fucking scissors!"

All at once she stopped in the middle of the room. A strange presentiment of disaster stole over her and left her trembling in the middle of the black and white linoleum floor. The filmy white curtains hanging at the dining-room window blew eerily away from the sill, like elusive, full ghosts' wings.

She rushed over to the ringing phone and put the receiver up to her ear,

"Hello," she whispered.

"Brandon is dead, Cybele," Crag sobbed. "Please come. Oh God, please don't hang up."

"I knew it," she said stonily. "I knew you were going to say something like this."

"Cybele, it's horrible. Oh, you. . . it's just horrible, Cybele. Somebody – they carved up his body – like it was a radish or something. You just wouldn't believe it."

He broke down and began crying wretchedly in her ear again.

"But where were you, Crag? Why weren't you there when this happened?" she asked suspiciously, with a thousand thoughts crowding into her brain.

"I was up at my parents' estate in Long Island. They offered me a Pleyel piano that's been in the family for years. I thought it'd be a good present for Brand's birthday. You know he just turned thirty-one yesterday? I came running upstairs to tell him I had a surprise for him." He stopped talking and sobbed brokenly into her ear.

"Oh Crag, Crag," she stammered, and sat down dizzily. "This can't be true."

"Oh it is, Cybele. It's very true. The windows were all open when I came in, and Le Chant du Roissignol was playing on the stereo. It must have happened a little while before I drove up."

He dragged heavily on his cigarette and coughed, choking from the smoke and his sobs.

"'At least that's what I thought at first before I understood that the record was stuck.

"Brand was sitting in a chair. I saw him from behind and thought he was listening to music. Then I realised that the same chord of music was playing over and over. The needle on the record was stuck. And Brand was so still.

"I felt a weird sort of foreboding for a second, but I thought it was just because I was so tired. Then I decided that a great thing to do would be to surprise him with the Pleyel piano.

"I closed the door to the study so I wouldn't wake him with the noise and ran back downstairs."

"Why didn't you shut the stereo off, Crag?" she asked, with a cold, obscure distrust flooding her words.

"The stereo?"

"Yeah, you said it was stuck," she reminded him. A relentless feeling of disbelief numbed her reactions of sympathy for Crag.

"Well. . . I. . dunno. I just didn't, that's all. Please, now will you let me finish the story and stop interrupting?" he said in a quavering tone that was a pale replica of his old, snappish self.

"I can hardly think anyway. I got Mason down in the antique shop next door to help me load the piano up the steps. That took us about an hour," he said, as if still exasperated by having exerted so much physical labour.

"You know how I hate to lift things or do anything like that," he reminded her.

His voice lapsed back into its former tone that it took on when he had confided petty personal grievances he held for certain people, and menial tasks that were imposed upon him by circumstances and life itself to her in the past. The words were expressed in his own inimical, stylish mode of speech, only now the confidence had lost its former charm or reason for being under the grim circumstances that had prompted his call.

"I got rid of Mason and then ran back to the study. Brand was still sitting there, only his head seemed to have dropped over to the side a little bit. I don't know, maybe I imagined it."

She heard him light another cigarette hastily.

"I ran around in front of him and yelled, 'Surprise!' Only it was me who got. . . surprised. I think. . . I. . . I think I fell down when I saw him. I – oh Cybele," he sobbed.

"When I came to my senses, I was covered with blood. I guess I fell on top of him or something. I remember picking up his hand and pressing it to my face. I always adored Brand's hands – especially when he played a piano."

He cried raggedly into the receiver.

"I was so looking forward to seeing his lovely fingers on the ivory keys of that piano. Then I noticed his hand. It was. . . Something horrible had happened to it," he said with anguish. "His little finger had been cut off. It. . . it wasn't there anymore. Oh, I can't take it. I can't. . . I'm not here. I want to get out of this place. It stinks like blood in here!" he shrieked incoherently.

She listened with horror to his voice then thought of Brand.

"Have you called the police yet?"

"No, not yet. I wanted to tell somebody first. Somebody who loves Brand – loved him, I mean – like I do."

His voice crumpled to a halt.

"Will you come?" he pleaded. "We'll call the police together."

She thought of Crag sitting in the apartment alone with Brand's mutilated body, and she shuddered.

"Are you in the study with Brand now?" she asked with a grisly curiosity. Sitting in a room with a dead man seemed unbearable to her.

"No," he answered, insentient to her tactless question. "I'm in the bedroom."

A long silence fell between them. Neither bothered to speak. They sat holding their respective receivers, each listening to the other's life breath pouring in through the tiny black holes of the phone.

"Are you coming or not?" Crag asked. "I've gotta hang up and call the police."

"OK, I'll come," she said listlessly.

"Right away?"

"I'm on my way, Crag. But. . ." she hesitated uncertainly. "I don't want to see Brand like that. Like he is now, I mean. I just don't."

"OK, I understand. You won't see him. I won't see him like he is now anymore either. Please come."

"Bye, Crag. I'll be there."

When her cab pulled up in front of the shop, a battery of police cars had already lined themselves along the street like shiny white bugs. Their tops gleamed white in the late morning sun, giving them the appearance of modern ghosts waiting along the black pavement of the street. In front of the Star Music Shop a flock of pigeons pecked hungrily at a pale yellow mound of bread crumbs that someone had thrown down for them on the sidewalk.

Cybele dug hastily into her purse for some money. The corded, black material of its interior lining scratched her hand roughly as she brought out several crinkly dollar bills.

"There you are," she said, and thrust the money into the cabby's dirty, plump hand.

She slid across the car seat and leapt out onto the boiling black pavement of the street, feeling the heels of her shoes sink into its soft, sun-melted tar. The front door of the shop looked fragile and small between the large glass display windows that flanked it, as if chastised by two huge bellows.

She breathed the sweet, matinal air of overripe summer leaves and secret, decaying moss deep into her lungs before pressing a small white button on the shop door. The straps of her shiny patent-leather sandals ground painfully against the sides of her feet, and she could feel the tightness from the elastic on her panties.

"Wonder why I wore panties today?" she said to no one as she pressed the bell.

A tall, slender police officer approached through the gloom of the shop, ducking his head when he passed under a long golden harp that Brand had hung whimsically from the ceiling. His brow wrinkled into a fresh row of creases when he squinted at her through the glass pane of the door.

"God, looks like Gary Cooper," she admired to herself.

"Can I help you, little lady?" the young man asked, smiling cutely with his small, compact mouth.

She hesitated before his clean-cut figure that swept through her dark, murky reasons for being there. She wanted to smile and tell him how attractive he was, how much he reminded her of her favourite movie star. Instead she lifted her foot out of her painfully confining shoes and said sombrely, "I'm here to see about Brand. . . Brand Star," she elucidated, looking at the neat edges of the man's mouth, at his narrow shoulders, and the arrowlike erectness of his body outfitted in his grey and blue police uniform.

"He's my friend. Crag is, too," she added disconnectedly. "I mean, that's why I came."

She looked at the officer's long slender face, at the fine wrinkles on each side of his intelligent, well-ordered mouth, and burst into tears.

"Crag wanted me to come," she sobbed, and leaned against the black, wooden edge of the door, pressing her head into her hand.

"You mean Cragmont Weatherby?" the man asked. His small blue eyes peered curiously at the girl while she cried weakly in the doorway.

"Yeah, Cragmont. Is he in here?" She looked up into the officer's face and was reminded of her tall, tubercular grandfather. She began crying harder from the memory.

"I don't know why I'm doing this," she apologised. "I guess I'm just tired," she said. She kept her forehead pressed into her hand in order to shield her face from the officer's eyes and she wiped tears from her dry, fatigued skin.

"Come on in," the man advised, and led her into the dark, cool shop.

"Wanna sit down?" he asked.

"I. . . I don't know," she said, looking around uncertainly at the musical instruments and Brand's empty wooden chair behind the desk that he had made.

She gasped when a long, dark pin dropped out of her hair and fell down on the floor by her foot. She grasped the officer's elbow involuntarily.

"Hey, steady there," he said, and patted her gently on her thin bare shoulder.

"You've had some real bad news, so just try to relax a minute."

He looked at her long dark hair hanging down richly on her smooth honey-brown shoulders, at the tears streaking her high cheekbones, and thought of a painting he had seen with his wife of a Magdalene. Her long-fingered, ample hands created an overwhelming feeling of tenderness in him as she held them up to her face. He was seized with an inspiration of warmth and languorous nights by the graceful contours of her arms.

"No, please. Please take me to Crag," she asked, looking at him imploringly. Her blue-green eyes shone gravely in the shadows.

"I know he needs me," she said, clutching at the material of her silky, orange blouse.

"You know that your friend is charged with murder?" the officer asked.

"Crag? I. . . I don't know," she said absently, looking again at Brand's empty chair.

She thought of the night Brand had begged her to meet him, of the rain beating against the window-pane in an insistent, splattering drizzle as they rode along in the cab to her apartment, and of what he had told her about Crag.

"Oh my God," she wailed. "It's his birthday! That's what Crag said on the phone."

"The phone? Did Mr Weatherby call you?"

"Yes, he asked me to come. He said that Brand had been murdered. That he had been mutilated. . . that. . ." She covered her face with her hands again.

"And he wanted you here?" the detective asked.

"Yes," she mumbled through her hands. "We were friends. I mean, I was more of a friend to Brand, at first. But then I got to know Crag."

She sighed wearily and accepted a large white handkerchief from the man. "Thanks, er?"

"Lowers, Officer Bob Lowers. And you are. . .?"

"Cybele Tashery," she said, and blew her nose violently into the soft muslin handkerchief.

"What do you know about Crag?"

"Oh, he's a character. He and Brand were lovers, you know. They were. . ." – she handed the large handkerchief back to Lowers – ". . .very close. Very close," she repeated, and relaxed, tired, in the straight-back chair. "In a strange sort of way," she finished.

"What do you mean?"

"Oh, just strange sometimes. The way all people are when they love someone. I guess we each play our own role with a person."

She rubbed her round, smooth knee with the palm of her hand.

"Could I beg a cigarette?" she asked suddenly.

"Huh?" Lowers said, staring down at her legs.

"Oh, sure, sure," he said, and grinned at her again with his small, pleasant mouth.

"Thanks," she said, taking the cigarette gratefully between her shaking fingers.

"What type of role would you say that Crag played in the relationship?" Lowers asked.

"Oh." She drew deeply on the newly lit cigarette. "He was sort of a sadist – I guess. He liked to think of himself that way, anyway. But Crag is actually very dear, a terribly understanding person when possessed of all his faculties. Ever noticed how he looks just like a Greek statue when he turns his head to the side?" she asked, adjusting her legs into a crossed position. "Of course, he effects that sort of hair style."

"How would you say that he and Brand got along?"

"Oh, erratically."

She smiled slightly, relieved momentarily by their confidences and the clearness of the man's blue eyes.

"At his worst Crag is a bully and a coward. He's so insecure, you know. His parents did that to him. But I guess we can all try to blame our parents, can't we?" she commented, looking wan and dissipated in the surreal surroundings of the music shop.

"But at his best," she breathed deeply and uncrossed her legs, "he has a subtle cunning intelligence that is always aware of what he is doing – and, I believe, is horrified by the path he has chosen. He is one of those people who chooses evil and suffers, but keeps right on choosing the wrong way, knowing ahead of time that he will suffer, but afraid – lacking courage, as it were – to follow another, more exacting rule of conduct."

She paused and inhaled the cigarette smoke brutally into her lungs.

"Let's just say he has style, and had a powerful psychological hold on Brand."

"When did you first meet Brand?"

"Oh, about a year ago."

"Was he with Crag then?"

"No. He had just come to town from California. He's lived all over the world, you know. Guess you've heard of the American Star Chili Company? That's owned by his family, among other things – like a few offshore oil holdings, race horses that paid off, homes in Palm Beach, Paris, a 30-acre estate in Georgia, a real live yacht – you name it, they-got-it sort of deal. Not just successful business people either. They came over from England. Anyway, we met right before I left my husband. He said that he was sick of the vapid life in California and the cold New York winters. He'd even got tired of the piquant charm of Paris. So. . ." she stubbed the half-smoked cigarette out in the familiar black ashtray on Brand's desk beside her, "he came to DC. He was a southerner, you know. Like me. And he thought this was a good in-between place to stop. He was so charming, so cute with his curly blond hair." She sighed. "And he was like a brother I'd never had. He understood me, and we were both lonely." She faltered in the unnerving quiet of the shop.

"Were you in love with Mr Star?" Lowers asked.

"Well, I. . . I loved him, like a brother. I didn't need anything more from him. I was in love with. . ." She stopped, thinking of Eric, Hadrian, and Pierre. "You might say I loved a lot of different. . . men. In different ways." She shrugged her shoulders helplessly. "It's the only way I know to do."

They heard footsteps on the stairs leading down from the apartment above and stopped talking abruptly.

Crag stumbled down the stairs between two plainclothes detectives, holding his handcuffed wrists before his legs like a man carrying a cross. His dark brown hair was curling in wild, matted whorls around his face, and he looked at Cybele with haunted, anguished eyes.

"Crag!" Cybele cried, and ran up to him and threw her arms around his shackled arms.

"Hey, step back, miss," one of the detectives ordered, looking at Officer Lowers uncertainly. "This man is under arrest for murder."

Cybele drew back from Crag a little, but still held his arms as if in a vain, uncomprehending entreaty.

"Oh Crag," she muttered, looking disbelievingly at his ravaged, ashen face. "Crag, this just can't be happening! It can't," she repeated dejectedly. A feeling of unreality swept over her. The police officers were like imagined trees in a fictitious forest. The giant harp and mahogany base viols in their midst turned into objects with other meanings. They were also displaced. Their function as musical instruments seemed to have disappeared and left them possessed of some other, more vital reality. She stared at the dark stubble of whiskers on Crag's cheek and reached out to touch his face, oblivious to the effect her gesture made on the men standing around them. Crag's tortured, brooding eyes stared into hers like a wild flying bird caught in captivity, but never possessed by it. As if reading her own thoughts, he clasped her hands strongly with his handcuffed hands and said, "Don't worry. I'm flying high and free, like an eagle. They won't touch me. Do you understand?"

His grey-blue eyes burned into hers like coals, and his red sensual lips pursed themselves determinedly into an expression she recognised from the past when he was in his normal "fighting form".

'Thank God something has remained of that old, logical strength,' she thought.

She felt his fingers grasping her hand with such a pressure that she had trouble not crying out. She wondered if he was trying to play his game of inflicting pain as a joke, as a secret bond between the two of them. Then she noticed his eyes and their expression of extreme alarm, and she grew terrified.

"It's *you* who can be shot down, Cybele," he warned her.

"Come on, lady, let us get out to the car with this guy," one of the detectives said grouchily. "I'm hungry, and the sooner I get this dude checked in to his new 'residence', the sooner I get those eggs and ham!"

He pushed Crag forward into the building heat of mid-morning.

"Don't go back to your apartment, Cybele," Crag beseeched her, jerking his head over his shoulder for one last look at her. "Listen to me, Cybele," he begged. "I'm the only person who can tell you this, the only one who can feel it. There's something evil in that apartment you live in, something gruesome and savage."

"Come on, bud, get cracking," the other fat detective ordered, and shoved Crag up against the police car.

Cybele ran out after them into the sun-dappled shade that splotched the sidewalk in front of the shop.

"You don't have to manhandle him," she protested.

The paunchy-bellied detective looked at her derisively. "Sister, you're a real freaky-looking dame. Got your eyes all painted up like

Cleopatra. You're really weird. You Georgetown freaks," he said, and shook his head admonishingly.

Cybele looked past his bulky, protesting figure into Crag's soul-haunted eyes. Again she saw a fierce eagle flying high over grey, lonely landscapes.

"Don't go back there, Cybele! Don't go back ever," Crag entreated her.

"Ah, get in the car and shut up, will ya?" the fat-knuckled officer drawled, and pushed Crag into the back seat of the car.

She stared hypnotically past the officer, not wanting to lose Crag's intent, prophetic gaze.

'He's right,' she thought. 'If anyone knows, if anyone can feel something this far out and subtle, it has to be Crag.'

"Remember what I told you, Cybele, for God's sake," Crag begged her from the back seat.

"Shit," the obese policeman said. "I used to think all you hippies were so colourful, so entertaining – sexy, and all that," he finished, running his eyes meaningfully up and down Cybele's bare legs. "But look where it's got you," he said with disgust. "You don't even know where you're at." He coughed and spit crudely on the kerb beside Cybele's feet. She stepped back as if she had seen a snake, and stumbled into the reed-slim chest of Officer Lowers.

"C'mon, Mrs Tashery, let us drive you home now," the gentle-voiced man advised.

"Oh no," she cried. "Didn't you hear him? I *can't* go home. I couldn't now, not since I know about this. . ." she ended vaguely.

"Are you sure you really have anything to worry about?" Lowers asked her. "I can always go back to your apartment with you and look around."

"No, no, that wouldn't do any good. You wouldn't find what he's talking about."

The young officer studied her worriedly with his sparkling blue eyes. "You need some rest. Do you know a friend you can stay with for a few days?"

"A friend? Oh yes, a friend. I have one!" she said.

They looked at each another and laughed with relief.

"Well, let's take you there – to your leader, as it were," Lowers said, and grasped her hand nervously.

At that moment they were aware that they shared the same attraction, that under different circumstances they might have been lovers. They let their eyes enjoy one another frankly, gaining a small reprieve from the grim situation.

"Oh, yes. My friend is near here – only a few blocks away. On Q Street."

"OK, lady, let's go. You look like you could use a good nap."

"I haven't been sleeping well lately," she admitted. "Maybe it's the company I've been keeping." She paused, pushing a long black strand of her hair back from her face in a characteristic gesture of nervousness. She let her eyes swim for a while in the clear blue prisms of Lowers' eyes. "Maybe you and your wife might invite me over for a drink sometimes," she asked wistfully. "I'll bet she's a very nice person, actually."

"Yes, she is," he replied.

"If I thought she'd understand, I'd take you home with me," he offered. "But. . . you're so beautiful."

"Forget it, that's what they all say. Ha ha, I mean. . ." she stuttered, when she realised what she had said.

"I can imagine," he replied. "Well, what's the address of this place? I'll have to be getting back to the precinct soon, or get hell from someone."

"Come on," she said, and pulled him towards his own patrol car. "I'll show ya."

She could hardly sit still on the hot black car seat until they pulled up in front of Eric's apartment house. She kept pushing her hands under her bare thighs to protect them from the scalding plastic seat cover. The fringe of her blue-jean shorts had become matted with dust and perspiration. Inside the patrol car, the frigid air-conditioning failed to stop droplets of perspiration from sliding down her honey-brown calves and keep it from beading on the fine blond stubble of whiskers above Lowers' mouth. She watched him push in the shiny car lighter perfunctorily, and imagined an automaton from another world pressing buttons on a spaceship. The man's detachment from his physical act of pushing in the lighter and the way the device sank into the dash was somehow comforting to her. She leaned her head back on the car seat in her first attitude of relaxation for more than three hours.

"You OK?" he asked as he pressed the red-orange coils of the lighter to his cigarette.

"Sure. With somebody like you taking me to a really good friend – I'm swinging," she replied, and smiled at him disarmingly.

She drew deep draughts of smoke from the freshly lit cigarette into her lungs, and thought of her grandfather again.

"Where're you from?" she asked abruptly.

"New Hampshire, why?" he answered.

"Oh, nothing," she said, disappointed. "Hey, here it is. My friend's house, I mean."

He swerved the car to a stop in front of the huge roots of a tree that had burrowed themselves under the kerb and buckled the cement like cracked, drying mud. The tree's large, fanlike leaves littered the sidewalk with their shapely shadows and fell across the slanting steps that led up to the black doorway of the apartment building. She looked at the door with relief, happy to see concrete evidence of some sort of refuge. She didn't know how Eric would react after what had happened the previous night, but she did know that he would come through for her when she told him about everything.

"All right, Cybele Tashery," Lowers said. "Run in and see if someone's there. Otherwise, I have to take you home." He saw her expression of consternation, and said, "Don't worry, I'll send a guard to stand by your door if worse comes to worse."

"No, Eric will be here," she said eagerly. "I just know he will."

She hopped out of the car and ran up the familiar stone steps two at a time. She pushed open the heavy black door and ran into the hallway to Eric's apartment door. The sign RING TWICE – ASK FOR PAUL' had been ripped off the door. She pressed the lighted doorbell button, and waited hopefully, leaning her shoulder against the rough wood of the doorway. She thought of Eric's compact hands making cabinets and felt comforted. Several minutes turned into ten before she realised that no one was answering the door.

'Everyone's still asleep,' she thought hopefully. 'After all, it's probably only about 11:30.'

She dashed out to the patrol car and said, "Listen, everything's great. I'll probably stay here with Wendy a few days."

"Are you sure, Cybele?" Lowers questioned her speculatively. "I don't want you to have any more trouble today."

"Sure I'm sure. These are my dearest friends," she assured him. "My very dearest," she repeated, anxious for him to leave.

"OK," he said, relinquishing his authority over her for the moment. "We have your home address and phone number. You'll be hearing from me in a day or so. Can you check your messages at your apartment building?"

"Of course. We're in a civilised country, aren't we?" she asked, and grinned at him impishly. The stinging sunlight etched a pattern of fine lines around her eyes that had not been there earlier that morning.

"I don't know, *are* we?" he asked sardonically. "In any case, rest," he advised her.

"Aye, aye, sir," she said, and brought her hand up to her temple with a playfulness that belied her impatience for him to leave.

She watched the shiny white patrol car pull off with relief, then ran back inside the darkened interior of the hallway. The other apartment doors lined the rectangular passageway of the apartment building like silent statues. She stood patiently by Eric's apartment door until her feet began to hurt. Finally she slipped down to the floor like a floating, feather and dozed off.

She awoke with a start when one of the adjacent apartment doors swung open. A yapping English terrier rushed up to her friskily and covered her with a flood of wet, pink-tongued caresses.

"Ugh!" she cried. "Fuck off, you. . . dog!

A woman whose fat behind filled a pair of white stretch shorts like rippling lard jerked at the dog's mint-green leash irritably.

"Come on, Arnold, don't bother the lady," the woman said.

The dog looked curiously at Cybele with his snapping black eyes. He obviously wanted to explore her for a longer period of time, but his silver-studded collar cut harshly into his grey, closely shaved neck with each tug the woman gave his leash. He gazed on at Cybele through two more painful jerks at his collar, then gave her a parting, sloppy kiss with his long pink tongue.

"Arnold, for Christ's sake," the woman said. "Everybody doesn't appreciate that you are Marlon Brando like me, OK?"

"The dog yapped along behind the woman like a small machine without a muffler.

"Oh God. What an alarm clock," Cybele groaned and yawned, tired. She stood up and brushed the seat of her shorts off, then groaned again. Her whole body ached from sitting for so long on the hard, carpetless floor.

'It must be at least one o'clock,' she thought. 'They oughta be up by now.'

She pressed the white plastic bell button twice and waited. After about ten minutes she pressed it again.

"Who the hell is it?" someone yelled. "If it's the cops, come back later!"

"It's Cybele," she said uneasily. "Is Eric around?"

"Is *who* around?" Jeff asked, as he swung open the door.

"Jeff!" she cried. "I've gotta see Eric."

Jeff backed sleepily away from the door, pulling her in behind him as he did so. "Eric ain't here, Cybele. But come on in anyway. You want some coffee?" he asked. His soft, Texas accent drawled coffee into "cawfee".

"No, I hate it," she refused ungraciously. "I've gotta find Eric."

"Hi, Cybele," a girl with tousled, curly red hair called from a bedroom.

"Oh, hi, Maria," Cybele said. She looked admiringly at the girl's white, voluptuous body lying like an inviting bowl of cream in the disarray of sheets on the water-bed.

"You wanna come and rest with us?" she asked, and patted the bed.

"No, not right now, Maria. I haven't got time," she declined.

"Night, night," Maria called sleepily, and fell back in a heap on the undulating water-bed. She stuck her short thumb in her bow-like mouth and immediately fell asleep. Her fine, pale eyelashes closed against her creamy pink cheeks wispily.

"Listen, Eric took off for the beach on a camping trip this morning."

"With whom?" she asked in spite of herself.

"Oh, just a bunch of kids," Jeff drawled. "Don't worry, he hasn't found another woman since you. You really got to him, you know."

She stood, tense, in the hallway, wondering what she should do next. Suddenly she thought of Porgy. His thick, blunt head and meaty body gave her a false sense of security that she needed acutely at that moment.

"Never mind, I've gotta get home anyway," she decided.

"Well, here. Take something good to start the afternoon off with," Jeff said, and pulled a joint out of his pocket. "You look too serious for this time of day."

She took the long joint and put it in her mouth. She watched placidly as Jeff lit its twisted, closed tip. She winced from the hot, ripping pain that seared her throat when she drew the marijuana deep into her lungs. It stung her eyes until they watered and burned her nostrils until she coughed, but she felt a heady cloud puff through her brain that accelerated her sensitivities like falling stars.

"Umm, so good," she sighed, and flexed her tingling fingertips like a cat extending its claws.

"You're a sweet chick," Jeff drawled pleasantly in her ear and blew strands of hair curling around her temples away from her face. The soft kiss he planted by her ear lobe exploded in her hearing like a sound studio filled with a recording of rushing wind. She touched the loosely-woven material of his Indian shirt dizzily, and noticed the chicken-like protuberances of his breastbones with dismay.

"You have a sculptured breastbone, Jeff," she noted kindly.

"You have some sculptured thighs, brown one," he returned the compliment. "Want to put my breastbones over your thighs and have a serenade on the sofa?"

She took another deep drag on the joint, letting the smoke explode through her brain in euphoric waves. She watched Jeff's powdery blue eyes shimmer through her teary, smoke-smarting eyes.

"What about Maria?" she asked.

"Oh, she's asleep. Come on," he said, and pulled her down the long hallway to the living room.

She looked around at the familiar furnishings of the room. They seemed haunted by Eric's ghost and all of the other people she had seen there. Her head felt light and her lips seemed swollen to her. She put her fingers on them and pressed their warm, spongy flesh.

"My lips feel like ribbons," she said.

"And your skin is like velvet," Jeff marvelled. He led her towards the black leather couch she had sat on with Eric so many times before.

"Are we going to do it here?" she asked, feeling disturbed.

"Sure, why not?" It's a comfortable piece of furniture."

He pulled her down on the cushiony seats of the sofa beside his bony white body. She stared at the long, sinewy muscles of his rope-thin arms and the tiny flexible bones leading down the middle of his wrists.

"You are so pale, Jeff. . . and thin. Look how fair and sparse your beard is," she observed. His angular legs cut into the tender flesh of her thighs like rough sticks.

"And you are so brown, child. Like one of those octoroons down in New Orleans."

"But I'm not an octoroon, you know," she said and scrooched her body up into a bow to escape the knife-like sharpness of his limbs. "I just masquerade as one."

She trembled beside his hot, wiry body in the air-conditioning. Stale cigarettes in an oversized pottery ashtray assailed her nostrils. She longed for a warm fur blanket and sleep; instead she felt Jeff's bony, rough-palmed hands on her body and smelt the stench of his armpits.

"I love to smell honeysuckle," she said slyly, looking at his fish-pale eyes and sallow cheeks. "Don't you?"

"Uh? Oh yeah," he agreed while studying her intently. "Where are you from, anyway, child?" he asked, then took a long hit off the joint of marijuana.

"Oh, I'm like you," she answered, and took the fast-disappearing joint that he had offered her. "I know what honeysuckle smells like."

"Southern, huh?"

"Oh yeah," she said. "Definitely."

"What sort of family are you from?"

"It depends on which sociology book you're reading."

"You seem like a lady to me," he said, watching her inhale the joint appreciatively. "One who's used to a lot." He pressed his hands around her hips and began a line of kisses down the side of her thigh.

"Yes," she agreed. "I'm used to a lot." The word 'lot' took on an ambiguous meaning.

"Does that mean you're a rich bitch?" he asked, and stuck one of his long, thin fingers into her cunt.

"I didn't know we were talking about money," she said, letting him invade her body with a detached, dreamy sensuality.

"Ummm, you have a lot, Cybele."

"Ha ha," she giggled, and let her hand flop back abjectly on the pillows. "That's what they say."

"Eric is obsessed by you," he informed her.

"Obsessed by me? Is that why he pulled out on me?" she asked dejectedly.

"Well, you teased him with another guy, you know. And the situation with your 'benefactor' was hard for him to live with, too."

"I adored Eric. I was so mad about his body, his personality, even his ignorance and stupidity that I was ready to leave Hadrian for him."

A tear trickled down her cheek. She drew her knees up under her chin, forgetting that Jeff's finger was up in her body.

"He enchanted me," she declared.

Her red, chapped lips pooched out in a charming pout. Her black, mascara'd eyelashes were matted with tears that sparkled in her green, gemlike eyes. Jeff contemplated her excitedly, then drew the top of her apricot coloured blouse away from her breast. The shiny white flesh of her bosom glowed like lustrous pearls under the line of deep brown tan that began where her bikini had left off.

"How special," Jeff said while he contemplated her breasts lovingly.

"He seems to be all around the room," she remarked and dragged her fingers along the roughly-constructed coffee table. "Oh!" she exclaimed when she felt Jeff's moist mouth on her flesh. She watched the top of his sparsely-haired head while he planted sticky, unpleasant-feeling kisses along her midriff and on up between her breasts. She felt the boniness of his finger inside her vagina and wondered if his cock would be as thin.

'Oh, why am I doing this?' she wondered desolately. 'Why?'

She felt his lips move onto her nipple and touch the teat with a nervous sucking motion, like a colicky baby trying to obtain milk.

"Oh, you're like sweetmeats, darlin' girl. I'm going to eat you up."

He put his head down to her cunt and began lapping hungrily at her pubis. She let the pleasant sensation of his tongue cajole her into a peaceful submission for a few moments, then turned her head wearily to gaze out through the balcony door. The leaves on the branches of a mimosa tree were lemon-green in the brilliant summer sunlight outside. They swirled and heaved in the breezes like myriad, reflecting jewels. The musky odour of the room overwhelmed her once more. She felt a sense of drowning, of being held down by a blanket of stale odours and unsatisfactory sexual approaches to her body.

Suddenly she struggled up from the couch, like one trying to surface from the depths of a deep, darkened pond.

"Oh Jeff – Jeff. I have to go," she announced, and squirmed out from under him.

"But sweetmeat, little tender flower," Jeff cried with his chin fallen down into the sofa cushions after being jarred away from her cunt. "We were just beginning to know one another!"

"I agree, Jeff. It's true. And you mustn't be hurt, really. We'll spend long afternoons together. . . sometime soon," she soothed him while looking with distaste at his sallow, weak features. "But I have to go right now." She snatched her shorts off the sofa and hopped into them like a gun-shy rabbit.

"Crap!" Jeff said sullenly, and pulled another joint from a cigarette package.

"Bye," she called as she ran pell-mell down the long, hallway.

The sun shone brutally in her eyes when she ran out of the apartment building; the same sun that had seduced her through the windows of the apartment.

'I have to get home,' she thought anxiously. 'What if something happens to Porgy? Crag said that there was something evil in that apartment. Oh, damn it, why didn't I go Mama's like I'd planned? It wouldn't have been so bad.'

She stumbled along the street. The marijuana clouded her brain like storm clouds and left her fingertips tingling with a strung-out sensation akin to vines creeping endlessly along old brick walls. The gay-coloured buildings of Georgetown looked like leftover party masks in the silently burning sunlight.

'How tired I am,' she thought as she passed a record shop. She looked at the stacks of record albums and thought of the countless singers enclosed inside their covers.

'God, I think I'll take a cab. No, first I'll have a coke – a nice, cold icy coke,' she decided. 'It'll be like down South.'

She ran into an old-fashioned drug store and dug into her purse for some change. She felt all around inside for money. Finally her hand fell on a cold, medium-sized coin.

"Christ, I forgot to bring any money," she exclaimed aloud in surprise. "How am I going to take a cab?" She plopped the coin into a large red coke machine. A bottle of pop rolled noisily down into the receiving slot.

A black-haired woman looked irritably at her with rock-black eyes. Her round, pallid face was framed between packages of Alka-Seltzer and aspirin bottles. The bottoms of her cheeks had folded in soft little wrinkles like a small collapsed cake.

'Reminds me of my first-grade teacher,' Cybele thought. 'The one who used to break rulers over my head or pinch me, ugh,' she thought disdainfully, and swallowed the gaseous liquid in thirsty gulps.

She walked over and sat down on the cracked leather fountain stools. Drops of water from the coke bottle fell onto her bare legs and trickled down into the dust covering the calf of her leg.

"What am I living for, if not for youuu," she sang and giggled. The grass kept sending little waves of euphoria through her brain, pushing her spirits up and down like pedals on a bike.

"You can't come in here barefoot anymore," the woman told her. She plopped a twisted wet cloth onto the counter emphatically and began swabbing it back and forth along the counter, following her own movements with her hard black eyes.

"Well, lucky for me that I've got shoes on," Cybele retorted smugly.

The woman looked over the counter past Cybele's bare legs at her feet.

"OK," she said grumpily and kept washing the counter with a mechanical, repetitive motion.

Cybele watched the last of the Coca-Cola surge in sudsy bubbles around the bottom of the coke bottle. A big, frothy burp forced its way up through her throat. She closed her mouth in embarrassment and looked at the woman behind the counter surreptitiously, hoping that she hadn't heard anything.

The woman's black, beady stare met her eyes like marbles hitting a target.

"Excuse me," Cybele apologised.

"Humph," the woman grunted, and went on swabbing the marble counter-top like a machine that had been set in motion by a computer for certain duties. Her graceless, jerky motions dragged the sour-smelling cloth back and forth in front of Cybele until she slammed her coke bottle down by the woman's hand and ran out of the door to escape the odour.

"God, how can she stand the smell?" she wondered aloud. "Why doesn't she wash the fucking thing? How can people bear to let themselves stink?" she muttered to herself, thinking of Jeff's acrid body odour that she had also had to escape from just a short while before.

"Baaalllooons, Balloons for the lovely lady," a tall, chocolate-faced man chanted. He swung a lavender gas balloon in front of her face.

"Ahhhh!" she shrieked. She pushed the rubber balloon away from her face and stumbled past the man. He dipped his body over to one side in an acrobatic movement that resembled the bouncing balloons over his head, then thrust his face into hers.

"Take this lovely balloon home with you, pleeassee!" he exclaimed.

"But I have no money," she explained, looking at his face with a clownish confusion.

The man kept holding the balloon in front of her invitingly. His white teeth shone pearly and luminous over the rim of the lavender-coloured balloon. The dark brown skin of his neck glistened exotically beside the neon whiteness of his shirt collar. A light, friendly line of dirt showed itself along its starched edges.

"You mean I can just have it?" she asked innocently. The monumental lines of his face and body reminded her of a Gauguin painting. She stood enjoying the colourful spectacle of the red and yellow and green balloons bobbing around his grinning, leering face, being more absorbed by his image than his words.

He nodded back and forth at her, rolling his eyes idiotically from side to side like an unmanned puppet. She reached her hand out for the balloon, still staring with delight at his macabre face. Just as her hand touched the long white stick attached to the balloon, it exploded with a loud pop.

"Oh!" she cried, and stepped back into the path of two long-haired freaks.

"Far out, man! Look what's landed my way."

"Manna from heaven," his companion praised.

Cybele felt the young man's muscular arms under her armpits and looked up into his smiling, perspiring face.

"My balloon popped," she said and laughed.

"Ha, you're right," he observed. He held up the piece of torn rubber as if to verify the fact. It hung down like lavender-coloured spaghetti between his fingers.

"Here," the other guy said, and handed the balloon man a dollar bill. "The lady wants a red one."

The vacant-eyed Negro handed Cybele a large red balloon as he chanted, "Certainly sir, maake the laady happy," as if none of them really existed, as if it were only his yolky, sonorous chant that had any reality in the afternoon's brilliant sunlight.

"Come on, babe," the taller boy holding her said. "Come and join Jim and me for a brew."

"But. . . I have to get home," she stammered, feeling dizzy from the marijuana and weak with hunger. "I would love a hot dog, though," she added plaintively.

"A hot dog! Hal!" Jim guffawed. "Oh Charles, this is rich – really rich."

He looked curiously at Cybele with large, spaniel-like eyes.

"You do look pale, little girl. Come on. We'll even take you for a cheeseburger, if you want," he offered generously.

"Oh, swell," she exclaimed.

They clasped their arms around one another's bodies like fellow football players and ambled along the street into the swinging, gold-barred doors of Clyde's.

"Whhaa, I don't believe it," Jim cried. "Look who's here."

Cybele looked at the tall, elegantly dressed young man that Jim referred to. His cream-coloured suit fitted on his handsome body with all the aplomb of a French silk scarf. They way his leg was draped over one of the wicker-backed chairs displayed his unconscious style and grace.

"C'mon, balloon gal," Charles instructed Cybele. "Sit yourself down."

She sank into a chair next to the young man who looked like Adonis. Her feet ached and the back of her throat was dry and scratchy-feeling. The grass Jeff had given her still seemed to be exploding out of her ears. Splotches of colour circulated in front of her eyes like red lights blinking. Their red circles made her think of Crag's blood-stained shirt.

'Brand is dead,' she remembered, and felt as if someone had just told her again.

"Which circus did you just leave?" the good-looking, young man asked her.

"I'm sorry, you'll have to check that balloon at the door," a waiter clad in a long white apron told her.

"OK, but make sure it don't break," Jim warned, and handed the big red balloon to the tall, black-moustached waiter. "I'll take care of things, don't worry," he assured Cybele. "What do you want to drink. . . what'd you say your name was?"

"Cybele."

"OK. OK, Cybele. We got it all taken care of."

"Whatcha been doin', Chad?" Jim asked the extraordinarily good-looking young man sitting beside Cybele.

"Oh, singing, you know. The usual. Got a big write-up in *The Washingtonian* the other day – 'the slinky, silky singer of the Dubonaes', they called me. Ha!" he laughed with an engaging, pleased vanity.

"Hey, ya'll ought to see that Warhol flick," he continued, delighted to have gained their attention. "It's so great. This guy will screw anybody just to get them to do what he wants." He opened his wide, shapely mouth and stuck one finger in it. His pale yellow eyes flicked around the table at everyone hungrily. All of his motions were cloaked in a voluptuous, cat-like grace that pleasantly disguised his need for attention.

"Anyway," he continued, "they just sit around shooting the shit like we're doing. You should go and see it. He makes it with this old lady just so she'll get him some groceries. He goes up to different women and says, "If I screw you, will you get me. . .?'"

"Where is that movie?" Charles asked. "Let's go and see it this afternoon."

Cybele looked at Chad's hands. They were long and thin around his drink glass, languid in the sunlight. His body relaxed her. She could almost forget about Brand and Crag as she basked in Chad's easy sensuality. His eyes gazed past them dreamily like two brown-yellow gems, unconsciously beautiful. He lowered his head to the steaming liquid in his white coffee cup, showing them clusters of silky brown curls.

"Chad, you're the most lovely little cat," Cybele said, and stroked the stranger's curly locks.

Chad eyed her warily. His expression of casual sensuality never left his lips while he watched her.

"No, you're an antelope. You can't be a cat – your lines are too angular for that," she decided.

She saw herself in the mirror behind the bar. Her tangerine-coloured blouse was like oranges on her brown skin. Her long, tangled hair waved around her shoulders like black silk.. The features of her face had sharpened into an almost blinding beauty and vitality.

"You're on something good today, lady." Chad grinned approvingly at her.

"Yeah, we found her with the balloon man. She'd just lost her balloon and we had to get her another one," Jim informed him. He took her by her chin and bit the bottom of it. "Ummm, child's so succulent!"

When Jim mentioned the balloon man, she felt a stabbing pain of grief between her ribs.

"Gosh, I've got to get home," she told them, remembering her predicament aloud.

"What happening with you, strange one?" Chad asked. "I see blood in your eyes."

Cybele shivered beside him.

"Oh no!" she said sadly. "Oh no!"

"I see the truth then?" Chad asked.

She took his long, pale fingers in her square, brown hand and sighed.

"I need this," a tall blond boy with startlingly blue eyes said, and he started pulling an empty chair away from their table.

"My God, look at his eyes," Chad exclaimed admiringly.

Everyone turned to look at the young man's eyes.

"Yes, they're fantastic," Charles agreed.

"If you knew who my father was. . ." the young boy said, grinning.

"Don't tell me, he's Paul Newman," Charles guessed.

"Oh God, discovered again," the boy confessed and he hit his forehead mockingly. He laughed helplessly at his companion.

"And you're Steve McQueen," Chad said to his companion, who looked like one of "Our gang". He held Cybele's hand in his seriously, while bantering back and forth with the guys. Every once in a while he put his large, loose mouth to her ear and asked, "You OK, weird one?"

"Actually, I'm more like little Lord Fauntleroy," the guy said, batting his curly eyelashes. "I couldn't ride a motorcycle as hard as Steve McQueen."

"Are you from California?" the blue-eyed guy asked Cybele. "You don't look like the East Coast."

"Yes, er – no," Cybele said absently. "I mean I've been there. You really *do* look like Paul Newman. *Are* you his son?"

"Well, I'd rather be in New York," Chad said before the guy could answer Cybele. "I mean for the music business – or Paris."

His voice stretched the word 'Paris' out as long and indolent as his hands were. Cybele sat half listening, ready to dash out of the door at a moment's notice. 'Jesus, Jesus,' she thought. 'What am I doing here? I've gotta get home and see old Porge.'

"I don't see how the music business could be any better here than in California," the boy who looked like little Lord Fauntleroy said.

"Listen, Jim – Charles," Cybele began with a hint of hysteria in her voice. "I've gotta get home. Can you loan me a couple of bucks for a cab?"

"But child, you haven't even finished your brew yet – not to mention your hot dog," Jim protested.

"I don't know if I'm hungry or not anymore," she said dolefully.

"I guess I'll go and watch TV," Chad said, looking at Cybele with disappointment.

"TV? Chad! It's three in the afternoon," Cybele said in horror.

"Yeah, that's when I like it best – between four and six."

"God," Cybele groaned, "TV depresses me. God, how it depresses me – when I think about it, that is."

"You're a crazy little lady," Chad remarked, and stroked her cheek like one would caress an animal.

"But sometimes when I watch it I like it," she contradicted herself. "Did you see Disneyland on Sunday? God, what a beautiful black cat!" She thought of the large television blaring out at Eric's apartment and sighed. 'Guess I should never have gone out with Sherman,' she thought. 'And he was such a lousy lay compared to Eric, anyway.'

"Wasn't he great?" Charles agreed. "And all those statues of Buddha."

"False face must know what false heart must hide," Chad said, slanting his eyes with his fingers. "I mean, which would you rather watch – Huntley-Brinkley or 'I dream of Jeanie'?" he asked everyone.

"Neither," the boy with brilliant blue eyes said. "I mean, I never watch the news. It's pretty depressing, isn't it? So I never watch it."

"Well, I mean *if* you did watch TV?" Chad persisted.

"I love Barbara McNair," Cybele offered.

"She died, you know," Chad informed her.

"Oh Chad, you're lying," Cybele screamed.

A group of freaks sitting nearby gave her the V-shaped peace sign.

"She did. I mean it – she had too many silicone injections," Chad continued.

"Oh, you're just saying that, like they said that one of The Beatles died," Charles scoffed. "I heard she was arrested for heroin, but it was a frame-up."

"Hey, Chad, look at this," Jim said and lifted some books up from a table where three girls sat sipping tall rum concoctions.

"Oh yeah, yeah. I love Chekhov. Sartre? He's pretty. . . Oh, hey," Chad exclaimed, and held one of the books up admiringly. "Stalvinsky. You girls into acting?"

An auburn-haired girl gazed at Chad, "He's like an exotic gazelle, with golden, brandy-coloured eyes," she said.

"Who *are* you anyway?" Cybele asked Chad.

"Oh I'm Chad, I'm the universe – anything," he replied.

"He's beautiful," the auburn-haired girl, and possessor of the Stalvinsky book, said.

"Yes, I guess you're right. He *is* beautiful – in his own way."

Cybele stared at his wide, handsome mouth, at his cascade of curly hair, and his vain, childish eyes that were hazel-coloured and a little red in one of the corners. He stared back at her with hard black pinpoints for pupils.

"I know someone who would love him," Cybele said, thinking of Brandon. "*Would* have loved him," she corrected herself as she remembered Crag's tormented face afresh.

Chad studied her intently and said, "I see blood in your eyes again."

"Who is this being, who *would* have liked me?" he continued. "Is it a he or a she?"

"It's a he." Cybele said, and smiled. "Where are you from, Chad?" she asked. "New York?"

"Actually, Chevy Chase."

"Oh Christ, another Chevy Chase brat," she christened him. She looked appreciatively at his beige gabardine suit and his striped silk shirt, partially unbuttoned down his chest. He opened his mouth and lolled his tongue about, then peered at her while laughing happily. His saliva had a milky quality that didn't quite repulse her. He had a slim, reedlike body with wide graceful shoulders. When he stood up to play some music at the jukebox, she noticed that his slenderness had made him appear much taller than he actually was. The heels on his shoes were high and mod-looking. He had the kind of body she liked, but then she could get into a lot of bodies.

"I love Johnnie Nash," he said as he walked back up to the table. "Do you like him?"

"Yes, I do, " Cybele said. "He has such a smooth voice."

"Yeah, yeah. I like that sort of thing," Chad said.

"But he's been around for so long," she added.

"Chad's voice is lower than his," Charles said. "It's more abrasive – you're the rock 'n' roll type, eh, Chad?"

"Are you the god— Can't think of his name, but he's beautiful," Cybele drawled flirtatiously at Chad. "The god from Chevy Chase?"

"I resent that," Jim protested. "I liked growing up in Chevy Chase."

"Yeah, ya know," Chad said. "Up in New York they say Harlem is so dangerous, what with people throwing one another off roofs and all, but when the kids get mad at their parents or somebody in Chevy Chase they just throw them into a pool. More people die that way out there than anybody knows."

"You're like that god – oh, what's his name?" Cybele asked anyone.

"Narcissus!" the beautiful young actress offered.

"Yeah, Narcissus."

"What's wrong with that?" Charles asked, running his fingers through his long wavy hair. "I like people who admire themselves. The first relationship always belongs to yourself."

"I agree," Cybele said, looking at her hot dog as if it were a peculiar, oriental dish. "You gotta like yourself to like other people, I think."

"You must be Echo," Chad said to Cybele. "Luring me on, right?"

"Sure, I'm Echo," she said tiredly.

She picked up her heavy mug of beer and sipped its tepid liquid without desire. A deadening ennui swept over her entire being. She sighed and looked out into the mellowing, mid-afternoon sunlight, squinting her eyes protectively.

"Hey, let's get married and go back to your place and watch TV," Chad proposed to her.

"Now, why does every guy I meet ask me that?" she questioned him jadely. She stroked his long, splendid fingers on the hand he had placed over hers.

"What?" he queried her teasingly.

"To marry them," she said. The memory of Brand's emaciated body and ravaged face loomed up in her mind's eye, painting a picture of him in the restaurant booth while he sat, half coherent, writing a proposal of marriage to her on an old envelope flap.

"I've got to go!" she announced and stood up suddenly, knocking her chair over backwards. She hustled out of the door without looking at any of them.

"Hey, wait a minute," Chad shouted as he ran after her. "You forgot your balloon!"

She stood outside the door of the restaurant, wondering how she would find the strength to walk home. Some pigeons shuffled around the tyres of parked automobiles like well-fed nuns, scratching at old peanut shells. A shiny black crow cawed piercingly in the afternoon heat, gliding overhead like a soaring aeroplane.

"Caw! Caw! Caw!" it cried stridently, dipping its wings gracefully for a turn over the rooftops. They glistened with a blue-black sheen in the midday brightness. She watched the crow with fascination as it settled abruptly on a chimney top.

"Caw! Caw! Caw!" she called to it happily.

"Caw! Caw!" the crow answered her back.

"Here's your balloon," Chad said when he caught up with her.

"Did you hear that, Chad?" she exclaimed.

"Hear what?" he asked, standing beside her with the stupendous red balloon.

"That crow answered me."

"If I was a crow, I'd do the same."

"No, listen, Chad," she said, holding onto the choice material of his suit with her hand fervently. "Man used to know the language of birds."

"Sure, I suppose so," he said, looking at the childlike expression of solemnity on her face with tenderness as she stood transfixed by the spectacle of the crow.

"Birds *served* man, Chad. Haven't you read what Solomon said about the lapwing?"

"Er, no. No, I haven't, Cybele."

"Well, the lapwing helped Solomon, Chad. That's what God created animals for – to serve man. But we lost that language, Chad. We lost it," she said sadly.

She staggered back against him weakly.

"Oh, I don't know. You seemed to have quite a rapport with the crow just now, Cybele."

"Yes, I do. Because I love him, Chad, I love that crow. I love his black shiny wings, and the way he can fly so free and graceful. Look how saucy, how wise he is sitting there. He hasn't forgotten the language, Chad, mankind has. The animals are wiser than the people today," she said and began to cry pitifully.

"Hey, hey lady. Beautiful lady," he began to croon.

"Say, aren't you Chad Westerly," a girl with long blonde hair asked Chad excitedly. Her blue, doll-like eyes stared at him voraciously. She put one hand on her companion's arm like a swimmer readying herself a shove-off in her most important race.

"Francine!" she screamed with absolute recognition of Chad.

"I know, I know. It's him!" her companion shouted shrilly.

"Let's get him," the blonde girl urged.

"Uh oh," Chad said. "Let's get outta here."

"Oh, Chad, I've got to go home," Cybele said, oblivious to the two enthusiastic girls. "I've got to go back and see if Porgy is all right. Someone told me there's something evil in my apartment, and I'm worried that it might hurt poor Porge."

"Sure, c'mon. I'll drive you home."

He steered her towards an old Rover, then opened the door and helped her inside.

"Uh oh," he said, when he tried to cram the oversized balloon into the back seat of the car. "Won't fit."

He stood beside the car hesitantly for a moment, wondering what to do with the balloon.

"Oh Chad, Chad!" the two admiring fans cried. "Can we have your autograph?" they asked slavishly.

"Hmm," he muttered as he watched Cybele intently, trying to understand what was torturing her so. "Oh. . . yes," he said. "Sure." He handed them the big red balloon and jumped into his car.

"Where to?" he asked.

" Massachusetts Avenue," she said. "I'll show you."

"Say, this Porge fellow. He's not your old man, is he?" Chad asked uneasily.

"My old man?"

"Your husband, or anything freaky like that?"

"Oh no. Porgy is my cat."

"Oh yeah. Your cat," he said, and pulled out into the heavy M Street traffic.

"Porgy is my most secret, most powerful companion, Chad. We live with one another and give each other strength. I love him like I love the birds. Birds speak to me and so do the stars. Trees show me their essence also. I feel the lines of things, exactly like Gauguin did. I hope to get that essence in my painting someday."

"You know, you're something fantastic," Chad told her. The material from his excellent suit draped itself over the leather-clad steering wheel of the old car as he rested his wrist that he guided the car with on the wheel.

"No, I'm not. I just believe in things," she said. "Even though my best friend was just murdered, I do believe in things."

"Murdered?" Chad exclaimed. He looked at her, worried.

"Yes, Chad. You were right about the blood in my eyes."

"Christ, what a freaky afternoon," he exclaimed as he braked the car for a red light.

"I have a lot of blood in my eyes actually," she informed him.

"Oh – have you been acquainted with many friends who were murdered?"

"Well, not exactly friends. But my husband shot a crow once. He shot it out of the window of a car while we were driving along. Then we ran out into a field full of pine trees to find it. But we couldn't find it. He did the same thing to a jack rabbit when we were driving through New Mexico."

Chad studied her anxiously while they paused for the light. Her perfectly shaped thighs were like honey-brown fruit under the fringe of her jean shorts. A light spray of threads from the fringe framed their flesh like unspun silk. Under the deep neckline of her orange blouse, the tops of her firm, round breasts were visible. She twisted a Chinese ring with an amber stone round and round on her finger while staring nervously ahead.

"It was awful. That poor rabbit suffered so." She pulled the ring completely off, then put it back on again. She looked at it carefully to see if she had put it on the same way she had taken it off. "He didn't kill it all at once – the poor thing,. So we saw it there in the headlights of the car, struggling in pain – God, God!" she said, and began sobbing.

"When you do that, Cybele, I can hardly drive," Chad told her. "Please, please don't cry."

"Oh really, Chad. I'm sorry," she said. "You're being so kind and everything, and you don't even really know me."

"Oh I know you, lady. Listen, did your husband have a bad childhood?" he asked.

"Because people often try to recreate things they experienced in childhood."

"How do you know that?" she asked suspiciously.

"Well, my father's a doctor. I mean, he's not a shrink or anything, but he's been into a lot of psychology."

"What kind of doctor is he?" she asked while thinking of what he had just said. She began to rummage around in her memories of Pierre's family and boyhood.

"Oh, he's an Ob Gyn. Not exactly what I'd want to do. It might be different if you always got the young, good-looking ones, but when you think about the older ones who've been through the menopause. . ."

"Still, I wouldn't want to do that sort of work if I were a man," Cybele said. ". . .I mean, the sort of man I'd want to be if I were a man. I guess it takes a certain type. Pierre's father was a real macho chauvinistic person," she added, still thinking of what Chad had said about childhood and recreating situations. "But I admired him, along with hating him. He was a good artist and a self-made man."

"My father says that all women are like chairs." Chad interjected.

"Chairs?"

"Yeah," he laughed, curling his mouth into an expression of sarcasm. Again she thought of a tender, hazel-eyed antelope. "I mean, in a way I know what he means. Because when you think of going out and having some fun and just talking – well, you think of a guy. I mean I'd rather go out with a guy. Wouldn't you rather go out with a girl?"

"No. No. I'd rather go out with a man. But I like women and going out with then – when I know I have a man who's in love with me somewhere around. There's magic between a man and a woman. . ." she began. "Something I'd miss if I were with a woman only. . ." Well, it's too bad that your father feels that way," Cybele concluded.

Chad shifted gears and the car shot on off down Wisconsin Avenue. "I could never think of a woman like you as a chair – that's for sure," he declared and laughed in embarrassment.

"Maybe when Pierre tried to run me down with the Jaguar, he was trying to recreate the feeling he had when his father used to stop his car and beat him," she said, without hearing Chad's remark.

"Christ, sounds like a real Faulkner type of family."

"But why did he kill the crow and the rabbit?" she puzzled. "Why do people kill things? To capture them?"

"I dunno, sweet child. I've never known any people like the ones you're describing. Your old man was definitely following patterns he learned as a child. Very bad patterns. But I do the same thing, don't I? I mean, my father is hostile towards women for his own reasons. And obviously, I am too. But not with you," he added, almost as an afterthought. "I could go 'straight' with a woman like you."

"We're almost at where I live now, Chad. It's been great meeting you," she told him.

"Not so fast, girl of the streets," he said and handed her a piece of paper. "Write your name and telephone number down for me, please."

She took the sheet of paper and pen he handed her.

"Oh, there's Porge," she said with delight. "Hi, Porge!" she called at her cat sitting on the old stone balcony of her apartment.

"You really dig on animals, don't you?"

"Yeah, yeah I do." She scribbled the information he had requested down hurriedly on the note. "I believe that all animals have a function – one that can serve man. But man has lost the secret knowledge of animals. We no longer know how to command them. Remember how cats in ancient Egypt were trained to guard the palace jewels – to fight to the death for them? And how the lion was a symbol that guarded the soul while a person was asleep – prevented it from leaving a person's body, or getting lost if it did while the person slept?"

"But don't you like steak?" he asked and smiled at her wryly.

"Yes, I admit it. I love it terribly – and I love it rare. The blood is so sweet in my mouth. I love lobster too – but it makes me sad when I see them all stacked on top of one another at the seafood market. They tape up their poor claws. Did you know they love to be stroked on their heads?"

"Listen," Chad began, then placed his ample mouth on her lips. She smelled a fresh, inspiring perfume from the flesh of his face and mouth. She felt the cool silk of his shirt under her hand and she realised that she had placed her arm around his waist.

"You'll see me again, won't you, Cybele?" he asked, holding her eyes with his golden, translucent gaze.

"Of course," she replied. She looked at his handsome, childish face appreciatively, then turned her attention back to Porgy.

"Oh gosh, Chad. Porgy's so good," she exclaimed breathlessly. "He's just so good and I know he'll protect me from anything. He just will," she repeated and stepped out of the faded blue Rover.

Chapter Sixteen

"Look over here, Flannagan. I got the murder weapon," the officer said as he stood in the harsh glare of the light streaming through the screen doors of the balcony.

Porgy looked at them with curiosity, silently blinking his large green eyes. He considered them carefully, then began to lick his blunt white paw. He was perched on the stone railing of the balcony, ready to leap off at a moment's notice. Every once in a while he looked at the white sheet with which they had covered her. All night he had guarded her, sniffing the blood on her face and licking it occasionally, then crying softly while waiting for her to open her eyes.

"Yeah? Let's see." Suddenly he felt a sharp pain on his scalp. "Goddamned cat's got fleas," he said, scratching his greying red hair. "Miaoooowwwww," he mocked at Porgy.

Porgy turned his wide, elegant head towards the Irish policeman. Cybele would have recognised the disdain in his piercing, oriental eyes with which he greeted this uneloquent man. Behind him the August trees swayed heavily, sighing from a frail morning wind. The cars crawled thick and dusty down tree-lined Massachusetts Avenue.

"'Sgonna rain, thank God," Mike said, looking around the spacious old apartment.

"What is it about this joint anyway?" Flannagan asked, scratching his fat, solid neck. "Makes me feel strange as hell for some reason. Christ, it's hot in here – smells weird, too." He glanced at himself inadvertently in the baroque frame of the living-room mirror, and assumed a position of offence before he realised that it was only his reflection that he had seen.

Mike plopped a curiously round knife with a short wooden handle into Flannagan's hand, then shifted one of his splinter-thin legs against the deep blue of his uniform as he watched his superior examine the instrument. Its parabolic blade glinted dully in Flannagan's ruddy palm.

"My wife might know better, but I'd say it's a potato peeler," Mike said. He towered down from his Celtic height over his short, squat companion.

"Ugh," Flannagan grimaced. A V-shaped line of sweat had formed over his lips like tiny, translucent peas. One of the drops fell onto the knife's blade. He rubbed it off cautiously with his blunt finger.

"Ow!" he cried, and drew back his finger bleeding from a tiny wound near his fingernail. "Goddamned knife's like a razor. Whoever used this thing liked to keep his cooking utensils in top working order. Here, keep it in the handkerchief, will ya? You can put it in the box over there. We can always hope for a good print on it somewhere."

He looked at the mound under the sheet once more, squinting against the heat and glare that filled the room. The whole apartment was bathed in it. Only an old pitcher full of withering yellow and lavender flowers sitting on the radiators that she had covered with a red print shawl lent a disparate technicolour to the black and white film of the bright morning.

He lifted the corner of the sheet. "Yep, some bastard sure had fun carving her up. Must not have had much trouble. Girl's so thin – looks like a nice night-gown, what's left of it." He touched the hem of Cybele's gown, then followed the line of her body up to her face. "Beautiful hair on her."

He looked into Mike's pale blue eyes, still holding the sheet up. Dark slabs of blood had dried like paint on her flesh. The two men stared at one another for an unremembered moment. They were both breathing heavily and their hands vibrated at their sides from their racing pulses. They looked away from each other quickly, embarrassed at their excitement – of the tension in both of their bodies that the scene had induced.

"Who found her anyway?"

"The old lady across the hall. She said that the girl's cat kept crying at her door – that he actually dug a small hole in the carpeting right under her doorway, he was so frantic to get someone's attention."

"The killer left the door open then. That's strange! – why would he do that?"

"I don't know – do you think he planned to come back?"

"For what? Some snapshots for his photo album?"

Flannagan sighed. "You say that the old lady talked to the girl before she died?"

"Yes – said that all she would say is 'Call Hadrian – it's about the rose garden'."

"Rose garden? Christ, this is a weird case." Flannagan looked blank for a moment. "Did she give the lady a number?"

"Yes, right before she died. The old lady called it and the man's servant answered. The old woman told the butler that the girl was dead – that she had been murdered."

"This man Hadrian – he's going to call back?"

"Yes. The butler took her number. He called the man's office and left it with his secretary."

"Get that address and send a squad car to his home – *now*."

"We did," Flannagan said, smiling.

"What's so funny?"

"Should have seen this Hadrian's wife's face when the butler showed the cops into the reception room. She had a bunch of old ladies there for a meeting of the Colonial Dames."

"Hmmm, hope the old gal didn't have a heart attack."

"The old gal is a beautiful young blonde. Didn't look more than 25 herself!"

"Damn! What money can buy," Mike said, thinking of his fat, middle-aged wife.

"Let's look in the bedroom before the squad gets here," Flannagan directed.

Mike followed him awkwardly through the long, arch-shaped hallway.

"Looks like this used to be a fairly swell place in its day," Mike observed. His voice sounded hoarse in his own ears. All around them an echo pervaded.

"Goddamn!" Flannagan exclaimed, and swished a Chinese mobile hanging down from the ceiling of the hallway violently from his face.

Suddenly Porgy darted between their legs, wild and frightened-looking.

"Jesus, mother-fucker Christ! What is it with this joint? Look in the closet for a skeleton, will ya, Mike."

"That'll be fifty *Hail Marys* for you, Flannagan, on Sunday!"

Mike was already searching for a light in the bedroom closet. He felt a long string with a little piece of ribbon on it and pulled.

"Hmmm, look at the clothes in here – wow! This dame knew how to dress. There's even a mink coat."

Flannagan glanced up from a drawer of papers he had found in the pale yellow vanity table. He said solemnly, smell this." He pinched a few half-burnt leaves in his fingers out of a tiny pipe.

Mike looked puzzled and shrugged. "Some women like to smoke cigars too. So what?"

"That's dope, you idiot. Didn'tcha ever smoke grass?"

"Nah," he said and grinned. "Anyway, I couldn't admit it to a police captain, now could I?"

"Quit clowning and bring me that black box again."

Mike started towards the living-room, then noticed that the bathroom light was on. He pushed the door open slowly. "She must have just got out of the bathtub," he said to himself. He looked curiously at a film of oily-like stuff floating on top of the bathwater. 'Expensive looking bath towels,' he thought and looked down at the blackness of his boots on the yellow bathroom rug.

When he came back into the living-room, Porgy was hunched mournfully at the body's feet. One toe with chipped red nail polish stuck out comically from under the sheet. Outside, the wind picked up dried summer leaves from the grey-white pavement of the street, whirling them in little eddies. Something tinkled close to his head, and he noticed for the first time an ornate chandelier hanging in the middle of the room, well secured to the ceiling but obviously not wired for lighting. It hung with an illogical beauty in the centre of the room. Its only purpose was for decoration. Its crystals tinkled softly again like little bells, and Mike noticed that the ones in the centre were lavender coloured.

Once more he was seized by a strange feeling that made the hair on his neck prickle – a feeling that made him halt to look over his shoulder, as if someone might be silently approaching behind him. Ever since he had entered into this incongruous menagerie he had felt the same watching, hidden presence. The wind howled in a shrill scream outside, brushing the thick branches of the evergreens flat against the windows. The whole apartment was opened by windows. It sat as in a treetop.

"WWWWWWRRRRRRROOOOOOOWW!" Porgy howled and spurted away from water cascading out of the pitcher of flowers that had been blown over by a whoosh of wind from the abrupt summer storm.

"Jesus," Mike said softly and looked at the water sinking slowly into the sheet. It had spilled over her body, flattening the sheet around her contours like a mould. The outline of her form was gentle and quiet underneath.

Flowers had fluttered over and around her, as if some impromptu funeral rites were being performed. Tears came to Mike's eyes, leaving him with an empty, drained feeling. He felt the loss all around him. Over in the corner he noticed a painting, half-finished, with some tubes of oil paint and brushes lying nearby. On the canvas, done heavily in maroons and mahogany browns, was a Madonna-like young woman holding a nude baby boy. Both the mother and baby had a dark, foreign quality. Beside them a delicate, blonde-haired little girl looked at the baby with delight. Mike shook his head, feeling a bit dizzy.

"Get in here, Mike," he heard his superior call. "I've hit the jackpot!"

He rushed into the high-ceilinged, spacious bedroom. Flannagan was reclining on the yellow bedspread, still sweating profusely, with a small, thin, black book in his hand.

"What is it?" Mike asked.

"It's her diary," Flannagan said excitedly. "Listen to this, will ya? *'Très interesting evening with Sherman.'*" he quoted. "*'Tall, big intern – silver Corvette – laughing yet? He got freaked out trying to place me and natch, he couldn't. It was a gas. He was in a pensive mood.'* Pensive! Get that, wouldja? Girl's got real class – education."

"*'It was the second time he had been to see the fireworks,'*" he continued reading from her diary. "*'At any rate, after they were over we stood by the bridge. I got high on the night and—'* – listen to this, will ya," Flannagan exclaimed – "*'I got high on the night, and the moon pulled me.'* The moon pulled her – what the hell is that supposed to mean? *'Then we had a glass of wine in Georgetown – I've been telling Brandon about this all morning – I got this guy all excited mentally and physically (not by touching – just the mood). He freaked me out when he said that I liked unkind men. . .'* Wow, this one liked to play games," Flannagan concluded.

"Yeah?" Mike said dully. "Looks like she was pretty good at it too, except for the last one."

"*'Then I got him in the bedroom. I went to the bathroom and changed into my kimono,'*" Flannagan read with fascination. "*'I came back and began to do embroidery. When he asked me to put down my sewing and seduce him, I said that would be too redundant.'*"

"Ha, how'd ya liked to have played that night, Mike, boy?"

"*'Eric rode his bike over – he was all hopped up on Mescaline. I taunted him with tales of Sherman – he even cried.'*"

"Listen to this, shit, wouldja?" Flannagan marvelled. "She was crying for what happened in there. Christ!"

"*'He was all beautiful and firm, like a tall, muscular reed, and he made love to me from three until six in the morning.'*"

"Ha, is this for real?" Mike asked.

"*'He said that I lit a fire in men's pants and gave them a little something for their brain but never enough, and that was all there was to me. He said that I liked to play with the meanness of men, and that someday I would end up dead because of it.'*"

"Looks like he turned out to be her most perceptive beau," Mike remarked cryptically.

"We'd better look around for more bodies," Flannagan said, making a grim joke. He held the small black diary in his beefy hands and stared around the room with his red eyebrows knitted together over his faded blue eyes like a consternated orang-utan. He opened the book once more and saw the name *Cybele Tashery* written in a bold, flowing script across the front leaf. *'New times, New loves, New hopes'* had been scrawled underneath.

"Yep, she sure had a flair for expressing herself – a little like *True Confessions*," Mike opined, "but nevertheless. . ."

"This Brandon she refers to must be that poor guy they brought in yesterday," Flannagan decided. "Tch! Did you see him, Mike? Christ, he was cut up a lot worse 'n' her."

"Yeah, a guy like that – rich, young, everything goin' for 'em," Mike said longingly. "And here I am, good old healthy me, working my ass off on double duty just to afford law courses whenever I can squeeze 'em in. God, Ann sure could use some of those fancy digs in that closet." He looked covetously in the direction of the clothes-filled closet. "Christ, what am I sayin?" he asked, shaking his head dolefully. "Is this beat turning me into a ghoul?"

"Yeah, you're just tired, Mike. Take the missus and kids up to Harper's Ferry this weekend and look at wide spaces," Flannagan advised. "That's what me paw always said. 'Ryan,' he says, 'anything ever gets you down, I mean way down, boy, just climb up atop a tall mountain and spit!' That was Paw's logic. But I never saw him sober enough to climb past the three steps to our house, dog drunk, and scream to Mama, 'Maureen!'"

A loud knock on the apartment door interrupted his reminiscences.

"Police officers, open up!" they heard a loud voice cry.

"Go open that, Mike, while I sort this stuff out," Flannagan ordered, using his rank as captain to remind Mike that he was in command. He drew his pudgy neck up stiffly in the rigidly starched uniform, and adjusted his position from the laxity of his childhood memories to one he thought more befitting an officer of his status. His bulging belly slipped a few inches over his belt when he held himself erect. He stood puffing and wheezing from the effort. He still held her diary in his hand, looking like Neanderthal man trying to fathom the zany antics of teenagers.

"God, Flannagan. What the hell's going on in this town anyway?" a tall dark-haired policeman asked as he strode over to the captain, pushing his shiny, hard-brimmed cap away from his perspiring forehead. "Is there a mad housewife at large in the neighbourhood?"

"Housewife?" Flannagan asked stupidly.

"Well, carving people up with a potato peeler ain't exactly the work of a football player. Although. . . the world's changing awfully fast," the young policeman declared.

He smacked the top of his hat nervously back and forth against his pie-sized palms, worried that he had overstepped his position of subservience by voicing his opinion so blatantly. 'The chief's a funny guy,' he thought. 'You never really know how to act around him'

"Who told you about that?" Flannagan snapped suspiciously.

"Mike here, sir," the young officer said apologetically.

The captain glared at Mike like an incensed bear, then smiled sheepishly. "Oh yeah. Christ, this case is getting to me. Makin' me jumpy," he explained.

The four officers who had entered the room chuckled with relief, then stood quietly, waiting for Ryan Flannagan to signal their next move.

"Lowers, you'd better get an ambulance for the body. Greg, go and call the morgue and tell 'em we've got a little beauty for them this morning. Sort of messed up, but that'll give 'em something to do besides sit around and pick their haemorrhoids all day." He looked around the room impatiently and shrugged. "There ain't nothing more for me to do around this joint right now. I've got about five other assignments today. Gotta talk to the Mayor about those lotteries for the blind, stuff like that," Flannagan intoned importantly. "Mike, go and talk to the landlord while you've got these guys here to watch over things, and pump him for all the information you can get. He seems really down on the girl." He put his swollen, fleshy hands to the prickly bristles on his chin bemusedly. "Guess she did have a wild lifestyle for this sort of joint."

The men stood in their tightly-buckled uniforms, sweating profusely from the late morning sun's increasing heat. Their high black boots made squeaking noises when they shifted the weight of their tense bodies from foot to foot for some sort of relief in the room's charged atmosphere.

"Peters, Monkton," Flannagan addressed the two officers. "You come with me. I need you to lend support in front of the Mayor. Ain't nothing harder than an educated politician, me paw used to say," he remarked loudly and clamped a fat cigar between his false teeth.

"Whew!" Mike said with relief after they had gone. He smiled sympathetically at the two cowed officers.

"Guess he's gone to spit off a mountain," Gregg offered sportily.

"Or a tall building," Mike agreed ironically. "Flannagan has been known to compromise."

"For the right amount," Lowers muttered.

"I'll pretend I didn't hear that, Lowers," Mike said. "Now you guys hang on while I go and talk to this old dude. Uh, wait a minute. Pick up the telephone over there and ask the desk what the landlord's apartment number is."

"505," Lowers called, holding his hand cupped over the old-fashioned telephone receiver.

"Stay cool till I get back," Mike advised as he opened the door. "Fifth?" he mused while walking along the hallway. "Say, must be right at the end of the hall. Guess he had a pretty good idea of everything she did."

He rapped briskly on the landlord's door, then stood back. He didn't want to frighten the old man by yelling out "Police officer".

Presently he heard shuffling footsteps and thought of worn slippers on hospital hallways, recognising the gait of a very old person. He heard a soft, slipping noise against the door and waited patiently while the landlord examined him through the peep-hole.

Mr Masters pulled the door open slowly and stood in the stark light of midday that streamed through his windows, without giving Mike any sort of greeting. He blinked his rheumy eyes like a mole, adjusting his sight for daylight.

"Good afternoon, Mr Masters. I'm Sergeant Dunster. I'd like to ask you a few questions about your tenant down the hall – Miss Cybele Tashery."

"*Mrs* Tashery," the old man emphasised surlily. "Though it sure didn't make any difference with her. Humph, what do you want to know?" he asked rudely.

"Well, just some general information."

"What's she done now?" he asked suspiciously. "Always one after another from her. She takes dope, you know. All of her friends take it!"

"Oh? What makes you think that, Mr Masters?"

"I seen 'er. Hauling a fella in here t'other night at two o'clock in the morning, staggering up the back drive. Thinking I wouldn't see her. Hummoh!"

He cleared his phlegmy throat loudly and grasped the apartment doorknob in a demented fashion, stretching, the pallid, unhealthy-looking skin of his hand tautly against its bones.

"Did you watch her often?" Mike inquired suspiciously.

"What're you talkin' about?" the old man demanded angrily. "Everybody in this building saw 'er. Her and all them men!"

The landlord tottered back a few steps from the vehemence of his statements. A small line of watery sweat had formed across the grey stubble of his beard like slime. An acrid, sour odour drifted up from his dirty white shirt, causing Mike to step back involuntarily in order to escape the sickly smell of Mr Masters' old body.

"Sittin' out there in my back yard sunning herself with them bikinis. Scandalising the whole place. I got forty families in this building to take care of, Mr. . .?"

"Dunster, Sergeant Mike Dunster."

"Mr Dunster," he repeated absently. "Not just anybody either. All of 'em's with the State Department, lots of retired diplomats – snazzy people. And what do you think they thought when that girl's husband came over here and sprayed 'KEPT WHORE' on her door in red paint?" The man wheezed from indignation, and took out an oversized handkerchief and coughed repeatedly with rasping noises into it.

'Certainly doesn't splurge any personal luxuries on himself,' Mike thought, looking beyond the man's substantial bulk and observing the worn furnishings of his apartment.

"Say, could I ask you for a drink of water?" Mike asked, trying to exact an invitation inside somehow, but feeling very obvious. "I'm just on my way back to the station, and I haven't had a chance to stop for even a glass of water all morning."

The old man hung in the doorway like a hovering bat, not budging an inch from his belligerent stance.

"What's going on anyway?" he asked, twisting his hand tighter around the white plastic doorknob.

"Mr Masters, Miss Tashery has been murdered – here in your apartment building. I'm one of the investigating officers. Now, could I get a glass of water or not?" he said adamantly, pushing his chance to get into the apartment as much as possible while a jolted expression of surprise crossed Mr Masters' pasty face.

"Murdered?" he repeated. "That'll ruin my building's reputation. I knew that woman was bad news the minute I laid eyes on 'er."

"May I come in?" Mike repeated.

"Oh, sure," he said dazedly. "I'll get your water."

He followed the landlord into his apartment, surprised at the dowdiness of the furnishings inside. A cheap, formica table sat against the dining-room wall, surrounded by four tasteless chairs. On the table's busy pattern of innumerable little boomerangs, stood a vase with large plastic flowers. Its severe turquoise colour jarred Mike's eyes. A brown, woolly sofa had been placed between two plastic-topped end tables in the living-room. Its gold and silver threads stuck out from the worn material. Hanging on the wall above the sofa was a picture of fruit tumbling from a cornucopia. Mike noticed an elaborate set of nut-cracking tools lying on top of a basket of walnuts that had been placed at the coffee table.

He walked towards the living-room window and looked outside. A trellis of old, gnarled vines had attached themselves to the window-sill. They clutched tenaciously at the brick side of the building like withered fingers. Suddenly a picture of Mr Masters as a macabre Romeo climbing up the vines from the courtyard below flashed through his mind, leaving an unpleasant, bitter residue in the detective's thoughts. He turned away from the window and breathed deeply from fatigue. The same acrid odour he had smelt from the landlord's stale body penetrated his nostrils. He shuddered with disgust and stared out at the colourful summer flowers blooming like natural bouquets around benches in the wide, rambling backyard.

'Christ, if he owns this place, he must have money. So why does he live like this?' he wondered.

"Here's your water, son," Mr Masters said. "Sorry the ice ain't made yet," he apologised, and handed the officer a jelly glass filled with water.

"You say she was murdered? Got any idea who did it?" he asked. His rheumy eyes peered out at Mike like discoloured window-panes.

"No, not yet. You got any ideas?"

"You better look for her husband. He was a real terror. Came over here and glued up her keyhole, then sprayed 'KEPT WHORE' in red paint all over the door. We had to paint the door over. She just left the paint up there for a week. Like she was proud of it, or something. She was with all different men, you know."

He wheezed asthmatically and went into another spell of coughing, then sat down weakly in a rocking chair beside the sofa.

"Yep, a real she-devil. People used to burn women like her." He wiped some mucous from his mouth, then studied it minutely. "Maybe they had the right idea."

"Did she ever talk to you about her husband?"

"Yeah. One day she was real sad, sitting out there in the backyard on a bench all alone. I watched her for a while from my window here, then I got to feeling sorry for 'er. So I went out and took her some soup. I'm a really good cook," he volunteered. "That was right when she first moved here, before I found out about her and all them men."

Mike moved uncomfortably on the sofa's prodding, broken springs, drinking a little of the warm, unsatisfying water.

"I asked her what was wrong, and she said that she missed her husband. 'Why don't you go back to 'im?' I asked her. And she said it was because he beat her all the time. Then she admitted that she loved another man anyway." He stuffed his used handkerchief deep into his pants' pocket, shaking his grey-haired head. "Humph, she was a mess, I tell you. Finally it commenced to get dark and I persuaded her to come upstairs with me. She followed me back up here like a little child and I gave her some aspirins and told her to go to bed early." He rubbed the side of his white bristled cheek and moved his false teeth against one another ruminatingly. "She acted like a baby sometimes. She really was like a person never growed up. I thought she was really sweet, truly beautiful, when she first came." His voice trailed off wistfully, then a dark, clouded look passed over his spurious features. "But that was before I found out about 'er."

"OK, Mr Masters, I'll leave you now," Mike said. "There may be some detectives stopping by in the next few days to ask you a few routine questions."

He set the jelly glass down on the table. The old man snatched it up and wiped the plastic-topped table meticulously with his dirty handkerchief. He squinted so much that Mike wondered if he could see what he was doing.

'Funny old coot,' he reflected.

"I always like to keep things nice and neat," he explained. "I cook a lot and you never can be too careful about germs. Causes cancer, you know. 'Course you're a young 'un and don't have to worry about things like that. Bet you ain't even married yet?" he prodded with a vulgar, hungry curiosity showing in his eyes.

"Married, with three kids," Mike replied.

"M'gosh. And on a policeman's salary. Bet you eat a lot of potatoes. Ha. Ha!"

"Well, we're vegetarians, Mr Masters. And we eat a lot of peanut butter."

"What, no meat?" the old man exclaimed incredulously.

"Well, you see, Mr Masters," Mike began as he walked towards the door, anxious to get away from the stifling odour emanating from the old man, "My wife hates the taste of blood, and she's got me to the point where I hate it too. Brainwashing, I guess!" he confided, chuckling through his impatience to get away from the doleful atmosphere created by the old man's personality and the décor it had inspired in the apartment.

"Women," the old man muttered, holding the jelly glass nervously.

Mike strode down the hall away from the landlord's collapsed-looking figure, back to the murdered girl's apartment. When he entered, the living-room had been emptied of the body and several 'Crime Scene and Search' men were taking specimens from the rug and making copies of fingerprints around the room.

He picked up the phone and dialled Flannagan.

"I'll think we've got a lead on the husband, Flannagan. Want me to check it out?"

"We've already called the university that he's with here in DC. They gave us an address in Louisiana – said he's been at his parents' house for several weeks before the autumn term starts. I talked with his mother and she says that he and his brother and his brother's wife are down in Biloxi deep-sea fishing on their pa's yacht."

"Mmm, looks like that's pretty airtight."

"Did you check on the sugar daddy?"

"Yeah, yeah. Ha, Christ, you should've seen his wife's face. She was in the middle of some kind of afternoon tea party with a whole bunch of old biddies when we let her have it."

Rocky laughed heartily into the phone. His caustic chuckles forced Mike to hold the receiver away from the raucous sound.

"The old man had an airtight alibi – he was with a governor and several senators at an embassy party."

"Hmmm, that leaves the bum she was living with and the young doctor."

"Forget it, we picked up the hippie. He had just come back from a beach party with a bunch of other freaks. Busted him on seven counts for possession of marijuana and cocaine. He told us the young doctor's name. He was very obliging with that piece of information, I must say. I think the kid was really hurt that she cheated on him – with someone besides her benefactor, that is!" The captain guffawed loudly into the phone again.

Mike stuck his finger in his ear and held the receiver out a few inches, still able to hear the captain's voice distinctly. The two remaining police officers winced sympathetically at him.

"Anyway, this Eric fella was more than glad to give us the dude's name. The young doctor – Sherman Stein – had been on duty for forty-eight hours at the hospital during the time period of the murder. He seemed to be more broken up about her than anybody. Said he had some gruesome evidence for us. So that's another one bitten the dust."

"Christ, who does that leave?" Mike asked, puzzled.

"I dunno. Maybe somebody she didn't write about in the book. One things for sure. The lady liked money and sex, preferably money with her sex! So we should look for someone with those qualifications. "OK, Mike, tidy it up and hop on over," Flannagan ended on a more official note.

Mike hung the old black receiver up belatedly, then turned towards the grim scene in the living-room. One of the 'Crime Scene and Search' men was closing a tiny plastic case he had filled with particles of hair and dust from the carpeting.

"We're going to be taking off now, Sergeant Dunster," the man squatting on the carpeting said. "We've got everything we need for our lab analysis."

His companion stood up, holding the small plastic container of evidence in his hand like a breakable egg, and waited with a preoccupied expression on his thin-lipped mouth. The austere light streaming through the windows whitened the man's features, as it had bleached all of the room's interior the colour of dried, banked bones. The complexions of the men appeared pebbly and desiccated from their nervous fatigue. Each face was like a differently shaped stone in the glossy white illumination of the room.

"OK then," Mike said to them with a note of finality. "Thanks." He stood woodenly in the hallway while the two detectives filed past him in tandem, stifling a yawn.

"I may be by your office tomorrow," Mike told them. "Why don't you— What the hell!" he cried as the large, tiger-striped cat shot between his legs and out of the door.

"Catch that beast, will ya?" asked Lowers. "Shit! Fucking cat!"

The men stood in the doorway and watched Lowers lumbering down the hall after the gracefully fleeing cat. He reached out several times to catch the cat's thick black-ringed tail, but each time Porgy dodged out from under his grasp.

"Ha ha, Lowers looks like a broken-down track star," the thin-lipped detective said. His paper-dry skin crinkled into wrinkles from his whining laughter.

The fat, ball-like cat reached the end of the hallway within a few seconds. He stood cornered with his pink tongue hanging out, panting and waiting to see what the running man would do to him before he made his next move.

"Gotcha now," Lowers exclaimed, and lunged forward to grab the cat. His two outstretched hands loomed menacingly in front of Porgy's eyes. As soon as they came too close, Porgy gauged the position of the man's legs, and, seeing an unobstructed opening, darted out between then.

"Oww," the man cried when his head clunked against the wall. In the moment before he had seen Porgy in front of him, and the split second that the disconcertingly agile cat had disappeared between his legs, Lowers had lunged with all of his might towards the cat and into the wall.

"Ah ha ha, ha ha. Oh, hee hee," the thin-lipped detective laughed. His hearty laughter was misplaced in the confines of his narrow face.

"You got a really funny bone on you today," his companion noted sourly, taking a crumpled cigarette package from his suit pocket.

"Get that cat, dammit!" Mike shouted. "We can't afford to lose any evidence – feline or human," he threw in cleverly.

Porgy scampered back down to the middle of the hallway with the sound of the officers' heavy-soled boots thudding closely behind him. He sprang round suddenly and faced the officer with a rebellious, stubborn courage, angered by the fear and intimidation he felt from being chased. He spat and hissed heroically, flattening his sensitive ears on the back of his snake-shaped head.

"Kitty, Kitty," Lowers called, making an unsuccessful attempt at approaching the cat.

"Wrrow, wrroww," Porgy howled, and spat forcefully at the man. Lowers stretched his hand out towards Porgy in a conciliatory manner. Quick as a flash of lightning Porgy's many-clawed paw flicked over the man's head, leaving a row of gaping, blood-filled wounds.

"That does it, you fucking bastard!" Lowers yelled. He stared incredulously at the razor-like wounds on the back of his hand. "I'm gonna break your neck!" he declared, and grabbed Porgy by his violently swishing tail.

"Wrrrowww!" the cat howled, and struggled savagely to get out of the man's grasp.

"What's going on out here?" the old landlord called garrulously, craning his neck out of the doorway to his apartment like a mountaineer guarding a still. "This is a respectable—"

Porgy wriggled out of the officer's hands and scampered into the open doorway, past the feet of the startled landlord.

"Blasted cat," Mr Masters scowled and swatted at the fleeing animal as it ran past him and into his apartment. "I always told that Jezebel that we didn't allow no pets in here. Especially cats. Hate 'em. They give me the creeps. So sneaky and all."

He stood back in the doorway, holding his slovenly-clad legs apart uncertainly, as if waiting for the cat to make his exit the same way that he had entered, and be gone. Instead Porgy ran under the threadbare sofa and hid.

"Sorry, sir," Lowers apologised, looking uneasily at the landlord's frowning countenance. "We're just trying to get this stupid cat."

Mike and the other officers came trotting down the long hallway like a battalion of Marines after a squirrel.

"Gee, we're awfully sorry about this, Mr Masters," Mike said fawningly. He looked at the old man's grey-whiskered face and once again felt a prescience of disease. "We'll try to get this dumb beast out of your way pronto," he said, trying to smile through the negative emotions running through his mind about the landlord.

The other policemen collected behind him, waiting expectantly for Mr Masters to step aside and let them enter. Instead he stood in the doorway like an immutable pile of rocks, glaring at them through his dim eyes. Only the black pinpoints of his pupils fastened onto their faces in a wizened, answering direction. He held onto the door handle tightly, unconsciously using his body to block their entrance into his apartment.

"I'll try to get him for you," he offered. "I just mopped up in here and I don't want the house getting all tracked up inside," he reasoned with them crudely. "Where d'he go?" he asked, wiping his bulbous nose and sniffing sensually at the flaccid flesh of his fingers afterwards.

"Er, behind the sofa, sir," Mike told him, and shrugged helplessly at his companions while they watched the old man shuffle over to the sofa.

"Kitty, Kitty," he called, bending down in a heap of old baggy trousers beside the couch. "Come on, Kitty!" He stretched his hand under the sofa cautiously and felt blindly about until he touched Porgy's tail.

"Ha! Gotcha now," he cried triumphantly, and pulled at the cat's tail like a fisherman reeling in his most precious catch.

The big cat came sliding out from under the couch backwards with each claw dug deeply into the rug as Mr Masters hauled him out mercilessly by his tail.

"Now, you creature," the landlord snarled, "I've got you at last!" He gathered the cat up against his surprisingly massive chest and looked into its farouche green eyes with a malicious hatred. "You miserable creature," he intoned with loathing, and squeezed the cat's paws cruelly.

"OK, easy does it," Mike said and walked over to the landlord's side. "You stay here, Lowers. Maybe *I* can handle the cat better."

"Kitty, Kitty, Kitty," Mike said and tickled Porgy under his chin. The frightened cat pushed his jaw out and enjoyed Mike's caress automatically, but glanced about the room frantically, hunting for an escape. His eyes lit on an open window as Mike attempted to take him from the landlord's arms.

"Nice kitty, come on, big thing," Mike cajoled and lifted the agitated cat easily from the old man's vicious embrace.

"Yeah, nice boy," Mike soothed, petting Porgy's wide, diamond-striped head gently. "My wife's got a cat just like you, but not as good looking," he flattered. "Yeah, love to be petted, don'tcha?" he spoke soothingly while still petting the cat's head.

"Cheez, I don't believe it," Lowers said, shaking his head. The officers watched apprehensively while Mike walked slowly to the doorway.

"Just gotta have the magic touch!" Mike smiled disarmingly at the other men.

"You oughta put that monster in a bag and throw 'im in the river," the landlord said with disgust. "It's what I wanted to do ever since I laid eyes on 'im." His cloudy eyes shone inimically in the pale flesh of his face. A mole on his nose protruded whitely from the angry red veins laced in an ugly design on the sides of his nostrils.

"Oh, I think everything's under control now, Mr Masters," Mike said placatingly. "Lowers, open the door, will you?"

Porgy's emerald-green eyes saw the door open and his supple body muscles tensed for an escape. He sprang agilely to the floor in one graceful leap and made his way through the men's legs to the open doorway.

"Oh, no, ya don't," the thin-faced detective cried and backed completely out of the room and slammed the door shut, so great was his enthusiasm to keep the cat captive.

Porgy looked at the abruptly closed door with stunned chagrin, then spun around, seeing an alternate escape.

"Catch 'im, catch 'im," the landlord cried, wringing his hands with a hysterical vexation.

"Take it easy." Mike cautioned. "Don't get him all excited. My wife taught me all about cats. You gotta appeal to them."

"I'll appeal to 'em," Mr Masters cried and snatched up a blunt, wooden cane. "I'll kill the bastard!" he threatened and raised the cane over Porgy's fleeing back.

"No, Mr Masters! For God's sake, don't hurt the cat," Lowers cried. "He's an innocent animal, you know." He looked quizzically at Mr Masters' twisted countenance, curious at his overwhelming animosity for the cat.

"Please, Mr Masters," Mike pleaded and reached out to grab his raised weapon-bearing hand. "You'll kill him with that!"

The landlord brought the cane down on Porgy's back and head with a sickening whap!, then sniggered feebly over the injured cat.

"Gotcha, now didn't I?" the old man leered into the cat's bleeding face. He stooped down to observe Porgy's crushed nose and eye with glee.

"Wrrrowow!" Porgy screamed with hate and leapt straight into the man's face with all four claws bared.

"Ahhh – help! He's killing me!" Mr Masters cried and staggered backwards, clutching his face in pain. He fell against a scarred mahogany table and knocked over a large vase.

"Cheez," Mike said in amazement. "I think that cat *would* like to kill him."

Porgy ran swiftly into the kitchen and sprang up on a window-sill overlooking the sink.

"No!" Mr Masters whimpered. Don't let him go in there. I just mopped the floor. Blood'll be everywhere."

The policemen hastened into the stark white kitchen after the cat.

"Go and get a blanket or something from the old guy, Lowers," Mike directed. "We'll throw it over the cat like a net. Looks like we ain't going to get him any other way."

Lowers ran into the living-room asked the landlord for a blanket. The old man hobbled up unsteadily from the floor and tottered into the bedroom after a blanket.

"Christ, it's hot in here," the fat-necked detective complained. "Can I get a glass of water?"

"Yeah, sure. Go ahead, Rocky," Mike said. "Only there ain't any ice made yet – or maybe there is by now."

The detective walked over to the high-legged sink and lifted a glass from the basin clumsily, then filled it with water.

"You could probably check and see about that ice," Mike advised with his eyes riveted to the crouched, bleeding cat.

"Gosh, that cat is bleeding badly," Rocky remarked, looking at a splattering of blood along the bottom of the refrigerator as he pulled the door open.

Mr Masters entered the kitchen with a blanket in his arms and cried out when the saw the officer in front of the refrigerator, "What're you doing?" he asked excitedly.

"Just getting myself some ice," Rocky replied, puzzled at the hysteria in the man's voice.

"I told your friend that there's no ice made," he said hostilely. "Now, if you don't mind. . ." he said and slammed the refrigerator door in Rocky's shocked face.

"This *is* my house, you know," he said emphatically.

"Sure, sure, Mr Masters. Don't get yourself upset over nothing. I'll just drink the stuff plain," the detective said nervously, looking with sympathy at the claw marks on the old man's face. "Whew, he really got you, didn't he?"

"Darned vulture," Mr Masters agreed and handed the blanket to Mike.

"OK, stand back," Mike said and threw the blanket over Porgy. He gathered the cat inside quickly and held the coverlet tightly around his struggling body. "There'll be no getting away this time, fat cat. Lowers, you'd better take the cat down to a vet. He looks pretty hurt."

Lowers gathered the bulky bundle that was Porgy to his breast and walked with surprising ease out of the room.

"Borscht, Nick, you guys can take on off too," he suggested. "We're through here for the day. You can wait around for five minutes, Rocky," he said to the burly detective standing next to him. "I might need you again."

The officers filed out of the room and left Mike and Rocky standing awkwardly in front of the landlord.

"Well, that's over," Mr Masters muttered. His face looked strangely chastised after his ferocious fight with the cat.

"Not quite, Mr Masters," Mike said, looking at the dried blood on the floor under the refrigerator door. "I'd like to see if there's any ice made yet."

"What?" the old man asked fearfully.

"Let's see what's inside the refrigerator, Mr Masters." Mike said and yanked open the refrigerator door. He pulled out the fruit storage bin and stared at its blood-soaked contents.

"My God!" Rocky exclaimed, "I think I'm going to throw up!"

A torn, bloody shirt lay over two blood-soaked towels, and visible in the far corner of the bin was a withered human finger.

"Handcuff him instead," Mike said dully. "Looks like that cat cooked your goose, Mr Masters."

Mike opened the freezer door. The eyes of two frozen heads stared out at him with strange expressions.

"Uhhh!" he cried out.

The old man's beady eyes looked around them wildly, hunting for an avenue of escape.

"She was evil, you know. Evil. Playing around with all them men!"

His loud pants were heard throughout the kitchen.

"Handcuff him, Rocky," Lowers told the young lieutenant again.

The old man whirled around to the sink and lifted one of the sharp knives up from its rack. He waved it menacingly at Rocky.

"There's a lot of evil people in this world, you know. I've got rid of a lot of them."

Lowers looked at the landlord with revulsion. "You've done this before, haven't you, Mr Masters? Only you got rid of the others."

"That's right," Rocky said. "The guy they booked in Georgetown said that the record player was still going when he came up the stairs. He must have surprised the old coot before he could haul his victim off." Rocky moved towards Masters with the handcuffs.

"You were going back for the girl too, weren't you?"

"I'll cut your hand off!" the old man shouted.

"A bullet is faster than your hand," Lowers warned him.

"It don't make me no nevermind now," the old man warned.

Rocky stepped back from the knife and looked at his superior quizzically.

"You were coming back for the girl's body when her old lover showed up, weren't you, Mr Masters?"

"He was another serpent I could have got rid of for you," the old man said dementedly.

Lowers shook his head incredulously. He felt a buzzing in his ears from the strain.

"Have many 'evil people' stayed in your place, Mr Masters?" he phrased his words carefully.

The old man's wide, flaccid lips curved into a smile.

"Trying to find me out, ain't cha?"

Rocky and Lowers looked at one another quickly, both aware that they were in the presence of a madman.

"Would you let me go iffin' I told you where the others are?" Masters asked, with the illogical cunning of an insane person.

"We could cut a deal." Lowers lied.

"Call your dog off then," Masters slurred.

Lowers motioned at Rocky with his eyes. Rocky stepped back from the landlord, but his hand was near his holster.

"It's back here in the bedroom," Masters told them. The officers exchanged puzzled glances.

"The bedroom?"

The old man shuffled through the living-room and into his bedroom. A curious array of old telescopes and magnifying glasses lay on a table by the windows. A blanket was drying on one window-sill. Flies buzzed around the room from the open windows.

"Just look out through these windows," he told them.

Rocky and Lowers followed the old man's pointing hand. A garden of golden yellow and red roses beamed their colours in the blazing sunlight.

"They're all under there," Masters told them as he leaned over the sill. "Fertiliser for my roses." He smiled at them happily.

Rocky gasped. The sound seemed to wake Masters from his happy reverie.

"That's what they were anyway – fertiliser. Fit for nothing else." The knife glinted in his other hand from the fierce sunlight. Lowers nodded at Rocky as he drew his pistol silently from his holster. Rocky grabbed Masters' hand that held the knife, but the old man twisted out of his grasp with a ferocious agility and flung himself over the window-sill. Rocky grasped wildly at Masters' shirt but it just ripped apart in his hand.

"Don't be crazy, Mr Masters," Lowers shouted. "We'll have to shoot you!"

Masters paid no attention to the two officers, but seemed intent on climbing down the gnarled old ivy vines that covered the back side of the apartment building. His foot hit a facing from one of the fourth storey windows when a large vine he clung to gave a loud, tearing sound.

"Help! Help!" the old man cried.

"Jesus!" Rocky said, as they watched Masters splatter onto the black pavement of the back driveway.

Hadrian came striding into his large suite of offices, talking animatedly with his business associate. "Hie, hie!" he said intermittently, sounding like a Chinese feudal chief. Laura, his secretary, looked up briefly and started to feel herself excited also by his infectious laughter. His dark eyes were sparkling with an audacious triumph, and his powerful hands moved in generous gestures as he talked with his partner. But she glanced at her stack of correspondence and shipping tenders to be typed, and remembered from long experience that her boss's enthusiasm was always for himself and meant good things for him, not her.

Hadrian stood in the door of his private office after Ishmael had gone, examining its walls as if he were about to take aim with a rifle. Suddenly he walked to the wall behind his massive executive desk and took something out of a bag he had been carrying. He held it up for a moment, then called to his secretary, "Oh, Laura, could you come here for a moment, dear?"

The dumpy, tweedily dressed girl came mincingly into the room. She stood before him humbly, her large, bovine eyes waiting for his command.

"Laura, how do you like my new Syrian medal here?" He looked down at the medal, congratulating himself again on his choice of where it should be placed, then back at his secretary.

"Oh, it's wonderful, Mr Abdullah, just grand," she said nervously, eager to say what would please him and anxious to get back to her place of safety behind the typewriter.

The woman stood limply in the doorway. She was a little afraid of Hadrian since she had often heard him yelling on the phone. She didn't want him to yell at her because she knew that she wouldn't have the nerve to come back to work the next day if he ever did.

"Do you think so?" he asked and looked back at the brightly coloured ribbons and elaborate scrollwork on the medal.

"Oh yes, sir," Laura responded, wishing she could go.

"Thank you, Laura. That'll be all then."

"Yes, sir."

"Er, Laura, would you please shut the door?"

"Of course, sir."

"Thank you."

He leaned over to his desk and took a small, substantial nail out of the drawer and used one of his Abraham Lincoln bookends to hammer it into the wall. After he had placed the gold-framed medal in the place that he had chosen, he sat down in his large, black leather chair, rotating it so that his back was turned to anyone who might come into his room, and he sat mesmerised by the medal.

Suddenly the phone rang. He whirled around to his desk and snatched up the receiver, looking like a ferocious bear just awakened.

"Hallo," he said flatly.

"Dear? I just thought I'd tell you I won't be home for dinner tonight." A female voice paused for some sort of cue.

"Oh?" he said, hardly hearing his wife.

"Yes, so please have Arjur serve you. The Colonial Dames are having a buffet and bazaar at the church tonight." She waited for a reply. "Dear?" she said again.

452

"Oh yes. That's very good. I'm busy now. Talk to you later."

He hardly remembered whom he had been talking to after he had hung up. The only thing that registered moments later was that he'd have a few hours alone at home. Maybe he could take a nap. He felt tired, yet too excited to sleep. He looked at his watch – 4:30. He decided to let Laura go home early.

He pressed the intercom on his desk and told her that she could go. Her "Oh, thank you, sir" was so grateful that he wondered for the first time what his secretary's life was like. But he forgot her as soon as his finger left the intercom button.

He leaned his head back into the plush, leathery-smelling chair and closed his eyes. He was tired, but he felt a deep, frustrated longing. – one that he would never again satisfy with Cybele. He wanted to call her and order her to meet him somewhere. He wanted to tell her about the medal more than anyone. He knew her reaction would have been honest.

"Aman, Aman!" he said, staring mindlessly out his window at the thickening Connecticut Avenue traffic, remembering the police at the door of his home in Bethesda, the awful ride in the back of a patrol car and the pictures they had shown him of Cybele's nude, slashed-up body at the police station.

Recalling those gruesome photographs reminded him of the picture he had taken of Cybele at her apartment with his Polaroid. Slowly he took his wallet out of his pocket and slid the colour snapshot of her from between stacks of credit cards and business cards. She was lying nude on the bed with her black hair spread out on yellow sheets. She had purposely raised one leg, coyly hiding herself, and she lay looking vulnerably at him. At the sight of her body and eyes, he felt himself grow hard and insistent in his expensive linen slacks.

"Oh, Cybele," he said and began fondling himself. He hadn't made love for seven days. She had been dead for six. The memories of the other photographs crept back into his mind, but the urgent, pleasurable sensations under his fingers made him forget everything except the smiling girl in the photograph.

"Oh, what a pussy you have, darling. I adore to fuck her," he said and moved his dick in his hand faster and faster. "Is she well fucked, darling? Can you come?"

He groaned and stopped. He sat for a moment panting while the room materialised in front of his eyes once more after his orgasm, then reached for some Kleenex on the desk. After cleaning himself, he looked at the picture again and felt an overwhelming urge to cry. Tears welled up in his eyes, making him feel silly and powerless. He grew angry at his weakness and stood up to leave the room. An eerie feeling of displacement passed over him as he walked through the darkened rooms of his offices.

"Good night," Ishmael said from the other suite of rooms adjoining Hadrian's office.

Hadrian raised his hand in a small salute, then walked down the long corridor to the elevator. His footsteps echoed hollowly behind him.

When he came out of the Boston Building late that afternoon, the sun was still scorching, as if it were spending itself for the last time before September came. Already, with his sharply trained eye for detail, he could see a hint that the leaves were about to lose their colour around the edges. He glanced back up at his suite of offices and saw his business associate continually talking on the phone, with two of their secretaries huddled close by.

The man he worked with was a brilliant young business dynamo – and his lust for money always reassured Hadrian that he could meet any competition with success. Hadrian tried to picture vividly the way they had underbid on ten 100-ton tankers that day, but for some reason he couldn't derive the keen pleasure he usually felt after a fight well done. Even the sight of his blue silk drapes hanging near his large, reclining desk chair did not inspire him. And when he looked back at his associate, the expression on his face seemed to have changed from animation to sheer greed. Or had it? He ran his fingers quietly through his dark, wavy hair, feeling a curious detachment towards everything usually familiar and rewarding to him.

He walked into his parking lot and immediately three muscular Negro men ran up to him, smiling unctuously and competing for the extra dollar he sometimes surprised them with. He stood smiling at them, enjoying being fawned over and the momentary pleasure of feeling superior. When his sleek white Continental came sliding down the concrete driveway of the parking lot, he felt another private surge of pride. It would have embarrassed him if anyone of his calibre had noticed his petty reaction of possession. But at any rate America was, as he had often agreed with his Arabic Ambassadors, so simple and unsophisticated. Who would notice anything like this in a parking lot anyway?

When he slid under the steering wheel, he had to adjust it upwards to make room for his stomach. The bulging muscles of his arms and extreme width of his shoulders seemed to belie his perfectly tailored sports coat, his doctorate from a famous French university, and his rich, successful business. As he bent down to adjust the car air-conditioner, squinting his large, fine brown eyes from the smoke of his cigarette, one could have imagined him to be just another swarthy sailor on some boat, dressed in a businessman's attire.

Riding down Massachusetts Avenue towards his immaculate house in Bethesda, he tried not to turn his head and look at the balcony of Cybele's apartment. But as he accelerated the car, something seemed to force him to look – as if he might see her there, like an apparition, smiling and waving at him. She would be perched on the old stone railing, waiting for him to pass by on his way home from work on those nights when he couldn't think of an excuse to get away from his wife. He was so upset when he thought of Cybele, that he flew through a red light without knowing it, abnormally absent-minded.

'She was so sweet, sitting there like an angel,' he thought and put one of his big blunt thumbs to his top lip in a habitual gesture of consternation.

He felt ashamed that tears were coming to his eyes again. He wasn't used to being ruled by his emotions, however strong they were. 'But fucking with everybody,' he thought grimly, trying to dispel the deep pain he felt at not having her anymore.

Suddenly he felt cold in the wide, luxurious, air-conditioned car and a little queasy in his stomach.

'Must have been something I ate last night at Ishmael's house. Saudis have good food but it's too rich,' he thought. He remembered the housewarming party at his associate's house, the rooms and rooms of pastel velvet furniture from Sloane's. Ishmael had been describing how he intended to knock out a wall and create arches in front of his second bar in the den. He had looked so earnest and innocent standing there, describing the finishing touches of a dream he had worked for all his life.

'Yes, Ishmael is a man I can trust,' he thought. 'And he's also properly humble and grateful to me.'

But Hadrian had tripped over an oriental rug as he walked towards Ishmael to see what he was describing more clearly. Instead of recovering himself immediately, as he normally would have done, he staggered a little. His associate ran over to help him, and as Hadrian steadied himself they had looked at one another with embarrassment.

Ishmael had known about Cybele and had often worried about Hadrian's safety and the reputation of their firm. Her death had certainly been horrible but maybe all for the best, he had decided. One couldn't escape kismet after all. But he saw how his boss was suffering and felt a little helpless in the presence of his grief. Hadrian had left the party early, adamantly advising Ishmael's wife not to take any more diet shots, then gulping down two diet pills himself with his last Scotch old fashioned and chewing the cherry slowly to get rid of the pill taste.

When he had come home from Ishmael's, his wife was already asleep. She had been sick that day with terrible cramps and couldn't come to the party. He used "her" bathroom in the other bedroom so as not to disturb her or himself by having to make polite conversation with her. As he stood in the harsh glare of the bathroom light, pushing his dick to the side to guide the stream of urine, he noticed Tampax in the trash can and felt a revulsion at the sight of them. They were too personal an item to be seen from a woman he hadn't touched for over two years now.

He quickly left the bathroom and went out into the garden. The flowers swayed and scented the air with a calming perfume. He collapsed into a patio chair and breathed the cool air of the garden deeply, hoping to relax. He reached for a package of cigarettes that he always kept on the patio table. As he did so, the cuff of his coat picked up the phone receiver like an inanimate hand. He replaced it and lit his cigarette. But then he heard her say, "Where are you?"

"In the garden."

"You've got a phone in your garden?"

"That's right."

"That's super," she said.

He had crushed out his cigarette as soon as he had lit it. Sleeping with his wife that night had been unusually depressing.

Well, he wouldn't let that happen tonight. He was going to find a way to dispel his depression.

He pressed the plastic garage control, and up came the garage door. His butler was waiting by one of the side entrances of his mansion to take his briefcase. 'Something else from Cybele,' he thought. She had sold one of her fur coats he had given her to buy a set of impressive Italian luggage for him. But as he strode into the den, he felt a comforting impatience with his constant nostalgia. After all, fate was fate. "She's dead, and that's it," he said to no one.

"Arjur, fix me a tall Bloody Mary – a double shot of vodka inside please," he said to his butler in Turkish and walked straight to the patio, followed by his yapping poodles.

Almost in an instant Arjur was there at his side like a robot moron with the Bloody Mary. Hadrian could tell that he wanted to chat with him for a while in his native tongue since he couldn't speak English well and grew lonely during the day. The butler's isolation made Hadrian feel that he worked better, and for some reason it made him seem more exclusively Hadrian's. Hadrian liked to own things. If he didn't, he soon lost interest in them.

But tonight he cut Arjur short, waving him away and complaining of a headache. The butler was timid in the presence of his boss's bad moods and disappeared.

Actually Hadrian was not in a bad mood. He was more nonplussed than anything else. He wasn't used to his game palling on him.

He sat drumming his fingers on the table, then glanced at his watch – 6:30. He had about an hour to think of how to escape for the evening before his wife came home from the bazaar. When he thought of her, it seemed odd that she was in fact his wife.

"Ridiculous!" he said suddenly and picked up the phone. He dialled a number quickly, then said, "Yolanda, how are you?" when a girl answered the phone.

"Still missing my 500 bucks," came the nasal reply.

"Oh, Yolanda, I'm sure we can discuss that."

"When?"

"How would you like to go for a nice dinner tonight? At the Rive Gauche," he proposed and listened for some sort of reaction confidently. "You'll have *carte blanche* of course."

"Well, I haven't eaten yet," the girl said.

"Then it's all settled" he decided. "What time can you be ready?"

"In twenty minutes," she replied.

Hadrian smiled at her anxiety for the dinner.

"Oh, Yolanda, by the way don't you bring one of your girl friends?"

"You mean one like Cybele?"

"You did introduce us, didn't you? I had forgotten," he lied.

"I not only introduced you – you promised me 500 bucks when I offered to get you two back together that time she tried to break it off with you and stay with the monster she was married to."

"I shall bring you a check tonight," he told her. He pulled his checkbook out of his coat and immediately began writing a check as if she were there waiting.

"Really? Wow!" Yolanda said.

"But about one of your girl friends," he said with his dick tightening in an unexpected erection.

"How about 500 more bucks?"

"If I like her, yes."

"How long does that take?" Yolanda asked suspiciously.

"Oh, a few nice dinners with you and the girl."

"Don't try to double-cross me this time, Hadrian."

"No, of course not. Now be ready. We're going to have a wonderful dinner together."

Hadrian got up hastily from his chair and ran upstairs to "their" bedroom. He splashed some Fabergé on his heavily jowled face and gargled with a mouthwash, then rushed back to his car. The butler watched him, puzzled, then went out to collect the drink that he had left half full.

'I hope this will be entertaining,' Hadrian thought and switched on his car stereo.

Chapter Seventeen

"If I were a carpenter and you were a lady. . ." Eric sang while he sat on a painter's bench hanging in front of the second story of a Georgetown apartment building. He chipped methodically at a rotting window facing, then leaned back to inspect his work and almost fell over backwards.

"Oh ho, steady there," he said to himself. "Don't want anyone to get the wrong idea – like I was on grass or something wonderful like that."

He thought longingly of his little grey scales. His fingers secretly itched to cut some dope. "A little pound here, a little pound there," he sang in a discreet whisper, "and I could have a nice velvet jacket instead of this paint and shit all over me."

He felt his fingers resting on the old wooden facing of the window and suffered from a momentary amnesia. He really forgot where he was. Eric's thought patterns, like his physical movements, were fragmented.

Since the rehabilitative services of the Police Department had given him three job choices – one in subway construction, one as a short-order cook, and another as a carpenter - he had chosen the job he felt he had some talent for. Also, it doubtless crossed his mind that he could be his own boss more readily working alone at some building or house.

"You gotta do your thing," he said aloud again, as if conducting his own private counselling. "And if you can't do your own thing, you can do something else at your leisure," he said, lighting a cigarette.

He looked down M Street from his perch towards Key Bridge and Canal Road. In a field below the George Washington Canal, long willowy plants billowed out in golden waves, blown by the wind in the direction of the Potomac River. His thin, faded shirt moulded the contours of his perfectly shaped shoulders and chest as it whipped against his body in the wind. It was the middle of September, and the first suggestion of autumn was swirling about him in the cool, invigorating breeze.

He squinted his eyes against the virginal sunlight of beginning autumn, and the field of golden plants became a crop of marijuana, blowing like a graceful gold mine for all to see.

He shook his head a little bit, then looked back at the field. It had returned to normal. "Jesus, far out Christ," he said, working his mouth back and forth over his gums as he did when he got upset or happy about something. "There I go with those. . ." He looked up into the sky, trying to remember what the counsellor had said: ". . .thought patterns. . . thought patterns conducive to delinquent behaviour."

Eric had been ordered by the court not to cohabit, support or in any way converse with hippies, nor effect their lifestyle ever again. Therefore, he often talked to himself these days for company as he didn't have a single friend who wasn't a hippie. Virtually the only acquaintance he had in DC who was not a part of the hippie community was Hadrian. And what did they have in common now that Cybele was dead? Besides, he had caused Hadrian a great deal of trouble. He smiled grimly. "Old bastard, but he got out of it and I didn't. Bet he's already got some broad a little dumber and more settled as a replacement." He clenched his square, small fists and began chipping violently at the wooden window facing him. "God, God, I'd like to tie an anchor around his neck and watch him drown slowly. I'd want it to be dirty water, too!" He looked back at the Potomac and again thought of owning his own beautiful field of marijuana.

"Hey, you!" someone yelled up at him.

The raucous voice sounded so accusing that it startled Eric until he fell over backwards from the painter's bench.

"My God, Eric!" the man who had yelled at him said as he came running over. "You're not on dope again, are you?"

Eric looked up at the man's long white apron and realised that it was the cook from the sandwich shop below.

"Shhh!" Eric warned, standing up painfully from where he had landed and looking cautiously about. "You can't trust these Feds – they might have a stake-out around."

"Eric, you ain't into that mess again!"

"Don't get your ass up on your shoulders, Mac," Eric said and grinned. "I'm an honest man today." He put one long, supple arm around the stooped old man. "I mean, I've got no choice what with the fuzz and all."

The old man chuckled and squeezed Eric's pencil-slim waist with his pudgy hand. He lived alone like Eric in a one-room flat, and had come to look forward to Eric's daily luncheons at the sandwich shop. He had even persuaded Eric to have dinner at his apartment one night. But Eric had felt uneasy throughout the meal. The old man had seemed so grateful for his company that he had felt embarrassed. And he had kept thinking all through the dinner, 'Jesus, a short-order cook at 60. That just ain't going to happen to me," and felt the same nervous anxiety that had begun to prod him since his 26th birthday.

Eric walked into the long, narrow shop and stood watching the old man making his usual corned beef on rye with mustard. "That's right, *with* mustard," Eric had emphasised the first couple of days he'd eaten there.

"Just like you like it," Mac said. He put the sandwich down on the counter and looked at Eric shyly.

"Thanks, Mac," he said and wandered out of the shop without carrying on his usual conversation with the old man.

He leaned back against the fading, pastel paint of the brick store front, feeling a baking warmth from the bricks on his back and finished the sandwich except for the crust. This he scattered around for the birds.

"Eric is a bird feeder," he heard a childish female voice say. He looked up from the masses of clucking pigeons and saw Flo and Kate waving at him.

"Right on," he shouted back, looking appreciatively at Flo's racoon fur coat. She came running nimbly across M Street, dodging the traffic with her super-long, black-stockinged legs, and dragging Kate behind her.

"Whew!" Kate said, straightening a brilliant green scarf she had tied around her curling brown hair in gypsy fashion. "I'm getting too old for this sort of thing, Flo," she exclaimed loudly. Eric caught a whiff of brandy from her breath that smelled like mellowing apricots in the expectant autumn air.

'Probably just got back from a really swell luncheon,' Eric thought, looking back at the birds happily gobbling up their crumbs.

"Yeah?" Flo said, turning her black-turbaned head towards Kate and inspecting her dramatically. "What are you anyway? All of twenty-one?"

"I'm twenty-two, my dear," Kate said, emphasising the 'two'. "Twenty-two," she repeated as if it were a magic catalyst for her life. They both stared at one another, oblivious to Eric and their surroundings, looking like two survivors from a remote tribe.

"Well, I just don't see how I can be very sympathetic with someone who is twenty-two, when *I* am twenty-three!" Flo said and propped one hand on her hip. Her long red-lacquered nails spread out like bright claws on the bushy racoon fur. The pale, porcelain skin of her face was heavily powdered, and in the sharp sunlight one could see fine blonde hairs on her cheek and over her top lip. The contours of her high cheekbones made small, delicate blue shadows in the sides of her face. She gazed down at Kate from her super height, perched like a colourful bird on the five-inch high heels that she wore. Her nose was long and thin, giving her a flattering resemblance to Neffertiti, but she often threatened to alter it with plastic surgery. When one looked into her light green eyes past this long, slender nose, they had the impression that they had been trysting in an unknown land and had come upon one of its beautiful, bizarre inhabitants.

"What if you were an old man like me?" Eric said, half meaning his remark.

The two girls stopped contemplating one another and trained their eyes on Eric, trying to judge whether he was acceptable to their "tribe" or not.

Kate walked up to Eric and flung herself on him, encircling his waist with her arms. She was from a large Catholic family and more accustomed to brotherly relationships with men than Flo, who stood haughtily by her side. Flo's expression was one of indulgence while she waited impatiently for Kate to step back onto their carefully construed stage of stylishness.

"You're the greatest old man in the world, Eric," Kate said. Her words were muffled because she had pressed her wide, pretty mouth against his chest. With her hair cropped short, she looked like an Irish version of Zelda Fitzgerald, yet younger, more vivid, and perhaps more "saved" by time and circumstances. Her long green midi stretched tight across her broad behind. Flo contemplated its girth with distaste, unconsciously clenching her round buttocks and touching her flat stomach with her savage red finger nails. 'How can anyone stand to be overweight?" she wondered, and remembered that it was time for her glass of grapefruit juice. She had had oysters on the half shell for lunch and a tiny glass of champagne while she sat watching Kate gulp French fries and a thick steak and wash it down with large, perspiring mugs of beer.

"Eric does look rather sheepish today. Wonder why?" Flo asked, and came closer to Eric on her long, shapely legs. "Eric, have you cut your hair?"

"*They* cut my hair," Eric said ruefully.

"They?" Flo looked blankly at Eric and pursed her red mouth prettily.

"You know who 'they' are, Flo!" Kate shouted with an unnecessary loudness. But it was necessary for her style of doing things, for her whole adaptation to life. When one grew up in a family of seven brothers and sisters, one had to be loud, or quick, or something.

"The Feds, of course," Kate told Flo impatiently. "How are you, poor darlin' boy?" Kate asked, stroking what was left of his curls. "You've been through so much since I saw you last."

"Yeah, they thought you were a murderer and everything," Flo said excitedly. "Must have been pretty far out, Eric."

"Nooo, they *didn't* think he was a murderer," Kate said. She and Flo turned towards one another, looking like two little girls arguing over mud pies. "They've got poor Eric here for sale and possession."

"Oh, I'm doing OK," Eric said. "Want to see my office?"

"Office?" Flo asked, with disbelief showing in her eyes.

"It's right over your heads," Eric told them, pointing towards his painter's bench.

Flo and Kate looked at the wide, horizontal board, uncomprehendingly.

"You dumb sissies, I'm a *carpenter*. A good, honest carpenter," he declared and looked proudly at the bench.

"Eric, that's wonderful," Kate championed him. "Cybele told me once that your second choice for a vocation would be as a carpenter." She stopped talking abruptly, conscious that she had mentioned Cybele to Eric and worried that it might upset him. Flo noticed Kate's hesitation with her perceptive green eyes and waited for her turn at Eric like an animal of prey.

"Hey, Eric, how do you get down from that thing?" Flo asked.

Eric laughed. "Oh I just fall over backwards, m'dear, and land on my ass."

"Oh, Eric, be serious," Kate said, and yanked irritably at the spaghetti strings of her black velvet bag resting on her knee. The alluring black material of the purse emphasised the ruddy health of her knee, dappled in colour from her own red blood underneath.

"I am serious, m'dear. That's exactly the way I got down for lunch."

Kate threw back her head and laughed like a young Irish washerwoman. Her blue eyes reflected the sky above them. "I'll bet he's even telling the truth."

"I never lie," Eric said solemnly, a little indignant at her sense of humour.

"Except to the Feds," Flo said. Her piercing voice cut into the soft afternoon air, making one think of a beak.

"You can't lie to the Feds," Eric said. "But you can try to avoid them – unless someone hangs the creeps onto your place." He pronounced the word 'Feds' like all of his friends did – as if it were some underground Gestapo or Soviet police, created solely to harass them and their particular style of life. For the freaks, the FBI was a net of ugly people peering into the fishbowl of a magic, untamed culture – a culture as superfluous as a summer daisy, flagrantly hedonistic and immersed in symbols and images, yet searching for a belief, or perhaps avoiding the discovery of one that might chain them to the same deadening rules they sought to escape from.

"That's right. Cybele came to your house the day she was murdered, didn't she?" Flo asked. "Too bad you weren't there. You might have saved her."

Eric started to reply, but changed his mind and just stood beside the flaking brick wall in an embarrassed silence.

"Flo! For Christ's sake, Eric doesn't want to talk about that," Kate admonished her friend. "I think your new profession is wonderful, Eric," Kate continued constructively. "And I want you to come to a party at my parents' house next weekend."

"Thanks, Kate," Eric said gratefully, and thought of Kate's large rambling home in the best section of Bethesda, of her genteel mother and her rich father, of her upcoming art show since her graduation from American University. Suddenly he felt swamped. 'Well, her father had to study and work hard a long time for what they have,' he thought pensively. 'Maybe I could go back to school too, if I keep this job up at a steady pace.'

Once more he looked longingly at the imaginary field of marijuana and thought of staggering sums of quick, easy money. He clenched his hands from the thought, then looked down at them with an odd feeling of being reminded of something. At that same moment he seemed to feel the coarse texture of the crumbling window-sills under his fingers. He was surprised to realise that the memory was pleasant. Amazingly enough, he felt anxious for Kate and Flo to leave so that he could go back to work.

'Jesus, can this be me?' he thought, but then reflected again on the warmth of the wood under his hands and the certainty of the chisel as he hammered it into the wood.

"Kate, come on, dear girl. They've got my latest pictures from *Style* tacked all over the Pie's walls. I'm dying to see them," Flo said breathlessly. Her innocent vanity lit up her face, enhancing its superb bone structure.

"You look like no Parisian model to me, gal," Eric mocked in a heavy Negro accent. "Mo lak a New Yoik who!"

Flo put out one of her long legs and rested the sole of her foot on his crotch.

"What did yo say, boay?" she asked, laughing.

"I said yo looks lak a Parisian model," Eric answered, feigning horror at the long, pointed heel of her shoe.

"That's what ah thought yo said, boay. Now go climb back up on your board," Flo said imperiously.

He walked over to the rope and hauled the board down, then hoisted himself back up to the second storey, watching the tops of their heads as he went up.

"Eric, you look like an early evening star up there," Kate said. "Doesn't he, Flo? You're poetic enough for me to do a painting of."

'Eric, Eric, Eric Star,' floated through his mind and landed like a knife in his heart.

"Come on, baby, I got no time to waste on a lowly carpenter. I gotta pick up my art from *Style* and get ready for Paris!" Flo said. She pulled Kate back across M Street impatiently.

Kate turned her head over her shoulder and 'blew Eric a kiss while he sat on his hanging office in the sky. But he was not looking at the two girls anymore.

He ran his hand carefully along the window-sill, searching for the place where he had left off chipping. He felt the last dip in the wood and fitted the chisel into place, then raised his hammer and brought it down on the head of the chisel. A neat piece of wood flew out from under the blade of the chisel, then another and another as he repeated the same motions over and over.

The sun grew hotter during mid afternoon, seeming to state that the summer had been a particularly intense one and that its remnants still held a fallen power over the early autumn day. Eric felt the sun burning into the muscles of his back and arms. He drew the hand that he was holding the chisel with up to his forehead and brushed crystal beads of perspiration from his brow with the back of it. He had a vivid picture of the cool, chlorinated pool water at the Hilton, of Cybele's black hair floating in its turquoise waters as she swam up to him. But it was drowned out of his mind by the honking of car horns.

Beneath him a steady stream of people had begun to mill about, riding bikes, looking into shop windows, or slouching down on the sidewalk rapping with one another. High school classes were over for the day and students had drifted into Georgetown from the Maryland and Virginia suburbs – some hitching, some packed into little shiny VWs their parents had bought as second cars in case something went wrong with their Cadillac or Lincoln. Many were like Eric – poor, colourful bums from lower- and middle-class families, searching for a bit of magic in the old cobblestoned streets of Georgetown.

Eric stretched and groaned. He had a crick in his back. He debated on whether to let himself back down for a drink or keep working a while longer. Automatically he placed the chisel securely into its last notch and hit it with the hammer. Each time a piece of wood flew out from under it, he felt a surprising sense of freedom. He didn't know why. Since he had started back to work he decided to keep on for at least another half an hour.

"If I were a carpenter, and you were a lady," he sang, "would you marry me anyway?" Bam! went his hammer on the chisel's head. "Would you have my baby?"

He thought of Cybele and all the tightly wadded hundred-dollar bills she had been carrying around with her the first day they met, of her white purse thumping against her brown thighs. He imagined his hands caressing her body, touching her skin, when – bam! – he missed the chisel's head and brought the hammer down on his finger.

"Eeoooww!" he cried so loudly that the freaks on the street stared up at him with alarm.

"Just shows you. Just goes to show!" he mumbled to himself while sucking his thumb. "What even thinking about that bitch can do to a guy."

"Yeah, well, I'm a carpenter, m'dear, but you weren't Mary – and I sure ain't Joseph," he said and steadied the chisel once more, eyeing it suspiciously before he raised the hammer.

Outside the long latticed windows of the Hotel Athenia the Mediterranean sparkled jauntily in the early September sunlight. Its brilliant turquoise waters shimmered along the white sand like melted emeralds, following the curve of a ladle-shaped bay. White bungalows dotting its sands wore their pink and blue roofs like the gay hats on the heads of young girls and old men sitting under multi-coloured umbrellas along the beach.

A jet black raven jerked his compact head over his shining, sooty-coloured shoulder when he heard the shriek of a little child who had upset her sand bucket. His small, dark eyes glinted like wet gems when he stopped his progress along the ledge of a hotel window to look at the child. He dipped his long beak forward several times to regain his former balance on the window-sill, then trotted over the white shutters with his small yellow feet and landed with a plop into a spacious hotel room.

It was the raven's custom to enter the rooms early, before the guests had awakened, and search for the succulent scraps of French bread, sweetmeats and pâté left on silver trays from the evening before. Once he had even drunk champagne from a crystal glass, holding a golden piece of bread in his sharp, wise beak and melting it a little in the bubbling liquid before letting it glide down his tiny throat.

This morning there was nothing to be found in that particular room as he hopped along the serving stand and off onto the bedside tables. He dipped his head under his wing and dug his beak into his feathers with irritation. Then he spied what he thought were some green leaves lying near the hotel guest's foot.

Dare he get that close to the man in order to investigate, he wondered? He contemplated the man's face, then realised with a start that his eyes were partially open. The bird cocked his little head to the right and looked at the man with his other flint-coloured eye. Something seemed different about this human being to the raven. He was not like the people talking and swimming outside the hotel window.

Suddenly one of the green "leaves" blew up into the air from a brisk sea breeze. The raven forgot himself in his curiosity and hopped brazenly along the bed in order to reach this new plant.

His little feet left small tracks of blood over the picture of Brand that Crag still clutched in one hand. The hundred-dollar bill that had caught the raven's attention swirled up into the air and stuck on the long sharp blade of a sword jutting up from Cragmont's back.

The raven lifted his wide black wings and swooped over to the green money. It crackled like dead leaves when he grasped it in his beak. The bird flew to the window ledge in excitement, holding his prey possessively. His black eyes darted back to the strangely still man before he dropped the money to his feet and began trying to savour its taste. After some moments he gave up disappointedly, when he realised that it was only paper he had captured for breakfast. He looked around the room once more before abandoning his search for food there, then flew to the next hotel window.

"Did you hear about the suicide up at the Athenia this morning?" a young man asked his mother as he contemplated a solitary woman with shining blonde hair sitting at the table next to theirs. 'She's French, I suppose,' he thought. 'Peculiar how their noses are always so long and straight.'

"No, anything special?" his mother inquired, pushing her *hors d'oeuvre* away and following her son's ardent gaze to the beautiful woman.

"Why don't you send her a glass of wine?" she suggested, and rolled her dark grey pearls between her fingers thoughtfully.

He smiled at his mother indulgently and raised his hand to signal the waiter. Since her latest cancer operation, he had used every source at his command to bring her happiness.

"Well, yes, it *was* rather glamorous, the way he did it and all," he replied in answer to her first question.

His mother raised one eyebrow and smiled at her dark-haired son with interest.

"The wine is so excellent today, Teddy," she declared. "And you know how I adore rosé – how thoughtful of you, darling boy!" She laid her hand over her son's with a tender affection. The diamonds of her rings sparkled deeply, enhanced, rather than dimmed by their age, as her hand trembled over his in the candlelight.

"The man was Cragmont Weatherby – does that ring a bell?" Teddy asked and took more of the sparkling red wine into his mouth.

"Well, the Weatherby family is well known in Connecticut," his mother replied. "At least the family I'm acquainted with. But one of them married a Jew. Pity," she sighed and began cutting the last of her smoked salmon weakly.

"Yes, well, the dead man is one of those Weatherbys in Connecticut. He was also in New York for two years. At thirty he was one of the youngest and most highly paid stockbrokers that town had seen for a long time. But. . . he had a weakness for liquor and for another very famous young man – one Brandon Starr. So he abandoned his career in New York and came down to live with this incredibly wealthy Mr Starr in Washington DC."

"Yes, I read about his murder last month – so grisly!" She put her fork down absently and shuddered, then dropped her beads against her pale grey dress and sighed again.

"Are you all right, Mother?" Teddy asked anxiously. "We can always take our after-dinner drink in your suite."

"Of course I'm all right, Teddy darling. I don't intend to die until I see you happily wedded and bedded." She blushed furiously at her last word, then said, "Go on with the detective story," in a charmingly flustered manner.

"Well, this Cragmont inherited a vast amount of money from Mr Starr – over forty million."

"Sounds like a fairy tale. Oh darling, here's the waiter."

"Yes, er – could you send the pretty lady at the table next to ours a bottle of champagne?" the young man asked. "Make sure it's *Moet* and very cold." He looked at the woman's pale shoulders with his dark eyes admiringly. A little smile had begun to light up her face from his attentions.

"Yes, a fairy tale, Mother. But very Gothic. Mr Weatherby was so much in love with this murdered Mr Starr that he came here and threw himself on a long sword to end his grief."

"Oouuff! How dramatic!" his mother exclaimed.

"Yes, I suppose you could say that he had quite a flair. That's why he was so successful with his sources for investments. They say a shop owner here in Greece sold him the sword yesterday. It was the same day that he flew in – so he must have made up his mind to do it on the plane."

"Good Lord, Teddy, let's not talk about it anymore before dinner," his mother begged.

"Oh, of course, Mum's love, I just thought it might entertain you. The sword. . . and all the money. There were thousands and thousands of dollars in cash blowing out of a suitcase. Some little children picked up hundred-dollar bills outside the window of his room."

"Wonder why he brought all that money with him?" she asked, puzzled, then glanced over at a waiter as he placed a bucket of ice beside the blonde woman. The champagne bottle's large capped head stuck out over its moist side like a shield of beaten silver.

"Oh, darling, look, she's got your present!"

Teddy raised his glass and toasted the woman. Her blue eyes brimmed with pleasure as she looked at the handsome young man.

"Well, I guess he thought it was something tangible – something he could hold onto," Teddy continued. "I mean, the weight of it in his suitcases and all."

"The weight? What do you mean weight?" his mother asked. "You talk like a French philosopher sometimes, Teddy – and, for an Irishman from Philly, that's inconsistent."

She drank the last of her rosé and held her glass up to him engagingly. "Pour child, pour it, do!"

He lifted the tall wine bottle and filled her glass with the sparkling pink wine.

"Everything else had vanished like vapour evaporating from a window in the morning. The money was the only thing left that he could see and hold."

"But Teddy, how could one carry that much money into a foreign country?"

"He came here with diplomatic immunity from the embassy. Claimed he planned to buy many antiquities for the Corcoran Museum of Art. Greece was a hobby of his all of his life. He was an expert on it. He had an official invitation from the Greek Ambassador – strictly VIP and all that."

"Look, Teddy darling, she's smiling at you," his mother said, forgetting their conversation about the tragic young man. "Why don't you invite her over for dinner with us?"

"After dinner, Mother, afterwards," Teddy replied, and patted her hand complacently.

"All in due time, eh, son?" she said and laughed conspiratorially.

"It usually does work out that way, doesn't it?" Teddy agreed.